ISLAND IN THE SUN

*A Story of the 1950's Set in the West Indies*

# Island
# in
# the
# Sun

## by Alec Waugh

FARRAR, STRAUS AND CUDAHY, NEW YORK

©

*To*

*Mrs. Edward MacDowell*

*who in tribute to the memory of her husband, the com-*
*poser, founded at Peterborough, New Hampshire, the*
*colony for writers, artists, and musicians where the second*
*half of this book was written*

*In gratitude, homage and affection*

# CHAPTER ONE

Maxwell Fleury rarely smoked. He was on that account peculiarly sensitive to the odor of tobacco. The moment he came into the house he was conscious of the scent upon the air of a cigarette stronger than those which his wife and sister used.

He crossed into the drawing room.

It was three o'clock on a February afternoon. The windows were open to combat the West Indian heat and a breeze was blowing from the hills. Yet the smell was stronger here. He sniffed. Turkish tobacco or Egyptian. Who would smoke that kind of cigarette, foreign, expensive, and exotic, in this remote obscure little British island?

He glanced at the ashtrays by the sofa; no cigarette stubs. Only someone with an acute sense of smell would have known there had been a visitor. Who had been here? At breakfast there had been no talk of plans. His mother was visiting in Barbados. His father had been with him all the morning, going over the estate accounts in the office. They had lunched together at the club. Who had been here besides Sylvia and Jocelyn?

He turned to go upstairs; he needed his siesta, but with his foot on the first stair he stopped. The smell had again grown pungent. There was a lavatory underneath the staircase. He opened the door leading to the toilet; the wood seat was raised; a man then: who?

From outside came the crunch of wheels. Then the sound of voices; Sylvia's and Jocelyn's. No third voice. They came into the hall, chattering and laughing; their hand-baskets bulged with towels; they were sandy and disheveled. He stepped toward his wife; he liked her this way; she seemed so much more approachable than when her blonde hair lay smooth above her ears, with her cheeks masked with make-up and her skirt falling from her waist in level folds.

He let his hand fall upon her shoulder; her skin was damp under her blouse; her flesh was soft and yielding; but he was conscious of a movement of withdrawal.

"I'm hot and sticky. I'm for a shower right away," she said.

"I'm set for a siesta too."

"I took mine on the beach."

1

"Were there many there?"

"The usual bunch. The Kellaways, most of the younger set, and Mavis." Mavis was her sister.

"How's Mavis?"

"Fine: her heart's nearly mended. I'll tell you later."

She bounded up the stairs; supple and slim and rounded.

"I'm going too," said Jocelyn.

He turned toward her. She must know who had been here this morning, but his pride would not let him question her. Besides, was she on his side? She and Sylvia had always been loyal allies: they had been known as the inseparables, she and Sylvia and Mavis.

In silence he watched her follow his wife upstairs. They should be such close friends, he and she. Just the right difference in age, three years, twenty to his twenty-three. Most men would have thought of her as the perfect sister, friendly, good-natured, easily pleased and easily amused, pretty and fresh and blonde, with a strawberry and cream complexion and very even teeth. Women liked her, men were attracted by her. Why hadn't they become the friends they should? His fault, he supposed, as usual.

Self-doubt and self-distrust fretted him as he undressed. What was wrong with him? What was there about him that put people off, that held people back? He stared at his reflection in the glass. He was tallish, athletic, strong; he had regular features, a pale complexion, smooth dark hair. What had Sylvia against him? He never flirted; he didn't drink. He was crazy over her. No one could call him "a bad match." The Fleurys might not be rich—who was in the West Indies now?—but they were one of the oldest families in the islands. Their estate house was quoted in every guide book as one of the finest survivals from the patrician days when the sugar islands of the Caribbean had been the focal point of European foreign policy, and the phrase "rich as a Creole" had been in general use. When Sylvia got bored with living in Belfontaine, she was always welcome here, in Jamestown, in his father's house. What more could she want? What more, as the daughter of a Barbadian bank manager, could she have hoped for, here in Santa Marta with its perennial lack of eligible males?

He stretched himself dejectedly under the mosquito net. There was a party at G.H. that afternoon to welcome the Governor's son on a vacation visit. He needed sleep, but his mind was racing.

The door-handle slowly turned and Sylvia stole in.

"It's all right, I'm not asleep," he said.

As she sat at her dressing table, brushing out her hair, he could

2

see her reflection tripled in the three-sided mirror. There was not an angle from which she did not charm him.

She began to talk about the party.

"I wish you could have been on the beach today. All the girls are frantic about H. E.'s son. Doris found a photo of him in a back number of the *Tatler*. He's certainly good-looking. They're all saying the same thing, that he can't have any entanglement or he'd not be coming here. They're so many Cinderellas; it's not surprising; he's not twenty-two yet and a title."

She chattered brightly on. No reference to that unknown visitor. Jealousy tore at him. She had never loved him, in the way that he did her. At first he had scarcely noticed. That kind of love, he had assured himself, came afterward, in a woman's case. It hadn't though. He had tried to content himself with what she gave him: a passive, nonchalant acceptance; but all the time there had been that niggling torturing suspicion, that sooner or later there would come, there must come into her life the man to whom she could respond.

Was this that moment? Why hadn't she mentioned that male visitor? Who had smoked that cigarette?

2

The Governor's son, Euan, had arrived in Santa Marta on the previous evening. For the last eighteen months he had been stationed in the Canal Zone on military service. His father had felt that after so dreary and at times dangerous an assignment he deserved a holiday before going up to Oxford in the autumn.

As Maxwell Fleury tossed with racked nerves under his mosquito net, a mile and a half away, in the long low colonnaded building half up the hill, on whose terrace from a tall white flagpole the Union Jack was flying, Euan's father, His Excellency Major General the Lord Templeton issued his final instructions for the party to his A.D.C. Captain Denis Archer.

Ostensibly the party was being given in the young man's honor but a secondary project was involved. The proprietor of the *Baltimore Evening Star*, Mr. Wilson P. Romer, was in transit on a winter cruise and it was desirable that so influential a personage should carry back with him to America a favorable impression of the island.

"The native West Indian," the Governor was saying, "is highly susceptible to American opinion. Harlem is to him what Mecca is to the Arab—the spiritual and cultural center of his race. He places higher value on a paragraph in a New York paper than a pronouncement from the throne. If we handle Mr. Romer tactfully, articles

3

may appear in the American press that will make our work here easier."

He spoke with the firm confident voice of one who is accustomed to giving orders. He was in the early fifties, gray-haired, of medium height with a trim, spare figure, and a military bearing. His chief feature was a long straight nose.

"But I'm not only concerned," he was continuing, "with the effect that Mr. Romer's articles will have upon the Santa Martans. I want the Americans themselves to be assured that we are pursuing here a democratic policy. Americans in the light of their own history distrust the colonial principle; many of them suspect, and naturally, that the money which they are pouring into Europe under Marshall Aid is being spent by us not in helping backward peoples but in strengthening our hold over them. I want to convince Mr. Romer that even if we are batting on a tricky wicket, we are keeping our bats straight."

Lord Templeton frequently illustrated his addresses with similes and metaphors from the cricket field. He had been a prominent and successful player. Many considered that he had only been prevented by his military duties from earning an England cap at Lord's.

"Mr. Romer," he went on, "can do us a great deal of good; he can also do us a great deal of harm. We must ensure that he does the one and not the other."

"Yes, sir."

The Governor looked at Archer sharply. Nothing could be more deferential than his A.D.C.'s manner, but, now and again, his voice assumed a tone that inspired misgivings. Had he been wise in his selection? For a widower such as himself, the need for a satisfactory A.D.C. was primary. Before World War I, it had been easy enough to find healthy, athletic young men of family and education, who were glad to occupy amusingly and inexpensively three of the dozen years that must be spent in relative obscurity before they inherited the family estate. But now, after the second war, it had become difficult to find competent, responsible, well-bred young men who were ready to give up three years to an occupation that had no future. The job needed very definite qualifications, and the fact that many of those qualifications were of a type more often to be found in women than in men, had led to embarrassing situations in more than one Colonial establishment. Templeton had been on his guard.

On the whole he was satisfied with his choice. Denis Archer had literary ambitions; that did not predispose Templeton in his favor, but it provided a reasonable alibi for a young man's readiness to spend three apparently purposeless years in the West Indies. Archer

4

had a good war record and played reasonable tennis; he was tall, blond-haired, and had an effective profile, but he did not look a poet. He washed, his hair was a little long, but it was tidy; his ties were uneccentric. Finally the General had learnt that his time at Oxford had been cut short on account of an injudicious friendship with a woman student. That clinched the matter. Whatever Archer was, he was not "one of those." He might, he decided, go farther and fare worse.

Three months' experience of Archer's capabilities had confirmed that first impression. He might have fared worse, but occasionally he felt apprehensive. "When in doubt, play back," he told himself, and continued his instructions.

"The color problem," he said, "is one on which Americans are touchy. Mr. Romer must be shown that as far as Government House is concerned, the various sections of the community meet on equal terms. The party must not, that is to say, be allowed to form itself into separate groups of white, near white, brown and black. If you see such groups forming, break them up. I want Romer to meet representative members of the community, men and women whom he can describe on his return as types. I shall of course make a certain number of these introductions myself; a man like the Attorney General is flattered at being especially selected to meet a visiting fireman. At the same time Romer must not feel that his hand is being forced; some introductions must be made by you."

An invisible attendant of the scene would have concluded, "Here, now, is a typical example of the Englishman who from the day of his birth until his death never questions, never needs to question the essential foundations of his faith. As a soldier, and as the eldest son of a fourth Baron, his path of duty and responsibility has lain clear. The crown, the altar, and the hearth, those three allegiances have ruled his life."

Up to a point that invisible attendant would have been correct. But only up to a point. Templeton may have had no qualms as to the ultimate purposes of existence, but beneath his impersonal military manner he was constantly harassed by uncertainty. "Am I talking too much?" he asked himself. You cleared your mind by talking out your problems, but he knew, how well, the dangers of that "talking out." He had been exposed as a junior staff officer to a Brigadier who had droned on and on at conferences, talking so that no one could interrupt his mental processes, lulling everyone into somnolence, then suddenly when he had arrived at a conclusion, pouncing upon his juniors with key questions. Templeton had vowed to keep that Brigadier's example as a warning. Had he now fallen into the same bad habit? It was very easy to go on talking once you were wound up and if you were a General your rank protected you from interruption.

Was he talking too much? He could hear himself talking but he could not stop. "Let us take the case of David Boyeur," he was continuing. "Some of our reactionaries will be surprised to see him here. They think he's dangerous. I don't agree. He's young and brash, but he'll only be dangerous if he's handled tactlessly. Power has gone to his head. You can't be surprised at that. He's under thirty and he's not only organized a trades union movement but got it in his pocket. I've nothing against the boy: he has as much right to be here as they have. At the same time, I don't want to give the impression either to them or to him that he's my protégé. He's not. It would be better if you did the introducing. Then I can say to Romer afterward, 'I saw you talking to young Boyeur. I wonder how he struck you?' I shall be surprised if Boyeur does not make a good impression. The boy's direct, forthcoming. Then I'll say, 'That is very interesting. That's how he strikes me. If he's our most dangerous revolutionary, I don't feel I've much to worry over.' You see my point?"

"Yes, sir."

"At the same time I don't want Romer to run away with the idea that our planters are tiresome reactionaries. They aren't, the better ones. Julian Fleury in particular. I'll ensure that Romer has a talk with him. Let me see the list."

It was a list indicative of the island's history and fortunes.

Fifty miles long and fifteen wide, with a population of a hundred thousand, raising sugar, copra, and cocoa, originally French—it had been captured by the British during the Napoleonic wars—Santa Marta, though never of great strategic or economic importance, had always been an asset rather than a liability on the Imperial sheet, and several of the old planter families had survived the slump that had followed emancipation in the nineteenth century. There were a hundred and fifty names upon the Governor's list and half of them had a Latin ring—Fleury had been once de Fleurie. The Governor ran his eye down the columns. All of the notables had been invited: the chief planters, the members of council, the government officials, the doctors, a few of the richer tradesmen. Invitations to Government House were a command, and against only two names was there the mark of a refusal.

"Why aren't the Prestons coming?" the Governor asked.

"He asked to be excused, sir. He's shipping his copra this afternoon."

"I see." Perhaps it was as well. Preston, who had come out since the war, was having trouble with the magistrate in his district. Better not to have to see him till the matter had been arranged.

He read on down the list.

"Colonel Carson, now that's a man you must have Romer meet. A new type of colonist; the retired soldier who's come out since the war because of high taxation and shrunken dividends."

Then there was Dr. Leisching. He was a new type too. An Austrian who had been taken prisoner during the war and had not wanted to go back to an occupied Vienna. Most islands had upon their medical staffs a German, a Pole, a Czech or Austrian. Leisching would interest Romer.

"And the Archdeacon. Be sure that they meet. You get the general idea, Denis. I've worked out the strategy. You're responsible for the tactics."

"I see, sir."

To himself Archer thought, This will be great copy one day.

## 3

Back in his office, Archer in his turn studied the list of guests. He had met them all, most of them several times; but he kept confusing them, particularly the colored ones, and most of them were colored; they all looked alike. At the end of each day he would summon a mental roll call of everyone whom he had met, visualizing their features, recapitulating the details of their careers and functions. But the next morning when he tried to repeat his homework, names, faces, and occupations blurred into one another. He stared at the list now, prescient of trouble. He was bound to make some mistakes that afternoon, he prayed that none of them would be serious. He had marked the most important notables. John Lestrange, the Attorney General. He knew him all right. But Mrs. Lestrange. He hesitated. Hadn't he confused her once with Mrs. Arundel? They were both corpulent, with ill-fitting dentures. Wasn't Mrs. Arundel's hair less crinkly . . .

"Am I disturbing you?"

He turned with a start. It was Euan Templeton.

"I'm always at the disposal of the Governor's son."

He said it with a smile and Euan laughed, perching himself on the desk and picking up the list of guests. It was now only a line of names; who could tell what some of those names might not have come to mean to him within a month.

"I'm relying on you this afternoon," he said.

7

"How do I take that?"

Euan flushed. He was very much his father's son, Archer thought: the spare straight figure, the long thin nose, but he had something his father lacked, had lost, or never had, a diffidence that belied the firmness of the clear-cut profile. It was an appealing diffidence that made Archer warm to him. The young man must have had a lonely boyhood since his mother's death in a motor accident in the blackout, spending his holidays with aunts, with his father's stiff, precise letters arriving from overseas with military regularity.

"If there's anything I can do," he said.

"There's quite a lot. The trouble is, I'm the Governor's son. I mustn't do anything that would let him down. At the same time, well for eighteen months I haven't seen a woman under thirty who didn't wear a yashmak."

Archer smiled. So that was it. He felt even better about Euan now. At the same time he would have to disappoint him.

"If that's what you're looking for, you've come to the wrong shop."

"But surely . . ."

"I know, I know: those magazine stories about midnight bathing parties, moons, hibiscus, all that glamor stuff. That's not the way it is, at least not here." He proceeded to explain. "In the first place," he said, "this is a small community; it's everyone's business to know what everyone is doing. There is no privacy. There are no doors to shut and most of us wear rubber soles; didn't you notice how I jumped when you came in? I'd no idea you were in the room. Anyone can walk into any bungalow at any time. That's point number one. Secondly there aren't more than half a dozen white girls here and they're intent on getting married."

"I'm not out for that."

"I'm sure you aren't. I'm not saying that these young women are not human beings; if they saw an opportunity for adventure without causing scandal they'd leap at it, but normally those opportunities only come when they're somewhere else. Antigua, Trinidad, Barbados. They're careful how they behave in their own island."

"What about the half-whites?"

"That's point number three. Some are very pretty. But they're a tricky proposition. They have the sound middle-class virtues; they are brought up to make solid marriages. I don't say that they don't have wild parties, because they do; but they are on their guard against white men. They know that white men won't want to marry them, will let them down if trouble comes. They've got both their

8

pride and chips upon their shoulders. They're afraid that a white man would despise them."

"But I've heard that they were flattered at having a white man paying them attention."

"They'd be flattered if he wanted to marry them, but they know he doesn't."

"You surely aren't going to tell me that white men in Santa Marta never have romances with half-white girls?"

"Of course I'm not, but it's not as common as you'd think. And when it does happen, it's unsatisfactory. It has to be a hole-and-corner business. He can't take her out in public, there's nowhere he can take her. It's not like London or Paris or New York, where you can lead a private life: everyone knows what you're doing, and if you cause a scandal... anyhow that's out for you, as the Governor's son."

"It sounded very different in books."

"This is not Tahiti."

"And think of me counting hours to getting here."

"Think of me on a three year stretch. It's only till the autumn as far as you're concerned, and you'll have a good time in lots of other ways."

4

The invitation cards had read 5 P.M. to 7 P.M. The party started in the garden, with tables set under the trees and tea, sandwiches, and ices being served; at sunset, at 6, the gathering would move indoors, for whisky sodas and rum swizzles.

Euan stood at his father's side while the guests filed across the lawn to be presented. Two weeks ago he had been living in a pastel world of sand and desert; everything had been flat and ochre brown under a film of dust, even the date palms and the oleanders. Here everything was lush and mountainous, with flowering shrubs flaming in red and yellow against wide branching trees. Government House was built upon a spur and from the terrace he could see the harbor, with its red brick, red-tiled warehouses that the French had built, and the schooners rocking against their moorings; beyond the harbor was a mile long curve of beach with a grove of coconut palms fringing it; a valley of sugar cane wound like a river broad and green between the mountains whose dark flanks were studded with the orange red flower of the *immortelle*. What a contrast to Suez and its flat sea of desert, to the drab mud houses, and the sullen river. His eyes were dazzled. What a contrast too between those

9

shuffling, silent, long-robed Arabs and these laughing chattering West Indians with their bright blouses and gaudy neckwear, their grinning glistening faces, and their shining teeth. And people talked of the tropics as if they were all one place.

As Archer announced the guests one by one by name, his father amplified the introductions. "Mr. Codrington is one of our health inspectors. He is also our best fast bowler.... Miss De Voeux is matron of the hospital.... Mr. Lestrange is our Attorney General. A very formidable person."

Nine-tenths of the guests had dark complexions; they were of every shade of color and every type of feature. Euan had read a West Indian history before coming out, he had learnt of the immense basic differences between the various West African tribes that had been ransacked by the slave traders of the Guinea Coast. He knew that in the mid-nineteenth century, following emancipation, Hindu labor from India had been indented. He had expected a mixture, but not one like this, every shade of color from sepia to olive gray, every texture of hair from short black curls to a smooth gleaming surface, every variety of profile from flattened nostrils and bulging mouths to aquiline noses and thin lips. He was fascinated. What a place to come to for a holiday. If only he were not the Governor's son fettered by all the obligations that that involved. If only he were on his own, alone, a tourist.

For twenty minutes there was a steady stream across the lawn, then there was a tapering off.

"I must stay at my post a little longer," the Governor said. "But you needn't, my boy. You can start campaigning."

Jocelyn Fleury, from the shade of a banyan tree, saw Euan move away from his father's side and stand on the terrace, hesitant, looking round him. I'll will him to look my way, she thought and stared at him. His glance moved across the lawn; it came nearer, reached her, checked. She smiled and he smiled back with recognition. So he *did* remember her. There was of course every reason why he should. There was a close family connection. Their fathers had been at school together, had come from the same part of England. The Governor had made a special point over their introduction. But even so, there had been so many introductions.

One up to me, she thought, as he stepped from the terrace.

As he came to her across the lawn, he looked like a character in a film: handsome and new and wholesome. Such a change from the men she had been seeing every day.

She was standing by the Archdeacon.

10

"I don't need to remind you, do I," she said, "that this is Father Roberts?"

"Of course you don't."

He looked from the one to the other, then spoke to the Archdeacon.

"It's a curious thing, Father, but I know more about this young lady than she does about herself."

He employed an artificial, mock-humorous, slightly facetious manner. He's most likely shy and doesn't want to show it, Jocelyn thought.

"How is that?" the Archdeacon asked.

"I was born within ten miles of her. I knew her grandparents. I know her cousins, I know all the people and the countryside that her parents knew when they were young. None of which she has seen herself."

"He's quite right, Father. I left there when I was two. I've not been back."

"I could tell her more about the country of her birth than her own parents could, and in just the same way, she could tell me a great deal more about my father's present country than he knows himself."

The Archdeacon smiled. He was on the brink of fifty. Tall and thin, with a long pointed nose and finely modeled mouth, he combined an ascetic appearance with an air of benign patrician worldliness. He gave the impression that life had treated him generously and that he was appropriately grateful. He was wearing a white soutane. He had long thin fingers and his nails were polished.

"I'm very sure she could," he said.

"Then don't you think I should be wise to put myself in her hands?"

"You'd be most wise."

Jocelyn turned toward the priest. It pleased and amused her that Euan should have adopted this device of addressing her through an intermediary. It was a game that had an undercurrent of accepted intimacy; moreover it enabled them to talk to one another without being rude to the holy man. She continued to accept the formula. "I wonder what he would most like to have me tell him, Father."

"I should like to get a day to day, hour to hour picture of the life that is led here by the upper crust young women of her age. Then I'd know how to organize my own day. Don't you think, Father, that that's a sound idea?"

"It would be a help."

Jocelyn laughed. "It would take me a very long time to tell him that."

"Perhaps it would be easier if she were to give me a demonstration."

"Now what, Father, does he mean by that?"

"If we spent a day in each other's company, by the end of it I should have at any rate a rough idea of how a girl spends her day here in comparison with the way she would in England."

"I'm afraid he'd find that very dull."

"Perhaps half a day then. I don't even know when she would go and swim."

The Archdeacon re-entered the conversation. "That depends, you will find, very much upon the day. On Sunday, for instance, I trust after Church, but anyhow before lunch, it is a general social custom to drink rum punches on the beach, but on week days, I think I am right in saying, the residents of the island bathe far less often than you in England fancy. You'd agree with that, Jocelyn, I believe."

"Most certainly."

"Then perhaps if Miss Fleury would let me know when she will swim tomorrow, I could call for her and drive her to the beach."

It was eventually decided that they should swim together the following afternoon. In ten minutes they had become friendly. This is fun, she thought. I like him.

There was a pause. He was probably feeling that he ought to be doing his duty by his father's guests. She'd make it easy for him.

"I mustn't monopolize you," she said. "There are a great many people here who want to meet you. Let's see now who there is."

They turned together, looking across the lawn. "There's Mr. Lestrange over there, and Mrs. Norman whose daughter married my brother. Then there's my brother . . ."

But his attention was already caught.

"Heavens, what a surprise. I'd never realized he was here."

She followed his glance. He was staring at a tall, wiry young man with short crinkly hair and an olive pale complexion.

The Archdeacon followed his glance too. "So you know Grainger Morris then?" he asked.

"I'll say I do. He was in the Middle East last summer. He told me he came from the West Indies, but Santa Marta at that time didn't mean a thing to me."

"Did you see much of him?"

"As much as I could. It wasn't easy. He was in too great demand. I don't know if you know the way it is out there, but the Welfare Authorities send out lecturers from England to boost the troops' morale: they're all right in their way, most of them, though some are dreary, but to get somebody like Grainger Morris who, as an athlete, was a hero to half the men before he started, now that was something."

There was a glow of hero worship in the young man's voice. The Archdeacon chuckled inwardly. This was a situation after his own heart. Grainger Morris was the son of a Santa Martan business man. He had won a state scholarship to Oxford and had recently returned to the island after seven years of spectacular success in England. He had won a blue for cricket and for rugger: he had been president of the Union. At Oxford and in London he had been a welcome guest in any house, but here because of his color he could not join the Country Club. His friendship with the Governor's son would frame an amusing social comedy.

"The troops were crazy over him," Euan was continuing. "He didn't speak down to them, he met them upon equal terms. I remember an evening lecture of his when they asked so many questions that I thought we'd never get him back to the mess for dinner. I must go across and say hullo to him."

There was no doubting the genuineness of his delight at finding Morris here. It would make, the Archdeacon decided, a pretty problem for the Santa Marta socialites. How would they react when they found that the man they wanted to fête held as his chief friend on the island a man whom they did not consider eligible for their club. He foresaw a good deal of quiet amusement during the next few months. It should provide the A.D.C. with some useful copy for that book of his. Where was that young man by the way? He wanted to be introduced to the American visitor.

The young man was having, as it happened, an awkward moment. The party had been in progress forty minutes and he had failed to put into action one of his chief's first instructions. He had not introduced David Boyeur to the American tycoon. He had not in fact seen Boyeur and he was beginning to wonder whether he had sent him an invitation. He could not, he told himself, have been so careless as to forget Boyeur of all people. But he knew very well he could. "I need a secretary," he told himself.

Looking ahead, he saw himself in five years' time with his novel of the West Indies a Book Society choice, on which M.G.M. had taken up its option. He pictured himself in chambers in Albany, in a long silk dressing gown, warm and glowing from his bath; his dark, slim secretary was sorting his correspondence. "Good morning, Mr. Archer, now don't forget that you're lunching with Lady

13

Forester and that you're being interviewed by Woman's Own at four." For the moment he stood stock still with the bustle of the party noisily surging round him, picturing that fate-favored mortal. Then he pulled himself together. He was not in Albany, he was in a West Indian garden, and he was not Denis Archer the brilliant new star in the literary firmament, he was Captain Archer, a dishwasher, a dogsbody, the lowest of all created things, a colonial governor's A.D.C. and a highly incompetent one at that. Where was that damned man, Boyeur?

He need not have been so self-critical. Boyeur had had his invitation. He was at that moment engaged in violent argument outside the Government House gates with a highly picturesque young woman. Little and lithe, dark, brown-skinned, with smooth straight hair, her features were delicate, her lips were thin, her nose almost aquiline. Her hands and feet were small. Her mother had come from Trinidad. She did not know who her father was. There was no sign of African blood in her appearance; she seemed a mixture of Indian and Spanish. She was twenty years old. Her name was Margot Seaton. She worked in the Bon Marche drugstore and for two years she and Boyeur had in the local phrase "been going steady."

"No," she was saying. "No, I can't go in. I've not been invited. I can't crash a party at G.H."

"You can if you're with me."

He spoke arrogantly, flinging out his chest. He was tall, broad-shouldered; he had little if any white blood in his veins. His lips were thick, his teeth very white and even, his nose broad at its base. He was dressed flamboyantly, with brown and white buckskin shoes, a chocolate colored pinstripe suit and a long thin canary yellow tie. He wore a Homburg-shaped hat made of straw, with a wide bandanna band. The colors harmonized on him. He was a striking creature.

"You bet it'll be all right. If you'd been my sister they'd have said, 'Why, bring her.' I'll say that you're my cousin. What's the difference."

"There's a big difference."

"Not where David Boyeur is concerned. They're afraid of David Boyeur. They don't want another strike."

He beat his fist upon his chest. He was enjoying himself immensely. A week ago she had remarked, "I wish I was going to the Governor's party." "That's easy," he had replied, "I'll take you."

He had talked her into it. He had bought her a dress for the occasion. He had enjoyed her delight in the preliminaries. But what he had enjoyed most had been the knowledge that at the last moment

14

her nerve would fail her. It was what he wanted. It would put him in a strong position. He would be able to tease her on his return. He would tell her whom he'd met, what he'd said to them, and how they'd answered him, even if he had no more than seen them across the garden. "You'd have enjoyed yourself. You were an idiot to stay away," he'd say, "and you could so easily. I told H. E. that you'd been afraid to come. You should have heard him laugh. Any relative of mine was welcome in his house, he said."

That was how he would put it, how he would chuckle at the disappointment in her face; she would feel humble, abashed, in the way that she never was. She never looked up to him in the way she should, she was always aloof. There was no question of his being her master, there were uncomfortable signs that it was the other way about, that she used him. This would teach her a lesson.

"Come on. Don't be a yellow-belly."

"Very well; let's go then." The suddenness with which she changed her attitude took him off his guard.

She noted his hesitation. "Are you quite sure that you want me to come?" she asked.

"Of course, why not?"

"It may get you into trouble with the Governor. It can't do me any damage, I'm far too humble, but it could damage you."

He threw out his chest again.

"It doesn't affect David Boyeur whether His Excellency the Governor thinks well of him or not. David Boyeur stands on his own two feet."

"Very well, in that case—" She paused, she was looking at him very straight. "Think again. You may regret my going in. If you say so, I'll go right home. I don't care either way, it's up to you."

She spoke on a note of indifference that roused him. It was he now who was being dared, and she did not appear to care two cents whether he called her bluff or not. His vanity was hurt.

"You're talking nonsense. What could hurt me, who could hurt me?"

"That's fine, then, if that's how you feel."

She still held his eyes with hers. There was in them an expression that he had not seen before: it was not hostility, it was more appraisal. He hesitated, vaguely apprehensive, as though a curse of some kind had been laid on him. He was superstitious, as most West Indians are.

"Would you rather not?" she said. There was in her voice an accent of contempt. That accent decided him. He had got to show her who the master was.

"Come along," he said.

The sight of them coming up the drive was a cause of unbounded relief to Denis Archer. Thank heavens, he thought, and hurried over. "You're very late," he began, then checked. From under the trees he had only noticed Boyeur, with his brown and white buck-skin shoes, and his chocolate colored pinstripe suit; he was vaguely conscious of a companion at his side, but he had taken no note of her. Now suddenly he saw her. He started, stared, and a shiver passed along his nerves. It was not the first time he had felt that shiver and he knew what it meant. Hell's bells, he thought; it was the last thing he had wanted to have happen here. Anyhow, with this kind of girl. Who on earth was she? It was the first time that he had seen her. He had thought that he knew everyone on the list.

"You're so late," he said, "that I was beginning to think I'd forgotten to invite you."

Boyeur laughed, a loud, self-confident laugh. "You need not have worried about that. I knew there was a party and if I hadn't received an invitation, I would have rung up to ask if there was some mistake."

"You would?"

"I should assume, naturally, that His Excellency would want me to this kind of party. I am sorry that I was late, but I have much work on my hands. I never know how I manage to get it done. By the way, you do know my cousin don't you, Margot Seaton?"

"No, I don't think I do."

Her hand was dry and cool; it had short lean fingers. At the same time the skin of her palm was very soft. Her clasp was firm. As they shook hands the bangles on her wrist shook together. Margot Seaton? The name meant nothing to him. He could not remember it upon the list. She was looking at him straight. Had she felt anything when that shiver passed along his nerves, or had it been only on his side? He turned to Boyeur.

"I know that your cousin will excuse us, but H. E. wishes you to meet Wilson Romer, an American newspaper proprietor. I'm sure Miss Seaton can look after herself. She must know everybody here."

"I shall be quite all right."

Her voice was deeper than he had expected, almost a contralto.

He led Boyeur across the lawn to the American, effected the introduction, started them talking, moved away.

He looked about him. Everything seemed to be going well. The more elderly who were seated had sorted themselves into strict color groups, white and near white, brown and black. Exactly what H. E. had dreaded, but how could it have been helped; nothing

16

anyhow could be done about it. You could not reorganize people once they had sat down; but as far as the standing and ambulatory groups were concerned, there was a sufficient mingling of color groups to impress the editor. There was a lot of noise. Everyone seemed happy.

He turned slowly round in search of anything that might be out of order, then he checked, conscious again of Margot Seaton. She had joined a group of youngish people; she was laughing and talking, but he had the sensation that she was watching him. He hesitated. Better not, he thought. Nothing but trouble lay along that road. Yet he knew himself too well not to know that when that kind of a shiver passed along his nerves he would have no peace of mind till he had learnt what it was all about. He walked across to her; as he approached, she moved away slightly from her group. So she had been watching for him. It had been on her side too, not only upon his. His heart began to pound. She took a step sideways, turning her back upon the group, so that he need not join in the general conversation; she gave him the impression that she knew what was in his mind, understood and welcomed it.

"How is it that I've not seen you anywhere around?" he asked.

"Probably because you buy your toothpaste at The Cosmos."

"What do I take that to mean?"

"I work in the Bon Marche."

"Oh." He did not know why it should surprise him, but it did.

"I'll change my patronage," he said.

"We'll appreciate that." She said it on a note of mockery; he felt very young. He could not think of anything to say.

"You're wondering what I'm doing here," she said.

"Well . . ."

"As a matter of fact, I haven't any right."

"How's that?"

"I wasn't invited. Mr. Boyeur dared me; he said it would be all right if I came in with him. I knew it wouldn't be. But I don't like being dared. So I came along."

"I see."

There was a pause. His heart was thudding, but he could not think of anything to say that would make sense.

"Next time I'll see you're properly invited."

"That's very good of you."

Her eyes never left his face. There was mockery in them still, but there was kindness too, as though she both liked him and were sorry for him. I must find something to say, he told himself.

Sharply across the noise of talk, silencing it, rang the first bugle

17

notes of "The Last Post." Dusk had fallen; the Union Jack was being lowered. Everyone stood to attention. As the last note sounded the Governor turned toward the house. It was the signal for the cocktail party to begin. Archer knew what his duty was. He had to get into that house before the Governor, to see that everything ran smoothly. "I'm sorry," he said, "but I've got to see that everything goes well in there."

"Of course you have." She said it as though he were a small boy afraid of being late for school.

From his vantage point on the terrace before the two small brass cannons that stood one on each side of the main entrance, the Governor watched his guests file through the French windows into the dining room. Although no alcohol had yet been served, they were chattering animatedly. They seemed to be having a good time; they wouldn't be having a good time unless they were happy coming here, and they wouldn't be happy coming here if their host wasn't a person whom they could trust. If they trusted him, he'd done half his job. The P.M.—a friend of long standing—had made it very clear to him why he had been chosen for the post.

"It is most important," he had said, "that we should have in Santa Marta someone whom the West Indians can like and trust; it's a help if that person has no ax to grind. They're touchy in these small places, they consider that in the past we've sent out second-grade administrators at the end of their careers, who want to avoid trouble at any cost, and finish with a K. You've got all the decorations that you want already. You couldn't get anything out of Santa for yourself. Then there's your cricket; the natives know about you. You've toured there with the M.C.C. They'll respect you before you start."

That was half a year ago. Having been here now three months, he felt that he had got his eye in. If trouble came, he would know how to deal with it.

As to the kind of trouble that might come, he had been carefully briefed by the Minister of State.

"Things are moving fast, possibly too fast," he had been told. "But nationalism is in the air. It's no use fighting it; we must work with it. Every colony wants Dominion status. We're committed under the Charter of the United Nations to a policy of developing backward peoples. In the past we've waited until our hand was forced, then yielded gracefully. That won't do any longer. We shall make mistakes, inevitably. But it's better that those mistakes should be the result of overconfidence than overcaution. As you know, we have agreed on universal suffrage for Santa Marta. They may not be ready for it, but it's something that must come. Better for it to come too early than too late. Then there's a new constitution drafted which will give a majority in the Council to the elected members; it's for you to decide how soon that can be implemented. But this is the point to keep in mind—move too fast rather than too slow."

It was the kind of advice that Templeton liked to follow; he had always believed in hitting a bowler off his length. Elections, the first since the introduction of universal suffrage, were shortly due, and the announcement of the new constitution a few weeks before would effectively illustrate the policy "too fast rather than too slow." Yes, he thought, as he watched his guests file amicably into his dining room, I've got the pace of the wicket now.

He was turning to join his guests, when a hand fell upon his elbow and a powerful transatlantic voice boomed in his ear.

"I appreciate more than I can say, Your Excellency, all you've done to make me feel at home here. I shall certainly carry back with me to America the warmest memories of your hospitality."

It was thirty-six hours since Wilson P. Romer had landed on the pier at Jamestown, and seven of those hours had been spent in the Governor's company, but Templeton could not yet think of him as an individual. He saw him as a type. In doing so, he was being, he readily admitted, imperceptive. But with a foreigner inevitably you noticed first only the divergences from your own norm. In Romer he marked the idiosyncrasies of dress and manner and appearance that stamped him as American; the pitch of his voice, the boyishness persisting into middle age, the neat well pressed suit of summer weight material, the nylon shirt, the "loafer" shoes, the gaudy tie. Romer was no doubt in the same way labeling him as typically English, recognizing the pattern, not seeing the individual beneath. With one's compatriots one did not notice the pattern, one saw the man as in himself he was. No, he thought, I've no idea what kind of a man Romer is. I like him, but I don't know what he's like.

"I saw you having a talk with our young revolutionary," he said. "How did he strike you?"

Romer shrugged. "Lord, that type! Young man fighting his way, no background, no idea where he wants to go. But has to amount to something. White or black, they're always the same. Wait ten years and see where they've got to, then they're interesting, for what they've done, or haven't. Up north we've Boyeurs on every bush. But there's one fellow here that does interest me—this Fleury."

19

"Which one, the son or father?"

"A fellow in the sixties."

"That would be the father. What struck you about him?"

"Couldn't place him. You said his family was the oldest one around here. When I was driving round the island someone pointed out his place, but he seems one hundred per cent English to me. Forty years in England, he says, married there, served in the first war in the British Army. How does all that add up?"

"I'll tell you."

Templeton was impressed. It was quick of Romer to have seen so much. The journalist's power of detection, he supposed.

"It's a curious story. This is the way it was," he said.

He outlined the Fleury saga. In many respects it was a typical West Indian story. The de Fleuries in the eighteenth century had been Plantagenets of the Caribbean, the French equivalents of the Warners and the Codringtons. After Waterloo, reluctant to return to a France so different from the one their ancestors had known, they changed their allegiance and anglicized their name. Then came emancipation and the slump in sugar. The Fleurys like so many others became absentee owners. Julian Fleury's great-grandfather bought a place in Devonshire.

"It was only a few miles from ours," the Governor said. "The friendship between our families was a close one. We were in each other's houses all the time. Julian was at Eton with me. I was half engaged to his elder sister. His wife is a distant cousin of mine."

"How did he happen to come back here?"

"That's what I'm coming to. His English estate was heavily hit by death duties when his father died. His West Indian properties weren't making the profits that he thought they should. His sisters were married to men without much money. The situation was disquieting. Julian came out here to see if his affairs were being handled properly. He brought his wife with him and his two younger children, leaving behind the elder son who was at school."

That had been in the early 1930's. Fleury had only meant to stay a year. But the slump had grown more acute, he had put off going back, first one year then the next; then there was the war making a return impossible. He never did go back.

"Well, isn't that something now, oldest family in the island and hadn't seen the place till he was over forty."

"Yes, in a sense, though actually he was born here."

"He was?"

"His father came out on a cricket tour, liked it, stayed on and married. But Julian's mother died in childbirth. His father brought

20

him back to England and remarried there. The sisters that I spoke of are half sisters."

"And the older boy? Is he still in England?"

"No, he was killed in the war."

"The last link cut then." Romer shook his head. "What about his wife? I haven't met her yet."

"She isn't here today. She's in Barbados. She seems to like it here."

"She does? I'm not surprised. One thing about your English women, they do seem able to adapt themselves. I'd like to talk with Fleury before I leave. By the way, will you point out his son to me before I go."

The son was by the buffet table. He had been one of the first inside. Standing by the bar he watched the other guests file through out of the garden. One of them almost certainly had smoked that Turkish cigarette. Everybody of any consequence was here. Anyone of sufficient importance to be smoking his own cigarette in the Fleury home would have been invited. The man who had smoked that cigarette must be known to him. Why hadn't he come up to him with some such remark as, "I was sorry to miss you this morning at your father's house." Why? For one reason only, the man hadn't wanted him to know. And on whose account other than Sylvia's. If the man was interested in Jocelyn and was unmarried, he would have wanted, surely, to make an ally of the brother; if the man was married, Sylvia would have made some comment to him. She'd have said, "I'm a little worried about Jocelyn. Frank's not right for her. It's not getting her anywhere." Something like that.

Why was he being kept in the dark? He looked about him angrily. Where was Sylvia? He had been watching her all the afternoon. Most of the time she had been in groups, either with Mavis, Jocelyn, or with Doris Kellaway. The fact that he had not once seen her talking with someone unexpected made him the more suspicious. She must be purposely avoiding the man whom she had seen that morning. Where was she now? Ah, yes, with Mavis and young Templeton.

He looked at his sister-in-law, thoughtfully. She was two years older than his wife, and every bit as pretty in a warm brown way, with soft rounded features and long-lashed eyelids over hazel eyes. At a first glance most people comparing her with Sylvia would have thought, So that's the serious one. Sylvia, blonde, animated, wearing more make-up than she needed, with crisp tight-set hair, looked trivial and charming, a girl who lived to be entertained. Actually it was the other way about.

It was Mavis who was frivolous and flighty, a birdlike creature, always involved in some flirtation. A few weeks ago she had been prostrate with a broken heart over a Canadian tourist who had left the island half engaged to her, only to announce six weeks later his imminent marriage in Montreal to his boss's daughter. Mavis had cried her eyes out then, but here she was now getting over her trouble quickly; its roots had not gone deep. She lived on the surface. As a wife she would be a friendly, affectionate companion: she wouldn't have moods, she wouldn't shrink away. Why couldn't he have fallen in love with her? She'd never be a problem to a man. She wouldn't tear a man's nerves with jealousy.

He moved over to their group. Why was it always he who had to join a group, to make the preliminary effort? No one ever came across to him. As he joined them, silence fell; the way it always did. It was always he who had to restart the conversation. "Are you as keen on cricket as your father was?" he asked.

A few yards away Julian Fleury stood beside Colonel Carson, the man whom His Excellency had described as a new kind of colonist. Carson was a man of forty; short, muscular, a little bloated, with a close-clipped mustache, who always wore a club or an old school tie. During the war, while he was in the Middle East, his wife had fallen in love with a Pole and he had made a complete break with his past. He worked hard on his estate and was making it pay, apparently. He was not a man for whom Fleury cared particularly. He was obtuse and self-assertive but at the same time there were subjects that he could discuss with Carson that he could not with anybody else. They had been born into the same kind of world.

They were discussing, as were so many others, the Governor's son's visit to the island.

"What a time for all these fillies," Carson was remarking. "The rivalries there'll be. How many of them will still be on speaking terms with one another by the time he leaves."

It was said in the patronizing tone that provided Fleury with one of his reasons for not completely liking Carson. But Carson was dead right. He had noticed in his daughter a mounting sense of excitement. All the girls were building daydreams about Euan Templeton. What else could be expected; there was a dearth of men. There weren't half a dozen of the old white families still resident in Santa Marta, and the livelier young men invariably sought their fortunes in the larger islands, went north to Canada or home to England. It was a problem that had been worrying him on Jocelyn's account for several months. Who was there for her to marry? He ought to send her back to England, to her aunt or cousins. He had talked it over with his wife more than once. Betty had not been enthusiastic. "Do you think they'd welcome her?" she had said. Then there was the cost. The estate wasn't making the profits that it should.

"I'm thinking of opening a book," Carson was continuing. "Four to one against Mavis Norman, six to one against Doris Kellaway. What odds are you taking on your daughter?"

By the buffet table the Governor, momentarily alone again, took a slow look round the room. Everything was going well. The right amount of noise, but not too much of it; the party had not split up into racial groups. Mr. Romer should be impressed. Euan looked happy. He had kept an eye on him; he had felt very proud of him, watching him move from group to group. Euan had grown up a lot during these last two years. He had a new manliness, a new assurance. They'd have more in common with one another now. He reminded himself that his subalterns had always thought of him as a kind of uncle.

His eye moved on. Was there anything he had overlooked, any professional aspect of the occasion that he had missed? Yes, he remembered now; something he had wanted to ask Fleury. He went across, detaching him from Carson.

"How well do you know Preston?"

"Not intimately."

"Well enough to drop in upon him casually?"

"Yes, certainly."

"Good."

Preston was another postwar colonist, a man in his middle thirties, of simple origin, an articled clerk before the war who had reached the rank of major in the R.A.O.C. through his familiarity with balance sheets. In that capacity he had met in the Middle East and married a W.A.A.F. who was definitely "county"; seeing few prospects for himself in England, he had invested his war gratuity and his father's life insurance in a plantation here. At one point his boundaries touched Fleury's.

"You know that there's been trouble on his place?" the Governor said.

"I've a rough idea about it." It was a typical village squabble. Some cattle of Preston's had escaped through a gap in a fence onto a neighboring estate, a colored man's, and trampled down some sugar cane. Preston had admitted the trespass, but there had been an argument as to the amount of compensation. The case had been brought before the magistrate, Graham, a white government official, who had fined Preston fifteen dollars. Preston on grounds of principle had appealed against this verdict.

"I'd like you to have a chat with Preston, and let him air his grievances," the Governor said. "Graham wants to avoid trouble. I've talked to Whittingham and he agrees with Graham. 'Keep them happy, let them think they are running their own show, but keep the reins within your hands.' That's what he says. A typical policeman's point of view. I see their point, but Graham and Whittingham have been here all their lives; they don't want trouble. Appeasement's their line, and it isn't mine. They may be right, in this case; I don't know. If I chose to put in a word with Preston, I could stop the appeal, but I won't unless I'm sure he's being tiresome. If you'd give me your angle on the case, I'd be grateful."

"I'll do that certainly."

"There's no hurry. The law's delays. The appeal won't be heard for at least two weeks."

"I'm going out one day next week."

"Fine." He paused. He laid his hand upon Fleury's shoulder. "I can't tell you what it means to me to have you here. Somebody I know and trust. One never forgets one's early hero worships, you were my first captain; you gave me my school colors. I shall never forget your saying to me after that Winchester game when I'd missed that easy catch, 'Don't worry, Jimmy, you'll get a century at Lord's.'"

Fleury smiled. He himself had forgotten the incident altogether till Templeton on his arrival had reminded him. He had given half a dozen "colors" during his year's captaincy. Yet he remembered vividly being given his own colors and still retained a veneration for his captain; though he was now an obscure solicitor in a small West country village, he still thought of him as his senior because he had been a prefect when he himself was a fifth former.

"We must have you all up to dinner one day soon," Templeton was continuing. "The others can play bridge and we can talk about old days. I'll get Archer to fix it; where is that A.D.C.? Oh, there he is bringing our editor across; I'll leave you to him."

Fleury had had one session already with Romer, and he was in no spirit for a second, but there was, he saw well, no hope of avoiding it. Romer was advancing on him with an air of purpose.

"I think I've got it straight," he was saying. "Let me see. This island is under the control of a governor, who is himself under instructions from Whitehall. The governor is advised by his legislative council and all legislation has to be passed by that legislative council."

As he spoke, he watched Fleury closely, seeing him in the light of what the Governor had told him. He was looking at a man of sixty, tall, thin, bald; with a sallow skin, thin lips, a thin pointed nose, and a short clipped gray mustache; Fleury's face was lined and tired, but it had an air of authority, self-confidence, and breeding. This is the kind of Englishman that I've read about, Romer thought. The man nobody sees, who's behind the scenes. Never shows himself in public, carries on with his job as a private citizen. Yet in a way we can't understand in America, he influences everything that happens: he has position and prestige with the big men, don't ask me how. They need him on their side, and can't get far without him. Just the man to know what's cooking in a place.

"That's right now, isn't it?" he asked.

"That's right."

"There's another concern called the executive council which carries out the laws passed by the legislative council, but can't pass any laws itself."

"That's right."

"And the legislative is composed of six members nominated by the Governor and six members elected by the people. The Governor has a casting vote, so G.H. runs the island."

"That's so."

"And there was a limited suffrage wasn't there."

"At the last election there was a literacy test and an income test."

"So that up to the present this has been an oligarchy."

"You could call it that."

"But I have heard some talk about a new constitution."

"I've heard about it too."

"From what I've heard, under this constitution and with universal suffrage there will be nine elected members on the council, so that through their elected members the people will control the island. That's so, isn't it?"

"I'm not sure of the exact facts about the new constitution, but that is roughly what I've heard."

"If that's the way it is, then sir, it's what I call democracy."

Fleury smiled. Democracy; he had heard that word so often since President Wilson had talked about making the world safe for it. All that talk in the second war about democratic principles. Russia had been called a democracy then, and so had China. What more did democracy mean in the long run than that a different group of professional politicians achieved their personal ends behind a different cover? In England and America the word might, the word did, have a significance, but what could it mean here to the laborers in the cane fields; they followed a herd instinct. The new constitution would look fine on paper, but its passing would only make it more difficult for those who recognized the islanders' real needs to get those needs fulfilled.

"Do you think His Excellency will promulgate this new constitution?" Romer was inquiring.

"I've no idea."

"He'd certainly be setting this part of the world a fine example if he did. Will he meet opposition?"

"I fancy so."

"Who from?"

"From several sections. It's not only the white planters who are afraid of letting these people have their heads too soon. Many responsible colored men are nervous too, the lawyers, the officials, the police."

"But surely, Mr. Fleury . . ."

Fleury interrupted him. It was late and he was tired; he had had a long and trying morning going over the estate accounts with Maxwell. He had had enough of being tactful. He said without violence, in a calm level voice, exactly what he thought.

"You've got to remember the background and history of these peoples. They were taken from their own countries and shipped here as slaves; they came from different parts of Africa, they are a mingling of different tribes and races. They had only one thing in common, a sense of bitter injustice against their masters. That sense has never died. A great crime was committed. And it is not only the victims of a crime that suffer. Its perpetrators do as well. The planters had a deep-rooted sense of guilt which made them vindictive first toward their slaves, afterward toward their laborers. They were frightened. They were so few, the slaves were many. All through the eighteenth century there were slave revolts. There were revolts even after emancipation. And emancipation is only a hundred years old. Two and a half centuries of an organized slave trade preceded it. The hatred, the fear, the longing for revenge still simmers underneath the surface. You can't tell at what point they will explode. There've been troubles all down these islands since they were first colonized. I'm not saying that they're serious outbursts nowadays, but property is destroyed and lives are lost. You can never tell where the explosion will come; the slightest thing will set it off, here, or in Grenada, or St. Kitts. But I'll tell you how

26

I feel, how a large section of us feel right through the islands. That we're sitting on a keg of dynamite."

He spoke quietly; and because he spoke quietly, Romer was impressed. Romer made no reply. But his brow was furrowed. An idea had struck him. It might be a good plan to have a man down here, to be on the spot when the keg of dynamite exploded.

# CHAPTER TWO

*1*

By ten past seven the last guest had been bowed out of Government House, but the party was still alive in the form of scattered groups. Rum swizzles and whisky sodas had only been served for an hour. West Indians need two hours of sundowners before they are ready for the dinner which will be succeeded by an almost immediate retiring to sleep and Jamestown possessed five establishments where conviviality could be continued.

Each establishment had a distinct and separate personality. There were two hotels, the St. James and the Continental. The St. James was patronized exclusively by whites: its bar did good business, but its rooms were often vacant and its dining room was like a mausoleum. It owed its prosperity, such as it was, to outside catering. It provided picnic lunches, wedding teas, and canapes for cocktail parties, and it sold wine and spirits by the case to selected customers at a lower rate than they would have had to pay by the bottle at the stores.

The Continental was much livelier and catered for all sections of the community. Visitors needed to book rooms in advance. Planters patronized the bar, usually without their wives. There was no formal dining room. Breakfasts were served in the lounge. At lunch and in the evening, snack meals could be had at the bar, on a buffet system. Most of the Continental's regular clientele were in low income brackets and took their meals with their friends and relatives.

In addition there were three clubs. The Jamestown was for men only, and no color line was drawn. It was in the center of the town, near the Fleury house, and had been built at the same time. Red brick, red tiled, rectangular, a relic of colonial France, it had been furnished with taste from the auctions of many estate houses. There was old mahogany and silver, its walls were decorated with eighteenth century prints of the Antilles; it had a bar, a billiard table, a writing and a dining room. It was crowded before lunch and lunches were served if ordered three hours in advance. Most of the business of the town was transacted there informally. It was less frequented in the evening and it closed at nine. No dinners were served. Its members were usually to be found after work with their

28

wives and families either at the Country Club, which owned two tennis courts, a croquet lawn, and a card room, and to which no one was admitted who could not pass as white, or at the Aquatic Club which was on the shore a mile out of town and to which no one who was not definitely dark could be elected.

In accordance with their separate positions in the social hierarchy, the guests at the Governor's cocktail party dispersed themselves among these institutions.

The Fleurys went to the Country Club. As they came onto the porch, Sylvia hesitated; a year ago she would have gone to the end of the veranda with Jocelyn and Mavis, to form a rallying point for the younger set. But as a married woman her place was in the bridge room or the matron's circle. She had felt very grown up and grand, the first time she had said, "I'll leave you children to discuss your beaux, me I'm for bridge." By the calendar Mavis was the elder by two years, but in experience she had been ten years older and it had amused Sylvia to have now a senior status. But that was twelve months ago; she would have given a lot now to have joined in the gossip about Euan Templeton with Jocelyn and her sister. But the end of the veranda was, on a night like this, no place for her.

She paused beside a cluster of middle-aged married people. Mrs. Hartley, the wife of the electrical adviser, was raising her voice in resentful, grumbling self-pity. She was a recent addition to the community. Her husband with three other technicians had been brought out from England on a short term contract to advise and assist local labor. The men had proved successes but their wives had been a problem, in particular Mrs. Hartley. Her house was three miles out and her husband usually had the car.

"Morning after morning, it's the same," she said, "no one drops in to see me. There isn't anyone to drop in and see me. I don't know what to do with myself. I'm used to neighbors. What does one find to do? At home I was always busy. I enjoyed the shopping, gossiping in a queue, wondering what you'd find at the counter when you reached it; shopping's so awkward here, doing all the buying from one shop, not knowing how it'll work out. In England you knew exactly where you were, you had your ration book, you knew what each thing cost, and how much of it you could have. But here where you can buy all you want ... No really, I can't get used to it."

It was the kind of conversation Sylvia had made fun of twelve months ago. "Wives' talk" they had called it, she and Jocelyn. Now she was a wife herself. She turned into the card room. She did not particularly care for bridge, but it had the merit of being a silent game.

From her seat at the bridge table she could see the girls at the far end of the veranda. She could imagine their conversation. Mavis and Jocelyn had been joined by Doris Kellaway, the daughter of one of the chief sugar planters who had recently been co-opted to take Sylvia's place. Doris was dark-haired, pale skinned: her genealogy obviously included an African ancestor, but in Santa Marta the phrase "passes for white" had supplanted the denigrating "touch of the tarbrush." She was pretty in a neat, trim way. She was only nine-teen and had been flutteringly excited at becoming "an inseparable." Mavis for years had been the object for Doris of a schoolgirl crush. Doris thought her marvelous. No wonder the men fell in love with her. She wanted to dress like Mavis, talk like Mavis, live like Mavis. From fifteen on, she had daydreams about Mavis, picturing scenes in which she would save her life, in which Mavis would be in desperate trouble from which she alone could rescue her. She could still hardly believe that she was an associate of Mavis'. Sometimes she would sit in entranced silence in awe of her own position. At other times she talked too much.

She was talking too much now.

"We're in for the time of our lives," she was asserting. "Think of all the parties there'll be given for him. H.E.'ll have to exert him-self. Did you notice Euan's tie, and the material of his suit? I've never seen one like it. It looked like shot silk. And he's so good-looking."

"I wouldn't say good-looking. I'd say nice-looking," Mavis inter-rupted.

They discussed what he was like inside himself. They compared what he had said to each.

"He asked me how we spent the day here, what our routine was," Jocelyn said.

"I did better than that," said Doris. "He said he was delighted that there were so many pretty girls."

"Girls, in the plural? I don't think you did so well. He wanted to know what I did, me myself."

"Did he ask you to do anything?"

"As a matter of fact he did. He asked me to arrange a bathing party for tomorrow."

"He did? Then that's why he didn't ask any of us. He knew he would be seeing us tomorrow."

"How did he know that? He didn't know that I'd be asking you."

"He must have had the sense to know that we wouldn't let you take him out without us, as early as this anyhow."

They laughed in unison. They might be "the inseparables," but they were rivals.

"Who shall we take along with us?" Jocelyn asked. "That A.D.C.?"

There was a pause; a dubious pause. No one was completely ready to say exactly what she thought about the A.D.C.

"I suppose he's all right really," Doris said.

"I suppose he is."

There was another pause. The ground had been broken and they were almost ready to say what they really thought. "I wouldn't say he was actually wet," said Doris.

"Nor'd I, though he does write poetry."

"What is there that we don't like about him?"

"I wouldn't use the word 'like'; 'trust' is the word I'd use."

"You've got something there."

"He's a dark horse."

"I wouldn't mind that if I knew . . ." Mavis hesitated. "He never looks at one in a very interested way. At the same time . . ." again she hesitated. "All the same I don't think he is, do you?"

She was shy of using an actual definition, but they all knew what she meant. They shook their heads.

"If he was, one would know where one was. But I'm sure he's not," said Mavis.

He had them puzzled. He had been here for three months. He had been cordial, gracious, but he had shown no preference.

"I suppose we shall have to ask him."

"I suppose we shall."

It was the conclusion to which they were invariably forced when they planned a party. This lamentable lack of men.

"What about Grainger Morris?" Jocelyn asked. "He and Euan Templeton know each other."

Again there was a pause. Each knew exactly what was in the others' minds. Color was not a topic that they discussed. It was a point on which they were subject to their parents' ruling. They talked in shorthand. "I don't see why we shouldn't ask him to a beach party," Mavis said.

"I don't see either."

"Perhaps it would be better if we asked Euan to ask him. We could say we don't know Grainger very well."

"We might do that."

They could not ask him to the tennis club. He could not ask them to the Aquatic. They could not ask him to their houses without asking their parents which they would not want to do, but there was something conveniently noncommittal about a picnic party on a neutral beach. "It's all very silly," Doris said.

They nodded in agreement. They did not say what it was they all thought silly. But it was, each one conceded, ridiculous in a high degree.

From his station at the bar, Maxwell Fleury could see his wife's face in profile. He watched her as she gathered up her hand, as she sorted out the suits, as she played the cards. No change of expression crossed her face. He could not tell if she was winning or if she was losing, if she was picking up good hands or bad. How could he, how could anyone, tell what she was thinking? Was she, even as she played her hand, reliving that morning hour with the man who had smoked a Turkish cigarette in his father's drawing room? Who had it been?

He rested the back of his hand against his head. He had been through too much today. He had come into town the night before so that he and his father could go over the estate accounts. The price of copra was going up, but the profits remained stationary. No one could understand it, there had to be a check up. But as so often happens on a first night in town he had taken too many swizzles at the club. He had woken in no mood for figures. He had talked to his father of contributory factors, the atmosphere of impending change under the influence of this new Governor, with upstarts like David Boyeur threatening you with strikes, with the peasants robbing you and the police backing them. His father had listened in his courteous patient way. "Yes," he had said. "Yes, yes," and then he had asked questions that had shown very clearly that he was not interested in vague theories, but was concerned with the tangible entries of a balance sheet.

Pestered by precise questions, with his head aching, how could he provide the answers that would satisfy his father. His father nodded, "I see," he had said, "I see." But he had not seen. How could he when the answers were so nebulous? He holds me to blame, naturally, and no doubt he's right. A black mood of mingled self-pity and self-contempt was on him. It was his fault that the estate was running at a loss. What good was he at anything? He couldn't even make his own wife love him. Was it his fault though? What chance had he ever had? He'd been brought out here at the age of four, sent to school with a lot of colored brats whom he'd so despised that he couldn't be bothered to set himself in competition with them. The colored teachers had exaggerated his mistakes; anxious to appear superior to a white boy. No one had taken any interest in him. No one had inspired him. His father had always said, "Don't worry. We'll be going back to England soon. You'll find it an advantage then to have seen something of the world."

He had tried to be patient when he had been forced to listen to accounts of how well his brother was doing, first at Eton, afterwards at Oxford. It was Arthur, Arthur, Arthur all the time. That was all his father cared about, how the elder son, the apple of his eye, was doing.

He had tried to be patient. One day he'd show them. He'd counted the months till he could go to Eton. September 1940. That's when his chance would come. September 1940, indeed. He laughed bitterly, ruefully. When that day had come, who was bothering about him. The war was all that mattered; and with the Caribbean infested with submarines it had been impossible to send him even to Barbados. He'd had to make do with the high school here. No wonder people compared him to his disadvantage with his family.

He knew what people said about him. "Fancy Julian Fleury having a son like that." Everyone admired his father. At the club, at every party, his father was the center of a group, not only of his contemporaries, but the younger people. They asked his advice. They listened to his anecdotes. Everyone kept telling him how marvelous his father was. Well, and why shouldn't he be? He had had every chance, had money spent on him, been sent to the best school, allowed to meet the most amusing people. No wonder his father was thought marvelous; no wonder Arthur had been too. Arthur had had every break: stayed on in England, gone to Eton. He hadn't been dragged up in this dreary island, taught by a half-caste in a class of nigger boys; in retrospect Arthur was a hero, naturally: but even when he was a schoolboy, when he had been an undergraduate, glowing reports about him had come back to Santa Marta, how charming he was, how modestly he bore his successes. The record of his achievements stood in black and white.

In comparison what had he to offer. Nothing. Nothing. He had done nothing; he was nothing. He had no polish, no real education. He had made no friends because he had not met the kind of man with whom he could be friends. He had been robbed of his inheritance. No wonder the profits dropped; no wonder Sylvia despised him.

At his side the familiar topics were being discussed: the price of copra, sugar, cocoa: the prospects of the West Indian cricketers beating the M.C.C., the political situation, the coming elections, the chances of West Indian Federation. Carson was holding forth.

"I'm not in a position to judge, I know. I've only been here three years. But the newcomer sees things with new eyes. What I'm wondering is this. Wouldn't it be a good thing if you tried playing these fellows at their own game?"

He spoke with a thick, full voice, slowly articulating every syllable. There were those who found him pompous, but to Maxwell he was a hero. He was everything that Maxwell wished he was himself. He admired Carson's county accent, the way he wore his clothes, the way in which he held an audience: to have all these men listening to him, and to be able to talk so slowly, to have the confidence that no one would interrupt.

"Why don't more of you fellows go into politics yourselves," he was continuing. "Until now you've had a majority in the Leg. Co. through nominated members, but you won't much longer from what I hear; the elected members will be outnumbering you; why don't you take up the challenge, fight these fellows at the polls, show the voters that you are cleverer than their Boyeurs."

He paused. He looked round the circle. His eye fell on Maxwell. "A young chap like you now. Why don't you stand in your own district. Your name means a lot there. You'd probably get in."

Maxwell flushed, flattered and excited at being thus singled out by a man he so much admired, and before all these others. The idea fired his brain. Why shouldn't he? Why in hell's name shouldn't he? He was a Fleury, wasn't he? This was his chance to show them.

2

Most of the guests at the party were distributed between the three clubs and the two hotels. Not all however.

At the Carlton cinema David Boyeur and Margot Seaton were about to watch from the most expensive seats the first showing in Santa Marta of *Christopher Columbus*. There were still five minutes to pass before the picture started. Boyeur was in high spirits. He had been made much of at the party. The Governor had shown him honor. The American editor had listened to his views. He had noticed Grainger Morris talking to two white girls. He had joined the group and the girls had been polite; no edging away. A triumphant evening.

He had also felt proud of Margot. He had kept his eye on her, and her poise had pleased him. She had never looked lost. She had never been unattended. He had been alarmed when she had called his bluff. He need not have been. She could hold her own.

"If anyone had told me that first evening I danced with you at Carnival that within three years you'd be a guest at Government House, I'd have roared with laughter."

"Would you. I shouldn't have."

"What?"

"Would you have been surprised if you had been told then that you'd be there today?"

"Heavens no, I've always known that I'd be in the big time soon."

"Maybe I've known it too, about myself."

"You?" He stared at her. She still looked to him the child who at that first dance had set his every sense alight. She was smiling, ironically.

"I was never quite as simple as you thought," she said.

He looked at her thoughtfully. Perhaps she hadn't been. Perhaps that was why she had laid so firm a hold on him, a hold he had not resented, that he had made no attempt to break. He saw her with new eyes. Not simply as a plaything to amuse his leisure. She could be more than that; a credit to him; an asset in his career. They'd make a good team, he and she. Why hadn't he realized that before?

"This is a strange place to be saying it," he said. "But I think we should be getting married soon."

He had expected to hear a gasp of surprised delight. He did not. She turned her head slowly and looked him in the face.

"I've never thought of you in terms of marriage," she replied.

"Then you can start thinking now."

She shook her head. "That wouldn't be at all a good idea."

"Now listen . . ."

The lights went off and the room was filled with the noise of music. A series of advertisements was flashed upon the screen. On all sides of them the audience chattered on with unabated animation. Boyeur alone was speechless. To have been turned down: for David Boyeur to have been rejected, and by a girl with whom he had been going steadily for thirty months! It was unthinkable. She must be joking.

He took her hand. It lay limp in his; there was no electricity in her fingers; they might not have belonged to her. An advertisement of a thermos flask appeared on the screen.

"I've thought of getting one of those," she said.

The subject of their marriage might never have been brought up. He felt indignant. She couldn't get away with this. He moved her hand sideways onto her lap. He pressed the back of his hand against her leg; she made no movement. He loosed his hold upon her fingers and let the palm of his hand rest upon her knee. He began to stroke her leg.

"Stop that," she said.

He took no notice. His touch became more firm. He'd teach her. He'd subjugate her, through her senses; as he had before. She might be able to outtalk him, but here he held the mastery. His hand moved upward.

"If you don't stop that, I'll leave."

Again he took no notice. His hand advanced. Its pressure tightened.

"Very well."

It happened so quickly that he did not realize that it was happening. She was on her feet: they were two seats from the aisle. Without fuss or hurry, she edged past the couple in her way. At her normal slow pace of walking, she left the hall.

His eyes followed her through the dusk. It was incredible. Had many people noticed her? His vanity prevented him from hurrying after her. He could not face a scene. David Boyeur quarreling in public with his girl friend; he would look ridiculous. There was nothing for him to do but to sit on and pretend nothing had happened. He would tell anyone who made inquiries that she had a headache.

### 3

Mr. Romer's liner sailed at half-past nine. The Governor had urged him to stay on to dinner, but he had refused. He had a sense of timing. It would be a hurried, interrupted meal; far better to leave in the warm afterglow of a cocktail party. Templeton drove him to the dock, where the government launch was waiting. The engineer saluted.

"I'm very sorry sir, something the matter with the engine. Nothing serious; it won't take a minute."

"Perhaps we had better take a boat."

"Oh no, sir, I assure you. Two minutes at the most."

They stood on the dock, Romer, Templeton, and Euan, while the sailor fiddled with the engine.

"A watched pot never boils," said Templeton.

Silence supervened. During the drive down the hill they had said all they had to say. Romer's timing was so exact that he was now speechless. The silence became awkward.

"This reminds me of an occasion . . ." Templeton began.

As he repeated the anecdote, he remembered the advice given him at the staff college many years ago. "The press is a great nuisance but it exists and you must co-operate; it can do you a great deal of damage: if you are in any doubt as to how much to tell, tell too much rather than too little. Journalists have chips upon their shoulders. They are grateful to the man who trusts them." Why not tell this fellow the advice he had been given by the Minister, take him into his confidence, tell him that he'd probably be implementing this new constitution in a week or two? It might pay a dividend.

"I've been most interested in your reactions to all you've seen today," he started. "The Caribbean is as much an American as a British problem. You look on it from a different angle, in terms of the Monroe Doctrine: that's why—" But at that point the engine sputtered into life, and the engineer saluted.

"That's that," said Templeton as the launch sped across the harbor to the anchored liner. He looked at his son thoughtfully. It was nearly two years since they had met. Euan had then been a freshly gazetted subaltern, on his overseas leave, full of inquiries about the Middle East. He had barely ceased to be a schoolboy. Now he was a man. He had exercised authority, assumed responsibility, faced danger. He must be a different person, yet he looked the same. I must remember that, the Governor warned himself. I mustn't treat him as a schoolboy.

"What did you make of it?" he asked.

"Fine. I enjoyed it."

"How did they strike you?"

"They were all very friendly."

"You don't think you'll be bored here?"

"Heavens, no!"

"I'm kept pretty hard at work. You'll have to rely on your own devices."

"I shan't find that difficult."

Euan said it with a smile; as though he were smiling to himself, at his own thoughts. What were those thoughts, his father asked himself? What had he himself felt when he was twenty-one? It was hard to put oneself back. Besides, his own case had been different. It had been in wartime. For him those years had been cut up into arbitrary divisions; his leaves, his periods in the line; he'd been wounded twice: there had been the weeks in hospitals, then the periods of recuperation at the depot. He had never had a holiday. What would he have wanted if he had? The same things, presumably, that he had wanted on his leaves—cricket and a girl to take out dancing. Euan probably wasn't so very different.

"Which of the girls did you find the most attractive?" he inquired.

"I'll be able to answer that question better tomorrow evening. Jocelyn Fleury's fixing up a bathing party."

"You should enjoy that."

The car swung round into the Government House courtyard.

"Dinner's at eight; we won't bother to change. What sort of cocktail would you like?"

"Shall we be having wine at dinner?"

"Of course."

"Then I'll wait till then."

"A sensible decision."

Archer was waiting in the hallway. "Any instructions, sir?"

"No, no, thank you. The party went very well I thought."

"I'm glad you did, sir. I think Mr. Romer saw everyone he needed to."

"Splendid. You managed very well. Euan and I won't be having cocktails, but help yourself to anything you'd like."

"Thank you, sir, thank you very much."

It would be much pleasanter, Archer thought, now that young Templeton was here and there'd be no more tête-à-tête dinners with H.E. His employer on the other hand was thinking, Dinner *à trois*. I wonder how much I really shall see of Euan during these six months.

### 4

The dinner *à trois* was on the whole a cheerful one. It was nearly finished when Euan was summoned to the telephone.

"You won't remember who I am," a feminine voice with a slight West Indian accent was informing him, "but you met me this afternoon. I was wearing a hat that wasn't really a hat at all; a posy of sham flowers kept in place by invisible elastic."

"I remember it very well. You were wearing a mauve scarf and a wide belt matching it and your name's Mavis Norman."

"Now I *am* flattered."

"But we talked for at least four minutes."

"There are several four-minute sessions in an hour; I'm flattered, very, and it makes what I was going to ask easier. It's about Grainger Morris; you're good friends, aren't you?"

"You bet we are."

"That's what we thought. The point is this: we'd like to ask him to this bathing party, but we don't know him very well, he might think us forward, we wondered if you wouldn't ask him for us. It might be better if the invitation came from you."

"I'd be delighted to."

"Good. You fix it up with him and we'll rendezvous at four at the Continental."

She rang off so quickly that he had not time to realize he was surprised.

"Wasn't that rather odd?" he asked his father. "Why didn't Jocelyn ring him up direct, or failing that why didn't she ring me up? It's her party. I don't see why Mavis Norman should be calling me."

His father smiled. He could think of at least one reason. It was a group decision of the girls; they wanted to disarm their parents with the half lie that Euan had invited Grainger. They would also be more punctilious with a colored man than they would be with a white, they would be afraid of "giving him ideas," so they'd tossed as to who should take on the chore. The issue turned, he was very sure, on color, but he did not want to suggest that to his son. Euan would have a far better time in Santa Marta if he did not become color conscious. Moreover he might be wrong and he did not want to invite the criticism that he saw everything in terms of color.

"I can think of several reasons," he said, "but I'll suggest this one— that you made an impression on Mavis Norman and she was curious to find out whether she had made one on you."

"Do you think that's likely?"

"Can you think of a likelier explanation?"

Euan did not want to think of one. Here perhaps was the recompense for those arid months in Suez? Mavis Norman had not made a vivid impression on him. She had seemed an agreeable, nice-looking girl and that was all. But now, in terms of her newly discovered interest in himself, he saw her with new eyes. He remembered that she had long eyelashes and a firm supple figure, that she walked with a smooth easy grace. He would not find it difficult to fall in love with her, if she showed a disposition to be courted. "I'd better ring up Grainger right away," he said. "Would I find him at home?"

"Almost certainly."

5

Grainger Morris lived with his parents in a section of Jamestown that had been fashionable before motor cars had come into general use. Now the rich planters and officials had moved farther out to a neat collection of houses set along a bay on the windward coast, while the bungalows on the lower slope of *Trois Frères*, the three-peaked mountain that made of Jamestown the stage of an Attic amphitheater, had been taken over by the better-class colored families. The Morrises were one of these. As a family, apart from Grainger they were typical of their day and origin.

The father, as part owner of the Bon Marche and one of the directors of the Carlton Cinema, was a man of a certain substance, but he was shy, retiring, had taken no part in public life, and was not invited to G.H. more than once a year. Grainger had three brothers and two sisters, all except one sister younger than himself. His elder sister who looked likely to remain unmarried was one of the chief nurses at the hospital; his younger sister Muriel was just seventeen, she was pretty and gay and likely to become a problem. The youngest brother was only twelve. Neither of his older brothers looked likely to make anything particular of their lives. They lacked drive.

After the Governor's party Grainger had gone to the Aquatic Club, but he had only stayed ten minutes. It was gay enough with a number of the younger set splashing in the water and the veranda crowded with chattering groups; the moon was three-quarters full; fireflies were hovering above the crotons; shadowy on the horizon across thirty miles of water was the cone-shaped outline of an island; but the contrast between the atmosphere of Government House and that of the club depressed him. It reminded him of how rigid still was the barrier between black and white.

His family had finished their evening meal when he arrived. "I've kept some soup hot for you," his mother said.

He shook his head. He had taken a good deal of nourishment at the party. He was in no temper to sit at table and make conversation. He wanted to be alone with his own thoughts: to sit on the veranda, looking out over the harbor, his mind abroad. In his study briefs that should be attended to were awaiting him, but he was in no mood for work. He would set his alarm clock for half-past four, and come fresh to them next morning.

He had been home five months now, but he had not realized until tonight to what extent those seven years in England had spoilt him for life here in the island of his birth. He had been as a child brought up to accept the fact of color, as something that separated him from the members of the Country Club, in the same way that in feudal times the son of an English peasant had accepted that the fact

40

of rank divided him from the squire and the doctor. He had accepted the fact, and it had not worried him.

In England, however, where nearly everyone was white, his dark skin had been disregarded. The English with their innate sense of superiority might be accused of classing alike as "dagoes" Italians, Spaniards, Indians, Africans, but he did not believe that he would have had any better time at Oxford if he had been white. Ceylonese, Iraqis, Chinese, Afghans had all been treated there on their deserts. As a rugger and a cricket blue, he had met his contemporaries upon equal terms. He had been a member of Vincent's. He had been president of the Union. He had met girls from Somerville at cocktail parties. Afterward they had gone on in groups, sometimes in couples, to dine at the Mitre or the George. There had been no awkwardness, no embarrassment. How different it was here.

This afternoon under the aegis of Government House there had been a general amnesty; everyone had talked to everyone; he had spent half his time with Jocelyn Fleury and with Mavis Norman; they had been open, friendly, and forthcoming. But had not they looked a little surprised at the warmth with which young Templeton had welcomed him? Had such an unexpected meeting of old friends taken place at a London cocktail party, the four of them would have teamed up and gone on to dinner. It was very different here, with one group going to the Aquatic, and another to the Country Club; probably next time he met Mavis Norman, though she might wave to him she would not stop to speak. There were two camps. He was in the other.

The breeze was warm upon his cheeks. It was scented with the small white flower of the night. The moon was high above *Trois Frères*, silvering the palm fronds and the ragged leaves of the banana, the frogs were croaking in the bushes, the lights of the town twinkled round the *carenage;* the honking taxi horns were faint. How often in chill bleak England, shivering over a stuttering gas fire, had he not felt homesick for those scents and sights and sounds, how often, on a winter evening, had he not wished himself back here upon this veranda; but now that he was here, with all this beauty spread before his eyes, his heart was heavy, he was homesick for England's freedom. His seven years there had spoilt him for this pigeonholed society; would he ever be able to adapt himself to this, having once known that?

"Telephone, Grainger."

It was his brother calling from the living room. He hurried to answer it. "Yes, this is Grainger Morris."

41

"It's me, Euan. Listen, are you doing anything tomorrow in the late afternoon?"

"Nothing that matters."

"That's fine. Then you can come out swimming with some girls."

"What girls?"

"Mavis Norman, Jocelyn Fleury and I don't know who else, that bunch that was up today."

"Now wait a moment, I must think. . . ."

He must think very fast. Those girls would not want to meet him on such terms. Euan had rushed them into it, or very likely he hadn't yet consulted them. It was the kind of mistake that visitors to the islands kept on making. They met members of different groups, then they gave a party and mixed up in one room people who for generations had tacitly and friendlily agreed not to meet one another and with whom they did not want to make social contacts that would subsequently embarrass them. He had often heard his father say, "It's all very well for these tourists; they go away but we have to go on living here." He must save Euan from that mistake.

"I'm sorry, but a bathing party's not quite my line. I thought you meant a quiet gossip in the Jamestown Club."

"We can have a gossip on the beach; you needn't swim, you can sunbathe if you like."

Euan was persistent but Grainger remained adamant. Finally Euan yielded. "I'm disappointed. So'll the girls be, they just rang up to ask me to persuade you."

"*They* rang *you* up? Who rang you up?"

"Mavis Norman. She thought I would have more influence with you than she would. She guessed wrong."

"But if she rang up . . ." He checked. It made all the difference if the girls had rung up Euan. Perhaps he had been fancying things; perhaps color had come to matter less here, in the same way that rank was ceasing to count in England. Perhaps it was only the old people who continued the old prejudices. If that were the case it would be churlish of him, it would be ridiculous of him to refuse. "I'll do my best," he said. "I can't promise definitely until tomorrow, but I'll do my best."

In a very different mood he returned to his chair on the veranda. Perhaps he had been wrong about Santa Marta. It might not be the same place that it had before the war. Ideas had changed, and when the younger generation took their parents' place, the island would become as liberal as England was.

42

# CHAPTER THREE

## 1

Santa Martans as a rule retire early: they rise at daybreak and it is rare for them to stay up long enough to hear the BBC news at ten. Within a few minutes of rising from the dinner table, Sylvia Fleury went upstairs, leaving Maxwell and Jocelyn with their father.

Julian Fleury was in a reminiscent mood.

"It was curious seeing Euan Templeton today," he said. "Seeing the two standing there together in the receiving line, I couldn't help remembering how Jimmy Templeton and his father had received their guests at his coming of age dance. Exactly the same scene thirty-five years later."

Maxwell smiled, wryly. That's how you'd have liked it for yourself, he thought; a son of whom you could be proud, of whom everybody would say "like father, like son." Instead of that you've me. It's too bad, isn't it?

Maxwell rose to his feet. All this talk of sons and fathers, of Eton and Oxford, and coming-out dances in English country houses. The heritage he had been denied. He'd had enough of it. But he'd show them one day.

"I've come to a decision tonight," he said. "I'm going to stand for the Leg. Co. in the next elections."

"My dear boy. . . ." The surprise on his father's face annoyed him, but strengthened his resolve. He'd show them. He'd show them all.

"What made you decide this?"

"Nothing in particular. It's something I've had on my mind for a long time. It's absurd the way we all sit around saying the island is going to the dogs and making no attempt to influence events in the one place where we can influence them, in our equivalent for Parliament."

Because he was quoting his hero, his words carried conviction to himself.

"I shall stand as an independent. I shall throw my vote whichever way I choose. That way I shall be of influence and power."

"You have to get yourself elected first."

"I'll manage that."

43

He spoke with confidence. He'd be all right. He was a Fleury wasn't he? But he couldn't argue it out now.

"I'm tired, father, I'm going up," he said.

"A whisky first?"

"No thanks. I've had enough. It's been a long day."

As long a day as he could remember. That tedious discussion of the accounts with a splitting headache, all those rum punches before lunch; coming back to find the smell of that cigarette; his brain racing so that he couldn't sleep, and then the party. A long, long day. Oh, but he'd show them yet, no doubt of that.

Sylvia sat before her mirror. He stood in the doorway watching her. Was she too reliving the day, incident by incident; was she brooding over that half hour in the morning with a man of whom she had not spoken to her husband?

Her back was turned to him, but in the mirror he could see her smile. What memory had inspired that smile?

"It's funny to think of all those girls going to sleep tonight dreaming about Euan Templeton," she said.

"Are you surprised?"

"Indeed not."

"You thought him attractive?"

"Certainly."

"Indeed not." "Certainly." The dreamy inflection of her voice struck rough on his raw nerves.

"I suppose you envy them," he said.

"Envy them?"

"Envy them their opportunity. Don't you wish that you were still one of them, that you could throw your bonnet into the ring and try your chances with the young Adonis?"

"Don't be absurd."

"That's not absurd. He's the most attractive man to come here in a dozen years; the most attractive man you've ever met. It's too bad that you can't try your luck with him."

"Now Maxwell . . ."

She swung round upon her stool. Her face wore a haughty, displeased look, as though she was saying, You're being childish. It was a familiar look, it never failed to madden him. He caught her by the arms underneath the elbows.

"Don't look at me like that. There's no need to pretend where I'm concerned. I read you like a book. I know what you're thinking about young Templeton: how you're envying Jocelyn and Mavis

44

and Doris Kellaway. The most attractive man that's ever landed and he's outside your reach, because you're married."

"Now, Maxwell . . ."

"No, don't deny it. Don't start 'Now Maxwelling' me. Of course you feel that way. 'Indeed not.' 'Certainly,' but you're mine. He's not for you. You're mine."

He shook her as he said it. Her flesh was soft under the thin dressing jacket. All the frustration, the doubt, the self-pity, the irritation of the day, culminating in his resolution to run for parliament, had reached their peak in a need for self-assertion. In her face was that look of faint revulsion that disconcerted and disarmed him: that made him ashamed of his own appetites. He could not face that look. The mirror was lit by a long narrow bulb; he switched it off. The moon might light the room, but it hid that look from him. He caught her under the knees and round the shoulders, lifted her from the stool, tossed her onto the bed. The mosquito net sagged, but it did not tear; he dragged it away from under her: he pulled off her dressing jacket, caught at her nightgown, ripping it, tossing it across the room.

"Mine, mine, you're mine. You're never to forget that, never."

He gloated in his possession; confident in his strength and mastery. She was his prey and powerless. He let his hands travel over her like a miser letting the golden coins run through his palms. His fingers met behind her head, moved upward through her hair, ruffling it forward. Her arms lay at her sides, her face averted, in profile against the pillow. He did not know whether weariness or resignation, disgust or hate were written there. He did not care.

Whatever his father reading in the study below might think of him, whatever they might say about him in the club, though the inseparables might pity Sylvia, though somewhere in Jamestown the man who had smoked that cigarette might be savoring the memories of a stolen hour; though Sylvia herself might in the daylight shrink away from him, might daunt him with her aloof contempt, whatever he might be elsewhere at other times, here in the dusk he was the master: supreme, unchallenged.

The long strain of the day, the drinks in the club that morning and that night, gave him a strength and a control of that strength that he prolonged with a deliberate relish. She was at his mercy. His hands closed on her shoulders.

"You're mine, mine, mine."

He shook her as he whispered it. She moaned, stirred, writhed beneath him; whether in response or revulsion he did not know. He did not care. He was concerned only with his mastery of her white

45

body; with the self-justification that that mastery conferred on him. He had no feeling for her, except in her subjection to him. A perverse impulse flashed on him to confirm that subjection by denying her her woman's victory when a man, his strength drained out of him, reveals himself in weakness, a Samson shorn before Delilah, the vanquished become the victor, the tyrant become the suppliant. Tonight at least she would be denied that moment. He rose and stood away from her. He took her hand, forced on it a recognition of his dominance.

"You're mine. You're never to forget that, never, never."

2

Across the passage Jocelyn undressed quickly. She had stayed only a few minutes with her father. She wanted to brood in the darkness over the day's events. So much had happened, so much that was the prelude to so much. Doris had been right. The time of their lives had started. A succession of parties, with Euan's own niceness making the whole prospect gayer.

She smiled, remembering the silly triangular game that they had played with the Archdeacon. It was the kind of silliness that was amusing. There was something unspoilt about Euan Templeton. It was flattering to her that he had made his approach to her. They had picked up each other's wave lengths right away, falling into the silly game with an instantaneous accord. Now steady, she warned herself, don't start fancying things. Don't start thinking about affinities. Haven't you got wise to yourself yet, and to this island, and the way things are here. Why can't you be like Mavis.

She had heard Mavis declaim her point of view so often. "This is a very small island. There are a dozen girls like ourselves, and there is a lamentable dearth of personable men. At the same time we're not uncherished. Men-of-war put in, there are pleasure cruises, yachtsmen look in on their way elsewhere. Quite a number of people come here, one way and another and with one main intention, to give and to be given a good time, on a short term basis. They get my full co-operation."

When she'd been asked "Where does all that lead?" she'd had her answer ready. "You don't get anywhere by looking too far ahead; someone who comes to trifle may find it sufficiently agreeable to make a whole time job of it."

And Mavis might well be right.

But that was Mavis' way, not hers. It would be all wrong for her.

46

Herself, she had to go on believing that somewhere she'd find someone who'd prove to her that he'd been worth the waiting for.

3

In the room below, her father's attention wandered from his detective story. Much was on his mind, too. It had been strange seeing the Templetons standing there together on the lawn backed by that Colonial portico, just as Jimmy and his father had stood on a July evening on the eve of the first World War, in the entrance to that Paladian drawing room under the vast Venetian chandelier, very much as he and his father had stood two years earlier at the dance given for his coming-of-age.

There had been very little difference then between himself and Jimmy Templeton. Their own house had been as impressive as Tavernslake though it had been in the family for two generations instead of six. Jimmy's father was a peer whereas his was not, but with the power of the House of Lords curtailed after Lloyd George's budget, the difference between a peer and a landlord had not been great. They had foreseen for themselves, he and Jimmy, the same kind of life. How different their lives had been.

Jimmy's name in a Brain Trust Quiz would have been picked up by nine in ten. It was fame too, not notoriety. No blot had tarnished his reputation, in public or in private life, as a cricketer or as a soldier. His name was more honored than his father's. In comparison how obscure had been his own life. Only the people he had personally known had heard of him. Yet he did not think of himself as a failure. He had performed his various duties as well as he could and not ineffectively; step by step he had done what had seemed the right and the wise thing to do; in his own world he was an object of respect and of affection. How differently though it had turned out from the way he had expected.

He had imagined that he would lead a life like his father's. The running of an estate in England had seemed a full occupation when he was a boy. What reason had there been for doubting that the lands which had provided his father and grandfather with an honored place in the community would fulfill the same function for himself? Money was coming in from Santa Marta. He had looked on that money as the interest from invested capital, as his friends looked on their dividends from diamond mines in South Africa.

He had never considered himself a part of West Indian life. Even though he had himself been born here. The West Indies had never been real to him. His father had rarely talked of them. Once, when

47

he himself had said, "I'd like to go there one day and see our estate and some of our relations," his father had shaken his head. "If you follow my advice, that's the last thing you'll do."

Had he been wrong to ignore that warning? How could he tell now? At the time it had seemed sensible, with the slump hitting simultaneously his English investments and his revenues from Santa Marta, with his capital depleted to meet the death duties under his father's will, with Arthur's school bills to be met and his brothers-in-law in difficulties: surely it had been prudent to see for himself what the situation was. And indeed what would have happened if he had not come out? With the estate badly if not dishonestly handled by an inefficient manager, he might have been bankrupt within ten years. He had had to get the estate reorganized. How could he have foreseen that the slump would become an economic blizzard.

Step by step he had done what had seemed the best thing at the time. Until now he had no regrets. But today, seeing Jimmy and his son together on the lawn he had realized suddenly, not so much what he had lost as what his children had lost through him. He compared Maxwell with Euan Templeton. What a difference; and Jocelyn: what future was there for her here? She was twenty now. The years went by so quickly. Something must be done about it soon.

But what? He felt inadequate. He had none of the instincts and capacities of the careerist. In a day when every Englishman of a certain class had been brought up to an assurance of security through the mere fact of having been born an Englishman, his duty had been clearly marked: duty to his family, his school, his country, "the white man's burden." On the map that hung above the schoolroom mantelpiece a sixth of the world's surface was painted red: there was no talk of a commonwealth or of self-governing dominions. He had his own foreordained niche in the empire. One day he would run the estate that his father had inherited from his father. Until that time, as an officer in the county regiment he would fit himself for his responsibilities. It was not for him to organize a career; his instinct, deep-rooted in his nature and his training, was to accept unquestioningly the responsibilities that each new day brought; but nowadays in a changing world that was not enough. Something had to be done quickly about Jocelyn. He had realized that today. When Betty came back, the question must be tackled seriously.

4

In the White House half way up the hill, the Governor was studying the three copies of the *London Times* that had come down by the morning's plane. He had a power of concentration that enabled him to detach himself from the day's events and discover by a quick turning of the sheets what there was of interest or concern to him. There was little as far as he could see. The birth and death columns contained no familiar names: no letters of condolence or congratulation to be written. He marked three answers to questions in the House on colonial policy for Archer to cut out and file. They were midweek issues; no football scores. He folded them and rose. It was time for bed. He was at peace with himself and with his world. It was good to have Euan here. It was high time that he and the boy got to know each other. Letters were a poor substitute, and he was glad that the period of rapprochement should take place here. He wanted to be looked up to by his son and there was all the difference in the world between a general who goes down to the War Office every morning in a bowler hat like any Whitehall clerk, and the Crown's representative abroad in whose presence everyone has to stand until he himself is seated.

Across the harbor he heard the wail of a liner's siren. Wilson P. Romer's ship. She was late in sailing. Trouble on shore, he supposed, with members of the crew. He must ask Whittingham about that tomorrow. He hoped nothing had happened to disturb the good impression that he wanted to color the editorials of the *Baltimore Evening Star*. He walked to the window. He watched the ship draw slowly from the quay. Its band was playing "Some enchanted evening." Its sound grew fainter, the ship grew smaller, like a toy boat in a bath, as it passed behind the spur of the hill that flanked the harbor.

5

In the lounge of the liner Wilson P. Romer, a cigar in his hand, a whisky soda on the table, was giving an account of his day.

"I only spent thirty hours ashore," he said, "but that for a journalist is ample. A journalist knows what to look for. In the same way that a camera can take in a second a picture that would require forty hours of an artist's time, a journalist can get a swift, vivid, accurate first impression; if he stays longer he loses that impression. He does not see the woods for trees. But in those first hours his perceptive antennae are alert. He misses nothing. His trained sense tells him what to accept and what to reject."

He outlined his technique.

"At that garden party of the Governor's I knew right off which were the men, and women, that it was worth my while to meet. I

49

picked the significant types. There was the Attorney General, a man almost completely black, well trained, wise, I've no doubt, but pathetically anxious to convince me that a colored jurist could be as impartial as a white; he was one of the older generation, brought up in a day when the colored man had few civic rights.

"Then there was the conservative *ancien régime* type of planter. He wasn't by any means the reactionary you might suppose. He wasn't intolerant; he wasn't unliberal, but he felt things were going too fast. Then there was the young labor leader who was afraid that things were going too slowly, a brash young man in some ways, but intelligent, oh yes, very definitely a young man of parts. He wants to have his island transformed tomorrow, or rather today, on what he believes to be the pattern of the English Welfare State.

"And then at the head of it all, holding in his hands the strings of these separate and often conflicting interests, is the Governor. Gentlemen, I was most impressed by him." He paused, dramatically. "I am myself a one hundred per cent American. I have no doubt that the future of the world lies with the American people, that out of our melting pot we have produced the finest race the world has seen. At the same time I must admit when you find an Englishman, cultured and informed, a man of the world, who has rid himself of insular prejudices, an aristocrat by birth but a liberal in politics who has kept abreast of modern ideas, I would be inclined to argue that as an individual type . . . well, gentlemen, all I can say is that Lord Templeton is all of that."

It came as the peroration to some fifteen minutes of uninterrupted oratory. There was a pause, each of his five companions waiting to see who would take the stage and how; manners demanding that a straight switch should not be made into another subject. The topic must be allowed to taper off.

"And what do you think yourself of the immediate future of the island? How would you compare its prospects with those of our own Virgin Islands?"

The editor smiled knowingly. "I've a hunch that it's all going to be much more interesting than anyone on that island thinks. And I'm going to back my hunch. I'll tell you how I propose to do it. I'm going to send one of my staff down there to cruise among the islands and keep me posted as to what's going on."

He said it with an air of finality; he had delivered his last word and was now ready to concede the chair. The permission was promptly taken up.

"A journalist I met last fall was telling me . . ." one of the group began.

Wilson P. Romer sipped his whisky, drew on his cigar, sat back in his chair, and followed his own thoughts. Bradshaw was the man to send. Bradshaw needed a change. He had been on one job too long. He was getting into a rut. He needed to be revitalized. Bradshaw had been on his mind for a long time now. Younger men were clamoring for his job. But it would break Bradshaw's heart to be pensioned off. Here was the solution. Bradshaw knew his oats. If there was a story here, he'd find it. He'd have no rivals, no younger men to beat him to it. Bradshaw for Santa Marta; that was how to fix it.

# CHAPTER FOUR

## 1

Travel agent folders of the Caribbean present the islands in terms of
unbroken sunlight, white gold beaches, and towering mountains. All
those things are to be found there, but rarely all in the same island.
Dominica is mountainous and majestic, but it has no sand beaches off
which it is safe to swim, and there is more rain than sunshine there.
Antigua and Barbados have beautiful beaches and steady sunlight,
but they are flat. A few islands like St. Lucia do, however, have
mountains, white beaches, and a dry climate. Santa Marta is one of
such lucky ones; its succession of beaches along the Leeward coast
not only provides admirable facilities for smuggling—it is estimated
that two-thirds of the rum that is shipped from Santa Marta finds its
way back to the groceries by small boats within forty hours—but
makes bathing picnics one of the chief occupations of the residents,
a fact which explains why the Country Club did not own a beach.
On Sunday mornings as the Archdeacon had pointed out there was a
general agreement to meet at *Grande Anse* after matins, but otherwise the patricians were glad to avail themselves of one of the few
opportunities for privacy that the conditions of their life allowed.

The beach that Jocelyn Fleury had chosen for her party on the
afternoon following the Governor's party was ten miles out of
Jamestown and one of the least frequented. It was for that reason
that she had chosen it. She did not want Grainger Morris to be embarrassed by the presence of her friends. It was also a very pretty
beach, edged with coconut palms, with a wide spreading mango tree
to whose shade you could retire when the sun grew too hot; there
was no village within two miles; behind it there towered the high peak
of the Diadem; on the horizon were the shapes of islands so shadowy
that you were not certain whether they were clouds or mountains.
It faced northwest.

"There's always a chance of seeing the green ray there," Jocelyn
informed the newcomer.

At half-past three that afternoon the A.D.C. was the victim of
nervous turmoil. He had driven the Governor to the cricket ground;
on his way back he had passed the Bon Marche pharmacy; he had

slowed down, and turning his head had seen Margot Seaton in its center, standing by a vitrine, demonstrating an article to a customer. Their eyes met, and she had smiled; he stamped on the accelerator.

Back in his office he discovered that his hand was trembling. He could hardly hold his pen. He could not concentrate upon his report. The sentences would not take shape. He sat at the desk motionless. He'd have to leave it to the next day. Steady, he warned himself. Steady. This is the danger point.

He knew the sky-signs. His experience in gallantry might not be extensive but it had been intense. Not only had it abruptly terminated his career at Oxford, but in London he had only escaped being cited as a corespondent because the defendant, an exceedingly free-hearted lady, had deserted him at the eleventh hour for a man better fitted to support her. Having read in a novel that there was always a point at the beginning of a love affair where you could withdraw yourself into safety, he had vowed when he joined the Governor's staff that next time, when he reached the danger line, he would stop on the safe side of it.

It had been easy to make himself a promise like that when he was high over the Atlantic in an airplane. It was very different here, when adventure beckoned. The minute hand on his watch pointed to the number nine. He tidied his desk, locked away a confidential document. The Continental was five minutes away. He had time to drive through the town.

He slowed down as he reached the drugstore and craned his neck; he could not see her; she must be behind the counter, or gone out for tea. His foot rested on the accelerator, but he did not press it. He reminded himself that he needed a new tube of toothpaste. He pulled on the brake.

She was standing behind the counter.

"I want a tube of toothpaste," he informed her.

"Certainly. What kind?"

"Do you have Eucryl?"

"Yes."

"Then I'll have that."

"The large size or the small?"

"What is the difference in price?"

"The large size is thirty-six cents, the small size twenty-four."

"How much difference in size?"

"The large size is nearly twice as large."

"Then the large size is the better bargain."

"Yes, it's the better bargain."

"I'll have the large size."

She took the tube from the glass case. He laid three shillings on the counter. He watched her pack up the parcel. The bangles on her wrists rattled as she folded the paper over. Her fingernails were painted a purplish red, they were rounded and short, the varnish matched her lipstick. As she leant forward, he could see her breasts. On this hot afternoon, her skin looked cool and firm. If he got out of this shop with nothing said, he'd have stayed on the safe side of the danger line. If he made no move now, he never could. Everything hinged on the next sixty seconds.

She fixed the package with Scotch tape.

"There."

She handed it across and their eyes met.

He felt weak, defenseless, chained; yet he was conscious of a vibrant, triumphant sense of power.

"I've got to see you again, somewhere not here," he said.

"That is up to you."

There was a moment of silence. Her glance met his steadily. He had not the slightest idea what she was thinking.

"Are you going to the Nurses' Dance?" he asked.

"Yes."

"We'll dance together then."

She nodded.

It was more of a relief than he had dared to hope. The danger line was passed; there was no going back. He was committed. The last two lines of a sonnet by Clifford Bax ran through his mind—

What bright spirit impelled towards delight
Was ever known to finger out the cost?

He drove to the Continental in what he described to himself as an anapaestic mood.

The others were already waiting. They all crowded into Jocelyn's car; Jocelyn drove, with Euan sitting between her and Doris. Doris, in one of her garrulous moods, acted as a guide, pointing out the landmarks.

"Isn't it curious how the French names stick, calling a bay an *anse*, a mountain a *morne*, a factory a *boucan*, the harbor the *carenage*. I wonder if it would have been the same if the French had taken Barbados from us, or if they'd have altered all the English names into French."

Euan scarcely listened. His attention was concentrated upon Mavis. He could see her reflection in the driving mirror. Now and again he looked round to ask her something. She was prettier than he had suspected. Had he really made an impression on her?

Jocelyn at the wheel was thinking, There was one thing certainly to be said for Doris; when she was in the mood she made a party go. Not that she was a substitute for Sylvia. The inseparables had been one thing. This new trio was another. Perhaps they'd made a mistake in trying to maintain it as a trio. They should have formed a group of five or six, with interchanging units. Archer sat silent in a corner. He was a dull dish, Mavis thought.

The car drew up beside a narrow bay; the sand was white, the water a faint blue deepening to dark. The girls changed in the car, the men behind a cluster of mangrove bushes. Euan was in the water first. How cool, how invigorating it seemed, after the tepid tideless Mediterranean. He stretched himself upon the sand and Jocelyn sat beside him. I must find out what he's really like, she thought.

What was he planning to do, she asked him, when he came down from Oxford.

He shrugged. He had no fixed plans, he said. "I'll have three years there. That ought to give me time to make up my mind."

"What about the Army?"

"Not for me, no thank you. There may be a war in the next ten years. If there is, there'll be only one thing for a regular army subaltern, to stay with his regiment and the men he's trained. Nothing could be duller. But as a civilian I might land myself something dramatic."

He was employing again in self-defense his artificial manner. Jocelyn was amused by it and intrigued. What lay behind this manner?

"That's a curious reason for not being a regular soldier."

"But it makes good sense. I've heard a lot of military talk, and a good deal of military grumbling, and I've come to the conclusion that three-quarters of the glamor jobs in the last war were performed by men who were civilians at the start of it."

She laughed, she was still intrigued. He had an original point of view. Was he an aesthete in disguise?

"Do you think you might be an artist of some kind? Do you want to write?"

"I'd like to write something one day, but I've noticed that the best books are written by men who aren't professional authors."

She laughed again. "You seem to think that all the best results are achieved by amateurs."

"Well, aren't they? Take medicine. Don't you think it would be more fun to be a psychoanalyst than a G.P.?"

"If you're so keen on being an amateur, you ought to go in for politics. That's a free for all."

"But that's what I shall do. I've an hereditary seat in the House of Lords waiting for me."

"I hadn't thought of that. So you do really have a profession after all."

She had talked banteringly, to match his manner. But suddenly he changed that manner.

"It's curious being a peer today," he said. "It's an advantage, I don't pretend it isn't. But it's hard to know how to make the best use of it. My grandfather had a cut-and-dried future. An estate to run with many responsibilities attached, an assured place as a legislator. The House of Lords had real power then; a peerage was a profession. It wasn't quite the same thing when my father was a boy. There'd been the tussle between the Lords and Commons; the Peers or People election, and the Commons won, but even so my father as a boy could look on Tavernslake as a career. If there hadn't been the war and he hadn't been such a success in it, I don't suppose he'd have stayed in the Army. He'd have concentrated on his cricket. But it's different now.

"In the first place I shan't be able to keep up Tavernslake. It won't stand another attack of death duties. No one knows what the House of Lords will amount to in thirty years. You can't bank on its amounting to a thing. At the same time it's something you can't ignore. It excludes you from quite a lot. Party politics for example. What could be more maddening than making yourself a career in the House of Commons and then having it cut short by your father's death. Then again there are quite a few jobs in which at the start, anyhow, it's a handicap. It's hard to begin at the bottom of the tree when you've a handle to your name. I realized that in the army. Before I had my commission there was a corporal who always read out my name in full, Private the Hon. Templeton E. J. Number six-one-three-nine. There'd be a sneer in his voice and someone would always snigger. People think you're different if you've a title and in a way you are. It's quite a problem."

It was the first time that she had heard him speaking seriously. A different tone came into his voice, a different expression into his face. She liked him this way. He was something more than a well-born playboy out for a good time. She realized now that she too had thought of him, because he had a handle to his name, as being not quite human.

"I'd never thought of it like that," she said. "The problem of being a peer, I mean."

"One wouldn't, unless one happened to be one. I had it drummed into me by a fierce Scots nanny. When I was seven years old, she woke me up to hear the Duke of Windsor's abdication broadcast. I didn't know what it was all about. I was more interested in the test match in Australia. But I'll never forget the lecture she gave me afterward.

" 'Prince Edward,' she said, 'has betrayed his country. He has put his own pleasure before his duty to his people. A King is different from other people. He must always put his duty to his country first. You must remember that when you are grown up. You will not be a King, but you will be a Baron. You will be different from other people. You have your duty to perform.'

"I've laughed at the old girl since; but that is the kind of thing that sticks in one's memory. She kept harping on that point, telling me that I was different, that I had a special duty to perform."

Jocelyn nodded. Yes, she could see that it would make him different. It was something she must remember about him.

She changed the subject.

"Tell me about Egypt," she said. "Was it very dreary?"

"In some ways, very. In eighteen months I didn't have one meal alone in feminine society."

"That's a long time."

"I'll say it was."

Sitting here on this beach, in this fresh green world beside this friendly girl with a soft breeze dulling the sun's heat and the trade wind churning the dark waters beyond the reef, it was hard to believe that only two weeks ago he had been in Suez: with a stale smell upon the air, and the pale pink oleanders drooping under their weight of dust.

He watched Mavis as she came out of the water. Wasn't this the dream that he had cherished in those arid days? She took off her bathing cap and shook out her hair. Her back was against the sun; the small firm breasts and full rounded hips were in silhouette.

"She's very attractive isn't she?" he said.

"I think so."

"She's not only so good to look at, she's amusing too; she's such good company."

"You should be telling that to her, not to me. She'd like to hear it."

It was said with a twinkle and again they laughed together. She would be a friendly and amusing confidante, Euan thought.

Mentally Jocelyn shrugged. So that was the way it was. Mavis again. Did she feel a twinge of jealousy? She didn't think she did. Not jealousy, but a sense of disappointment in herself. Men liked her, felt at ease with her, confided in her; but it was for girls like Mavis that they fell. She ought to feel glad and grateful. Mavis was always getting into trouble, always being let down by someone. This Canadian tourist was only the last of several. People felt sorry for Mavis. Poor Mavis, they kept on saying. She didn't feel sorry for Mavis in the least. She'd like for a change to have someone let her down; have someone sufficiently involved with her to treat her badly.

Mavis settled herself beside them on the beach

"Have you a punch in that thermos?" she inquired.

She had a sudden feeling that she could use a drink. She had been conscious of Euan's glances in the car; she had noticed his sudden start, the way his eyes had opened as she came to join them. She had seen that look before: she knew the symptoms; that's how it had been with Rickie. It was exciting, but she wasn't in the market for that kind of thing, at least not yet.

"When I was in Suez," Euan was saying, "I'd lie out on the beach and close my eyes and make a prayer to Allah, 'Please,' I'd say, 'when I open my eyes, may I see a pretty girl walking across the sand toward me.'"

Yes, here it came again. Why was it always this way, with her; why couldn't it be the other way round; with a man whom she'd known for three months saying, it's an extraordinary thing, but I've begun to realize that I'm in love with you. You grow on one. There'd be so much more likelihood of that lasting.

From a rock by himself Denis Archer was throwing stones into the water. Doris was swimming with Grainger Morris.

"I really don't know why we bother to bring that A.D.C. out with us," Jocelyn said.

"To ensure our keeping on the G.H. party list," Mavis said.

"I hope you don't feel you need that still," said Euan. "Grainger," he called out. "Come and join us."

He wanted Grainger to talk to Jocelyn so that he could talk to Mavis. But it was next to Mavis that Grainger stretched himself.

"I often used to wonder when I was in England how you'd look when I got back," he said.

She raised her eyebrows.

"I shouldn't have thought you knew that I existed."

"That means that you weren't aware that I existed."

"I knew there was such a person."

"But you don't associate me with anything, any time or place, any particular occasion?"

"I can't say I do."

"And I could remember you so clearly. Do you remember that children's party at G.H. when you won the obstacle race?"

"Of course. I was eleven then."

"You looked so triumphant when you went up to take your prize, you were wearing green openwork mittens. I remember how you held out both hands to take it. It was a book I think."

"I've got it still. Lamb's *Tales from Shakespeare*."

"You were taking such a fresh, happy pleasure in it all. I was so glad for your sake. I've often thought about that day. I hoped life was turning out for you the way you wanted it."

She looked away: she felt herself surprisingly near to tears; how it all came back; the white frock with the green trimming and the book that she had stood up that night beside her bed so that it should be the first thing she saw when she woke up. It was nice to have someone remembering her as she had been that day.

Doris also had noticed Euan start when Mavis ran across the sand: had also been aware of the glances that he had flung over his shoulder in the car, but she had felt no jealousy, no sense of self-inadequacy: on the contrary she felt pride, excitement, exaltation. He had fallen for Mavis. Mavis was wonderful. There was no one like her. It was the same every time: no man could resist her.

2

There were no guests that night to dinner at G.H.

"We must work out our plan of campaign," the Governor said. "These next months must be gay. Denis, what would you suggest, as *arbiter elegantiarum*?"

"There's the Nurses' Dance next week, sir. Why not a dinner party first?"

The Governor agreed. Whom should they invite.

"There're the girls we were with this afternoon."

"Then let's ask them. Do we need to have their parents?"

"I don't think so, sir."

"What about Grainger Morris. The girls like him."

It was Euan who suggested that. His father's hesitation before agreement was so swift that neither of the young men noticed it. Normally, Templeton would not have invited a man of color to meet white girls at a small dinner party, but since this was an accepted friendship, and they were going on to dance in public, it was a good opportunity of showing the community that Government House admitted no racial distinctions. But if he was going to ask Morris, he must ask at least one girl of color, too. These people were touchy: he could not have them saying, H. E. asks the men but he won't have the women to his party. Not sufficiently ladylike, I suppose. While if he were to ask the women without the men, he'd have them saying, He has our women up; treating them like courtesans to amuse the gentry, the old fashioned *droit de seigneur*. But our men aren't gentlemen.

"Can you think of any girl who's respectable and not, shall we say, too African, who'd help make the party go?"

"I'll think, sir."

A wild idea had occurred to Archer; so wild that he did not know whether he dared put it to the proof. He had a moment of panic, then he knew that he'd despise himself if he didn't risk it.

"Do you know Margot Seaton, sir?"

"I don't think I do."

"She was up here yesterday. She's pretty and quick-witted."

"What does she do?"

"Work at the Bon Marche."

"What about her people?"

"She's a cousin of David Boyeur."

"We don't want him here."

At the same time, the Governor reflected, to invite a relative of his might prove a salutary lesson to the young demagogue; it would diminish his self-importance.

"Ask her, certainly, if you are convinced that she won't disgrace us."

"I can promise you that, sir."

And that, he told himself, was that.

Next morning Archer sent out the invitations. He invited Jocelyn, Doris, and Mavis by telephone, but for Grainger Morris and Margot Seaton he made out official invitations on Government House cards. He sent round Grainger's by the chauffeur. Margot's he proposed to deliver personally.

On his way to the Country Club he drove past the Bon Marche. Margot was standing behind the counter. "The Cosmos seems to have lost a customer," she said.

"I've not come to buy shaving soap. I am on official business."

"Shall I fetch Mr. Martin?"

"My business is with you."

"Oh."

"Are you going with a party to the Nurses' Dance?"

"Naturally."

"Then I'm afraid your friends will have to find someone to take your place."

"Yes?"

"This envelope contains a Royal Command that can only be declined in the case of illness."

He handed her the envelope. It was embossed with a crown.

"What does it say?"

"Look inside and read."

She opened it, took out the card. His Excellency the Governor requested the honor of Miss Margot Seaton's company at dinner on Tuesday, April 15, at 8 P.M.

She read it slowly. Her face showed no change. He was impressed by her lack of surprise.

"I will see that someone calls for you. I had better have your address," he said.

She gave it to him. It was in St. Catherine's, a section a little out of Jamestown that he scarcely knew.

"I will let you know the final arrangements on the day."

As she watched him drive away, her lips parted and the tip of her tongue passed slowly over them.

That evening David Boyeur called at the Bon Marche pharmacy.

"I've come to apologize," he said.

"O.K."

"It was a very good film."

"It was. I went to it last night."

"There's a new film tomorrow. Would you like to come?"

"I would, very much."

"Have you decided which party you'd like to join for the Nurses' Dance, the Salmons' or the Levasseurs'?"

"That's something I want to talk to you about. I shan't be able to go with you."

"Why not?"

"The Governor has invited me."

"The Governor's what?"

"I warned you, didn't I?"

"Of what?"

"That you might regret having dared me to go to that garden party."

The next morning the Governor was taking a visitor to inspect the sugar factory; they were to lunch with the manager. Archer drove them out; on his way back he made a detour through St. Catherine's. It was a typical West Indian village. A haphazard collection of shingle huts, perched on boulders, straggling below the main circular road in a small valley on either side of a shallow stream that in the rainy season became a flood. It was picturesque, shaded by mango and by breadfruit trees, with canoes drawn up along the beach, and fishing nets hanging up to dry. There was a cheerful farmyard atmosphere about it all, with chickens and pigs and children tumbling over one another among the stones; yet actually the very characteristics that made it picturesque made it unhealthy: it was damp and airless and mosquitoes bred there. It was one of the villages that worried the health authorities, and it was in this village that one at least of Margot's grandparents had been born.

Half a mile away, on higher ground and above the road, was a series of one-storied bungalows with glass windows and wide verandas, a recent building project, sponsored by the government. It was in one of these houses that she now lived. He thought of the Georgian Manor House in Somerset in which his great-grandfather had lived at the time when Margot's ancestors were tumbling in the picturesque squalor of the ghut, with its flies and dysentery and malaria. The house in Somerset was now a preparatory school, his father had sold it to meet death duties in the 1920's and settled in the Hampstead Garden Suburb. He compared that pleasant, compact, semi-detached villa, under the shadow of St. Jude's, with Margot's neat trim bungalow on the hill. In a novel, one could draw an effective parallel, showing how the course of change had brought the two of them from such different backgrounds to a present that was not dissimilar. One lift was going down, another lift was going up. He sat pensively at the wheel, looking first one way, then another.

If you don't write a real novel one day, he adjured himself.

# CHAPTER FIVE

## *1*

Three days later Julian Fleury found himself with a convenient opportunity to fulfill his promise to the Governor. He needed to have a talk with Maxwell. He could call in on Preston on his way.

He was in a thoughtful mood as he drove out. His son's surprising resolve to stand for election confirmed his suspicion that all was by no means well there. Maxwell had always been a problem. As a boy he had been jealous of the brother; not unnaturally. But he had been no less moody after Arthur's death when he became the heir.

Julian had hoped that marriage and responsibility would supply a medicine. He knew himself the relief and inspiration of returning at the end of the day to somebody whose lot was yours, to whom you could talk openly. Sylvia was sweet, Maxwell was in love with her, and he had overborne the Normans' objection to an early marriage on the grounds that Sylvia was too young. He had given the young couple Belfontaine as a wedding present. But things had not turned out the way that he had hoped. The estate was not showing the profits that it should. Maxwell was discontented and what else was this ridiculous plan to run for council but a gesture to convince himself that he was somebody.

He was worried about Jocelyn too. She ought to be got back to England. But her problem would not be solved by checking her in upon a homebound boat. What kind of a welcome would she receive from the aunts and cousins who had daughters of their own to marry off? Conditions were difficult, so everyone assured him: the only people with money to spend were those with capital to cut into; or those with expense accounts—the new privileged class that could charge their entertainment "against the house." Jocelyn would have no common ground of shared experience with the girls who had been to English schools, and done a London Season. The young men might find her "naïve."

The obvious solution was, of course, for her to go back with her mother. But that he knew would not work. Betty, as she said, had lost touch with England, and did not want to be reminded of that lost world. Moreover, and he had to face the fact, she had never got on well with Jocelyn. They had not quarreled, but there had

63

been no sympathy between them. They had never enjoyed doing things together. He could not picture them alone together on a six months' trip. If Jocelyn went, he would have to go back too; he could afford the trip, there was a boom in copra. But was he justified in leaving Maxwell behind to run the estate alone at a time like this.

Times were difficult, and likely to become more difficult. He had only spoken the half of what he felt the other night to that American journalist. He distrusted Whitehall courtiers who drew up blueprints for colonial development with no firsthand knowledge of the countries for which they legislated. In London they only met cultured and educated West Indians: how could they appreciate, untraveled as they were, the backwardness, the superstitious ignorance, the basic savagery of the average peasant? How could they gauge how easily those peasants could become the prey and victim of corrupt self-seeking politicians? It was highly inflammable material. Every present day situation in the Caribbean came as the climax to a long and bloodstained history.

There was much to remind him of that history as he drove out to Belfontaine. The main road was a firm, macadamed thoroughfare, but the side roads were rough and rutted, and on the hillside the squat rounded windmills long since wingless, the skeleton houses, the crumbled masonry of walls and gateways, silently testified to the days of departed grandeur.

There were signs everywhere of decay. Large stretches of land had gone out of cultivation, and were used for grazing. There was no sign of bustle on the estates. The cane had been already cut, the coffee already planted: here and there a peasant or two would be collecting cocoanuts; a squad of convicts was clearing the ditches by the road; casual domestic occupations like weeding and charcoal burning were in progress. There was little traffic along the road. The sun was shining; pale dove-colored clouds drifted across the sky; in the rivers women were washing their clothes, beating the damp cotton against the stones. At the foot of every ghut was the collection of wooden shacks that was called a village; women sat on their doorsteps, chattering. There was an air of placid and contented apathy. Nobody was working hard. No one had worked hard since emancipation. Thanks to their small gardens, the peasants managed well enough on their small wages; they had no wish to better themselves. If you raised their wages, they did less work. Occasional men like Boyeur had ideas of grandeur. There were exceptional men like Grainger Morris. But for the rest...

What meaning could Democracy have to this friendly, feckless people. Trouble was bound to come if power was put into their hands too soon.

So he mused as he drove along the curving road under the bright February sun.

## 2

The Prestons' estate was four miles from Belfontaine and Fleury had planned to arrive there at about eleven. He had an idea that Mrs. Preston was as much responsible as her husband for the way in which the situation had developed, and he was anxious to see her alone. At eleven Preston would certainly be in the fields.

He was right in his assumption. Mrs. Preston was on her veranda, knitting. He honked his horn and swung round into the drive. As she rose to greet him, his spirits sank. He had forgotten how her company depressed him.

She was a type that is produced only in rural England and by the county families. Of medium height, freckled, with sandy hair, she had a long, thin neck. In England she would have worn tweeds, woolen stockings, and stout shoes; in winter her nose would have been slightly red. In the tropics barbaric colors might have suited her but she preferred pastel blues. She was the mother of two children, but her figure was flat. She kept her hands half closed and only at the card table did you realize that her nails were bitten to the quick. She had a high-pitched voice that was slightly inflected by a whine.

She was not popular in the island, her manner conveyed that she felt herself superior to her environment. Fleury, because of his West Country background, was the only islander whom she accepted as an equal. They had one or two acquaintances in common, and whenever they met she would invite or provide news of them. Whenever she saw him in the club she would, the moment there was a pause in the conversation, proceed to tell him the latest social gossip from the Blackmoor Vale. She would talk about people whom no one else in the group knew personally and she had the exasperating habit of referring by a Christian name to anyone who was at all well known, particularly when the owner of a title was concerned; only at the end of the anecdote would she casually permit the uninstructed listener to appreciate whom she had been discussing.

At the sight of Julian Fleury her face lit up. "I was thinking of you this very morning. I received such an amusing letter from Lily Percival. She tells me that the National Trust is refusing to take over Matchett. It's a great blow to Victor. You know Victor don't you?"

"I've met him."

Victor was the Duke of Wessex and Fleury had occasionally shot at Matchett but he did not know him as Victor. He would have been inclined to doubt if Mrs. Preston did, had he not, on one occasion, taken the trouble to check up on her, only to learn from a mutual friend that she was in fact a very close friend of the politician with whose name she had one evening peppered her conversation. Carson had summed her up pithily. "She's bloody but not bogus, damn her."

He listened to the news about the Duke, then changed the subject, asking her about her husband.

"He's happy enough. Why shouldn't he be? He's in the open air, he's busy with his hands: he likes his laborers, I can't think why. They drive me mad: they steal, they're lazy, they need flogging. We daren't leave the place for half a day. They've no feeling for the animals. They'd let them starve if we didn't watch them. Would you credit it, we've actually caught them eating the food we put out for the pigs. They've no gratitude. At first we tried to be good neighbors. Twice when one of them came round to say his wife was sick Frank drove into town in the middle of the night to fetch a doctor. There was nothing wrong with the woman. The man wanted to get a sack of copra into town. They're terrible. You can't trust them."

"I hear you're having trouble with one of your neighbors at this moment."

"Indeed we are. Some of our cattle got through a gap in the fence; and how did that gap get there I should like to know? It was a new fence and a stout one. Frank put it up himself. It was the nigger man himself who made the gap. We can't prove it but I'm convinced. If you give them an inch, they take an ell. It's the thin end of the wedge. That's what I've told Frank. If you give way now, you're laying up a mint of trouble for yourself. Whenever they want a few more dollars, they'll let our cattle through onto their land. It's a racket. But you don't need telling that, you know these people."

Half an hour earlier he had been thinking along very much the same lines himself, but he resented the criticism coming from Mrs. Preston. They were his people after all.

"Was there much damage done?" he asked.

"I wouldn't know; that's a technical point. Frank could tell you about that. It's the principle of the thing that worries me. If Frank takes this lying down, anything may happen."

Fleury nodded. All this bore out what he had thought.

"Will your husband be back soon?" he asked.

"He'll be in for his morning punch. You'll join him, won't you?"

"I'd love to, thank you very much."

Preston returned shortly before noon. He was a short stocky man with a close-clipped military mustache. He was wearing a khaki shirt, khaki shorts and gray-green stockings. His hair was matted by heat and dust, and his hands were dirty. He started at the sight of Fleury. "This is an honor and a surprise."

"I was on my way to Belfontaine. Your wife very kindly suggested that I should stay on and join you in a punch."

It was a good punch, not too sweet, made with fresh limes and bitter oranges.

"What I wouldn't have given for one of these when I was in the Western Desert," Preston said.

His four years in the Middle East had been the big adventure of his life. He was always referring to it. He missed not having more people in Santa Marta with whom he could "talk over old times." Colonel Carson was the only other Santa Martan who had served there and Carson disliked war talk.

"I told you, didn't I, about that week when we lost those tanks at Knightsbridge. . . ."

Fleury had heard the story several times, but he encouraged Preston to continue. He wanted to get him into a good mood.

Preston's voice began to glow. He was once again the officer in charge of men, in command of other officers: he had forgotten for the moment that he was now become a planter, uncertain of his future; fretted by his wife's disapproval. He had long since ceased to be in love with her, no doubt. But he respected her opinion. He respected the things she stood for. He could only feel self-confident when she was pleased; and that she rarely was. She had been taken out of her niche and she blamed him for it. She made him feel inadequate.

Fleury let him have his talk, then brought up the reason of his visit.

"I was talking to your wife about the trouble you've been having with that neighbor of yours. I hear you're appealing against Graham's verdict."

"I should say I was. The most disgraceful affair I ever heard. The man has no right to be a magistrate."

"It does not seem to me a very heavy fine. Fifteen dollars, and there *was* trespass."

67

"That's not the point. A deliberate attempt was made to exploit the incident."

"In what way?"

"I'd better put you in the picture."

"I'd be most grateful if you would."

"It started off as a straightforward case. There was a gap in my wire. I don't know how it got there, but there was a gap. My cattle got into his property. I was prepared to make reasonable amends. He said he would be satisfied with a hundred dollars. Now that was quite absurd. It was old cane, stubble. A herd of cattle couldn't do that amount of damage. I asked to see the damage. He showed me hoof marks, but I couldn't see that anything had been destroyed. I wasn't going to argue with him. I wasn't going to haggle. I won't haggle with that kind of person. 'Very well,' I said, 'we'll get the agricultural advisor to make an inspection and estimate the cost of damage.' I acted in good faith. I put in my report to the Agricultural department.

"You know what Harrison is like. He took four weeks to make his visit. By then the new cane had grown. He asked to see the damage and Montez told him that you could not see it now. 'In that case,' Harrison said, 'there is no damage,' so I refused to pay. Montez then proceeded to sue me before the magistrate for fifty dollars. He'd come down, you'll notice, from a hundred to fifty. Graham came round to see me. You know what Graham is. He wanted me to settle out of court. He thought Montez would be happy with twenty-five. But I wasn't having that. I stand by my rights. Graham argued that it was well worth saving all the trouble there'd be for twenty-five West Indian dollars which was only five pounds after all. But no, I wouldn't agree. I went into court, and I brought with me Harrison's report that he could see no damage.

"Graham did not like it at all. He wants to keep on the right side of these nigger men. He doesn't want to have his car tires slashed. Do you know what he said at a cocktail party the other day, that he wasn't going to retire with a bunch of ulcers. That, I ask you, from a Government official. Well, there he sat in court, looking at Harrison's report: he found a quibble in it. It didn't say there was no damage, but only that Harrison could see no damage. So Graham said, 'I will call on the Agricultural officer to make an official report. Until then the case is adjourned.' An official report, mind you, from my own witness."

"What happened then?"

"The worst thing of all. There was a long delay, there always is, where the law or at any rate where Graham is concerned. Finally a date was fixed. On that very day I had a touch of fever. I caught malaria in the war. I sent a message down to Graham. He told me that my attendance wasn't necessary, that he had heard my evidence. Then in my absence, in my absence mark you, he fined me fifteen dollars. I never heard of such a breach of justice. I won't stand for that."

"Did you see the agricultural officer's report?"

"I did not, for the very good reason that there never was one."

"Are you sure of that?"

"As sure as I can be of anything. Harrison wasn't going to put in a report against Graham. They're all hand in glove. But a clerk in Graham's office heard the two of them discussing it. She heard Harrison say, 'How can I make out a report after a three months' delay? The cane is six foot high. You can't see anything.' There wasn't any damage, I can assure you that."

"Will that clerk go into the witness box and swear to what she told you?"

"I shan't ask her. I don't want to get her into trouble with Graham. She's no right anyhow to be telling me what goes on in a government office."

"Which lawyer have you go to handle your case?"

"I haven't one."

"Isn't that unwise?"

"I don't trust these colored lawyers. They're all hand in glove. I want to have my day in court, say my say before a judge. Probably I shan't get justice, how can you expect to in a place like this, but I'll have made my protest."

Fleury made no reply. As Preston talked, he had felt his irritation rising. He could see Graham's point of view. Trespass had been committed. Trespass presumed damage. An ignorant peasant would feel entitled to compensation. He could not tell how much. One hundred dollars and fifty dollars were much the same to him in a case like that. It would be an occasion for a bottle or two of "mountain dew" with his friends round him, and the steel band for an hour. Graham understood that. He was the magistrate; he knew his people and he had to keep the peace. In terms of practical politics he was right. At the same time, legally he was probably at fault. No damage had been proved. In England he had been always told as a boy that if you were caught trespassing you were safe if you handed over sixpence and told the landlord he would have to prove that more than sixpence worth of damage had been done. Preston knew that, and Preston was the kind of man to stand upon his rights. He had the temperament of the small official with his regard for rules and regulations; and with this wife of his undermining his self-confidence, it was not surprising that he was making an issue out of a sum as ridiculously small as fifteen dollars.

"If Frank doesn't fight this case," Mrs. Preston was saying, "if he doesn't show these nigger men that when an English gentleman says a thing he means it, I shan't be able to hold my head up in the village."

It was precisely the kind of remark that would inflame the resolution of a man like her husband.

"There's another thing too," she said. "If they once find they can get money out of us that way, we shall have them pulling our fence down every week."

There, Fleury recognized, she had a point. The peasants were crafty and dishonest: or rather they did not regard stealing as dishonest. The rights and wrongs in the case were evenly divided, but he himself, living in the district, had no doubt that Graham had acted in the general interest. Himself he didn't want the laborers discontented, as they would be if they believed that one of their people had suffered an injustice at a white man's hands. A white man's cattle broke loose over a colored man's property and the colored man had got no compensation. That's how they would see it. They were so easily swayed. They were sunny, friendly, happy when everything was going well, but when they got a grievance, when that sense of hereditary grievance was played upon, anything could happen.

He would advise Jimmy Templeton to suggest to Preston that he let the matter drop.

He rose to his feet. He had learnt all he could.

"I must be on my way," he said.

3

Belfontaine, with its avenue of palms, its "welcoming arms" stairway, its dignified colonnaded portico and two-storied frontage is as familiar an illustration in West Indian guidebooks as Josephine's statue in Martinique. It is one of the few estate houses in the Caribbean that have survived hurricanes, earthquakes, and the neglect of absentee ownership.

As Fleury turned his car into the drive, his son cantered across the paddock. Maxwell was hot and dusty and he was frowning.

"That tractor's broken down again," he said. "They're the most hopeless people; all they're good for is cutting cane with a cutlass.

God, but I need a drink. They drive me mad. Sylvia," he called, "I'll be ready in five minutes. I'd like a sour cocktail."

Sylvia came out of the house, looking very cool and fresh, in a light cotton frock, with her hair smooth and shining. It would cheer a husband coming in from a long morning in the fields to find her waiting there, his recompense and reward.

As her father-in-law came up the steps, she ran to meet him. She lifted herself upon her toes and flung her arms round his neck; her cheek was soft and cool. There was a pleasant scent of lavender. A young man ought to be happy with a wife like this.

"Would you like a sour cocktail too?" she asked.

He shook his head.

"I've already had a punch. I'd like a lime and soda."

"A punch already. Where've you been?"

He told her. He was beginning to explain the situation when Maxwell came down, his hair still damp from his shower, his shirt changed, wearing a pair of freshly pressed gray gabardine trousers; he looked fit and healthy; surely he was a husband to be proud of. Was Sylvia bored? What did they do with themselves when the quick evenings fell. There was no club here.

"I don't suppose you see much of the Prestons, do you?" he inquired.

She shook her head.

"Not oftener than we can help. She tires me."

"Me too." He turned to Maxwell. "You know all about that trouble of theirs with Graham don't you?"

"Who doesn't? It's their only topic of conversation."

"What's your view of it?"

"That Graham's a coward."

"Has he any cause for being one?"

"He probably has now, after letting the peasants get out of hand. They think they can do anything they like."

"If Preston wins his case, will it make things difficult for the rest of you?"

"It might, but it's high time we had a showdown."

Maxwell spoke in the resentful tone that was now habitual with him.

They went in to lunch; into a high cool room, darkened by closed shutters. The long walnut table was well polished; the silver shone. The fish soup was cold without being iced. Sylvia was a good manager. A radio was playing dance music. Did they have it on, Fleury wondered, to take the place of conversation? They seemed to have little to say to one another. It was only because he was

71

here that the ball of talk kept moving. What were they like when they were alone together? More than once he noticed his son fixing on Sylvia a pensive look he found difficult to describe.

"Have you wondered what effect your going in for politics will have upon our own laborers?" he asked.

"That's the last thing I should consider."

"Twenty years ago it was considered beneath the dignity of our class to offer ourselves at the hustings. We would never put ourselves in the position of having to solicit from them."

"That was all very well when the nominated members had a majority, but when this new constitution comes into force, the island will be run by the legislators whom the islanders have chosen themselves; some of us will have to convince them that we are the right people to run the island."

"Do you think it'll increase your prestige to argue with them?"

"I'm not going to argue with them. I'm going to give them the facts. I'm going to tell them not to be silly fools. I'll tell them they're uneducated, that they'd better place their trust in men who are."

His father let that pass. There was little chance as he saw it of his son being elected. It might be as well for him to learn his lesson. But his heart was heavy as he lay out afterward for his siesta. He felt tired and old and lonely. Thank heaven, Betty would be back tomorrow.

When the heat had slightly lessened they went round the estate. It was mainly coconuts, but sugar cane was planted round the house with a little cocoa in the foothills. The hillside looked very lovely with the immortelles covering the tender shoots with their orange-red parasols.

A couple of laborers who were supposed to be collecting coconuts were siting on their haunches, smoking. Maxwell blazed out at them.

"Lazy sods, what you need is an overseer with a whip! That's the only way you can be got to work. Come along now, on with it."

There was venom in his voice. He doesn't like them, his father thought. And that was the one thing a West Indian would not forgive. He'd forgive anything in the long run to the man who liked him. Probably that was what was wrong with the estate. The men didn't like Maxwell; they wouldn't work for him. It was as simple as all that.

A little farther on Fleury noticed that there had been a minor landslide and a ditch was dammed. A pond of stagnant water had formed.

"Mosquitoes'll breed there," he said.

"I suppose they will. I must get it seen to."

72

"Is anyone responsible for keeping a special lookout for that kind of thing?"

"I am myself: but I can't be expected to go round the estate every day."

He spoke casually, with indifference. His father made no comment. Maxwell had flown into a fury over an idle laborer when everyone knew that a West Indian laborer spent half his time squatting on his heels, yet he was not checking stagnant water. That was what was wrong out here: scenes over trivialities and no attention to what really mattered.

"No," he said when the tour was finished, "I won't stay on for tea. I want to be back before it's dark."

He also wanted to look in at the Jamestown Club. Colonel Whittingham, the chief of police, was usually in there at that time. He would like a word with him before reporting to the Governor. Whittingham was noisy, garrulous, and drank his full share of swizzles, but he knew what was going on.

His views coincided with Fleury's own. "I'm a policeman," he said, "and I don't like trouble. Which is exactly what we're likely to get in Santa Marta, with this damned fellow Boyeur telling them all that they're exploited. And your section of the island is as inflammable as any."

It was close on seven when Fleury got back to his own house.

As he came into the house, the telephone bell rang. It was Denis Archer.

"I'm sorry to trouble you, sir, but I think that you went to Preston's place today."

"I did. Yes."

"Fine. H. E. has to go to Antigua tomorrow for a conference. He wanted to have your views on that affair before he left. He wondered if you could dine here; it's very short notice I'm afraid."

"It isn't that, but Jocelyn's here alone."

"He'd thought of that: he'd be delighted to have her too. If you both can, then I'll beat up another girl. You could? Oh splendid. H. E. will be delighted."

It was a successful party, in the way that impromptu parties so often are. The talk flowed easily. But Fleury did not fail to notice that though Jocelyn and Euan Templeton had a lot to say to one another, the young man's eyes kept glancing across the table at Mavis Norman; she was very obviously his choice. Not surprisingly, he supposed. She had the glamor of experience. The eloquence of

73

those glances across the table strengthened an idea that had come to Fleury during the drive back.

He turned to Mavis.

"I saw your sister today."

"How was she?"

"As always, very pretty."

He paused, looking at Mavis thoughtfully.

"Would you say she really liked it there?"

"How do you mean, liked it?"

"Do you think she's bored ... no, let me put it this way: if you were out there, would you miss the clubs and parties?"

"I'm very different from my sister."

She said it with a twinkle. She's a nice girl, he thought. What was going to come of her? What was going to come of any of them, for that matter?

"Suppose you were in her position, would you welcome a chance of being brought back into town?"

"I'd leap at it; but then I'm me."

He nodded: the sisters were very different. But would any girl of twenty enjoy living on an estate, with no neighbors, no child, no real responsibilities? It was easy to get servants in Santa Marta. Sylvia only had to issue orders. How did she spend her days; reading, listening to the radio? Was that one of the causes of Maxwell's restlessness, the knowledge that his wife was discontented? It might make all the difference if they came into Jamestown; why shouldn't Maxwell undertake the office side of the work, and let someone else run the estate; Preston for example? Their properties adjoined: then he and Betty could take Jocelyn home.

It might work out. But Maxwell would need careful handling. He must not feel that he was being displaced.

"And now," Templeton was saying, "what would you young things like to do? Your father and I, Jocelyn, have one or two matters to discuss. Would you like to play bridge, or turn on the gramophone, or go for a drive?"

They voted for the drive: the moon was nearly full. They would take their bathing suits. The Governor led Fleury into his study.

"Now," he said, "tell me about it."

He listened attentively, without interrupting.

"What kind of a chap is this Preston? Would you say he was a solid citizen?" he asked.

"I would."

"He had a good war record. I've checked up on that. We want

74

to do all we can for our ex-officers. Crown colonies aren't much use if they don't give a chance to our own nationals. Would he feel ill-used if I asked him to drop his appeal?"

"His wife would."

"Wives can be the devil." He paused. "I take it that you, in his position, wouldn't have appealed?"

"In my case the situation would not have arisen. The matter would have been stopped at the start. I don't quite know where or how, but I'm sure it would have been. A peasant wouldn't have tried to take advantage of *me* that way."

"Then you do think it was sharp practice."

"You know what these people are. They don't think it dishonest to cheat a white man."

"The sooner they learn it is the better. I don't see why an ex-soldier should be given a raw deal because of the custom of the country."

"In two years' time he'll probably be grateful to you for intervening."

"You think if I don't intervene, there may be trouble."

"There's a possibility."

"You do, now that's most interesting. I'm very grateful to you. I've said it before and I say it again, it means more than I can say to have one person whom I know and trust. How little I guessed forty years ago when you led me onto the field at Lord's that we should be meeting under these conditions. Do you know I don't think there's a single other person on that side about whom I know for certain if he's alive or dead."

"I'm sure that I don't."

They told you when you were at school that you were making friendships that would last your life. But it wasn't true, the Governor thought. You were limited at school by your age group and the house you were in. There were only a dozen or so boys with whom you stood a chance of being a friend, and the things you had in common with them were matters of immediate association. It was different at a university, where a freshman could meet a graduate on equal terms: when you were yourself mentally developed, knew your own tastes and plans: you could take your pick out of an entire generation. At a university you did make friends that lasted you through your life. At the same time curiously enough there were few links greater than those that held together those who had been at the same school, even if they had not spoken ten words to each other during their five years there, or had indeed not even

75

been contemporaries: there was such a wide common ground of joint experience.

For an hour they talked of masters and boys that each had known. When finally Fleury rose to leave, Templeton repeated what he had said before. "I don't know what I should do without you here."

Fleury left believing that the Governor proposed to take his advice. He would have been surprised could he have known what the Governor was thinking. When I was sixteen Julian Fleury was my captain, he was thinking. And I looked up to him. I mustn't forget that's forty years ago; our positions are now very different. I have a far wider experience of life than he has. My judgment is the likelier to be sound. He can tell me a lot, but I must be on my guard against being overinfluenced by him because he was my senior then.

# CHAPTER SIX

## 1

On the following afternoon Julian Fleury drove out to the airport to meet his wife. She had been away two weeks, and he was conscious of a quickening excitement. It was good to feel like this after thirty-five years of marriage. He was lucky, very lucky.

As she came down the gangway of the plane, he had the same sense that he had had in their days of courtship of seeing her afresh, for the first time. She waved, and her mouth was smiling; a warm and friendly smile, very like Jocelyn's: perhaps too much like Jocelyn's; perhaps that was why they had never been wholly natural with each other.

Betty had kept her figure. Had he half closed his eyes, he would not have known whether it was she or her daughter that was coming across the asphalt to him.

"Darling. It's lovely to be back."

She came into his arms, and there was again under his nostrils that faint scent of lilac. It was a real kiss of welcome.

"I feel incomplete when you're away," he said.

The plane had grounded at four o'clock.

"Is anyone home?" she asked.

He shook his head.

"Sylvia and Maxwell are at Belfontaine. Jocelyn's out with Euan Templeton."

"Now that's something I want to hear all about."

They had so much to tell each other that it was hard to know where to start.

"This is the best part of going away," she said. "All the time I kept saying to myself when anything amusing happened, 'how I shall enjoy telling Julian this.' "

They had so much gossip to exchange that they had finished tea, and the sun had already sunk behind *Trois frères* before they began to talk about their children.

They had left that last, because it was something serious. They were neither of them completely happy about their children. Yet they were conscious that they did not see their joint problems from the same angle. It was the one issue on which they did not see eye

77

to eye, and they avoided it as much as possible. Without wholly recognizing that they did, they resented their children's having disturbed their harmony; the father feeling resentful toward the son, the mother toward the daughter.

"Have you heard from Maxwell?" he asked finally.

"No."

"He's planning to run for council."

"Why?"

He did not try to explain. He gave her the bare details.

"Poor little boy," she said.

There was a note of pity in her voice that irritated him. Why should Maxwell evoke that warmth? What had he done to deserve sympathy? He'd had the best there was.

But it was not against his wife but against his son that he felt that irritation.

"Does he stand any chance of getting in?" she asked.

"I shouldn't say so."

"Won't that make him feel worse than ever about everything?"

"It needn't. No other white man will get in. He'll not be out of things. It may make him feel less alone. He'll be in the same boat with others."

"That's always been his trouble hasn't it, being out of things?"

It had been, but why had it; others hadn't felt that way. Why couldn't Maxwell have accepted the West Indian pattern. He did not want to discuss the boy: it made him angry. He couldn't let that happen on Betty's first evening home. He switched the subject.

"I'm worrying about Jocelyn too," he said.

"Oh."

There was a bleak lack of interest in that "oh" that matched, on her side, the irritation that her "poor little boy" had stirred in him; an irritation not against him but Jocelyn. He steeled himself. He had too often skimped a discussion of Jocelyn's problems, so as to avoid a tension with her mother. He was guiltily aware that more than once he had failed to fight Jocelyn's battles, out of a reluctance to disturb the harmony between himself and Betty. They talked of the injuries done to the children of an unhappy marriage, but the children of happy marriages were victims too: the parents resenting having their children come between them. Had not that happened to Maxwell and to Jocelyn? He'd got to be firm now.

"She must be got out of here. She must be sent back to England."

"We've discussed that before. She'd feel very lost."

"She would, if she went alone. We must go with her."

"We?"

"You wouldn't want to go alone, I wouldn't want to be six months without you. We need a change."

"It will cost a lot."

"We can afford it."

"What about the estate, what about Maxwell? Do you trust him to run it single-handed?"

"I've thought about that."

He told her what he had planned.

"I suppose it's all right if you say it is. If you seriously think six months for Jocelyn in England is worth all this bother."

It was said grudgingly. Confound the children, he thought. Why can't they leave their mother and myself alone. A second later he was despising himself for thinking that. They were his children. He must fight Jocelyn's battles.

"It's absolutely essential in my opinion. Who is there for her to marry here? We don't want to have her turn out a Mavis Norman."

"Do you think that's likely?"

"She might do even worse. She might become a shriveled spinster."

"It's your decision, Julian."

There was a pause. They had said all they needed, more than they had wanted.

"Have you talked to the children about this yet?" she asked.

"I wanted to see you first. I did not want to say anything to Jocelyn till I had talked to Maxwell. It might improve matters between himself and Sylvia."

"It might."

"We can discuss it on the night of the Nurses' Dance. Jocelyn is dining at G.H. We'll have them to ourselves."

"That's a good idea."

"And now don't you think we should be going to the club. They'll all want to hear your gossip."

As they walked through the hall toward the car, he slipped his arm through hers, pressing it against his side.

"Nothing must come between us. Nothing."

She returned the pressure.

"Nothing," she said. "Not ever."

2

On the eve of the dance Sylvia bathed and in her dressing gown lolled back in a long chair, while Jocelyn dressed for the G.H. dinner.

"Do you know who'll be there?" Sylvia asked.

"A mixed crowd, the usual ones and one or two unlikely ones."

The usual ones.

Fifteen months ago she would have been one of those. Now she was a matron, and only went on young people's parties as a chaperone.

"Who are the unlikely ones?"

"Grainger for one, and then a cousin of David Boyeur's, someone I've never heard of, Margot Seaton. Denis asked me to be nice to her. He said she might be shy."

"Margot Seaton. I know her. She works at the Bon Marche. My, isn't G.H. getting democratic."

"I suppose H. E. thinks his son must see every side of our society."

"From what I hear he spends his whole time with the inseparables."

"We see him most days."

"What's he like?"

"I think he's very nice. Wholesome without being dull. He's flippant in self-defense, but he's really a serious person. I fancy he's a little overawed by being the son of somebody so important as H. E."

"What does he talk about?"

"Mavis, half the time."

"What does he talk about to Mavis?"

"Not about me, I gather. I'm due for a T.L. from her."

T.L. Trade Last. A nostalgic word. It was eighteen months since she had used it. What fun they had had, the three of them, ringing each other up the morning after. Mavis and Jocelyn were still having that kind of fun.

"Do you gather that he's at all serious about Mavis?"

"As serious as a young man can be who knows that he's leaving soon."

"With Mavis content to have it that way?"

"You ought to be the first person to know how Mavis feels."

"Ought I? I'd say I was the last."

Sylvia said it laughingly, but it was in large part true. Her sister puzzled her. "I'm not going to miss any fun that's within my reach," she'd say.

"But do you really find it all that fun?" Sylvia had asked her once.

"Heavens, yes, don't you?"

Sylvia had laughed; that was just the point. She didn't. She had enjoyed flirtations; at least she had enjoyed all that accompanied flirtations; the dressing-up, the competition, the telephone calls, the comparing of notes afterward, the flattery, the presents, the attentions; but when it went beyond preliminaries, that was another matter. She had been curious, inquisitive; but her experiments had left her with no inclination to repeat them. She had married for the dramatics of being married. Now as a matron, she envied the other two. She wished that like Jocelyn she was dressing for a real occasion, spurred by a rivalry in which nothing ultimate was at stake. What was the fun of dancing with middle-aged married men who held you too tightly when their wives weren't looking?

There was a shuffle of bare feet on the landing.

"Car here, Mistress Jocelyn."

Jocelyn took a long slow look at herself in the glass; then circled before Sylvia.

"Do I look a dream."

"I wish I were a man. Have a good time. I'll see you later."

Sylvia rose lazily to her feet. Quarter to eight. She supposed she must start dressing. Whom for, what for, in heaven's name?

## 3

Betty Fleury had not seen her son since her return. She had made that fact the excuse for inviting no other guests. "It's too long since we were just ourselves," she said.

She had planned in advance with Julian when and in what way they should raise the question of the English visit. They had both agreed that it would be better if she brought it up, taking advantage of the first convenient pause.

The opportunity came when they were starting the main course, with little likelihood of immediate interruption.

"Your father and I are worrying about Jocelyn," she began. "She ought to meet more eligible men. She ought to spend six months in England; but if she went there alone, it might not work out well; she needs to be sponsored by someone closer to her than aunts and cousins whom she has never seen. We want to take her back ourselves. But I don't want her to think that she's the reason for our going. I am going to say that I am worried about your father's health, he needs the change of a cool climate and the advice of a European doctor; moreover I want to see my cousins. Jocelyn must be made to feel that we have quite strong personal reasons for wanting to go back to England."

Betty Fleury paused; she looked interrogatively at her son. It was his feelings not her daughter's that she was considering. But Maxwell wouldn't realize that: he was too wrapped inside himself to appreciate another's point of view.

"Do you agree with me?" she asked.

81

"I do, but how'll you manage about the Jamestown office?"

His father intervened.

"That's the very point. The work in town is tricky; it could only be carried on by someone in whom I had the most perfect trust. There is no one employed in the office in whom I have that trust."

"Then I don't see . . ."

"What I suggest is this, that you should come into Jamestown, live here, and run the store until I come back. I know it's a lot to ask, giving up your home, but it wouldn't be for long."

He paused; he looked from one to the other. He noted an eager flush in Sylvia's eyes. She was in favor of it clearly, as he'd thought she would be. He had been right in guessing that she was bored at Belfontaine.

Maxwell had noted that look too. Anger shot along his nerves. Did she want to come into town, so that she would have more opportunities of seeing the man who smoked Turkish cigarettes?

"This needs thinking about," he said.

## 4

The Nurses' Dance was held in the St. James. The placards announced that it would start at 9. The Governor's party was not expected until 10, and when the band started to play at half-past 9, no one took the floor though a number of men stood round the bar, and half the tables were occupied.

Ten chairs had been set round David Boyeur's table. He was not the host, but he was behaving as though he were; wherever he was, he made himself the center of conversation. Whenever he found himself unable to do this, he moved to another group. By and large he had a good sense of audience. He did not often need to move.

"In a few weeks' time," he was saying, "we shall have our new constitution. All will be smooth sailing then. Our own representatives will pass the laws that will raise the standard of living; income tax will be raised to meet the rise in wages. We shall nationalize the sugar factory: the power will then be in our hands; that's what I tell the laborers. I've got them where I want them. They listen to me. A strike, I tell them, is something that you may threaten, but must only use on very rare occasions when you are sure you'll win. It's like a right-hand punch, keep it for the knockout. Once we've got our constitution we shall not need to strike."

He kept his eye upon the car park. He was anxious not to miss the arrival of the Governor's party. He wanted to see out of which car Margot stepped. He had not seen her for a week. The game was up, and he knew when to cut his losses. When a woman was through with you, there wasn't a thing to do. He had his pride. He wasn't going to have people saying, "Look at David Boyeur hanging round the Bon Marche when the bird has flown." He had spoken openly to his friends. "We've had two good years, and at our ages that's enough. We can both use a change; but we've stayed good friends, naturally. Why shouldn't we?"

He was most anxious that everyone should have a chance of seeing this evening that he had not spoken idly. And indeed he bore her no ill will. He was glad of a change and his self-esteem was flattered by her success. It would suit his book in a couple of years' time when she was married to someone grand, to have people say, "Oh, don't you know about her? She was David Boyeur's girl for quite a time."

Tonight he should learn who his successor was. She would never have been asked to a G.H. party unless she had been vouched for by someone with influence at Court. Grainger Morris? No. He wouldn't have had that much influence. The Governor's son? If that was the case, a useful lever would have been placed within his hands. Margot was an ally he did not propose to lose. For him she was still the pivot of the evening.


The arrival of the G.H. party was like the raising of a curtain on a play; there was a general feeling, Now we can start to enjoy ourselves: at the same time its immediate effect was damping. Many West Indians do not touch alcohol; music is their stimulant, and it is only after the rhythm of the music has beaten along their nerves for half an hour that they become worked up. For a quarter of an hour they would be too busy observing His Excellency for that to happen.

His Excellency was aware of their attention and it pleased him. It was a new experience for him. As a soldier he had sought, whenever possible, the anonymity of civilian clothes. At Lord's, since most of his cricket had been played in India, he had not been well known by sight. Small boys had not rushed across the field to get his autograph. He felt now like a film star.

He looked round the room complacently. It was bare and large; divided by screens, normally it served as a dining room and a lounge; the screens had now been removed, and flags had been draped about the bar; there were over two hundred people in the room, half were coal black: a third were coffee colored; there were a dozen Syrians; but only three white tables. One of them was Fleury's. That reminded him. But later on, he thought, not now.

It was time for him to open the ball. He looked round his table. His glance rested upon Margot. Everyone would be wondering whether he would choose Jocelyn Fleury first or Mavis Norman. He would surprise them. He had scarcely spoken to this pretty little girl. It was time he did. He rose to his feet. He walked round the table. He bowed. "Will you give me the pleasure of this dance."

David Boyeur watching from his table raised his eyebrows. An idea that he immediately dismissed crossed his mind. The Governor was a widower, but that surely was an impossibility. Even so it was impressive. He watched them as they danced. His Excellency was five inches taller than Margot. He danced stiffly, yet there was a jauntiness about his movements. He was smiling. He seemed to be enjoying himself.

He was. He had expected that Margot would be tongue-tied and a little coy. He had counted upon a simper. To his surprise she chattered away, naturally.

"I did enjoy myself at dinner. I've never been to a big party like that before. I didn't know whether I should bow or curtsey. Everyone told me something different. They said I mustn't speak unless I was spoken to, but how could I have done that. I don't think that Mr. Lestrange would have spoken at all, unless I had drawn him out."

His Excellency chuckled. The Attorney General either remained silent or delivered half-hour-long speeches. If this child had got small talk out of him, it had been a feat.

"Tell me about yourself," he said. "You're a cousin of David Boyeur, I believe."

"A distant one."

"He's a young man for whom I prophesy a very brilliant future. You must all be very proud of him."

"That's what he keeps telling us we should be."

Again His Excellency chuckled. That A.D.C. of his had sense.

"They also tell me that you work at the Bon Marche Pharmacy."

"For the time being, but I've taken shorthand and typing classes. I'm a qualified stenographer. I suppose you haven't a place for me."

That took the great man's breath away. He looked at her quickly, then felt reassured. She was not being impertinent; she was not presuming on her presence at his party. She was someone who said as a matter of course whatever was in her mind. It would be fun to have her around.

"I didn't think you'd dance as well as this," she said.

That decided him. He needed some lightness in his routine. He'd have her shorthand and her typing checked and if she made the

84

grade, a place would be found for her; and a place that lay "under his eye."

When it was seen that the Governor's first choice was not to be Jocelyn Fleury, Euan Templeton caught her eye across the table. "Shall we?" his look said; she nodded and they rose together. Their steps fitted well. It was the first time he had a chance of talking to her. It was a relief to be with her again; at dinner he had set next to Mavis. Mavis had looked pleased when they had met that evening: they had started talking fast as though they had so much to tell each other that one party was not nearly adequate, but before they had gone in to dinner, the pace of their conversation had begun to flag. They had not much common ground. She had never been out of the West Indies; she had only left Santa Marta for occasional holidays in Barbados and Antigua. She evinced an interest in anything he had to tell her, about London, about Devonshire and about the Middle East. She was ready to answer his questions about the Caribbean, but she was chiefly interested in personalities, and he knew few of the people in whom she was interested. With Jocelyn on the other hand there was no lack of common ground. He could talk to her about the Wessex that she had never seen, about the cousins and the aunts whom she knew only by name and about whom she could not ask too many questions.

He looked for Mavis. She was dancing with Colonel Carson. They were attempting, at least he was attempting—she was executing—a form of boogie-woogie. Her movements were provocative. Euan's eyes lightened. Another quarter of an hour and they would dance together. It would be easier when they were dancing.

"How'm I doing?" Carson was inquiring.

"You're doing fine."

He felt that he was doing fine. This was one of his good days. He'd slept well after a tranquil night. His ulcers weren't worrying him. There were days when he woke feeling sixty-eight, when he was ready to snap anybody's head off, when he said the first mean thing that came into his mind; he'd abused his system and the abuse was paying dividends; but now and again there was a day when he felt under thirty. This was one of them. Why couldn't he always feel like this? Maybe what he needed was someone young, to pace him down the course, someone like this filly. Then he wouldn't spend all those evenings in the club, with men as old or older than himself, with rum the only means of rendering their talk tolerable.

The music quickened its rhythm and he quickened his: hands

raised, shoulders shaking, feet moving fast. He wasn't out of breath. There was nothing wrong with him.

The music stopped; the Governor looked round the table. It was time for refreshments. Champagne would not only dress the table, but keep the party sober; a girl wouldn't feel justified in drinking more than a couple of glasses; none of the men would switch into spirits with champagne available. He caught Archer's eye: the A.D.C. hurried to the kitchen.

Archer returned to find Margot by herself. It was the opportunity for which he had been waiting. He held his hand out to her. It was the first time that they had danced together. He knew nothing about her, at the same time he knew everything: as she did about him. There was no pretense between them: they did not speak, there was no need, each knew what was in the other's mind. His heart was pounding. If he missed this chance, she would despise him. He'd never make up the lost ground.

Their steps fitted in an easy rhythm. He was not holding her close: his right hand rested, but did not press, against her shoulder; the palm of his left hand lay level against hers. But even so that light touch was a courtship: a courtship that grew keener as their feet moved faster.

"It would be lovely to make love to you," he said.

She smiled; her smile was an acceptance.

It was as simple as all that.

As the music stopped, once again he caught his boss's eye. What was it now? A title for a book crossed his mind: H.E.'s Lackey, or the Unprivate Life of an A.D.C.

"Yes, sir."

"I want to talk to Julian Fleury, but I don't want it to seem that I have especially asked him over; will you invite his wife as well, and the two young people."

The manoeuver was carried out. "I want an excuse for not dancing for at least ten minutes," he said to Julian. "I think two old fogies like ourselves should be allowed a gossip."

He brought the talk round at once to what he had in mind.

"I wanted you to be the first to know, I'm telling Whitehall that I propose to implement the new constitution right away. There will be three nominated members on the Legislative Council. I want you, my dear fellow, to be one of them. I need somebody in whom I can have implicit trust. I hope you will accept. You will be doing me a great kindness if you will."

"I'm honored and I'm touched."

It was indeed an honor and he was very touched. He would also enjoy the exercise of his duties. There was only one obstacle. If he took Jocelyn back to England, he might have to resign his seat. He could cross that bridge when he came to it. He did not want Jocelyn to know what he had in mind: he did not want to announce prematurely plans that might never be carried out.

"And to show you what a contrary person you are going to find me," the Governor was continuing, "I'll break it to you now that I'm not taking your advice in the Preston case."

"No?"

"No. You're probably right, in fact I am sure you are right in feeling that Preston made a mistake. At the same time I don't feel sufficiently strongly about it to interfere. Justice should be allowed to take its course. And I must confess that I'm a little curious to see what course it takes."

"The betting is fifty to one against anything happening."

"That's rather what I thought and it will be educational for me to see how things work out in what I suppose may be called 'a pretty point.'"

"Very likely Preston won't win his case."

"In which case everyone will be pleased. It can't cost him much and he will have the satisfaction of knowing that he has made his gesture. Is he here this evening, by the way?"

"I haven't noticed him."

They both availed themselves of the excuse to halt their conversation and look round the room. The atmosphere was warming up: the dances were longer, the musicians had been well primed with rum. More and more couples were breaking into boogie-woogie. Euan Templeton had not, however. He was dancing with Mavis Norman, holding her very close.

She was conscious, acutely conscious, of the mounting excitement in him that made his touch electric. She in part responded; her vanity was flattered; at the same time she was depressed; the same routine again; so soon after the last.

On the other side of his father, Maxwell sat glowering and silent. Sylvia was dancing with Grainger Morris. The sight of it made him want to vomit. That dark hand against his wife's white skin. But what could he do, since that was the way things were.

"One more dance," the Governor was saying, "and then I go. I've an idea that though they like me to come, they're relieved when I go away. Like a Corporal's dance."

He rose to his feet and moved round the table. The Fleurys were left alone. Julian turned to Betty.

"My dear, I've been paid a compliment. I'd like you to be the first to hear. I'm going to be one of the nominated members on the Legislative Council."

"Darling, that's wonderful!"

"Congratulations, Daddy."

Maxwell said it with enthusiasm, the ring in his voice was genuine. But there followed a raw aftertaste. His father was offered things like this, himself he had to fight for them. Why—because his father's position here was backed with achievement. He'd done things. He was someone. Whereas *he*—what had he done? What was he? No wonder Sylvia thought nothing of him. He'd show her though. This election was the test. When she saw him sway an audience she'd realize there was something to him.

Mavis and Doris were in the Ladies' Room, alone: they stood side by side, fixing their faces in the mirror. Doris was highly voluble.

"I saw him dancing with you. There's no doubt is there? He's fallen for you flat. I knew he would. They all do. You're marvelous. The way you dress, the way you move, the things you say. I wish I was like you. When I was a kid at school I used to look at you. If only I could be like that, I'd think."

Their eyes met in the glass. In Doris' there was a look of adoration that moved the elder girl.

"I used to have daydreams about you, of how I might save you from trouble, blackmailers, or someone who was jealous of you. Such silly childish dreams about my being injured in defense of you: things that I'm shy to tell you even now. How little I dreamt that one day I should be your friend."

Doris looked away. A dreamy note had come into her voice. "You'll tell me about it won't you: the things he says, the things he does, so that I can share it with you, so that I can be a part of it, so that I can feel it's happening to me."

There was a hypnotic quality about her voice. Her head was in profile now. Mavis put her hand under her chin, turning her face to hers. She wanted to meet again that look of adoration. It was still there, but deeper now. No one had ever looked at her in quite that way. It was a compelling look. She raised Doris' chin, then very gently kissed her. It was a soft warm mouth and she let her lips linger there. She drew back and patted the young girl's cheek.

"Don't worry, Kitten. You'll have all the fun of that kind you can use before you've finished. Yes, I'll tell you everything."

Once again Archer had his eye caught by the Governor. So the old man wanted to go home. He was himself dancing with Jocelyn. He looked for Margot. She was across the room, with Carson. He steered toward her. They danced side by side.

"I've got to see H.E. home," he said, "but I'll be back in half an hour."

She nodded. He had the heady knowledge that she knew exactly what was in his mind.

That's that, he thought. He danced Jocelyn back to the table.

"Yes, sir, shall I get the car?" he said.

He was back within twenty minutes. Margot Seaton was now dancing with Maxwell Fleury. He caught her eye, raised his eyebrows, interrogatively. She gave a sign of recognition. A moment later she and Maxwell came back to their table.

"It's hot. Let's take a drive," he said.

She rose and followed him. Boyeur saw them go. So that was who it was. On the whole he was content. Archer was a bright young fellow: no fool either. It soothed his vanity to have his taste confirmed by an A.D.C. When they came back, if they did come back, he would dance with Margot; so that everyone should recognize that the episode had his approval.

Denis had returned, not in the small Austin to which he was usually restricted for his errands, but in the Governor's Cadillac. It was large and heavily upholstered. It was, he presumed, the first time that Margot had driven in a car of such caliber, but if she was impressed she did not show it. He drove in silence along the coast, climbing to the fort that had once guarded the harbor. A waning moon was rising about *Trois Frères;* it cast a ruffled stretch of silver on the water that mingled with and confused the reflection from the boats anchored against the *carenage.* He stopped the car, switched off the engine, turned toward her.

"You know how I feel about you."

"Yes."

"Let's sit in the back."

She settled herself in the far corner of the seat.

"No, that won't do," he said.

He bent, put his hands round her ankles, swung up her legs and sat beside her, one arm round her shoulders. With the other hand under her chin, he turned her face to his. Her lips were soft and smooth. There was no passion in her kiss, but the touch of it fired his blood. She was wearing a strapless dress; he pulled it down and was aware of something snapping; he unhooked her brassiere. She

89

raised her arms, crossing her hands behind her head, tightening her pectoral muscles. He bent his head: her breasts were small and firm: their points grew firm; she was wearing a heavy perfume with a scent of musk.

With an English girl he would have invested his courtship with a wind of words, but instinct counseled him that Margot would have no use for that. She would consider delay a reflection on the power of her charms. She did not hinder him. She did not help him. She did not close her eyes. She made no movement. She kept her hands crossed behind her head. It did not last ninety seconds. He felt both fulfilled and foiled.

"I think we should go back," he said.

"I think so too."

"I hope I didn't tear your dress."

"Let's look and see."

It was nothing that five minutes with a needle would not put right. She had a safety pin in her bag; she turned her back to him and he fixed it. He rested his cheek against her skin: it was soft, so soft and firm.

She turned, looked at him, took his face between her hands, then slowly, very gently, with closed lips set her mouth on his.

Boyeur noted their return. Thirty-five minutes. Nothing could have happened in that time. He knew Margot too well to have any doubts on that score. If she once let anything start, it would last a lot, lot longer. Archer was no doubt one of these timid Englishmen who called cowardice chivalry. He smiled. It gave him a reassuring feeling of superiority. In a quarter of an hour he'd ask her for a dance.

Mavis was sitting next to Grainger.

"Do you mind if we don't dance," he said.

"Not in the least, I'm tired too."

"It isn't that. I'm not tired. I'd rather talk to you."

She raised her eyebrows. As far as she could remember it was the first time that any man had said that to her. When a man had said he did not feel like dancing, it was the opening gambit for "a drive somewhere, where it's cool."

"We don't have so many chances, after all," he said.

She knew what he meant. They could never meet in each other's houses; he could not belong to the Country Club, nor she to the Aquatic. They could never go out alone together. The scandal would be fantastic. They could only meet at an occasional intimate picnic or at semi-formal occasions such as this.

"You'd be surprised how often I thought of you when I was in England," he was saying. "You symbolized so many of the things I love best about the islands."

"What kind of things?"

"Wholesomeness, openness of heart; a natural, a patrician quality of graciousness that comes to people who've been born to rule; most people have chips of some kind on their shoulders. The real patrician hasn't. That's such a relief, after the strain of walking in spiked shoes."

"Why should I have stood for that to you."

"Something about you, the way you looked and spoke. You were so friendly to all those other children. I remembered how you looked. I wondered what you had become. Shall I tell you what saddened me, that time when you were twelve? We could have been friends as children, but when I went back, now you were grown up, we couldn't be."

He said it without any bitterness, without a sneer. He hadn't a chip on his shoulder either. He accepted as an inevitable fact the difference that color made between them.

"There's another thing too I used to think," he was going on. "We could have been friends in England. There's no feeling about color there. Everyone knew that I was a West Indian. It's obvious, but it didn't make any difference. It didn't worry any of the girls; there was one in particular, who would have been very glad to come out here and marry me."

"Why didn't you bring her back?"

"Would that have been fair to her? Think of her position here, unable to join the Country Club; never being able to meet the people that she would think of as her own kind."

"Were you unhappy over it?"

He shook his head. "I knew from the start it was impossible."

"Did you ever consider marrying her and staying there? You could have built up a practice in England, couldn't you?"

"I considered that."

"Why didn't you then? Perhaps you weren't in love with her."

"It may have been that, but I don't think it was. I felt I had a duty here, to my own people."

He said it quietly, undramatically. It impressed her as much as anything that had ever been said to her. This is somebody very fine, she thought. As fine a person as I've met. And to that thought there came an afterthought that sent a glow along her veins, that this so fine person should want to talk to her, should have singled her out for his confidence. She must be something more than the obvious girl whom visiting firemen took for car drives in the moonlight.

In his study at Government House, Lord Templeton reread the report that he was submitting to the Minister of State, announcing his plans to implement the new constitution. It was short and concise, not unlike in form and manner the operation orders that he had issued to his company commanders. The concluding sentence ran: "I do not anticipate that any serious friction will result from the implementation of this policy."

He sealed down the envelope, then took a sheet of note paper and began a personal letter to the Minister.

"Dear Bunny, I am sending by this same mail in a separate envelope my situation report. I think it puts the matter clearly, but what I can never expect to convey in an official document is the essential *opera bouffe* atmosphere that colours every least event here. They are all of them comics, these West Indians, even or rather especially my legislative councillors; and like all true comedians they behave with the utmost seriousness. One must never let them think that their acting has not convinced one. And it's not only the coloured West Indians who behave in this way: 'the Sugar Barons,' as Olie nicknamed them, have caught their tempo. Let me give you an example of a case in which I was asked to intervene."

He described the Preston incident. "Could you imagine anything more ridiculous. A few miserable cane stalks stamped upon by a few mangy cows and a stake of fifteen depreciated West Indian dollars. But of course I must not allow them to think I consider it all ridiculous. Oh, dear me, no. I am telling them that the principles of British Justice are at stake; I am making a high issue of it. And indeed quite seriously I do feel that it would be most improper for me to intervene. The people here must learn that the same treatment must be given to everyone irrespective of the political impact of a decision. If politics run the courts, where is one?

"Did I tell you, by the way, that one of the chief figures in the island is my old friend Julian Fleury? I say old though I haven't seen him for over thirty years, but it's odd how one never in later life makes such firm friends as one does at school, and in one's first years in the regiment. One knows men as they really are at school. Later on they learn to cover up.

"Fleury incidentally does not see eye to eye with me in this case of Preston. He thinks it may lead to trouble, but I extracted even

92

from him the admission that something very unusual would have to happen first."

He reread the letter: folded it, put it in the envelope, but did not stick down the flap. It was his practice to leave an important letter open overnight. Not that he felt that he would need to alter it. The matter was well in hand.

From his bedroom window as he stood looking out over the harbor, he could hear the music of the dance. It sounded fiercer, tenser, more barbaric. He smiled. He had thought that they would let their hair down once he'd gone. He hoped Euan was having a good time.

The dance had not only become wilder, but the separate parties had disintegrated. Groups had split up and had reformed. At the Government House table the supply of champagne had ceased.

Carson was at the bar. "What a relief to get back to whisky," he was saying.

Maxwell was at his side. For Maxwell it had been a reasonably satisfactory evening. Nothing had happened to disturb his vanity. Sylvia had been friendly, almost affectionate. He had watched her carefully. She had shown no signs of exaggerated interest in anybody else. Perhaps he had been fancying things. Perhaps it would be a good idea if they accepted his father's suggestion and came to live in Jamestown. It must be lonely for her out there.

The tempo of the dance heightened. Euan Templeton was dancing again with Mavis. He rested his cheek against hers. She did not move away. It would be fun at that, telling it all to Doris.

Maxwell watching from the bar noted them with a smile. "Those two don't seem to be wasting time," he said.

Carson guffawed.

"The punters at the Aquatic Club were laying four to one on her this afternoon. The odds will shorten when this gallop is reported."

He put his hand into his hip pocket and brought out his cigarette case. It was a large case; he was a heavy smoker. He took out a cigarette, then offered it to Maxwell. Each flap was divided into two sections; one of these sections contained thicker cigarettes. Maxwell hesitated, then took one of them. He read on the thin paper, in gold lettering, *Laurens Alexandria*.

"Do you often smoke these?" he asked.

"Occasionally. On occasions."

Maxwell's hand was trembling as he lit a match. He hardly dared to kindle it. He took a whiff. There was no doubt about it.

It was like no sensation that he had felt before: rage, impotence, horror, sickening apprehension. Carson was the last person he would have expected: the last person he would have had it be. What chance did he stand against Carson? He looked desperately round the room. Sylvia was with Jocelyn; standing beside that agitator fellow and that pretty half-caste from the pharmacy. He hurried over. He was blind with misery. He had to get Sylvia home. He could not stand another minute here.

"It's time we were going. Let's be on our way." He ignored Margot, ignored Boyeur; to his sister he said: "Are you coming with us or will you stay on? Mother and Father have gone back."

"It's late. I might as well come too."

"Right. Then we're off." He put his hand under Sylvia's elbow.

Boyeur clenched his teeth. To be ignored in this way; and in front of Margot. To have no notice taken of him: at the very moment when he had been explaining something: and in front of Margot. Never had he felt more humiliated. I've a score to settle there, he thought.


Back in their room at his father's, Maxwell once again watched through the mosquito-netting Sylvia brush out her hair. She was chatting, brightly, about the evening.

"You much prefer it here in Jamestown, don't you," he said.

"It is more fun."

"You'd like to fall in with my father's plans, and have me take over the town side of things."

"If it would suit you all right."

"It would suit me all right."

It would indeed suit him very well. He could keep track of Carson's movements; lay traps; catch them out in lies. Now that he knew whom he was fighting, the road was easy. Yes, it would be much better if they came into Jamestown. He'd bide his time and when he got the evidence . . . His hands behind his head clasped one another with an angry, exulting promise: as though they were making a pact with one another. When the time came, they would know what to do.

# CHAPTER SEVEN

## 1

Lord Templeton's report reached the Colonial Office on a Friday afternoon. The Minister was going away for the week end early the following morning. He was a youthfully preserved man of middle age who had been too young for the first war and too old for the second. He had kept his figure and his hair. He was photogenic and married to an attractive and titled woman ten years younger than himself; the illustrated weeklies contained more photographs than his actual achievements warranted of Mr. Robert Marsh "forgetting affairs of state" at Lord's, Newbury, or a film premiere. Brisk, hearty, hail-fellow-well-met, he tended to make snap decisions, a tendency that forced him to rely more heavily than he liked on his parliamentary secretary, Purvis, a precise, scholarly young man, whom Marsh, an old Harrovian himself, described to his friends as "you know the type, old boy, one of those typical bloodless Wykehamists; etiolated; yes, that's the word, etiolated."

Purvis was not going away for the week end. He rarely did. He worked all Saturday. The office was quiet then and he was able to clear up work that had accumulated through the week. Though he slept late on Sunday, he took papers home with him. He lived with his parents in St. John's Wood.

Purvis glanced quickly over Templeton's report, and got its general gist; it looked straightforward; then he read the covering letter and pursed his lips. He wondered about this man Fleury. He would have preferred to make inquiries, and draft a memorandum. But it was after five o'clock. The Minister would not like to be left without a piece of information of this kind over a week end.

It was his custom to pay a final visit to his chief every evening at half-past five. He rang through to the personal secretary, a pert dapper little minx whom Purvis considered highly unsuitable for so confidential a position.

"O.K.," she said. "His nibs is ready."

The Minister looked up with his quick automatic smile.

"Any trouble this evening, Purvis?"

"A report from the Governor of Santa Marta, sir."

"Fine. What's he got on his mind?"

"He considers the island ready for the new constitution."

"Excellent, that's one problem settled."

"There's a covering letter."

"Oh," the Minister frowned. He wished people would not complicate his position by resorting to a personal basis of communication. Questions were asked him in the House which required cut and dried answers. He needed to quote from a Governor's report, not from a private letter.

"What does it say?"

"I think you'd better read it, sir."

"Right, let's see it then."

He read it quickly. Why on earth did the old man have to write this rigmarole about a local law case. Had he any idea how many papers a Minister had to read? It might amuse Jimmy Templeton with time upon his hands to write letters home, but he might consider the busy people who had to read them.

"There doesn't appear to be anything that concerns us here," he said.

"I thought you might like to make some inquiries about this Mr. Fleury."

The minister smiled. The indefatigable Purvis. There he went again. Leaving no stone unturned. No wonder it took such a long time to get an answer from the Treasury. One mustn't discourage him.

"I'll be very grateful for anything you can find out," he said. "Now, there's a question coming up next week about a tribesman in North Borneo . . ."

2

The Marshes were giving a cocktail party that evening. Marsh had promised to be home on time, but he had no intention of being so. In the days when he had been in Opposition, he had performed his duties as a host punctiliously. But now as quarter-past six became half-past six, he liked to picture Marjorie welcoming her guests with that fussed frown of hers.

"I must apologize for Robert. He promised to be here on time, but you know how it is."

Beneath the assumed anxiety in her voice there would be a smug complacent purr at having a husband with a legitimate excuse for unpunctuality. That purr was the greatest reward that office had brought him. He was devoted to Marjorie, and he enjoyed their life together. A little while ago he had had anxious moments. They had been married fifteen years and there had been danger signals. She was getting restless. The purr in her voice was reassuring. She liked being the wife of a senior Minister. It was all right now. Big Ben struck half-past six. Time to be on his way.

His house was in Brompton Square. He arrived there at quarter to seven. The party was in full swing. At the start of a party Marjorie turned on the radio to make people raise their voices and give to a three-quarters empty room a sense, through volume of sound, of its being full. The radio was now switched off. Marsh stood in the doorway, looking round him, waiting for Marjorie to notice him. He wanted to make an entrance, and he needed her help to make it. He had not long to wait. Her eye was always on the door till his arrival.

"Darling," she called, and ran across to him.

"Your host at last," she said.

She raised her voice; it was not a large room and conversation ceased. She made quite a thing of it. She slipped her arm through his. "Don't you pity me with a husband who can never be at home on time?"

She addressed the room at large. In her voice was that soft smug purr. He pressed her arm and she looked up and smiled. Success had brought them close.

"Settled the affairs of state satisfactorily?" said a man beside her.

There was a tinge of envy in his voice. It pleased Marsh as much as the purr had done. Its owner, a contemporary, and a banker, had been prominent in immediate postwar years on several economic missions, and had tended to patronize the Opposition M.P. who had no access either to an expense account or top secret files.

"Darling," Marjorie was saying. "There's a young man whom you should meet. Frank Lambert. The London correspondent of the *New York Sun*. Matilda brought him. Here he is."

Two paces away stood a tall sandy open-faced young man.

"I'm certainly glad you've made it, sir," he said. "I was just getting ready to check out. My weekly article goes in tomorrow; I've got to tap a pipeline or two before I hit the hay."

"In that case let's see if I can't give you material for a paragraph that will justify your staying here half an hour longer."

During the war Marsh had worked in the Ministry of Economic Warfare. Many top secret files had passed his way. He had acquired a nose for what was really confidential and what could be safely told. He liked to help a journalist when he could. It usually paid dividends. He ran his mind over the last three days: Malaya and Rhodesia were dynamite. Borneo was too parochial. But the Caribbean was an American sphere of interest.

"This might be of interest to you," he said. "I had a report tonight from the Governor of Santa Marta. I expect you know more about the island than I do."

"I wouldn't say that, but I have been there."

"I'll bet you have. That's the great advantage you fellows have over us; you know places by sight; we know them only from a dossier; but about Santa Marta, they're being given a new constitution. They've already got universal suffrage, now they'll have a majority of elected members in the council, a practical application of the Point Four principle; encouragement of backward peoples. There might be something there, I think?"

"There might indeed, sir, I'm most grateful."

Not a great deal though, Lambert reflected, as he moved away, his audience finished. He remembered Santa Marta clearly. He had spent a day there, on a pleasure cruise: they had done fifteen islands in three weeks. They had docked at Jamestown before lunch and sailed at seven. Someone on board knew someone on the island and there had been a party. They had had rum punches on a beach; there had been plenty of sandwiches and afterward no one felt like lunch; so they had driven round the island; he had been drowsy after all those punches and had fallen asleep, to find when he awoke his head on the shoulder of a quite pretty girl, a Mavis somebody, who'd been very amusing about the incident. They'd bathed again and gone back to the club for swizzles; and he and that Mavis Somebody had stood on the veranda looking out over the sea, waiting for the sun to sink, watching for the green ray, and suddenly he had found that they were holding hands and there's been something about her, he couldn't quite say what, something malleable and tender, yes, malleable was the word, a need to be taken charge of and be molded; something that had made him think, Why not stay on, let the boat sail, see what she's really like. Hop a plane back later. Why not, he'd asked himself. And then there'd been someone shouting, If we're going to make that boat we'd better hurry. They'd faced one another, he and that Mavis Somebody, and her eyes had said, It would be nice if you could stay on here but of course you can't. And the impulse had been very strong to counter back, Why shouldn't I? I'm a free man aren't I? But there was that voice insisting, We *must* go now. Where is young Lambert. Hell, he had thought, I can't do things like this. I'm a journalist. I've got to see all I can.

That had been Santa Marta: not so very different, in essentials, from the other islands, Antigua, St. Kitts, St. Lucia: he only remembered Santa Marta so vividly because of that Mavis Somebody and that wasn't a good enough reason to devote twenty lines of his weekly column to its new constitution. He'd better go, he thought. There was another cocktail party on his circuit; then he'd dine at Bolton's, a small intimate club frequented by politicians; if he kept his ears open there, he might hear something. He'd look in at his office afterward and see if there were any cables; then he'd go back and do his piece and wake fresh in the morning to revise it.

He was planning a kaleidoscopic series of vignettes of London life showing the variety of its different interests and strata, and how they were knit into homogeneity by the news, by the public events that made of seven million scattered Londoners one corporate body. It was an ambitious idea. He wanted to get it right. He'd better go.

He turned toward the door, but as he did, he saw at the head of the stairway something that made him check. She was, he guessed, in the middle twenties; she was of medium height. She was not plump but one day she might be fat. She wore a tight-fitting green dress. She was pale skinned, and had what it was contemporary to describe as "a pushed-in face." She moved smoothly. She was not a girl that men would turn round to look at in the streets, but she was a type he liked. Their eyes met and he checked his stride. Her impression was not so much sulky as lowering: if anyone annoyed her she would smack his face. The look excited him. He walked across to her.

"I was going to leave," he said, "but I've changed my mind. You're the most attractive girl I've seen in a long time."

She blinked, and her expression changed. He had accurately diagnosed her mood. She had had a bad day, starting with a headache, and an account rendered bill from a shop where she had planned to buy a new hat that morning. At her Whitehall office, she had been snapped at by the D.A.G.'s secretary. Finally she had been stood up at lunch by a man whom she had recognized for quite a long time now as a bad bet. This healthy looking young American presented a pleasantly wholesome contrast to all that.

"Do you know what I told myself as you came up the stairs?" he asked.

"You tell me what you told yourself."

"That there's a girl who puts a 'no' to all that talk about Englishwomen not knowing how to dress."

Her eyes were hazel and they sparkled. She could use a line like this.

99

"You can fetch me a martini, then you can tell me some more about myself," she said.

Eight hours later Frank Lambert paid off a taxi outside his flat in Westminster. No pipelines had been tapped, no cable had been studied. His head was light and his heart was singing. His typewriter faced him accusingly. He waved his hand to it. "Bide your time, my friend." He set his alarm for ten. His lunch date was for one. He had to be punctual. She only got an hour off. He wanted to look in at a jeweler's on the way. The kaleidoscope piece could wait. He could beat out some routine stuff round that idea of Marsh's; the West Indies, Santa Marta, Truman's Point Four. My, but life was good and unexpected. How little he'd thought last night when he'd started out for that cocktail party that he wouldn't be back here for nine hours, and in this mood.

### 3

Lambert's article on Santa Marta was snipped from the *New York Sun* by a sub-editor on the *Baltimore Evening Star* and sent up to his chief's secretary with the comment, "In view of W.R.'s recent trip, this may interest."

It interested but it irritated Wilson Romer. This should have appeared in his own paper. Why hadn't it? It was a reflection on his own power of intuition. He had heard rumors of this new constitution, had indeed discussed it with Mr. Fleury, but he had no idea that its implementation was immediate. Why hadn't he got on to it? Was he losing his grip? He felt angry with himself, and sought an outlet for his irritation. It was the Governor's fault far more than his. The Governor should have told him. He had appeared to be taking his guest into his confidence. Why should that confidence have stopped halfway? That was the trouble with the English. You never knew where you were with them. They had so many layers of reserve. You thought you had got to know them but you never had. Their real selves lay under yet another layer. Damn them and their diplomacy. This settled it. Bradshaw should go down there.

On his return to Baltimore he had reconsidered his decision. The Caribbean had seemed important when he was actually there, among people whose horizon was bounded by it, but back home there was so much else important. Why waste a man down there? He had half changed his mind. This article sent him back to his first intention. No titled Governor was going to hoodwink Wilson P. Romer. If there was any news in that trumpery little place, he would be the first with it: and if any of that news was hot, he'd know how to make it hotter.

## 4

Romer's cable to the Governor read: "Sending Santa Marta-ward senior reporter Carl Bradshaw leave absence stop rest cure not assignment stop appreciate your help."

The Governor chuckled. The gentleman did protest too much. Did Romer think he was a fool because he was a soldier. He handed the cable to his A.D.C.

"This is your pigeon. Show him everything. Invite him to dinner his first evening here; but bear in mind that everything you say will be cabled back to Baltimore; behave as though you didn't know it would."

Archer had not been to America. But he had read many American novels and seen a great many American films, among others *The Front Page.* He knew what to expect of an American journalist. Bradshaw would be untidy; he would wear a battered hat indoors; he would shave at night; his pockets would be filled with packs of cigarettes; he would breakfast off a two finger shot of bourbon. As his day began so would it continue; yet he would never appear the worse for liquor. He would have a way with dames.

Carl Bradshaw was not at all like that. Bald, cherubic, rosy-cheeked, shiny with soap and redolent of eau de Cologne, he wore a freshly pressed brown and white striped rayon suit; his bow tie was narrow-ended and neatly knotted. He spoke in a high-pitched voice, with a Boston accent, his large hold-all type bag was new. A portable typewriter was the only indication of his calling.

He arrived at half-past three in the afternoon. "I expect you're thirsty after your trip," said Archer. He had a bottle of Canadian Club whisky in the car.

"I am. I should enjoy a cup of tea," was the unexpected answer.

Archer had booked him a room at the Continental.

"H.E. wanted to invite you to G.H. at any rate for the first few days, but as you are here for a rest cure he thought you might prefer to be on your own. H.E. has to do a good deal of official entertaining you might have found exhausting. But if later on . . ."

"I appreciate His Excellency's concern, but as you say I am run down. I shall be better on my own."

"At the same time H.E. very much hopes that you will be able to dine with him tonight: not a large party; half a dozen or so representative people whom he thought it would be of interest to you to meet. It won't be a late evening, but if you don't feel up to it . . ."

"I normally take a rest between five and six. With that refreshment I find myself able to stay up till two or three in the morning."

"You won't find many people ready to stay up with you that long. People pack up soon after dinner; they take their exercise between five and six."

"In that case I shall have to adjust my schedule. Ah, here's the tea. Sandwiches, but no cakes. I wonder if they have any eclairs. Would they send out for some?"

He put three spoonfuls of sugar in his tea. After one sip he put in another.

"I'm surprised that your sugar isn't sweeter. Perhaps it's exported in a more concentrated form."

"Would you like to look over the sugar factory?"

"Not particularly."

The reply surprised Archer and impressed him. He was used to visitors who let themselves be victimized and patiently inspected housing projects that must surely bore them. This man was at least original.

"You're very wise," he said, "and we realize, of course, that you are on a rest cure. At the same time H.E. would like you to take back an overall picture of our life here. We were wondering, by the way, we should know of course, but we don't see the American papers as often as we'd like, what kind of article do you write."

"Feature articles."

That didn't help Archer much.

"Is there anything you'd particularly like to know about?" he asked.

"I'm a little curious about the religious life."

That was another surprise for Archer. "In what way curious?" he asked.

"The island was, I believe, French originally. That usually means a strong Roman Catholic element."

"About ninety per cent of the peasants are Roman Catholic."

"But officially the island is—what is your English phrase for it— Episcopalian?"

"They call themselves Anglo-Catholics."

"That means high church?"

"Incense and all that, yes. Red robes for the choir. You know how Africans love dressing up."

"Do you have a bishop here?"

"No, only an archdeacon. There aren't enough churches for a

102

bishop. There's a bishop in Antigua. We're in his diocese, and in Jamaica there's an archbishop for the whole British West Indies."

"Are the congregations large?"

"Very."

"That's very interesting. Yes, most interesting."

He really did seem interested too. This was better copy than Archer had dared to hope. He rose to his feet.

"I'll leave you to unpack," he said, "and to your siesta. I'll call for you at a quarter to eight. Black tie."

Back at G.H., Archer slowed his pace as he passed the secretariat. He glanced into the room, and his spirits lifted. Margot was alone. Her presence within fifty yards of him for eight hours of the day was proving a considerable strain. He kept making excuses to cross the courtyard, to see if she was by herself. She seldom was. He quickened his pace toward her door.

She looked up with a casual smile as he laid a package on her desk. It contained a length of yellow silk that he had bought on the way to the airport at the Syrian Bazaar.

"You might be able to make yourself a dress with this," he said.

"That's very kind of you."

She opened a drawer and put the package in it. It pleased him more than it disappointed him that she did not tear back a corner of the package to see the color and to feel the texture.

On her desk was lying an anthology of modern poetry that he had lent her.

"What do you make of them?" he asked.

"A lot. Now you've read them to me first. If you hadn't I'd have missed their rhythm."

"Which was your favorite?"

"I liked several."

She picked up the book and turned its pages. "This for instance—" and began to read out loud a poem by Nigel Heseltine.

> That autumn when the partridges called in the stubble
> I waded the wet beet to my knees and angrily fired
> At birds who had no part in my trouble
> And blew them apart and walked all day till I was tired.

She read it rhythmically. Yes, she'd got its measure. It was extraordinary that she had, she who had scarcely read a line of poetry a month ago; but perhaps it was only natural that she should. Modern poetry was on the wavelength of its day; addressed to its day, saying things for that day. And those who were of that day should be able

103

to pick it up. It was those who had been taught to listen on the wavelength of an earlier day, who had been bred in the tradition of Milton, Wordsworth, Tennyson who could not hear the rhythms of Spender, Day Lewis, Dylan Thomas.

Margot read on:

> Gnawing in me that drove my feet on, her face in every wall
> her walk upon the hill, her voice, her tall
> body below the trees. The hot September sun was like a
>     prison
> binding me in parched heat where I trod up and down and
>     never could reach the horizon.

Her voice was rich and melodious. He had not realized before how good the poem was. She put down the book.

"I wish you'd show me some of your own poems," she said. "Read them to me first, as you did these ones, then let me take them away and read them by myself."

He hesitated for a moment. He was shy of showing his poems. He had no idea if they were any good. He was confident in his capacity to write. He believed that he would make his mark as a novelist or a critic, but he was uncertain of himself, as a poet. His poems had been published in Oxford magazines, but that might be only because poetry of his kind was in the fashion, and editors liked to play for safety. When Jocelyn Fleury had asked to see them, he had shaken his head. He could not have stood the comments she might have made, about not being "educated up to it." With Margot it was different. She had the direct vision of a primitive painter; he would like to know what she thought about them. If he heard her read them he might have a better idea as to whether they had any quality.

"I'll bring some in tomorrow."

There was a pause.

"When are we going to meet again?" he said.

"You are the busy one."

It was said uncoquettishly. She was never coy. She never flirted. Her directness was one of her chief attractions for him. They had met several times since the Nurses' Dance, briefly for snatched moments, drives along the coast sandwiched between two engagements, fretted by the knowledge that anyone driving by would recognize his car. He recalled the warning that he had given to young Templeton on the afternoon of that first garden party. It was ironical that he should have been so prescient.

"It's maddening, this seeing you and yet not seeing you," he said.

"I know."

She said it simply.

That was another of her attractions for him, the feeling that she knew what was in his mind. She did not have to have things explained or veiled. He could not see her alone in Government House. He could not take rooms in town.

"Don't your parents ever go out?" he said.

"Sometimes."

"Couldn't I see you there?"

"I don't see why not."

"Next time they go out will you let me know?"

"I will."

Her eyes were looking straight into his. He had the breathtaking certainty that she would. There would be no need to pester her with questions. One day she would say "tomorrow."

In the meantime when did he see her next? It was four days since he had been alone with her. Tomorrow he would be out all day. The day after seemed a century away. He was thinking fast. The party at G.H. would break up early: he would have to see some of the guests home.

"Are you going to the pictures tonight?" he asked.

"Most likely."

"Then if you do, lose whoever you're with as you come out. If I can manage, I'll be parked behind the Continental. If I'm not there, don't wait."

"O.K."

His heart was thudding as he crossed to the Governor's study.

"What was the spy like?" asked Templeton.

"More like a spy, sir, than a journalist."

Archer described the meeting.

"In that case, see if the Archdeacon is free for dinner. Apologize for a last minute invitation.

5

Carl Bradshaw's description of himself as a feature writer was misleading. His function as New York representative was to keep the paper in touch with the big city. He contributed twice a week a signed column of paragraphs and to the Sunday supplement a full page diary, "The Week in New York." He was a gossip writer rather than a columnist.

It was work for which he considered himself admirably suited, and it allowed him to lead the kind of life he liked. He was gregarious, he enjoyed the theater; he was interested in personalities. He was spared direct editorial supervision, he had a three room apartment on the river, he was invited to cocktail parties, he entertained at his paper's expense, he lunched at the Coffee House three days a week. His work gave him a special status. Hostesses liked to think that their activities were being recorded in another city and authors and playwrights felt they were being given national publicity. He had his own niche in Manhattan's life. He had held the post now for twenty years, with complete satisfaction to himself. Until a year or so ago he had considered himself an example of the happy man.

Recently, however, he had become aware that the satisfaction which he was giving to a certain section of the editorial staff of the *Baltimore Evening Star* was incomplete. It had been suggested that he might widen the range of his contributions. Why so little about the United Nations: it was questioned whether the efforts of seaboard society hostesses to maintain their prewar traditions of hospitality under the present strain of income tax were quite as interesting as the struggle of their children to adapt themselves to "this brave New World." Scott Fitzgerald's heroines had been grandmothers now for quite a while.

Carl Bradshaw knew what they were thinking—that he was old-fashioned, out of date, no longer in the swim. It was a criticism that made him petulant. How could he at his time of life start to make new friends? He could not drop his old ones, there were only fourteen meals in a week. And where were the new "pipelines"? The children of his friends? It had been one thing to take them to the zoo when they were ten-year-olds; but to pick up those threads now —he corrected himself, to try to pick them up; how hopeless. They were now mothers-of-families; they classed him with their mother's friends, they thought of him as a nice old fogey; they had friends of their own; the last thing they wanted was to have their homes littered with their parents' friends, who'd carry gossip "home to mother." He considered that he had shown admirable tact, admirable good sense in not attempting to exploit them. He would have made himself ridiculous. At the same time he had become acutely conscious of the mounting irritation in Baltimore. His present assignment might not be the sack, but it was the embroidered bag. This was a last chance, he told himself, as he dressed for the Governor's dinner party.

He was in a resolute, determined mood. He knew what failure would involve: not destitution; nothing as dramatic as that; he had been prudent, he had invested wisely the money that he had saved. He was in a position to resign from the paper if they made him an

106

offer which would insult his pride. But what would his life be without his work: no more seats for openings, no more lunch parties "on the house": no more opportunities of doing things for people; no more being solicited for this or the other project. What would he be able to contribute to the talk round the octagonal table at the Coffee House? New York was a place where people worked: you were graded by the social status that your work accorded you. Apart from your work you were a nobody. In London it was different, so he had been told; there it wasn't so much what you did, as who you were. A retired man would be listened to with deference at the Athenaeum. But not in New York. His life would not be worth living if he lost his New York post.

He was not going to lose it if he could help. Romer might have sent him down here as a prelude to retirement, but it was still within his power to send back an article, a series of articles, that would show those young fools in Baltimore that he knew a story when he saw one. He no more believed that Romer had sent him down on an assignment than His Excellency believed he was on a rest cure.

### 6

It was the first time that Bradshaw had dined at Government House in a British colony. He was impressed. These Englishmen had something. They had lost their Empire, their coinage was debased, their mines were obsolete, their navy was minute, yet they still behaved as though they owned the universe. Lord Templeton's descent of the wide curving staircase was like a film scene. Only Hollywood would have botched it. They would have given him some elaborate decoration, a sash across his shirt front; Hollywood would have missed the dignity of that slow descent with one man in a plain white uniform with four rows of medal ribbons concentrating in his person the "might, majesty, dominion and power" of a far-flung empire.

Archer had put him at the extreme right of the line; he was the first to be welcomed by the Governor.

"It is a great pleasure and a real privilege," he said, "to welcome you, Mr. Bradshaw, to our island. We hope you will be happy among us, and we hope that you will go back to your work in your own country refreshed and restored by your rest cure here."

Bradshaw winced at the words "rest cure." So Romer had told him that. It was like the letter that Claudius had sent by Gildenstein; it was as good as though Romer had said "this man is of no concern to us any longer, but I shall be grateful if you will pay him the deference due to a member of our staff." Romer had not taken the precaution of telling Bradshaw how he had worded his cable and with what intent.

7

Carl Bradshaw had one great merit as a gossip writer. He was a good listener. As a young man with his way to make he had earned a reputation as a raconteur. As he dressed for dinner he would think out epigrams and plan how he could lead the conversation so as to employ them. He liked to think that next day half the guests would be saying at other tables, "That young fellow Carl Bradshaw was at Molly Winn's last night. He's an engaging scamp!" He had pictured other hostesses making mental notes, "Carl Bradshaw. I must remember to put that name upon my list." It had worked very well when he was twenty-five.

In the early forties, however, he had changed his technique. He had read a story by Osbert Sitwell called *The Machine Runs Down*. He had recognized that there are few bores more tiresome than the middle-aged raconteur. No one has an unlimited repertoire of stories, and as the years went by, he had come to find it increasingly difficult to remember in which company he had told which story; so he stopped telling stories and encouraged other people to talk about themselves. The easiest way to being considered a good talker is to make it easy for others to talk well. Nowadays, after a dinner party he had attended he pictured the other guests saying the next day, "I had such an interesting talk last night at Molly's with Carl Bradshaw. He's so wise, so understanding."

He glanced at the place card of the lady next to him. He had been introduced to her, but the A.D.C. had in the English manner dropped his voice at the end of the sentence. Thank heaven the young man's script was legible. He read the name—Mrs. Norman. She was an attractive looking woman in the middle forties; brown hair, brown eyes, pale skin; in a few years time she would be plump; the kind of woman with whom he felt most at ease.

"I want you to tell me everything about everybody here," he said. "But first of all I want you to tell me all about yourself."

"There's not much to tell."

She had been born here, she said. Her father had a cocoa and sugar estate on the leeward side. Her husband was a Barbadian, in Barclay's Bank. "That's him over there." She indicated a tall thin balding sandy-colored man across the table. He had come to Santa Marta as junior cashier. "He was twenty-five and I was seventeen.

108

He came here for three years as an apprentice; he's been here ever since. That's all there is to it."

"It sounds a very satisfactory story."

"I'm not complaining."

"Have you any children?"

"Two daughters. The younger one's married to Maxwell Fleury, the son of the man next to the Archdeacon."

"Indeed, that's interesting."

In the briefing that he had been given by his chief, he had been advised to concentrate on Fleury. He was impressed by his appearance. Fleury had an air of dignity and indifference. He would be, Bradshaw reflected, suave, affable, but reserved. I'll probably learn more about Fleury from his daughter-in-law's mother than from himself. He might do worse than concentrate on her.

"Is your husband manager of the bank?" he asked.

"Among other things. He's several irons in the fire. He runs my father's estate, in all but name. Daddy's getting past it now. He's also one of the directors of the St. James Hotel. It's actually too much for him. I'd like him to give up the bank and concentrate on the hotel; I believe there are tourist possibilities here if the right men worked on it in the right way; what do you think, Mr. Bradshaw?"

"I've only been here a few hours."

"I know; but you got a bird's eye view of the island coming in to it on the plane. You saw the beaches, you saw . . ."

As she dilated on the special and varied attractions of Santa Marta, Bradshaw followed his own thoughts. All these islands wanted to cash in on the tourist trade; the rewards were so great and certain islands had cashed in so handsomely. Jamaica, Bermuda, the Virgin Islands. The trouble was to get things started. It was not only that Americans wanted "States side comfort," hot running water and chilled orange juice; they wanted to meet other Americans when they traveled; on their return they wanted to be able to talk about places that their friends had heard about: to compare notes with Frank and Mary. If you could get six American tourists to Santa Marta, you could get sixty. But how to get those six?

"What do you think Mr. Bradshaw?"

As she talked an idea had struck him.

"I'd advise you to concentrate on a summer season," he advised. "Between January and March you're in competition with luxury resorts, and luxury hotels. You're trying to attract a plush clientele and the rich go where the rich are. In July and August you can aim at a different, simpler clientele. The plush people are in Maine or Newport or the South of France, but there is a large group of school

109

teachers, students, parents whose children have gone to camp, who want a holiday in the sun. The climate in those months is very good down here: it's not too hot. The only bad months are September through November. Why don't you concentrate on trying to get American tourists in the summer?"

As he talked, his own plan began to rise in his estimation. Santa Marta might get in on the ground floor.

"A summer in the West Indies may be a thing of the future," he continued. "Fifty years ago no one thought of the South of France in August. Now the winter season is almost dead." He spoke with conviction. It sounded feasible. He could see that it had appealed to Mrs. Norman.

"You must tell this to Jim," she said. "You must come round one evening for a cocktail."

It was exactly what he had wanted. She might prove a useful "pipeline." He looked across the table at Fleury: as he did so he was aware of the Archdeacon looking at him. It was almost a stare. His own eyes met it. The Archdeacon held his glance, then with a half smile as it were of recognition, looked away. It was for Bradshaw a dramatic instant.

The party as Archer had prophesied broke up early.

"I'm sure," the Governor said, "that our guest from Baltimore needs a full night's sleep. And I'm sure he'll soon learn to adjust himself to our early hours."

He walked beside Bradshaw into the hall.

"You're here for a rest, but at the same time as a journalist you'll want to see as much of the island as you can. I'm only too anxious to help you; if there's anything you're in doubt about, get in touch with Archer. There's one thing I'd particularly advise you not to miss—a case that's coming on in the Courts next week; about a planter whose cattle strayed onto the neighbor's land. It'll give you a picture of our Island life."

On the other side of him the Archdeacon waited. "We've had no chance of a real talk this evening. I wonder if you could take a dish of tea with me one afternoon. You could—delightful. Would Thursday suit you? I shall look forward to it. In the meantime may I give you a lift back to your hotel."

Bradshaw was about to accept but Archer interposed.

"No, Father, that's right out of your way. I've got our car waiting. Really, I insist. I'd enjoy the drive."

His eye had been on the clock for the last twenty minutes. It was half-past ten. The cinema would be out at quarter to. It was essential that he should leave when the others did. Otherwise the old man would keep him talking.

He turned to the Governor. "Will you be wanting me again this evening, sir?"

"No, no, my boy. That's everything."

Archer's heart beat fast as he took his seat at the wheel. In a quarter of an hour's time, he thought.

The Normans drove the Fleurys back. Jocelyn had taken the family car for a bathing party. Mrs. Norman drove, with Fleury at her side.

"Did you have any talk with him?" she asked.

"Scarcely a word."

"Did you hear what he was saying about the possibility of a tourist summer season?"

"It made sense to me."

"There, do you hear that, Jim? That's what I thought too. I'm always telling you that we could make more out of the St. James. Three-quarters of the rooms are empty. It's ridiculous that Mr. Bradshaw should be booked at the Continental. Just because it's got a reputation for being livelier. You're on the Council and you run the Tourist Board. If anyone could do anything you could. Don't you agree, Julian?"

"You may have got something there."

"I've asked Mr. Bradshaw for a drink on Friday. We won't make it a big party. Six or seven. We'll find out if he's anything to suggest."

They drew up outside the Fleury house. The car was already in the drive. "It's early for them to be back," Mrs. Fleury said.

There was no downstairs light on in the Fleury house, but at the Normans' the drawing room was lit up. Mavis was stretched in a long chair, smoking, a glass of milk beside her. She did not get up as her parents entered. "Hullo," she said. Her voice was listless.

"You're back very early," her mother said.

"Euan was feeling tired, so was Jocelyn."

"Did you have a good time?"

"It was all right."

She rose languidly, stretching her arms above her head. Her parents exchanged a glance. Mavis was a problem they preferred not to discuss. Each knew what the other thought. But there were some things better not put into words.

In the doorway Mavis paused, turned slowly round to face them.

111

"I wonder what you would say if I were to ask—no, there's no point in asking. I know the answer."

No point at all, she told herself, as she walked upstairs. Oh, she was so tired of it all. What a fit they would have if they could know what she had it on the tip of her tongue to ask them.

Carl Bradshaw stood at his window, looking out over the now silent town. He had slept badly on the plane the night before. He had had a siesta, but his mind was racing. He had made a good start. He had learnt a lot. He had seen how the field was set. Mrs. Norman would prove useful; she was garrulous; she had children; she was in several camps. But the Archdeacon, that was a different matter. There was a kinship there, different though they were in age, in race, in calling; they could talk in shorthand. He looked forward to tea on Thursday.

From the courtyard below came the purr of a revolving engine. He craned his neck. A car drew out of the shadows and drove toward the shore. It looked very like the car in which he had been driven down. It was a quarter of an hour, at least, since he had been dropped. What on earth had the A.D.C. been doing? The bar was closed. He must check up on this.

*8*

The Archdeacon surveyed his tea table with approval. He had an English idea of how a tea table should look. Old china, a silver tray, thin-cut cucumber and marmite sandwiches, hot scones, a fruit cake. He fancied that his guest's tastes were similar.

He had guessed correctly. Bradshaw's eyes brightened.

"I am being indulged."

"We try to maintain our civilized *oubliettes*."

Bradshaw looked round him. The Archdeacon, he had been informed, had the best house in Jamestown.

"Now and again," Archer had told him, "you get a first class example of Georgian architecture in the Caribbean, particularly in Antigua. Have you seen John Summerstown's book? H. E.'s got a copy, I'll lend it you. There are not too many houses left, of course, there've been so many hurricanes, and fires and what not, and the atmosphere here is French. The Archdeacon's house is one of the best examples. It was built after the English took over: being a Catholic island there was no Anglican establishment; they had to build one. They meant it for a bishop. It's called the Palace. Have a good look when you go there, compare it with some of your New

112

England colonial styles. There are some features that may be new to you: the long low arched fanlights over the doors for instance."

Bradshaw had been prepared for a gracious harmony of line, but he had not expected that Georgian paneling would serve as a background for a Venetian mirror, a cutglass chandelier, Chippendale chairs and Doulton china.

"The Church seems to treat its Archdeacon far better than the Commonwealth treats its Governor," he commented.

The Archdeacon chuckled. It was the kind of compliment he relished.

"It is not so much the Church that tempers the wind to the Archdeacon, as the Archdeacon's aunt. The old lady was, I venture to say, extremely fond of me, but she had an unfortunate experience in youth. She was, I think it is the correct word, jilted, by a curate. She cherished as a result an unfortunate prejudice against the cloth. She was distressed when I took holy orders. I was her favorite nephew. I had always believed I was to be her heir; I proved to be, but only on condition that I preached the gospel to the heathen. It was a pretty point for the lawyers to decide, whether or not the West Indians could be classed as heathen. Finally it was agreed that my aunt had meant anybody with a dark complexion. So I came out here.

"Was it a life sentence?"

"A ten years' sentence, with ill health as a waiver clause."

"Yet you've been out here over twenty years."

"I've come to like it here."

"For the climate's sake?"

"Not altogether. Every climate has its disadvantages: even this one. Its advantages are obvious. It is never oppressively hot; there is no rainy season. It's a little sticky in October and November; but that is all. There are no diseases. For the first two years one feels one is in the Garden of Eden, then one finds one would give anything for a sharp September morning with a mist in the valley, the leaves turning yellow and frost in the air. I have leave every three years. I always arrange it so that I shan't miss a day of an English autumn."

"Why have you stayed on here?"

"Motives are mixed. The more confessions I hear—and for certain members of my congregation I strongly recommend confession, it clears the minds, take burdens off the shoulders—the more confessions I hear the more I realize that people do not recognize the causes of their actions, even to themselves. It may be that I've stayed on because the climate had made me lazy, perhaps it's because I have

113

more than a suspicion that if I went back to England I should find myself out of touch with my old friends: those were I daresay factors in my decision, but I should like to believe that I stayed on because I felt that I could do more good here."

He paused and his voice took on the same slow tone that it reached in the peroration to his sermons. It was not a theatrical, mannered, sanctimonious manner. People liked his sermons because he was direct, simple, and sincere. "These people are good at heart, they are lovable, gay, good-natured. But they have no roots; they are featherdown in the wind, and the winds blow strongly. Their lives are drab; they are born and live and die in squalor. They need badly what the church can give them, the pomp and pageant of its ritual, the majesty of its language, its reminder of a world elsewhere, of values beyond their own. I know that they go to church because they like dressing up, because they meet their friends there, because they enjoy singing hymns; they don't understand the meaning of the words they use; but those words repeated Sunday after Sunday through a lifetime do create, as the passage of time creates a patina, a subconscious armor of faith. One knows one's doing good here."

He paused. A twinkle came into his eye and the tone of his voice changed.

"When I go back to England and see my contemporaries in their Georgian rectories and fashionable city churches, I don't envy them their congregations. Established religion in England today, well shall I put it this way, I can't honestly say that in England I should care to choose my personal friends from the churchgoing section of the community."

Bradshaw chuckled. This was a man after his own heart. And what a relief after those sour swizzles and savory canapes was this profusion of scones dripping with warm butter, and cakes layered with cream and coated with almond icing. The tea too, though Indian, was slightly scented, with a Chinese aftertaste.

"I'm not saying," the Archdeacon was continuing, "that a great deal of very noble work isn't being done in the slum areas of England, but we must accept the limitations that the good Lord has chosen to impose on us, and can you picture me, my dear Mr. Bradshaw, in a dockyard parish."

They laughed together. Yes, this was a man after his own heart. They did not need to explain themselves. Bradshaw had been right in gauging that look across the dinner table as one of recognition.

"Even so," Bradshaw said, "it does a little surprise me that you should have taken holy orders in the first place."

"Another case of mixed motives possibly." The Archdeacon said

114

it in a tone suggesting he would prefer to evade that question. But Bradshaw was insistent. He had documented himself carefully on his man before coming out. Father Roberts was well connected, with titled cousins, there was money in the family, he had gone up to Oxford in the early twenties. Bradshaw was an anglophile. He spent at least an hour a week in the Holliday Bookshop. He knew what that period stood for.

He was not, however, prepared to let the Archdeacon know how carefully documented he was. He assumed a semi-knowledge.

"They tell me you were at Oxford; judging from your age you were up at what must have been the period of the Bright Young People. I shouldn't have thought that the religious atmosphere was strong there at the time. And I should have thought you were the kind of person who would, as a young man, be in the swim."

The Archdeacon smiled, nostalgically. Yes, he had been in the swim all right. And what a period to be in the swim of. Oxford in '22 and '23. The Hypocrites Club and all those feuds between the aesthetes and the hearties. A halcyon period. The wartime lot had all gone down, and the young men who had been submerged at their public schools during the war with the indifference shown to anyone who was not in the war—"Don't bother us with your petty problems when your uncles, brothers, and fathers are in the trenches"—the young men who had begun to think when the war was over that they were of no account because they had been too young to fight, a generation that had grown up with a chip on its shoulder, rebellious and self-distrustful, had at last had a chance to spread its wings. How it had spread them, and what wings.

From a distance of three thousand miles, he had watched his contemporaries one by one make their mark in public life. Christopher Hollis and Hugh Molson in the House of Commons, Peter Quennel as a critic and a poet, Anthony Powell as a novelist, Cyril Connolly that captious arbiter of taste, Harold Acton that elusive aesthete, Patrick Kirross as a keen, quick-witted traveler, John Sutro as a voice behind London films, the mysterious Henry Green, Claud Cockburn with his live pen and many pseudonyms, Anthony Bushell on the stage, Terence Grenidge with his eccentric publications, Robert Bryon—what might he not have achieved if the war had spared him, and how much he had achieved before that untimely end; and finally, as first the mouthpiece of the period, and its highest peak—the author of *Vile Bodies*: A halcyon period; so halcyon that he did not dare to think of it now, too often.

It was true that there had not been much talk then of religion, and for that very reason it had been an amusing conversational line in tune with the temper of the day to announce that he was proposing to take holy orders; in the same way that when it was "the thing" to be a socialist, it had been amusing to make Tory speeches at the Union. But that had been a very partial, a very superficial reason for his acceptance of a calling.

He had been always what his contemporaries had labeled "serious-minded." He had always needed a solid rock under his feet. He had never doubted the general tenets of the faith in which he had been raised. When his contemporaries were seeking for panaceas in Marx and Bernard Shaw he had believed sincerely that the Established Church offered a sounder answer. Social reform alone would not satisfy the hankerings of the human heart for something that could not be explained in terms of material improvement. He had in addition a deep-rooted social sense of obligation toward his fellows. He wanted to help others to find the road that had led him to a peace of spirit. But he was not prepared to take this highly agreeable American into his confidence to the extent of explaining quite all of that.

"I agree with you," he said, "it was a wild bright time; in which religion was a negligible factor. But within a few years many of my contemporaries had come to feel need for authority and guidance. A number became Catholics, and quite a few, you may remember, became communists; though most of them, I fancy, have recanted since. Perhaps I was a little ahead of my friends in feeling that need for authority and guidance in 1924 instead of 1930. Perhaps because I felt it earlier, I was not forced to the same extremes. I could satisfy that need in the faith of my forefathers."

He said it simply, but directly; Bradshaw was impressed. This was a far deeper, more complex man than he had suspected when he had been aware of that pensive glance fixed on him across the table. He must put in a lot of time on Father Roberts.

Slowly he worked the conversation round to the island's more general problems.

"You probably see more than anyone," he said. "The people relax with you. Would you say there was any danger here of communism?"

The Archdeacon shook his head. "They've not reached that stage yet. There's the usual conflict of the haves and the have-nots, but they are very backward; they have stayed backward because the intelligent ones go to the larger islands, Jamaica and Trinidad, and to British Guiana; that's where you'll find communism, where there are highly intelligent educated men who feel that they can't advance because of the inequalities of the social system under which they live. That's a thing you've always got to realize about this place. The best people go somewhere else. Take a fellow like David Boyeur, whom you'll be meeting soon if you've not already met him. He'd never amount to anything in Jamaica. He has no real education. He's forced to cultivate his own back yard. Communism isn't a problem here; it may be in twenty years but it isn't now. The party is too busy organizing its cells in Trinidad, Jamaica, and B.G. to worry about Santa Marta."

This information disappointed Bradshaw. He had thought there might be an article on the communist menace as presented by British West Indians who were coming up to the States. It might have made a three day sensation. It still might, at a later date, and in another place, but his present assignment was the Windward and Leeward Islands.

"What would you say then was *the* issue here?" he asked.

"Color, my dear fellow, color."

A mischievous look came into the Archdeacon's eye: he was a good man, devout, sincere, an idealist, but he had a leavening humanizing share of malice.

"For three hundred years," he said, "Europeans have been settling in these islands. There has been marriage and intermarriage and every variety of irregular alliance. Nobody can be sure of their precise ancestry. How many Englishmen know the maiden name of their mother's maternal grandmother. We all carry in our veins blood of whose nature we have no suspicion. In England that does not matter, since our skins are white; but here where skins are brown, it's a different matter. There used to be a phrase, 'touch of the tarbrush.' Now its place has been taken by 'passes for white,' and there isn't a family that does not try to pretend that as far as itself is concerned, those two words 'passes for' do not exist."

"Does it matter so very much?"

"More than you as an American from the North can begin to realize. A Southerner would not ask that question. You don't have our situation in the North. Your colored folk are segregated in different parts of your cities. You aren't meeting them all the time, as Southerners are, and we are here. When I first came out I was astonished to realize how much that trace of color meant, how many social barriers it creates. There was a time, as you won't need reminding, in Haiti before the French Revolution when Moreau St. Mery drew up some two hundred different classifications of mixed blood. That spirit still persists. The man with an eighth mixture considers himself the superior of the man with a quarter; though the man who's completely African thinks himself the superior of

117

the man of mixed blood. But the pure white and pure African among the educated classes are the exception. Among the vast majority this question of color affects every official, social, and political issue."

"Indeed."

Bradshaw was listening attentively. He was on to something now.

"It would amuse you," the Archdeacon was continuing, "to know the trouble to which these patrician families put themselves to conceal what everybody knows. You noticed the Kellaways for instance at G.H. the other night. It's obvious to everyone that she has some African ancestry. But will she admit it—no of course she won't. And the grandmother who might give away the secret is kept well out of sight, tucked away in a nice little villa in the hills and never allowed to come into Jamestown."

The Archdeacon chuckled. The malicious side of his nature was in control.

"Old parish records are most illuminating," he went on. "I was something of a scholar in my day. I had a taste for research. I get few opportunities of indulging it today. But I have derived much entertainment from tracing the genealogies of our leading families: when I visit other islands, as I often have to, I continue my research there. Several members of my congregation would be astonished by the information I possess about their antecedents."

Again he gave that ripe, rich chuckle.

"I'm having cocktails with the Normans tomorrow. Is there a skeleton in that cupboard?"

The Archdeacon shook his head. "Norman is a Barbadian; the French never touched Barbados. It lay outside the cock-pit arena of the eighteenth century. It lay too far to the east and with the trades winds blowing against them, the French in Guadeloupe and Martinique could never launch an attack against it, so the rule of the whites was never disturbed. The same thing happened in Antigua in a lesser way; and that's where Mrs. Norman's mother came from. Her father's family has a clear record too, at least as far as her father's concerned. He's a nice old boy; built the St. James Hotel. You'll probably meet him there tomorrow."

"Will you be there?"

"One of the advantages of my calling is that I have an excuse for not attending cocktail parties. I consider them one of the most barbarous inventions of our day. Evensong is sung in the Cathedral every evening at six o'clock. If ever you need an alibi, my dear fellow, there it is."

# CHAPTER EIGHT

## 1

The Archdeacon was right in thinking that Mavis' grandfather would be asked to meet Carl Bradshaw. Mrs. Norman wanted the American to meet new people. She discussed the party's composition with Mavis.

"We'd better ask Euan. He wasn't at G.H.," she said.

To her mother's surprise Mavis shook her head. "Euan sees quite enough of us."

Her mother made no comment. She remembered Mavis' manner on the previous evening. They must have had a tiff.

"Who else would you suggest? Doris Kellaway?"

"She's always fun."

"We want some men."

"That's a perpetual problem."

"What about Denis Archer?"

"There's always Denis Archer."

It was said with an eloquent absence of enthusiasm.

"Don't you like him?"

"He's all right."

"Who else is there?"

"It's no good suggesting Grainger Morris is it?"

"Well, darling, after all—"

"I know, I know."

"It would only embarrass him, now wouldn't it?"

"Sure, sure. What about Colonel Carson?"

"Well, what about Colonel Carson?"

It was a question that the elder group often asked themselves. The Colonel was, in a very special way, an odd man out. He was too old for the younger set, yet as a divorced man, he did not fit into the adult married group. In Santa Marta, a Catholic island, divorce was rare. Carson introduced a discordant note. He was neither one thing nor another. Though he had an estate which he was working with success, he chose to live in town, driving out every morning. He was neither a planter nor a townsman. He had no intimates. There was no mystery about his past. He came of a sound Hampshire family; he had been to Marlborough and to Sandhurst. He had served in his county regiment and been mentioned in dispatches. Yet even so he was a dark horse, and Santa Marta was on its guard against dark horses. It liked people to keep their private thoughts and opinions to themselves, but it liked them to be transparent; packages hermetically sealed in cellophane.

"Yes," Mrs. Norman said, "there's always Colonel Carson."

At lunch she mentioned the matter to her husband. He hesitated, as she herself had done when Mavis brought up his name.

"He's always at the club, you could ask him when you see him there tonight," she said.

"I could."

But when he arrived, and saw Carson leaning against the bar, Norman was tempted to go back upon his promise. He was late and several of his friends were grouped around tables on the veranda. Carson was by himself. That was one of the things about him that put people off. He was self-sufficient, often preferring his own company to his fellow members. At an annual general meeting he had caused considerable resentment by proposing a non-treating rule. "A man's club should be like his home where he can please himself as to how many drinks he has. There's no reason why because he wants to sit at a table with six other members he should have to have seven drinks." He had argued the case at length. "It's very hard on the young fellows. They don't come up, except on dance nights, because they can't afford to. They're shy of not standing their rounds, and they don't like to appear spongers. So they stay away. That's not what we want at all. We had a non-treating rule in my regiment, and a very good thing it was."

That final remark put people's backs up. Airing his military rank, treating a colonial club like an Army Mess. A non-treating rule undermined the whole fabric of West Indian hospitality. Carson did not find a seconder for his proposal. A number of harsh comments had been passed. "Trying to make out that he was thinking of the young men. He wasn't at all. He was thinking of himself. He's unsociable and thinks he's Lord God Almighty. He likes to pick and choose, to stand up drinking by himself, then before he goes home he'll condescend to sit at a table that suits him for a final drink."

Norman seeing him alone at the bar was tempted to pass on down the veranda. Why should he bother to ask to his house a man who was clearly so well satisfied with his own company? But at the last moment he thought better of it. You never knew what people were thinking under their façade. Maybe the man was shy. He walked across to him.

"We're having a few people in for drinks tomorrow, to meet this

American journalist, Carl Bradshaw. We'd be delighted if you could join us."

"I'd love to. Thanks a lot. What's yours?"

Norman could scarcely refuse, though he did not want to drink at the bar, though he wanted to join a group; that was one of the damned things about Carson: he always put you in a false position. "I'll have a pony rum and water, thanks," he said.

"That's very modest."

Carson turned to give the order. "One pony rum and water. I've only just started mine," he added. He had a long drink in his hand.

Norman finished his drink quickly. "Come over to one of the tables for the other half," he said.

Carson shook his head.

"I'm on the point of leaving."

He had had three whisky and sodas and he did not want to switch into rum: which he would have had to do, since whisky was expensive and he did not care to sting anyone for the extra cost. That was one of his objections to this treating rule. You could not drink what you wanted. Sometimes he felt like beer, and Dutch beer cost the earth. He liked to drink in terms of his own purse strings, not the other man's. Why should he have to drink a pony rum and water if he didn't feel like one?

His glass was still half full. He sipped it appreciatively. He did not believe in hurrying his drinks. Norman, who had finished his drink, felt awkward standing without a glass in his hand. He wished Carson would either come over to one of the tables or finish up his drink. But that was another of the troubles about Carson. He moved at his own pace.

He took ten minutes finishing his drink, then, "I'll be on my way," he said. "I'll be seeing you tomorrow."

Norman watched him go with mingled relief and irritation. He felt frustrated, and irritated with himself for feeling so. He disliked being stood a drink without being allowed to stand one back: which was illogical, he fully recognized. Tomorrow he would be standing Carson four or five rum swizzles, to say nothing of a whole plate of "short eats." Highly illogical; but that was the effect that Carson had on one. Norman recalled a jingle he had learnt at school:

> I do not love thee, Dr. Fell,
> The reason why I cannot tell;
> But this alone I know full well,
> I do not love thee, Dr. Fell.

That summed up Carson.

Carson lived within five minutes' walk of the club, behind the police station. It was the quietest place in Jamestown, and he had chosen it for that very reason. During the war he had spent six months in Baghdad and had learnt the necessity for privacy; particularly if you proposed to indulge in gallantry. He was delighted when he had found this small brick-built eighteenth century house, within fifty yards of a main road, in a cul-de-sac, screened both from the main road and from prying eyes by a cemetery on one side and the blank wall of the prison on the other. No one could see his front door and visitors could park their cars behind the club.

A light was burning in his hall. Through the open doorway of the dining room he could see his table, set for a buffet meal; a pile of plates, a potato salad, a chafing dish and a bowl of eggs, with cheese and bread and a row of tins that he could open if the occasion needed. The table was set like that most evenings, in case he returned with guests. Sometimes he would get into a poker game at the club, they would sit on late, and the best way to break it up was to say, "one more round of jackpots, then let's go back to my place and have food."

He never made any set plans for the evening; sometimes he would go to a chopsuey; sometimes he would miss dinner altogether; he made his big meal in the middle of the day. He sent his boy back early. He did not want to keep him up. He paused, looking at the preparations of a meal. It was barely seven. He did not feel hungry yet. He probably would not by the time he had had another whisky. Better clear everything that needed clearing. He took the salad, the cheese, and butter and shut them in the Frigidaire. He lifted the lid of the large thermos flask. Ice there all right: he took it with the tantalus, a glass, and a bottle of soda water into his sitting room across the passage.

He switched on the light and winced. How dreary it all looked. What they had called a man's den, in Edwardian novels: a roll-top desk, a table with magazines; bookshelves that were mainly empty, pictures of school and regimental groups. How different from that other room, with its bowls of flowers, its fresh, crisp chintzes and the firelight flickering upon old china and polished rosewood. How long was it ago? Twelve, fourteen, fifteen years. Sometimes it seemed to be yesterday, sometimes it seemed to belong to another century, to a life upon another planet.

He poured into his glass a two-finger peg of whisky; filled it three-quarter way with soda, took a long steady sip and put the glass down upon his desk. He was restless and did not feel like sitting down. He liked walking up and down a room, then coming back to his drink; you could keep your hands in your pockets and your ice didn't melt too fast. He was used to walking. He had spent many hours pacing a parade ground, trying to keep warm while the N.C.O.'s drilled their sections. He could think better walking.

He paused in front of a framed school photograph of a cricket side. He was sitting on the left side of the captain. The captain held the challenge cup upon his knee. It had been taken his last week at Marlborough. He had regarded the winning of the house cup his last term as a happy augury for Sandhurst. What would he have thought then could he have foreseen that photograph hanging here?

Beside the Marlborough picture was a regimental group; the officers, thirty of them taken outside the mess, three years before the war. They were just home from India. He'd been engaged three weeks: he was to be married in October. How good life had been, how alive he'd felt; the green fresh fields of England after the arid plains, and Daphne. . . . After the masculinity of those years in India he had been ready to fall in love with the first white woman whom he met. What crazy good luck that that first person had been Daphne; Daphne who was so witty, was such good company, sat a horse so well, shared all his tastes; who was in every way the jackpot.

It had all been so unplanned, too. He had no idea when he had met her at that first regimental dance that she was, if not an heiress, halfway to being one. He'd noticed her across the room; the fresh coloring, the air she had of combining delicacy and strength. He hadn't known who she was. He'd watched her as he danced; he had noticed how smoothly she moved, then suddenly he had been aware that she was watching him; it had sent a shock along his nerves. The music had stopped. She was standing beside her partner at the buffet. Her eyes were on him. I can't go up to her like this, he thought, but knew he could. He knew he had to. "We've not been introduced. But I'm Hilary Carson. I think you're the most attractive girl I've ever met. When will you dance with me?"

"The next one would be as good as any."

It had been as easy as all that. Before they had taken three steps together he had known it for a settled thing.

Should he have been warned by the easiness with which it went? He had been so dizzily in love, it was so much the once-in-a-lifetime miracle for him, that he had never doubted it had not been the same for her. And perhaps it had been too, at that.

Backward and forward he paced up and down his study. He ought to stop brooding about the past. It was done and over; it was the present and the future he should be thinking about now. But how could he help living in the past when it was much more alive?

He looked again at the regimental photograph. How boundless had seemed then the boundaries of the future. For several years the battalion would be at home. He had a small private income. He had passed his captain's exam. Her father had bought them a house in Devonshire. Daphne had in her own right half as much money again as he had. They would not need to bother over pennies. For a few years they need not bother about anything. They would incur no responsibilities. A family could wait. They could do every amusing thing they wanted, throw a gay party, dash over to Le Touquet, buy a hunter. He did not know what he had done to deserve such luck. What would he have thought had he been told when that photograph was taken that he would finish up like this, alone, in a twopenny-ha'penny West Indian island?

His glass was empty and he refilled it. This was the last. He had some accounts to go over. He must keep his mind clear for them. As he paced the room, he looked about him with disfavor. Why couldn't he make something better of it? Why couldn't he buy some decent furniture? He could well afford it. He looked with irritation at the vase of flowers. That idiot Sam had merely jammed them in. Why didn't he do the flowers himself? He'd seen Daphne arrange flowers often enough. He remembered her great masses of mixed flowers, ferns and leaves and every kind of flower. She ought to have been married to a painter, he had told her. That big vase of Waterford glass that she had always kept in the corner of the drawing room. Once again there rose agonizingly before his eyes the memory of that drawing room as he had seen it last in the spring of 1940.

He had been posted in March as a replacement to the second battalion stationed then at Malta. He had been sent home on a week's final leave. It had been a bitter winter of cold and snow, but the fires had been banked high at Taviton. Their hearts had been light: the phony war was on, Italy was neutral. His posting to Malta was merely one of those routine nuisances inseparable from a soldier's life. Soon Daphne would come out and join him. They had still thought of war as that—an exacting form of peacetime maneuvers. All the same, since they might be separated for a year, it might not be a bad idea for them to start that family they had been postponing. It would keep her occupied. When he came back or when she came out to join him, they could pick up the threads of their earlier carefree life.

That final leave had been a second honeymoon. They had felt

utterly at peace, fulfilled, very much one person as they had sat on that last evening, before the fire. They'd call it Hilary, boy or girl, they had agreed. Hilary was a girl's name too. How little he had guessed that that was the last evening he would ever spend at Taviton, that he would never again sit alone with Daphne before a fire.

It was all a very commonplace story, he supposed. It had happened to how many hundred others. There had been that first letter beginning, "Too sad, darling, but no little Hilary, there's plenty of time though, isn't there." Then there had been a spate of letters, sometimes two a day, arriving in great batches, that he had tried in vain to sort into their proper order. Soon the letters had become less frequent, less ecstatic, but that after all was only natural. So had his too. You could not live on that high plane forever. You had to get down to ordinary living. The war became suddenly intense. The fall of France, Italy joining in, the siege of Malta: then his own posting to the Western Desert, to take over command of a territorial battalion: there'd been the long chases back and forth; halfway to Tripoli, back to Alexandria; finally Alamein, with the wounds that had kept him in hospital for seven months, then when he was convalescent there had come, out of the blue, that letter starting, "Dearest, this is the hardest letter I have ever had to write."

He had never seen her again. The divorce had taken place through the usual channels. He had not been in any hurry, when it was through, to return to England. He had refused repatriation when his four years were up. By the time he had got home, she was in South Africa, and Taviton was sold.

It might have been easier if he had seen her again: if some later picture had exorcised those earlier pictures: if he could have seen her with her new husband, when she was no longer in love with him, when her voice had lost the special inflections that it had for him. Then he could have consoled himself with the thought, She's a different woman now: the Daphne that I knew has vanished. But he never had. Nothing had come to shatter the picture of that earlier Daphne, of their three years' marriage, of that embarkation leave. He still felt married to that Daphne.

He had said that to H. E. once, and a look of surprise and interest had come into the Governor's face. "It's curious that you should say that. It's what I've felt about myself." He had thought about that afterward. Perhaps in their different ways he and H. E. were in the same boat. H. E. had lost his wife during the war. H. E. had been accustomed to long separations. His wife's death had not suddenly cut the thread of livelihood. His routine had continued, unchanged. The Whitehall official who loses the wife whom he has been accustomed to seeing every day of his life for a dozen years, is for a while distracted, broken, rudderless, but gradually he becomes acclimatized to a new way of existence: he becomes a new person and that new person is able to form new attachments. It was altogether different if your run-of-the-mill routine was undisturbed as his, as H. E.'s had been. In that case you remained loyal to your bonds and vows. He had often heard people wonder why H. E. had not remarried. That was the reason. For himself, as for H. E. He felt himself still married to his wife.

His glass was half empty now; high time to eat. He went into the kitchen and cut a sandwich. He swung a leg over the table and munched it slowly. What a way to dine, for a man who was used to the ritual of a mess. He looked at the clock: quarter-past eight: early yet. Plenty of time to get down to that stack of figures. Come on, he told himself, back to the other room. Show a leg now, Carson.

He returned to his study. Once again he winced, at the sight of it under the hard glass of the single central light. He must alter that, buy a chandelier. Against the wall was the mahogany bookcase that had stood in the drawing room at Taviton. Everyone had admired it, when it was there; it amounted to nothing here: just as he himself had looked so right there, and amounted to so little here. The whole life here was wrong for him. He was not the man for it. He ought to be in England, the colonel of a regiment, with a wife he could be proud of, with a son at Marlborough, a daughter at Roedean, another son at a preparatory school. Horses and golf and the regiment and a home of his own, that's what he was meant for. . . . As for this—

He finished his whisky, turned toward his desk, hesitated, turned back to the decanter. Those figures could wait until tomorrow.

2

To his relief and very considerably to his surprise Carson woke the next morning as the room was lightening, in fine fettle. Well, there it was, you could never tell. If you were someone like himself, who had been blown sky high by high explosive, whose system was a conglomeration of unexplained reactions, the outcome of this nerve pressing on this tendon, you never knew how alcohol would affect you. It might release this pressure, close on that. After a quiet tomato juice evening you could wake with a cracking head, every joint stiff and your mouth like a bird's cage. On the other hand, with a ruin of Scotch around you, you could wake as though it was your seventh birthday. He drove out to his estate, after breakfast, in the highest spirits.

It was as well he did. He arrived to find an atmosphere of high confusion. Outside the estate house, which was occupied by his manager, and where he stayed on the rare occasions when he had to spend the night on the plantation, was a group of chattering, gibbering peasants. It was like a monkey house.

"What is all this about?" he demanded.

There was a twittering silence. Fingers were pointed at the bungalow. He stared and understood. The wirework mosquito screen round the veranda was spattered with white feathers. On the grass round the steps leading to the veranda was a semicircle of white feathers. An Obeah spell had been placed upon the house.

"How did this come about?" he asked.

There was a movement at the back of the group and the manager's wife was pushed forward to the front. She was a tall, handsome young woman, who was always laughing and with whom Carson indulged in flirtatious badinage; today she was bowed, she seemed to have shrunk into half her height, her face was shapeless with crying; her story was interspersed with gulps; she kept her head averted. He could scarcely hear what she said. Her husband interpolated explanations.

At last Carson was able to discover what had happened. Her niece, her sister's daughter, a child of six, was visiting with them. The girl had gone out swimming with a villager. They had gone out too far and the villager's daughter had been drowned. The mother blamed the manager and his wife. They ought not to have allowed the children to go swimming. She had gone to the Obeah man and he had put this curse upon the house.

Carson's face grew grave. This, he knew, was serious. The peasants believed in their Obeah man. Something must be done, and quickly, or there'd be idle hands on the estate for weeks. He thought fast, and an idea came to him. It was the kind of situation that he liked; for which his training had equipped him.

He raised his voice.

"Now listen, all of you," he said. "The woman whose child is dead is angry. I will see her. I will give her money. She does not work for me, but she lives in the village where you work. I want no one in that village to be angry."

He spoke slowly. He used short and simple words. He had listened to the Archdeacon's sermons and had noted, for his own use, his avoidance of long words and his repetition of essential phrases.

"The woman has suffered; she is sad and she is angry; but why

127

is she angry against John and Helen? Are they to blame? How can they be blamed? It was not Helen's sister's child who led this woman's daughter to the sea. Helen's sister's child is younger than was the daughter of this woman. It is the elder one who is the leader. Helen and John are not to blame. This house is not to blame. The woman is angry. She takes her anger to the Obeah man. Was it right of her to do that? No, it was not right. No blame lies upon John and Helen, no blame lies upon this house."

He paused. He looked round him; he had placed himself on the second step of the flight that led to the veranda: the peasants stood on the far side of the half-circle of white feathers. Their faces wore a rapt, mesmerized expression.

"The woman is angry and she wishes to bring harm upon John and Helen. She wants to bring harm upon this house. She goes to the Obeah man. Is that right of her? No, it is not right. Was it right of him to have placed a spell upon John and Helen who have done no wrong? No, it was not right. And was it right of him to have placed a spell upon this house that had done no wrong? No, it was not right. But though it was not right, he has laid this spell; upon John and Helen, and upon this house. What are we to do?"

Again he paused. The silence was complete. He had got them where he wanted.

"A spell has been laid," he said, "and it must be broken. It must be broken because it was wrong to lay it. It must be broken and I will break it. The Obeah man is wise, but I am wiser. The Obeah man knows many spells, but I know more spells. My spells are more powerful than his spells. I have traveled far, in Baghdad, Jerusalem, Damascus. The wise men of those countries know many spells. They taught me their spells. They taught me their magic. The spell must be broken. I will break it."

He was speaking now for the mere sake of speaking. The longer he talked, the more they would be impressed. He kept repeating the refrain: "John and Helen have done no wrong. This house has done no wrong." He also kept repeating, "His spells are powerful. My spells are more powerful." He would be unwise to disparage the Obeah man. The peasants believed in him. The Obeah man was clever. He had proved his powers. It was for himself to show, not that the Obeah man was puny, but that he was mightier.

"I will break the spell," he said. "You wait, all of you."

He kept a dispensary in the bungalow. He took from it a hypodermic, an ampule, disinfectant, cotton wool. He held up the hypodermic. A gasp went up. The hypodermic had great prestige value among the peasants. It was the new magic of the atomic age.

It had relieved sufferings and cured sores. The villagers felt proud when they could say on their return from hospital that they had had injections. They felt cheated when they were given medicine.

"The spell has been laid upon this house. I am the owner of the house, but John is the master of the house. I will kill the spell that has been laid on John. Then there will be no spell upon this house and no spell upon Helen."

He was standing now upon the veranda. He filed off the cap of the ampule, filled the syringe, and laid it on the table.

"John, come here."

He wheeled forward a divan couch. He was resolved to make a parade of the occasion. The peasants were used to injections in the arm, he was going to make this one intramuscular.

"Slip down your trousers and lie upon your stomach."

A ripple of interest ran along the crowd. Not so many of them had seen an intramuscular. He held up the hypodermic. "I am going to drive this two inches into John's seat, but he will feel no pain at all."

He rubbed disinfectant on the spot. It felt like rubbing leather. He prayed that the needle would not break. It was a question of timing, like a short pitch to the green. He hoped he had learnt the knack. He struck. The needle quivered but stood firm. He emptied the syringe slowly.

"That's all," he said. Then gave the other cheek a slap.

The slap removed the tension. A laugh went up.

"Did it hurt?" he asked.

John shook his head. He was a tall, stalwart fellow in his later twenties. Thirty minutes ago he had been scowling; now a great grin lit his features.

Carson faced the crowd.

"The spell is broken."

He walked down the steps, he picked up two handfuls of feathers and tossed them over his shoulder, then he turned to Helen. She had shed her woebegone expression. She looked quite pretty. How quickly these people went from one extreme to another.

"That Obeah man said he would make John sick. I will prove to you how sick he is."

He took her above the elbow and his eyes twinkled. "How long have you been married?"

"Two years, sah."

Carson grinned. He broke into patois. "John, *bien bon au cabane?*" Which meant in the vernacular of a first war private soldier "John pretty good jig-a-jig." Had he said it in English, she would have

129

been embarrassed, but said in patois, she was delighted. She flung back her head and gave a cackling laugh; the others joined her.

"I'll wager you are not too bad yourself," said Carson.

She covered her face in her hands and turned away in simulated coyness. She giggled behind her hands, a series of cackles spluttered round her.

"Now you listen carefully, Helen," he went on. "Tonight you leave John alone. My spell will be fighting with Obeah man's spell. You sleep in another room. And tomorrow again, you sleep in another room. John will be tired after the fight between the two spells: very, very tired. You leave him alone, but the next night, Saturday, you go to him. Then you tell all this folk on Sunday whether he's sick or not. You got that? Good. Now back to work, the lot of you."

Carson returned to town that afternoon to the Normans' party in the highest spirits. He was glad that the American would be there. It was a story that a journalist would appreciate.

Bradshaw listened with appropriate attention.

"What was in the ampule? Don't tell me you injected water?"

"Heavens no, I injected hormones. Mystotesterone, fifty milligrams, and that young fellow likes his wife. Helen won't get a wink of sleep on Saturday. That Obeah man's going to be the laughing stock of the whole neighborhood. He won't monkey around again with my people in a hurry."

Bradshaw chuckled. He had only been in this island half a week and every hour he learnt something new: each new acquaintance was a window opening onto a different aspect of the island's life.

"We hear a lot about Haitian Voodooism. I hadn't realized how far spread it was."

Carson corrected him.

"Voodoo and Obeah are two separate things. There's much confusion on that point. Journalists' fault in the main, I'm afraid to say. I'd describe Obeah as necromancy, as the art of the witch doctor. But Voodoo is a religion. It's come straight from Africa. It's genuine, in its way. But I don't know very much about it. I'm not even sure if there is much of it here."

"Would you say Obeah was all quackery?"

"Indeed no, not at all. Those boys know their stuff. They know the local herbs. And that was our own medicine, after all, five hundred years ago. They can poison you if they want to. Some of their love potions are genuine aphrodisiacs, they can cure some ailments: why shouldn't they be able to, after all."

"And there's the power of suggestion."

"There's very much the power of persuasion. I don't disbelieve these stories of sticking pins into clay models. Doesn't modern medicine prove that the witch doctors were nearer to the truth than the Edwardian G.P.? Aren't they proving that half our illnesses are mental?"

"Won't that Obeah man try to get his revenge on you?"

"If I started to worry about things like that I wouldn't get much sleep."

To that there was no answer. But it gave Bradshaw a slight shiver down his spine to reflect that at this moment, sitting on his haunches, in some hut under the palm trees, was a man endowed with curious and uncalculated powers who in three days' time would have only one desire, to be revenged on the white man who had made him an object of ridicule to his neighborhood. He looked thoughtfully at Carson. In his different way this man might prove as useful as the Archdeacon.

"You like your laborers, don't you, on the whole," he said.

"One can't help liking them: at least I can't. They're comics, they make me laugh, they drive me mad at times. I can understand how in the days of slavery, their masters tortured them, even though they were damaging their own property. They can be maddening. But at heart they are thoroughly good-natured. They bear no ill will, provided they know you like them. That's the important thing, to make them realize that you like them, even though you swear at them. They have such capacity for enjoyment too. You'll have a chance of seeing that at Carnival."

"When is that?"

"The two days before Ash Wednesday. Three weeks from now. Trinidad is the place to see it, at least people will tell you that it is, but in Trinidad the Carnival's too organized for my taste, too commercial. It's more intimate in a small place like this. You mustn't miss it."

"There's something else I've been told not to miss. The case that one of the planters is bringing about some cattle of his that strayed onto a neighbor's land."

"That'll be interesting all right."

"Will you be going?"

"I expect so."

"Could I go with you? I'd enjoy it much more if I had someone to tell me who was who."

"I'll be delighted."

"I'm most grateful."

131

On the evening after the case he would write his first article. It would be as well to start writing before his first, clear impressions became blurred. It was an axiom of travel writing that you learnt more in your first five days in a new place than you did in the next five months. You began to learn too much. Everything he was seeing and hearing now made a fresh impact.

"I must have a word with our hostess's daughter," he told Carson. He wanted to make a few inquiries about that A.D.C. He was curious to know more about that car that he had seen driving away from the Continental two nights before.

# CHAPTER NINE

## 1

On the eve of the Preston case, Carson went to bed early and completely sober. He had played a round of golf in the afternoon, given the club a miss, gone to the first show at the cinema, and on his return had scrambled himself a couple of eggs and made a pot of tea. He woke, however, with a searing headache. Better take a shower, he told himself; the cold water would revive him. But as he stepped from under it, he nearly fainted. Back to the beaters. He lay supine, wondering whether he was going to be sick. The wound in his hip was aching, and the ball of his right toe—the toe that he had lost at Alamein—began to throb. If that shell had pitched one fraction of an inch nearer him . . .

Why hadn't it? What had his life been for the last ten years? What would it be for the next twenty?

Lying with his eyes half closed, with aching limbs and thudding temples, he faced a self-imposed confessional. He had not one friend in the place. He had no illusions as to how they felt about him: he was surly, off-hand, ungregarious; then when they had written him off as a sour impossible person, he would disarm them by being genial, good company, generous. He'd talk amusingly, he'd collect a group round him in the bar, take them back with him to supper, fix them something pretty good in his chafing dish, open a bottle or two of wine and have a cracking evening: they'd part on the best of terms. And that stood him in worse stead than his surliness. People went away from one of his parties saying that after all the old colonel wasn't a bad fellow if you got to know him; flattering themselves that they had been specially selected to be shown "his real side." It only made it worse next day at the club when he retired behind his mask: they felt they had been cheated.

He was hopeless, hopeless, and he knew it. Sick in body, sick in mind: poisoned in mind and body. So poisoned that unless he had taken the counter-poison of alcohol, he felt like death; so poisoned in mind that unless the glow of alcohol was on him, he felt savage, bitter, ready to snap at anyone; and half the time alcohol made him even bitterer. He knew what he was doing but he could not stop it when he came into the club, feeling like murder; he couldn't join in that everlasting shop about the price of copra and the price of cocoa, and their trivial gossip about who'd said what at the last G.H. party. If people came up and spoke to him, when he was in that kind of mood, he couldn't help snapping off their heads. He could hear himself saying these things and he couldn't stop himself. Why hadn't that shell pitched an inch farther to the right?

When his boy brought him his cup of tea, he shook his head. Whisky, that was the medicine that morning.

2

At the same time that Carson was refusing his morning tea, Maxwell Fleury was taking his, perched beside Sylvia's bed.

"I'm going into Jamestown to hear the Preston case. What about you?" he said.

"You know me. Any excuse to get into town."

He frowned. Any excuse to see Hilary Carson, was that what she had meant? It was ten days now since she had had a chance of seeing him. He had watched her closely; he thought that he had known what she was doing at every hour of the day. But maybe he was only fooling himself. He had no check on Carson. Carson could swoop down at any moment in his car. Maybe they had found some ingenious meeting place. It would be easier when they were both in Jamestown, then he could check upon joint absences. Then he'd know the truth, one way or another.

"I'll ring up Mavis. She'll probably be going," Sylvia said.

"I'm sure she will."

That's where Sylvia was so clever; always this hunt in couples; Jocelyn or Mavis or Doris Kellaway. This posing as a chaperone for her sister. Wasn't it likelier, far likelier that she was using Mavis as a cover? Jocelyn had been with her that first time.

"As far as I can see the half of Jamestown will be at this trial," Maxwell said.

It certainly seemed so three hours later. The courthouse, an adjunct of the police station, was a square thick fort-like building that had withstood hurricanes and earthquakes and that standing at right angles to the prison, helped to screen the cul-de-sac that led to Carson's house. It was here that the Legislative Council sat. Cool and whitewashed, it had a sense of dignity with its dais and dark benches and gilt-framed portraits of eighteenth century governors. As the seats by the door began to fill, there settled on the room the kind of hush that steals upon a theater as the musicians take their places in the orchestra. Various officials with an air of self-importance conferred together over sheafs of paper. There was an atmosphere not of bustle but of things being about to happen.

Carson pointed out to Bradshaw such of the local notables as he did not already know.

"Do you know that barrister in the front row to the left?"

Bradshaw shook his head. "A wig is a very good disguise, besides I'm ashamed to have to admit it, but I find it very hard to tell one colored gentleman from another. The Chinese have the same difficulty with regard to us."

Carson chuckled. "All the same," he said, "this chap is worth taking note of. He's Grainger Morris." He provided a succinct biography. "In England he went everywhere, knew everyone, but here because he's colored, because he's not in the stud book, they wouldn't let him join the tennis club. Amusingly enough the Governor's son knew him in England so now Mr. Morris gets asked to all the smartest parties. I couldn't be more amused. You ought to make a point of knowing him. I'll introduce you afterward."

"I'd be most grateful if you would." Another pipeline here. "Which is Mr. Preston by the way?"

"He's not come yet. I'll point him out to you when he does. Ah, here he is. Oh damn, he's coming next to us."

Preston was one of Carson's pet aversions. Preston would talk to him about the war. As a fighting soldier, Carson considered officers in the R.A.O.C. as "uniformed civilians," and as a regular officer he had resented the way in which during the war civilians had been put into uniform with flannel on their lapels. Lawyers had become brigadiers overnight.

As he had expected, Preston met him once again on the presumably shared ground of military experience. "First time I've been in court since I was president of that court-martial in Ismalia. I told you about that, didn't I?"

"You did."

"Never thought then that I should find myself in this kind of set-up."

Carson did not answer. The effect of his breakfast whisky was wearing off. If he had spoken, he would have snapped.

"My case isn't the first," Preston was continuing. "There's one before mine that needs a jury, some typically ridiculous situation about a man biting off his sister's finger."

Carson turned to Bradshaw. "There's copy for you, old boy."

Mavis was sitting two rows in front beside her sister, behind Grainger Morris; she had been surprised to see him there.

135

"On whose side are you?" she asked.

"I'm afraid I'm not figuring in the *cause célèbre*. I came down in case any of these poor devils need a counsel."

"Isn't that a waste of time?"

"Not if it's in someone's service."

If anyone else had said a thing like that she would have felt it sanctimonious, but he said it naturally. There was no one like him, she thought: no one, no one. It was the first time she had seen him in a wig. The tight white curls made him look ten years older, they gave him an air of distinction, of authority: below his wig there showed only a brief fringe of dark hair. You could not see its crinkly texture. If her father had put on a wig and gown would anyone have seen the difference?

A fist was thumped upon a desk. A voice announced "His Honor!" There was a shuffle as the attendance rose, and the judge walked slowly to his seat upon the dais. He was a short, squat man three quarters colored; he had an air of considerable dignity.

Carson leant across to Bradshaw. "Say what you will, there are some remarkable characteristics about the British Empire; here's the descendant of a slave, sitting in judgment on his captors; without any revolution, with a direct succession of authority at Westminster: the same royal family upon the throne. It's something you can't shrug away."

"Silence in the court."

The prisoner had been brought into the dock. He was a thin, weak-looking negro who might have been thirty, who might have been sixty years of age. He looked about him with a furtive hangdog air. The charge against him was read out. He had bitten off the top joint of the fourth finger of his half sister's left hand and the lobe of her right ear.

The judge looked round the court. "Has this man any counsel?"

Grainger rose.

"I shall be very glad to offer my services if the prisoner agrees."

The judge turned to the prisoner.

"Mr. Morris, a very distinguished member of the bar, is offering you his services, at no cost to yourself. This is an act of great generosity on his behalf. I consider you very fortunate. I presume that you will accept his services."

The prisoner looked round vaguely. His eyes rested upon Grainger. Then he looked back at the judge. Carson leant across to Bradshaw. "Hasn't a clue, poor fellow."

The selection of the jury started. Twenty men had been told to present themselves. As each man's name was read out, the judge turned to the prisoner and said, "Have you any objection to this man?" The prisoner stared stupidly and made no comment. He did not nod or shake his head. The judge tried to explain to him his rights under the jury system.

"If there is a man here who will not, in your opinion, judge your case fairly, some man who dislikes you, who has quarreled with you, you may object to his presence on the jury."

The prisoner's face wore the same blank stare.

"Typical British justice," Carson whispered. "We keep to the drill of it, even if the business is completely pointless, because one is dealing with a half-wit."

Eventually the twelve jurors were chosen, and the prosecution opened its case. The first witness was Leisching, the Austrian doctor. He was tall, heavily jowled, clean shaven, bald, with a scar across his forehead. On such a day and at such an hour the plaintiff, so the doctor informed the court, had come into hospital for treatment, with the top joint of the fourth finger of her left hand severed, and with the lobe of her right ear torn and bleeding. He gave his evidence in a precise Teutonic manner. He had a strong German accent. "Square-headed bastard," Carson whispered. Counsel for the prosecution asked the doctor what in his opinion had caused the accident.

"The woman told me that her brother had bitten her. The condition of the wounds was consistent with her story."

Grainger rose. Did the doctor think the wounds could have been produced in any other way? Could an instrument have made them? No, the doctor did not think so: it was not a clean cut. There was no appearance of crushing.

"Suppose that the woman had not told you that she had been bitten. Would it have occurred to you at once that that was how the wounds were made?"

The doctor hesitated. "I might have been puzzled for a moment. It is not after all a usual occurrence. I have never had to deal with such a case before; but I think that in a very few minutes I would have realized that the injury could not have been inflicted in any other way."

"Could an animal have done it?"

"I cannot think it could have done. A dog's teeth are widely spaced. There would have been separate teeth marks."

"Wouldn't it need considerable strength to bite off the top joint of a finger? Think how tough one finds a piece of meat occasionally."

The doctor agreed that it would have needed considerable

137

strength. He informed the court that the victim had been kept in hospital five days.

The plaintiff was now called. She was a tall, slim, not unhandsome creature. She wore a bright red blouse, and a yellow skirt; a bright orange and black handkerchief was knotted round her head. She was, she explained, the half sister of the accused. They had the same mother but different fathers. The accused did not live in her house, she said, but came and stayed there sometimes. No, she was not married. She lived with her mother who had once kept house with the accused's father, who now was dead, as her own father was. Her twelve-year-old half brother by another man lived with them. Where was the father of this half brother? She did not know. Had her mother been married to any of these men? No, she had not.

"Sixty per cent of the births here are illegitimate," Carson explained to Bradshaw. "Half the time the parents can't afford to marry. Half the time the woman wants to keep her independence. The children are brought up by the mother. It's a form of matriarchy."

They lived, the plaintiff was continuing, in a two-roomed shack in Jamestown. On the day in question the accused had arrived in the morning. At what time in the morning? She did not know; it was before she had got back from market. She returned from the market to be told that the accused had arrived and was lying down. He had brought some food with him. What kind of food? Some meal and some peppers. She had looked to see what he had brought. Then she had started her own cooking. While she was at the stove, the accused had woken up: he had accused her of troubling his food.

"Troubling his food?" Bradshaw whispered.

"That means stealing; a polite synonym. Just as we'd say drawing a long bow, instead of lying."

From that point the plaintiff's story became confused: an argument had gone on right through the afternoon until at five o'clock the plaintiff had arrived at the hospital with a bleeding ear and severed finger. The argument had had its peaks and its intermissions. Once at least the accused had retired and gone to sleep. When he awoke, the argument had been renewed. At one time he had had a fit.

"What kind of a fit?"

"Like so."

The plaintiff gave an imitation in the witness box, shaking her body and waving her arms. The spectators roared with laughter. The sergeant at arms banged his hammer. The judge threatened to clear the court. The plaintiff grinned with delighted pride as she resumed her story. There had been, she said, a succession of outbursts and recriminations: finally there had been the fight. But for her small brother's intervention she would have been surely killed.

"But your brother is only eleven years old," the judge reminded her.

"Yessir, he let fall a stone."

"Another polite synonym," Carson explained. "You don't throw a stone at a man. You let it fall on him."

The brother had "let fall" the stone, the accused had relaxed his hold and the woman had broken free and rushed screaming to the hospital.

Counsel had finished his examination. He looked interrogatively at Grainger. Grainger rose.

"I presume, my lord, that my learned friend is going to call the younger brother as a witness."

"Yes, my lord."

"In that case, my lord, I should prefer, with your permission, to delay my cross-examination of this witness till we have heard her brother."

The permission was granted, and the brother took the stand. He was tall, wiry, sturdy. He looked round him with pride. This was a big day for him. He had got off school. He was standing up before all these people, before white folks too, to tell them how he had saved his sister. Yes, he said, he had heard screams; he had run in from the street; his sister was on the floor, her brother was on top of her. He had looked for a weapon, could not see one, had run out into the yard, had found a stone, had let it fall upon his brother's head: "like that," he said and showed how he had crashed down the stone.

"The word 'let fall,'" Carson whispered, "has a wide range of meaning."

The examination by counsel was a brief one; too brief in the boy's view. He turned expectantly to Grainger. Everyone had told him that his cross-examination by the defense would be much longer.

"Your sister has told us that the accused has fits. Have you seen one of these fits?"

"Yes, sir."

"What was it like?"

"Like so."

His imitation was less dramatic than his sister's and the spectators received it decorously.

"Does he often have these fits?"

"Yes, sir, often."

"Does he fall down when he has these fits?"

"He falls about."

"Have you ever seen him faint?"

"No, sir."

"When he has these fits, do you notice anything unusual about his face?"

"How you mean, sir?"

"Does the color change; does he froth at the mouth?"

The boy looked puzzled. "When I let fall the stone . . ." Grainger interrupted him.

"I don't want to hear about that for the moment. I want to know about these fits; how often does he have them, how does he behave when he has them? Tell me in your own way what you can remember."

The boy looked disappointed. He had expected to be asked questions about the stone, how hard he had let it fall, and on which side of the head. He had seen many gangster films. He had expected to have the judge say, "Now show the court exactly what you did." He had not expected to be questioned about these fits. Why should anyone be interested in that? He did his best to remember, to tell the lawyer what he could, but his heart was not in it.

"And now, one last question," Grainger said. "When you came into the room and saw your sister on the floor, tell the court exactly what you saw. Tell us exactly what her brother was doing."

The boy brightened. This was the kind of thing he wanted.

"I hear her scream. I see her on the floor. I run into the yard. . . ."

"No, no, please, I don't want to know what you did, I know that already. You've told us very clearly. You showed great courage and presence of mind. But what I want to know now is what her brother was actually doing; was he struggling with your sister?"

Reluctantly the boy let himself be led back to the point in which the defense was interested. Yes, they had been struggling. Good. What form did the struggle take? Was he beating your sister? Was he trying to throttle her? Did you actually see him biting her? The questions followed one on top of the other. The boy looked puzzled. How could he remember? It had been such a long time ago. He had run out into the yard to find a stone.

"Yes," Grainger said. "You ran out into the yard to find a stone. When you came back was there still a struggle; was her brother beating her: did you actually see him biting her? Are you absolutely sure that he was not motionless: that he had not fainted, that he was not in some kind of a collapse?"

"Me lud, I object." Counsel for the prosecution was on his feet.

"My learned friend is leading my witness in a most improper manner."

"Bumping and boring. I thought as much," said Carson.

The objection was sustained, and the jury was instructed to ignore that final question.

"But he made his point," Carson whispered. "I see what he's driving at, don't you?"

Bradshaw nodded. Mavis too saw what he was driving at. She had followed the case with mounting interest: ever since the Nurses' Dance she had been looking forward to seeing Grainger in court in his wig and gown. She would then be seeing the real man; it would be like seeing for the first time in uniform a soldier whom she had only met in mufti. She had never imagined that he would look so impressive. Next to the judge he was the most impressive person in the room. It had been fascinating to listen to his cross-examination, wondering whither it was leading, then gradually getting a glimpse of his intentions. But it was not so much his cleverness that had moved her—she had known that he would be clever—as his gentleness, his patience, his fairness. He could so easily have tied this boy in knots, confused him, made him contradict himself. But he had not done that. He had tried to get at the truth, feeling that the truth was the best defense. The small boy left the box, a little disappointed that he had not been able to explain quite as fully as he had liked how he had let fall the stone, but even so he had been placed high in his own esteem. He had been called brave.

The plaintiff was now recalled. Mavis' interest quickened. Her evidence had been diffuse, the sequence of events was hard to follow. Moreover there was that first cause of complaint; had she been stealing her brother's food? She was a witness whom it would be easy to discredit. But Grainger made no effort to discredit her. He concentrated with her, as he had with her brother, on the fits—how often had she seen them, how long did they last.

"When you say he falls about, could you explain what you mean? Does he roll on the floor?"

"Yes, sir, he roll on the floor."

"Would you describe that rolling as a kind of convulsion?"

"Convulsion, what is that?"

"Does he behave like a drunk man?"

"Yes, sir, like a very drunk man."

"You have seen men when drunk suddenly collapse, fall down, go to sleep, so that you cannot wake them."

Yes, she had seen that.

141

"Have you ever seen a man when drunk froth like a horse at the mouth?"

Yes, she had seen that too.

"Have you seen a man when drunk catch hold of something so that you could not get it away from him?"

"Yes, sir, for certain sure."

"Have you heard it said that a man when drunk is twice as strong as a man when he is sober?"

Yes, she had heard that.

Had she seen any case of that?

"My mother say when my father drunk, he sure beats her up good."

There was a roar of laughter in the court. Once again the sergeant at arms beat his hammer on the desk.

"If this happens again, I will clear the court," the judge proclaimed. "This is not a cinema; this is not a place of entertainment."

The hubbub subsided. The woman preened herself in the witness box, catching the eye of one of the jurors and giggling behind her hand. Her delight with herself irritated Mavis. She only got that laugh because Grainger let her get it. She thought she was cleverer than he. Tonight she would boast to her friends of how she had humbugged the clever Mr. Morris. She had no idea how silly he could have made her look if he had chosen. Mavis wished that Grainger would take his revenge, that he would trip up this woman, make her contradict herself, humiliate her. She resented his refusal to take his revenge. Yet she would have regretted it if he had.

"Now tell us," Grainger was continuing, "when you have seen drunk men behave that way, froth at the mouth, grasp hold of things, then suddenly collapse on the floor, unconscious—when you have seen drunk men behave like that, have you sometimes thought, 'That is very like my brother in a fit'?"

She deliberated for a moment, then nodded. Yes, she had thought that.

"Then that is all I have to ask you. Thank you very much."

He sat down. The girl was puzzled. This could not be the end. He had hardly started yet. If her own lawyer had questioned her for half an hour, the lawyer on the other side would question her for an hour. She stared round her, perplexed, turning an inquiring look to the bench. The judge nodded. Yes, that was all. She stepped out of the witness box, sheepishly, resentfully. She felt she had been cheated. Her big day should have been a bigger one. Her ear had been torn; her finger bitten off. She should have got more out of it than this.

Grainger was on his feet again. He would like to ask the doctor one or two further questions. The doctor was not in court, but the hospital was within half a mile. A policeman was dispatched for him, and the court adjourned. The spectators drifted out into the street to stretch their legs.

Mrs. Preston was in a fretful mood.

"At this rate our case may not come on at all today. It certainly won't have come on before lunch. We've wasted a whole morning and we shall have the discomfort and expense of an excruciating luncheon at the St. James."

She said it in the direction of her husband; but her voice was raised. Her complaint was addressed to the group at large. Carson came across to her. He was leading Bradshaw by the arm. "Mrs. Preston, here is a newcomer whom you should meet. An American journalist who's down here for a holiday. I've been telling him how charmingly you've arranged your house."

He had actually said nothing of the kind. But he had an idea that Mrs. Preston was the kind of woman that Bradshaw might not dislike, and he wanted to be rid of Bradshaw for a little. He needed a drink badly, and Bradshaw was almost a teetotaller. His house was only round the corner. He looked to see if there was anyone to take in with him. He preferred not to drink alone. It was a habit he had to guard against. He noticed Maxwell Fleury beside his wife. He hesitated, then thought better of it, waved to them and turned away. Maxwell noted the hesitation. It struck him as suspicious. Why hadn't Carson come across? Was he nervous, was he shy of meeting him? He looked quickly at Sylvia. Her face wore its invariable impassive mask. What was she thinking? What was she feeling? The sooner she was in town, so that he could keep close check, the better.

"I do hope, Mr. Bradshaw, that you will come out and see our place," Mrs. Preston was saying. "It's nothing remarkable. You know what these estate houses are; a veranda round a box of rooms, but we have nice furniture. People say it's ridiculous to bring out good furniture to a place like this, all the damp and wood rot; but good things were made to be enjoyed. It makes such a difference for children, to be brought up with beautiful things round them. They acquire taste without realizing it. Don't you agree with me?"

"It's what I've been saying in my articles for a quarter of a century. That's one of the great advantages that your young people have over ours. They are surrounded by the culture of the past. Beautiful buildings and planned gardens; silver and china that have been in the family for generations."

143

"You feel that? I'm so glad you do. So few people care about such things these days. And to have an American saying that. You must come out and see us. We must fix a day. Now where is Frank—oh, there's Doctor Leisching's car: we'd better be getting back or we'll find our places taken."

Dr. Leisching looked aggrieved. He was annoyed at having been brought back to court. He had already given his evidence. This interruption in his morning's work would involve the loss either of his siesta or his tennis. He was in no mood to be co-operative.

"I've told you all I know," he said.

He said it rudely. Mavis' nails bit into her palms. Dr. Leisching was an arrogant bully where those weaker than he was were concerned. He would not talk to a white man that way. Yet two hundred years ago, for all anyone in this room might know, Grainger's ancestors were Princes of Dahomey while the doctor's were servile serfs of a Junker landlord. Who was Dr. Leisching to think himself superior to Grainger? And why, oh why must Grainger be so patient?

"I'm sorry to have inconvenienced you, doctor," he was saying. "But there are one or two points on which we should very much value your opinion. You saw the wound that had been inflicted on the patient. Would you say that it needed exceptional strength to inflict such an injury?"

"It would need strong teeth."

"Would it not need more than that? I have strong teeth myself, but I should not have believed myself capable of biting off anybody's finger joint."

"Perhaps that is because it has never occurred to you to attempt such a thing. You are a sensitive, civilized, educated man. You have inhibitions, checks on your impulses which would prevent you doing things of which you are in fact capable physically. A poor bewildered savage has no such inhibitions."

He underlined the words sensitive, civilized, educated, savage. It was as though he were saying, "We'll admit for the sake of appearances to the existence of this veneer of culture that you assume. But we know, perfectly well, that under that veneer you are as much a savage as that prisoner in the dock."

Mavis' temper rose. If only Grainger were not so patient. Why must he keep turning the other cheek. There was an infuriating Christlike quality about him that was at the same time the core of his attraction for her. Why was he not more self-assertive? Yet how she would have loathed it if he had been a loud-voiced, aggressive

144

upstart like David Boyeur who was lounging back now in the corner of the back row, in a light slate-gray-blue double breasted suit with a blue and pink bow tie, his white and brown shoe planted on the bench in front, with a look on his face that said, "Don't forget me. I may be in the background but I'm the one that counts." She was glad Grainger was not like that. If only, though, he had something, a fraction, a leavening of that drive of Boyeur's.

"May I put my questions in another way," he was saying now; there was no trace of irritation in his voice, nor was there, that she had to admit, the least subservience.

"Would you agree," he asked, "that every now and then a man or woman can be subject to a fit that gives them great power for the brief time that that fit is on them?"

He paused interrogatively.

"Naturally, of course."

"What kinds of fit would give a man this power?"

"In the first place, epilepsy."

"Would you consider the possibility of the prisoner being subject to such fits?"

Dr. Leisching looked at the prisoner. The prisoner was leaning forward across the dock, a blank, uncomprehending, uninterested expression on his face. He had the air of being a completely retrograde type. The doctor shrugged.

"I should find it hard to say. I should have to make a thorough investigation."

"Would you say that he was a robust person?"

"Indeed I wouldn't."

"If, for instance, to take a frivolous example, we were to have in this court, a tug of war, eight men on either side, and you were one of the captains, he would not be, I take it, your first choice."

There was a titter in the court, but so slight that it brought no protest from the bench. The doctor grinned.

"I should say I wouldn't. Looking round this room I would say he was the last."

"Then in that case, wouldn't you say that it was only under the influence of some very strong compulsion, under some such compulsion for example as an epileptic fit, that as poor a physical specimen as the prisoner could have the strength to bite clean off the top joint of a human finger?"

"I don't know. I . . ." The doctor hesitated, flushed: he had been trapped and saw it. Mavis exulted. He had got what he deserved. He had been arrogant and insolent and he had been humbled. Grainger was wonderful. He wasn't mild and meek. He could hit back when he was roused, when he had been challenged, by an equal or by a bully. It was only with the poor, the helpless, the underprivileged that he was patient, gentle, infinitely tolerant.

How she admired Grainger. If only she could have met somebody like that in her own world, three years ago. If only she could meet someone like that, in her own world, now. Surely it wasn't too late. She was only twenty-two. She closed her eyes. She needn't have been the way she was, she thought, if she had met someone to look up to, someone to whom she could have given her real self. But she never had. She was warm-blooded: she had thought, why not? and she'd enjoyed it. She had felt no regrets. She had had bad moments, naturally: with Rickie in particular. But she had shrugged it off. It was just another thing. She would get over it as she had before. It was only during these last weeks that she had begun to wish things different.

As a schoolgirl she had joked about "Mr. Right." But as far as she had thought of any Mr. Right, it had been in terms of the young men off boats with whom she had flirted; one of whom would turn out to be Mr. Right because he was in "a marrying mood," was good to look at, and had money. It was not till the last two weeks that she had realized her need for a quite different order of emotion.

How shallow in comparison with that need seemed now that sequence of flirtations, in particular this final one with Euan. Why on earth had she gone into that? He was not her type: she was not even sure that she was his. Why had they started it? Boredom, propinquity: because there was no one else? That was the trouble about a place like this, one had to make do with what there was. Of everything that she had ever done, this final exploit was the shallowest. The only kick she had got out of it was the prestige of having annexed the Governor's son; that and the talking about it afterwards to Doris. . . . Doris, that was another thing. How helpless she was when temptation beckoned.

She opened her eyes. They had been closed for a bare thirty seconds as that spate of thoughts flowed through her mind. Grainger was on his feet, addressing the judge. His face was in profile. It had a clean-cut line, thin lips, a straight nose. Had a bust been made of him, now as he stood in his robes, with his tight-fitting wig, no one would have thought of him as being anything but white. It was only his skin and his crinkling hair that betrayed his African ancestry. And was his skin so very dark? Here everyone knew who his father was. But in another island, in Jamaica say, could he not have passed as white?

"It is nearly twelve, my lord. I would like to have a conference with my client, and I would like to read over my notes."

"Certainly. I agree, Mr. Morris. The court will be adjourned until two o'clock."

Mavis waited outside for Grainger. His wig was in his hand, his gown over his arm. He was wheeling a bicycle. Without his wig there was no questioning his background; it did not disappoint her. She was glad to have seen him in uniform, but she preferred him, he was more himself, like this.

"It's more exciting than a film," she said. "It's been fascinating, trying to guess why you were asking a certain kind of question, then getting the reason. You caught the doctor out all right."

"He was pompous, wasn't he?"

"Will you get your man off?"

He shrugged. "These juries are incalculable. You can never tell what they may have in the back of their minds. Very often they know something that never comes out in court. That's something one must remember. Everyone knows everybody here. It's not like England where no one on the jury has heard of the prisoner before he actually walks into the box. Sometimes a verdict will astonish you, but you always know that there's a reason. Anything may happen this afternoon."

"I'll be here to wish you luck."

"That'll make a difference. It has made a difference having you in court. It put me on my mettle."

He said it lightly. But she felt he meant it. He jumped on his bicycle. She watched him ride away. Couldn't he afford a car? She looked round for Sylvia. Sylvia would no doubt want to make an occasion of it; it was her first visit to Jamestown for a week.

"Where would you like to go?" she asked her.

"The St. James. We shall see all we want of the club tonight."

"Where's Maxwell?"

"With the boys. In the Jamestown Club. He'll have a heavy head this evening."

He was not the only one who might be expected to have a heavy head. The club was crowded; the noise was deafening. Bradshaw looked round him with discomfort. He had not wanted to come here. He disliked drinking. It was an unfortunate occupational hazard of his profession that the best way to get a story was to sit about in bars. One of the things he had liked best about his New York assignment was the being able to spend more time in drawing rooms than in bars. All the same he might find something here. He looked round him inquisitively. It was not the first time he had been in the club, but it was the first time that he had been here before lunch. He was surprised at the number of colored members and at the ease with which they were mixing with the whites. Was the color line a matter of feminine influence, or was it that though white men were quite happy to mix with colored men, they wanted to keep their women away from them? Something of both most likely. He was not, he reflected, seeing enough of the colored community. He sought out Carson.

"Is David Boyeur here?"

Carson looked round. "Yes, over there, by the fireplace."

At the sight of Boyeur, a little start ran along Bradshaw's nerves. That was a very personable creature.

"I'd be very grateful," he said, "if you'd introduce me."

### 3

Mavis was back by five to two. She knew what line of defense Grainger would adopt; that the prisoner was subject to fits that were either epileptic or of an epileptic nature, that a fit had seized him when he was struggling with his sister and his teeth in the spasm of the fit had closed upon her finger. They had talked it over at lunch.

"Doesn't that sound very reasonable?" she had asked her father.

"Up to a point, but that torn ear will need to be explained. You can only bite in one place at a time. One of those bites must have been deliberate."

The point had not occurred to Mavis. She wondered how Grainger would argue round it, or if it had not occurred to him. She had arrived early so that she could warn him.

"I'm looking forward to your address," she said.

"I wish I were."

"Don't tell me you are nervous."

"It isn't that. I wish I knew what form my speech will take. A maddening thing has happened. The idiot prisoner is resolved to make a statement. Heaven knows what he'll say; but he'll almost certainly run opposite to the defense I'd planned."

"Can't you stop him?"

"I've done my best, but you know what these people are, they want to be the center of attention. He can't resist the chance of having all eyes turned on him. And it's his legal right. I couldn't stop him."

148

"Then I hurried my lunch in vain."

"What do you mean by that?"

She told him. "I wondered if that point had occurred to you."

"You thought of that yourself?"

She smiled. If it had been anyone else she would have taken the credit for her father's perspicacity, but she could not lie to Grainger. "I wish I had. We were discussing it at lunch, my father raised that objection."

He looked at her thoughtfully. "I'm more touched by this," he said, "than I've been by anything since—I can't remember when I was touched so much. I shan't forget it."

There was a look in his eyes that told her that he would not.

4

The court was fairly empty after the resumption: empty at least of the upper crust members of the community. For them the chief interest of the session lay in the Preston case which would not come on for a half hour yet. They preferred to linger over their coffee. But the back benches were crowded with the proletariat; and the prisoner, looking round him from the dock, brightened at the prospect of addressing so many friends. It was a gala day for him.

"My Lord," he began, "I would like you to understand..." He took it slowly, explaining how there had always been friction between his sister and himself. Her father had always hated him. Her father had been jealous of his father. His mother had preferred his father. His sister had insulted him, her father had told her to insult him. If he had tried to hit her, her father had thrashed him. Her father was dead now and she could not take shelter behind his strength. She deserved what she had got. She had "troubled" his food. When she was a child she had insulted him. Her father was here no longer to protect her. She deserved what she had got.

"He's running off the course," said Carson. The tale trailed on: a mixture of self-pity and self-vindication. It tore Grainger's defense to shreds. There was no chance now of his pleading the unconscious violence of a fit. Mavis saw him exchange with the judge a glance of histrionic and amused despair. She felt very sorry for him. He had given up his whole day to this case, and this was his reward. Yet perhaps in the long run it would not be wasted. It would show the Santa Martans that there was such a thing as justice: that even if a man was penniless, a member of the bar would argue in his defense.

149

"She deserved it," the prisoner was continuing. "When her father was alive . . ."

The judge interrupted him.

"You have already told us that: according to your account your sister during her father's life took advantage of her father's strength to insult you. On this particular occasion she had troubled your food. That is what you have to tell us isn't it?"

"Yes, that is what I have to tell you. She deserved it. When her father was alive . . ."

Again the judge interrupted him. "You have made yourself very clear. Unless you have anything to add, and I do not think you have, I will call on your counsel to address the jury on your behalf."

The prisoner nodded. He had had his say. He looked round the court. A friend waved at him. He saw a row of intent faces. He had never been listened to for so long before. They would remember how he had talked before the judge and these men with wigs, and how the judge had said that he had made things very clear. He was well content. He relapsed into apathy.

Grainger rose. There was nothing that he could do but extend a plea for mercy: to ask the jury to consider the squalid conditions under which persons like the prisoner lived. He did it quietly, undramatically, without emotion.

"Life is very different in these small shacks in airless back streets from what it is in the pleasant bungalows in which you live. You cannot declare my client innocent. He has confessed his guilt. It was a ruthless brutal act. But I think you would be justified in view of what the prisoner has told you in attaching a plea of mercy to your verdict."

But he did not get his plea of mercy. The prisoner was too well known to members of the jury. A verdict of guilty was brought in. The judge asked to see the prisoner's record. There were three previous convictions, two for theft, one for robbery with violence. He received nine months and a lecture from the judge. "It was a beastly thing you did," he was informed.

It was now half-past two, and once again the body of the court was crowded. There were several new arrivals. Denis Archer had been sent down by the Governor. Euan had come with him. Bradshaw was feeling faint. It had been a strenuous morning at the club. If only people would sit down at a table instead of standing at a bar; if only they would eat more. He had been very bored as they had gone on declaiming their opinions, their voices getting louder as their sentences grew less grammatical. He did not know how they could take so much to drink on an empty stomach. He had had one punch, and then made a rum and soda last him through a succession of fresh rounds. In the end they had only left themselves time for a hurried twenty minutes lunch. An exhausting morning. Still he had met David Boyeur, and Boyeur was coming to tea with him that afternoon. Tonight he would begin his article. He had so much to say that his problem was one of compression, not expansion. Now for the *cause célèbre*, he told himself.

He was sitting two rows behind the Prestons. On an occasion such as this he made use of a hearing aid, and he was able to overhear the advice that Mrs. Preston gave her husband.

"Don't be diffident, that's one of your weaknesses. And don't get flustered, that's another of them. It's the obverse side of your diffidence. Tell your story in a straightforward way. Even if the judge won't give you justice, you'll have made it very clear to these people that you won't be trampled on. It's your turn: keep your head."

Preston was placed in what had been the witness box in the previous case. His neighbor stood in the dock. His neighbor wore a tight-fitting dark blue suit, a stiff white collar and a bright yellow and blue American tie arranged in a pattern of spheres and rhomboids. The neighbor was represented by counsel and had brought down ten witnesses from his estate, who stood against the wall in eagerly restless anticipation.

The judge consulted his papers.

"Now this is an appeal made by you, Mr. Preston, against a decision of the magistrate in your district in connection with a fine imposed on you, because of the trespass of your cattle on your neighbor's land." He turned to the man in the dock. "That neighbor is you, I take it?" The man in the dock nodded.

"Good, now let me see."

The judge restudied the papers then turned to Preston. "Are you represented by counsel?"

"No, sir."

"I see. Usually an appeal turns upon a technicality, and I wonder if you wouldn't be well advised to consult with counsel. There is one other matter to be heard in court. If you cared to defer your case until tomorrow, I'm sure . . ." He paused. He looked at Grainger and Grainger nodded back. "As I thought. Mr. Morris, who is, I may say, a very talented member of the bar, would be only too glad to give you the benefit of his special knowledge. If I may say so, I think you would be wise to accept his offer."

Preston hesitated. He looked toward his wife. She shook her head emphatically.

151

"I'm sorry, sir, it's very generous of Mr. Morris, but I would prefer to handle it in my own way."

"Very good."

Mrs. Preston turned to Mrs. Norman. "A white man is perfectly capable of making his own case. We can't have these local lawyers fixing our cases between themselves." It was said in a stage whisper, not loud enough to reach the bench but loud enough for everyone in the body of the court to hear. Mavis flushed. Grainger must have heard. He could not have helped hearing. Her indignation rose. It was outrageous that he should have to endure a thing like that: as though anywhere in the world except this twopenny-ha'penny island he wasn't worth fifty of Mrs. Preston and her upstart husband.

Mavis was so angry that she could scarcely follow the conduct of the case.

As the judge had prophesied, it turned upon a technicality. The judge was satisfied that Preston had acted in good faith, and had made every effort to discover how much damage had been done. He could appreciate Mr. Preston's fears that this kind of thing might become a racket, but according to the evidence given and accepted at the trial before the magistrate there was an admitted trespass and the commission of a trespass assumed damage.

"But I didn't attend the trial. I do not accept that evidence," Preston protested.

"In that case your appeal should have taken a different form."

It hinged, so it seemed to Mavis, on a verbal quibble. She could not be bothered to listen to it. She was following her own thoughts. They were angry, rebellious thoughts. Here they sat, the Mrs. Prestons of Santa Marta, smug and complacent and superior, thinking themselves a heaven-appointed aristocracy, for no other reason than that their skin was white. To what would they have amounted anywhere but in a place like this? Who had ever heard of any of them outside the Caribbean? Everyone in England had heard of Grainger Morris, anyone who followed sport at least, and wasn't the sports page the first one to which every Englishman turned automatically? How long did people like Mrs. Preston think they would be able to give themselves these airs and graces? Did they realize that they were outnumbered here by one hundred to one?

"As you were not represented by counsel," the judge was concluding, "I have allowed you greater freedom of expression than I should have done. Much of what I have let you say could not have been admitted in this court as evidence. And I have been at particular pains to explain why I have reached my opinion, that the magistrate's decision must be allowed to stand."

He spoke quietly, friendlily; with an air of dignity and authority. He was a colored man, Mavis told herself; there was not a single white man in the smaller islands with sufficient brains and enterprise to be entrusted with such a post. Yet people like Mrs. Preston thought they belonged to a superior race.

"But, my lord, I do entreat you..." The intensity in the voice broke her reverie. An argument was going on. The neighbor's counsel was on his feet. He was asking for costs and the judge had refused him costs. "But, my lord, there are counsel's and legal costs. Ten witnesses have been brought from the estate."

"There was no need for them to have been brought. They gave their evidence before the magistrate. That evidence is on record."

A smile was flickering in the corners of the judge's mouth. He knew his people. Whether or not a deliberate racket had been plotted, whether the fence had been removed and Preston's cattle driven in to trespass at a point where no damage could be done, he knew very well that Montez, the peasant, had been resolved, once the trespass had been done, to take all the profit possible. Montez had asked in the first place for a ridiculously high recompense. And now he had thought that the appeal which he had been certain to win provided an excellent opportunity to bring ten of his friends into town for a day's festivity. Montez must not get away with that.

"There will be no costs. There was no reason for their having been incurred," the judge decided.

The decision filled the tennis club section of the audience with jubilation. Montez must have promised his witnesses a reward. Though he had been awarded fifteen dollars for damage to his property, he would be substantially out of pocket. It was a Pyrrhic victory; if a victory at all. The tennis club was delighted.

In the street outside there was a clamor of indignation. Montez was surrounded by his witnesses. They were insisting that he had promised them five dollars each. He was arguing that that promise had been dependent on his obtaining the five dollars from the court.

"You never said that, boss."

"I did not say it, but I meant it. How can I give you money I have not received?"

Boyeur listened in the background. The estate hands were members of his union. He let them talk, he always let them talk; while they were talking, he made up his mind. He could turn this to his own advantage. He waited for a while, then interrupted.

"Listen boys, you've had an unlucky deal, all of you. You should

153

have had five dollars. You were promised five dollars and you should have had it. You feel that you've been humbugged; naturally."

"He said five dollars. He must pay five dollars."

Boyeur raised his hand.

"Let's look at it like this. A colonel says to his men during a war, 'We are going to take that town. We will plunder it. There is much money in the bank, much jewelry, much silver in the houses. When we divide the spoil, each man will receive a hundred dollars.' That is what he says. But suppose the town has been warned, suppose the money, the silver and the jewelry have been sent away. What to do? The colonel cannot give them a hundred dollars each. He has not got it. They have deserved it, but he has not got it. He cannot give them what he has not got. What to do?"

Boyeur paused. He was following the same technique that Carson had, a few days earlier. If you went on talking, using one phrase as a refrain, you mesmerized your audience.

"What to do? There is only one thing to do. The colonel makes a pile of what he has captured and divides it equally among his men. That is fair, that is just, that is all he can do. That is what you do now. How much money has the judge awarded you. Fifteen dollars. There are ten of you. There is also Montez. Montez has suffered damage to his land. He had also to pay his lawyer. It is fair that he should have the biggest share. What to do? I say five dollars to Montez, one dollar to each of you."

He looked round him. They were not yet wholly satisfied, but they were feeling better than they had. Ten minutes ago they had been afraid that they would get nothing.

"One dollar is not as good as five," Boyeur was continuing. "But you have had a day in town. Montez drove you in. You have seen your friends. It has been a party. If someone had said to you two weeks ago, 'I drive you into town, you see your friends, you do no work, you drink mountain dew, I give you a dollar to spend,' you would have been delighted, wouldn't you?"

They agreed that they would have been delighted.

"Montez has done you no injury. He has said 'What to do.' He has done the best he can. He is not to blame. At the same time you have been humbugged. When you go back tonight, they will laugh at you in the village. Your girls will say 'Where is that handkerchief. Where is that scent you promised me?' You will look silly."

He paused. It was a point that had not occurred to them. They would look silly. They had been thinking only of their five dollars. They had not realized that the girls would laugh at them. They would look silly in the village. That was much worse than losing five dollars.

"You will look silly. And whose fault is it that you will look silly? Not Montez'. He did his best for you. Shall I tell you whose fault it is? Come close, I whisper."

They gathered round him and he dropped his voice.

"It is a white man's plot, to make the brown man look silly. Have you not heard that Preston is going to manage Belfontaine for Maxwell Fleury? It is Maxwell Fleury who wanted to make you silly, so that the village should be afraid of the white man. It was Maxwell Fleury who made Preston bring this case. It is not Preston's fault. He is a little man. Maxwell Fleury is a big man, the son of a big man. It is Maxwell Fleury's fault. You have been made to look silly because of him."

The argument, Boyeur knew it well, had no basis of truth whatsoever, but they would not recognize that. In their present mesmerized state they would believe anything.

"You have been made to look silly. It is Maxwell Fleury's fault. Shall I tell you what I do when a man makes me look silly? I wait my time and then I fix him good."

Across the street stood Maxwell Fleury talking to his wife and sister-in-law. He looked very handsome and at ease, laughing and chattering with a smug self-satisfied expression. I'll teach you to ignore me in public, Boyeur thought.

Smug was the word that had occurred to Boyeur looking at Maxwell across the street. Smug was the word that occurred to Mavis, as Maxwell gloated over the outcome of the case.

"It's the best thing that could have happened for the neighborhood," he was saying. "It'll show these nigger-men their place. They thought they were going to exploit us, now they're in a worse state than when they started."

Mavis disliked his manner. It did not amuse her that an ignorant, ill-educated colored man had been discomfited. The case should never have been allowed to come into court, the appeal should never have been made. They were children, these people: they should be treated as children were, firmly no doubt when the occasion warranted, but kindly, with forbearance. She had no patience with this atmosphere of enmity. They were all Santa Martans weren't they? There should not be two sides, there was only one side—the island's welfare. It was this atmosphere of enmity that made possible a remark like Mrs. Preston's. She was still incensed over that. She wanted to make amends. She watched for Grainger. The moment she saw him in the doorway, she hurried over.

"I want to apologize, on behalf of all of us, for what Mrs. Preston said. I felt hurt on your account; but ashamed on mine. I felt humiliated that such a thing could be said, that nobody protested."

The words poured out; she was overwhelmed with an imperious need to subject herself, to make atonement by her own sacrifice for the intolerance, the narrowness, the injustice of her world.

"We are not all like that," she said. "I'm not the only one who is disgusted by that kind of talk, that way of thinking. It's only the older ones who are like that. We, the younger ones, don't draw these lines, don't make these distinctions."

"I know."

"And it's because you know that, that you're so different: you haven't any chip upon your shoulder. We can be natural with you. You don't know how hard it is for us to be natural with the others, some of the others."

"I can guess that."

"We don't blame them. It's our fault, not theirs: ours in the long run, because of what we did in the past, ours too for what some of us are doing in the present, people like Mrs. Preston; we don't blame your people for being difficult. But can't you see what a relief it is to have some like yourself whom we can use as an example, of whom we can say, 'Is there one point on which he isn't the equal of any man we know?' "

She paused, breathless, flushed. She had never talked in this way in her life; she had never suspected that she could talk like this. She had become a new person to herself. Was she making herself ridiculous? She didn't care. She had to get it all said, now; once and for all. She would have liked to have stood at his side and flung out a challenge to her world; a demand of it to find his equal.

"I think you're wonderful," she said.

He did not answer. He held out his hand. It was a firm cool handclasp, more eloquent than any verbal answer. She watched him as he mounted his bicycle and rode off. Something irremediable had been said, something that could never be unsaid now, that was a part of them for ever, their own secret. It was one of the biggest moments of her life. She felt reborn.

And it was at that very moment that a hand took her arm above her elbow and a voice whispered, "What about a drive?"

She turned and there was Euan Templeton. There was a hot look in his eyes; his thumb moved against the soft flesh of her upper arm. That touch, that look symbolized everything in herself that she despised, that this new-found self of hers rejected. She pulled herself away.

"Leave me alone. Can't you see how sick I am of that."

It was said in a low tense voice, so low that no one heard it. It happened so quickly that only two people saw it. But they were the two people to whom the seeing of it mattered most. Carl Bradshaw and Jocelyn Fleury; to both of them in a very different way, it had a special meaning.

From the other side of the street Denis Archer was waving to young Templeton.

"Do you want a lift? I promised your old man to hurry back."

"O.K."

"That's exactly what the old man wanted," Archer said. "Nobody really won, no one's completely satisfied. The magistrate's face is saved, and there's a general feeling everywhere that it doesn't pay to bring one's grievances to court."

Euan made no comment. Huddled in the corner of the car, he looked away from Archer. What's biting him, Archer thought. He dropped Euan at the front door then drove round to the garage. He looked into the secretariat, two dark heads were bent over their desks. Margot was not alone: there was no real point in his going in, but the impulse to be near her, to hear her voice if only for a moment, was insistent, and he had an excuse for going in; they would want to know about the case.

They listened with interest and amusement to his recital.

"Serve Montez right," said the other girl.

Margot made no comment. There was an air about her that he had come to connect with the harboring of inner thoughts. He looked at her interrogatively.

"I reread your poem," she said. "I'm beginning to understand it. But there were four lines I didn't get."

"Which ones?"

"These."

She slipped a sheet of paper in the machine and began to type. He stood behind her shoulder. It touched and flattered him that she should have learnt his lines by heart. He was surprised too. They were lines of which he had himself been doubtful.

He watched the lines appear upon the sheet. She tapped three spaces, then a line of dots, then the words "My parents will be away tonight."

She pulled out the sheet. "There," she said, and handed it to him. There was no change in her voice, no change in her expression. The

157

other girl seated three yards away could have no inkling that anything unusual had transpired.

5

Carl Bradshaw, on his veranda, sipped at his strong, sweetened tea. It was a relief to enjoy a civilized drink after all those punches. Across the tea table David Boyeur lounged back in a long chair, recounting the story of his rise.

"I wasn't going to live the way my parents did, in a small house, with no money to spend on clothes or parties. My father had worked hard, passed exams, learnt to be a good clerk in an office. But where did that get him? There were fifty others like him in this island alone, the pay is poor, there are no prospects. He has to wear neat clothes. The little money he has must go in keeping up appearances. All my childhood it has been the same thing. No fun because no money. That wasn't good enough for me. No, sir."

He stretched out his legs; his eyes rested with pleasure on his thin silk socks and his highly polished brown and white shoes: he was a Balzac character, Bradshaw told himself; a West Indian de Rubempré. Had anyone understood young men better than that coffee drinking Frenchman? That phrase of his that George Moore had quoted as the key to every young man's ambition; the urge "to be famous and to be loved." That goad had driven Boyeur.

"What made you decide to go in for politics?" Bradshaw asked.

"I had to find something that I could do better than the others could. I found that I could speak. We had a debating society at school. I could get people to listen to me. I could get them to vote the way I wanted, even against their own calmer judgment. All I had to do was talk. They followed. That was what I had to rely on, that was my one gift, apart from being good at cricket. How was I to make the most of it? I saw that quickly. By getting their trust and confidence. I had to do something for them, then when I had them behind me, the 'big shots' in Jamestown would have to take notice of me. I had to take a short cut somewhere. I hadn't time to wait."

Bradshaw nodded. It was pure de Rubempré. Balzac himself had waited. Poor and squat and ugly, he had taken the long slow way; triumph had come when he had no longer the heart and youth to savor it; but his young men one and all had been the exact reverse. They had been tall and handsome. They had snatched at success when they were young, when they could wear it like a buttonhole; they had taken their short cuts; and the account was registered in the long ledger of the Human Comedy. Boyeur was one of those.

158

"I've always heard," Bradshaw said, "that the first ten thousand dollars of a fortune are the hardest earned, that it's the first step that counts. What was yours? How did you get started?"

"I went to Trinidad."

"What did you do there?"

"Two things. I played cricket. I'm a good cricketer. I made a lot of runs. I played in the state trials. I was offered a job in one of the stores so that I could play for Trinidad. I refused. I said I was a Santa Martan, that I wasn't going to desert the island of my birth. That was reported in the papers here. It sent up my stock."

"What was the second thing you did?"

"I met the Left Wing politicians, men like Uriah Butler. Everyone here has heard of him. I wanted to quote him on my return, to be able to say 'My friend Uriah Butler.'"

"How long did you stay away?"

"Not long, two cricket seasons. They mustn't have time to forget me. I was given a big reception when I returned. They asked me to captain the island cricket side. But I refused. That was my short cut. I told them that there were more important things than cricket. At least for me. I hadn't time for cricket. I had other things to do. I had come back to raise the living standard of the islanders, to devote myself to the Santa Martans. They believed me, because they saw I had made a sacrifice on their account. You know how they worship cricket. They thought there must be something special about a man who could have played cricket for Trinidad, but preferred to return and work for them. I had them where I wanted them."

Bradshaw listened, sympathetically. It was Balzac, all the way.

"They tell me that you are running for a seat in the local Parliament. Doesn't that mean that you'll have to toe the party line?"

Boyeur laughed boastfully. "Not me. I'm an independent. I'm not taking orders. The Left Wing want me on their side because I've got organized labor under my thumb. They can't afford to quarrel with me."

"What'll happen when you and they don't see eye to eye?"

"That won't be happening. I shall know what's my business and what isn't. I'll let them run their show, but when it's a question of labor, they'll do what I tell them."

"Is there such a thing today as an issue that doesn't turn on labor, whether it's education, housing, anything you like?"

Boyeur grinned. "That's what the boys are going to discover. I shan't push myself. But they'll soon find that at every turn of the road I'm the important person. Up to now I have played their game,

159

I shall appear to go on playing it. In all these other islands, Grenada, St. Kitts, Antigua, there have been serious strikes. Here there has only been one strike; a short one, and we won it. I have stopped strikes. I have told my chaps that they have only to wait for the new constitution, then they won't need to strike. They will be given their raises legally, through the Leg. Co. The party members know how much they owe to me. I've kept this island quiet for two years."

"Do you think that below the surface there is discontent?"

"Naturally, why not. 'The haves' and 'the havenots.' They know that Whitehall has lost its power. They have seen what has happened in India, in Egypt, in the Persian Gulf. Other peoples are free, they say, so why not us?"

"Do you think they are ready to govern themselves?"

"That's another question. They think they are. That's what they're clamoring for. They want to run their own show."

Bradshaw nodded. It was the same story everywhere, people preferred to run their own show, even if they ran it badly: how many thousand Indians had not been slaughtered by fellow Indians when the British troops went out of India, but the Indians preferred it that way.

He sipped his tea, helped himself to another slice of cake; what a good meal tea was. He had enjoyed reading in English novels of returns home after golf in winter, drawing the blinds and sitting down before a fire to tea and crumpets. There were many very admirable things about the English and their way of living.

He let Boyeur talk on; he encouraged him to talk. Everything Boyeur said was copy. He had been hurt, angry, aggrieved when his chief had given him this assignment. He was grateful now. He was alert, stimulated, eager, impatient to get it down on paper: he'd show the boys in Baltimore that he wasn't finished.

From the street below came the clatter of a steel band, preparing to parade the town. Carnival was only a few days distant, and tension was already mounting: shops were filled with costumes and the children had started to run in bands, with their faces painted. Bradshaw walked to the edge of the veranda.

"It'll be quite a show I reckon, on the day."

"For three days the whole place goes mad. On the last day anything may happen. You'll have a good view from here."

"I see more than you might imagine from up here. The other night quite late in the evening I saw a Government House car drive away from here. I assumed that that young A.D.C. doesn't waste his time."

"From what I've heard he doesn't."

160

Boyeur chuckled as he said it. There was a knowing twinkle in his eyes that Bradshaw did not miss.

"That sounds as though you knew the form that those amusements take."

"I'd say I do. She's one of the secretaries at G.H. She was my girl for a couple of years."

"Indeed." Wheels within wheels, and with a vengeance. "What happened between you two?"

"Time. One of those things, we both felt that we could use a change."

"You didn't quarrel."

"No, no. Mutual agreement. We've stayed the best of friends."

Did the Governor know that, Bradshaw asked himself? Every moment the plot got thicker. Unless he wrote his first article quickly he would not be able to get all he had to say into a single column.

6

Bradshaw would have liked to begin his article the moment Boyeur left him; but his professional instinct warned him that on a night like this he should put in an appearance at the club.

As he had foreseen, the Prestons were the center of attention.

"We all owe you a real debt of gratitude. These fellows will think twice before they try that trick again," Mr. Norman was assuring them.

There were a dozen or so round a table. Carson was one of them. He looked morose and sullen. He had pushed back his chair so that he was half outside the circle; in but not of it.

Dr. Leisching joined them. "You are right. They are out of hand; Did you see how that impertinent puppy Morris talked to me today?"

The doctor had had two punches; it was an airless evening; his face was flushed, and the pleated skin tissue of his scar stood out white and livid.

"That fellow needs a lesson too," he said.

"Why didn't you give it him when you were in the box?"

It was from Carson that that came, and it was said on the note of aloof superiority that those who knew him well recognized as a danger sign. He had felt ill all day. His wound had ached, from under his armpit right down his left side to his ankle; there was that twitching sensation in his severed toe. Alcohol alone could dull the pain, and now the periods of immunity were getting briefer. For the

161

last ninety minutes he had been drinking fast. He was in a belligerent mood, knew it and did not care.

The fact that Carson was sitting put Leisching at a disadvantage. It embarrassed him that the Englishman should loll back there, while he was standing. He felt like a subaltern had up before his colonel. He looked for a free chair and did not see one. He tried to be haughty too.

"I am a very busy man. I have work in the hospital. I have my private patients. It was a great inconvenience for me to have to give evidence at all. In a case like that, it should have been sufficient for me to give evidence in my own house, in my own time, on oath."

"It must be nice to be able to consider yourself and your own time as important as all that."

"My time is anyhow too important to be wasted by a bumptious young colored lawyer."

"At any rate he's a Briton."

"What does that mean?"

"That this is his country and his parents' country and his grand-parents' country; that for a hundred years, since emancipation, his people have been brought up in a country where justice is respected. He hasn't cashed in late."

"Are you trying to insult me?"

"Am I? I don't know. I'm telling you the truth. You should con-sider yourself very lucky to be allowed to live in a society such as this, every night and morning you ought to go down on your knees and thank your Maker that the British have been so magnanimous as to allow you to enjoy their laws and liberty."

"I'm a British subject."

"I know you are. There's an American phrase for that. 'A johnny-come-lately.' If you and your pals had had your way there'd have been no British laws and liberty for you to shelter under."

Carson's voice remained as calm and as aloof as ever. He had not lost his temper. He was not drunk. He felt like death; his wound was aching, but he knew what he was doing. He was enjoying himself. If this square-headed bastard wanted to pick a fight he could. These bloody Germans, how he hated them. They'd spoilt the world for everyone, with their insufferable arrogance, born of that chip upon their silly shoulders. Always rattling their sabers and starting wars. They had ruined life for his father's generation, now they'd ruined it for his.

He half closed his eyes. How different everything would have been for him if there'd been no war. He'd never have lost Daphne; his side would not be throbbing. He'd be in England, in the prime

162

of manhood, colonel of his regiment, with a wife, a home, two children . . . the way his kind of Englishman should live. But here he was, a second-rate expatriate in a third-rate colony; because of these damned Germans, who thought themselves so important that they couldn't be called away from their work to give evidence in a court of law.

"It is most unjust of you to say things like that," the doctor was protesting. "No one objected more than I did to the excesses that were committed under the Hitler regime."

"What form did your objections take? You kept out of the concentration camps, I gather."

"Why should I have been in a concentration camp? I am not a Jew."

"A great many Germans who were not Jews found themselves in a concentration camp."

"I would remind you that I am not a German, that I am an Austrian."

An Austrian, not a German. There it went again. They always had an excuse. It was never their fault, always someone else's. They weren't Prussians, they were Bavarians; they weren't Nazis, they were liberals; they weren't Germans, they were Austrians. Always an excuse. Their sniveling self-righteousness was more tiresome than their saber rattling.

"It suited you all right to be Germans when Hitler was winning battles, when Hitler was bringing you plunder from France and Belgium, when you were fed, with money in your purses, earned for you by him. It was great gravy then. It was a very different thing when he started losing battles, when your cities were bombed, when food ran short; then you became Austrians. I can't say I've much use for fair weather patriots. There is a lot to be said for the old British motto 'My country right or wrong.' "

"Sir, that is too much."

"Is it? I don't think it is. When my father was fighting against your people in what is now called 'The Kaiser's War,' they had a phrase 'There's only one good German, a dead German.' That wasn't very complimentary. It wasn't such a polite war as this last one's been. I'd use that phrase in another way. I'd say that the best Germans are dead."

He was still keeping his voice on a level note. He was angry, very angry, but he had not lost his temper. He was in control. He had rarely enjoyed himself so much. Leisching was flushed and angry. There was silence along the whole veranda, not only at his table, but at the other tables. Everyone had turned to see what was happening, but that was because Leisching had raised his voice, not because Carson had. No one would be able to say next day that Carson had got drunk, lost his temper, and made a scene.

"I'd put it this way," he went on. "When I say that the best Germans are dead Germans, I am referring to the men of the Afrika Corps, to the men who were sacrificed at Stalingrad, to the men who made their last desperate effort in the Battle of the Bulge; they were brave men and honorable soldiers. As a soldier I can respect and honor them. I can't say I can have feelings like that for men who disown their country when things go badly with it. There's a lot to be said for going down with a sinking ship."

"Sir, I insist."

Leisching was scarlet; his voice was strained, with its guttural quality accentuated. "You may say what you like about my country, but in my country, when a man insults us, we slap him across the face, and next morning his seconds call on us, and we fight a duel. Look at this proof of that."

He pointed to the scar on his forehead. There was a little murmur of approval. The doctor had made a point, and Carson knew it. He had to make a comeback. He rose to his feet.

"You and your scars. I call them self-inflicted wounds, scratches kept open with salt so that they shan't heal. When an Englishman fights a duel, he makes a job of it."

He paused. He took a quick look round him at the circle of smug faces; they were all secretly loving it, yet were all prepared the moment it was over to say, "What terribly bad form." He longed to shock that smug look from their faces. They couldn't guess what he was feeling. What did they know about wars and Germans: what had they done, any of them? With about two exceptions they had been indispensably employed out here, sitting in the sun, with all the rum they wanted, and an American naval base to keep them supplied with Chesterfields. What did they know about wars and Germans? He'd show them, once and finally. His hands went to his belt. He undid the buckle. Eyes widened in the circle round him. No one could guess what he had in mind.

"This is how we fight duels."

He pulled down the zipper of his fly and his trousers fell in a pile about his feet: he turned his back upon Leisching, raised his shirt, bent slightly forward and displayed his rump. "That's the kind of scar we carry in my country."

It was an immense wide scar; the flesh drawn and puckered, sunk in where a bone had been extracted. It was simultaneously impressive and repulsive.

164

"That's what we call a scar. And I got that from real Germans, from the Afrika Corps at Alamein; you can go down on your knees and kiss it."

He stood there for a quarter of a minute, then straightened up, pulling up his trousers as he did so.

"Good-night ladies and gentlemen, I'm sorry to have had to make this exhibition."

Leaning against the veranda rails, Carl Bradshaw thanked his stars that he had had the prescience to come up this evening.

7

After breakfast the next morning, the Governor sent for his A.D.C.

"Were you at the club last night?"

"No, sir."

"Have you heard what took place there?"

"No, sir."

"Then go to the Jamestown Club before lunch this morning, and keep your ears open. Don't ask questions, but if anyone starts talking, encourage him. Got that?"

"Yes, sir."

The Governor gave him a close look.

"Are you feeling all right, Denis?"

"Yes thank you, sir."

"You don't look as though you did. You look—" His Excellency paused. "I don't know how a person looks after a shot of cocaine, but I imagine he'd look much as you do now."

Archer laughed. For that in point of fact was how he did feel. He was in a trance and knew it; in a trance and gloried in it. Never had he felt more alive. For ten days he had been thinking if only he could have Margot to himself for a whole evening, not for a snatched moment, he could make her really his. Now that a whole evening lay behind him, an evening that had been more of a dream than he had dared to dream, he had the exciting but disconcerting knowledge that whether she was his or not, he very certainly was hers.

From His Excellency's study he went straight to the Secretariat. The two girls looked up. He addressed the other one.

"H.E. wants to dictate a draft. Could you go along to him right away."

As the door closed behind her, he crossed to Margot's desk. Her eyes were watching him. Was there a fonder look in them? He did

165

not know. There seemed a closer one. I must keep this light, he thought. I mustn't be intense.

He sat on her desk, picked up her hand, turned it over in his, ran his forefinger along her nails.

"They don't seem so sharp this morning. You wouldn't have thought they could do all that damage."

"It was your fault wasn't it they did?"

The tone on which she said it sent a flutter of flattered vanity along his nerve.

"I don't know how I'm going to go bathing at *Grande Anse* next Sunday with a back like mine."

She smiled, but she said nothing. She had a capacity for eloquent silences. "In some South Sea islands," he went on, "a man isn't considered a man till he has scars of that kind on his shoulders, but this is the Caribbean."

He turned over her hand; raised the palm, laid it against his cheek. He felt a slight roughness underneath her thumb. A film of new skin lay over a small cut. She saw him glance at it.

"No," she said, "that was afterward."

The undertone of meaning set the blood pounding through his veins. He had never known anything like this; he had never suspected that there was anything like this. He could not rely on chance occasions when her parents were away.

"I've thought of something," he said.

"Yes?"

"There's a summerhouse in the garden, a chalet where Governors' wives do their sewing and keep their children out of mischief. It's not used now. I could tell H.E. that I want somewhere quiet where I can do some writing. We could meet there, couldn't we."

"Why not."

The summerhouse lay out of sight of the windows of the house. It lay off the main path leading to the secretariat. No one would ever see either of them going there. They could meet there, nearly every day, at some time or another. Excitement bubbled in him. He wanted to make her a long speech; but this was not the time for speeches.

"I'm going to write a poem: it'll be a very good poem. People will say it must have been a very wonderful girl who inspired so good a poem."

"Do that," she said.

On his way down to the club he saw Bradshaw coming out of the post office. He drew up beside the curb.

"Like a lift? I'm going to the club."

166

Bradshaw had just mailed his article. He was in the best of tempers. He was in one of the moods rare with him when he could use a drink. "Fine. I'd love to."

He was also feeling garrulous. By the time they reached the club Archer was at least partially briefed as to what had transpired the previous evening.

## 8

Bradshaw's article reached Baltimore forty-eight hours later. The Foreign News sub-editor whistled as he read it.

"The old man had better see this hadn't he?" he asked his chief.

"He certainly had."

Romer raised his eyebrows as he read it. His hunch had been correct.

"Is that all right sir?"

"It's very much all right." He hadn't realized Bradshaw had it in him.

"What about this bit about the Governor's son?"

Romer reread it. The incident outside the courthouse had been quoted as an example of the electric atmosphere beneath the surface. Anyone was ready to snap at a moment's notice. It prefaced the scene at the club later that same evening. It was not strictly necessary. The article could stand without it. Romer hesitated. He was a family man. He would not like having a thing like that appearing about his son. At the same time he was a journalist. News was News. Only under very exceptional circumstances did you kill a story that was news. Was this one of them? He did not see how it was. He had been the Governor's guest. But you had to abuse hospitality, on occasions. Your host, unless he was an idiot, recognized that fact. He asked you to his house knowing that you would write him up. Nine times in ten he would be disappointed if you didn't. Feelings were hurt occasionally. Sometimes a genuine confidence was betrayed. Was this one of those occasions? He did not think it was. The Governor had entertained him at the expense of the British taxpayer. The Governor had placed no particular confidence in him. The Governor had not told him that he was planning to implement the new constitution right away. He had had to read it for himself in a New York paper. No, there was no reason why he should consider the feelings of His Excellency, Major General the Lord Templeton. "Let it stand," he said.

If the engine of that launch had remained stalled five minutes longer, he would have been taken into the Governor's confidence and that passage about the Governor's son would have been erased.

"Let it stand," Romer repeated. "And send Carl a cable of congratulation," he added.

Ten hours later a copy of that cable lay on the Governor's desk.

At one point in his military career, Lord Templeton had been employed in Intelligence. He had learnt there the routine of security checks; road, rail, mail, cable, air. Spread a net with a strand at each key point, know what was coming into the country and what was going out and you would learn if anything funny was afoot. He could not check the mail. There was no censorship. But he had methods of his own of keeping a check on cables. Romer's cable to Bradshaw interested him. He wondered what the old quean had said. He cabled a friend in New York asking him to send down every copy of the *Baltimore Evening Star* that carried an article signed Carl Bradshaw.

# CHAPTER TEN

## 1

The final words of advice given to Lord Templeton by the Minister of State for the Colonies had been, "When in any doubt produce a simile from the cricket field." His Excellency remembered that advice when he prepared the speech with which he was to announce the new constitution.

"I came to the islands first," his speech began, "over a quarter of a century ago, as a member of an M.C.C. eleven. It was not a particularly strong eleven, by the standard of international cricket: if it had been, I should not have been a member of it. We took our cricket casually, we regarded the tour as a holiday, we delighted in your scenery, we enjoyed your hospitality, we appreciated your friendly, gay, large-hearted way of life, we were struck by the enthusiasm with which you played cricket and the excitement, I must add the intelligent and sportsmanlike excitement, with which your crowds followed the play. But at the same time I do not think one of us imagined that we should live to see a day when a West Indian cricket eleven would beat the full strength of England at Lord's, and in a Test match."

He paused. He looked round him. He was seated in the chair that the Judge had occupied for the Preston trial. He was wearing the uniform of office, dark blue, braided with silver; four rows of medals above his heart; on the table beside him was his plumed cockaded hat; behind him was the Royal coat of arms; with the standard of Santa Marta beside the Union Jack. Immediately in front were the members of the Legislative Council, the seven nominated members on his right, the five elected members on his left. There were the representatives of Government, the Attorney General, the Colonial Secretary, the one in wig and gown, the other in white uniform, with gleaming Sam Browne belt. Three of the nominated members were white men; two were slightly colored, two were completely black. The five elected members were all very dark: they looked highly uncomfortable in their dark suits and stiff white collars.

In the body of the hall, by invitation, were the island notables; the civil servants, the officials, the planters, the lawyers, the business chiefs; at the back, standing, and round the walls, were such of the proletariat as had managed to crowd the passage. Dark faces peered through the windows; from the boughs of the mango in the courtyard, and from the broad high wall round it urchins were gazing into the dark cool room.

Templeton was conscious of his audience. For this one hour he was speaking for this people, the mouthpiece of its ambitions and aspirations. The island expressed itself through him. The feeling lent his voice sincerity.

"The strides made by West Indian cricket in the last thirty years have astounded and dazzled the cricket playing world; but equally astonishing have been the strides made by the West Indians in culture, housing, education, in raising the standard of general living. Thirty years ago I should not have thought it possible that within my lifetime I should talk of Dominion status for the West Indies. I thought of you, I must confess it, as an essentially backward people. I thought the West Indians would need many years of tutoring. I anticipated a process of gradual development. I did not believe that universal suffrage was a practical proposition. Certainly not universal suffrage with a majority of elected members in the Legislative Council. Yet that is what this new constitution gives you. Universal suffrage and nine elected members to three nominated members in the Assembly."

He explained the details of the constitution. He announced the date of the elections. He reached his concluding paragraphs.

"This constitution," he said, "gives you considerable powers of self-government, but it does not give you self-government. You must remember that. Certain powers are retained by the Governor. I have the right of veto. I can dismiss a minister. I can even suspend the constitution. But I would remind you that I am not myself in the position of a dictator. I am the Throne's representative. I am responsible to the Throne, and through the Throne I am answerable to Parliament. I can be dismissed. You have the right to petition the Throne against my administration. I say this, confident that no such situation can arise here, but to remind you that Santa Marta is not yet a self-governing Dominion; it is a Crown Colony; subject to the privileges and obligations that a Crown Colony enjoys. At the same time, in view of what has happened in the immediate past, in view of the immense recent progress in every walk of life, I have no doubt that in a very short while the West Indies will be federated in one self-governing Dominion, and in that Dominion Santa Marta will play a significant and valuable part."

He had ended. He rose, picked up his hat. Outside in the sunlight he could see his Guard of Honor forming. The gathering had risen too. He walked slowly down the passage between the benches. He had known many proud moments, but none prouder than this. He was lucky in having had this full rich wine prepared for his final banquet. He was lucky in having his son here to savor its bouquet with him.

He paused in the doorway, standing at the head of the short flight of steps that led to the square in whose center stood the war memorial. It was a bright clear morning; with an occasional cloud drifting across the sky; the high peak of the diadem was unveiled. The sunlight poured in mild amber radiance onto the mildewed stone of the custom house, onto the yellow and green shutters of the houses, onto the dull red brick of the old French buildings. Beyond the roof tops he could see the sea. The square was crowded, with boys, girls, men and women, old and young, all of them in their brightest clothes, the women with handkerchiefs knotted in their hair, some wearing the long traditional French skirt, the boys in their blue jeans and bright beach shirts. How did they all manage to be here? It wasn't a holiday. If they were able to afford these gay clothes, how were they not working? It was a question that he had often asked himself in England, seeing the cricket crowds at Lord's and at the Oval on a week day.

His heart warmed at the sight of them. They were chattering and laughing. They did not cheer, that was not their way, but they were here on his account. On a morning such as this, it was hard to believe that there was such a thing as trouble in the world.

2

Mails from England via New York came in by air twice a week. A large official mail awaited the Governor's return. The private mail was small. He rarely wrote a personal letter nowadays, except in sympathy for a bereavement or to congratulate an old friend upon an honor or a grandchild's birth. How your personal life dwindled in the last third of your life. You no longer had friends, only professional contacts. If you were ambitious that was to say. It started, he supposed, with your first staff appointment. Until then you were part of a community, family, school, village, regiment; you were at one with a hundred others: then you were on your own, part of somebody's staff, someone in transit, on your way to another staff, to a staff of your own: making close friends with the men with whom you were associated for a period; forgetting them, or at least losing touch with them when you and they passed to another post, to become identified with another group: like passengers on a transatlantic crossing separating when the ship docked, like actors and actresses in a cast scattering when the final curtain fell. Someone in transit. That's what you became.

He shrugged. He was probably an exception. He was a widower. It would have been different without that car smash in the blackout. Marjorie would have maintained a central core of living for him. There would have been his home, and all that gathered round a home: a fire at which others could warm their hands. He ought, he supposed, to have remarried. He wasn't sixty yet. There was still time. But he knew there wasn't. At least not for him. He was too committed. He began to work through his letters, quickly, methodically; arranging them in their separate trays according to their urgency. There was no out mail for two days. He had not to hurry about answering. He turned to his newspapers. There were four copies of the *Times*: there was also a copy of the *Baltimore Evening Star*. That was, he reminded himself, an official sideline. He opened it first.

"I sit on a volcano." That was the heading across double columns.

"I sit on a volcano," he began to read; "one of the peaks of a now submerged range of mountains that curved in prehistoric days in a semicircle from the tip of Florida to Venezuela. Geographically, geologically I sit on an extinct volcano, but socially, politically I sit on an active, a very live, volcano here on the veranda of a hotel in the charming British West Indian island of Santa Marta. I can hear its rumblings beneath me.

"These are the chemical ingredients that cause those rumblings: a proletariat, ignorant and resentful, maintaining a bare level of subsistence; a small patrician class, ignorant and backward, unaware of the changes that have taken place in political thought during the last twenty years, still thinking in terms of the nineteenth century, hating the proletariat and afraid of it, ridden by a sense of guilt for their ancestors' treatment of that proletariat, knowing themselves powerless and outnumbered. There is also a small clan of intelligent, educated colored men who resent the color bar and the secondary position in which it places them; who feel themselves ill-used by these distinctions; there is a demagogue anxious to stir up unrest and to exploit unrest. Resentment, fear, distrust, a need for revenge, these are the ingredients that create an electric inflammable atmosphere. Sooner or later there must be an explosion. Will the spark be applied this week or next week, this year or next? I do not know. But the trail will very certainly be laid next Thursday, when the Governor of the Island, His Excellency, Major General the Lord

Templeton, drives down in state to the Legislative Council to announce a new constitution for the island.

"By this new constitution power will pass out of the hands of what the Governor of another island called 'The Sugar Barons' into the hands of a few colored politicians, who will be able to exploit the voting power of a credulous inflammable proletariat that has no political education. It is idle to call this democracy. It is the substitution of one oligarchy by another. An enlightened oligarchy is probably the best form of government for a backward, agricultural community such as Santa Marta. But will this new oligarchy prove more efficient, more long-sighted, more disinterested than the last? Before we answer that question let us consider the financial position of Santa Marta."

Carl Bradshaw had studied the colonial reports issued by the Stationary Office for the last dozen years; these reports contained profit and loss statements of the island's finances; they showed that the island was entirely dependent on its three main crops of sugar, copra, cocoa, and that its economy was tightly linked with that of Britain. Britain purchased its sugar at a price fixed in relation to the price paid for sugar in other parts of the Empire. Santa Marta could not sell its cocoa in the open market. Britain bought it and resold it. The island was under the control of the Colonial Office and the Board of Trade.

"The island is not genuinely self supporting," Bradshaw argued. "Income tax, which is by American standards cripplingly high, and customs duties which are also high, pay for its administration and support the upkeep of Government House. But the money that supports the various welfare schemes comes out of the Imperial treasury. In time of war the West Indian islands are an asset to Britain, but in time of peace they are a liability. This is a fact that the proletariat does not realize. Do the leaders of the new oligarchy realize it? Does David Boyeur, for example? And many consider David Boyeur to be the key to the situation. David Boyeur . . ."

There followed a pen picture of David Boyeur. The Governor read it with a mounting measure of appreciation. There was more to Bradshaw than he had thought. The fellow had got around, understood what he had seen. Up to a point Bradshaw's view of Boyeur coincided with his own.

"Boyeur is in his own field all powerful. He can organize a strike, and Santa Marta cannot afford a strike. If the cane is not cut, if the cane is not shipped, the island's economy will be thrown out of gear. Boyeur has obtained more than one rise in wages by threatening a strike; but there is a limit to which the wages of a cane cutter can be raised. The price of sugar must be kept to a level at which it can enter the world market side by side with sugar not only from Barbados, St. Lucia and St. Kitts, but from Mauritius and Ceylon and Cuba. Boyeur has promised his followers that when he is in the Assembly, he will raise their wages another five per cent. Will he be able to keep that promise? Will he have the sense that is ingrained in every practicing politician of being able to go back on his promise once he is in power? Boyeur is young and vain. Has he learnt how to eat his words, without loss of face? A great deal depends on that."

Bradshaw then talked of some of the other men who were likely to get elected to the Council: the lawyers, the landowners, the men in trade. "They are sound, sensible men, or at least they appeared to be when they were in the minority, when they were in opposition, but it must not be forgotten that they have been trained for three hundred years to see their lot in terms of subjection to the white man. How will they behave now that they are in control, that they have the bit between their teeth?

"There is another point, a final one, but a most important one. We must not forget the climate, which is something that is so often forgotten by those who are not familiar with the effects of climate. How many of the officials who administer the fortunes of a remote dependency from Washington, London, Paris, take into account that difference of climate?

"At a first glance the West Indian climate seems one of the most beneficent on the globe. There is no winter, as we know it; there is no torrid heat; there are no diseases; malaria is under control; the trade wind blows throughout the year. The vacationist flying south from our frostbound northern streets will consider Santa Marta a terrestrial paradise. 'Is it like this all the year round?' he asks in amazement. The answer is, yes, it is, and that is precisely why for those who live here all the year it is not a paradise. For fifty-two weeks, one day is like another. There is rain most days. There is sun every day. Between January and December there is only an hour's difference between the length of a day. The temperature varies very slightly. November is supposed to be the wet hot month: March is supposed to be the dry cool month. But landing at the Santa Marta airport without a calendar you could not guess in which month you were. There is the danger of hurricanes in August and September. But that is all. One day is like another, too like another.

"This constancy of climate gets upon people's nerves: it drives them to do things that in a cool climate they would never do. When we read of the brutalities that were inflicted by the old planters on their slaves, we ask ourselves how men can have been so foolish as to

174

damage their own property; a slave was worth two hundred dollars when a dollar was twenty modern dollars. There is only one answer to that; the climate. Tempers are frayed. In a second men lose self-control. Two incidents took place today that prove how very near to the surface tempers are. They both concern white people. The first incident concerns the Governor's son, who has come out here for a summer's holiday at the end of his military service, before going up to Oxford in the autumn. He is a good-looking agreeable youth. This is what happened this afternoon outside the Court House."

He described Mavis' behavior. "Would you expect such a girl to behave like that in England? The second incident is far more remarkable. It concerned a colonel, a career soldier now retired." The incident was recounted. "When members of the white ruling class can behave like this, is it not natural to wonder what will happen when the demagogues of an undisciplined proletariat are in control. I sit, I repeat, on a volcano."

At the reference to his son, the Governor started, but he went on reading. He must let this sink in, he must think of something else. He turned the sheet. On the leader page an editorial was headed "Trouble in the Caribbean."

"On page 15 we print a highly significant article from Carl Bradshaw, our New York correspondent, who for reasons of health is now vacationing in the small British West Indian island of Santa Marta. When he took off, he had no plans to write, but the situation there has interested him so much that he felt compelled to write the article we print. We believe it will be appreciated. Some readers may contend that the domestic fortunes of a small British colony are no concern of ours. To that we would retort that anything that happens in the Caribbean is our concern. The Caribbean lies at our back door; by examining this present situation in Santa Marta we can better gauge not only the problems that await us in Puerto Rico and the Virgin Islands, but problems that we cannot ignore in Jamaica, Cuba, and the Dominican Republic. Anarchy in that area is a menace to our own security. We trust that the charming little island of Santa Marta will not become the victim of the explosion of which our correspondent has heard the rumblings. But even so his diagnosis of the various ingredients of these inflammable conditions has a meaning and a significance for us all. We have suggested to Carl Bradshaw that when his holiday is over, he should regard an extensive trip of the Antilles in the light of an assignment."

His Excellency grunted. That was sound enough, but obvious. Which was, of course, the object of an editorial, to state the obvious in such a way that it would appear profound: to sum up the news of the day in terms of the mentality, tastes, prejudices of that paper's public, so that the average commuter reading it on his return from work would see his own ideas confirmed and expressed for him, so that he would close the day elevated in his own esteem.

The Governor turned back to the double column article. He read the penultimate paragraph. He had flattered himself that he was well posted on the various facets of the island's life. But he had no inkling, so it seemed, as to what was passing under his own roof, had no idea what was passing in his own son's mind. Five weeks ago when he had seen that plane, circling in the sky, he had looked forward to the chance that the next months would give him of getting to know his son. But how much had he really seen of Euan; they had been in each other's company half the time, but had they had one real talk? They had discussed the day's events, the local gossip; they had talked of friends and relatives in England. Euan had described service conditions in what was euphemistically called peacetime conditions in the Middle East. They had discussed Euan's career, and had agreed that it was wise to make no decision till he had a chance of looking round at Oxford. "That's the great thing about a university," he had said. "However much you learn or don't learn, you'll find out the kind of person that you are yourself." They had talked easily; there had been no embarrassment, but had they once gone below the surface? As the colonel of a regiment he had prided himself on his ability to be "a father confessor" to his subalterns. But there was all the difference in the world between a subaltern and a son. What do I do now, he thought; knowing even as he asked himself that question that there was nothing, absolutely nothing that he could do. If Euan came to him for advice, he would meet him three-quarters way. But he could not force sympathy upon him. There was one thing, thank heaven, he could rely upon. Euan would never see the article.

### 3

There was a lunch party of forty guests that morning at Government House, for the retiring members of the Council, their wives and a few of the head officials. It was a buffet meal.

"There's no need for you to come to this unless you want," Templeton told his son. "You might find it boring."

"I don't think I shall. I usually manage to get some fun out of this kind of thing."

"You really are having fun out here?"

"Of course. I sometimes can't believe I'm here. I wake up and say to myself, 'Another desert patrol tonight.' Then I remember that I'm not there."

Euan certainly looked happy enough. No sign of a broken heart; probably it had only been a flirtation. Euan had been living like a monk for eighteen months. Maybe he had been too enterprising. At the moment there was nothing to be done.

"Have you made any plans for Carnival?" his father asked.

"We thought we'd go out into the country and see what it's like in the smaller villages."

"Who's we?"

"The usual crowd. Jocelyn, Mavis Norman, Doris Kellaway."

The usual crowd. It didn't look as though the scene outside the Court House, whatever its cause or nature, had broken up the family atmosphere of the inseparables. It was probably not anything to worry over.

"That's a good idea," he said. "I should go out on the Tuesday itself if I were you, then come back here late in the evening to see the last parades. Mardi gras is something not to miss from all that I've been told."

He had been also told that there was a danger of trouble during carnival. It was the last fling before the long Lenten calm. The natives would be drinking fierce illicitly brewed rum for a week on end. With everyone "running mask" there were easy opportunities for the paying off of old scores behind the anonymity of a carnival disguise. In some of the islands, the precaution had been taken of insisting that all masks be removed by six o'clock. Once in the past a similar restriction had been placed on Santa Marta; but that was ten years ago. There had been no real trouble lately. Only a few broken crowns, a few car tires slashed.

Colonel Whittingham was one of his guests at lunch. The Governor was glad of the chance it gave him to have a few unofficial words with him.

"Do you think there's any real danger of trouble during Carnival?" he asked.

"There's always that danger, sir."

"I take it that's an official answer. What's the unofficial one?"

The colonel grinned. "You know what the police are, sir. They want to avoid trouble. They want to cover themselves. If there is trouble, they like to be able to say, 'I warned you, sir.'"

"So you'd like to impose a curfew on the evening of Mardi gras."

"Frankly, sir, I would."

"Would you say that there was more likelihood of trouble this year than any of the last five years?"

177

Whittingham hesitated. He would have liked to have said "Yes," but he could not honestly.

"It's much the same as it always is," he said.

"In that case I don't think it would be a very popular act for me, as a new Governor, to abandon the practice of my predecessors. By the way," he added, "have you heard much talk about that scene at the club the other night with Carson?"

"Half the talk I hear is about that one thing."

"What's going to happen?"

"Leisching has put in an official complaint to the Committee. The Committee hasn't met yet. They're playing for time. They won't do anything till after Carnival."

"Do they hope it'll die of its own accord?"

"That's just about it, sir."

"From what I know of the German temperament that's the last thing Leisching will allow to happen. Germans are very persistent when they consider they have a grievance. I take it the Doctor has."

"I wasn't there, sir, but from what I heard, why, yes."

"I suppose I may have to intervene."

The policeman made no comment.

It was simpler, the Governor reflected, to command a division against Rommel in the Western Desert than administer a small Crown Colony. Across the room, he saw Carl Bradshaw in conference with the Attorney General. He had asked Bradshaw, as an afterthought, as a corollary to that cable of congratulation from Baltimore. He walked across to him. "I hope you're finding your holiday is having the results you hoped."

"I have rarely felt in better health, sir."

"It must be a great relief to be freed of the strain of writing two articles a week. I think you told me that that's what your ration was."

"Two signed columns, a weekly article, and occasional news items."

"I can imagine how quickly those two articles follow one on the other's heels. No sooner is one done than you have to start the next. You probably don't feel free of that responsibility even here?"

"Well, I . . ."

The Governor ignored the interruption. He was enjoying the dramatic irony of the conversation. "I wonder if you ever met the *Daily Express* cartoonist Strube: I'm sure you must know his work. He created 'the little man' of the 1930's. I sat next him once at a Saturday Night dinner at the Savage Club. He told me a curious thing. He was so used, he said, to producing a cartoon every day that when he went on a holiday, he dreamed one every night. Do

178

you, Mr. Bradshaw, dream an article every Tuesday and Friday night?"

"On the contrary, Your Excellency, I'm very glad to be able to say that I am deriving the fullest benefits from my holiday."

Templeton chuckled inwardly. Bradshaw had clearly no idea that his article had found its way to the house upon the hill. He did not intend to let him know. During his service in Military Intelligence he had learnt to let a suspect run free through the bazaars, if he were causing no great danger and one could watch his movements. One day he might find it convenient to administer a rude shock to Master Bradshaw. But in the meantime it was intriguing to wait and wonder what future rabbits Bradshaw would pull out of his hat.

*4*

No one is consistent. And when His Excellency had felt relieved at the knowledge that his son stood no chance of reading the article in the *Baltimore Evening Star*, he forgot that only a short time earlier he had been telling his A.D.C. that it was important to have the right kind of article about Santa Marta appearing in the American Press, since Harlem was to a West Indian what Mecca was to an Iraqi Moslem, and that Santa Martans were more affected by a paragraph about themselves in a New York paper than by a tribute from the Throne in a Christmas Day broadcast.

When he had told Archer that, he had assumed that the articles that Wilson P. Romer would sponsor in the *Baltimore Evening Star* would eventually find their way back to Santa Marta. He had been right in that assumption. A large number of Santa Martans had relatives in the United States and the same plane that brought the *Baltimore Evening Star* to Government House, carried clippings of Bradshaw's article to the offices of the island's daily paper, *The Voice of Santa Marta*.

The editor's eyes widened as he read it. This certainly was something. The editor, Marcel Tourneur, was a colored man in the early thirties. His father owned a store and a plantation on the windward coast. The Tourneurs were one of the richer families. Marcel was very much the son of a rich man. He knew he could lead a comfortable life without overworking. He had never kept regular hours when he worked in the store, and when his father had put him in charge of the estate, he had spent most of his time in Jamestown. His father had bought up *The Voice of Santa Marta* entirely to provide his son with an occupation.

The paper was an expression of its editor's personality. It was

179

the paper of a man with a sense of mischief and a sense of fun. It had a daily four sheet issue. Its front page carried general international news that was a precis of the B.B.C. news bulletin. The back page carried advertisements, the third page shipping news, lists of arrivals and departures; local cricket and football scores: reports of Police Court cases and of the meetings of the Council.

The second page was the lively one. It was Marcel's direct responsibility. He wrote the editorials. He chose the leading article from a London or New York paper. Whenever possible he chose an article that was likely to cause controversy.

When the *Baltimore Evening Star* reached his office, Marcel whistled. This was too good to be true. His first impulse was to print it right away; to make a splash, to give it a build-up; to have posters printed. He could make a sensation with this piece. At the same time he had the same detective's instinct that the Governor had. Let your prey run wild a little, give the criminal his head, don't let him know that he is being watched. The second or a third article might be a good deal livelier. By waiting he might make a bigger splash. If he printed this article now he might scare Bradshaw into prudence. Much better for Bradshaw not to know that his articles had found their way back to Santa Marta. He placed the clipping in a drawer to which he had a key.

# CHAPTER ELEVEN

## 1

The sun on the morning of Mardi gras rose into a cloudless sky. Jocelyn, seated at her window beside her morning tea, looked forward to the day with mingled anticipation and anxiety. There might be awkward moments. It was the first picnic since the scene outside the court house. As far as she could observe, there had been no patching up. Mavis and Euan had met in groups, at the tennis club and at *Grande Anse* on Sunday. They had not avoided one another. They had talked naturally: there had been no sign of friction; but that had been in groups. It would be different today, in a small party, on their own.

She felt sorry for Euan. It must be difficult for him here, with no established friendships, and the constant knowledge that he had to comport himself in terms of his father's position. As a safeguard against unpleasantness she had arranged a larger party than usual: twelve of them instead of six. Since Sylvia and Maxwell were in town, they had three cars. If things got difficult, they could break up into small groups.

They met at ten at the Continental. From the veranda Bradshaw watched them arrange themselves in three sets of four. Archer, he noticed, was not with them. He had fish of his own to fry presumably. Young Templeton did not get into the same car with Mavis. Did that mean that the quarrel was still on; or was it farsightedness on Euan's part? It would give him a chance of saying to Mavis in the evening, "I've not seen you once today. Let's get in the same car now." Then driving back together in the dusk, he could make his peace with her. Was that the way it was?

He saw Jocelyn get into a car with some Barbadians who had come over for the Carnival. He saw Mavis with Doris and Doris' brother join up with Grainger Morris. Grainger—that was a possible pipeline that he had neglected. He watched the three cars drive off. He would give a lot to be around when those cars returned, to read the expressions on those twelve faces. He settled himself back in his deck chair. He repeated the phrases of that Baltimore editorial. It was the first time he had been referred to in an editorial. It need not be the last, if he played his cards correctly. The world was a good place.

Mavis too was thinking that as she drove at Grainger's side. It was a perfect day; the air was so clear that she could see shadowy on the horizon across sixty miles of water the outline of Guadeloupe. It was hard to realize on a day like this that a hundred and fifty years ago men were watching anxiously from here for French ships to attack across the channel.

Grainger smiled when she said that.

"They never did, you know."

"Never did what?"

"Attack across the channel. They were always threatening to, but the trade winds were too strong. The English could always sail from Antigua and intercept them."

It was only by a fluke, he said, that the British captured Santa Marta. A squadron of Rodney's, sailing for English Harbour, got driven south by a hurricane and as Santa Marta lay in their path, they took it.

"I'd never realized that before, about the trade wind, I mean."

"Because they don't teach history and geography simultaneously. They leave the climate out of their text books. And everything turned on the trade winds in those days. That's why there was so little fighting here, the attack came where it was not expected. That in the long run is why there are so many old feudal families still left here. Like the Fleurys. In Grenada and St. Lucia they were all wiped out by the revolutionaries. But the French Revolution didn't touch Santa Marta because by then the British were in possession here."

"But there were slave risings here, too, weren't there? Lots of them?" she said.

"In ten minutes we'll be passing a house that was destroyed in one."

It lay on the slope of a hill, two hundred yards back from the road. Only its carcass remained, the walls with the gaps for windows and the "welcoming arms" flight of steps. In the roadway was the crumbled masonry of the gateway. Three royal palms marked the avenue that had led from it to the house; higher up the road was the rounded tower of a windmill: shrubs grew out of the interstices between the bricks: there was a broken archway, the ruins of a *boucan*: the ground between the gateway and the house had been planted with coffee; the last yellow petals were about to fall: the picking of the feathery buds would be starting soon. It all looked very calm and peaceful.

Grainger stopped the car. She had passed the house innumerable times, she was familiar with the legend that surrounded it. But she wanted to have him tell it to her. She liked the sound of his voice, and the knowledge and authority that lay behind it.

"When did all this happen?" she asked.

"In eighteen sixty-three," he said.

"After emancipation then."

"There was more trouble after emancipation than before."

Santa Marta during the eighteenth century, he said, had been a happy island mainly through its lack of history. It had been prosperous in an unobtrusive way and the slaves were treated well. But after emancipation, when the landlords were no longer responsible for their workers' health and comfort, there was poverty and unemployment.

"The slaves," he said, "could not get the idea of a day's pay for a day's work. A great many of them haven't yet. They think that their boss should provide them with food, clothing, and a house; it's smart to do as little work for him as possible, and steal when they get the chance; they put in their real work on their own small gardens where they grow their vegetables."

She had often heard the same sentiments expressed by her father's friends. But with them it had been said angrily, sneeringly, spitefully. "Treat them like mules, dangle a carrot in front of their noses and keep a stout whip in a strong right hand." She had heard hatred in the voices of her father's friends. But in Grainger's voice the mockery was friendly. He liked these people; they were his own people after all.

She looked at the ruined house upon the hill.

"Why did it happen? What was it about?"

He shrugged.

"Can one ever tell how those things start? It may be a single insult, a single injustice; it may be the accumulation of small incidents. But the basic cause is constant: a part of the community is ill-housed and underfed; there's a grievance; and a scapegoat's sought; there's an inflammable situation; the first spark touches it off. You know what these people are. How excitable, how quickly worked up they are."

"What happened to the owners of the house?"

"They were found burnt."

"Were the people who did it caught?"

"How could they be? No peasant will give evidence against

183

another where a white man is concerned. Everyone in the village had an alibi."

She looked across the green stretch of the coffee crop, at the three solitary palms and at the crumbled walls. She shivered. It was hard to believe, on a day like this, that ninety years ago when those palms had been three units in a long, proud avenue, the shrubberies had quivered with creeping figures, vowed to vengeance; that the blackness of the night had been lit suddenly by towering flames, with dark, distorted faces glistening in the glare, that human screams had broken through the noise of crackling wood.

"Let's go on," she said.

A mile farther down the road they reached the houses in which ninety years ago that pack of murderers had laid their plans. It was a straggling village, almost a township, at the foot of a valley with a river running through it to the sea; a jetty ran out into the water; produce was shipped from here to Jamestown; sloops called from the other islands; boats were being built and repaired along the beach, the village was sufficiently large to own a police station and a post office. Today it was hung with flags. Every shack was decorated. The main street was crowded. There was scarcely a villager who was not "running mask." Sometimes they paraded in groups, similarly attired; sometimes they were in couples, sometimes alone. There were men dressed as women, waggling their posteriors as they danced. From the porches of the shacks that lined the road old men and women yelled encouragement, children jigged up and down on the edge of the road in imitation of their elders. On the veranda of the police station, a ten-piece steel band was beating out its jagged rhythm.

The noise was deafening and the car was forced to slow down till it was scarcely moving. Children jumped on the footboard. Men and women peered through the windows, waving whatever they carried in their hands, laughing, shouting, gesticulating. Some of them carried bottles. But it was only the minority who did so. By and large West Indians do not take alcohol. They were drunk not with rum but with the music. Their teeth shone white in the gash their mouths made in their painted faces. Beads of sweat percolated through the paint. There was a powerful pervading smell of brilliantine and coconut oil that overlaid the smell of sweat, but did not any more conceal it than the paint concealed the beads of perspiration. The car was below the level of the parade. The sun beat down upon its roof. The airlessness was suffocating.

"It's seven years since I was here. I'd forgotten it was like this," said Grainger.

184

Mavis made no reply. She was thinking of that day ninety years ago. The great-grandparents of these men must have looked very much like this as they pranced round that guttering building, waving their cutlasses, the glare of the fire illuminating their gloating faces. They were happy now, these people: gay, good-natured, laughing, but they were out of control. They were as drunk with happiness as their ancestors had been drunk with hatred. She turned toward Grainger. His eyes were on her face.

"We're thinking the same thing aren't we?"

"More or less," he said.

2

The rendezvous was a beach on the north point of the island. They could be sure there of solitude. The patricians would be at *Grande Anse*; the proletariat would be "running mask." They arrived, in their separate cars, hot and soiled and tired, eager for the cool fresh water. They sat on the sand under the palms and drank punches out of thermos flasks. They were too tired to talk. After the first two punches, most of them went back to swim again. Then they opened their lunch baskets. Each had brought something different: there was lobster mayonnaise, there was "soursop," chilled in a wide-necked flask; there was a rabbit pie and a sponge roll and cheese: mangoes were not yet in season, but there was a pawpaw and a pineapple. They overate a little, as one does at picnics. After lunch they stretched themselves on rugs, so tired that even the sandflies could not stop them sleeping.

The heat of the day was over when Euan woke. The sun was sinking toward the hill. Another three-quarters of an hour and the beach would be in shadow. He was the first to wake. He felt sluggish and heavy-eyed as he always did after a siesta. Another swim, he thought.

That did the trick. On his return to the beach, he saw that Jocelyn too had woken. The others would be waking soon. That meant more punches. He could dispense with that.

"Is Belfontaine far from here?" he asked.

"Three miles."

"I've never seen it properly. Could you show me round?"

"I'd love to."

They looked at their slumbering friends.

"Will they be driving past the house on the way back?" he asked.

"They may do, but it's a longer way."

"It doesn't matter, though, we've got three cars."

185

It was the first time she had been beside him the whole day. It was the first time they had been alone for at least a week. As always she felt cozily at ease with him. And it was good, after the noise of carnival to be driving round the tip of the island in the quiet, past a long grove of coconuts, with grazing ground stretching toward the foothills. This was the least populated parish in the island because the least protected; but it was one of the most charming.

"I can see why your ancestors chose this place," he said.

It was the first time he had approached Belfontaine from this side. It looked very dignified, white against the green of the surrounding cane fields, with the avenue of palms leading to it from the road.

Jocelyn honked the horn as she turned into the avenue.

"I'll bet that wretched guardian has taken the day off," she prophesied.

The windows were shuttered and the front door locked. No sound came from the outhouses.

"What did I tell you? They're the most casual people. You can't rely on them."

"Does that mean we can't get in?"

"No, no. I know where they keep the key."

It was in a small flowerpot on the veranda.

"It won't take a minute," she told him.

She had parked the car to the left of the drive, in the shadow of a mango tree. It was out of sight of the house.

A ten-year-old urchin who had been squatting on the edge of the cane field since midday, noted its position with approval. He slunk back to the main road, keeping out of view. The moment he was out of sight he began to run. There was plenty of time still to "run mask." Perhaps the man who had sent him there would give him fifty cents. The man who had posted him was one of those whom Boyeur had exhorted to "fix that bastard good."

It was less than thirty hours since Maxwell and Sylvia had driven into town, but already the shuttered house carried a damp smell. Jocelyn wrinkled her nose.

"Do you wonder that nothing lasts here? Worms eat through books and furniture. It's not worth having a good piano. They eat the felt. Let's let in some fresh air, quick."

They moved from room to room, opening windows, throwing back the shutters. In five minutes a transformation had been effected. The fusty, frowsy atmosphere had been dispelled, sunlight was streaming through open windows onto rosewood and mahogany, onto silver and Venetian glass; onto family portraits in dull gilt frames. From the windows you saw the fresh green of the cane fields and the cotton crop.

"In the tropics all you need is a roof supported at the corners, and a floor to stand beds and chairs and tables on," she said. "You don't need any decorative furniture or pictures. Look at that."

She pointed toward the windows. The series of views seen through them made the walls look like the corridor of a gallery lined with pictures.

"Perhaps that's why these people have produced no art," he said. In the north you had to have pictures on your walls; nature gave so little; you had to create beauty in protest against the niggardliness of nature.

Even so it was a relief to have all this, he thought as he looked about him, at all the evidence this house contained of a long-based family life, pictures and photographs and chairs and tables that had been bought and cherished over two hundred years, the residue of changing tastes sorted out from one generation to the next. It reminded him of the Queen Anne house on the edge of Dartmoor in which he had been born, the house that had been requisitioned by the Army during the war, that had only been partially reopened, that had been offered to the National Trust and been refused; that in all human probability would never be a home again.

He looked at a collection of West Indian prints, collected by Jocelyn's great-great-grandfather. He had been shown them when he had been brought out to lunch, but he had no time to examine them. They had a charming eighteenth century quality; a sense of leisure, a lack of hurry; with the slaves either elaborately clothed in Sunday raiment or naked, except for a loincloth, in the cane fields and at the sugar mill. They reproduced the scenery, the landscape and foliage of the tropics, but they did not present the tropics. They were the tropics seen in terms of an English country house. The heat and humidity of the tropics had been left out.

In what had been her father's study the walls were hung with photographs. "That's grandfather," she said.

It had been taken on the steps of the house in Devonshire that Euan had known so well in boyhood. The house had been acquired, during the slump, by a rich man in the city, who had children of his own age and had given lavish parties.

"It's funny to think that you've never been in that house," he said.

He looked more closely at the photograph. Her grandfather was wearing a Norfolk jacket, with a handkerchief tucked sideways into the long pleat; the pockets sagged; he had a gun under his arm;

187

there were cartridges most likely in his pocket; his breeches fitted tightly at his knees. He was wearing boots. There was a spaniel at his feet.

"I've got a photograph of my grandfather looking just like that," he said.

"There's one of Daddy with his father."

It was a cricket group. They were both wearing I.Z. blazers. They were very obviously son and father, though the son was thinner, smaller, with finer features, and the darker hair cut short. They were seated on the steps of a pavilion.

"That's the Sidmouth ground," he said. "I've played there often."

"That's Mummy."

"She's the image of your aunt Cicely."

"It's strange your knowing all these relatives that I've never met."

"That's what I told you at that first garden party."

They looked at other photographs. He told her about the people in them, the places that were in the background. "This one, I've seen before," he said. "In my aunt Julia's house. Isn't it strange to think we've been brought up with the same things round us, living all these miles apart."

They reached the final photograph.

"Haven't you one of your father's mother?" he asked.

"Daddy's got one somewhere. Only a snap. You can't see her at all well. She's wearing a floppy hat. Her face is in the shadow."

"He was born out here wasn't he?"

"Not in this island, in Jamaica."

They returned to the veranda. The shadow of the palms had lengthened, the blue of the sky had darkened, the green of the cane stalks deepened. All day their waving spearheads had been like polished metal reflecting the sun's glare; now in the declining light they resumed their own rich hue. There was not a cloud on the horizon.

"We may see the green ray tonight," she said.

They stood side by side on the veranda, leaning against the railing.

"The others ought to be coming by now any moment."

"Unless they've gone the other way."

"That's probably what they would do, isn't it?"

"There are more villages on the leeward side, there's more for them to see."

"We don't need to feel guilty about them, do we?"

"They'll be all right."

It was very quiet. The nearest village was two miles away. The beating of the steel drums carried faintly against the wash of the waves upon the shingle, the croaking of the frogs, the rustle of the palm fronds.

"Why don't I make some tea," she said.

"That's an idea."

"Sylvia's very wasteful. We'll probably find a cake in the bread tin."

They did not find a cake, but they found a box of biscuits. Sylvia had an electric kettle. "We'll switch on the current," Jocelyn said.

The electric plant was housed in a stone cistern, fifty yards away. It was connected with the house by an outside wire.

"It's a funny Heath Robinson contraption," Jocelyn said. The handle was concealed behind a mirror. She pulled it gently, but no answering throb came from the cistern. She pulled again. There was no response.

"It keeps going wrong. We'll have to use the stove," she said.

They brought the tea and biscuits onto the veranda. The hot, sweet tea was infinitely refreshing.

"They won't be coming now," he said.

"No, not now."

"I'm glad they won't. I want to see that emerald ray."

They had not long to wait. The sun grew rounder and redder as it dipped. First the tip touched the horizon; a quarter was submerged, then a half.

"Be careful not to blink," she warned him.

He wanted desperately to blink. The sun dried his eyeballs. Three quarters were under now. He blinked fast, twice. Now he could hold out surely. He stared, fascinated. He had heard so much of the emerald ray, the last flash of vivid green as the sun submerged. But every time when the sky had been cloudless, the horizon had been hidden behind a hill. Whenever he had had an uninterrupted view, the sealine had been banked with clouds, and the sky streaked and torn and glorified with streamers of gold and orange, green and blue. This was the first time he had a clear chance to see the ray. He stared, resolved not to blink: the sun had almost vanished. One moment it was there and his eyes were smarting: another moment and it had gone and he was blinking hard.

"Well?" she asked.

He laughed. "I don't know. It was a blur. I'll say I saw it."

"That's what most people do."

He looked back at the horizon. " 'Evening's after green,' " he quoted. It was very lovely; the air was cooler now; a breeze was blowing from the mountains; the white flower of the night was opening, spreading its sweet heavy scent. The croaking of the frogs grew louder.

"Oughtn't we to be going soon," he said.

"I suppose we should."

But she made no movement. The dark fell quickly. There is no twilight in the Caribbean. Stars began to stud the sky.

"What time does the moon rise?" he asked.

"It's three-quarters full. It should be coming over the mountain in about an hour."

"Let's wait a little. It'd be nice driving back by moonlight."

"We'd better put the tea things away first. The light's not working."

They moved the tea things down into the kitchen.

"In England we'd have to wash them up," he said.

"That's one of the advantages of living here."

They fastened back the shutters, closed the windows; locked the doors opening onto the veranda. The road was unlighted except on the outskirts of each village. The circling cars provided their own illumination. It was not exactly dark. The sky was starlit, and the moon mounting on the leeward coast was heralding its approach behind the mountains, but it was dark enough for them not to be able to see each other's features. Conversation became difficult.

"Perhaps we should be going back," he said.

"Perhaps we should."

"Before we're quarter way there we'll have a moon to light us."

"In less than that."

"We might stop on the way and have some supper."

"That's an idea."

"Then we're on our way."

They walked down the short flight of steps into the avenue. The steps were narrow and they were very close. She got into the driver's seat.

"Would you rather I drove?" he said.

"It's Maxwell's car. It's got its idiosyncrasies. I know them."

She pressed the starter. There was no response.

"I suppose that's one of them," he said.

"You wait. It's got plenty of others."

She pressed the starter again. Again there was no response. She sat back, rested; pressed again; the same result. Another pause; another attempt; still silence.

"This time it's got me puzzled."

"I'll try the jack."

But the jack was no more effective.

"I hope you've got a torch," he said.

"I have."

He lifted up the hood, and flashed the torch. "Well, well," he said, and let the hood down. "I hate to break it to you, but your carburetor's gone."

"What?"

"Your car, lady, has no carburetor."

"What?"

"Come and look."

She got out of the car and peered. "You're right, it's gone."

"Is that a carnival idea of humor?"

"You could call it that."

"What do we do now? Ring up your father?"

"We can try."

He took the key out of the flowerpot, and opened the main door. "You're better at your machines than I am."

She spun the handle, lifted the receiver, stood with it against her ear. There was a minute's silence. She hung the receiver back, swung the handle; stood again with the receiver against her ear. Silence again.

"It's no good. It's dead."

"It's carnival, remember, the girl at the exchange may be on a jag."

"I know when a line's dead." She paused thoughtfully. "The electric light engine, the carburetor, now the telephone. Three things can't be a coincidence."

"What does it mean?"

"It might mean anything. Grudges get paid off at carnival."

"Against you, against me, against my father?"

"They don't know it's me. They don't know it's us. They only know it's Maxwell's car. He may have put their backs up. Or Sylvia may have done."

"We need a drink."

"You couldn't be more right."

The refrigerator was worked not from the electric battery but by gasoline. They brought up ice and limes, rum and sugar and a bottle of angostura.

She mixed the ingredients.

"One of sour, two of sweet, three of strong and four of weak."

She spun the swizzle stick. "It's very dry. It must be sipped. But you've learnt that by now."

He had. A dry swizzle, the rum heavily drenched in angostura, looked pink and frothing after it had been beaten up, as sweet as grenadine but it had a bitter aftertaste. He finished his cocktail

191

in a couple of quick gulps.

"What do we do now?" he asked.

"There's nothing we can do."

"That's what I was thinking. The others must have taken the other road."

"They must."

"They won't start worrying about us for hours yet."

"Not till tomorrow morning."

"If they did, they'd decide there was nothing they could do about it. That's what they'd want to decide anyhow. They wouldn't start driving back to look for us when they were hungry and wanted dinner."

"If they thought about us at all, they'd feel it wasn't any of their business to find out where we were."

"That's much more likely."

"In which case, since there's nothing that we can do about it, we might as well have another drink."

"That's an idea."

"Let's make it a long one this time. Let's get some soda. There must be a bottle in the icebox."

There was also in the icebox, half a chicken pie.

"We'll be able to have a good supper later on."

Their search for the soda had not taken them three minutes. But they returned to a world transfigured and transformed. In those three minutes the moon had risen over the shoulder of the hill. Three-quarters full, its soft cool light burnished the palm fronds, throwing long shadows along the avenue; they could see the expressions on their faces.

"I'm beginning to enjoy this," he said.

They sat back in their long chairs on the veranda, sipping at the long, weakened, sour-sweet punch. How happy I always am with him, she thought.

"How much longer have you got here?" she asked.

"I'm supposed to have four months."

"Supposed?"

"I don't go up to Oxford till October. My father wanted me to spend all the summer here, but I've been rather wondering . . ."

He paused. She helped him out.

"Has Mavis made all that difference?"

"No, no, it isn't that, it's . . . But what did you know about Mavis?"

"I was in on it from the start wasn't I?"

"I suppose you were."

192

"At the beginning you were always talking about her, then you stopped talking her, so I assumed something was happening. I was there that afternoon outside the court house, so you see."

"I see."

"You don't mind my having mentioned it?"

"Of course I don't...." He did not want to discuss it, at least not now. He frowned.

She hesitated. Was there anything to say that could lessen the blow for Euan, that could restore his self-esteem. She knew the way Mavis thought, the way Mavis acted. She had her own explanation of what had happened. Mavis resolute to make the most of any opportunity for a good time provided by chance visitors, preferred to play the game on her own terms. She would call the tune and pay off the pipers when she was in the mood; and the fact that she had been humiliated by Rickie would make her all the more anxious to rehabilitate herself in her own and in the general esteem by walking out upon the Governor's son. Jocelyn had no idea how far the thing had gone. But it was not impossible that Mavis had "led Euan up the garden path" to make his discomfiture the more complete. Euan had been sacrificed to Mavis' injured vanity. His position as the Governor's son made him the more desirable as a victim.

She could hardly explain that to him without being disloyal to her friend. Yet she wanted to make it up to him.

"Then if it isn't on that account that you're thinking of cutting your visit short..." She paused, interrogatively. It was an opening if he chose to take it.

"Well, I suppose..." he started.

But the sentence was never finished. Right in front of them and right along the cane field sprung shafts of fire that rose and roared; fanned by the wind, crackling, sweeping up the hill, tossing their sparks into the sky.

For a moment they stared transfixed, then simultaneously they jumped to their feet and ran to the veranda rails. They stood there side by side, dazzled by the utter beauty of the sight; the orange and red flames, the clouds of smoke with the moonlight silvering their fringes; the dark backcloth of the sky, with the stars that studded it; the flickering glare upon the palm trees. He had never seen anything more lovely.

"Somebody's got it in for your brother right enough," he said.

She made no answer. He felt a sharp hot sting against his cheek.

"Better stand back," he said. "The sparks are flying."

But she did not move.

"That's the only danger," she said, "that one of the sparks might set the house on fire."

"How far does the cane go?" he asked.

"For half a mile, but the stream runs that way. The stream will stop it."

"Then it'll turn south. How far do the fields go that way?"

"For a mile or two, but there may be a field that's been ploughed up."

"We ought to cut an avenue that the flames can't jump across."

He asked her a succession of quick, practical questions. What chance was there of getting any of the villagers, was there a bicycle? Were there two bicycles? He wouldn't want to leave her here alone, but perhaps they shouldn't leave the house unguarded. The house was surrounded by a drive and garden. There was little danger of a spark landing on the veranda, but there was that danger.

"They'll probably see the fire won't they? If they do, they're bound to come and see what's happening."

She laughed. "They'll know about it right enough. You've heard of coconut wireless. They'll soon be flocking round from everywhere."

"We might as well wait for them."

They had not moved since they had left their chairs: it was scarcely five minutes back, but it seemed that they had been living in another world when they had lolled back in the moonlit dusk, sipping at their long, cool, sour-sweet punches. The heat from the fire flushed their cheeks. He was conscious of an excitement mounting along his veins and nerves: there was the incredible beauty of the raging fire against the tropic night, and the spice of danger was intensified by his sharing of it with this girl. His arm was round her waist.

"You're not frightened are you?"

"No, I'm not frightened."

"It's like the air raids in London. There was danger, but a very slight one. You never expected a bomb to pitch where you were. Yet the fact that there was a danger gave a zest to everything. You enjoyed everything more because of it."

"I shouldn't have thought you would have been there for the raids. Didn't your parents keep you in the country?"

"Daddy was in the Middle East. The house was shut. Mummy was in London. I didn't want to stay with aunts."

"Tell me about it."

There was not a great deal to tell. He had been in London on that first Saturday in September when the first raid came. He had

194

stayed on through the week, had seen that incredible Sunday, the 15th, when all day long the sky had been lined with the white trails of aircraft, when he had watched dogfight after dogfight right above his head; when he had seen a German plane crash wingless in circles to the ground. Then he had gone back to school. When he had returned for the Christmas holidays, the worst was over: there had only been the one big Sunday fire raid just after Christmas, when half the city had been in flames. That had been the end of London for him. During the Easter term his mother had been killed. After that he had spent the holidays with his aunts. He had not seen another raid. But that fortnight of raids during that first September was among the most vivid experiences of his life.

"It wasn't unlike this in a way," he said, "though it couldn't be more different. But it was beautiful in its own way too. The complete darkness of the city; the searchlights in the sky; the star shells scattering and growing brighter as they fell. I'd never realized how beautiful London was till I saw it in the blackout. You can't see the lines and the proportions of the buildings when there are all those street lamps and neon signs, but when you see a London square suddenly emerge out of the darkness in the light of a star shell, you can't see its base; it seems suspended in the air, then the shell fades and it slowly vanishes. It looked like a magician's trick."

As he spoke it seemed to him that she drew closer to him, as though they were not here on a West Indian night looking onto a grand-scale bonfire, but back in London, sharing London's proudest hour. He shifted his arm, adjusting it to her changed position; his fingers brushed against her breast and lingered there.

"There was one very strange thing about it all," he said. "When I got back to school after that two weeks of bombing, I didn't, as you'd have expected, sleep as I'd never slept before. I was restless. I kept waking up all night wondering how things were in London."

His hand was cupped now about her breast. He was vividly conscious of its smooth soft roundness under the thin brassiere. She did not move away. She appeared to be unaware that he was touching her.

"I've been told," he was going on, "that a lot of Londoners felt like that; that they'd go out of London for a weekend, hoping to get some sleep, and couldn't sleep at all: they worried about what was happening in London."

His hand was moving now, softly, slowly over her breast, stroking it, caressing it. She leant a little closer to him. The blood pounded through his veins. The nipple lifted and hardened under his caress. He went on talking about London in the blackout, in the bombing, pretending that nothing was happening. He was watching and listening for the villagers' arrival, with one part of his mind praying that they would hurry, with the other half praying that they would delay: praying for time to stay its hand, yet wishing for this moment of taut expectancy to be broken by some outside agency.

The fire was now roaring up the hill, and turning southwards: immediately in front of them it had burnt low, and its heat was lessening, but its glare still flickered on the outhouses and on the palm trees. Her face in profile below his was soft and glowing.

"How little I thought when I stood at my bedroom window on that first September night that one day I should be standing on a West Indian veranda, looking out on to a fire, talking about it to a girl."

She made no answer. She seemed to be as unaware of what he was saying as she was of the slow movement of his palm and fingers. She might have been asleep. Then suddenly she started.

"Look, they're here," she cried.

In the avenue there was a horde of them. Twenty, thirty, forty, he could not tell how many. They looked fantastically barbaric in their carnival costume, with the glare of the conflagration on their painted, glistening faces. More seemed to be coming every moment: boys, women, girls, half a village. The men were carrying cutlasses.

"We must get this organized," he said.

He became in an instant the officer he had been until six weeks ago; taking control, giving orders confidently, with assurance, knowing they would be obeyed: finding the leaders, splitting up the villagers into teams, sending one party here, another there: giving them their instructions.

"Come on now, all of you, let's get to work," he shouted.

She was seeing a new side of him: the officer, the practical efficient leader.


Within an hour the fire had been controlled: on the edge of a ploughed field a quarter of a mile down the road, the cane had been cut back and cleared. The fire could not spread. It was still raging up the hill, but it could not cross the stream. It would burn itself out. Immediately in front of the house stretched a smouldering, blackened mass. There was nothing more to be done. The villagers were grouped before the steps.

"I had better give them some money hadn't I?" he said.

"It would be a good idea."

"How much, twenty dollars?"

"Ten's ample."

196

The villagers were delighted. For them the whole adventure was a footnote to carnival. They cheered, shouted, waved their cutlasses: dispersed as quickly as they had come, hurrying back to their steel bands. Once again he was standing beside Jocelyn, leaning against the veranda rail. He was exhilarated and exhausted; excited by the evening's drama; with an air of triumph; the fire conquered. But it had been hard work. He had started to feel very hungry.

"I'm not surprised. It's after nine," she said. "You go and shower while I raid the kitchen. If you could only see yourself."

"Am I very filthy?"

"I can't think what you would be like if there was a light to see you by."

He cleaned himself as best he could by the light of a candle, then followed her into the basement. She had set out a pile of plates and tins on the kitchen table.

"You move these up, while I shower," she said.

He set them out in the dining room. There were candlesticks with hurricane glass covers. Jocelyn had chosen some of the better glass and china.

"What about the wine," he called.

"I've unlocked the cellar door. You choose."

There was quite a cellar there. There was champagne, he noticed, but that perhaps would be making too much of an occasion of it. Besides it would take a long while to cool and there was a good red Burgundy.

He returned to find her in the dining room. She had changed into Chinese pajamas. The high neck with its severe line suited her.

"It makes you look sixteen," he said.

"Daddy gave it me for my sixteenth birthday. I always keep a few things of my own out here."

While he had been in the cellar, she had rearranged the table; it looked quite different.

"This doesn't feel like a picnic at all," he said. "It's like a banquet."

"It is rather an occasion isn't it?"

They had brought up the chicken pie, some cheese, some salad and a bowl of fruit. A quarter of an hour earlier he had been ravenous, but now his appetite had left him. He had to force himself to eat, as a counter measure against the full rich Burgundy.

"Will the fire have done much harm?" he asked her.

"Not to us. We're insured."

"Does it often happen?"

"Most months there's a fire on one or other of the estates."

"Is it always done on purpose?"

197

"No one can tell. Tonight it was obvious: the engine, the telephone, the carburetor. All that couldn't happen on the same night by chance—particularly the carburetor."

"Doesn't it worry you living in a place where something like this can happen at any moment?"

"One gets used to it. One knows it's going to happen one day, like a hurricane. You have to accept things here."

She leant forward across the table to take an orange; the long loose sleeves of her Chinese jacket fell back over her elbows. Her arms looked very white and soft against the stiff black silk. Her cheeks in the candlelight were smooth and rounded with the bloom of fruit on them.

"You were born within twenty miles of me," he said. "It's strange that we should have led such different lives, that you should have got acclimatized to a thing like this. But for mere chance, we'd have been brought up together. We'd have been going to the same dances, played tennis together at the vicarage, ridden in the same hunt; had the same friends; yet even so meeting you here now for the first time, I don't feel I could have known you any better if we'd been going to the same parties all our lives. I've got the feeling that I've known you all my life."

"I'm glad you feel that. That's how I've felt too."

She smiled: no one had smiled at him in quite that way before.

"This cheese is very good," he said.

It was a dry, hard cheddar. It brought out the bouquet and flavor of the Burgundy. He was glad they had finished with the pie; that he hadn't to force himself to eat, that he could nibble at the cheese and sip this noble wine.

The grandfather clock began to strike. Nine, ten, eleven. "I suppose we ought to clear away," he said.

"Don't bother, this isn't England. Matilda will be here at daybreak—or at least she should be. Dirty plates will tell her she's got work to do."

They rose and faced each other.

"It's late," she said.

"It's very late."

"Shall we toss for rooms?"

He spun a coin in the air.

"Heads," she called.

The coin fell on its edge and rolled into a corner. "There it is." They went down on their knees to pick it up.

"Heads. I win."

They straightened up. There was a bare yard between them.

"I'll have the room on the right," she said. "I always wanted it when I was a child. It's a funny thing, I always promised myself when I grew up that I'd move into that room. I loved the view from it. And the furniture; the gilt on the wardrobe and the bed. They match. I promised myself that I'd take it over on my seventeenth birthday. But I never have. I've never slept in it. Not once. What luck my winning the toss."

She was talking for the sake of talking. But there was no nervousness in her voice. He was scarcely listening. He was vividly, acutely conscious of her nearness, in this empty house, remembering how they had stood side by side against the veranda railings, with the fire raging a hundred yards away; his fingers remembered the smooth soft firmness of her breast.

He took a step toward her and she moved to meet him. His arms went round her. She was talking still. "There's a clock on the bookcase of that room I always loved, and there's a picture between the windows."

He loosened one arm about her shoulders; he put his hand under her chin; he lifted her face to his.

It all seemed the most natural, the most inevitable thing that had ever happened.

The moonlight lay in a wide broad stream across the room.

"It is a pretty clock. Even from here you can see that it's a pretty clock," she said.

She stretched herself, lazily, luxuriously. She raised her arms above her head, closing her hands under her neck.

"When you do that, you make your breasts disappear," he said.

"I'll bring them back."

She lowered her arms against her side.

"Look, there they are."

"I could play with them for hours."

"They'd like that."

She sighed, a long, deep, happy sigh.

"It's funny that I've always had that feeling about this room. I must have known that one day something very lovely was going to happen to me here."

"I'd never believed anybody could look as beautiful as you look now."

"Please go on saying things like that."

"There are so many things I want to say."

"Say some of them."

199

"I'd like to be able to say that you were the first girl I'd made love to ever."

"I could hardly expect that, could I?"

"Why not?"

"You're twenty-two and you're attractive."

"There's not been very much but if there'd not been anything . . . in a way I'm rather glad there was."

"Why's that?"

"If there hadn't been, I shouldn't be able to say, because I know something about other girls, I know how wonderful you are."

"I'm glad you can say that. . . . All the same—" she paused. "I'm very glad to be able to say 'this is the first time ever.' "

"It is?"

"Darling, didn't you know?"

"I half guessed. I wondered."

"I thought that was the kind of thing men always knew: that's the warning they gave to us at school: how would we feel on our wedding night when our husband realized. To think that you didn't know. How they do fool girls, don't they?"

She chuckled. Once again she stretched out lazily, clasping her hands under her head.

"I'm so glad now I waited. I used to think sometimes that I was being silly; that I was missing a lot of fun. I used to envy Mavis. Was I being a coward, I'd ask myself. But all the time I knew somewhere deep inside myself that there was a thing worth waiting for. And, darling, so there was."

He could not speak. A sense of pride mingled with humility stifled him. His arms went round her and she turned to face him.

"Darling," she whispered. "Oh my dear, my darling."

She was speaking in a voice that he had never heard before.

"Dear one, it must be late. The moon's gone down."

He blinked, sat up, the room was so dark now that he could not see her.

"I must have been asleep."

"You were."

"Didn't you sleep too?"

"No. I've been watching you."

"What time is it?"

"Nearly five."

"I ought to go into the other room."

"I think you should. Matilda will be turning up at daylight."

"Not for five minutes though."

"No, not for five minutes perhaps."

"Or even ten."

"Maybe not ten."

"It's funny in the dark not seeing you."

"Is it nicer in the dark?"

"It's different isn't it?"

"Is it? I wouldn't know. Oh, darling, this is the loveliest ten minutes."

He woke, it seemed only a moment later, but the room was warm with sunlight, and a maid was at his bedside with a cup of tea.

"Half-past seven. Breakfast be ready eight o'clock," she said. He blinked; for a second he did not know where he was: then he remembered.

"Miss Jocelyn awake?" he asked.

"Sure, yes, Miss Jocelyn dressed."

He walked out on the veranda. She was seated in a long chair with rockers, her foot against the railing.

"Hullo," he called.

She turned and a shock of delighted surprise passed along his nerves. She looked radiant. He could not believe that only two hours ago they had been whispering in the dark. She pointed to the smouldering cane field.

"They made a job of that all right."

They had indeed. It stretched for half a mile along the road and for a hundred yards up the hill, a sodden, blackened ruin.

"I feel rather like that cane field looks," he said. "Do you suppose Maxwell has a razor?"

"You can always look. Sylvia should have one if he hasn't."

She had. It was very small. But he made a job with it. He had scarcely slept: he was surprised how fresh he looked as he combed his hair after the shower.

"Breakfast's ready," Jocelyn called.

There was pawpaw with a slice of lime beside it. The coffee was hot and strong.

"I suppose the telephone's not working yet."

She shook her head.

"I've sent one of the boys in to the police station. I told them not to hurry out, but I didn't want to have them worrying at home."

"Your brother's going to be furious about the car."

"He'll be tearing mad, about that and everything. He can lose his temper very easily."

"I scarcely know him."

"I sometimes wonder if I do."

"I'd have thought you'd have been so close, coming out here together, being a little different from everybody else."

"You'd have thought so, wouldn't you?"

"And there's the right difference of age between you too—three years."

"It's not turned out that way."

"I'd have given anything to have had a sister."

"It would have been nice to have you as a brother."

"I'm glad that we're the way we are though."

"I'm very glad."

Ten hours ago, she thought, we were sitting here over our picnic supper, talking as we are now about little casual things, intimately but not seriously. Anybody who had seen us then and were to see us now, would not recognize any difference between us, would not guess that anything had happened in those ten hours, that everything is different now, that we've been transformed.

"What would be jolly about having a sister," he was going on, "is that you'd always have girls about the house, pleasant, friendly girls by whom you set no store, whom you could get to know as friends; because if you haven't a sister the only girls you see are the ones in whom you are interested in what they call 'that way.'"

"I've never thought of that. Yes, I suppose that must be true. And it's true with girls: if they have brothers, there's always a crowd of boys around the house whom they can treat casually, not as 'dates.'"

"But it wasn't that way with you and Maxwell?"

"No, it never was."

"I wonder why."

She shrugged. "He's an awkward person. I don't quite know how. He's secretive; he bottles things up; then suddenly he flies into a rage. He was terrifying as a child. I remember once . . . no, I'll forget that one, but if you'd once seen him lose his temper you were on your guard with him."

To anyone listening, it would have sounded exactly the same kind of talk that they had exchanged the night before. Only they knew the difference, knew how close those hours in the dusk and dark had brought them to each other. Marriage must be a very lovely thing, she thought. Two people gossiping across a breakfast table, making no reference to that whispering in the dusk, yet with their whole outlook for the day conditioned by it.

"I certainly shan't be going back to England till the autumn now," he said.

"We might be going back in the same ship then."

"In the same ship?"

"It's something I didn't tell you. Daddy's very keen on going back to England for six months. He wants to see a doctor there. He's taking me along. He wanted to go back in May. He thought the summer would be better. Then he thought he needed a cold climate. I was delighted. I'd like to know what snow is like. We might have a great deal of fun over there together. You could introduce me to your friends. It's an idea."

"It's a marvelous idea."

"Or would it be a better idea if we went back in May?"

"It depends on how difficult we find it to find alibis." He remembered the warning that Archer had given him that first afternoon.

"We'll find ways," she said.

### 3

Maxwell and Sylvia drove out to fetch them, bringing a mechanic with them. On the surface Maxwell was very calm. But beneath the surface Euan could recognize the bubbling of that temper to which Jocelyn had referred.

"You can see what's happened. It's plain, isn't it," he said. "They had a grudge against me. They thought it was my car. They saw a chance of paying off old scores. That shows the kind of people that they are. And to think that they are going to be allowed equality with us. Ridiculous, ridiculous."

He spoke with a sneer. Sylvia made no comment. She stood aside, a look of indifference on her face. Euan and Jocelyn let him talk. It relieved Jocelyn that Maxwell should be so completely concerned with the destruction to his property. He had no interest in the other aspect of the matter, that his sister had spent an entire night alone with a man in an empty house. It gave her a useful clue to the attitude that would be taken generally in Jamestown.

"Nobody's going to worry about us at all," she said to Euan, as they drove back to town in the car that Maxwell had brought out.

Her mother was on the doorstep awaiting her. "What's happened? Was there a great deal of damage?"

That clearly was the angle by which everyone in Jamestown would be affected. A rising on an estate was part of the West Indian tradition. For three hundred years there had been that constant fear in the hearts of the white planters. They were outnumbered fifty to one. Resentment was always smouldering. Gossip would concentrate on the car, the cane field, the cut wire. The fact that she and Euan had been all night alone in that empty house was incidental. We're lucky, she thought, we're very lucky.

"Lucky, very lucky."

She repeated it to herself as she stood in her room before her mirror. Did she look different? She had read in books that you looked different afterwards. She did not think she did. But she felt different, oh, so completely different. The blood beat through her veins at a different pace; how glad she was now that she had waited. She remembered all those hours of self-questioning and self-doubt; remembered how she had envied Mavis; or rather how she had wished that she was more like Mavis. She did not now. If she had been like Mavis this would not have happened. If she had been like Mavis, she would not have been able to appreciate a thing like this. Her palate would have been cloyed.

She sighed, a long deep sigh. She walked over to the window. There it lay, the familiar curve of the *carenage*, with its anchored schooners, and the red brick warehouses, the line of the hills beyond, the white sand of *Petite Anse* with the grove of coconut palms flanking it: unchanged yet at the same time different.

It had become the setting now of high adventure. It was against this backcloth that the drama of the next weeks would be played. March to September. Half a year. By the time she sailed for England every aspect of the landscape would hold its own special memory for her. Whenever she looked through this window afterward, whenever she drove out to Belfontaine, she would be able to relive the enchantment of these six months. She was lucky to have this limit set: it would not drag on, die out. And at the end of that six months there was not the necessity of parting. They would return to England, they would meet in England, no doubt once there they would find themselves caught up into their separate lives, they would drift apart, without realizing that they were: there would be no sharp, sudden severance. But she did not want to look that far ahead. She did not need to look that far ahead. She could be indefinite. She was lucky there. She could live in the moment, for the moment, in the belief that it might be prolonged. I'll be seeing him at the club tonight, she thought. Then they'd discuss when they'd be meeting next. The need for secrecy would add its special relish to the adventure.

*4*

At the club that evening Jocelyn was the center of attention. No one wanted to discuss anything else. Doctor Leisching's case was shelved. It was amusing to have so much notice taken of her, and all the time there was the dramatic irony of knowing that no one guessed the story that lay behind the story. Carl Bradshaw was particularly inquisitive. His eyes had lit when the news reached him. His second article was taking shape.

"There can be no doubt, can there, that it was a plot against your brother?" he said to Jocelyn.

"I don't see what else it could be; the telephone wires had been cut."

"Have you any idea why anyone should have borne a grudge against your brother?"

She could think of a great many reasons. She had no illusions about her brother. She knew that he was unpopular with his laborers, that he was tactless with them, alternately overindulgent and overstrict. But she was not going to tell Bradshaw that.

"You can never tell with these people," she said. "They get a fancy in their heads. They brood and it breeds."

It was the precise answer that Carl Bradshaw had hoped for. It suited his theme that the island was in a restless state whose exact nature no one could diagnose. He did not want to have to give precise reasons. His articles would be much more effective if he could use the simile of a sick body that broke out in sores, now here, now there; sores that were not local but organic. He crossed to Colonel Whittingham.

"Have you any explanation for this incident?" he asked.

He received the same answer from the policeman.

"Do you stand any chance of finding out who did it?" he inquired.

The colonel shook his head. "Everyone will have an alibi. I shall strengthen my police post in that area. I may hear whispers. I may learn who needs watching. But that's the most that I can hope for."

"Were you surprised?"

"I'm never surprised by anything that happens here."

It was again the answer Bradshaw had been hoping for. Across the veranda he saw Euan Templeton. There was nothing that young Templeton could tell him but his training had taught him to tap every line.

"I was wondering whether this business would be an indirect way of attacking your father through you," he said. "Could anyone have known in advance that you were driving in that car?"

"I don't see how they could, seeing that I didn't know myself. We were a party of twelve. We had three cars."

Bradshaw nodded. He had watched them drive off himself.

"But a hundred people must have seen you driving out."

"They may have, but we changed cars after the picnic."

Of course they had. Why hadn't he spotted that himself? He should have realized that something must have happened for Euan Templeton and Jocelyn Fleury to have been alone. He ought not to have missed that point. He wondered what had happened. He docketed the fact in his mind's reference file.

"I don't think anyone can have known I was in that car," Euan said. "We drove round the north part of the island. I don't think that we passed a person on the way. It must have been premeditated. They planned to burn the cane on Carnival night. They knew Maxwell would be in town: they cut the telephone wire to make sure that no one could send out a warning. When they saw a car there, they took the precaution of throwing away the carburetor, so that whoever was in the car couldn't drive away and give a warning. They probably recognized it as Maxwell's car. It's being there was an unexpected dividend. Can you see any other explanation?"

Bradshaw shook his head. He couldn't. It was motiveless malignity against a planter. It suited the temper of his article.

Euan, as he had been talking, had caught Jocelyn's eye. He raised his eyebrows, and she nodded. Her heart was light. How she was going to enjoy the private drama of these conspiratorial glances flashed across crowded rooms.

He made his way to her.

"I've an idea for tomorrow," he said.

"What's that?"

"There's a film at the Carlton. We could start out to go to it, and not go to it. I've seen it already. I can tell you what it was all about."

"All right." She nodded in agreement. Her parents were dining with the Normans. "We could have a snack at our place first," she said.

She felt no qualms when she told her mother that Euan was taking her to the cinema. Would her mother care if she knew the truth? She did not think she would: she would not want her daughter to be involved in a scandal, but she had never cared for her daughter in the way that she had for her sons. The appearance of the thing was all that counted with her. Jocelyn would see to the maintenance of that.

5

The cinema began at eight; Jocelyn left the house a few minutes before her parents.

Euan drove up the hill.

"Where are we going?" she asked. She had expected that he would drive along the shore.

"You wait," he said.

He was by now above the town.

"It looks as though you were going to G.H."

"I am."

He drove through the main gates. There were no lights in the lower rooms.

"The old man's dining with the A.G.," he said.

She was perplexed and puzzled; surely he was not planning to look at photograph albums in the drawing room. He parked the car in the garage.

"Out we get. There's a side door here."

It opened onto a long dark passage at the end of which was a glow of light. He slipped his arm through hers. "Straight up. Don't make a noise."

She tiptoed up a flight of uncarpeted wooden stairs. It was like that nursery game "I spy." Her heart was beating fast. It would have been exciting to steal into any house this way with a lover, but to put the sacrosanct premises of Government House to such a purpose was very special.

The stairway branched at a narrow landing.

"To the left," he said.

It was a short flight of seven steps leading to a door. "I'll go ahead, you wait."

He looked both ways, then beckoned her on to the wide thickly carpeted gallery that led round the center hall.

"To the right," he said.

The door was already open. She slipped quickly through. "Safe," he said.

She was in what seemed to her a small study annex, furnished mainly with a desk. On the table were a cake and a decanter.

A door beside the desk led into a bedroom. It was high and wide, with a mahogany fourposter.

"This is where I live," he said. As a frequent guest, she was familiar with the general geography of the house, but this was new to her.

"I've never been here before," she said.

"I'm not surprised. It's the Governor's private quarters. It's completely shut away; that stairway's never used. I'm lucky don't you think?"

She nodded. She had been excited but she had been frightened too, as she tiptoed up the stairs. Now she felt reassured, like a kitten that has licked the butter off its toes. She looked slowly round her. It was cozy here. Lucky. It was not only he that was lucky, she was too. One of the things that had always held her back when she had toyed with the idea of following Mavis' example had been the fear of a squalid setting. Particularly in a place like Jamestown, with its lack of privacy. They were lucky to have this hideaway.

"Would you like a glass of port?" he asked.

She shook her head.

He stepped toward her.

"Do you mean 'not yet'?" he asked, as his arms went round her.

"Yes, that's what I mean," she said. "Not yet."

The moon had risen, filling the room with twilight. She held his head against her shoulder under her chin, her hand stroking his hair. She had never guessed that there could exist a happiness like this. She had read in a novel that it was the second not the first night that was important. She had wondered what the writer had meant. Now she knew. And it would go on getting better. She knew that too.

She hated to disturb this trance-like rapture.

"Oughtn't I to be going back; won't your father be home soon?"

"It won't matter if he is. He's in the other wing. I can smuggle you out any time."

"But I mustn't be too late. My mother mustn't get suspicious."

"The cinema does not come out till half-past ten. It would be natural wouldn't it, to go for a drive afterward?"

"I suppose so. Yes."

"And when the moon's nearly full, one might be tempted to go swimming."

"One might."

"So that if you were back by one o'clock..."

"By half-past twelve."

"Anyhow, as it's only half-past ten..."

"And the cinema's just ending: don't you think you'd better tell me what the plot was."

"Right now?"

"Why not: oh darling, yes... no, perhaps, not right now."

"I think now you might," she said.

"Might what?"

"Tell me about that film."

He outlined the plot. It sounded very silly.

"So that's how it ends up does it?"

"It's the way most films end."

"How?"

"With people getting married. Where are we going to get married, by the way, here or in England?"

She smiled. She had half expected this. In Victorian days when a man kissed a girl, he felt bound in honor to say he loved her, and in those days to say that you loved a girl was to propose. Now in a modern day, a man who had spent a weekend with a girl felt himself bound to mention marriage. And in each case the girl's obligation was the same; unless she was quite sure that the proposal was serious, to shrug it off. It was a convention as the other had been. On both sides face was saved. She was grateful to Euan for having fulfilled his side of the bargain, so early and so deftly.

"If we were married here," he said, "we'd have two marriages. There'd be the ceremony in Jamestown, then there'd be all the parties for us when we got back home."

She made no answer. He was being nice about it. The proposal was not a serious one, but it was said in a way that made it seem it was. It was now up to her to fulfill her side of the bargain.

"I think it would be more amusing to be married here," he said. "There'd be a public holiday for it. It would be a second carnival."

She recalled Maxwell's wedding. Half the island and three-quarters of the police force had come into town; the church was packed, the windows lined with peering faces. She had been one of the four bridesmaids. As she came out of the cool dark church into the bright hard sunlight, she had been dazed and dazzled by the crowded color of the scene: necks were craning from every window, urchins had clambered up every tree: the men were wearing their gayest shirts, the women their brightest turbans. And that had been for a planter's son; what would it not be for a Governor's son. A second carnival. Yes, it would be that all right. She pictured the scene. Then she blinked. It was too fond a pipe dream.

"Darling, let's not talk of it," she said. "Never again, not ever."

"But what am I to tell my father?"

"Your father?"

"I've already told him that we are half engaged."

"You've what?"

"Told him that we're half engaged."

"But you hadn't proposed to me."

"I'd assumed that was assumed."

"You had."

"Why, naturally."

His head still rested on her shoulder. She could not see his face.

His voice was light and bantering. She could not believe that he was serious; yet if he was not serious he was taking a joke too far.

"What did you tell your father?"

"That I was in love with you, that I thought you were with me."

"What did he say?"

"That if he'd been told on my christening day that his son would one day marry the daughter of two such trusted friends, he couldn't have wished a happier fate for me."

"He said that, did he?"

"He said a good deal more. Shall I tell you some of it?"

"No, please don't, it's quite impossible you know."

"That's the last thing it is."

His voice was confident and masterly. He was serious, there was no doubt of that. For a moment she let that dream picture flicker before her eyes. It was not true. It could not be. It was too like her schoolgirl dreams of marrying a Duke or a foreign Prince. She had never thought of Euan Templeton in terms of marriage. They had separate destinies. She could not adjust the reality of her lover to a schoolgirl's dream world.

She temporized. "It's not sixty hours since that picnic."

"I know."

"The last thing that you imagined when we drove to Belfontaine was that you'd be talking like this to me tonight."

"I know."

"Don't you think it's very silly to let the events of a single night upset the plans of a whole lifetime?"

"Shall I tell you what I think?"

"You tell me."

"Yesterday morning, as we drove back into town, I told myself that if I lost you now, my whole life would be empty."

His voice had lost its bantering tone. His cheek still lay against her shoulder. She could not see his expression. She was glad that it should be this way, his voice coming to her out of darkness. She stroked his hair, her eyes half closed.

"You don't know what my life's been," he said. "I didn't realize what it had been myself till we drove back yesterday. Can you realize how alone I've been since my mother's death? No atmosphere of home; no brothers and sisters; living with aunts and cousins; my father away all the time. Can't you see how someone brought up like that builds a defensive covering for himself, goes behind a screen; so much is bottled up.

"That's what happened to me. I lived behind reserves. That's why I behaved the way I did when I came out here. I'd had those eighteen months in the Canal Zone. I was due for a good time. I wasn't looking for anything that went deep. I was living on the surface, as I had been for a dozen years, and when you have been living like that, it needs something violent, something sudden and unexpected to break through the crust. That's what happened two nights ago at Belfontaine. I was taken off my guard. I did not know that there could be anyone like you, that anybody could do to me what you have done; I'm defenseless, wide open now. That barrier is down. I'm a new person: the person that I've become now, can't exist without you."

He spoke slowly, quietly, undramatically. She had no doubt, there was no reason for doubting, that he was speaking out of his very heart. She could not trust herself to speak. In all her girlhood dreams, as a corollary to those reveries of grandeur, as a counterbalance there had been the dream of hearing such words spoken, of finding herself adored and needed by someone whom she could revere and love; words that would count more to her than the proud position, words for whose sake she would forsake tiaras. And now miraculously she had heard those words spoken, and by one who at the same time fulfilled that other dream. She could not believe that it was true. She continued to stroke his hair while she recovered control over her voice.

"Whatever happens, never forget this, never. You'll never be more loved than you are this instant." She said it fondly, tenderly, but her voice was sad.

It wasn't possible. She knew it wasn't, deep in her heart she knew it.

It was close upon two o'clock that he left her outside her parents' house.

"I have been accepted haven't I?" he said.

She smiled, ruefully. "There's nothing I wouldn't give to be able to say 'yes,' but there's one thing, no . . . I can't be certain yet. I've got to discuss it with my parents."

6

Jocelyn came down to breakfast to find the Belfontaine incident being discussed in the light of Maxwell's candidature.

"It would be both wise and dignified for him to retire," her father was saying, "but I know he won't."

"Isn't that exactly what they want him to do?" her mother said.

"By no means. They've their own remedy, not to elect him, as of course they won't. But if he told them that he didn't care to

211

represent such a group of thugs, some of them would feel humble. But he won't. And because there's been this attack upon his property, he'll say something during his election speeches that will stir up bad feeling. The trouble's only half begun."

Jocelyn listened in silence, waiting for the moment to break her news. It was a moment that she had often dramatized in her imagination, visualizing the scene against many settings: sometimes she had pictured herself announcing an alliance that her parents would regard as disastrous, sometimes one of such glamor that it would take their breath away: at other times in a gloomy mood she had seen herself announcing some dreary "better than nothing at all" engagement, to which her parents could only say, "Of course, dear, if you really are sure that it's for your happiness."

Now that at last that scene was to be enacted, she felt apprehensive. This time yesterday morning she had been vivid with anticipation, chuckling over her secret. If only she could be in that mood now. If only she and Euan could have played their truant roles a little longer. Everything was changed and wrong now, though she could not tell why.

She waited for the pause in the conversation.

"I've news that may surprise you," she remarked. "I've been proposed to."

She said it in a way that made her parents believe that she was treating the occasion with levity.

"Who by?" her father asked.

"Wouldn't you like to guess?"

"I'd need to know first what your answer was."

"I answered like a well brought up young lady in a Victorian novel. I said I must ask my parents."

"That sounds as though you'd like to answer 'yes.'"

"I would."

"So you're in love with him?"

She would have liked to have quoted from a musical hit, "If this isn't love, the whole world is crazy," instead she said, "Won't you guess who it is?"

There was a pause. Her father looked puzzled. She knew what he was thinking: that it was Grainger Morris or somebody like Grainger Morris. It wasn't fair to tease him.

"Don't look so alarmed," she said. "It's Euan Templeton."

"Darling, how wonderful."

It was from her mother that that exclamation came. But it was at her father she was looking, watching to see if his expression changed.

"If you are in love with Euan Templeton then it's all plain

sailing," her mother was continuing. "I know he's young, but nowadays it's quite common for a married man to go up to Oxford, and Euan isn't perhaps in the same situation as other men, as regards his career, I mean. Examinations won't mean as much to him as they do to the young men who have to make their own way in the world. You wouldn't be a hindrance to him."

Jocelyn let her mother talk. She waited for a pause, she watched her father.

"Mother's right," she said. "Euan is in a different position. He has a name to carry on, he has duties, obligations. That's why I have to be quite certain. Is there any reason why I shouldn't marry him?"

"What do you mean? What reason could there be?"

It was her mother who spoke, but her eyes were on her father. Did he hesitate or only seem to hesitate?

"Father?" she said. He still stayed silent. So she had been right then. She repeated her question. "Is there any good reason why I shouldn't marry Euan Templeton? Is there any reason why I shouldn't be the mother of his children?"

Her father shook his head.

"No," he said. "There's no good reason why you shouldn't marry him."

"In that case then..." Jocelyn hesitated. She should, she knew, be feeling jubilant. From every worldly point of view, no one could be more suitable than Euan. Had she been told six weeks ago that she would find herself in such a situation, she would have felt that life was pouring all its riches into her lap. All this and heaven too. Yet her heart was heavy with a vague foreboding. She looked back nostalgically to the eager mood of anticipation with which twenty-four hours ago she had begun the day.

# CHAPTER TWELVE

*1*

The news of an imminent engagement between Jocelyn Fleury and
the Governor's son reached Carl Bradshaw on the morning that he
had finished his second article. The article started with the line:

"On Mardi gras as dusk was falling, while the streets of Jamestown
were thronged with prancing revelers, fifteen miles away a white
man and his white companion stood on the veranda of a bungalow,
facing a furnace. The cane fields had been lit, the telephone wires
had been cut, their car had been put out of action; they were
prisoners, cut off by fire from the road: victims of a terrorist
assault. The white man was the Governor's son."

The news of the engagement reached him in the club. On his
return to his hotel he reread the article. It was shorter than his first
one had been, a bare thousand words. Should he add a postscript.
He hesitated, then decided no. It was better to keep to one main
thread. This new piece of information could make the pivot of
another article. He had not forgotten his first conversation with
Father Roberts.

*2*

Four days later Bradshaw's second article was headlined in the
*Baltimore Evening Star*. Its main points were cabled back to London
by the Reuter service. The editor of the *Globe*, the foremost Opposition paper, read it with interest. He was looking for a whip with
which to flog the Government: this seemed as good as any: the
pinprick of a picador. He called up his news editor. "The line is
this," he said. "The Government has appointed as Governor a man
without Colonial Office training; this is an injustice to the service
that is only justified by success. Templeton has only been in Santa
Marta for five months and for the first time in the island's history
they are having trouble. Make a particular point of the fact that the
Governor's son was the object of a terrorist attack."

Next day the leader page of the *Globe* lay blue-penciled on the
desk of the Minister of State for the Colonies. The Minister read
it with a frown.

"Has Purvis seen this?" he asked.

"Yes, sir, there's his minute."

The minute read, "Suggest we should ask His Excellency to forward a report."

The cable asking the Governor for a report reached Santa Marta before the copy of the *Baltimore Evening Star* did.

"I wonder what our journalist has told the world this time," he thought. He rang for Denis Archer.

"Is Colonel Whittingham in town?"

"I'm not sure, sir. I'll find out."

"Do that. I'd like to see him as soon as possible."

Whittingham was in the police station. He was round within ten minutes. The Governor handed him the cable.

"What am I to say to that?" he said.

"How do you mean, sir?"

"Have you any further information?"

"No, sir."

"What is your personal opinion; do you think I should be justified in saying that Carnival always provides an opportunity for the paying off of grudges, and that this incident means neither more nor less than that?"

"That, sir, is my belief."   ·

"You don't think that my son was the object of this attack?"

"I don't see how he can have been. No one knew that he was in that car."

"You are convinced therefore that the whole incident was the paying off of a grudge against young Fleury."

"Yes, sir."

"Do you know what is the reason for this grudge?"

The Colonel hesitated. Belfontaine had always been a tricky district. He did not like to play an 'I told you so' part. Even so . . .

"I have heard, sir, that a number of the peasants held Maxwell Fleury to blame in that Preston case."

"But the local man won the case."

"That didn't help the peasants. They didn't get the five dollars they had been promised."

So they were still harping on that point, were they? They still believed that he should have intervened. They were sticking to their guns. He let that point pass.

"I haven't yet read the article by Bradshaw that's responsible for these inquiries," he said. "But his point appears to be that there's a general atmosphere of unrest of which this incident is symptomatic. You don't agree with that?"

"No, sir."

Neither did Templeton for that matter. How could Bradshaw know? There was an idea nowadays that journalists by hanging around bars knew more than ambassadors who received top secret reports from twenty confidential sources. He knew more of what was going on than Bradshaw. Two weeks ago Bradshaw had been saying that Euan was in love with Mavis Norman. Now Euan was unofficially engaged to Jocelyn Fleury. That showed how much Bradshaw knew.

"Thank you very much," he said. "I'll explain this to Whitehall. By the way, what's happening about the Carson incident?"

"The Committee haven't decided yet. I believe they're going to ask him to apologize."

"Will he do that, do you suppose?"

"I don't think so, sir."

"Neither do I."

There was a pause.

"We can cross that bridge when we come to it," the Governor said. "And there seem quite a few bridges ahead of us at the present moment, with these elections coming. Do you anticipate any trouble there?"

"I shall be very glad when they are over, sir."

"Don't you think I shall, too?"

They laughed together. As he rose to indicate that the interview was ended, the Governor pressed the bell upon his desk that rang in Archer's room.

"I want you to fix an evening soon when Colonel Whittingham and his wife can dine here for an informal party. Oh, and by the way, I'm lunching with the Fleurys, Euan is too. That means that you can make what arrangements for yourself you like."

"Very good, sir."

Archer kept his expression calm, but his heart bounded. That meant a meeting in the summerhouse.

"When will you be back, sir?"

"Not before half-past three."

Half-past three. That meant at least two hours; two hours of picnicking, of gossiping, of reading poetry, of playing the gramophone, of making love. The Governor's wife who fifty years ago had built this chalet had chosen the site wisely: out of earshot, out of sight, it was a secluded paradise. No one could see you going there, but from its windows you could observe approach. He had wondered sometimes whether the lady who had built it had not had some ulterior motive when she sited it. He wondered who she had been. He had looked through the records, but there was nothing to show when it had been built. There had been so many Governors during forty years. "I wish I could find out who she was," he had said to Margot. "I'd like to write a poem about her."

"You don't need to know who she was to write a poem."

"I'd like to have a peg to hang it on. I'd like to think of her watching over us, a friendly ghost."

"I find that very easy to believe."

It was over a series of enchanted hours that the ghost of the forgotten Governor's lady had stood as sentinel. Denis Archer had an eye for decoration. He had brought down three eighteenth century prints from the lumber room at Government House; he had found some chairs, a few rugs, a table, and a divan day couch: within a few hours he had made it a personal apartment. He had told the Governor that he needed a place in which to work, and to perfect his alibi he had fallen into a routine of going there, before breakfast, lunching there when he was not on duty, and returning there three to four times a week when the office closed. Quite often he went after dinner and worked there by the light of a hurricane lamp.

"If ever you find yourself with half an hour free, you are more likely than not to find me there," he had said to Margot. Quite often she did come on the off chance, without prearrangement. He would have thought that the knowledge that she might come unexpectedly would make it impossible for him to work, that he would be restless, impatient, striding up and down the room. Yet to his surprise it was not like that at all. He found it easy to concentrate upon his manuscript.

A year back in London he had known the strain of a liaison: the constant watching of a clock on this and the other mantelpiece, the jump every time a telephone bell rang: he had felt enslaved. "The white implacable Aphrodite." There was nothing like that now: there was no greedy snatching at stolen minutes, no sense of haste or hurry: no uncertainty.

On days when they had a definite rendezvous, Margot would arrive punctually but casually: on the table there would be fruit, a cake, perhaps some cheese. She might turn on the gramophone, she might pick up a book, she behaved as though she lived here: as though this were her home. They would talk, and share their picnic: sometimes they would dance to the gramophone, suddenly they would find themselves making love. They always did make love: yet it was never, at any time, suggested or inferred that she had come there on an assignation. Lovemaking was part of the rhythm of their joint lives, a long deep rhythm.

On the morning that the Governor had interviewed Colonel Whittingham, Denis Archer was so absorbed in his writing that he never saw Margot walking up the path toward him, never heard her open the door: he was conscious suddenly of a scent beside him, the deep strong scent of jasmin; he turned and her hand was on the desk beside him. She was reading over his shoulder.

"I think that's good," she said. "But will you read it to me?"

She perched herself on the desk while he read his poem to her. He finished and she took the sheet. She read it back to him, in her musical singsong voice. She looked at him questioningly when she reached the end. She never made a criticism. She waited for him to make it, but always when he heard her read one of his poems, he became aware of its deficiencies.

"I don't like the sound of that passage, right after the beginning," he remarked.

"I'm not sure I do. Read it to me again."

As he reread it, he saw where the passage failed.

"I must work up those four lines," he said.

She crossed to the table, cut a slice of cake, opened a Coca Cola.

"I heard a new calypso record; if you like, I'll bring it round," she said.

"I'd like you to."

She sat on the table swinging her legs. It was the most natural thing in the world to see her there, yet he had as little idea of what was passing in her mind as he had had the first time he had walked into the Bon Marche pharmacy. She picked up the manuscript book in which two or three times a week he jotted down impressions of what he had seen and heard; she turned the pages.

"What will you make out of this?" she asked. "A novel?"

"Perhaps, I don't know. It might be more original to do it as a diary. It might be an idea to publish it anonymously."

She pouted. "But you want people to know who you are, don't you?"

"If the book was a success, I'd announce who I was."

"I see."

She turned the pages. "It's the kind of book I'd like to read," she said.

When she read, a frown invariably came between her eyes. It made her look very solemn and very young. He sat beside her, his arm round her, reading over her shoulder.

"It doesn't seem too bad," he said.

"It's very good."

They read in silence. She began to laugh. "That's very funny."

218

It was the description of Carson's treatment of the Obeah man. "But it's dangerous to make fun of the Obeah man," she said.

"Do you believe he can do you damage?"

"Of course."

"You believe that he can put a spell upon you."

"I know he can."

"If you wanted something very much would you ask an Obeah man for it?"

"If I wanted it very much."

"Even though your priest told you it was very wrong?"

"Even if my priest told me it was very wrong."

"You would have more faith in your Obeah man than in your priest?"

"It's different."

"Have you ever been to an Obeah man?"

"My friends have been."

She was not laughing any longer now. Her face was serious. He hesitated. He had a feeling that she did not want him to question her, but he was inquisitive.

"Your friends have told you what happens when they visit the Obeah man?"

"They have."

"When do they go to him?"

"When they want something very much."

"What kind of thing?"

"When someone has done them harm."

"Or when they are in love?"

"Yes, when they are in love."

"And do they get what they want from the Obeah man?"

"If they do what he tells them."

"What would he tell them to do?"

"Different things."

"For instance."

"He might ask for a piece of the loved one's clothing."

"What else?"

"He might say 'a piece of cloth with the loved one's blood on it.'"

"And you believe all this."

"We all believe in it."

He was standing beside her now, in front of her, his arms round her waist. He drew her to the edge of the table. She twisted her ankles round his calves.

"I sometimes think you've put a spell on me," he said.

She smiled. She raised her arms. She twined them round his neck,

219

lifted her face under his. That first afternoon in the Bon Marche pharmacy, when he had hesitated on the brink of the first step, he had felt himself to be on the threshold of sinister experience. Yet nothing could have been more natural than this lovemaking.

### 3

In the town in the Fleury household lunch was ending. It was a family party. The parents, Jocelyn, Maxwell and Sylvia and the two Templetons. It was an engagement party though it had been agreed that there should be no official announcement yet.

"It would be far better for Euan to have at least one term at Oxford," said Lord Templeton. "He will get to know his contemporaries far better if he does. Jocelyn could come over to England. They would be able to see quite a lot of one another. They could be married at Christmas. I feel that is the better way."

"And we can stick to our original plan," Julian said, "and sail together in October."

And that, Maxwell thought, left constant the position as regards Belfontaine. He watched his wife. Did she seem relieved? He thought she did. How did he know what was passing behind that smooth calm mask? Was she adding up her opportunities of seeing the man who had smoked that Egyptian cigarette, or was she pondering on her own bad luck in not having been free when young Templeton had paid his visit? He would surely, might she not be thinking, have preferred her to Jocelyn.

"I must be back to my duties," the Governor was saying. "I expect that you'd like to be left here, Euan."

"I think so, father."

Euan looked at Jocelyn.

"What about a swim?" he said.

"I'd like that."

She turned to Sylvia. "Why don't you and Maxwell come with us?"

"You don't want us. Don't you want to be alone?"

Jocelyn shook her head. A week ago she would have been scheming for every opportunity to be alone with Euan, but things were different now. It had been amusing to outwit parental scrutiny, but now that they were trusted, it would be cheating. She felt almost awkward now when she was alone with Euan.

"Let's have a short siesta, then drive out to *Petite Anse*. There's a fine long chair on the veranda, Euan, that you can use."

She was glad to be alone in her room. Her brain was racing. Too much had happened to her, too quickly. She ought to be radiantly happy, but that sense of apprehension still remained.

Across the passage Maxwell lay under the mosquito net, his hands under his head.

"This is going to make a difference to us when we go to England," he was saying.

"Why should it?" Sylvia said.

"Having one's sister the Hon. Mrs. Euan Templeton, having her later on Lady Templeton."

"I hadn't thought of that."

"Nor had I at first. But it will make a difference. Think of all the people we'll be related to."

"They won't be our real relations, only connections."

"That's so, as regards us, but not as regards our children. Jocelyn'll be our children's aunt. Her children will be our children's first cousins. It will make an immense difference to our children when they go to England."

"You're looking a long way ahead."

"One has to look a long way ahead."

Looking up at the ceiling, he imagined the houses to which he and Sylvia would be invited, the photographs in the *Tatler* and the *Sketch*, the paragraphs in the gossip columns; their children would go to Court, might become the friends of royalty, would marry into the peerage. The news reels would show him walking down the aisle, his daughter on his arm. He pictured the christening photographs: himself standing as a grandfather beside a Peer of the Realm. Royalty might accept the role of godparent. There was no limit to the future's possibilities. Sylvia would live in the reflected glory of their children's prominence. Surely then Sylvia would appreciate him; there would come into her eyes the look of respect, of devotion that he longed for. He would have become a person of consequence, somebody to whom she could look up. The future was lit with hope, now.

On the veranda below Euan Templeton was drowsing, slipping into sleep. He was without a trouble in the world. He would have laughed, incredulously, had he been told that a mile away in a hotel bedroom an article was being tapped upon a typewriter that would shatter the plans that had been made so confidently across his future father-in-law's lunch table.

221

The article reached Baltimore three days later. It was headed, "The Color Problem in the B.W.I." It began, "Everything in the last analysis turns on color. It is the subject that everyone avoids but it is at the back of every social and political issue. To understand the B.W.I. you have to understand how the situation stands in the British Islands. That is a difficult thing for an American to understand, because we tend to see the British problem in terms of our problem, but there is no resemblance between the two. In the first place in the British Isles themselves there is no color or racial problem; there is no colored proletariat; the only colored people that the average Briton sees are men of distinction either intellectually or as athletes who come to Britain as 'visiting firemen.' They are treated with respect and deference; they meet English men and women upon equal terms. Very often they marry English women. In the West Indies on the other hand the completely white man is as much an exception as the black man is in Europe. These islands have been colonies for three hundred years; there has been a long tradition of irregular relationships. Slavery was abolished over a hundred and twenty years ago. Emancipation created a depression and the old families one by one went back to England. In very few islands now are there any remains of the old feudal aristocracy except the names. Nearly every family has some trace of colored blood. You would think that this would result in a classless society, but that is not the case. Each class is graded according to the percentage of dark blood in its veins.

"In Haiti before the French Revolution, Moreau St. Mery drew up a list of the various combinations of color that might exist; he showed how a marriage between a man who was one-fifth colored and a woman who was three-eighths black produced a purer product than when a man quarter white married a half colored girl. In the plantation days color was the badge of rank and the tradition still persists.

"In almost every island there is a club that colored men cannot join and another that is barred to white man. All those who pass for white try to make out that they are completely white. In most families a dusky aunt or cousin is kept out of sight on the far side of the island. Everyone has a secret. That is the key to island life: everyone has something to conceal. Let us consider certain typical examples . . ."

The examples followed.

"In every issue, social and political," the article concluded, "color is the deciding force: it inspires jealousy, malice, and distrust. It is a malady that you cannot cure by legislation."

The sub-editor who read the article raised his eyebrows. This was even more atomic than that first article which he had queried. He penciled a memo to the news editor "Surely we can't print this." The news editor also raised his eyebrows, but he sent it without comment to the boss. It reached Wilson P. Romer shortly before he left for a family conference. His elder daughter had announced her intention of leaving immediately for Reno. Romer was upset. He had suspected for some time now that all was not well with his daughter's marriage, but he liked his son-in-law and the boy's father was a classmate of his. For him the break-up of the marriage would mean the end of a twenty-five years' friendship.

He read Bradshaw's article quickly. Where his juniors had raised their eyebrows, he whistled. This was going too far. He supposed Bradshaw was certain of his facts. Was there a risk of libel? He did not see how there could be: it was not libelous to say that a man living in the West Indies had colored blood. It would not damage him professionally: it did not in a modern enlightened community expose him to hatred, ridicule, and contempt. Would he, as a father, have liked to have had such a thing written about his family? Not at all, of course; but the families concerned no doubt knew already: that was the whole point of Bradshaw's article, everyone did know everything down there. If an editor started to worry himself about what parents felt, there would be no newspapers. He had not been spared trouble with his children. He could visualize the paragraphs that would attend his daughter's arrival at Reno. He glanced again at Bradshaw's article. It was a sound, solid piece: the kind of piece that conferred credit on a paper. Let it appear the way it had been written.

5

The airplane that brought the copy of the *Baltimore Evening Star* to Santa Marta carried on the Governor and his son to a conference in B.G. The copy with Bradshaw's article was to lie therefore unopened on his desk for half a week. A second copy, however, reached the offices of *The Voice*. The editor started at the title; this looked like something. He read with mounting interest and irritation. As a journalist he was delighted to be the recipient of such good copy, as a West Indian he resented having his country's foibles paraded before the public gaze. He read on then suddenly he started: just as the sub-editor in Baltimore had done. This was more than he had bargained for. He stared incredulously at the printed paragraph. Was it really true? He supposed it must be. Now he began to think of it, he was surprised that it had not occurred to him before. But that bore out Bradshaw's argument. It was the kind of thing one never spoke of: it was an affair of whispers. Well, it was in the open now.

What was the best use to make of this? The paper went to press in the afternoon; copies were on sale on the following morning. Nothing could be done for twenty-four hours. Nothing material, at least. He leant forward across the desk; he took a sheet of paper: on it he printed in large block capitals "Look out for tomorrow's issue. Sensational article by an American Journalist on Santa Marta's Socialites. No one will be talking of anything else tomorrow evening." He handed it over to the compositor. Now he had a whole day in which to think out the best use he could make of his material.

### 6

When Bradshaw saw the announcement set in big type, surrounded by white space in the center of the paper, he took a quick short breath. He had not expected this. He had enjoyed the illusion that he could publish what he liked about the island in another country, and no one in the island would hear of it; an illusion that was the reverse side of the belief so common among travelers that they can behave in any way they like away from home since no one at home will know of it. He remembered with concern the third article that he had dispatched a week ago. He must look into this.

He went round to the editor.

"I presume," he said, "that your paragraph in this morning's paper refers to me."

"It certainly does."

"May I ask what you are printing."

"The first of your three articles in the *Baltimore Evening Star*."

"Have you permission to print it?"

"We have an arrangement with A.P. and U.P. allowing us to print anything from an American or English newspaper, provided we acknowledge it. We pay an annual subscription for this right."

"I see."

There was a pause.

"As far as I can remember," Bradshaw said, "there was something in the first article that is now out of date."

224

"We've noticed that. It has been cut out."

"It might have offended His Excellency."

"You can trust us to print nothing that would in any way embarrass His Excellency."

"I had a feeling that perhaps in the third article there was something too, about the Governor' son."

"I noticed that too: it shall be erased."

Bradshaw left the office confident that he had no cause for worry. As soon as he was left alone, the editor picked up the copy of the *Baltimore Evening Star* that contained Bradshaw's article on Color. He reread the passage that Bradshaw had no doubt had in mind. He could edit it in such a way that he could keep his promise to Bradshaw—he did not want to have Bradshaw trying to obtain an injunction—avoid the suspicion of *lèse majesté* and at the same time maintain his scoop. He erased two sentences, then settled down to a first drafting of the leading article that would accompany the final article.

7

The daily issue of *The Voice of Santa Marta* did not reach Belfontaine until lunchtime. On the morning that the second article appeared Maxwell Fleury rehearsed his first speech to his constituents. He had written it out in full, timed its delivery, memorized the salient lines and made a list of the subject headings. He had it now word perfect. The speech was to be given that evening in front of the police station. Sylvia was to come with him. It would be the first time she had heard him speak. The temptation to read over the speech to her had been a hard one to resist. But he wanted to surprise her. He wanted her to be swept away, in the same manner that the crowd would be swept away. She would surely realize then what he amounted to, she would recognize him for a leader. She would see the future that, with him as a husband, might be hers. At last she would be proud of him.

Their servant brought in the copy of the day's Santa Marta paper. He ran his eye down the double columns of Carl Bradshaw's article, and saw his own name there. He read it closely. It was an account of the carnival outrage on his property. He was flattered to find himself the central figure of an incident that had been publicized throughout the United States. It should prove to Sylvia that he was not negligible. He marked and memorized two of Bradshaw's phrases for use in his speech that evening.

In Jamestown, David Boyeur was reading the same article. Its predecessor had given him solid pleasure. It had starred him as one of the foremost personalities of the island. The second article was giving him less pleasure. It contained no reference to himself. There might have been, there should have been one: it was at his instigation that the Fleury cane fields had been fired. Bradshaw did not know that, but there should have been some reference to his influence. He would have to give the old boy the tip-off. The sight of Maxwell Fleury's name gave him an idea. Fleury was making his first speech tonight. If his own plans held, that first meeting should be a meeting to end all meetings. He'd advise the old boy to go there.

*9*

Carl Bradshaw drove out alone to Belfontaine. It was a cloudless night and though the moon had not yet risen the road was not really dark. He told the chauffeur to park the car a hundred yards outside the village. He did not want the Fleurys to see the car. The Fleurys would be coming from the opposite direction. He walked slowly past the shuttered huts. It was seven o'clock. He wondered why Maxwell had chosen to hold the meeting so late. Perhaps because he had not wanted to disturb the work in the fields.

The road was empty, but a little farther on he could hear the din of a steel band. He was surprised to hear it. Normally steel bands did not play during Lent. A palm tree twenty yards away stood in silhouette against a glow of light. The road turned into the square before the police station. On the veranda in front of the building, which was reached by a short flight of steps, a row of chairs had been arranged behind a trestle table. There was a hurricane lamp at each end of the table. In the room behind, a spotlight had been arranged; it shone with blinding brilliance upon the crowd. Bradshaw stood in the shadow, away from its glare. He did not want to be recognized.

The crowd moving in and out of the light reminded him of the early vorticist paintings, which conveyed a sense of movement through abrupt anglings and curves. There seemed to be several hundred people here: not only the village of Belfontaine but the entire neighborhood. In front of the station, the ground rose from the road toward the foothills; a narrow path lined with two-room shacks led up to them; the doors of the shacks stood open; they were lit with lamps, revealing the bright colors of scarves and blouses. There were three shops, decorated with paper streamers. One of them was licensed to sell liquor. In front of it a five-man steel band was beating out a cacophonous calypso; ragged urchins were dancing round it. There was an air of carnival.

The darkness of the road leading away from the square was pierced by the headlights of a car. The car honked and the crowd divided. The car drove through the square and round to the back of the police station. A minute later Maxwell came on to the veranda, with Sylvia at his side. Behind them followed a tall thin man in clerical dress, the parish priest presumably. Bradshaw wondered if he was an Anglican. He supposed he was. He did not think a Roman Catholic would have attended a political meeting. There was no applause as the three of them took their seats before the table. The steel band ceased, however, and the crowd filtered away from the stores and doorways of their huts, to gather in front of the veranda. The priest rose to his feet and silence fell.

"I am here this evening," he said, "as chairman of a meeting in which Mr. Maxwell Fleury, who is offering himself for election as your representative in the Legislative Council, will explain his position to you. As you know, the Church stands aside from politics. We support the authorized government of the country. At the same time the Church cannot be uninterested in anything that concerns deeply the members of our congregation. We are anxious that you should have the best possible opportunities of judging for yourselves who are the men by whom you want to be represented. It is for that reason that I stand before you now, to ask you to listen carefully to what Maxwell Fleury has to say. Maxwell Fleury does not need to be introduced to you. Few West Indian families bear a name as honored. His father . . ."

There was a silence while the priest was speaking; at the same time there was a great deal of movement in the crowd. At first Bradshaw could not realize what was happening; then he understood. The single spotlight was so strong that anyone standing in its direct glare was dazzled. You could only see the speaker on the veranda by moving into the shadow. As a result the crowd was splitting into two separate sections with a bright channel dividing them. It reminded Bradshaw of the pictures he had seen in a Victorian Bible, of the Israelites crossing the Red Sea with the waves rising into two walls on either side of them. It would be an awkward audience to address. How good a speaker was young Fleury? Again Bradshaw wondered why he had chosen to hold this meeting in the dark.

227

Surely he could have captured an audience more effectively when it was light. Was it nervousness?

"And now," the priest concluded, "I will ask Mr. Fleury to address you."

There had been silence while the priest was speaking: there was silence as he sat down. There was no applause when Maxwell rose. He glanced from one side to the other. He appeared disconcerted by the empty avenue of roadway facing him. He would look, Bradshaw thought, like a spectator at a tennis match: his head turning first one way then another. Maxwell leant forward, his hands upon the table.

"The elections for which I stand before you as a candidate," he began.

The silence was abruptly shattered. From the liquor store came the clattering din of the steel band. It was deafening. No voice could have made itself heard above it. Maxwell tried, but the audience was only aware of his mouth opening and closing. Then as suddenly as it began, the music stopped. Maxwell's voice, breaking into the silence, was like a shrill scream of hysteria. There was a roar of laughter. Bradshaw could not see the expression on Maxwell's face. His head was in shadow, but the light from the hurricane lamp distorted Sylvia's features, she seemed to be grinning too. Maxwell waited for the laughter to stop, then began again.

"I stand here as a candidate in the elections . . ."

Once again the din of the steel band broke out. This time Maxwell did not attempt to shout above it. He waited. The band went on. He leant down and whispered to the priest. The priest stood up. There was instant silence.

"This," the priest said, "is a disgraceful exhibition. Mr. Fleury has come here to address you in your own interests. You should listen to what he has to say. I insist that you should listen. Some of you may not want to hear, but others do. Those who do not want to hear have not the right to prevent those who want to hear from listening. I insist on silence."

The priest sat down. Maxwell began once more. "I stand before you as a candidate . . ."

A voice from the side called out, "We heard you the second time."

Maxwell started on another tack.

"The elections that will take place in a few days are an event of the greatest importance in the history of Santa Marta: they are a unique occasion. Santa Marta is now a self-governing community. It is for you to prove that you are worthy of self-government. It is

228

for you to prove that you are worthy of the trust that has been placed in you. It is for you to show the world . . ."

He was speaking in a slow schoolmaster's voice. This won't do, Bradshaw thought. He ought not to be saying "you"; he ought to be saying "we." They won't like this, if they understand what he's saying, which probably they don't.

"It is for you to show that you are capable of running this island for yourselves. And how can you do that? There is only one way of doing that, by choosing the right men to govern you."

Bradshaw winced. Oh no, he thought, oh no, no, no. It was all wrong. He'd put their backs up.

"It is for you to find . . ."

The sentence was never finished. The clatter of the steel band burst out again, fierce, barbaric, mandatory. For a minute it continued, then it stopped as abruptly as it had begun. The complete silence following upon the noise was as disconcerting as the interruption. Maxwell hesitated. He had lost the thread of his argument. He began a sentence, abandoned it; stammered, then started on another.

"The duty of a Government," he said, "no, I don't quite mean that, the duty of the electors of the Government is as great as the duty of the Government to the electors. There is a mutual obligation. You owe it to the Government to choose the right men to form the Government."

Now what does that mean, Bradshaw asked himself. He could see what had happened. Maxwell was an inexperienced speaker. He had lost the thread of his argument. He could not improvise. He had fallen back on a passage that he had memorized, so as to recover his confidence, to get back into his stride, to get used to talking. No doubt that passage about "duty" and "obligation" would have been pertinent in its proper context. It was meaningless now.

"That is the joint purpose of Government: the interrelationship of obligation between the governing and the governed."

Maxwell paused. He had regained his confidence. He knew where he was standing.

"You will ask me how this affects you," he began again, "where this affects you, the voters of Belfontaine, who will soon be casting your votes here in this room behind me. You will ask me . . ."

Now this is better, Bradshaw thought. He's making it personal. He's got on to a "you and I" basis.

"You will be going each one of you to the polls, many of you for the first time in your lives. . . ."

Once again the sentence remained unfinished. Once again the din

229

of steel broke out; to cease again abruptly ninety seconds later; to leave Maxwell once again uncertain, hesitant, off his guard. Once again it took him three or four stammering sentences to recover his composure; and then once again as soon as he had begun to speak with confidence, the steel band interrupted him.

There was no doubt whatsoever that it was prearranged, and that David Boyeur, if he had not actually planned it, had been in the plot. Where would it end, Bradshaw wondered; had any climax been prepared: or was it to be a war of attrition, an endless series of interruptions until finally Maxwell was forced to abdicate?

Bradshaw watched, curious and interested, forming in his mind the sentences with which he would describe the incident in his next article. Romer had thought himself to be pensioning off an old retainer; he was now learning how little use he had made of one of the best writers on his staff. When he returned to Baltimore it would be on his own terms. What terms would he dictate? A pipe dream flowered as the din of the steel band beat on.

Once again the noise ended without warning in the very middle of a passage. Once again Maxwell stood, silent on the veranda, his face in shadow, his hands clenched upon the table. It was the sixth time that this had happened, and his nerve was shattered. He was inarticulate. At that moment into the channel of light that divided the two sections of the crowd walked David Boyeur. He checked in the very center and looked up at Maxwell. He was illuminated by the spotlight. He was wearing a white and blue check coat, a bow tie and dark blue trousers. He looked very handsome. His face wore an expression of amused contempt. He laughed, then turned his back on the veranda. He raised his voice.

"This isn't amusing any longer. Let's go." He walked back into the crowd and the crowd started to disperse. There was the shuffle of feet, a purr of voices. Within two minutes there were barely thirty people in the audience. Maxwell glared at the remaining few.

"You don't deserve a vote," he said. "I'm going."

He drove back to his house in silence. How differently had he foreseen this hour. He had seen himself returning home in the glow of victory, with Sylvia proud of him, he himself confident and masterful. The priest's house was half way back to theirs.

"Will you come in for a moment?" the priest asked. Maxwell shook his head.

"It's too late. Thank you very much. It was very good of you to come. I wish we had given you a more satisfactory evening."

"Don't be depressed. These people are incalculable. They're like their climate; one moment the sun is shining; the next it's raining."

"I know, I know."

Or rather he should have known. They were impossible. There was nothing to be done with them. It had been madness to give them the vote, to change the constitution. They couldn't run anything on their own; they were savages. He'd been a fool to run for the Council. It was only a moment's mood; because of what Carson had said that evening. Carson. What did Carson know. He'd only been here three years. Carson! He had admired him once, but that was before he'd known. Carson, Carson, Carson. Carson was at the back of everything that had gone wrong with him these last two months. He drove on in silence.

"Are you hungry? What would you like?" Sylvia was asking.

They had had a late substantial tea before they started. They had agreed that they would not know how they would be feeling till they returned. There was a cold chicken pie in the refrigerator with a half bottle of champagne beside it. He had planned it as an occasion.

"I'm hungry. We'd better have that pie," said Sylvia.

He had been too excited to eat before he left; but he had no appetite.

"What would you like to drink?" he asked.

"We might as well have the champagne since it's there," she said.

He did not feel in a champagne mood and the wine struck sour on his palate. Sylvia cut herself a large helping of the pie. She ate with gusto. The evening's fiasco had made no difference to her appetite. He resented her ability to enjoy her supper.

"I think I'll withdraw my candidature," he said.

She looked up from her plate incuriously.

"I never quite understood why you put yourself up," she said.

"I explained it didn't I, at the time."

"It never made much sense to me."

She spoke on a note of unconcern. She did not care whether he ran or not: whether he failed or succeeded. She did not share his life; she was not a wife in the real sense of the word. A wife was someone with whom you talked your problems over, in whom you confided, to whom you brought your triumphs; who offered you consolation when things went badly. If he had had a wife like that, he wouldn't be the pitiable failure that he was. He was no good here. He never would amount to anything in a place like this. It might be different in England. Here he was laboring all the time against the handicap of being white. No one trusted him, nobody believed in him. No one was on his side. How could he show these people what he was worth?

231

"I'll tell my father what happened here tonight," he said. "I'll withdraw my candidature. When he hears what's happened he'll refuse to serve as one of the nominated members. It was a put-up job tonight: that was obvious wasn't it? How could my father serve with men who have treated his son like that."

So he talked: angry, resentful, self-distrustful, on the night when Bradshaw's third article stood in type, on the printing press of *The Voice of Santa Marta*.

# CHAPTER THIRTEEN

## 1

The morning paper did not reach the Fleury town house until Julian Fleury had left for work; a second copy was delivered at his office. Ordinarily he did little more than glance at the arrival and departures column. On this morning however, the headline above Bradshaw's article caught his eye. He had better see what the fellow had to say. But even so, it was not until close on noon that he found time to study it.

He read the opening paragraphs with interest. It was well and clearly put. "Let us take some typical examples . . ." Two inches below his eye he saw his name. He had read of a sick feeling in the pit of a man's stomach. Now he knew what that meant. He closed his eyes. Pull yourself together, he adjured himself, and take your medicine. He opened his eyes.

"The Fleury family," he read, "provides a pertinent example of this mixed situation. The Fleurys are one of the oldest families in the Caribbean. Their estate house at Belfontaine is historic. Its present owner, Julian Fleury, was brought up in England. He was educated at Eton and at Oxford. His great-grandfather, as an absentee owner, had bought a house in Devonshire. The Fleurys are as well known in the West of England as they are in the West Indies. A distinguished Wessex family was delighted when Julian Fleury proposed marriage to their youngest daughter. Presumably they did not know, and if they had known they might not have cared that Julian's mother who died in childbirth was a Jamaican, with colored ancestry. The wheel has now come full circle and the Fleurys are resident once again at Belfontaine."

The lines that the editor had erased had linked Jocelyn's name with Euan.

Julian Fleury stared at the paragraph: that this should have been brought up after all these years. Thank heaven Arthur had never known. Betty, Jocelyn, Maxwell, how would they take this? Had they read it yet? He called up his house. Jocelyn answered.

"Is your mother there?"

"She's here. Do you want to speak to her?"

"Yes, please."

He could hear Jocelyn calling, "It's Daddy, Mother." Then there was Betty's voice, "Yes, darling?"

"Have you read Bradshaw's article?"

"Yes."

"I'll be right back."

They had read it, had no doubt discussed it. A sense of guilt bore down on him. It was outrageous that they should be subjected to such a shock; that he should have brought this on them.

Yet he had brought it in all innocence. He had had no idea of his real background when he came out here. He had never suspected it. His father had never told him.

Their voices dropped as he came onto the veranda. He looked first at Betty. There was sympathy and fondness in her smile. As at all times in their joint life she was standing by him. The knowledge gave him courage. Jocelyn's face, however, was set and stern; as it would be naturally.

"Is it true?" she asked.

"It's true."

"And you told me that there was no good reason why I shouldn't marry Euan Templeton."

"I can see no good reason."

"How can you say that? Euan's heir to a title. Can you picture a black man sitting in the House of Lords?"

"There's no need to exaggerate. My mother was three-quarters white. I've only one-sixteenth of colored blood; your children will be completely white, all but a thousandth part."

"What about a throwback."

"That's an old-fashioned theory. It's been disproved: the blood gets whiter all the time."

"That's what the scientists are saying now, but have they proved it? The risk's too big, in Euan's case. If he were an ordinary person it wouldn't matter, but he's not. His being a peer makes all the difference. You can't pretend it doesn't. Even in these democratic days. A colored man in the House of Lords. That fear would poison everything."

She spoke quietly, but accusingly.

"Why couldn't you have told me years ago," she said. "Then I wouldn't be in this fix. I'd have been on my guard. I've always wondered. One wonders about anyone who's born out here: I've compared photographs of your father and yourself. There's a different cast of feature. I've looked at myself in the glass. I'm exactly what mother was at my age. I can't see a trace of it in myself, but Maxwell's dark, like you. I've always wondered. Why was there so little

234

talk about my grandmother? Mr. Bradshaw's right. All this whispering and secrecy. Why wasn't I told? I had a right to know."

Julian Fleury looked toward his wife. There was nothing but fondness in her eyes. If only it were just the two of them they could brave this thing through so easily. It would be an added bond between them. Once again, as so often in the past, he found himself resentful of the children who had come between them, who had disturbed their harmony.

"I never knew it myself till I came out here," he said. "There was nothing to make me suspect. My father toured the West Indies with a cricket team, he fell in love and married. Within eighteen months he was back in England as a widower; a year later he had married again, a girl he had been half engaged to before he sailed. That was all I know. My stepmother was a mother to me. Why should I have felt any curiosity about a mother that I'd never seen, about an island that I never heard discussed. It was something I fancy that my father and stepmother wanted to forget. It was a brief episode in their lives. Perhaps my father should have told me, but I don't see why he should. I might have been worried by it. He never expected that I'd come out here. He warned me against coming here. He acted as he thought best, as I've acted as I thought best."

He did not elaborate the story. His mother, so he had learnt since, had belonged to one of those quiet, respectable middle-class families who were educated with care, whose sons worked in Government employ. He had always imagined that his father and mother had had the kind of romance that can so easily happen with a visitor to an island, that there had been no talk of marriage till his mother had found that she was pregnant. To a girl in her position an illegitimate baby would have been a great disgrace. His father had behaved honorably. No doubt his father had thought of his wife's death in childbirth as a merciful intervention of providence. He could then go back to England, to the life for which he was fitted by taste and training, to the woman he really loved. His conscience had been clear. How could he have foreseen that sixty years later a situation such as this would arise?

"I never knew till I came out here," he said. "I don't suppose I ever should have known if I hadn't met a remote cousin in Antigua."

Betty smiled.

"I wasn't certain if you knew."

"So you knew then."

She nodded. "An anonymous letter."

"You never mentioned it?"

"If you didn't know, it was better that you shouldn't."

Ah, there it went again, thought Jocelyn. Secrecy. Whispers. Anonymous letters. Nothing in the open.

"I didn't think it mattered," her mother added.

Jocelyn stared at her. Not matter, when her own life was being ruined by it.

The maid announced that lunch was ready.

"When does H.E. get back?" her mother asked.

"This afternoon. It'll be a nice surprise for him."

"Before you decide on anything . . ."

Jocelyn interrupted her. "Let's lunch," she said.

They seated themselves round the table. It was a curry luncheon. Julian's favorite dish. The sight of the high piled plate filled him with nausea. The telephone bell rang.

"I'll answer it," said Jocelyn.

Anything to be out of her parents' company.

"It's Maxwell," she announced on her return. "He's seen the paper. He's coming in right away."

Her parents exchanged a glance. Maxwell would take this badly.

"How did he sound?" asked Mrs. Fleury.

"Hopping mad. I couldn't get a word in edgewise."

"Poor little boy."

Poor little boy indeed. Jocelyn's temper rose. Why should Maxwell deserve pity. His life was not being spoilt. His die was cast. She would not worry if she were in his position. Poor little boy. She couldn't look her mother in the face. She was too resentful. Her mother had never cared for her. It was Maxwell, Maxwell, Maxwell. Just because he was disagreeable and ill-tempered. The mother's affection for the ugly duckling. Poor little boy.

2

Maxwell arrived soon after three, seething with indignation, vowing vengeance.

"We must break this fellow, we must sue him in America. That's where we can get big damages. You can't trust our juries. Besides they'd say that it wasn't doing any damage. In America it's different. To call a man colored is to ruin his career. We must sue in Baltimore."

He was on the brink of hysteria. Bradshaw's article exacerbated the humiliation of the previous night. Jocelyn was ashamed of herself for taking a sadistic pleasure in the foreknowledge of the shock that the truth would be to him, but she could not resist it. What was

236

he making all this fuss about; why should he get all this sympathy? Her parents exchanged a glance; she read the meaning in her father's nod. Her mother rose, put her hand on Maxwell's arm.

"Darling, it's true," she said.

Jocelyn noted with satisfaction the expression of incredulous dismay that wiped the indignation from her brother's face. Poor little boy, indeed.

## 3

The discussion dragged on and on. Jocelyn had missed her siesta and her eyes were aching.

Maxwell turned to his sister.

"How will this affect your engagement?"

"It's the end of that, of course."

"Now wait . . ." It was her mother once again who intervened, but once again she checked. What was on her mind, Jocelyn asked herself? She seemed to be keeping something back. Her brother did not notice the interruption. He was too absorbed in his own predicament. In a way that Jocelyn could not guess the revelation of his heritage was catastrophic.

It was the end of the dream picture he had cherished of a return to England under Templeton's protection. He had seen himself re-established under the patronage of his English cousins. He had seen his sons as the nephews of a peer carving for themselves careers that had been denied their father: he would be justified by his children. That dream was over now and the memory of his humiliation before the villagers returned to him with heightened violence. How could he face his friends in the light of this fresh exposure? How they would be chuckling at the club tonight. How would they treat him? Would they cold-shoulder him? Membership of the tennis club was restricted to white residents.

"Are you going to resign from the club?" he asked his father.

"Don't be ridiculous."

"It might make it easier in the long run if you did. It throws the responsibility on them. They can't say 'Unfortunately the Fleurys *do* belong. If we'd known about them in time we wouldn't have elected them.'"

He could hear himself talking. He was being silly, but he could not stop. He was easing his own disquiet by magnifying his trouble. He enjoyed masochistically making out his position to be worse than it was.

Jocelyn watched him in silence, in contempt. No wonder Sylvia

237

despised him. What a fool he was making of himself. What did it matter to him, whose life was rooted here, whether he had a twentieth, an eighth or a quarter of colored blood. He was not seeing, as she was, a whole life in ruins. He was thinking only of himself, of his minor malady.

"Did you hear about the scene last night at my meeting?" he was asking.

"No, I didn't."

"They wouldn't let me speak. They howled me down. It was a put-up thing. They had a steel band. Whenever I was reaching a key argument they began to play; they drowned my words. I couldn't go on. I had to stop. It was a put-up show, organized by Boyeur. He was there himself. He gave himself away, at the very end."

What on earth was all this about, thought Jocelyn? He was crazy, hysterical. What had all this to do with her engagement, or a newspaper article announcing that their father had colored blood? There were times when Maxwell was barely sane.

"It was an insult to me. It was an insult to Belfontaine. It was an insult to the family. It has to be avenged. We have to prove to these upstarts that we can't be pushed around. There's only one thing to do, convince H.E. that the decent elements in the island won't stand for this. I'll tell you how you can prove it, by refusing to sit on the Council with a man like Boyeur. You must refuse to be a nominated member."

"Now, my dear boy, do listen to me quietly for one moment. . . ."

Patiently, slowly, stage by stage, Julian Fleury explained to his son the impossibility of his suggestion.

"At the start of any misfortune one thinks that the end of the world has come. But it's only one step in a long journey. You know how it is at golf. You slice an approach into a bunker. You'll be unlikely to get on to the green with your next shot. You won't get your four but you've still a chance of a five if you lay your chip dead: anyhow, with any care, you should be certain of your six. You have two shots to make up during the rest of the round. That's all there is to it. The important thing is not to lose your head when you see the ball lying in the bunker. That's what we must do now: keep our heads. You and Jocelyn, your mother and myself. It's an unlucky business, but it's not as bad as you or Jocelyn think it is. The great thing is to do nothing hasty: behave as though nothing extraordinary had happened. If we behave as though a calamity had befallen us, people will say 'Look at the Fleurys. They don't dare hold up their heads in public.' People are always glad of an oppor-

238

tunity to say malicious things behind your back, but if you behave normally, if you show that you do not care, that you are not concerned, they say 'What was it all about after all?'

"I should for instance advise you to go to the club this evening. Behave quite naturally. Don't avoid people. At the same time don't be ostentatious. Don't start standing drinks to everyone. Don't refer to the article unless someone else does and you can be very sure they won't."

How very wise he is, Jocelyn thought. She felt guilty, ashamed, remembering how she had turned against him. This must be bad for him. But he was not thinking of himself. Only of his family, her mother, Maxwell, and herself. He must have a sense of guilt about it all, blaming himself, though actually he was not to blame. In one way he was the one to be most pitied.

"I shan't go to the club myself," he said. "It shouldn't be made to look as though the clan were mustering in force. I'd suggest that Jocelyn waited till tomorrow. Then I'll go up with her: we don't want to seem to making an occasion of it. Behave as though nothing had happened. That's the line."

Maxwell nodded. His father was quite right. He must face the music. He'd control himself. His blood was hot and his mind seething. He longed to be avenged on someone or on something: to get his own back somehow. But he must hold himself in check.

Through the window he saw a plane circling above the town. It was the plane from B.G. that was bringing back the Governor and his son. Maxwell said exactly what Jocelyn had. "He's got a nice surprise waiting him."

### 4

Denis Archer was thinking the same thing as he stood beside the runway. How would the old boy take it?

The plane circled, settled, taxied up the airstrip. The ground staff hurried forward with the steps. The passengers started to file out, not in order of protocol, but as they had chosen to seat themselves. There was a dapper colored man in a neat summer weight suit; an untidy man with a rumpled collar, his jacket over his arm, a tourist probably, looking hot and grubby; a couple of shapeless negresses, with trailing skirts and bright scarves round their shoulders, carrying wicker baskets piled with fruit. How could they afford a passage? Then framed in the doorway Archer saw the Governor, a panama hat bound with an I.Z. ribbon set at an angle over his left eye. He looked very spruce and laundered as he came down the steps. Euan was behind him: as they came onto the asphalt, Euan caught up with his father and they walked side by side; not talking, not exactly smiling, but with the air of finding life enjoyable. It was not a smug look: it was one of wholesome healthy enjoyment of the things life offered. For Archer the moment had a deep content of dramatic irony. Would they look back to it with a "last time" feeling. It might well be that never again at Santa Marta would they know that feeling. A pang of pity for them ran along his nerves. I must like them more than I thought, he told himself. It was unusually hard to resist taking a malicious pleasure in the misfortunes of one's acquaintances: particularly if they were persons in high office.

"Any news?" the Governor was inquiring. Archer shook his head. He could not tell him, not at least directly.

"There's been a mail in since you left. It's sorted out," he said.

"Fine, fine. Then probably I've more to tell you than you have to tell me. In the first place . . ."

As the car drove them to G.H. the Governor outlined the salient features of the B.G. conference.

"They are all very curious about our elections," he concluded. "They regard us as a guinea pig. They're waiting to see how things happen here before they make their own decisions with regard to Caribbean Federation. It's odd to think that a small island like this can set a lead. It gives one a pleasant sense of responsibility and importance. One feels that one's the spearhead."

It was nearly four when they reached G.H. H.E. looked at the pile of letters on his desk and hesitated. "Aren't I seeing Carson sometime today?"

"Yes, sir. At five."

"Then I'll leave those till afterward. I'll take a rest. I missed my siesta. What about you Euan?"

"I'll take one too."

"Fine, then I'll see you later."

Archer touched Euan's elbow. He owed it to his own generation to put Euan on his guard. "Can you spare me a couple of minutes."

"Certainly."

He took Euan into his office.

"You'd better read that," and handed him Bradshaw's article.

He watched Euan closely as he read it. Would it be a great shock to him? How would he take it? How far had he absorbed the local prejudice about color? At G.H. there were no distinctions drawn. Euan had seen a good deal of Grainger. Unless Grainger had talked to him on the subject—and the probability was that he had not— Euan might very well be unaware of the extent and nature of the

240

problem. Euan had spent eighteen months in the Middle East, an experience that must have countered his insularity. He would not think of an Arab as being inferior to a European. He would see no reason why an Englishman should not marry an Egyptian, a Turk, a Syrian, a Lebanese. Why should there be any complication about the granddaughter of a quarter African?

Whatever Euan might be thinking, his face remained impassive.

"Thank you for showing it to me," he said. "I'll call Jocelyn right away."

It was Maxwell who answered him, however.

"Jocelyn's gone out," he said.

"Do you know where?"

"She didn't say."

"When do you expect her back?"

"I've no idea. She won't be at the club this evening; that's all I know."

Euan hesitated. It might be difficult to ring her later. Telephones were difficult in this kind of thing. There might be a misunderstanding. He wanted to see, to talk to her. Better to leave a message, to make a date, after he had discussed it with his father.

"Tell her not to worry. Tell her it's all right," he said. "Tell her that I'll call for her tomorrow and we'll go and swim."

# CHAPTER FOURTEEN

*1*

The Governor had asked Carson to come up so that he could discuss the scene with Dr. Leisching. He had kept in touch through Whittingham with the development of the case. The committee was trying to stall, was hoping that by delay a decision would be first postponed and then avoided, but they had counted without Teutonic thoroughness. The doctor was resolved to have his pound of flesh. Sooner or later there would have to be a general meeting and the Governor suspected that the publication of Bradshaw's article would hasten action. It was no good any longer trying to pretend that nothing had happened.

As he waited for Carson in his study, the Governor wondered what Bradshaw had said in his latest article. While he was in B.G. he had seen a copy of that first issue of *The Voice*, and had noticed that the editor had cut out the remark about Euan and Mavis Norman. He was glad of that, he was grateful for that. But he wished he had been in Santa Marta when the article appeared. He would have liked to have read the next two articles in proof. It might have been as well to make some further cuts; he could have brought pressure to bear upon the editor. There were ways of doing things. It was lucky that he had made this appointment with Carson before he left.

He went as always straight to the point.

"I asked you up here, as you've probably guessed, for a special reason. It's about that quarrel you had in the club with Dr. Leisching. I've heard about it as, naturally, I hear about nearly everything on a small island such as this. But unofficially I'd like to hear how you feel about it."

Carson grinned.

"I made a fool of myself, sir. That's all there is to it."

"Have you taken any action?"

"No, sir, none."

"You've been to the club since the incident?"

"Naturally. I don't mind standing at a bar alone."

"I suppose you've read this article by Carl Bradshaw."

"Yes, sir."

"It will bring things to a head. Everyone in the island knows about it. It'll strengthen Leisching's hand. He'll consider himself entitled to redress."

"I'd thought of that, sir."

"What do you imagine will happen then?"

"They'll ask me to resign."

"That's what I had thought."

Templeton looked thoughtfully at Carson. He put himself in Carson's place. Carson in one way would rather enjoy being expelled from the Santa Marta Country Club. It would make a good story. He could tell it to tourists in the St. James' bar. "A very exclusive club," he'd say. "They'll blackball anyone who they think might be unkind to Germans. They've taken that song of Noel Coward's seriously." Carson had no real friends in the island. He'd probably have more fun in a hotel. Templeton had to find an argument that would appeal to Carson.

"It would be an embarrassment for me," he said, "if you ceased to be a member of the club."

"For you, sir?"

It was said in something that was very near a gasp: Templeton had attacked on the right line.

"When I came here, as a stranger, both to this island and to the West Indian way of life," he said, "I looked round me for the kind of men I could rely upon, men who came from the same world, who understood the things I stood for, to whom I could talk in shorthand. In many ways I was very lucky. There was the Fleury family. Our families grew up side by side. Julian Fleury and his wife gave me many invaluable sidelights on the island's way of seeing things. I had another piece of good luck. I found you here."

"Me, sir?"

"Exactly. You. You are a regular officer. We don't need to explain ourselves to each other. When I learnt about you, and later when I met you, I recognized in you one of the potentially solid elements of the community. I knew what I had to build up here, a sense of solidarity, the team spirit. So that each person in the island would feel himself one of the many working toward a common goal, the island's good. I saw at once that there had to be for a time distinctions of color. You can't merge the Aquatic Club and the Country Club; but G.H. can act as a catalyst. They can all meet each other here, as sergeants meet officers at a regimental dance or cricket match.

"I was more happy than I can say to know that there was someone here who had been trained in the same tradition as I had, who had been taught to realize that all men were not equal, that there were differences of class and birth and rank and race. The man is a fool who says there aren't. At the same time those differences don't affect the unity of a unit. When I've said that, I hope you'll understand me when I say that nothing could make me unhappier than the news that you had left the club."

He paused. He had watched Carson carefully as he had talked. I've got him, he thought. I mustn't let him slip. He followed quickly on.

"I have been thinking of what would happen if you left the club. You would make your base at the St. James. You are a man who enjoys company. You would go there every evening. Because you were there, others would start going there. It would split the community. You have English friends who will be calling here as tourists. It would seem strange to them if you could not take them to the club. What impression would they form? Would they consider that you were to blame; of course they wouldn't. They know you, they like you and they trust you. They would think that there is something wrong with the island. The club is the center of the life of a British colony. 'Santa Marta is a funny place,' they'd say, 'if a man like Hilary Carson can't join the club.'

"It's bad for an island to get the reputation of being odd. These small communities are very touchy. It doesn't do for them to get chips on their shoulders. During my service I've had a good many opportunities of seeing how British Colonies work. I remember an occasion in Africa when the Chief Justice and the Administrator were not on speaking terms. It split the community in half. What I'm saying, my dear fellow, is that I regard you as one of the most influential figures in the island. This is a very small place, very cut off from the big world. What might seem trivial in Jamaica is important here. I repeat, in my opinion it would be a calamity for Santa Marta if you found yourself forced to resign from the Country Club."

He paused again. He had watched Carson as he had talked. He was used to handling men of Carson's type. He knew which strings to play on. He had touched his vanity, he had also played upon his sense of loyalty, of duty, of responsibility, upon Carson's strongest instincts as a soldier. He waited for Carson to reply, for the kind of reply that as a colonel he would have looked for from one of his company commanders.

He got the kind of answer he had expected.

"What are you suggesting that I should do, sir?" Carson asked.

"I'm suggesting that you should do something that you will find very difficult, that you should go up to Leisching in the club when there are a number of others there, that you should apologize, and offer to shake hands. If I know him, he won't be able to refuse. Germans regard appearances and form. They're as keen as the Japanese are upon saving face. If you can bring yourself to do that, the incident will be closed. Do you think you can? You'd be doing a big thing for Santa Marta. You'd be making my job here a great deal easier."

"If you put it that way, sir."

"That's how I do put it. I've only been here a little time but the newcomer brings a fresh viewpoint. He very often sees more than men who've lived in a place all their lives. The next weeks are going to be very difficult with these elections. I need all the support I can get. I've spent these last days at the Governors' conference in B.G. From what they told me there, this is of course in the strictest confidence... Look here, let me fill your glass."

He made Carson's second drink a strong one. He wanted Carson to leave in a good temper, with no sense of having been upon the mat, proud of himself, in a glow of confidence and self-esteem; ready to make his peace with Leisching in a way that would throw the German off his guard.

"There's something else I want to talk about," he said. "About the general spirit in your district. Do you feel that there is any genuine communism there, or is the unrest simply the natural resentment of the 'have-nots' for the 'haves'?"

"I'd say it was that, sir, with the resentment played up by agitators."

"You wouldn't believe that there was a communist cell there?"

"No, sir."

"Nor would I. That's what I told them in B.G. In Jamaica and Trinidad and in B.G. very specially, the Communist Party is genuinely active. But the communists haven't started to bother yet about these small islands. What I expect will happen in the elections..."

He explained his point of view.

"No, don't hurry away, my dear fellow," he said, as Carson showed signs of moving. "It's so rarely that I get a chance of talking to someone of my own type. Let me fill your glass. I could use another whisky myself. I hate drinking alone. I have to much too often. I get very lonely sometimes. I expect you do too. I must say I'm surprised at your not remarrying."

"I'm a bit old for that, sir."

"Nonsense, how old are you? Under forty surely?"

"I'm thirty-eight."

"Heavens, man, that's nothing. If I was thirty-eight and unattached, with all these good-looking girls around, Mavis Norman, Doris Kellaway..."

"They're children, sir."

"Oh, no they're not. Most of them are over twenty, and you know as well as I do that a great many young women prefer men older than themselves. Besides there's a man shortage here. I'm sure that several very personable young people have asked themselves questions about you. In a place like this, a man's better married. For that matter a man's always better married."

Ah, but don't I know that, Carson told himself. His head was aching and his limbs were weary. He had been on the wagon for a week. He had meant to stay on it longer, as an experiment; but it hadn't done any good. He had felt worse if anything. Perhaps that was because he hadn't tried long enough. He had always heard that people who went on that orange juice cure at Tring came out in spots after the first week. He had meant to keep on the wagon for another week. But he couldn't have faced an ordeal like this without a couple first. It had tasted so good too, that first long swallow. It had sent such a warm peace along his nerves, but now once again there was that stabbing, intermittent pain that only ceased at the actual moment that the rich sharp liquid ran over his throat.

"In a place like this," the Governor was going on, "where there's so much to irritate you, the climate, the mosquitoes, the stupidity of the peasants, the narrowness of one's acquaintance, a man needs someone to relax him."

Carson smiled ruefully. Did he need telling that? Couldn't he remember in detail after cherished detail those two years with Daphne? He had been exposed to a pompous second in command with whom every day he had come into some kind of conflict. He had seen red at the sight of that perky little man with the short brushed-back mustache, and the meticulous tone of voice. "There's one item in your training program, Carson, that frankly I can't understand."

He could recall every inflection in that voice across a dozen years. At moments he had been on the brink of mutiny. Yet all the time he had known that at the day's end Daphne would be waiting for him in their Georgian drawing room. Firelight would flicker on the glass of a Queen Anne bookcase. Daphne would be fresh and gay and scented in contrast to the gravel of the barrack square and the mud of the rifle range, and the bare orderly room with its trestle tables. There would be a bowl of ice on the side table. "Hurry down," she would say, "and I'll have your cocktail ready."

He would find her standing by the fireplace, the tall steaming shaker in her hand. The glass would have been chilled. Daiquiris were her specialty. There was a bite of bitters through the sweetness. One sip and the harshness and impatience of the day dissolved. They would stand side by side, his arm about her waist; she would be soft and fond and pliant. This moment was his reward and recompense for all that he had known of strain and irritation through the day. Did he need telling how a wife, the right kind of wife, relaxed you?

"An unattached male in this kind of place can't help drinking more than he should," the Governor was continuing. "He sees the same people, night after night in the same place, discussing the same topics. He can only get a kick out of their company through alcohol."

Again Carson smiled ruefully. He knew the geography of that road.

"I sometimes wonder why you picked on an island like this. I should have thought you would have more to stimulate you in a bigger place, Jamaica say."

"Jamaica's too expensive, sir."

"It needn't be. There's the smart playboy group that hangs round Montego Bay, but there's no need to mix with that set. There is a large resident community that leads a pleasant life on their estates, entertaining one another, never meeting the socialites."

"That's what I didn't like the sound of: there being a whole section of the island's life in which I did not mix; I'd have felt so silly when my London friends asked me about Sunset Lodge and I'd have to confess I'd never been there."

"I don't see why you should. In London you don't stay at Claridge's. In Jamaica as in London you can find a life that suits your tastes and income. If I'd been you, I'd have picked Jamaica."

Suddenly Carson felt upon his guard. Was there, he asked himself, a note of insistence in the Governor's voice? Is he suggesting that I clear out of here, that I'm a nuisance and a responsibility, that I'd be wise to sell up, clear out? Has all he's been saying to me so far been so much soft soap? Is this what he's been working up to, was this the real point of having me up here?

His head was throbbing, his wound ached. He was in for a bad night. He finished his drink and rose. "I must be going, sir. I've stayed too long. I won't forget what you've said."

Templeton accompanied him to the door. "I've enjoyed our talk

247

more than I can say. We must meet oftener. We must have a quiet evening sometime. I wish I hadn't so many official obligations. There's so much protocol in a job like this. Everyone's so touchy about whom they're asked to meet and if I ask one person more often than another they get jealous and say I've favorites. Let's see now, where's your car?"

"I came on foot."

"That's a long walk."

"The exercise does me good."

"Mayn't I send you back?"

"No, thank you very much, sir. I'll enjoy the walk."

It had been a gray, cloudy afternoon, rain seemed imminent and Carson was walking with a limp. He knew his own business best, the Governor supposed, and returned to his study and to the pile of papers that Archer had arranged for him on his desk. At the top of the pile was that morning's issue of *The Voice of Santa Marta.*

2

Carson reached the club shortly after six. His back was aching. He had been a fool not to take the Governor's offer of a lift. He had thought a walk might do him good, take away the stiffness; sometimes it did. Tonight it hadn't. He went straight to the bar.

"A whisky soda, Joe."

The soda was well iced but the liquid was warm against his heart. He forgot that his head was throbbing, and that a knife was cutting at the big toe that was no longer his. He looked about him. The club was fairly full, but he did not see Dr. Leisching. Leisching usually came late. Or perhaps he was playing bridge. There was no one he cared to talk to. "A whisky soda, Joe."

Two girls came along the veranda, arm in arm, whispering. Doris Kellaway and Mavis.

"Hullo there, have a drink," he said.

They checked, surprised. It was the first time he had spoken to them, other than casually and when they were in a group.

"What'll you have?" he asked.

Doris was wearing a light scarf over a low-cut dress. Her shoulders were very smooth and rounded. H.E. was right. There *were* some striking girls here.

"Something with gin or something with rum?" he asked.

Doris looked questioningly at Mavis. They were anxious to join the girls' table at the end of the veranda. They wanted to have a long gossip about the article in that day's paper. They were anxious to know what everyone else thought. How was this going to affect Jocelyn and Euan? Had anyone seen Jocelyn? What were they to say when they met her? They did not want to stand here at the bar. At the same time they could not be rude to Colonel Carson.

"I'd like a dry swizzle," Mavis said. "I expect Doris would like the same."

A swizzle could be gulped, had to be gulped in fact.

"Fine, and another whisky, Joe."

He turned toward the girls, addressing himself to Doris. "You're looking very pretty tonight," he said.

Doris was too surprised to answer.

"Can't think why I haven't noticed it before," he said. "Funny how quickly a girl grows up. I've been here three years now; when I came here first you were a schoolgirl. So I've gone on thinking of you as a schoolgirl. I haven't realized that you were growing up; that you'd stopped being a schoolgirl. Do you know that when I saw you coming along the veranda, I said to myself, 'Now who is this extremely pretty girl?' then suddenly I realized that it was little Doris Kellaway grown up."

He said it on a bantering note. Doris felt awkward. She did not know what to say. She was not used to being spoken to like this by men nearly old enough to be her father.

"Now that I have realized it, we must do something about it," he was continuing. "We must have a party. You haven't seen my place since I took it over. We might have a picnic. Collect some of your friends, Mavis here, and that A.D.C., and that young Barbadian at the bank, what is his name, I can't remember it. Let's fix it now. What's the best day for you?"

Doris looked helplessly, appealingly, at Mavis. Carson saw the look and understood it. You're being a fool, he told himself, rushing your fences. This isn't the way to treat this kind of filly; patience, tact, that's what you need. A light hand on the rein. But that was precisely what he could not do, once he had begun.

"What day would suit you best? A picnic bathing party, or what about coming out for a bathe in the afternoon, then coming back to my place for dinner? That's not a bad idea. Let's choose an evening when there's a moon. There'll be a new moon next week. Why not the week after?"

The expression on Doris' face became more puzzled, more embarrassed. You're being a fool, he told himself. You've never taken any notice of this girl before; then without any warning you start showering her with fulsome compliments, asking her on a party, before she even knows you. You must be mad. Snap out of it. So he adjured himself, but he could not stop. He heard himself speaking and his voice went on.

"Personally I think an evening party would be better. I need a siesta after lunch myself. That breaks up the afternoon. What about Friday week? That's my pay day. I need a relaxation when that's over. Your glasses are empty. What about the other half?"

That gave them the break, the chance to get away they needed.

"No, really," Mavis protested. "Two drinks an evening are as much as I can stand. And I've promised to join some people."

"Have you? I see your point. Quite agree with you. You're very wise. Don't believe in young girls taking too many cocktails. Leave that for retired colonels."

Heavens, he thought, I'm talking like a caricature. I'm making myself ridiculous. But he couldn't stop.

"Run along and enjoy yourselves. But Friday week's a date now, isn't it?"

"Of course. Thanks for the swizzle."

They were gone before anything had been decided, the place, the time, the other guests. Tomorrow, he told himself, Doris would be ringing up to say that there was something she had remembered, or else there would be a letter. More likely there'd be a letter, then he wouldn't have a chance of saying, "Too bad but if you can't manage Friday what about Tuesday, any day in fact."

They hadn't wanted to be tied down. They didn't want to come. Why should they, with a man whom they'd dismissed as one of the grown-up set. Why had he asked them? Why had he let his mood run away with him? Too much to drink, following on what H.E. had said. The idea had been planted in his mind. Then suddenly the sight of those white shoulders. He was under forty after all. That wasn't anything. Younger than Antony when he met Cleopatra. H.E. was right. Lots of young girls preferred men older than themselves. Girls wanted to be married. They'd rather be married to a man of forty than not married. Yes, but he'd started it the wrong way round, rushing his fences.

He felt deflated, depressed, angry with himself. Why couldn't he have advanced slowly, got to know the girl by stages, it would have been so easy; first make her like him, interest her in him: he'd been about, she hadn't; he could tell her things, then gradually lead her from liking to affection, and from affection to something warm enough to justify the risk of marriage. He didn't expect to inspire a grand passion, but was that necessary? Many of the most lasting marriages had begun this way. H.E. might have held the key, the solution to his problem. Marriage to Doris Kellaway. Two hours

250

ago the idea had never crossed his mind, but now with the idea once planted...

He looked at her across the room. She was in profile. She had one of those amusing squashed-in faces. She was smiling. She looked fresh and gay. Life would be a picnic with her sharing it. If only he had played his cards correctly. Why had he been such a fool? He wouldn't be again. But it was not too late. It was drink. Everything was the fault of drink. He wouldn't be drinking if he were married. He hadn't drunk when he had had Daphne: if only he had Daphne still. If only he could find someone to take Daphne's place. Why shouldn't he? Other men did, older men... "A whisky soda, Joe."

He leant back against the wall, his eyes on Doris, visualizing life as it might be, as it would be if he married her. He saw that life in terms of his days with Daphne. Doris waiting for him with a planter's punch when he came back at lunch, at the end of a long morning in the cane fields: Doris at his side as they drove into town on Saturday evenings to "beat it up." Glimpses of Doris across a crowded room, at cocktail parties, a quick smile that said "the best part of all this will be talking it over afterwards." He was happy, confident, at peace. His headache had stopped. His wound throbbed no longer. He felt as he had fourteen years ago on the brink of marriage. The best of everything in front of him. Life gave you a second innings; an opportunity to repair the mistakes you had made first time, to consolidate your first advantages. This time there'd be no mistake. "A whisky soda, Joe."

Through the doorway of the card room a four that had broken up was making its way onto the veranda. Dr. Leisching was among them. Ah, the doctor. That promise of his to the General. He'd get that settled now. Then with the slate clean, he could begin that second innings. He levered himself forward from the wall. Leisching was standing beside his wife and another couple. They were indulging in an uncontentious post-mortem. He walked toward them. He was very conscious of his limp. Curious how it became more marked when the wind was in the east. He stood beside the doctor. The doctor was turned away, occupied with his discussion.

"But surely you must have recognized when I discarded the six of clubs..."

He explained his point with Teutonic thoroughness. The other man interrupted him.

"But as you had declared three hearts, I assumed that the six of clubs..."

Carson grew impatient. He couldn't wait here all day. He tapped

251

Leisching on the arm. "I'm sorry, Doctor, to interrupt this learned disquisition, but there's something I want to say to you. I behaved very stupidly the other night. I want to apologize. Let's shake hands and have a drink and forget all about it."

He held out his hand, but the hand that he held out was folded round a glass of whisky.

"Now that's funny, isn't it," he said.

He moved the glass over to his other hand. But his left hand as he leant against the wall had been in his trouser pocket. It was hot and sticky. The glass slipped, fell to the floor and broke. The clatter silenced instantly every conversation. With his right hand still held out, Carson stared down at the floor, at the broken glass and the trickling liquid.

"I'm very clumsy, aren't I?" he said.

The German smiled. It was his chance and he was not missing it.

"No, my friend," he said. "You are not very clumsy, but you are very drunk. It is generous of you to want to make me an apology for your very curious behavior the other evening, but in the condition that you are now in, I am afraid that by tomorrow morning you will have entirely forgotten the whole incident. I shall be in the Jamestown Club tomorrow morning at twelve o'clock and if you would care to make your apology to me there, I shall be delighted to accept it, but in the meantime, as a doctor, I should prescribe for you an early retirement preceded by a Bromo-Seltzer."

There was a general tittering laugh. Looking round, Carson had the impression of fifty staring faces turned toward him. They all seemed to be grinning. He was conscious of nothing but that grin, a single gaping maw. How they're enjoying this, he thought: then the many faces blurred, and one face only was distinct. Doris Kellaway's. She was laughing too, louder than anyone; with contempt, disgust, delight in his discomfiture. He felt immensely tired; tired and ill. There must be something for him to do, to say, some gesture he could make. He could not think what. Was there a flicker of friendship there? No, not any. Why should there be? He turned away. He walked back to the bar.

"I've smashed a glass, Joe, you might clear it up, then give me a whisky soda; yes, a large one."

It was not two minutes since he had been leaning here against the wall, since he had glimpsed Leisching coming from the card room. In that two minutes the whole structure of his life had collapsed about him. Blank and utter despair settled on him. H.E. had been right. He'd told him to get out. The old boy had put it friendlily, had wrapped it up, paid him compliments first. The old boy knew how he had got like this: and knowing, sympathized. But it was quite clear what he had been saying. "You're a nuisance in a small place like this. In a big place it wouldn't matter. You'd pass unnoticed. But everything one does in a place this size is everybody's business. You carry too many guns to be overlooked. You are an embarrassment."

That's what the Governor had been saying. The Governor was right. No one liked him here. How they had gloated, taken that German's side. In all that mist of faces was there one that was not hostile? H.E. was right. He knew men, he was used to commanding men. How often in his years of service had he not said to a difficult officer, "There's a vacancy at Division for a Staff Captain 'Q.' It's the kind of work that you'd do very well. If you like, I'll be only too happy to recommend you." That was what H.E. had been saying tonight. "Clean up the mess you've made and then either clear out or find yourself a wife."

Find yourself a wife, indeed. What a mess he'd made of that. He looked toward the far end of the veranda. Doris was leaning forward across the table. She was no longer in profile, she was directly opposite. There was an eager expression on her face. How young she was, how fresh and wholesome. She had thrown the scarf off her shoulders. He could fall in love with her very easily. Strange that he had not realized it until this evening. How one's subconscious worked when one was not watching it. His instinct told him that if he played his cards correctly, he could turn this evening's calamity to his own advantage. At the moment she was thinking of him as a silly old man who had made a drunken approach to her and then made an idiot of himself. But, if handled adroitly, an attitude of contemptuous disgust was a far better starting point than one of negative indifference. It created a situation. It would make it possible for him to talk to her about himself.

Suppose the next time they met, he were to make a point of speaking to her alone, of saying, "I made an exhibition of myself the other night. I want to explain. I don't care what the others think, but I want you to understand me." If he could make her feel that she was someone special, that she was selected, picked out, she would feel herself enrolled under his standard. She would find herself compelled to take his side. "I know he's difficult. I know he's tiresome, I used to feel the same way about him once, but when you get to know him . . ."

It was no bad thing to make a bad first impression. It was much more dramatic to have a friend of whom your friends disapproved, far more exciting to fight battles on that friend's behalf than to sit in a circle agreeing with everyone how marvelous he was. Everyone wanted to feel someone special. He could do that for Doris. In a flash of intuition he foresaw the whole course of his courtship. This evening's incident could be made the perfect prelude.

For a moment he allowed himself to be dazzled by the prospect. Then despair returned. It was no good, it was too late. He mustn't fool himself. "A whisky soda, Joe." He must face the looking glass. It wasn't that Doris was seventeen and he thirty-eight. It wasn't that he was a widower; that he'd been badly wounded, that his system had been shattered, that he wasn't likely to make old bones; those were handicaps, those were disadvantages; but they could with another kind of man have been surmounted. Himself he was in a different pass. Something had died inside him. Something had gone with Daphne, something irrecapturable.

He looked back to the days when he had known her first. He had been a different person then. That person existed in the world no longer. He lived again the tumult and rapture of the honeymoon. How completely he had given himself to Daphne. Nothing had been held back: no part of himself had been denied. And that was woman's birthright, that a man should give himself to her completely, that they should become one person.

He looked again at Doris. What could he give her in comparison with what he had given Daphne? He could take what she had to offer, and she had much to give: he could take it and gloat over and relish it. But what had he to offer in return? In his heart he was married still to Daphne. He still belonged to her. He would be cheating Doris of her birthright. Remembering what he had given once to Daphne, he would find no relief in Doris, take no real happiness in such a burglary: and in the perverse way that the human mind worked, he would hold it against Doris that he had robbed her. He might be cruel to her, when the black mood was on him, when his head ached and there was that throb in his right toe. "A whisky soda, Joe."

It was no good. He must face the fact. The old boy was right. Things had turned out awry. He was an encumbrance. What was more tiresome than the retired, bad-tempered soldier with a ruined liver? All those jokes in *Punch*. "He's not young enough to be young, poor fellow, and he's not old enough to be old." Marry or clear out. That was the ultimatum. And he couldn't marry: not with any dignity. Go while the going was still possible. Tomorrow he'd keep his promise to the Governor; go to the Jamestown Club at noon, eat humble pie; make his apology to that pompous Hun.

Tomorrow. He'd wake with his head aching, with agony in every limb, with shame in his heart. How he'd hate himself tomorrow. If only tomorrow hadn't got to come.

He leant his head back against the wall. He closed his eyes. For a moment he lost consciousness, in a mist of sleep. He was all washed up. Daphne. He would never have got like this if he had not lost her. How had he come to lose her? The war. The separation of the war. Their not having had children. She'd never have left him if they had. Why hadn't they? They had tried. She had had children all right that second time. Why couldn't he have had the luck, on that embarkation leave, that second honeymoon? She'd never have left him if there had been a child. All along the dice had been loaded against him. Why, why, why?

Once again he closed his eyes and once again a veil of sleep slid over him. From a waking dream he heard himself repeating Why. His opening eyes noticed the Archdeacon, seated at the nearest table. He'd have an answer, he supposed. And even as he said it he knew what the answer would be: "You tried to get it both ways," the priest would say. "You tried to take nature's gift which is God's gift, on your terms, not on nature's. You thought you had solved the problem of the universe with your little books. You thought you could have children when you chose. You thought you had fooled nature, but nature took its revenge on you; nature which is God. You weren't unlucky. You didn't deserve good luck. You can't hedge your bets."

That's what the holy man would say. And maybe the holy man was right. At any rate it was too late now; everything was too late now. And tomorrow morning at noon he would go into Jamestown and in a room full of colored men apologize to a German renegade. What would he have thought on the eve of that last attack at Alamein—against real Germans who were men—if he had known that one day he would be doing that. Tomorrow, in less than eighteen hours. If only tomorrow hadn't got to come. Tomorrow and all the tomorrows after it. He must be going. It was getting late.

He looked across the room toward the young girls' table. At that moment Doris raised her head. Their eyes met. Again a shiver passed along his nerves, but a shiver this time of a different quality; he had a sense of leave-taking. He lifted his hand and waved. He smiled. Did he fancy it or was there in her eyes a flicker of response? A wave of nostalgia struck him. If they'd met at a different time, at a different place; if the years by some miracle could have been telescoped. But it was too late now.

He turned aside. At that moment the Archdeacon pushed back his chair and rose. They were standing within three steps of one another. The Archdeacon had not been here when he had had the scene with Leisching. The Archdeacon smiled in his usual friendly way. This was the last time that anyone in the island would smile at him like that. Within a few hours everyone would know about the incident. They would feel embarrassed when they met him. They would avoid him or be over-friendly. This was his last chance of meeting an acquaintance on the old, on equal terms. A sense of leave-taking, of finality, urged him to make the most of it.

Affection for the Archdeacon struck him. Silly old Father Roberts, but all his faults were on the surface. He was a scholar and a gentleman. He was a good man. Carson wanted to say something to him, half in appeasement, half to placate the fates that pestered him. The chance would not come again. His head was aching, there was that throbbing in his toe and thigh. He had drunk far too much, but he had a sense of clarity, of seeing into the root of things. He knew now why things had turned against him. He knew and the Archdeacon knew. You couldn't hedge your bets, not in the things that mattered.

He needed to make his peace. He laid his hand on the Archdeacon's arm.

"You mustn't think, Father, that because I don't go to church too often I don't appreciate all you stand for, all you do. I don't know how we'd get on without you. We all feel that really, though we never say it. Don't forget that we do realize it. Good-night, Father."

His hand pressed for a moment on the Archdeacon's arm, then he turned quickly, before Father Roberts had a chance to answer. He wanted to make his exit quickly. Tomorrow. If only tomorrow had not got to come.

3

At that moment Maxwell Fleury was hurrying with angry strides toward the club. He had delayed his arrival as long as possible. He wanted to reach the club when it was crowded. He wanted to make an entrance. He did not want to stand at the bar, greeting each new group as it arrived, noting each fresh expression. He wanted to meet them all at once, to enforce his own atmosphere on theirs, to storm a fortress. When he came round the corner of the veranda there would be an immediate hushing of every conversation, every head would turn toward him, the same question would occur to everyone at the same moment, "How is he taking it?" He wanted to show them all, in a single flash, that he did not care a damn for any of them, that he was behaving as though nothing at all had happened. He was roused, belligerent; spoiling for action.

He turned into the road that ran past the police station. At the end of it he saw, in silhouette against a street lamp, a figure walking with a limp. Only one man limped like that. Carson. His temper mounted. Carson, the man who had smoked that cigarette. In the light of Bradshaw's article he understood Carson's conduct. Carson had known about that Jamaican ancestor. Carson had thought that Sylvia was fair game, the white man's *droit de seigneur*. He'd show Carson where he got off. He was in a mood for the settling of accounts. Here was one that he could settle. He waited at the corner of the dark, unlit lane that led to Carson's house.

"There's something I want to say to you," he said.

"You do. Who are you?"

"Fleury. Maxwell Fleury."

"Are you? So you are. What do you want? A subscription for the Belfontaine Committee?"

Belfontaine Committee, what was that, thought Maxwell. Then let the matter slip. "I want to talk to you alone. There's something that needs settling between us."

"Is there? I can't think what. You'd better come inside."

They walked in silence past the blank wall of the police station, turned into the blind alley at whose end stood the entrance to Carson's house. Carson was carrying a torch. He flashed it on, guiding Maxwell's steps over the uneven flagstones. The light in the hall was off. Carson closed the door behind him as he switched it on. Through the open doorway Maxwell could see the dining room table set with plates and glasses. In readiness for some girl most likely. His fists clenched against his sides.

"We'll go in here," said Carson.

He walked ahead into the sitting room. The college and regimental groups upon the walls fed Maxwell's anger. What chance did he stand against a man like Carson? In the back of his mind he still admired Carson. Carson was everything that he would like to be himself; everything that he was not, that he could not be. The extent of his admiration goaded him. Why could not Carson, who had so much, have let him alone? Why had Carson interfered with him? There was a look on Carson's face that maddened him: a look of superior indifference. How dared Carson look at him like that?

"You leave my wife alone," he snapped.

"Your wife?"

An incredulous, puzzled look came into Carson's face. What was this idiot talking about?

"Yes, my wife. You needn't think that you've fooled me. I've had my eye on you, sneaking round to the house when I'm not there, thinking yourself so clever. You weren't clever enough though, were you; making the place reek with those fancy cigarettes of yours."

"Have you gone mad?"

"Mad. I should say I hadn't. Come to my senses. That's what I've done. I've had enough of this, do you get me? Kindly stop sneaking round my house in future."

It was more than Carson was prepared to stand. He had been through too much during this last three hours. He was not prepared to be patient with this young maniac.

"Are you suggesting that I've been making passes at your wife?"

"I'm not suggesting it, I'm stating it."

"Then you can bloody well unstate it, and you can apologize to me, right now. I never heard such damned impertinence. I'm not the kind of man who chases after married women. I don't share my women."

He was so angry that he could hardly get the words out. Some dirty Polish sneak might have stolen his own wife from him. He wasn't that kind of a person. He didn't take a part share in a woman. He might buy a woman for a night: but even so he had exclusive rights in her for that one night. That he should try to seduce the wife of a man fifteen years younger than himself! He had never felt so insulted in his life.

"Get this into your dumb skull," he shouted. "I'm not the kind of man who makes passes at the wives of his acquaintances. And even if I were . . ." He paused, searching for something to say that would be really wounding, sought and found it in the memory of that morning's issue of the local paper. "If I were," he said, "I wouldn't be taking the leavings of a man like you, with a tarbrush rubbed across his face."

It was the last coal of fuel on Maxwell's mounting fury. The clenched fist against his side shot out. Carson saw the blow coming and stepped back; the blow caught him on his cheek-bone, with quarter force but he was off his balance. He staggered and the rug slipped under him; he flung out his arms in an attempt to save himself, but his hand missed the back of the armchair and he fell spreadeagled on the floor, his arms flung wide. Maxwell leapt down on him, kneeling across him, pinioning each arm beneath a knee, his hands upon his throat; he lifted Carson's head and banged it on the ground.

Choking, half stunned, Carson through dimming eyes saw glaring down at him a face distorted by hatred, from which it seemed to him every trace of white blood appeared to have been drained away leaving the negroid features.

"Tarbrush, I'll teach you. Tarbrush, I'll teach you."

The words repeated like a chant, beat through Carson's fading consciousness. The fingers were tightening at his throat. His head was again banged against the ground. He tried to raise his arms, but he was powerless under the heavy knees, he could not breathe, his chest was bursting; a mist was before his eyes. The face above his blurred. He was conscious of his head being raised again. There was a roaring in his ears, through which beat the refrain, "Tarbrush, I'll teach you. Tarbrush, I'll teach you." Then once again the hands at his throat plunged forward: his head cracked against the floor. There was a roar of cannon, like that night at Alamein; then silence.

4

"Tarbrush, I'll teach you. Tarbrush, I'll teach you."

Maxwell's fingers tightened their hold upon Carson's throat, as he beat the head rhythmically against the floor. He was in a trance, unconscious of what his fingers did, rocking as he chanted, like a drummer in an orchestra, his knees pressing on the pinioned arms.

"Tarbrush, I'll teach you. Tarbrush, I'll teach you."

Slowly he came out of his trance. His fingers felt cramped. He stretched them, and the lifeless head fell back. He stared at it. Carson's eyes were open, but they were glazed. They had lost their power. The person whom he had known as Carson was no longer there. He moved his knee, so that the right elbow joint was free. He lifted the arm; it fell back like an object. He did that, because he had read in books of people doing that. But there was no need. Carson was dead. He knew it.

He rose to his feet. His heart was thudding. A man had insulted him and he had killed him. That would show those idiots at the Country Club. They'd thought him a no account ineffective, the runt of a fine family. He chuckled. He knew what they had said about him, how could such a father have produced such a son. At this very moment they were discussing him, talking of his humiliation at the meeting, explaining it and his whole record in terms of Bradshaw's article. Bad blood will out. They'd be talking the other side of their mouths tomorrow evening. He could hear the incredulous intonation in their voices. "What, killed Carson, with his own hands, Maxwell Fleury."

He looked down at the vast stretched frame. Carson might be older than he was, but he was taller, heavier, a fighting man. No one could say he had attacked a weakling. Carson was the man he had most admired, most looked up to, most dreaded as a rival. No one could despise him for what he had done. They would all be impressed. They were laughing contemptuously about him now, but tomorrow night...

Tomorrow night. Where would he be then? The question sent the first chill shudder along his nerves. He had killed a man. This was not the kind of offense for which you deposited so much bail. This was manslaughter. It might even be called murder. Would it be called murder? He could plead self-defense. If only there were some mark upon him, some sign that Carson had tried to pull a weapon. Carson lay dead upon the floor; the back of his head battered, his throat bruised. But himself he did not bear a mark. He had struck first. His knees had pinioned Carson's arms. His face did not show a scratch. There was nothing to prove that he had been in a fight. Nothing at all. He could walk into the club and no one would make any comment; no one would say, "How did you get that black eye?" Wasn't that how murderers got so often caught, some bruise or scratch that they could not explain. He carried no such clues. In one way that might tell against him, but in another...

His thoughts were racing. He had read of this kind of incident in a dozen novels, had seen it depicted in fifty films. A scuffle and a fight; a head that in falling strikes a fender. A sudden corpse, and a man wild with terror, deciding to make a bolt for it, and always inevitably leaving behind him the one fatal clue. Reading that kind of novel, seeing that kind of film, he had thought, what a fool the man was. If he had gone to the police and told his story, he would have been believed. He would have been charged with manslaughter and would have been acquitted. But as it was, by behaving stupidly, he was in the dock on a charge of murder. If I had been in that position I'd have known what to do, he had thought. Well, here he was, in that position, and he was hesitating. He knew what he ought to do. Walk round to the police station. But suppose he didn't....

Suppose he didn't. Who would connect him with Carson's death? No one had seen him come here. They had met at the dark turning into this narrow lane. A blank wall faced that lane. The windows of Carson's house were shuttered. No one could have seen in. There was that one moment when he and Carson had stood in the lighted hall, but who could have seen them? He had left no fingerprints. He had touched nothing. He had come in by a stone-flagged pathway. He had left no footprints. There was no motive for his killing Carson. No motive that would occur to anyone. No one knew about Sylvia and Carson. When Carson's death was announced, no one would connect him with it. No one would wonder what he was doing at that hour. If Carson's body was found dead and robbed, the first thought would be, He came back and found a burglar, and the burglar went for him.

Now steady, Maxwell adjured himself, you must think this out.

Suppose that he were to walk straight round now to the club, and behave there as though nothing had happened. He would excite no comment. He had only been in Carson's place a quarter of an hour. His father would not know when he had left the house; he had been alone in the drawing room for an hour. It was unlikely that anyone at the club would remember exactly when he arrived. No clock was displayed with any prominence. It would only be remembered that he had arrived shortly after Carson had left. A post-mortem would no doubt give a rough idea when Carson had died, but there was no expert surgeon on the island. The precise moment would not be decided. There would be an hour or so to play with. A visitor might as easily have arrived before as after his return from the club. Two hours to play with. There was nothing to connect him with Carson's death. Nothing.

His former mood of exhilaration revived. Did not they always say that the hardest murders to spot were those unpremeditated sex crimes when a man leapt upon a girl whom he had never seen? When a murder was premeditated, the murderer stood to benefit from the victim's death and the police could endlessly cross-examine those who had profited. Usually in a premeditated crime, the murderer had been too clever. But in the case of a sex crime, the police had nothing to go upon.

Did not this present accident provide an exact parallel? A quarter of an hour ago he had had no conception that such a thing could happen. Because he had made no plans, thought out no alibi, he had left no clue. If he had meant to murder Carson, he would have thought it out too carefully. He would have had a story that sounded too pat. But as it was, he might very well have committed the perfect crime. Provided no one saw him coming away from the house now, he was surely safe. He knelt down and felt for Carson's wallet. It had got to look like a burglary. The wallet was in his hip pocket. It was not bulky. He looked inside; it was mostly money, he stuffed the wallet in his pocket. There was a gold watch on Carson's wrist. He took it off and put it with the money. Now, he thought.

The sooner he was out of here the better. He looked round him. Was there anything worth stealing, anything that would attract a thief. He saw nothing. Those silver cups upon the mantelpiece? A thief who had been surprised would not have bothered about those.

He walked into the dining room; there was a dramatic irony about this carefully set out appetizing meal that nobody now would eat. The sliced chicken under the glass cover looked very good. He had had no appetite at lunch. He was hungry. He felt tempted. No, he told himself, he might leave fingerprints. But wouldn't a West Indian thief have taken something? He hesitated. Better not risk it. With his handkerchief round his hand, he switched off the lights; in the sitting room, and dining room and then the hall. He did not want to show himself in silhouette in the opening doorway.

I'll walk quickly down the lane, he thought. If I see no one, then I'm safe. If I do see anyone then the game is up. I'll walk straight round to the police station and confess. I'll hand over the watch and wallet. I'll say, "I didn't trust one of you boys not to steal them." That would be a gesture. He stood in the darkened hall, his hand wrapped in his handkerchief upon the doorknob. He felt like a child playing hide and seek. Would he be able to get down that lane without being seen? One, two, three, go.

He opened the door and stepped onto the pathway. He had never been more excited in his life. He turned into the lane. At the end of it he could see the roadway. Could he get there without being seen? Sixty yards, fifty yards, twenty yards, less than a cricket pitch now. He lengthened his stride, without hastening it. He must not attract attention. He reached the dark corner where he had waited for Carson; everything depended on the next three seconds. He stepped into the road and swung toward the right. Now he was on safe ground, provided that no one had seen him come out from the lane. No one was ahead of him; was anyone behind? He looked over his shoulder. There was no one there. I'm safe, safe, safe, he told himself. He shortened his stride. No need to hurry now. He was where he had every right to be; on the road leading from his father's house to the club. It did not matter who saw him.

At the end of the road he saw the flash of a car's headlights. He stood aside to let the car pass him. He could not see who was inside. In twenty-four hours' time its occupants might be saying, "Do you know what? We went past the lane leading to the house just before seven. At that very moment Carson may have been being murdered."

Maxwell chuckled. He had got away with it. All he had to do now was to keep his head. Never had he felt greater exhilaration, greater self-confidence, greater sense of power. A man had taunted him and he had paid the price. No one would ever know, but the fact that he himself knew would make all the difference to his contacts with his acquaintances. How he would chuckle when he heard them discussing the case. How wide their guesses would go. He would feel so superior when he listened. He'd have the laugh over them all. He'd only got to keep his head. He'd only to behave as though nothing out of the ordinary had happened.

He walked through the main gates. The carpark was crowded. A big night clearly. He'd have fifty witnesses to testify in his defense. He could hear his counsel's voice. "It surely will not be believed that a man of Maxwell Fleury's type could walk into the club within five minutes of committing such a ghastly crime and calmly discuss the West Indians' chances in a test match?"

He turned onto the veranda. As he did so, he was conscious of a hush, of faces turned in his direction. It was so unexpected that he hesitated, taken off his guard. No one could know yet surely. Then he remembered. Bradshaw's article. They were all wondering how he would take it. "Behave as though nothing out of the ordinary had happened," that was the advice that his father had given him. It was precisely the same advice that he had been giving to himself. Two birds with one stone. He'd show them.

He smiled as he walked toward the bar. Bradshaw was standing there. He waved at him. Did a look of embarrassment cross his features? He thought it did. It might well have done. Bradshaw had betrayed the hospitality of the island. No family was anxious to have its antecedents examined closely. Few families would stand even a cursory examination. Look at the Kellaways. Half a dozen families must be wondering anxiously whom he would pounce on next. Probably it was that sense of guilt that had brought Bradshaw to the club this evening. He did not come very often. He had felt a need to brave it out, to see how the land lay. Just as he himself had done. Quite a few people had something on their minds tonight.

Did he fancy it, or was there a timid look on Bradshaw's face? There might well be. There should be. There'd be more than anxiety in his heart if he knew the caliber of the man with whom he had to deal, if he knew what had happened ten minutes ago in the house off the dark lane behind the Court House. A giddy sense of superiority and power flushed him as he met Bradshaw's look. He was more than a match for this pansified old journalist. An idea struck him. "Behave as though nothing had happened," his father had counseled him. But his father had been thinking in terms of the ineffectual manager of an estate, who couldn't show a profit, who'd been jeered at at the hustings. His father had never realized the kind of man his son really was. No one had. They would soon learn. He walked across to Bradshaw and held out his hand. "Congratulations."

Bradshaw started, surprised. He looked down at Maxwell's hand; hesitated, then put his own into it. It was a flabby handshake. Maxwell's was firm and vigorous.

"That's a fine series of articles. The best things I've read about the island; as for that one today, it certainly was the goods."

He paused. He was conscious of a gathering hush behind him and round him. On Bradshaw's face there was an expression of complete astonishment. There would be a similar expression on half the faces that were turning round to him, but he did not look to see. He was talking for effect, but he must not allow the others to see that he was.

"You've said things that needed saying," he went on, "that conspiracy of silence: those great-aunts that are kept out of sight over the mountains, you've brought it all into the open. You've cleared the air. We shall all be able to meet each other on more straightforward terms. From my own point of view I can't tell you how grateful I am."

"In what way, may I ask?"

"In every way. Up to now, you see—" He paused. He had meant to shrug it off, with some remark about being able to meet his acquaintances on equal terms, but a fresh idea had come to him. "Behave as though nothing out of the ordinary had happened." But his father had only said that because he had not trusted his son to carry off a difficult part skillfully. He had his cue now, he needed no prompter in the wings.

"I'll tell you how it'll help me. In fact I can give you a very good example. Aren't I right in thinking that you were at that election meeting of mine last night?"

"As a matter of fact I was."

"It was a fiasco, wasn't it?"

"It was hardly a success."

"I'll say it wasn't, and I'll tell you why it wasn't: they didn't trust me: they thought of me as a Fleury, one of the old feudal planters who had bought their ancestors in the market place. They don't want that kind of man to represent them; my standing up before them appealing to them to vote for me, gave them the opportunity they'd been wanting for three hundred years. They had been the slaves

264

of Belfontaine, but now they could reject me. As they did. You saw how they did. But it'll be different now, after your article. Now I'll be one of them."

It was only in that moment that the idea had come to him, but in this hour of illumination, his mind was moving fast and clearly.

"I'll tell you what I propose to do. They think they've scared me off. Far from it. I'll hold another meeting. This time in the daylight. I'm going to take your article as my text. I'll say to them, 'You thought because I carry the name Fleury that I'm one of the tyrants of your people; that isn't true. As this article tells you, my grandmother was of African ancestry. I am one of you. I combine the new and the old, both races, the black and white.' I shall explain to them that though the future lies with the brown race, they can only achieve their ends by working with the whites; that they should, for a while at any rate, rely upon men like myself who have a foot in both camps."

As he spoke, he visualized the scene: himself standing on the veranda of the police station where twenty-four hours back he had endured such humiliation. This time it would be different. He saw their black upturned faces. They could be swayed easily if you knew how to sway them. Crowds in the mass had neither mind nor memory. He'd get them, now that he had this card to play.

"Your article will make all the difference. Until the story had broken, I couldn't very well have got up and said, 'As a matter of fact I'm not quite as white as you imagine.' I suppose I could have, but I don't know that my father would have liked it. And as far as that goes, I doubt if I'd have had the guts myself. That's where your article has done so much good. It's brought the subject out into the open. I'm very grateful to you. I'm sure everyone in the island should be too. Though I suppose there'll be one or two of them who won't be."

He said it with a chuckle. He was conscious of a stir behind him; partially of disapproval, he suspected. They didn't like this. Well, let them dislike it. It would do them good. They'd see him in a new light anyhow. "Behave as though nothing had happened." In terms of his own dilemma, his behavior could not have been more effective. He had shown, incontrovertibly, that he had nothing on his mind except the article in the paper and the effect it would have upon his election.

"You must come out when I make my next speech," he said to Bradshaw. "It'll be in the afternoon this time. Perhaps you could have lunch with us before."

"I'd enjoy that."

"Fine. I'll ring you up. Will you have a drink? I feel I owe you one."

"Well, thank you, yes. A pony rum and soda."

"A full-size one for me."

He ordered the drinks, raised his glass to Bradshaw. "Here's luck and gratitude."

5

Maxwell had left his car outside his father's house. He had chosen to walk so as to clear his head. He returned by the same road on foot. He slowed down as he passed the dark lane behind the Court House, turning his head to the left. With what trepidation forty minutes ago he had hurried down it. His future, perhaps his very life, had depended then upon the emptiness of the road. Now it did not matter. Anyone could recognize him. Above the wall of the station, he could see the roof of Carson's house. How many people would pass here in the next twelve hours? How many people would glance toward that roof? How astonished they would feel tomorrow when they learnt that under that roof at that moment a man was lying dead.

He pictured the scene tomorrow morning. The cordon of police, the gaping crowd. It was as well he would be in the country. He could not have resisted going round. That was a temptation he must resist, the criminal's return to the scene of his crime.

He reached his father's house shortly before eight. Jocelyn was home. They were sitting, the three of them, on the veranda; they looked sad and tired. They were probably still discussing the same subject.

"It's all right," he told them. "I've fixed it. I took the bull by the horns."

With his back against the railing he described the incident. His high spirits in contrast to his parents' and Jocelyn's despondency might be a solecism. But he could not be bothered about that. There had been times enough in the past when they had been cheerful and he glum. Jocelyn would get over this. There were lots of other men. She was a nice-looking girl. There was no reason now why she should not marry a man of color: Grainger Morris possibly. Why not? What was the difference between a quarter and a six-teenth of color? She was one of them now, as he was. She would have a much wider choice.

"I told Bradshaw," he asserted, "that that article will do more good than anything that's happened in this island since emancipation. I didn't realize it at first, but I do now. It's brought the whole

266

question out into the open, but I mustn't stay here gossiping. I must get back to Belfontaine."

"Won't you have dinner first?"

He shook his head.

"No. Thanks very much. Sylvia will be waiting. I rang her from the club. She'll have something cold for me."

"When will you be back here next?"

"I've no idea. I'll have a lot to do these next few days. Possibly not before the elections. I'm going to canvass that district, you'll see how I'll canvass it!"

He waved his hand. He could not stay and talk: their gloom depressed him. He hurried toward the door; in the hall he paused. That wallet in his pocket. He needed to have a look at it. He turned into the lavatory below the stairs and took it out. A sudden memory returned to him: the smell of that cigarette, the raised seat. His clues to Carson. Here was where it had begun. Here was where it had finished; this wallet in his hand. He opened the wallet. There was a wad of five dollar notes. They were old and worn; had passed through several hands. No bank would have a record of them. He put them in his own wallet.

He looked into the other pockets; a driving license, membership card to a night club in San Juan, the photograph of a girl: no one he recognized. He put them back into the wallet. No thief would bother about those. He wiped the wallet carefully with his handkerchief, inside and out. No fingerprints. He took out the wrist watch. It was ticking cheerfully. How little had Carson thought that morning that he was winding it for the last time. Would it ever be wound again?

His heart was buoyant as he took his seat in the car. He wanted to sing. It was as though he were rid of the burden that oppressed his boyhood. He had forgotten Euan's message for Jocelyn. Should he go back and give it? Would his forgetting of it awake suspicions? He did not see how it could. The message could not matter, surely, and he was anxious to get away.

The moment he was out of Jamestown he began to sing. The road for a mile or so would be dotted with bungalows, then there would be the cane fields and the coconut plantations that divided the clustered ghuts. There was no moon, the sky was clouded. Soon he would be on a bare stretch of road. A scud of rain dashed against the windscreen. All the better. If there were any footprints on the flagstones this would wash them out. You could rely on a shower most days at this time of year. There were no headlights ahead, there were no headlights behind. He was in open country.

He slowed down the car, but did not stop it; there must be no sign of a car having stopped along this road. That was the kind of thing that gave a man away. With one hand on the wheel, he took Carson's wallet from his pocket. It was wrapped still in the handkerchief that had wiped it. Using the handkerchief as a sling, he flung it toward the cane fields. It was so dark that he could not see it in the air. Would anybody find it; most likely someone would. Would the finder hand it in to the police: possibly, but more likely not. Perhaps some peasant would be caught with it in his possession. But if he were, it could not harm him. He could prove an alibi. He would not have drawn attention to himself by spending money. If I hadn't kept the money, Maxwell told himself, I might have got some peasant into trouble. In how many detective stories had not the criminal's conscience been pricked by finding an innocent man accused of the crime he had committed. He had insured against that happening.

The watch though, was another matter. A watch would be hard to explain away. Why should anyone who had bothered to steal it throw it away. Perhaps he had made a mistake in taking it. He must get rid of it so that it would be lost irrecoverably, so that its disappearance would be a mystery, so that the police would waste time searching for it. He could take it out with him tomorrow when he swam. He had a small pocket in his bathing trunks. He could drop it well out to sea; yes, but was that safe? He would have to have it in his possession for the night.

Suppose he had a car accident and was knocked unconscious. The watch would be found on him. The betting was a million to one against that happening, but it was those million to one chances that brought men to the scaffold. And even if he concealed the watch till tomorrow, how could he be certain that the watch would not be washed ashore, brought in by a fisherman, near his house, so that the locality was defined. It was another million to one chance, but an outside chance could happen. There was that shark that had been caught in Sydney with the arm of a man undigested in its stomach; the arm was identified by a signet ring and round the wrist was the mark of a rope showing that the man had been flung bound into the harbor; a man had swung for that. You could not leave things to chance. He had to get rid of the watch at once.

He put himself in the position of a thief who had been surprised by Carson, and had in a moment of panic taken his accuser's life. Being a thief, he would, before hurrying away, have taken whatever of value he could see. What was there of value but the watch and wallet? He would take them, surely. And then surely when he began to think, he would realize that the watch was something which he must not keep. He would fling it away. It was no use hiding it. He could never use it. Fling it away. That's what the thief would do. That's what he must do. He took it out of his pocket, wiped it carefully and flung it wide. The last link with Carson gone. He breathed deeply. That was that. He was safe and free. He began to sing again. He was still singing when he drove up the drive to Belfontaine.

Sylvia was on the veranda reading. She rose to welcome him.

"Well?" she asked.

He looked at the clock. It was after half-past nine.

"You must be starving," he said.

"I'm not. I've nibbled. How about you?"

"I'm ravenous."

He was not, but he felt that he should say he was. He ought to be. He had not eaten since lunch and he had eaten little then. As they moved to the dining room, he passed his arm around her waist. How pliant and soft she was. Her hair smelt of jasmin. He faced her across the table. She was very neat and trim, with her hair firmly waved, under a smooth mask of make-up. Perhaps after all he liked her better this way; it was good at the end of a long day to return to something delicate and artificial, someone who would provide a contrast to mundane actualities. He leant forward across the table.

"It's true," he said.

"What's true?"

"About my grandmother having an African ancestor."

Sylvia made no comment.

"Doesn't it surprise you?"

"No."

"You mean you knew, all the time."

"I can't quite say; I suppose I did. I . . ."

"Does everybody know?"

"I've never heard anyone discuss it."

"How did you know then?"

"I didn't exactly know. I guessed."

"You guessed?"

"It seemed quite likely, likelier than not."

Likelier than not. So that was the explanation of her coldness, her indifference, her revulsion.

"Didn't your parents mention it when we were engaged?"

"No, no one mentioned it."

Of course not, no one would. How true Bradshaw's article had been. That conspiracy of silence.

"But you yourself, you must have thought over it."

"I didn't, really."

269

"It must have made some difference."

"No, honestly, it didn't. You see . . ." She paused, she hesitated. She wanted to put it, he felt, in a way that would not hurt him. "The point is this: people who have got colored blood, whether it's a little or a lot, fuss about it, they get self-conscious, but people like myself who know we're completely white, it's something that seems unimportant."

She said it slowly, with a smile. Was that really the way that it had been?

"While I, on the other hand, I've not only never known, it never occurred to me to wonder. But perhaps all the time I have known subconsciously. I might have overheard it from a nurse. It may have worked in the dark like a secret poison."

"It may have done."

Was this the secret of his moodiness? Had the high drama of this day been like a lancet cutting a hidden abscess? Was that why he had sung in the car driving back, why he had felt himself rid of the burden that had oppressed his boyhood? For the first time in his life he could carry his head high. Was this the explanation? At last he knew what he was and who he was. He stood square upon his own two feet. Wasn't this the miracle that psychoanalysts performed for you? They found out what was the secret reason for your problems. Then when you found out, your mind was clear. He had thought it all nonsense when he had heard it talked about. Why should a man feel any different because he learnt that his moodiness was due to his having been jealous of his nurse's flirtation with a chauffeur at the age of three? But perhaps those psychos had something after all.

All his life he had been fretted by his hatred of the colored people, he had resented having been put under a colored teacher; he had carried a chip upon his shoulder. Might not that have been due to an unconscious knowledge that he had colored blood? Now that he knew the facts he could toss that chip away, he could accept himself for what he was. That fight with Carson had been the vindication of his newly discovered self. He had found his manhood. He could look anyone in Santa Marta in the face.

"I expect that's what's been wrong with me all along. I've known but I've refused to admit to myself that I've known."

He looked at her thoughtfully across the table. They had sat here alone so often, facing each other, during their year of marriage. This was the first time that they had really talked to one another: there had always been a barrier.

"I must have been very difficult at times," he said.

"I wouldn't say that."

"I would. I must have been. I'm sorry. I'll be different now. Everything'll be different now."

He had a sense of his whole life starting again, in his new-found confidence.

"It's going to make all the difference to my candidature for the Leg. Co. That's what I told Bradshaw at the club tonight."

He recounted the conversation. She listened, interested.

"That was clever of you," she said. "You'll disarm them that way."

In her voice there was a note that he had never heard before, a note of pride. He told her about the meeting he planned to hold, of what he proposed to say. He talked quietly, uncontentiously. He had never talked to her like this, she thought. Where previously he had been arrogant, boastful, intolerant, he was confident, self-assured. If only he were like this oftener.

"It's getting late," he said. He stood beside her as she rose, he passed his arm about her shoulders.

"I'm sorry," he said. "You've had a wretched deal. It'll be better now."

There was a new tenderness in his voice. The exhilaration, the sense of power and achievement that had made him sing as he drove back was still upon him. He must make amends to Sylvia.

Later when he took her in his arms there was a new tenderness of word and touch; an exulting adoration in the hands that fondled, the lips that wandered in lingering caresses. Before he had been fierce, tyrannical, insistent, greedily gloating over her. He had revolted and disgusted her. She had felt that she was no more than a receptacle for passion. Now she had the feeling that she was a shrine: there was devotion, there was worship in his wooing. For the first time she felt a need to give; to meet, to reward his ardor. She wound her arms round his neck, let herself relax, let herself respond, meeting the rhythm of his courtship as though she were his partner, unconscious but acutely conscious, submerged yet dominant, dictating in her response the speed and tempo of his wooing with a new-found delight in her own powers. It was like music rising from one peak of harmony to another, till at last the shuddering, shattering excitement of which she had read but disbelieved in, finally convulsed her.

# CHAPTER FIFTEEN

*1*

Maxwell woke with the room filled with daylight. Sylvia was turned toward him. He raised himself upon his elbow. She had never looked lovelier than now, in profile against the pillow. He bent and kissed her. She stirred, opened her eyes, blinked, then smiled a long, slow smile of recognition and remembrance. She raised her arms, folded them round his neck, drew down his face to hers.

"Darling," she said.

At last, he thought, at last.

It was a peace, a happiness such as he had never known, then suddenly, shatteringly, he remembered. That body in the room behind the Court House. At this very moment Carson's servant would be letting himself into the back room, to light the stove, to prepare the morning tea. At this very moment the alarm was being given; policemen would soon be in the house, searching here, searching there, finding heaven knew what. How did he know that he had left no clue?

Panic struck him, with a sense of the dramatic irony of his position. Here he was, in this soft warm bed with his wife's arms round him, secure and loved and cherished, for the first time at peace, at the very moment when the structure of that happiness was threatened. His arms tightened about Sylvia's shoulders, desperately, as though she were an amulet. "You're everything I've got. Everything I care about in the world."

Once again she felt herself relax, respond to these new accents in his voice, to this new tenderness of tone and touch. There was a tap upon the door. The maid with the morning tea. She drew back with a laugh. "Too bad," she said.

She chattered happily as they sat up side by side, sipping at their tea. Usually she sat in silence: "I'm never alive till breakfast time," she'd say: he'd hurry out to his early chores as quickly as he could. But today she was awake, bright-eyed, talkative, wanting to know who had been at the club and who'd said what. It was part of the dramatic irony of the situation that she would want to talk on this one morning when he had to be alone, to think. But he must not show her that. He mustn't behave as though he was worried. In a month, a week, perhaps a few hours' time, she might be forced to take stock of his behavior during the day ahead. He could hear counsel for the prosecution saying, "Now think back carefully, Mrs. Fleury. Wasn't there anything in your husband's behavior that night and on the following day that seemed unusual?"

Sylvia would of course deny it, but she had to deny convincingly. The jury must have no doubt that she was telling them the truth. He must behave as though nothing out of the ordinary had happened, nothing except this miracle of self-discovery, of self-revelation.

"How I wish I were a gentleman of leisure; that I could idle here. Confound these planter's chores," he said.

Those chores began with the half-past seven roll call at the *boucan*. In the shade of a ruined aqueduct, he watched his laborers file past as the overseer called their names. There were over thirty of them, the men with their cutlasses, the women with their baskets: the men in their blue jeans, the women with their bright blouses and their heads tied round with yellow and red handkerchiefs. For each one he had a word of greeting. Among them he presumed were the men who had fired his cane, cut his telephone wire, put his car out of action. How little that mattered now. Was he standing here for the last time, was the evidence already mounting against him, down there in Jamestown? A girl whom he had known as a child went past. He remembered her as an untidy urchin making mud pies in the road. She was now on the verge of womanhood, rounded and slim, with a straight proud carriage. She was a handsome creature.

"What a big girl you're getting Julie."

"I make sixteen next month, sir."

"All that and not a husband yet?"

She gave a cackling laugh and turned her head away. They were gay, inconsequent, all right. In the light of yesterday's knowledge of himself, he felt a kinship with them. If only he had had this knowledge earlier. Had it come too late? What was happening in Jamestown?

As he rode round the estate, he recreated the scene with Carson. It had lasted a bare seven minutes. Surely he could have forgotten nothing. What clue could he have left behind? If he had made a mistake he would know about it in the course of that day, surely. If he had left anything behind, the article could be identified quickly. The scope was limited, here in this small community. If he had made a mistake this was the last time, for how many months, perhaps forever, that he would ride round his estate, that he would watch the men snipping off the cocoa pods with their long knives, the women

273

piercing them with a stroke of their pointed cutlasses and dropping them off into their baskets. They worked in pairs, husband and wife. He watched a couple squatting down beside their basket, the man cutting open the pods and the woman shelling them. A mood of envy touched him. It would be good to share one's work with a woman in that way, as those faraway ancestors of his had done. A partnership, two people become one person.

What was happening in Jamestown? It was after eight. The news must be out by now. Everyone must be discussing it. How soon would the news reach Belfontaine? How would he hear it? He had got to be careful about this. He must show the right kind of surprise, the right kind of concern; but he must not overdo it. He must be inquisitive, but he must not ask too many questions. He must ask the right questions. He had read enough detective stories to be on his guard on that account. How often had he not read of a detective swinging round upon a suspect with the question "How did you know that?"

How would the news come to him? It wouldn't, it couldn't be in that morning's paper. Tomorrow's paper would not reach him until lunch time. But the news would be in the village before then. Three or four buses passed every day; the first one had already been by: had it brought the news and if it had, how would it get to him. Who would tell Sylvia? She did not gossip with her maids. They were much likelier to learn from someone motoring past who paused for a gossip and a punch. He would have to be on his guard. The conversation might run on for ten, fifteen minutes before Carson's name came up. When would that car drive past? All day he would be on edge, awaiting it. Sometimes two or three friends would look in in a single day. But sometimes three or four days would pass without a car stopping at their door. The whole village might know about Carson, while he and Sylvia remained in ignorance. What a day it would be. Would his nerves stand the strain?

He paused at the sheds where the cocoa pods were being trodden in large circular cauldrons by laughing, sweating laborers with their trousers rolled above their knees. He examined the shallow trays where the pods were laid out to dry. It was a good cocoa crop. It should set the estate in the black. One of his overseers came across to him. A piece of ground where water had been lying stagnant had been drained. Would he care to see it?

"You've been quick about that," he said.

He had given the order only yesterday. When he had given it, Carson had been still alive. If only he could turn back the clock to

274

yesterday. If only none of this had ever happened. A whole new life might have begun for him. He had found the truth about himself, found too the way to Sylvia's heart. Oh, to erase those seven minutes. If only he had driven to the club instead of walking there. On how casual a hinge the door of one's fortunes swung. You spent your whole life working to a certain point, to achieve a certain object, and then you walked instead of drove the half mile from your father's house; the first time in a year that you had done so, because you said you wanted to clear your head, and the whole structure of your life was threatened.

Threatened but not destroyed, he told himself. He had only to keep his head. Thank heaven, he was here and not in Jamestown, where the news would have been sprung on him without warning: where he would be listening to talk of it at every moment of the day; it would have been so easy for him there to have given himself away. He was much safer here.

It was half-past ten when he returned to the bungalow. The news must have reached the village. He would let Sylvia break the news to him. She was lying in a long chair on the veranda. A book lay on the table, her knitting by it. There was not a single cigarette stub in the ashtray. She raised her eyes to him and smiled.

"No book, no knitting, no cigarette?"

She shook her head. "I was feeling idle."

There was a brooding, tranquil expression on her face. For the first time since her marriage, she seemed completely happy. At last he had made her happy. And because she was happy, she could make him happy. A new life was starting. If only this cloud could lift.

"No one been by?"

"No one that I've noticed. I've sat here brooding."

Brooding. And all the time cars had passed along the road, the bus from Jamestown had brought out its gossip. Everyone in the village knew, while he, the one person who needed to know, did not.

What was happening in Jamestown? The temptation to drive in was acute, but he must resist it. He knew that. It would be the worst thing for him to do. There was no excuse for him to go. And today was Friday: pay day. His absence would cause comment. The telephone. Wasn't there someone whom he could call, someone who in the course of a talk about something else would interrupt with a "I suppose you've heard the news?"

Whom could he call? His home: he shook his head. His father would be out. What had he to say to Jocelyn? His mother would not understand. He never rang her up to gossip. No one did in Santa Marta, with such an appalling exchange and everyone in the country

275

on a party line. Who was there he could call? The office? It would surprise his father. That was the one thing that he must not do. He thought back over yesterday: the evening at the club. Whom had he talked to? Bradshaw? Wasn't that the answer? He had promised to ask Bradshaw out to hear his election speech. He could ring up to confirm the date for it.

"I'll be back in a minute," he told Sylvia. "I've got to telephone."

As always there was a long delay. He fidgeted beside the box. What a backward place this was. At last an answer came. A very West Indian voice, one of the hotel servants almost certainly. He had to repeat Bradshaw's name twice and his own three times. "O.K. sir, I go look."

There was another long delay. These people were infuriatingly inefficient. No wonder it was so hard to get a number. Every call took three times the time it should. Numbers were invariably engaged. At last Bradshaw's voice, fluted, high-pitched, came over. "Yes, yes?"

"It's about my new election speech. We talked about it last night if you remember?"

"Indeed, I do."

"I'd very much like to give it when you could come. Tomorrow's Saturday. That's really the best day. Would that suit you, in the afternoon?"

"It would suit me very well."

"Lunch then at half-past twelve."

"I'll be there."

Maxwell pictured Bradshaw at the other end of the line, in the coffee room at the Continental. Ten yards away from him on the porch would be a group discussing the morning's news. If only he could hear what they were saying. If only the wire of the telephone could be stretched ten yards. There was a half-second's pause. Bradshaw was going to ring off. Panic seized Maxwell. He must keep Bradshaw on the line, must keep him talking long enough for Bradshaw to tell him about Carson, so that he would have the information, would be in a position to go down to the post office and say, "What is this about Colonel Carson?" He must keep Bradshaw talking.

"If you could get out by twelve . . ."

A clink came in his ear, a buzz, silence, then a confusion of voices. He'd been cut off. This infernal exchange, this maddening party line. He shook the receiver, swung the handle, then thought better of it. He would only wake suspicion. He had said all he had to say.

276

He hung the receiver back. It was no good. He would have to wait till the news reached him in the normal course of events. Surely soon, someone would drive along the road.

At the other end of the line Bradshaw shook the receiver, held it to his ear, listened to a buzz of voices. This telephone, he thought, and hung it back. He rejoined the group upon the porch and picked up the thread of talk where he had left it.

"Is there no doubt at all about its being murder?" he inquired.

"There's not the slightest. The marks at the throat, then all those bruises on the back of his head. He must have had his head banged a dozen times. I've just seen Whittingham."

"Who could it have been."

"It might have been anyone."

"What does Whittingham think?"

"He was noncommittal."

"Were there any clues?"

"He wouldn't have told me if there were."

"Who could it have been?"

There were half a dozen of them. Each had his own theory, but they were all agreed that the chances were a hundred to one on its having been some casual thief, who had been surprised and got into a fight with Carson. The chances were high against finding such a person. "Unless he does something silly," Bradshaw said. "Wears something that he's stolen, or starts spending money that he can't account for."

"He might very well do that. You know what these fellows are. They can't resist showing off."

"And they're so dumb too. If they aren't caught within three weeks, they think they're safe."

Norman was one of the group. He was worried about the repercussions that this would have outside the island. He had taken Bradshaw's advice and had started to publicize Santa Marta as a summer resort. He had had a poster printed. He had issued a folder to the tourist agencies. He had invited a party of American journalists, friends of Bradshaw's, to come down for a week as guests.

"It'll all be wasted if the idea gets around that this is a place where visitors get killed and robbed."

He looked thoughtfully at Bradshaw.

"I suppose it's no good asking you not to mention it in your articles."

"What a thing to ask a journalist."

"I know, I know. But all the same can't you play it down . . ."

277

"You needn't be afraid. The way I write it up is more likely to bring tourists down here than to scare them off."

An idea for a highly dramatic article had come to him. He remembered Carson's story about the Obeah man: it might be the Obeah man's revenge? Americans were interested in Obeah. Carson's Obeah story was a good piece of copy. He had kept it up his sleeve. That had been wise. He'd go out to Carson's place this afternoon and make inquiries. He would get the background of the Obeah man.

2

At Government House Templeton was discussing the funeral with his Chief of Police and Dr. Leisching, who had performed the post-mortem. Leisching stated that Carson had been killed early on the previous evening. He was insisting that the corpse be buried that day.

"The regulations say that in the tropics a body must be interred within twenty-four hours."

The Governor was anxious to have the funeral postponed. Carson must be buried with full military honors. The notables must be warned. It was very short notice.

"The climate here might surely be described as subtropical. More like Cannes than Cairo. It's not the hot season. Wouldn't it be possible to delay it till tomorrow morning?"

Leisching shook his head.

"The regulations, sir, define the tropics as the area between Capricorn and Cancer."

"Don't you think you might make an exception in this case. It's only half a day. Do you genuinely consider that there would be any danger?"

"That is not for me to decide, sir. The regulations definitely state twenty-four hours in the tropics."

Templeton controlled a twinge of irritation. This everlasting Teutonic reverence for regulations. But he could scarcely criticize a member of his staff for too strict a regard for them.

"Very well then, doctor, we'll have the funeral this afternoon."

As the doctor left the room, he exchanged a glance with Whittingham.

"He seems in a confounded hurry to get this fellow underground."

"That's what I thought, sir."

"I've never seen these regulations that he talks about, but I take it he's right."

"I haven't seen them either. They are probably in some medical handbook, but there is a general agreement in the islands that burials should take place within twenty-four hours. We tell the peasants that, and if we keep the rules ourselves, it's a good example."

"And Leisching has no doubt that he was killed last night."

"Leisching may not be an expert, sir, but there is a great deal of evidence to support that time. According to Leisching Carson had had no food for several hours. The supper on his table was untouched. Carson had had a great deal to drink, but there was no glass in the room. The whisky decanter was full. I wasn't in the club myself last night. I don't know exactly when he left, but from what Leisching tells me it was before seven and after half-past six. I'll check up and see if he went anywhere after the club—the St. James or the Continental. But if he had had a great deal to drink before he left, he was likely to have gone straight home."

"Would you say so? I've found that home is usually the last place a man goes to when he is in that condition. A soldier certainly goes somewhere else, as long as he is capable of movement."

"That's very true, sir."

"He may not have gone to the hotels or to the St. James but a man like Carson might have his special hideouts. Was there a woman anywhere?"

"Not that I know of, sir. I'm making inquiries."

"That might be the answer, mightn't it?"

"It might, sir, very well."

"Was he a friend of yours?"

The policeman hesitated. "We were on friendly terms, sir. Shall I put it that way?"

"I suppose that's how everyone else would put it, isn't it?"

"I rather think so."

"It's very sad, you know, when one thinks of what his life must have been fifteen years ago, with a wife, in a regiment, part of a community. I was inquisitive about him. I made inquiries. Everyone spoke very highly of him. And now he dies out here, like this. And there's not a single person in England to whom we have to send a cable. There isn't, is there?"

"Not that I can find, sir. I suppose we should send a notice to the *Times*."

"Yes, we should do that. Archer, that's your pigeon."

"Yes, sir."

"And he left the club some time before seven, you say. He left here at half-past five. He was walking back. It's curious but you know I felt worried on his account when I watched him go. He was

279

limping. That wound of his, I supposed. But it may have been whisky. Yet he made the club. How did he behave there?"

"Well, sir, from what I've heard . . ."

The policeman again hesitated.

"Was there a scene with Leisching?"

"A kind of a scene, from what they tell me."

"But Leisching stayed behind in the club?"

"Oh yes. I've checked on that. He and his wife dined with the Normans; they were together the whole evening."

"But if Carson didn't go straight home?"

"That's something I must check on."

"I mustn't interfere. But you know what an old soldier is; he likes to meddle. And we are accepting Leisching's time from his own post-mortem. But I must leave that to you. I know you'll see the point. You'll keep me informed won't you. In the meantime this funeral. Shall we say four? You'll arrange the parade, Whittingham. Let me know the details later. About the announcing of it, Archer, I'll leave that to you; I'll ring up the Archdeacon personally. I'd suggest that you send notices round to all the hotels, to the three clubs; then you'd better ring up the local notables; the members of the Leg. Co. for example; as many as you have time for anyhow. Send me in one of those typists. I want to dictate a draft."

Archer and Whittingham went out.

Templeton and his son were left alone. "This is pretty tough for you, Dad."

"All in the day's work."

The Governor was not displeased at his son having an opportunity of seeing how he coped with a situation; but it could not have happened at a more inconvenient time. When he had read Bradshaw's article he had welcomed the opportunity it would provide Euan and himself getting to undetstand each other. So far they had been on surface terms with one another. They would have to have a real talk now. But last night their guests had stayed on late. They had both been tired after the journey from B.G. They had barely skirted the subject. They had postponed a full discussion of it till after breakfast. Now this business had arisen. It had been like this all his life. He had never had a chance of being a good father. He had always been under the pressure of official duty. When Euan's mother had died, and Euan had really needed him, he had been chained to the Middle East. He had to say something now, but he had only time to brush the subject.

"Have you talked to Jocelyn yet?" he asked.

"I'd meant to take her for a swim this morning, but it might be better to postpone it."

"I think it would. We'll all feel a little different once the funeral's over."

There was a tap on the door. It was his secretary with her writing pad.

"Right, Dad. I'll get on with that. See you at lunch."

Euan crossed over to the office buildings. His father would be wanting the G.H. private line. He found the A.D.C. dictating to the new and rather pretty typist.

"Do you mind if I telephone from here. My old man's using ours."

"You can use the one in my own office."

He had some difficulty in getting through. Everyone in the island must be trying to telephone this morning. At last he heard Jocelyn's voice. It had a tired sound.

"About our date," he said.

"What date?"

"To swim this morning."

"Did we make a date?"

"I left a message with Maxwell."

"I never got it."

"Never got it?"

"No."

"What must you have thought?"

"Thought about what?"

"My not ringing you up the moment I got back."

"I supposed you were busy about something."

Her voice was listless. He was filled with guilt; that yesterday of all days, he had failed to get in touch with her at once. How could he have been so careless as to rely on a brother delivering a message? What can she have thought? But there was no point in going into all that now. He could smooth that later. He'd best be flippant about it all.

"You'd better warn that brother of yours to keep out of my way for a little time," he said. "But actually I was ringing up to suggest that we postpone our date."

"Yes?"

"You've heard I suppose about Colonel Carson. The funeral service is this afternoon at four. The old man's going. He'll expect me to go with him. Perhaps you'll be coming too?"

"I suppose I shall. I didn't know about it."

281

"It's only just been decided. I was going to have called your father later."

"You needn't bother. He'll be in to lunch. I'll tell him."

"In view of all this, don't you think it would be better if we met after the service, rather than this morning."

"I dare say it would."

"I could meet you outside the church and we could take a drive."

"We'll be in formal clothes."

"I'll put my bathing things in the car. We could collect your things on the way."

"All right."

"And you'll tell your father?"

"I'll tell him."

"Till this afternoon then."

"Till this afternoon."

The receiver at her end clicked back. We might have been strangers, he told himself. But perhaps it was only because they were so very close that they could talk as strangers did.

He returned to the office. Archer was still dictating.

"It's all yours now."

"It had better be. I've got a lot to do."

Archer looked at Margot in mock despair as the door closed behind Euan Templeton.

"This ruins our chance of a siesta in the chalet."

"I'm afraid it does."

"Do you know that'll make three whole days."

"That's what I was thinking."

"It's much too long."

"Two days too long."

"I don't know how I could exist without you."

"Why try?"

There was an air of authority in her voice that he found attractive. Now and again he felt that he was being managed. He rather liked the feeling.

"You'd better start that telephoning while I type out the notices for the hotels and clubs," she told him.

Jocelyn put the receiver back and walked into the drawing room. Her mother was reading a novel.

"Colonel Carson's funeral is at four. That was G.H. ringing up. We'll be going won't we?"

"Of course."

"We can tell Daddy at lunch."

"He'll probably hear about it at the club."

"What about letting Maxwell know?"

"Would he want to come? Was Colonel Carson at all a friend of his?"

"If we don't warn him he will feel aggrieved."

"I'd forgotten."

Maxwell was so touchy. Why should he be? Poor little boy indeed. "I'll ring him up," she said.

She went back to the telephone. She had to wait several minutes before she got an answer from the exchange.

"I'll do my best but everyone's ringing up this morning," the operator said.

"You'll do your best."

"I sure will, Miss Jocelyn. I'll call you back."

Ten minutes passed, quarter of an hour, half an hour.

"I'll try again," Jocelyn told her mother. But there was the same delay, then the operator's apologetic "I do my best, Miss Jocelyn. Every line's engaged. I try three times. Everyone telephones this morning."

"Don't bother then. It's not all that important."

"It's no good," Jocelyn told her mother. "Everyone's ringing everyone this morning."

"They would be."

"We can tell Maxwell that we've tried."

That was all that mattered. Maxwell hadn't been a particular friend of Colonel Carson's. It was a long drive in. What should she wear that afternoon? Would that dark blue look dark enough?

Thirty miles away at Belfontaine, Maxwell fidgeted on the veranda. If only something would happen soon. The delay was maddening. If only the telephone would ring, a car swing round out of the road. Sylvia was sitting in a brooding silence, that tranquil smile upon her lips. He felt foiled and cheated. Today should have been the happiest of his life. She turned her head, her eyes met his and the smile deepened. If only he could put back the clock to yesterday.

"Would you like a punch?" she asked.

"I'd love one."

Anything to calm his nerves. He strode impatiently back and forth while she mixed the drink. If only something would happen. This waiting, waiting, waiting. Unless something happened soon, he'd be driven to do something. And that was the one thing he mustn't do. He must behave as though nothing out of the ordinary had happened.

# CHAPTER SIXTEEN

## 1

The Fleurys were among the first inside the church. That was Jocelyn's doing. She did not want to have to meet people on the way in. Colonel Carson's death had no doubt driven out of everybody's mind the article in the paper yesterday. But the moment they saw her, they would be reminded of it: they would feel awkward and embararassed. She couldn't bear that, yet, not today anyhow: not till she had seen Euan.

There were only a dozen people in the church when she arrived, but outside a crowd had gathered. They would stand there, waiting, watching the white folk and the notables arrive; then at the last moment, after the Governor's arrival, they would swarm into the back pews and into the gallery and if there was not room they would perch themselves in the window sills.

The Fleurys' family pew was in the front, immediately behind the Governor's. Euan would be in sight of her all the time. What was he feeling, what was he thinking? It was worse for him than it was for her. What would he say to her, how would he put it? She must make it easy for him. She owed him that.

The coffin under its purple cloth was a bare four yards from her. It was strange to think that inside that wooden casket lay a man who twenty-four hours ago had been walking, laughing, drinking. How little Carson had suspected this time yesterday that within twenty-four hours' time he would be lying in a coffin, high-piled with flowers, guarded by six uniformed policemen with their arms reversed. What had he been looking forward to, what had he been worrying over? How quickly those dreams, those fears, those causes of resentment had been dissolved. Euan would soon get over it.

From the windows in the vestry the Archdeacon watched the congregation arrive. He had rarely seen so many people in his church. The island was predominantly Roman Catholic. Everyone in Jamestown seemed to be here today. He noticed David Boyeur, very correctly dressed in black shoes, a dark blue suit and a black tie. His face wore an appropriate expression. He saw the Normans, the Kellaways, the Leischings, the Morrises. He looked at his watch;

284

twenty to four. They were coming thickly now; another few minutes and there would be only stragglers. Then the G.H. party would arrive.

He glanced toward the choir. The trebles were whispering excitedly. He was himself a little nervous, as a colonel would be before a general's inspection. Nothing should go wrong but he was afraid something might. He wished it could be a more impressive service; that the funeral could have taken place in the morning with a requiem mass and a long ornate ritual. That was what the islanders enjoyed. He was doing the best possible in the circumstances. He had arranged for several hymns and for two psalms, the ninetieth and thirty-ninth. It would be a thirty minutes service, but he wished it could have been postponed. Ah, here was the Governor.

The car with the Union Jack flying from its bonnet swung round the corner. The A.D.C. stood by the door. His Excellency followed in his full dress uniform, with his four rows of ribbons. Euan followed in a dark suit.

"We'll give them three minutes," he told his chaplain.

The music of the organ swelled and eddied. He watched the chaplain line up the choir. They looked very smart in their dark purple surplices and wide white collars, the candles held high before their faces. The voluntary ended. "Now," he said. As the first file of choristers turned into the nave, the music swelled from the organ. The voices of the choir were raised in the Dies Irae. In that moment he was concerned only with the drill of it. As he himself came into the nave, the incense was swung high. Its thick, heavily sweet fumes were fragrant in the air. The sunlight gilded its thin smoke.

> When the Judge his seat attaineth
> And each hidden deed arraigneth
> Nothing unavenged remaineth . . .

The music ceased. He stood beside the coffin. His voice rang through the church.

"We brought nothing into this world and it is certain that we can carry nothing out."

Doris Kellaway bent her head low above her hands. All that day she had been in a trance; haunted by Carson's last look as he left the club. What had he been saying in that look? She had never seen such an expression in a man's face. Only a moment before she had been laughing with Mavis and the others at the ridiculous exhibition he had made; the fulsome compliments and then the broken glass:

285

how they had laughed at him. Mavis had been mocking her about her conquest: then she had raised her eyes and she had seen him standing by the Archdeacon, about to leave, their eyes had met and there had been a startling eloquence in his look. What was he trying to say? To ask her forgiveness, to explain that it had not been mere alcoholic gallantry, that he had genuinely seen her with new eyes that evening? "I'll explain next time we meet." That was what he had seemed to be saying; and then he had turned away, had gone to meet—who knew what he had met, how, why, under what conditions. Perhaps she was the last thing he thought of. She laid her forehead against her hands. She'd never forget him, never, never. . . .

"A thousand years in thy sight are but as yesterday."

"Are but as yesterday." David Boyeur rolled the phrase round his tongue. A noble phrase. As a Catholic, he only on special occasions attended an Anglican service. He wished his own services were in English, in this proud, rich language.

From halfway up the church he looked through latticed fingers to the left, to the right, then straight ahead. He did not move his head, only his eyes: no one should say that his attention had been wandering. Grainger's sister Muriel was two rows in front of him at an angle of sixty degrees. He could see the curve of her cheek and tip of her nose in profile. He had noticed her lately at the Aquatic. She swam well and had a pretty figure. She must be eighteen now. Had she a serious beau? She did not seem to have. She was always in a group of girls. He had talked to her once or twice. She had seemed friendly, ready to be more friendly. Why didn't he cultivate her? It was time he married. "Marry fair," that's what his mother had always told him: if your children were whiter than yourself, people thought of you as going up the ladder.

Margot Seaton was sitting in the front, with the G.H. staff. She was wearing a white hat trimmed with black. It was set at an angle over her eye. What style she had. He felt nostalgic. He often missed her. It was better though the way it was. She wasn't the wife he needed, too much the girl friend. He needed a solid marriage, something that would establish him; somebody with money for preference. The Morrises had money. He wasn't in their class, but he had a future. The elder sister had not married. It was not too easy for that kind of girl to get the kind of husband that she wanted. Their own class wanted to marry someone with a "better skin." Muriel would have the example of her sister as a warning. She'd be afraid of spinsterhood. She might jump at the first proposal; best get her young before she recognized her attractions. He'd speak to her coming out.

> Now the laborer's task is o'er
> Now the battle day is past.

Another hymn. The congregation was on its feet. Colonel Whittingham, his eyes upon his policemen, noted their immobility with approval. They were good at this kind of thing, took a pride in their own performance. Everything was going well. What a day it had been. Since that hysterical servant had brought the news into the police station just as dawn was breaking. What luck that he had been there himself. He was not there as early as that once in a month; he had gone there to make a check-up, to ensure that his men were on the mark. By that lucky chance he had been there first. He had not had the clues interfered with by his well-meaning but muddled subordinates.

There was a shuffle of feet behind him. The congregation was seated. The lesson was being read. The Archdeacon's voice was full and slow and rich.

"The last enemy that shall be destroyed is death."

Archer at the Governor's side, following his own thoughts, had his attention caught. So that's where Richard Hilary had got his title. When had he seen Carson last? He could not remember. De Quincy had said something about never doing a thing consciously for the last time without sadness of heart, but how often did you know that it was the last time? He remembered a poem called "Close of Play" about a casual cricket match in August 1914, written by somebody called Kenneth Ashley of whom he knew nothing except that one poem. He had memorized the opening lines.

> I wonder if Life is kind or callous,
> When it fails to warn us of final things,
> When we make an end, and no revelation
> Informs the heart with forebodings.

How little had he himself guessed that last night at Oxford that he was seeing Ruth for the last time. How could he have guessed that fate would intervene within thirty hours, with so much unsaid. If only he had known.

From the pew behind he caught a whiff of mignonette. Was that how it would end with Margot, suddenly, out of a clear sky; a plane to be caught. The thought tore at his heart. Life without Margot. Mentally he turned his head away. He must waste no moment. Never run the risk of being forced afterwards to think

287

he had been casual. "Look thy last on all things lovely." Live in the moment fully. "This day as if thy last," encompass eternity each fleeting moment.

> No more the foe can harm
> No more of leaguered camp
> And cry of night alarm
> And need of ready lamp.

The Governor had chosen that hymn personally. He had heard it for the first time at Sandhurst at the funeral of a cadet in his own company. He had heard it many times since by many graves, in France, in India, in the Western Desert. It was a soldier's hymn. Carson might well have chosen it himself. Only twenty-four hours earlier he had been preparing himself for his talk with Carson. As he had planned his argument, he had found himself thinking of Carson as a war casualty. Carson's life had been ruined by the war; his real life had ended in the war. The war had left him without the health and energy and faith to make a real thing of his life. When he had seen during the thirties what had happened to some of his brother officers who had survived the Somme and Passchendaele, he had envied on their account those who lay in Flanders beneath white crosses. Carson must have sometimes wished that the shell which wounded him at Alamein had pitched a yard further to the right.

Carson had been spared a lot. He began to phrase the report that he would send to Whitehall tomorrow.

> What matters now grief's darkest day
> The King has wiped those tears away?

In a semitrance Mavis listened to the words. Twenty-four hours ago she and Doris had been laughing over the Colonel's discomfiture and now he lay in that coffin, motionless, beyond ridicule and censure. How near to one's elbow death always stood; one did not know the day or hour.

Grainger Morris was two pews in front of her. What must be think of her? How much did he know about her? Something certainly. Everyone knew about everyone in a place like this. Grainger had thought about her while he was in England. He remembered her as a child. It must have been a shock to him to discover into what manner of adult that child had grown. She'd changed since he'd arrived, but how could he know that? She must prove to him that she had changed. That coffin so close to them was a sign, a symbol, a warning. I will be different, she vowed, I will, I will.

288

"Man walketh in a vain shadow and disquieteth himself in vain: he heapeth up riches and cannot tell who shall gather them."

The Archdeacon, too, was remembering that last evening at the club. He had arrived as Carson was making himself ridiculous. He had not known what was happening. He had learnt the details later. What had transpired in Carson's mind during those two minutes to make him pause beside him, to look at him in that way, say what he had said?

He had often heard it said that soldiers in wartime knew when they were starting on their last attack. Did God send a warning before sudden death, a summons to make one's peace with him? Was that what that last gesture of Carson's had meant, an equivalent of the Catholic's need for extreme unction?

Death, he had seen it so often, in so many guises. He had prayed by so many deathbeds, delivered so many funeral addresses: the words had become automatic. It was like putting a record on a gramophone. What did he really believe, in his heart of hearts? When he assured the bereaved that they would meet their loved ones in heaven, did he actually believe in such a place? Once he had, he must have, or he could not have presented himself for ordination; he had surely believed then in a savior who took the sins of the world upon him; who made there by his one oblation of himself once offered, a full, perfect, and sufficient sacrifice. He had believed that then: one believed in so much in youth; but how far had that faith survived the wear and tear of a long ministry, with all its parochial problems, its weighing of the politics of this and that, the conflict of personalities, the stage-management of a career.

There were moments when he did not dare to put himself in the confessional. Was he any more than a gramophone, repeating the same recordings? What did he believe, what was it possible to believe in face of the mounting tide of unbelief? Might not the Leninists be right; might not religion be no more than the opium of the working classes; an opium they had learnt to do without or rather that they had displaced with another opiate, the beneficence of the Welfare State?

He doubted sometimes. Then as a reminder, there came a moment such as this: that worldly, sensual man standing on the brink of a death, violent, unforeseen, unforeseeable, impelled in the last hour of his life to make his peace with God. What could this be but a sign of grace, of mercy, a proof that God existed?

"Lord, now lettest Thou Thy servant depart in peace."

The long service was at an end; the procession started, the troops leading the way, their arms reversed; the band playing the Dead March in Saul, the Archdeacon and the two chaplains following; then the coffin borne on the shoulders of the six policemen.

The Governor led the procession as chief mourner; it was a long, straggling silent group; they had only a hundred yards to walk, then the files broke and divided, forming up in a circle round the grave. The sun was low now in the sky and the trade wind was blowing gustily. The cemetery was on a slope and the choir stood above the grave, the dark purple of their surplices billowing in the wind in rich and somber contrast to the bright green background of the cane fields. The Archdeacon waited while the shuffling of the crowd was silenced, then he raised his voice.

"In the midst of life we are in death, to whom may we turn for succor...."

I wonder what everyone's thinking, Archer thought, how I'd like to be inside their minds. Is Carson's death the shock to them that it's supposed to be. Are they frightened: thinking how near death may be to them; how any moment a car may skid, a plane spin into a nosedive, a wave overturn a canoe. Or are they following their own thoughts; just as I am doing. Or are they thinking of three things simultaneously: Carson and death and what they are going to do tomorrow? That's what we all do, don't we: think of three things simultaneously.

"Thou knowest, oh Lord, the secrets of our hearts..."

Jocelyn smiled wryly. The secrets of her heart. She felt cheated, robbed. Everything had been spoilt by that talk of marriage. What should have been an exquisite idyll that would have colored and warmed her memories had been dirtied and made dingy, becoming something that she wanted to forget. Why had Euan been so insistent about marriage? Why couldn't they have been left alone. She thought of all the discussions and arguments that she would have to live through during the next weeks. Every time she left a room she would feel that when the door closed behind her people would start discussing her. If only she could go away for a few weeks, till it had all blown over. That was the worst of living on an island. You never could get away.

The grains of earth rattled on the coffin. The bugle sounded. The rifles volleyed their final tribute. Jocelyn turned away. It was over: or at least that was over. Now her battle began.

Euan was waiting for her at the gate leading from the cemetery. "I've parked the car in the club," he said.

It was only a couple of hundred yards away.

"Let's go to that beach where we went the first afternoon."

She was grateful to him for suggesting that. Let it end where it had begun.

"We'll get there as the sun sinks," she said.

"Perhaps I'll see the green ray at last."

"So you haven't seen it yet."

"Not yet. Whenever there's a chance of seeing it, I blink at the last moment."

"Like that night at Belfontaine."

"Like that."

He had brought the small Austin. It was a cozy car with a bucket seat in front. Would she ever drive in it again? She supposed she would. The thing would taper off. There'd still be picnics, dances, parties. The sooner she got out of Santa Marta the better. Why couldn't her parents revert to the original plan and go back in May?

"This business of Colonel Carson must be worrying your father a good deal," she said.

"He takes things in his stride."

It was lucky that they had this to talk about: something dramatic, of interest to them both; so that they hadn't to make conversation. "What do you feel about it yourself?" she asked.

"About Carson?"

"No, about the effect that it'll have outside the island. It'll be reported in all the papers."

"I imagine so, with Bradshaw here."

They laughed together, with a certain ruefulness. The same thing was in both their minds. It was cozy that they were able to make a joke of this. They really were in tune, talking the same language. It should not be too difficult when the showdown came.

"I suppose he's afraid that tourists will be scared away," he said.

"If you were an American going on a holiday, wouldn't you think twice about going to an island where a white man had been murdered?"

"I suppose I should."

"Have you heard of a similar incident happening in any other island?"

"Not since the days of the slave revolts."

"That's just my point. What's the general idea at Government House about how it happened?"

"That it was a thief, surprised by Carson's coming back sooner than was expected."

"That makes it worse from the tourist's point of view. If it had

291

been a *crime passionel* it would have been quite a different matter."

"And it couldn't have been that, could it?"

"I don't see how it could."

The talk flowed smoothly. They had always felt at ease with one another; right from the very start, from that "welcome here" party at G.H. They genuinely understood each other. It was a pity things had gone the way they had.

It was close on six when they arrived. The sun was sinking fast into the water. It was a cloudless day.

"We should see the green ray tonight," she said.

They sat in silence, looking toward the horizon. The sun grew larger, redder, yellower; the pace of its descent increased. The sky grew paler as the sun's color deepened. The edge of the sun touched the sea.

"Only another minute now, don't blink," she said.

"I won't."

It was less than a minute: the sun was cut in half then only a quarter showed: an eighth, a segment and then unmistakably there was for a second's span the flash of emerald.

"I didn't blink," he said.

"You really saw it?"

"I saw it."

"So now you'll admit it wasn't an old wives' tale?"

"Haven't I always believed everything you told me?"

It was ironically appropriate that on this last day they should see the green ray together.

"Let's go and swim before it's dark," he said.

But she did not move. She had had enough of this. It was time to put him out of misery. Besides she wanted to see his expression. She had to make it as easy as she could for him.

"I suppose you and your father discussed that article of Bradshaw's."

"Of course."

"It upset him, didn't it?"

"On the contrary he seemed relieved."

"Relieved?"

"He said that it had forced all our hands and that he was very glad about it."

"What did he mean by that?"

"It always paid, he said, to get the blow in first. There'll be a lot of gossip in the town. Everyone will be wondering what we're going to do. We can stop all that gossip by telling them right away.

We'll announce our engagement at once and have a celebration party."

"He said that, did he?"

"That's what he said to me last night. I asked him at lunch whether Carson's death would make any difference. He said heavens, no, we weren't having public mourning. Carson wasn't a relative of ours. It's Friday today. He said we'd cable the announcement to England over the weekend. It should be in the *Times* on Wednesday. We'd announce in that day's *Voice of Santa Marta* that we were having a party at G.H. on the Saturday in celebration."

"And what did he say about our getting married?"

"I asked him that. He said, 'First things first. Let's get this engagement settled, then we'll begin to think about what heroes in Victorian novels called "naming the day." ' I thought that rather a neat way of putting it."

She smiled through the fast falling dusk. Neat. It was much more than that. H.E. was no fool. He'd not only disarmed criticism but with one gesture he'd got the whole colored population of Santa Marta on his side. No one could say after this that G.H. drew a color bar. But that did not mean that he was going to run the risk of having a grandson, the eventual heir, with thick lips and crinkling curls. When it came to marriage he'd stall, he'd raise difficulties, devise separations, play for time, hoping that when Euan got back to England he would find somebody more suitable: not only more suitable, but suitable.

"Let's go and swim," she said.

The sea was warm but its fresh cleanliness was a relief, a solace after the long tiring day. She came out of the water first; sat on the sand where they had sat on that first picnic. Much had happened since. Then he had been concerned with Mavis. He was a young man on a holiday; after eighteen months' active service he had wanted a lighthearted casual romance. Mavis had seemed accessible. He had not been looking for a wife.

He was not in a marrying mood. It was all a mistake this talk of marriage. She had known it from the start. For a little, she had let herself be dazzled by the prospect of a new way of life. But the dream had faded now. In one way she was relieved.

She rose. The sand flies were beginning to sting.

"I'm not going in again," she called.

She dressed quickly. It was the bad hour for mosquitoes. She raised the windows of the car. She had a sense of peace, completer than she had known since that day he had proposed. All along since then she had felt in a false position. Now she was in control. She knew exactly what she wanted.

"Have you got to be back at any fixed time?" she asked him.

"I told my father not to wait if I wasn't home by eight."

"There's a grocery store three miles farther on. We could get a tin there and some biscuits and some rum."

They drove out to a strip of headland. There was no moon, but it was a cloudless evening; the stars created a dim twilight.

"Are you hungry?" she asked.

"Not desperately."

"Then let supper wait."

She switched on the radio, twiddled the knob, picked up a dance band in Puerto Rico. He might want to talk; she did not want to have him talk. There was nothing that needed saying. She lifted up her feet and tucked them under her, leaning against his shoulder. When she had seen herself as his future bride, she had felt herself restrained by a sense of loyalty, both to her parents and to his father. You could not cheat behind their backs those who had trusted you. It was different now. She had made a pact with herself. She was never going to marry Euan. She was going to do what she liked.

# CHAPTER SEVENTEEN

## 1

At Belfontaine, Sylvia and Maxwell sat alone on the veranda. The long slow day had passed with no car swinging round out of the roadway. Maxwell had started each time that he heard the drone of the engine, his ears alert, hearing it roar louder and then die away. In Jamestown they were talking of Carson's death; in the village they were talking of it: in every bungalow along the road it was the first topic of conversation. To this house alone no news of the drama had penetrated, the one house where it mattered.

"Shall we have one more swizzle?" Sylvia asked.

He rose to stir it; any action was a relief. Enforced inaction had set his nerves ajangle. He must do nothing out of the ordinary. He could not drive around to see the Prestons, even though he had a reasonable excuse to discuss the changeover when Jocelyn and his parents went back to England. It would be so unusual an occurrence that the Prestons would remember it afterwards; "As a matter of fact," Preston might say, "young Fleury did strike me as being in rather a curious mood that night."

He had a reasonable excuse for going down into the village to the police station, to arrange about his speech tomorrow. But he had thought it safer not. He had sent a message by his overseer. He had told his overseer to have the speech announced in the village and to send a boy on a bicycle round the estates that lay within his area.

The overseer had come back an hour ago.

"Everything fixed?" he had asked.

"Yes, sir, everything O.K."

"Has the boy started out?"

"Yes, sir, that boy has gone."

Maxwell had looked at him, waiting, in the hope that he would make some addition, start a conversation, but nothing came. The man seemed in a hurry to get away; probably to continue the argument about Carson's death. He would have to wait till the next day; perhaps till the paper came.

He spun the swizzle stick, beat the rum and ice with its flavoring of lime and angostura into a froth, then filled the glasses. He remained standing as he drank it. He could see the lights of the village twinkling across the bay; the wind rustled through the palm fronds; the bullfrogs were croaking by the stream; far away in the hills he could hear the beat of drums. Life throbbed and pulsed on every side of him, yet he had the sense of being completely isolated here with Sylvia; all this life and living round him, with he and she apart from it.

"Shall we have dinner now?" she asked.

"We might as well."

She rang the hand bell at her side. A minute later the maid came onto the veranda. "All ready, mistress."

As she rose from the chair, tonight as on the previous evening, he passed his arm round her waist. "You're all I've got, you're my whole world," he said.

There was a tremor in his voice. He means it, she thought. What had happened to him these last two days? He was a changed person. Before he had wanted her, now he needed her. It made all the difference.

2

It was after twelve when he rode back next morning from his tour of the estate. Had Bradshaw arrived yet? He looked for his car but did not see it. He was glad he hadn't. It would be easier if he learned the news from the paper. The paper must have arrived by now. Had Sylvia already seen it? Most likely not. He rode round to the stables, handed his horse over to the groom, entered the house by the back door.

"Hullo there," he called out.

"Won't be a second."

The answer came from the bedroom. He hurried through onto the veranda. No, no paper there. He turned into the dining room; not there either, nor in his study. He paused, puzzled, on the brink of calling out to ask where it was, but checked himself in time. He had never before shown any anxiety about the paper. He had to watch himself all the time. He went into his dressing room to shower before lunch. Perhaps the paper was in the kitchen, tossed there by the carrier, and because there had been no mail, Matilda had not bothered to bring it up. "I'll get the punches ready," he called out to Sylvia. That gave him an excuse for going down into the kitchen.

His guess had been correct; the paper lay on the kitchen table; he started, half stretched out a hand, then checked. Would he do that normally? No, of course he wouldn't. He'd tuck it under his

296

arm, laying it aside as he set out the drinks, then opening it out later with some such remark as "Why one bothers to get this rag at all, I can't imagine."

To test his self-control, he took as long as possible setting out the glasses, the savory biscuits, the nutmeg, the angostura, the freshly squeezed lime juice. Then he returned to the veranda.

"I hope that journalist isn't going to be late," he said. He opened out the paper. Now.

He blinked. There it was, right across the front in one black streamer. "Murder of Colonel Carson"; then a line of single columns. "Governor Attends Funeral." "Police Refuse Interview." He stared transfixed, then pulled himself together. He could not sit here staring; that would not be the normal thing to do.

"Darling, something appalling's happened, look."

At that moment a car honked in the road; "Ah, there he is." He handed her the paper. "Have a quick look at it. I've not had time to read it. We'll get the dirt from Bradshaw."

Bradshaw could not have come at a better time.

It was Sylvia not he who was asking the first questions. Her voice expressed a mingling of horror, excitement, curiosity.

"It's terrible, Maxwell's just shown me this. We haven't read it yet. Tell us all about it."

Maxwell looked at her quickly. Did her face, did her voice express anything but the obvious emotions? He didn't think they did. And she had been taken off her guard. If there had been anything between herself and Carson, she would have betrayed it surely at this moment. Carson, too, had looked surprised in that moment of accusal. Perhaps there had been nothing in it. His jealousy had invented the whole thing. None of this need have happened.

"Tell us all about it. When did it happen, how, where? Is anyone suspected? Who discovered it?"

Her questions rattled one on top of the other with an eagerness that could not have been feigned. No, there'd been nothing in it. There couldn't have been. He had the proof now of that. None of this need have happened.

He handed Bradshaw his punch and sat beside him. "Is there no possibility of its being suicide?" he asked.

"None at all. It's quite clear how it happened. He had his head banged against the floor while he was being throttled."

"What is the police theory?"

"They are refusing to commit themselves, but the general idea is that he surprised a thief, and the thief turned on him."

"Had he anything to steal?"

297

"I don't suppose he had. But the thief wouldn't know that. He'd think any white man's house was worth an attempt, and that the best time to try was between six and eight, when he'd be at the club. And so it would have been ninety-nine times in a hundred. I don't suppose Carson has ever left the club so early since he's been here."

"Why did he leave so early?"

"You heard about that, surely."

"Heard about what?"

"His scene with Leisching."

"No, I heard nothing."

"But you were in the club that night. We had a talk."

"Carson wasn't there then, at least I didn't see him."

"But didn't you hear about the row?"

"No, I heard nothing. Tell us."

Bradshaw recounted the incident. If there hadn't been that row, Maxwell thought, Carson would not have left the club so soon. They would never have met, he and Carson, at the corner of that unlighted lane. It had been a question of two minutes either way. And if Carson had not got involved in that ridiculous scene with Leisching, he would not have been in the belligerent mood from which the quarrel had sprung.

"I must have only just missed that scene at the club," he said.

"By about a quarter of an hour I should say."

"Then if what the police think is true, and Carson surprised a thief when he went back, I must have passed within earshot of his house at the very moment when the fight took place." He turned to Sylvia. "I never bothered to mention it to you, but I walked that evening to the club. I was worrying about that article of yours, Mr. Bradshaw. I knew that they'd all be wondering how I'd take it. I wanted to clear my mind; I may have been walking past the house at the very moment . . . to think of it—if Carson had shouted I must have heard him, but of course he couldn't shout, because he was being throttled."

"That's so. He couldn't shout."

"But if he had, and I had heard him. It's strange, isn't it? I might have saved his life."

He was watching Sylvia closely. Her face had expressed no sense of personal shock. She had been startled, amazed, curious. But nothing in her manner suggested that the bottom had fallen out of her world. There probably had not been anything between her and Carson. It was something he had imagined in view of her coldness to him; a coldness that he realized now was simply a confirmation

298

of the old adage that love came afterward. In the light of the last two nights he could not believe that Carson had meant a thing to her. He should have let himself be convinced by the incredulity in Carson's voice. But he had been in no mood then for reason. None of it need have happened.

"If I'd left home a few minutes earlier I'd have met him in the street," he was continuing. "We'd have stopped and gossiped. He might have asked me in for a drink. Probably he would have done. He must have been feeling lonely, after that scene at the club. He would have wanted to talk it over with someone. We were quite good friends you know, although he was so much older. I expect he would have asked me in; then we'd have found the thief there. It so easily might not have ever happened."

Bradshaw nodded. "That's how things usually appear in retrospect. There was a case in Baltimore . . ."

The incident was appropriate to the situation. Maxwell's blood pounded as he listened. He had got away with it; the perfect crime. He had fooled them all. Here in Bradshaw he had his witness that he had received the news with equanimity. Nothing in his manner could have aroused suspicion. He had carried it off. Once again his spirits were carried high, on a tide of confidence. He'd show these fellows in his speech this afternoon what he amounted to.

"Let's ring for lunch," he said. "Two punches are enough before a speech."

3

Bradshaw was back in Jamestown before seven. Maxwell had wanted him to stay on to dinner. The speech had been a great success. There had been no organized heckling and Maxwell had met his audience on a "you and I" basis; he had talked to them as one of them. He was jubilant, he wanted to relive his victory, like a golfer recounting his medal round, hole by hole and stroke by stroke. It was a mood with which Bradshaw was familiar. It would mean his having to listen to the whole of Maxwell's speech a second time. That was more than he could take. He excused himself on the grounds of work. He was only in part evasive. He wanted to write his article tomorrow and he needed Whittingham's advice.

A light was burning in the policeman's office, and he stopped the car. "If I'm not out within five minutes, you can go back home," he told the chauffeur. Whittingham was in and disengaged. He was seated at his desk, he had pulled out the lowest drawer and was using it as a footrest. It was a position he adopted when he was thinking.

He smiled when Bradshaw was brought in. He did not like journalists and Bradshaw did not seem to him a particularly attractive specimen of the fraternity, but he recognized Bradshaw as a man of consequence.

"So you've come to the fountain's source," he said.

"I'm thinking of diagnosing it as an Obeah case. Would that be too ridiculous?"

"It depends on the angle you select."

"I suppose you've heard how he made a ninny of that Obeah man on his estate?"

"I have."

"Could it be a case of vengeance?"

"I don't think so."

"Why not?"

"That's not the way they work."

"They give potions to the natives, don't they?"

"Yes, but those potions are mainly effective because the villagers believe in them. It's faith healing and faith killing. I've known cases in the New Hebrides of strong, healthy men who have nothing whatsoever wrong with them, turning their faces to the wall and dying within four days because their vanity has been hurt. These Obeah men are astute. They know when a man is seriously ill. If they lay a spell on such a man, and his friends tell him, it's in the cards he'll die. On the other hand, a man with a basically strong constitution who is told he is going to recover will get well nine times in ten. That's how these fellows work. They aren't Chicago gangsters. They wouldn't tell one of their followers to bump off an enemy."

"Shall I give those reasons for its not being Obeah?"

"If you want to write about Obeah. And perhaps you do."

"Can you suggest any alternative theory?"

Whittingham reflected. Anything he told Bradshaw would appear in Baltimore, and afterward be reported in the local press. Use might be made of Bradshaw. The murderer, if he was an educated person, would read the article. It might be advisable to lull him into false security. On the other hand it might be more useful to make the murderer feel anxious. An anxious man often gave himself away. The second course was perhaps the better.

"You might say this," he said. "You might suggest that though the obvious explanation is that Carson interrupted a casual burglar who set upon him, the police are not blind to the possibility that a clever murderer would try and make it look like the work of a casual thief. A criminal can sometimes be too clever."

300

"Do you think that's probable?"

"It's possible."

"Had Carson any enemies?"

"Everyone has enemies."

"Maybe that's so; but it can hardly have been premeditated. Carson wouldn't have left the club as early as that once in a month. There's another thing, it was the merest chance that Carson didn't meet Maxwell Fleury on the way."

"How could that have happened?"

Bradshaw repeated his talk with Maxwell.

"He and young Fleury were good friends. If they had met, he'd probably have asked young Fleury in. If he had, nothing would have happened the way it did. It's a curious coincidence. Fleury may have passed the house at the very moment that Carson was being throttled."

Whittingham made no reply. He was following his own thoughts. If Fleury had passed along that road by foot, he might have noticed something of no significance to him that would help the police.

"Is Fleury a particular friend of yours?" he asked.

"Not particularly."

"Yet you went all that way out there to lunch. . . ."

"He wanted me to hear his speech. I'd been there the other evening, when he was hooted down."

"How did it go this time?"

"Very well. He met them three-quarter-way. He reminded them that he had colored blood. He kept repeating, 'I am one of you.' I think he'll be elected."

"It's going to be a very curious Leg. Co. The A.G.'s going to be made a judge. That means a new A.G. and heaven knows who they'll choose. How long are you proposing to stay on here, by the way?"

"As long as there's material I can use."

"You may find quite a lot."

"I shouldn't complain if it turned out that way."

The following morning Bradshaw began his article. "A month ago I wrote that I sat on a volcano. The eruption has begun. Three mornings ago one of the chief white planters in the island was found on the floor of his study, murdered."

*4*

Two days later in London, Carson's death was announced in a four line paragraph at the foot of a column in an evening paper. It could scarcely have been accorded smaller prominence, but it caught the eye of the Opposition, and a question was tabled for the following week.

The Minister of State for the Colonies had also seen the paragraph. It was accompanied by a memo in Purvis' precise, small handwriting. "Shall I cable for fuller information?"

The Minister reread the paragraph. He had a great deal upon his mind. He wanted to concentrate on Kenya. He did not want to be bothered with a small West Indian island. He pressed the bell that rang in his secretary's room. "Tell Mr. Purvis that I'm going to telephone Santa Marta: then put a call through to the Governor. Mark it high priority."

There was a five hours difference in time between London and the Caribbean. Lunch in London was breakfast time in Santa Marta. The call reached Templeton as he was on the point of leaving G.H. on an afternoon tour of inspection of a housing project. It had been one of his boasts as a soldier that no news took him off his guard. He never expressed surprise. It was the first time he had been rung up from London, but he treated the call as a routine occurrence. His voice through a buzz of static sounded firm and clear.

"There is nothing to worry about," he reassured the Minister. "It is a tragic business, but it has no social or political implications. I shall be forwarding you a full report by air mail tomorrow. I am anxious that as little as possible should appear about it in the press. I don't want to scare the tourists. We are expecting a number of American journalists in July. I mentioned that in my last dispatch. We are trying to develop a summer season here. The less said the better. But you'll get my dispatch before the end of the week. It'll cover all these points."

"A question is going to be asked about it in the House."

"My dispatch will provide you with all information that you require."

The Governor was speaking to his chief. But his manner was that of a colonel reassuring his second-in-command. The Minister hung up the receiver with relief. If Templeton had had any qualms a sudden call from London would have brought them to the surface, and Templeton's composure had been complete. There could be nothing to worry about in Santa Marta. He could concentrate on Kenya.

At the other end of the line, the Governor hesitated. They must be worried over there. Did his dispatch need redrafting? He rang for Archer.

"You're a man of letters. Take away this report, read it, then come back straight away and tell me how it strikes you."

It was a one page report. It recounted the incident in succinct straightforward language. There was nothing literary about it, but it set out the facts and drew a conclusion from them, there was no possibility of misunderstanding the writer's point of view. Archer was impressed. He had been accustomed when he was in the army to disparage the intellectual caliber of the average professional soldier. "The army," he would argue, "has drawn upon the least intellectual section of the upper middle classes. Look at the Army Class in the average Public School. If a boy comes from a reasonable home, is a reasonably decent fellow, reasonably good at games, with no pretensions to scholarship, then his housemaster suggests that he should join the Army Class. You do not expect a J.C.R. standard of conversation in an Army Mess."

That was how he had talked six years ago. Yet here he was now being forced to recognize that the Governor's report was written in better because clearer English than that of a leading article in the average London newspaper. He followed his own thoughts. The Governor had been trained to use his pen as a medium with which to convey commands and information. His sentences had to be read by busy, harried men in action or on the brink of action. There could be no room for ambiguity. The senior and junior officers who read his reports must never be forced to read them twice to see what exactly he had meant. Could you have a better training for the writing of good English? How often in point of fact were not the best books written by men who were not professionals, by soldiers, administrators, engineers, who had something of interest to say and had learnt through necessity how to convey exactly what they had in mind.

He reread the report. It told exactly what had happened and gave the Governor's reasons for believing that there was no occasion for alarm. Why had the old man shown it to him? It couldn't be out of author's vanity. Many brother officers had forced their poems on him. "Just a little thing I tossed off the other day. I know it's no good of course." But H.E. wasn't that kind of person.

Archer carried back the draft.

"It looks fine to me," he said.

"Put yourself in the place of the man who'll read it. The Minister of State for the Colonies. He has to answer questions in the House. He has to cover himself, remember; to give an answer which may have to be interpreted two ways. He wants to be able to say in a year's time, if occasion arises, 'I must remind the Honorable member for East Stepney that I did point out the possibility of such an unfortunate eventuality as has in fact occurred.' You see my point, Denis?"

Archer saw it very well. Once again he got an angle on the school in which H.E. had been trained. Whereas the professional writer was concerned with the saying of something for his own satisfaction, a man like H.E. had always to have his audience in mind, since his audience would be taking action on what he wrote. Objective as opposed to subjective writing.

"I wonder if the report should be less unqualified," the Governor said.

He looked interrogatively at his A.D.C. Himself he did not think it should be. He believed, as a soldier, in deciding on a course of action and then pursuing his aim in blinkers. At the staff college they had told him that there were three ways of winning a battle, and that once you had decided on the way you preferred, you must not think about the other two. But he was dealing now not with soldiers but with politicians.

"What about asking Whittingham what he thinks, sir?"

"You might do that. Not that I'll follow his advice. He always plays for safety. Did you ever get involved during the war with any of those security fellows?"

"Only the F.S.P., sir."

"You're lucky. Some of the top boys drove me mad. They were so keen on their security that they'd have liked to have stopped us attacking, in case the Germans should discover the type of tanks we used. But you are quite right. We ought to know Whittingham's views, if only so that he'll have a chance of saying later on, 'I told you so.' "

5

Archer found the policeman in an expansive mood. No, he said, he had found no clues yet, but that was not worrying him. The police played a waiting game. Sooner or later the other man made a mistake. Something unusual happened and it caught one's notice.

"It's not unlike fishing. You throw out a net, and sooner or later a string will tighten. The efficiency of a police organization depends on how finely drawn are the meshes of the net. We are understaffed here, and half my constables are fools. But we've one great thing in our favor. This is an island. No one can get away without my knowing it. You see that map there on the wall. I look at it when I feel depressed. It reminds me that Santa Marta is only fifty miles long and fifteen wide: that there are only a hundred thousand people on it; that among the hundred thousand is the man I'm looking for, and that he, poor wretch, is shivering with terror, wondering what I'm doing, wondering what I know.

"Time's no problem," he went on. "That's another factor in my favor. I'll be waiting, I or my successor, for twenty years if need be. I'm in no hurry. I'm the spider in the center of the web. Sooner or later the fellow that I'm waiting for will become desperate or overconfident. At least that's what I tell myself. What now can I do for you?"

Archer handed him the Governor's report.

"H.E. would like your comment upon this."

He watched Whittingham as he read it. The policeman's expression did not change. He always looked the same, bland, bucolic, indolent. There was nothing sinister, nothing intimidating about his face. But how would one feel if one were a criminal sitting in this chair, trying to guess what he was suspecting, wondering if he had been fooled? It was difficult to credit Whittingham with quick perceptions. Perhaps that was in part his strength, that he did not look a sleuth.

Whittingham handed back the paper.

"It's fine as far as I'm concerned."

"H.E. wondered if you wanted anything qualified."

"I don't see what."

"You don't think then that there are any political complications here."

"Carson wasn't political."

"You don't think his laborers are getting their own back over something."

"He was popular on his estate."

"You don't link this up with that fire at Belfontaine."

"That was Mardi gras. Belfontaine is a trouble spot. Young Fleury isn't liked."

"H.E. will be relieved over what you say, so will the Tourist Board."

"Is that what's worrying him?"

"Among other things."

Whittingham pursed his lips and remained silent. He seemed to have said all he had to say. Archer stood up. "Shall I be seeing you at G.H. tomorrow?"

"You bet you will. I'm counting on champagne."

"You won't be disappointed."

# CHAPTER EIGHTEEN

*1*

The party in honor of Jocelyn's engagement was an after dinner occasion, with a band and dancing: a hundred invitations were dispatched and there was a small family dinner party first. Sylvia and Maxwell had arranged to come in early. Whittingham had suggested that Maxwell should call at his office next time he was in town. Maxwell had expected such a message. That busybody Bradshaw. But he was glad Bradshaw was, otherwise he would have been forced to call on Whittingham. It would have been suspicious if he had not. Whittingham would have said, "Didn't it occur to you that you might have information that would be of use to us?"

He was glad Whittingham had written, and he was glad that the party at G.H. had given him a definite date for coming into town. Otherwise he might have seemed too eager or too dilatory. He would have had to pick on precisely the right day. "Dear Colonel," he had written, "I'll be in town on Saturday for Jocelyn's engagement party. If I don't hear from you to the contrary, I'll look in at about eleven. I can guess why you want to see me, but I'm afraid I shan't be able to help you much." How luckily everything was turning out.

They left in the cool of the morning, shortly after eight. Maxwell was filled with the same exultation that he had experienced a week ago when he had driven out from Jamestown, through the rain. He was alive, alert in every nerve, in every fiber. How fresh and glowing Sylvia looked.

"You look more attractive every day," he said.

She made no answer, but her eyes were fond. It was like a second honeymoon, no it was not, it was like a first one. She leant against him, responsive to the pressure of his arm.

"Hurry or we'll be late," she said.

She didn't need to tell him how she felt. She had told him that, in the dusk, not in words but in her response to him. He must know. Why else would he look so radiant? He seemed reborn. He took his hand from the wheel and laid it over hers, pressing it then replac-

306

ing it upon the wheel. It was the kind of thing that he had never done before. It was a miracle, there was no other word for it.

She began to sing a song that her nurse had taught her,

> I gave my love a cherry
> Without a stone.
> I gave my love a chicken
> Without a bone.
> I gave my love a story
> Without an end.
> I gave my love a baby
> With no cryin'.

It was a song that he too had learnt in childhood and he answered her,

> How can there be a cherry
> Without a stone?
> How can there be a chicken
> Without a bone?
> How can there be a story
> Without an end?
> How can there be a baby
> With no cryin'?

How in tune we are, she thought.

Round a bend of the road Maxwell saw the cane field where he had flung Carson's watch. By now it must lie deep in mud. There had been heavy rain. Would it be ever found? Most likely not. The cane would be cut and the stubble burnt. Then the ground would be ploughed over. The cane would sprout again.

Sylvia was singing the response,

> A cherry in the blossom
> It has no stone.
> A chicken in the egg
> It has no bone.
> The story of "I love you"
> It has no end,
> A baby when it's sleepin'
> Has no cryin'.

They were passing the field where he had flung the wallet. Long before the cane was cut, its leather would have swelled and blistered under the rain and sun: the seams would have burst, the lining rotted, the papers pulped. The watch might one day be found, the wallet never. He had got away with it. He had no qualms about his interview with Whittingham. He had only to keep his head. He had been warned by many detective stories.

As he drove through the market place he noticed David Boyeur leaning out of an M.G. convertible talking to a girl. The car was brand new, the girl was only slightly colored.

"Isn't that the Morris girl?" he asked.

"I think it is. She's pretty, isn't she?"

"I'll say so."

A traffic light held him up. He had time to look at them. Boyeur was talking fast, the girl's lips were parted and her eyes were bright. He's cutting himself a swath, he thought. He remembered how Boyeur had strode into that path of light at his first meeting. Was it only ten days ago? It seemed a happening in another century. He chuckled. The light changed to green and he drove on. He checked by the M.G.

"Why didn't you come out to my meeting the other afternoon?" he said.

Boyeur turned quickly, surprised, taken off his guard.

"I made a mistake the first time, holding it in the dark. One needs to see one's hecklers face to face." Maxwell's tone was easy, self-confident, contemptuous. "I look forward to our meetings in the Leg. Co. It'll be very amusing. It's one thing to make promises at the hustings, quite another to get them carried out in parliament. It's all going to be most entertaining."

Before Boyeur could answer he had driven on. That's a point back for me, he thought. Boyeur had humiliated him in front of Sylvia. Boyeur had been paid back in his own coin, humiliated before that pretty girl.

"Will you be lunching at the club?" Sylvia asked.

"I expect my father'll want me to." Actually he had planned to go there. He wanted to show himself, to assert himself: to make the others recognize what he amounted to. He dropped Sylvia at his father's house, then drove to the police station. He was taut, expectant; as he had felt sitting in the changing room, waiting for a football match to start.

2

Whittingham was seated in his swivel chair, the bottom drawer of his desk drawn out and his foot tucked into it. He was holding a leather wallet, turning it over between his fingers. It was a pigskin wallet. It must have been expensive, but it had been subjected to

308

rough treatment. The leather was discolored and warped. Maxwell stared at it. Could there be two wallets like that in the colony? Whittingham put it down on the top of the desk, then swung round to face his visitor.

"It's good of you to come round," he said. "I don't suppose, as you say, that there's anything that you can tell me, but quite often something that seems unimportant to one man may have a meaning for another. Heavens but I feel ill this morning."

He raised his arm and laid the back of his hand against his forehead. "Fell among friends, I'll say I did. A losing battle with the sherbet. I ought to know better at my age. They talk about the last drink doing it, but it isn't the last drink, it's the fifth. Up to four you are all right. From the sixth onward you are lost. Refuse the fifth. That's what I always tell myself, but I keep forgetting. And it's too early for the hair of the dog yet."

With his high bald forehead, his fresh pink complexion he looked like a disgruntled baby, crying for its bottle. He was not a person you could take seriously, Maxwell told himself: an amiable old fossil who by slow processes of seniority had become a colonel. But all the same his nerves were tingling. That wallet! What was it doing here? Was it Carson's? There might be, there must be several pigskin wallets in the island; but why should there be another wallet that had been exposed to rain? A pigskin wallet was expensive. Its owner would take care of it. No one in this island was rich enough to be casual about a pigskin wallet. And anyhow why should any wallet but Carson's have found its way into the police station?

Maxwell longed to look at it, but knew he mustn't. It would be suspicious. How could he recognize it as Carson's in its discolored state? He was not supposed to know that Carson's wallet was missing. All he knew of the case was what he had read in the paper and what he had been told by Bradshaw. Had Bradshaw mentioned it? He could not remember. Perhaps Bradshaw had not known. He must not show a knowledge that he could not have come by naturally. That was the way criminals got caught.

"Suppose you tell me all that you can remember about that evening. The most trivial incident may be the one piece needed in a jigsaw puzzle. What time did you leave your father's house?"

"It might have been after six. It was almost dark."

"You were alone."

"Yes."

"Where was Sylvia?"

"At Belfontaine."

"So you came in alone. Isn't that unusual?"

"Yes, but it was the day that article of Bradshaw's was printed in *The Voice*. The one about our having colored blood. I wanted to discuss it with my father. It was a shock to me. I had no suspicion of it. That's why I was going to the club alone. My first appearance there would be important. Everyone would be discussing the article. They would wonder how I'd be taking it, how the family'd be taking it. We agreed that it would be best if we didn't arrive in a body. That's why I didn't drive. I wanted to clear my mind, by walking."

Whittingham nodded. With eyes half closed he was rotating himself in his swivel chair, from the leverage of his foot against the drawer. He seemed half asleep. Maxwell was desperately tempted to turn his head, to look at that wallet on the desk, but he mustn't. He knew he mustn't. He had no excuse for being interested in a battered wallet.

"I suppose you were pretty upset inside yourself, I mean you were all worked up?" the colonel asked.

"Of course, naturally. That's, I suppose, why I never discovered at the club that Carson had had that scene with Leisching."

"What's that?"

"You know that Carson had made a fool of himself, tried to apologize and dropped a glass."

"Yes, I heard that."

"It must have happened only a few minutes before I arrived; normally I should have stood around a little, caught the atmosphere of the place, listened before I began to talk, but that night I had to attack. I went straight up to Bradshaw. I thanked him for his article: I congratulated him on it. I told him how much easier it would make it for all the Santa Martans like myself who could pass for white. I took the wind out of his sails. I took the wind out of everybody's sails. I made myself the center of the evening. I was excited; as you say worked up. I stood drinks all round. But you heard all that, you hear everything."

Whittingham smiled, rocking himself in his chair.

"You walked back by the same route?" he asked.

"Yes."

"And when would that have been?"

"I can't say exactly: quarter to eight roughly."

"Did you see any lights in Carson's house?"

"No, but then from the road you can only see one upper window."

"Indeed, is that so, I hadn't realized that. You saw no one in the street outside his house."

"No."

"And on the way to the club, did you see anyone hanging outside Carson's house? It's important this, because you must have passed at about the time he was being killed."

"I saw no one. There was only one car that drove by afterward."

"Afterward. After what?"

"After I'd passed the turning to Carson's house."

"Ah, I see. And that was all."

"Yes, that was all. I'm afraid I haven't been much help. I warned you, didn't I?"

"Negative information can be quite useful. It precludes certain possibilities."

"You mean that you know certain things didn't happen, therefore others must have done."

"That's roughly what I meant. Oh God, my head. And I wanted to feel well too for your sister's party. The fifth drink. Never forget that. It's the fifth that counts."

Maxwell stood up. There was clearly nothing more to say. As he rose, he allowed himself for the first time during the interview to turn his eyes toward the desk. He blinked. It must be the wallet he had taken from Carson's hip. Whose else could it be? He longed to touch it, to turn it over in his hands. The very wallet.

He pulled himself together. "I shall be seeing you tonight," he said.

In the passage outside he closed his eyes. His knees felt weak. His heart was pounding. He leant against the wall. He had been exposed to a greater strain than he had realized. But I got through all right, he reassured himself. I was natural. I didn't give away a point.

In the room behind him, Whittingham swung back to his desk and took up the wallet. It was empty and he filled the pockets with paper. He gauged its weight in the palm of his hand. That was about right. He rang the bell and a corporal appeared. "Is Albert there?"

"Yes, sir, he there."

"Good, have you got the car?"

"Yes, sir, I have the car."

"Then we're on our way."

In the outside office, a ragged, frightened peasant was seated beside a constable. Whittingham beckoned to him. "Come."

The man followed whimpering and blustering. "I steal nothing, Colonel sir. I find purse in cane field. No money in purse. I keep purse. Why not keep purse, Colonel sir."

"It's all right, Albert. Don't fuss. No one's blaming you. You show me where you found that purse, then you can go home. Come."

They drove along the road to Belfontaine.

"Here, Colonel sir."

"Right. Out you get. Walk to the spot where you found this purse."

The man crossed the road and walked five yards into the cane.

"No farther than that?"

"No, Colonel sir, me saw it from the road."

"O.K."

Whittingham stood at the edge of the road and with a backhand flick flung the pocketbook toward the peasant. It carried ten yards over his head. The corporal had some difficulty in finding it.

"O.K., stay where you are," said Whittingham. He got into the car, put it into reverse, stopped, then drove back toward Belfontaine. As he neared the spot, he flung the wallet through the open window. He had the road between him and the cane field. His right arm was not free, his left hand was on the wheel; his attention was partially upon his driving. The wallet did not quite reach the peasant. So, he thought. It didn't prove anything, but it was an indication.

"O.K.," he called out. "Back we get."

He drove Albert to his village. "Don't fuss yourself," he said.

He put his hand into his pocket and pulled out two single dollar bills.

"This'll make up for the day's work you've lost."

He drove back, with the corporal in the front seat beside him.

"What did you make of that?" he asked.

"Make of what, sir?"

"My experiments. You saw what I did."

"Yes, sir, sure, sir. First you throw the wallet from the roadway, then you throw it from the car."

"Exactly. And what did I learn from that?"

"Learn from that, sir?"

"Yes. What did I learn from that?"

"Well, sir." The constable pondered, his face puckered and puzzled. "I can't properly say, sir," he said at length.

Whittingham shrugged mentally. This constable was responsible enough when he was given work to do, but he would be helpless on his own. That was the trouble about these people, they were only effective when they worked under precise instructions.

"The experiments," he explained, "prove nothing. They could not be produced as evidence in a court of law. But they can be useful to us as indications of what may have happened. It is probable, but not certain, that that wallet was flung into the cane field by the

312

murderer, after he had taken from it anything of value. We can assume that the murderer was a man. No woman would have been strong enough. There is the possibility that a pair may have worked together, but the actual murder was the work of one man unaided. If there had been a partner, I believe there would have been some sign of his presence. I cannot say what it would have been, but I think things would have happened differently if there had been a partner. Let us assume anyhow that the murderer was a man, alone, and that he wanted to get rid of the wallet as soon as he had emptied it. That cane field is three miles out of town. Why did he wait so long? That wasn't the first cane field, the first empty stretch of road. Why did he walk so far carrying the wallet? It was a wet night, remember. Isn't it likely that he was in a car?

"Let's see how those experiments bear that out. We can assume that a man wanting to get rid of a wallet would throw it as far away from himself as possible. He would go to the side of the road and throw it into the cane field. If he had done that the wallet would have carried far beyond the spot where it was found; though again we have to face the possibility that Albert did not stand in the spot where he found the wallet. All the same we must remember that he did see the wallet from the road. I can see no reason why he should have lied. If the wallet had been thrown by a man standing near the ditch, it would not have been seen from the road.

"Remember now what happened when I threw the wallet out of the car window. A man driving a car would throw an object through the right hand window. As he is driving on the left side of the road, he would therefore have the roadway between himself and the cane field. His right arm would not be free: his attention would be distracted by his driving. You saw what happened when I threw the wallet from the car. It did not reach Albert. Though this is largely guesswork, we can assume for our own purposes that the wallet was thrown from a car traveling north along the windward coast road. You realize the significance of that?"

"Yes, sir."

"What would you deduce from it?"

"Well, sir."

Once again the puckered, puzzled look came into the policeman's face. Whittingham had learnt patience. There was only one way to teach these people, through a friendly forcefulness.

"How many private cars are there on this island?"

The answer came back pat. "Three hundred and seventeen, sir."

"And how many trucks?"

"Eighty-seven motor lorries and forty buses, sir."

"Then if we are right in believing that the wallet was thrown through the window, we can limit the field of our inquiries to the four hundred and forty-four car-owning families. Instead of searching among a hundred thousand people, we have to search among seven hundred. What do you propose that we should do?"

"Check up on what every car was doing at that time, that night, sir."

"Exactly. And will you bring me a list of the car owners who live on the windward coast, north of that cane field."

"And check the taxis, sir?"

"Yes, check the taxis."

They were now on a point of routine and Whittingham had complete confidence in his constable's capacity to carry out his instructions with accuracy and speed. He had remembered the number of car licenses in the island and he would be thorough and systematic in drawing up his report. West Indians made first-class lawyers. They had regard for authority and precedent and order. They were an odd mixture. "Delegate all other work," he said, "till this job's finished. And I'd like that list of car owners by this evening. I'll find out who was at the Aquatic Club; then try and trace their movements."

As they reached town, an idea struck him. Instead of driving straight to the police station, he made a detour by the offices of *The Voice*.

"I won't be three minutes," he told the constable.

He found the editor in. The young man rose hurriedly. He looked nervous. Had he got into trouble over those articles? It was a free country, a free press, but even so. Whittingham guessed at his reaction.

"It's all right," he said. "I'm not here to arrest you. I'm bringing you a news release."

"That's very kind of you."

"I've an ulterior motive. You don't need telling that. So before I give you a piece of genuine hot news, I want your promise that if you do use it, you'll use it the way I want."

"I agree, naturally."

"The news is this. Carson's wallet has been found, in the possession of a peasant. I want you to say that the police regard this as a most valuable clue and that they are keeping the peasant in question under close observation."

Whittingham chuckled as he walked down the steps. The paragraph would appear tomorrow. One member of those four hundred car-owning families would be enjoying his last carefree sleep tonight.

# CHAPTER NINETEEN

*1*

"As you have no doubt heard," His Excellency was saying three hours later to Grainger Morris, "our old friend Lestrange is being promoted and is to become a judge. That leaves vacant the post of Attorney General. If you will accept the post, my own work will be made a great deal easier.

"The Attorney General's," he went on, "is the key position in our administration. Whatever reforms we make must be made legally: the law is above politics. That is the strength of the British people: that is the great gift we have brought to the countries we have colonized—a respect for law, a certainty in the minds of the governed that they will receive justice before the bench, a judiciary that is independent of the executive. I need the best man. You are the best man. I hope you will accept my offer even though it is to your financial disadvantage."

Grainger Morris was able to answer without hesitation. If he appeared to hesitate, it was only because the offer had surprised him. He had been confident that one day the post would become his. It was an obvious, an inevitable stage in his career. But he had had no idea that it would come so soon. Attorney General at twenty-seven.

"I'm flattered and honored, sir. I'll do my best to justify your faith in me."

"That means that you accept."

"Of course, sir, naturally."

"I'm delighted. You have put my mind at rest. And may I say how much I welcome the opportunities with which this appointment will provide me of seeing you in this house more often. It will be a genuine pleasure: it is rare that the doing of one's duty pays a personal dividend."

The Governor rose with his hand outstretched.

"I shall be seeing you here tonight, of course."

"Yes, sir. Thank you very much."

"Fine. I can't say how happy I am about this engagement: the daughter of one of my oldest friends. Euan is a little young. I'd rather in one way it had happened later, but there are some things

315

in which prudence does not pay. Jocelyn's a delightful girl. It's a wonderful thing for Euan."

His voice rang sincerely. Did he really mean it, Grainger asked himself? Was H.E. genuinely unaffected by that streak, faint though it was, of African ancestry in the Fleurys. He himself, raised in an atmosphere of racial discrimination, found it impossible to believe that Bradshaw's article had not shocked the Governor. But things were different in England and H.E. had spent many years in India where no one of culture and intelligence could think for long that there was any innate superiority in what E.M. Forster had called "a pinko-grey" complexion. Perhaps H.E. really had read that article without a qualm.

The Governor accompanied him to the porch. "Is David Boyeur a friend of yours?" he asked.

"I wouldn't say a friend, sir, but I know him."

"He may be a problem to us, in the next Leg. Co. He's bound to be elected and it may go to his head at first. We shall have to ensure that he doesn't break the standing orders. But he'll learn. He's a good fellow, at heart. Goes for the bowling. I like that. See you to-night, my boy."

Grainger's spirits were high as he drove away. Attorney General and at twenty-seven. It was due to luck far more than it was to merit, he knew well. It would never have happened if Euan and he had not made friends in the Canal Zone. During the three months before Euan's arrival, he had only been twice invited to G.H. and then on formal functions. It was only through Euan's sponsorship that H.E. had become aware of him. Through Euan he had taken a short cut.

It was luck, fantastic luck, all along the line. It was luck that he had made that lecture tour in the Middle East; luck that he had visited Euan's unit. On the night in question he had had a touch of sandfly fever, with a temperature of 100°. He had been advised not to go. One should watch a temperature in that climate. But he was reluctant to let people down, particularly soldiers; a sore throat did not relieve you in the trenches. He had gone and because he had been feeling ill, he had made a special effort to counterattack his headache. It had been a highly successful evening: and it had led to this. He had got to show himself worthy of his good luck.

2

Grainger arrived home in the middle of a family discussion. His sister Gertrude's voice was raised.

316

"This is the second time this week. You ought to stop it. Muriel's much too young to go about with a man like David Boyeur. You know what his reputation is."

Her voice was shrill. It often was these days. He remembered how soft it had been, fifteen years ago, when she had sung hymns by Muriel's cradle. He took a seat on the veranda. His parents were there and two of his brothers, the eldest and the youngest one.

"David Boyeur's thoroughly unreliable," Gertrude was continuing. "He's been involved with any number of young women. He's an upstart. His parents are nobodies. He's earned a cheap notoriety through his trade union, but it can't last. He'll go too far and they'll disown him. It's fatal for Muriel, at the start of her life to get her name linked with his."

Grainger made no comment. Let Gertrude get it off her chest. Then he would interpose, tactfully, in a way that would not offend Gertrude, but that would leave Muriel with her freedom.

One had to treat Gertrude gently. She had been a true friend to him when he was a boy; she had encouraged and inspired him. She had watched every cricket match he had played in. She had heard him his lessons, gone over his mathematics with him. It was to her first that he had brought the news of each fresh triumph. She had been his judge and audience. He had admired her, she was his ideal. He had dreamed of finding a girl like her to be his wife. Gertrude had been handsome, tall, athletic. She had played tennis for the island. She sailed. She was good company. Everybody liked her. During his years in England they had written to each other every week. It had been a shock to him to find on his return how time had soured her.

Letters were deceptive. Writing to each other every week their relationship had been static. The big proud sister, the admiring brother. They had played the same parts to one another: the changes in each had been unapparent, for he had changed too, of course, though in a different way. He had passed from boyhood into manhood. He was an adult person, poised and proved. For him it had been a period of progress. For her it had been a time of slow sad recognition of the tether by which her life was bound. She was thirty and it was unlikely that she would marry. She would inherit very little money. She had not put on much weight, but she had lost her suppleness. Working in the hospital, accustomed to giving orders, her manner had grown authoritarian. Her voice was no longer soft.

He had seen the same thing happen to many English women who were doomed to spinsterdom because they would not marry out of

317

their own class. Ambitious young men went abroad, or regarded marriage as a stage in self-advancement. They wanted to better themselves. In England they married a girl with money, in Santa Marta they married a girl with a better skin. And Gertrude was the dark one of the family.

Gertrude had faced the Gorgon during these seven years and it had made her bitter. In another ten years she would have perhaps become adjusted. She would fill then a position of high respect in the community. She would be matron of the hospital. She would have built up her defenses. But at the moment she was in turgid waters. She was a young woman still. She had not completely abandoned hope of matrimony. There was still a chance that the right man might arrive, and the fact that she had not abandoned hope, made her resentful of Muriel's acceptance of a solution she had herself declined, and that subconsciously she criticized herself for not accepting.

She turned for support to her eldest brother.

"You agree, don't you, that David Boyeur's impossible as Muriel's husband?"

"Is there any question of his being that. Has he proposed?"

"I don't say he has. That's not the point. A girl of Muriel's age ought only to go about alone with the kind of man with whom it would be suitable for her to fall in love, a man whom she could marry if she wanted."

"What men for instance?"

"Michael Forrest. John de Boulay. Eric Des Voeux."

They were all of them so little colored that in England they could have passed as white.

"You agree don't you," Gertrude persisted, "that David Boyeur is impossible as Muriel's husband."

"I shouldn't be pleased about it."

"What have you got against him?" Mrs. Morris asked.

"The same things that Gertrude has, I take it. He's brash, he's boastful; politically he's a subversive influence."

"Exactly," Gertrude said.

But when he said "the same things," were the reasons he had given the actual ones? Wasn't Boyeur's color the decisive point? Wasn't that what was worrying them both, in the last analysis? He transposed the situation to England; the daughter of a college professor, say, falling in love with a Left wing Trades Union leader. The professor and his wife would describe the young man as dangerous, an enemy of the realm. Would they dare to voice their real objection, that he was not a gentleman? In such a case, he himself would have

argued that in a democratic day it was good for a girl to link herself with the future, with a man of courage, ambition, vigor, somebody who was alive, even if he was common. But here, in his own
country, wasn't he imitating the professor, concealing his real opinion: talking about "boastfulness" and "brashness" and "subversive
influence."

Color, color, color . . . How it ran through everything. How ingrained in every West Indian was that predilection for the "better
skin." Even in himself, who in England had met on equal terms and
outpaced in studies and on the field the pick of England, who knew
intellectually that all men were equal, who had it confirmed for him
by the English attitude that in the mid-fifties a man stood on his
own feet to be judged on his own qualities, by his own performance,
even so, even in himself this prejudice persisted.

"I agree with Gertrude," he said, "but if we oppose Muriel, we'll
put her back up. I suggest that we should welcome Boyeur to the
house. We'll disarm them both that way. But let's invite at the same
time young men like de Boulay and Des Voeux: give Muriel a
chance of comparing the one group with another. We've not done
nearly enough for her in my opinion. We don't give girls a coming
out dance here as they do in England. In a small place like this
where everyone knows everyone it isn't necessary. But we should
entertain for Muriel, have young people to the house, show Muriel
off against her background. It'll give her confidence, send up her
stock. Why don't we have a cocktail party dance for her."

They were still discussing the project when they went in to
dinner. They had their meals in the drawing room. Their living room
was the veranda that ran three sides of the house. The drawing room
was littered with assorted furniture, china and silver cabinets: a
bookcase with the bookcovers eaten through by worms; highly decorated tables carved out of local wood; a Chippendale armchair
bought in the auction of an old estate. Some of the articles were
good, the majority were worthless. Nothing had been flung away.
The walls were decorated with oleographs and enlarged photographs; there were two plates emblazoned with pictures of Edward
VII and Alexandra at their coronation. It was a dark room, lighted
by a central lamp, draped with silk, that could be raised and lowered.
As a child, Grainger had loved examining the various objects. As a
boy he had looked forward to the day when he could transport
these treasures to his home. In England he had closed his eyes, visualizing the house, each piece in its own niche. But now, remembering rooms that he had seen in London, he found his home tasteless
and tawdry. It irritated him to be surrounded by so much junk.

The Graingers kept two servants, a maid of all work and a cook that had been with them for twenty years. She had prepared the kind of dinner that he had been eating for as long as he could remember. A thin chicken soup that was tasteless without a sprinkling of chili sauce, was followed by roast beef: the meat was tough. It always was in Santa Marta since meat was cooked on the day the animal was killed. The joint was accompanied by starchy vegetables, yams, mashed taros, sweet potatoes.

"Only a very little for me," he said. "I've got to dance and there'll be a supper."

But that was not the only reason. He was sick of West Indian cooking; it had no personality. In Trinidad through the East Indian influence you got curries and the callalou. In the Middle East he had enjoyed meat dishes like kibbe and cool bitter salads like tabouli. In India and in the Middle East a cuisine had been evolved in keeping with the climate and the people's faith. There was no such tradition here. Breadfruit had been brought from Tahiti and the slaves had been told to eat it. That was typical. West Indian cooking did not spring from the soil and climate, from a personal way of living. It was superimposed. As everything in every way was here. Superimposed was a key word to West Indian life.

He had seen in England the confidence and security that the English derived from their long past. On every side of them, in their buildings, their schools, their churches, their parks, their local customs, they had reassurances of survival. And at the apex of the social pyramid was the Crown, the symbol of continuity.

Himself a schoolboy in Santa Marta in the autumn of 1940, he had failed to see how the British Isles could survive against the overwhelming might of Germany. In England he had asked a number of Englishmen if they had felt the same. They had without exception smiled. They had not considered the possibility of defeat. A country whose streets and fields for nine hundred years had been untrodden by foreign feet could not at that late hour be overthrown. At the very hour when the invasion barges were collecting in Northern France, a committee in Whitehall was calmly considering the report of the Moyne Commission on the West Indies and was allocating to the Caribbean colonies an annual sum of a million pounds in welfare services. The English because of their past were confident in their future. Each Englishman saw himself as the torchbearer in the race. How could a West Indian with his untraced roots in Africa feel like that?

Sitting now at his father's table on what should have been one of the proudest evenings of his life, he was vividly conscious of his isolation. This was the house in which he had been born, which was the setting of his childhood's memories, yet he had not here the sense of family that his English friends living in their furnished flats had. Years ago as a schoolboy he had brought back to Gertrude the news of each new success. If anyone had told him on his seventeenth birthday that within ten years he would be the colony's Attorney General, he would have pictured himself as rushing home proudly to proclaim his triumph. Yet here he was discussing the guests' for Muriel's cocktail party. He wanted to tell his parents, but the words stuck in his throat. This appointment meant much to him. To them it would mean something altogether different. Their delight, their congratulations would jar his nerves. They would be happy for the wrong reasons. He did not try to particularize, to explain to himself what those reasons were: but he knew they would upset him, that they would destroy the deep interior happiness he felt. Let him brood on his happiness alone for this one night. He would tell them tomorrow. Tomorrow would be time enough.

3

The party at G.H. was scheduled to begin at half-past nine. Grainger planned to arrive at ten. He had a couple of briefs to study. Then he would shave and shower and change into evening clothes. He left the family and went into his study bedroom. The walls did not reach the ceiling, and he could hear, though he could not distinguish their actual words, his family talking on the veranda. His younger brother switched on the wireless, and it half drowned the talk. It was turned onto a Puerto Rican station that transmitted dance music. The music provided a congenial background to his thought, but the incessant commercials maddened him; there was an irritating quality about the voices of all announcers whether an Englishman was smugly deploring the death of a politician, or an American was recommending a new brand of toothpaste. The knowledge that at any moment that voice might interrupt made concentration difficult. He would have to get an apartment of his own. He could afford one now. The Governor had suggested that the acceptance of a Government post would be to his financial disadvantage. That might be true when a prominent silk went on the bench, but for an unestablished barrister like himself the appointment would mean a very great improvement in his scale of living. He would be able to afford a number of things that he could not previously. A car for instance. What kind should he get.

His thoughts began to wander. It was no good his trying to work

321

tonight. He'd set his alarm for half-past four. He'd take his shaving slowly and get to G.H. by quarter to.

As he came out from the shower, he saw the outline of a head through the veranda screen.

"Hi, who's that," he called. It was his younger brother who had wanted to watch him change. Grainger was the only member of the family who possessed evening dress, and his opportunities of wearing it were few.

"I want to see you in your armor," the boy said.

Though he wore a white dinner jacket, Grainger was one of the few Santa Martans who wore a stiff white shirt. It was cooler, he said, because it stood away from the body. But the real reason was that he possessed a pair of platinum and ruby studs that he liked to wear.

"Come in and sit down," he told his brother.

The boy sat on the bed, staring at him with wide admiring eyes. Grainger knew what he was thinking.

"Are you looking forward to the day when you can wear a shirt like this?" he asked.

The boy nodded quickly.

"Do you know what you'll have to do to wear one?"

"Grow up."

"No, that's not enough. You'll have to work. This shirt is a uniform. It is only worn in a certain kind of house, a certain kind of restaurant. You do not get invited to that kind of house unless you are someone who has passed exams. If you are born rich, you will be asked to that kind of house, you can go to that kind of restaurant without passing exams. But you and I are not born rich. We have to earn our right to wear this armor. It isn't a question of money for us. We don't need to be rich. We have to show that we have good brains and know how to use them. You remember the parable of the talents."

"Yes."

"That applies to us, to you and me. We've got to make use of our talents. To turn four talents into eight, then in ten years time you'll find yourself wearing armor too."

He said it lightly, anxious that it should not seem a sermon. You never knew what things affected a young man. You might send him a long, carefully thought out letter for his confirmation and he would forget that you had ever written it, while the casual remark of a stranger might make a deep impression. On his own tenth birthday, a schoolmaster for whom he had no personal regard had said, "What, ten today Grainger. You're in double figures. When I'm

322

batting and get my tenth run I say to myself 'Now I've really started.' Ten looks so much more than nine in the score book. It's a real innings."

He had thought that over carefully that afternoon. He had thought it over during the days that followed. Ten looked much more than nine. He was in double figures. His innings had started. The time had come for him to work really hard.

"So that's what you've got to do, young man," he said.

*4*

The band was playing when Grainger arrived at Government House, but only half a dozen couples were dancing. The dining room had been cleared and a buffet set under the royal portraits, but no one had patronized it yet and the drawing room was half full. Grainger looked round him, wondering which group to join. Then he saw Mavis. At the same time she noticed him. Her eyes brightened. As he walked toward her, she moved from the group that she was in.

"Shall we dance?" he asked.

She shook her head.

"Let's talk a minute. It's years since we saw each other."

It was barely a fortnight. Yet it seemed a long time to her. He was touched and warmed.

"What have you been doing? Have you had any thrilling cases?"

"Nothing sensational in that line. But something exciting has happened to me, personally."

"You're going to be married?"

"Heavens no, no likelihood of that. I'm going to be Attorney General."

"Grainger, how wonderful."

Her delight was too spontaneous to be feigned.

"How marvelous for you. What a difference it'll make. There's nothing you can't do now."

Two hours ago in his father's dining room, he had felt he could not talk about his appointment because he had known that their reaction to it would jar upon his nerves. It would mean, he had known, something different to them from what it did to him, but he had not attempted to examine that difference. Now sitting by Mavis he knew what it was. His parents would see the event in terms of prestige and of emoluments. So did he, too, of course, but there was another aspect, in the last analysis a more important aspect of

323

which he could not have spoken to them, but of which he could to Mavis.

"It's my chance to show the Santa Martans that one of their own people is as effective as any European. But I want to make it more than that, I want to create in these people a respect for law, a respect for justice. I want them to realize that the law is something that they have created themselves for their own use, for their own protection, that the law is something which they can alter themselves through their own elected representatives. They must cease to think of the law as something imposed upon them by a European master. Do you see what I mean?"

"I see what you mean."

"There's so much a lawyer can do. I've heard Americans say that that great judge of theirs in the eighteen twenties, Mr. Justice Marshall, did as much for the country as the actual framers of the Constitution by the decisions with which he interpreted and illuminated the Constitution. A single lawyer giving honest and wise decisions can create a new mentality among a people. I've a chance of doing that."

His voice was glowing. His eyes shone. In such a spirit, she felt, had knights in the high days of chivalry set out on a crusade.

"You'll do it," she said. "You'll do it."

"Let's dance. We must get this party moving," a voice was saying. It was Euan Templeton. She rose. She was grateful for the interruption. Euan had come at the right moment. Anything that followed would have been an anticlimax. She followed Euan onto the dancing floor.

"Will you buy a house of your own when you get back?" she asked. He shook his head.

"Not till we decide how we want to live. I don't even know what kind of a job I'll find. There'll be at least two years at Oxford first. It's a good idea to live from day to day as long as one is able to."

"You're very wise."

They discussed his plans amicably as they danced. It was strange to remember that only a month ago there had been that thing between them. How trivial and shallow it had been. And now there was a kind of cousinship between them; they would have the same brother-in-law. Not she supposed that she would see much of Euan, when he and Jocelyn had settled down in England. If she herself went over ever, there would be an exchange of letters, a weekend invitation, a theater in London; but they would not have much to talk about once they had finished reminiscing and asking what had happened to old so-and-so.

You couldn't remake a friendship in a different setting. So many West Indians had told her that. You met English visitors over here, you entertained them, established friendship with them, exchanged Christmas cards, "You must come over here and see us," they insisted. But when you went, it was always the same thing. They were away or busy; they sandwiched you between two important dates. You felt you had been a nuisance and the memory of a pleasant acquaintanceship was spoilt. It was not that the English were inhospitable, but that they had lives of their own, and whereas they fitted into one's life here, one didn't fit into their lives there. Noel Coward had written an amusing play *Hands Across the Sea* about it. Perhaps when she went back to England, she would not even bother to let Euan know. She would not like to think of his saying to Jocelyn afterward, "Mavis was a lot of fun over there, but do you think she'd contribute much to that house party we'd arranged for Ascot." Leave things in their setting. Treat friendships as you treated love affairs. That was the wise technique.

"I suppose your father will be retiring when he's finished his appointment here," she said.

"If they consider him a success, he might be sent somewhere more important. Kenya or Malaya. He's not old yet. He'd hate doing nothing." The music stopped.

"What about a drink now," he said.

"If you could get your guests toward the buffet, it would start things moving."

Mavis looked round the room. Sylvia and Maxwell were grouped with the Kellaways in the center of the drawing room. "Let's break that up," she said.

She slipped her arm through Sylvia's. "We both need champagne, at least I do. You look as though you were on the crest already."

"Only two swizzles before dinner. Nothing during it."

"Really?"

There was a glow, an alertness about Sylvia that she had rarely seen during these last months.

"One of the things about living in the country is that when you come in to town you do enjoy yourself," Sylvia said. "Two years ago I was a blasé party-goer. Now I'm not."

Wasn't she? Had she been? That did not square with Mavis' recollection. Sylvia had brought a zest to parties in those old days that she herself had lacked. It was recently, not before, that Sylvia had seemed bored. Mavis remembered how limp and listless her sister had looked at the Nurses' Dance.

"You look as though something had happened to you since I saw you last."

"I can assure you nothing has."

She said it with a laugh, but she knew she lied. She had been transformed, rejuvenated, recreated. As the music began, she turned to Maxwell. She raised her eyebrows and he nodded. He danced superbly. His dancing was a form of courtship. He did not hold her close. But the touch of his hand upon her shoulder was electric. Each fingertip was tingling. Soon, soon she thought, we shall be alone together; she sighed when the music stopped. They had not spoken as they danced. She was grateful to him for that. Words interfered with feelings. He had made no reference to the change of heart between them. She was grateful to him for that too. There was no need for words. Both knew, in the deep core of their beings.

Sylvia looked around her. Jocelyn and Mavis were chattering with Doris Kellaway. She had no wish to join them. That evening at the club after the Governor's cocktail party, she had felt resentful because she could not join the young people's group on the veranda and share their gossip. She did not want to now. She had outgrown that, she had outgrown them. She looked for a group of the young married set. That was where she belonged. She felt married now, as she hadn't then, and after all in the truest sense she hadn't been. She hadn't known what marriage was, the belonging to a man, possessing and possessed.

"Let's join the Des Voeuxes," she said.

"This must be a great night for you," Mavis said to Jocelyn.

"But of course."

Jocelyn smiled, aware of the dramatic irony of the moment. Yes, it was a great night for her, but not in the way that anybody guessed. She had made up her mind now. She would live in the moment, savoring a happiness which would know no tomorrow. Euan came across to her.

"I've deserved this, haven't I," he said.

She knew to what he referred. The dance he had just completed with the former Attorney General's wife.

"You've done your duty nobly. I was most impressed," she said.

He held her closely, his cheek resting against hers. He had a fresh, wholesome smell. Why was she in love with him? Or rather why did she love him? For she loved him, more than she was in love with him. She did not know him well. He was not quite real to her. Perhaps he was not quite real to himself; perhaps he had not become a real person, yet. He stood for certain things, cleanliness, decency, breeding: an essentially honest and honorable attitude to life. You could not imagine him doing anything that was not straight. He could not lie, he could not cheat. But life had not formed him yet. Perhaps that was his charm: his malleability. The knowledge that you would make an impress on him, that he would be a different person because of you.

I shall watch him, she thought, across an ocean, follow his career, see photographs of him, note how he's changing, what he does, thinking to myself "Perhaps it's because of me that he's like that." He won't know what I've done, but I shall.

That was perhaps why one wanted to give him things, to do things for him, because he was so essentially worth while, because one day he would be a person of importance, because what one gave would be valued, would not be wasted. Wasn't that one of the things one was so afraid of, that the gifts one gave, the gifts of value to oneself would not be valued, might just as well never have been made; were so much water poured through a sieve? He must have nothing from me that won't add to him, she thought, nothing that he won't be able to look back on happily, without regret, with pride. I must give him all I have, the best of me, in the best way possible.

"Darling, I've an idea," she said. "It's hard for us to see as much of one another as we'd like, in the way we'd want. We're so hedged round here. Couldn't you say to your father that you'd like to see something of the bigger islands, Trinidad for example? I could tell my father that I need to have my teeth done. My dentist's in Barbados. I could take the opportunity of going there, while you were away. Then you could get bored with Trinidad and think you'd like to see Barbados. You could arrive there while I was still there. Don't you think that's an ingenious scheme."

She had no qualms of modesty. The device would not have occurred to him. He could not know that it was the standard practice in the Caribbean, that "having ones teeth fixed in Barbados" was a joke line.

Her parents seated across the room, noticing Euan's face light up, turned to one another.

"You saw that?"

"Yes, I saw that."

"They really do seem happy together, don't they."

"I don't think we need to worry about them."

"And Sylvia seemed happier this evening than I've ever seen her."

"I thought so, too."

"Maxwell seems satisfied with his second election speech."

"I've heard from other sources that it was very good."

"Do you think he will be elected?" she asked.

"It's not unlikely."

"Will that make things awkward for you?"

"I don't see why it should. He'll be on the same side as I am as often as not. He's nothing against me. At least I don't think he has. He hasn't gone into this to even out a score. It was only a need for self-assertion. He had his brother on his mind. That's been his trouble all along."

"I think you're right." She paused, thoughtfully. For so long Maxwell had been a problem to her. Now, suddenly it seemed as though that problem had been solved. And Jocelyn, that was a responsibility relieved. She had always had a guilt consciousness with regard to Jocelyn. She was quit of that now. She looked at her husband fondly.

"It's good isn't it, being on our own again, just the two of us."

### 5

The invitation card had read 9.30 to 12, but it was close on one before the governor signaled to the band to play the national anthem. Everyone seemed to be having a good time. Why break it up? He stood on the doorstep, bidding the guests good-night. It was a night he had looked forward to often: a night of which he and his wife had dreamed; their son's engagement party. In a sense it was bitter that she was not here to share it with him, in another he wondered if he should not be glad; would she be happy about this marriage, would she be thinking he had acted wisely, was acting wisely. In early days they had had, he and she, the occasional flare-ups of disagreement that occur inevitably between two young people, but they had always been in accord on final issues. Would they have been here?

The Fleurys were coming toward him now. How like her mother Jocelyn was. His heart gave a sudden quirk. He might very easily have fallen in love with Betty Erskine. She was one of the half dozen girls round whom he had woven dreams during the long nights in the trenches. It had been a shock to him when he had read of her engagement. He remembered the night well. They were in a quiet part of the line, refitting after the third battle of Ypres, where they had lost half a company in the mud of Passchendaele. There would be no more offensives for a while. He was due for leave. He had gone down to the ration dump with his runner. He had stood with a light heart waiting for the tinkle of the pack mule's harness.

There was a large mail for him. "You must be writin' to yourself, sir," the driver said. Half a dozen letters, proofs of the good time that was waiting him next month. The largest was from his father. He left it till the last. It was full of gossip. "Several local engagements," he had read. "The one that'll interest you most is Julian Fleury's to Betty Erskine."

He had let the letter fall onto his table. It was only now, when he had lost her, that he realized how much she had meant to him, how much his hopes for the next leave had been bound up with her. How blind, how slow he had been. Julian Fleury and Betty Erskine. Julian had been wounded in May at Bullecourt, had gone home on sick leave, in the role of a wounded hero: his courtship had been framed against an English summer.

He called his runner. "We'll go round the line," he said.

It was a bleak but rainless night: the dark stretch of shell holes, lit every few moments by the flickering incandescence of a Very light matched his mood.

Three weeks later a splinter from a chance shell tore through his thigh. As he was driven, drowsy under a shot of morphia, to the casualty clearing station, he thought of what would have happened if he and Julian could have changed roles, if he had been wounded in May and Julian in November. How little he had guessed that by a turn of fortune's wheel, Betty's grandchildren would be his own.

The memory of that long, numbed drive to the C.C.S. was very actual to him as he stood now on his doorstep, wishing his guests good-night. How like her mother Jocelyn was, no trace of Julian. He put his arm round her shoulder.

"This is a very happy day for me," he said. "When I was Euan's age your mother was to me the ideal English girl. You look so exactly like her that you might be her. I can't begin to tell you how happy and proud I am for Euan's sake."

He tightened the pressure: to his surprise he found that his voice was trembling. She looked up quickly, hesitated, then raised herself upon her toes and, for the first time, kissed his cheek.

"You're a dear," she whispered.

There was a mist before his eyes. He did not know whose hand he was shaking next.

### 6

Mavis, standing in the courtyard, waited for Jocelyn to come through. Her parents had not been invited. It was as far as possible a young people's party. She had come with the Fleurys.

"You'll probably make some date there," Sylvia had said. She had half expected that she would herself. Parties usually led to other parties, particularly when there was a moon: suggestions had been made to her, but she had met them barely quarter way. She was preoccupied; for her the climax of the evening had come at the beginning in that talk with Grainger.

She watched the guests file out. This might have been her party if she had played her cards cleverly. She smiled wryly. She was glad that she was not the kind of girl who played cards cleverly. She preferred to be the girl to whom a man like Grainger Morris brought the first news of his success; she was glad to be the way she was.

7

Back at his parents' home Grainger sat on the veranda, tired but not sleepy, as he had sat only a few weeks earlier on the night of the Governor's cocktail party. What would he have thought then, could he have foreseen that within five weeks this high honor would have come to him. How little he had suspected when he had left home that morning that he would be sitting here in this mood tonight. As long as he lived he would remember this evening. Looking back from ten, twenty, thirty, maybe fifty years, he would see this night as the beginning, the crucial date in his career. From what ultimate point would he look back toward this evening?

He recalled a lecture he had heard at Oxford on the structure of tragedy. "The end," the lecturer had said, "is foreseen in the beginning. When the denouement is reached the audience recognizes that no other climax was possible, that given those characters, in that situation, against that background, the drama could not have worked to any other close. Yet at the same time in the working out of the plot, each new step, each new incident must surprise the audience. The audience must be kept guessing all the time as to what is going to happen next, even though it knows subconsciously how the threads will be unraveled.

"If you will look at your lives as you live them day by day, week by week, month by month," the lecturer had said, "you will feel that everything in life is unpredictable, that we are all the victims of chance: that because we start out one morning without an umbrella, because a telephone bell rings when we are leaving the house and we decide to run back and answer it, because we wear a light suit instead of a dark one, because we travel by a bus instead of by a tube, we meet by chance the person who for good or bad will revolutionize our life. It all seems to turn on chance.

"Yet ninety-nine times in a hundred when a man of forty looks back on the last fifteen years, he sees that he is in more or less the position and condition that he might have expected for himself. It has worked out according to plan. And when he looks at the lives of his friends, he will see that very few of them have surprised him, that they have all more or less followed the road on which their feet seemed set when they were young. Yet for them as for you each day has brought its own unexpected rewards, problems, and discomfitures. Life is an adventure because every day is different: that is why a good play must be exciting, but never forget that it is one of the functions of the play to show behind that hour by hour, day to day excitingness, the eternal forces that control the wind and tides of human action, working out their own inevitable pattern."

It was strange to reflect that when he ultimately did look back toward this night, he would see his progress to that point in terms of an inevitable logical process of effect and cause.

From the road outside came the sound of brakes: then of two low voices. Female and masculine. The female voice was Muriel's. He glanced at his watch. Quarter to two. But there was a moon, bathing picnics lingered on; the voices hushed, but he heard no sound of feet upon the stairs; of a door opening; no creak of boards on the veranda. He ought to go, he did not want to spy. Yet he did not want to interrupt them. The minutes passed. Then there was the sound of a car being put in gear. A male voice whispered "good-night," then a soft footfall on the stair. Perhaps she would not come out here.

But Muriel was feeling the need of quiet reverie. He saw her in silhouette against the sky. She came toward him with a slow, gliding walk.

"Hullo," he said.

She did not start. She pulled a chair forward and sat beside him. She stretched out her legs and crossed her hands behind her head. She looked out over the sea, across which a waning moon drew its long line of ruffled silver. He could not read the expression of her face. But her profile, her whole pose had an air of calm. They sat there silent, side by side; conscious of one another, grateful for the knowledge that they did not need to speak, that they were in tune, respecting each other's problems if not understanding them, savoring the beauty of the night.

Peace lay upon their hearts, as it lay upon the hearts of so many who had been distracted a few weeks earlier on the night of the Governor's cocktail party. Euan and his father and young Archer, Maxwell and Sylvia, Jocelyn and Julian Fleury, Mavis and Margot and

David Boyeur, they had all been in their separate ways distracted, frustrated, perplexed that evening. Tonight they had each in their separate ways found their way to harbor, at the very moment when in the offices of *The Voice of Santa Marta* high bundles of the next day's issue were awaiting delivery at daybreak.

# CHAPTER TWENTY

## *1*

Maxwell left town early. He wanted to drive in the cool, he also wanted to surprise his laborers, to see how much they did in his absence. Within ten minutes of his return, he had changed his clothes and was on his horse: he did not get back till half-past twelve.

"I'll be ready as soon as that punch you're fixing is," he shouted.

"Hurry," she called back. "For once there's some real news in the paper."

"What is it, tell me."

"They've found the wallet."

"What wallet?"

"Carson's."

He was glad that she could not see him at that moment. They talked in novels of bleaching under your tan. He felt as though every drop of blood had been drained out of him. He walked round to the stables, slowly; mechanically undid his pony's girth.

"Hi, George, unsaddle Susie," he called out.

Carson's wallet. So it had been Carson's wallet on the Colonel's desk. How had it got there? What did its presence there purport? Why had it been reported? There must be a reason. Who had found it?

He must not hurry, he warned himself. He must not look over-interested. He would shower at his normal pace; behave as though nothing of concern to him had happened.

He picked up the punch and sipped.

"Fine. I needed that," he said. "Let's see the paper."

It was headlined across three columns. *Colonel Carson's Wallet. Finder detained.* Then across double columns. *Sensational Discovery. Police have clue at last.*

He put down his glass. He rested his hand against a chair. He pressed down on it. Steady, he told himself, steady. Keep your head. He read the paragraph. It was only six lines long. The meat was in the headlines.

"It doesn't tell us much," he said.

333

"It tells us that there was a wallet missing. We didn't know that before."

"Didn't we?"

"How could we have?"

Indeed, how could they have. He knew. They didn't. That was the trouble. He kept forgetting what they knew and what they didn't know: what Whittingham knew and what the public knew. He remembered hearing an officer who had worked in intelligence during the war remark on the difficulty of remembering whether you had acquired a piece of information from gossip, a newspaper, or a top secret source. It forced you, he had said, to discuss in public nothing but gallantry and athletics. That was his problem now. He knew everything, while the public knew practically nothing.

"It's very vague about the man who had the wallet. I wonder why they don't give the name," she said.

"I suppose they want to keep the real man guessing."

"The real man. But why shouldn't the man who had the wallet be the right man?"

"If he were, he wouldn't be carrying it around with him."

"Then what's your explanation of his having it?"

"I'd say that the man who killed Carson took his wallet, took out the money, flung away the wallet, and this laborer discovered it. Then one of the police found it on him."

"It's very ingenious of you to have thought of that."

Was it, or was it too ingenious. Surely it wasn't. Wouldn't this explanation have occurred to any reasonable person who read detective stories. Sylvia never read them. That was why it had not occurred to her.

"But if that's the case, why do the police say that its discovery is so valuable," she said. "The paper says 'sensational discovery.'"

"Papers always say that kind of thing. It's their busines to exaggerate."

"I know, but in a case like this . . ."

She hesitated, dubious.

"The paper must have got this news from the police. The police must have encouraged them to think it was important."

"That's to stop the public worrying. The police like to throw out sops to keep the public quiet, until the public has lost interest."

"In England, possibly, but not here surely, where everyone knows everybody. The paper says it's a valuable clue. If what you say is true, I don't see that it's a clue at all."

He thought fast. In what way could it be a clue. He didn't see

that it was any use at all, unless . . . a sudden frightening thought had
struck him.

"If they know where the pocketbook was found, they know
where the murderer went that night. That gives them some indication of the area in which he lives."

"It doesn't say where they found it."

"Doesn't it?" He reread the paper. "No more it does. But it must
have been some help to them to know."

The knowledge that it must have been disturbed him. It would
limit the scope of their inquiry. Or would it? Why should they
think that it had been flung there by the murderer on that night? He
could have kept it on him, waiting for an opportunity to throw it
into a cane field, far from where he lived.

He might have; but that's not what I did, Maxwell told himself. I
wanted to get rid of that wallet and watch as soon as possible. I did
not want to have them found on me. I was afraid that I might have a
car accident: I didn't even drive home by the longest road, if I had
it would have looked suspicious: to be found late at night on the
leeward coast road. How would I have explained that? I did what the
average man would have done in my position; made for home by the
quickest road and got rid of the watch and wallet at the first available
opportunity. That's what ninety-nine in a hundred men would have
done in my position; Whittingham unless he's an idiot knows it. And
he's not an idiot.

He picked up his glass and sipped at it. He would have given a lot
to gulp at it and then ask Sylvia for another. But that would be unusual. He must not do anything unusual.

"As I see it, the discovery of that wallet is really of no use to the
police at all. If they had had a lucky break in some other direction,
it might help; but not otherwise."

He said it as much as possible to reassure himself. Sylvia was still
unconvinced.

"You may be right, but I believe you are assuming that the murderer is cleverer than he is. You are trying to imagine how you
would have behaved if you had done the murder."

"What?"

"You are thinking, how should I behave if I had gone into Carson's that night as a thief, and then been disturbed and got into a
fight and killed him. And I'm sure that you're right in saying that
that's how you would have behaved if you had found yourself in
such a predicament. But you are not a thief. You did not break into
Carson's house. It was another type of man who did. And that man
would have behaved differently because he was a different type. The

average thief is stupid and ignorant. If he hadn't been stupid, he'd have gone to the police straight away and told them that he killed Carson in self-defense. If he'd done that, he'd only have been charged with manslaughter. You know how the courts always take the side of the colored man. That's what you would have done in his position. Think of all the films you have seen in which a man has killed someone by mistake and has got into all kinds of trouble by running away, by trying to hide the traces. You'd never have made a mistake like that. This man did. He was a stupid fellow. He ran away and then held on to the wallet and was caught with it."

"Then why do you think the police haven't arrested him?"

"Because they haven't enough evidence. They prefer to watch him. He may have an accomplice."

"You may be right."

She might indeed be right. So many of the things she had said were true. Why had he thought that he could get away with it? Why hadn't he followed his first impulse and gone to the police? She had guessed three-quarters right and quarter wrong because she had assumed that a sensible man always acted sensibly. Whittingham had more experience of the irrationalities of the human mind. Whittingham would also recognize that there were additional possibilities; he could afford to wait. But was there any reason to suppose that he had not to some extent argued along the same lines as Sylvia. Perhaps he had been inclined to assume that the man with the wallet had come by it illegally. He might see the wallet as a clue.

Whoever had found the wallet would have certainly contradicted himself under interrogation. Though the whites and the near whites believed that the courts took the side of the colored man, the colored man talked of the white man's law. In the plantation days a dark man was not allowed to give evidence in court against a white. Whoever had found that wallet must have lied. His manner would have bred suspicion.

Suppose sufficient evidence accumulated to warrant his arrest? It would not be the first time that an innocent man had been tried for murder. How would I feel, Maxwell thought, if an innocent man were in the box for a crime I had committed? It was the kind of situation that occurred in novels, that you never expected to have happen in real life, not in your own life. Would he have the nerve to sit in court while a man was being tried for a crime he had committed; would he have the patience to await the verdict, banking on the man being acquitted? Was he to be exposed to that test?

The maid stood in the doorway. "Lunch is ready mistress."

He finished his punch with a quick gulp.

"I'm thirsty. I'd like a beer," he said.

"I'll have one too."

He held out his hand. She took it and drawing herself to her feet, let her weight rest against his arm. She lingered there, smiling up at him. Never had he felt so close to her. Never had he felt so far away.

## 2

Two mornings later Preston returned from his round of the estate to find a constable seated on the veranda, talking to his wife. He had called, he said, to ask Mr. Preston if he could remember what he had been doing on the night of Carson's death.

"I can't recall that we did anything," he said. "That means that we did nothing, that that night was the same as every other night. We remember the few occasions when we do anything unusual."

"Have you any method of checking up on that?" the constable inquired. He had risen to his feet as Preston came onto the veranda. He was tall, stiff, formal. In his white tunic, with the high collar buttoning at the throat, the blue serge trousers and heavy thick-soled black leather boots, he looked very incongruous against a background of palm trees and bougainvillea.

"I don't keep a diary myself but I think my wife . . ."

Mrs. Preston laughed.

"Every Christmas I receive from my Aunt Eleanor a Smythson pocket diary. Every Boxing Day I write to tell her that it is exactly what I needed and every December thirty-first I find that I have made not a single entry on its pages."

"Wouldn't your servants remember if they had been given the day off. Do you yourself, sir, check the morning roll call at the *boucan?* Wouldn't your overseer's roll call help?"

"I suppose it would. But it would be a great nuisance. Is it all that important?"

"Colonel Whittingham, sir, considers that it is most important. He wants to know who was in town that evening and who was in the country; and what everyone who was in the country did."

A checking over of the estate muster roll and of the grocery books eventually satisfied the Prestons that that night had been for them like three hundred and fifty other nights of the year, quiet and eventless.

"Did no one call on you?" the constable asked.

"Who is there that could call on us. We have no neighbors, except the Fleurys, and we rarely see them except in town."

"Did anyone borrow your car?"

"No."

"Could anyone have taken it for the night, without your knowing?"

"I keep the keys locked inside my desk."

"Then that, sir, answers everything. Thank you very much. I am most sorry to have inconvenienced you."

He took out his notebook, flipped over a number of pages and made a mark against an item on a list.

"You seem to have set yourself quite an investigation, constable."

"I am calling on every house along the windward coast whose owner possesses a car."

On the following afternoon Preston passed Maxwell driving to the point. He stopped his car.

"How did you manage with the constable?" he asked.

"What constable?"

"The one who was out here yesterday, asking what each of us was doing the night Carson caught his packet."

"He never came to me."

"Didn't he? He said he was calling on everyone who has a car."

"What did he want to know?"

"Whether I was in that night, whether anyone came to see me, whether anybody could have used my car. He was asking everyone, so he said."

"He didn't need to ask me. He knew where I was. I'd been to Whittingham about it. I'm in a peculiar position. I passed Carson's house, at the exact time when the murderer was in it. With any luck I should have met the man. Whittingham and I checked over my movements thoroughly."

Had his voice sounded as casual and offhand as he had meant it should? His brain was racing, he wanted to close his eyes, to lie flat on his back in the dark and let the river of this distracting mood flow over him. But he had to sit here on his pony, erect under the midday sun, composed and indifferent.

"I never knew that," Preston was saying. "To think of your actually passing the house at the very time. Perhaps you should consider yourself lucky; if he had killed one man, he might have killed another. Fancy my not hearing that. It shows how out of touch I get, down here on the estate."

"You ought to get into town more often."

"How can I with Jane and the two children. I can't leave them alone out here. This is the most unsettled section in the island."

"It won't be after the elections. There'll be a New Deal then."

"So you think you'll be elected."

"I know I shall."

"From what I hear . . ."

"From what everybody hears. They're volatile. They were so much against me a month ago, that they can't help being all for me in three weeks' time. I shall sweep the poll. You wait. See you at the hustings."

He tightened his reins and pressed his knees against the saddle. His pony moved and he waved his hand. He wanted to spur his pony, to gallop it up the pathway to the hills, to exercise his problems by violent exercise; but he knew he mustn't. It was close on noon. Sylvia was on the veranda; the nutmeg and the limes were waiting by the jug of ice. It was the hour of the morning punch. He must do nothing unexpected, nothing that would arouse suspicion: nothing, nothing. How long had this perpetual self-watching to continue. It would drive him mad if it did not stop.

### 3

Usually after lunch Maxwell took his siesta in his dressing room, but today he joined Sylvia in her room. He had never needed her so much. If only he could pour out his troubles to her. In one way they were so close; he could have talked now about himself as he could never have done before; any problem that had been his a month ago he could have talked about freely now—his difficulties with the estate and with his father, his diffidence and lack of confidence, his sense of grievance against the world, his feeling that life had cheated him, his jealousy of his brother. All those sources of irritation that he had bottled up, had concealed beneath a mask of arrogance, had ceased to be troubles in the light of this one all-shadowing trouble.

If only he could speak of it to Sylvia, now when he needed to be unburdened, now when he could have revealed to her any other secret, no matter how obscure and shaming. The need to speak heightening the knowledge that he could not speak, deepened his need of her. The knowledge that because of this shadow he could not yet give himself to her completely, gave him a new and intenser eloquence. As his arms went round her, his words struck a deeper note.

"You are the whole world to me," he told her.

He meant it, and she knew he did. She was his sky, his ocean, his sun, his stars: he took reflection from her.

"Without you there is nothing, nothing."

He had never needed her so desperately, so utterly, with his heart and spirit. Never had he felt such an overpowering need to give himself, to be encompassed by her. For the first time in his life, he crossed the boundaries of passion, and found love.

He slept with his head upon her shoulder. She stroked his cheek slowly, as she would a child's. If only a child could be born out of this afternoon, she thought.

He slept till late afternoon, while she lay motionless, unsleeping.

That night, however, he lay awake, his mind beset by questions. Why had Whittingham instigated these inquiries? Why now, and not three weeks ago? Something new had happened. There must be some fresh development in connection with the discovery of the wallet. What had the wallet told him? What had it suggested? Why did Whittingham want these facts. Was this laborer who had found the wallet really in danger of his life. Would his own conscience allow him to go free when another man was suffering for his sake.

What was this wretched laborer thinking now? The man knew that he was innocent, but what comfort was that to him if the court thought him guilty. Was he undergoing mental torture at this very moment. What did Whittingham suspect? What had Whittingham had in mind?

Unless I have some inkling, I shall go mad, Maxwell told himself. He'd got to see Whittingham; find some excuse for seeing him; then lead the conversation round to the murder, to the investigation, the wallet, evoke some confidence: find out how the land lay. Unless he knew that he would go off his head.

### 4

Next morning Maxwell rang up Whittingham.

"It's nothing important. But I'd like to have a word with you when next I'm in town. I'll be in next week, which day would suit you best—Tuesday or Wednesday. Tuesday. Fine. I'll be round about eleven."

He found Whittingham as he had found him on the previous visit, his foot rested in the lower drawer of his desk.

"What can I do for you?"

"Not a subscription for the Belfontaine Committee."

Whittingham gave a start.

"What do you know about the Belfontaine Committee?"

"Nothing in particular. I have heard it mentioned."

"Who by?"

"I can't remember. Someone in the club."

"Indeed. You're the last person I should have expected to have heard of it."

Whittingham's surprise was manifest. The Belfontaine Committee. How had he come to mention it? It had slipped out suddenly. Belfontaine Committee. What was it after all? Where had he heard of it? He pondered. Suddenly the scene came back. Carson's house. The sneer on Carson's face. Carson's first question. "What can I do for you? Not a subscription for the Belfontaine Committee?"

"What can I do for you?" Whittingham had used the same words as Carson, and out of his subconsciousness an involuntary reaction, outside his control, had brought the identical response. That's what the psychoanalyst did, asked you what certain words made you think of first.

Once again terror struck him. Had he given himself away? In this instance he did not see how he could have done, but the fact that the words Belfontaine Committee had automatically sprung to his lips was terrifying. What might not the subconscious self over which one had no control reveal another time?

But that lay in the future. He must hurry on now as though he had not said anything unusual.

"I've come to ask about my property during the elections. Do you think it's safe. Ought I to take special precautions. You've always said that my parish was the most unsettled in the island."

"It is."

"Do we need special precautions then?"

"I've made arrangements with the local police officer that he can get help quickly if it's needed."

Whittingham explained what the help was and how quickly it could reach a given danger point.

"Everything's under control," the colonel said, "but I may be flattering myself. It's like the dams that one erects to keep out a flood. One doesn't realize till the flood comes, how strong they are."

"What danger is there?"

"Your bet is as good as mine."

They discussed the temper of the district. As always Whittingham was bland, talkative, congenial. With his pink cheeks, his white fringe of hair about his ears, his high damp forehead, he looked like a contented baby. It was a disarming manner. When you talked of a man having a poker face, you pictured him as thin, gaunt, long-chinned, with deepset eyes, but Whittingham with his cherubic face was the most redoubtable poker-player in the club. The only time

Maxwell had caught him off his guard was this morning when he had spoken of the Belfontaine Committee. What was the Belfontaine Committee, hang it all. He'd have to find that out.

For a quarter of an hour they sat talking, then Maxwell pickèd up his hat. "I must be on my way," he said. Then as though struck by an afterthought, he added. "I see you've found Carson's wallet."

"It's been found."

"I suppose that that was Carson's wallet on your desk the last time I was in here."

"Was it? I don't know, it may have been. When were you here?"

"Thursday of the week before last."

"What day would that have been?"

"The day of the G.H. dance. Next day I read about it in the paper."

"Then it very likely was Carson's wallet. What made you think it was?"

The moment that he had mentioned the wallet, Maxwell was afraid that he had made a mistake, but he had to go on with it now.

"You were holding a wallet in your hand when I came in. You put it on the top of the desk."

"Did you recognize the wallet."

"Of course not, how could I, I'd never seen his wallet, or at least I'd never noticed it. But reading that article next day in the paper, I put two and two together."

"Naturally. Of course."

"I remember thinking it probably was his; after all it's only a few of us who can afford pigskin wallets."

"So you could recognize it as being pigskin."

"I thought it was pigskin. It was pigskin wasn't it?"

"I can't remember. It was ruined by rain. It didn't matter. I knew it was Carson's because of the papers in it."

"You'd have thought he'd have destroyed them."

"Who?"

"The man who found it."

"Yes, you would have thought so, wouldn't you?"

"Isn't the fact that he had the papers on him, a proof that the man who had the wallet couldn't have done the murder."

"Why do you say that?"

"The man who had done the murder would have surely destroyed everything that could connect him with the crime. He might have kept the money. Money's anonymous after all, but a thing like a wallet or a watch."

"A watch?"

"Or a ring or perhaps a fountain pen."

Watch. Why did I say watch, Maxwell asked himself. There'd been no mention of a watch. Why should the watch have occurred to him: again that subconscious reflex. Had the colonel noticed? He had repeated the word watch, but he had not followed it up. That fat babyish smile had remained unruffled. What did he think behind that mask? Was he past thinking—a genial figurehead whose juniors covered up and did the work for him?

"Whichever way you look at it," Maxwell said, "the man that you caught with the wallet was a stupid fellow."

"Or else he was too clever."

"How do you make that out?"

"People nowadays have seen so many detective films and spy films. They may not be able to read, but their wits are keen in what concerns themselves. They all know about the doublecross. Did you read that book *Operation Cicero*?"

"I saw the film."

"Then you'll understand the point I'm making. During the war each side indulged in deception campaigns, to mislead the other side as to their intentions. As you may remember, an actor, dressed up as Montgomery, was sent to Gibraltar on the eve of the Normandy landings. The Germans could not believe that an invasion was imminent in Northern France when the Commander-in-Chief was in Gibraltar. Sometimes the deceptions were so elaborate that we could best deceive the Germans by putting out the truth by a source that the Germans distrusted."

"How do you mean?"

"Suppose we capture a wireless set by which a German spy is transmitting information to the Germans. The Germans don't know we have captured it, so we continue to operate it, sending out the kind of information, most of it false, that is likely to deceive the Germans. Then the Germans find out that we have captured and are operating the set; they promptly discount all the news that comes through on it. We then find out that the Germans know about it but they don't know that we know they know. What do we do? We start telling them the truth, because they'll disbelieve it. You see how complicated it gets: particularly when the Germans find out that we know they know. Then we have to start telling lies again."

"Where is all this leading to?"

"Operation Cicero. A German spy captured from a British diplomat the plans of the Normandy Invasion. The Germans refused to believe that the plans were genuine. They could not conceive that

343

any British diplomat could be so stupid. If they had acted on that spy's information, many thousands of allied lives would have been lost. The war might have gone on another year."

"But how does this bear on the Carson case?"

"I'm wandering. I'm sorry. I get vague, I start digressing. That's middle age. It starts in the middle forties: earlier sometimes in the tropics. Where did I begin? Operation Cicero, deception, yes that's it: deception. Criminals practice deception too; they try and throw us off the scent by acting, on purpose, more stupidly than you could expect any sane man to. Have you seen *The Voice* today?"

"No."

"Then you've not read our American friend's latest article."

"No."

"Here it is, run your eye over it."

It was the article that Bradshaw had sent to Baltimore three weeks ago. It began with a section about Obeah, exploiting the author's knowledge and giving his reasons for disbelieving that Carson's was an Obeah murder. It then mentioned the loss of the watch and wallet, and suggested that these might have been taken so as to make the crime look like the outcome of theft and violence. As he read, Maxwell was conscious of Whittingham watching him with his lazy, seemingly indifferent stare. It made him feel uncomfortable; he wanted to look up and meet that stare but he felt he shouldn't.

"Finished?" the colonel asked.

Maxwell nodded.

"See what I mean about a thief being too clever. You hadn't read that article before, you say."

"How could I? I left before the paper came."

"Of course, of course. It's rather curious, you know."

"What's curious?"

"Doesn't anything strike you as curious about that article?"

"No, what?"

"The watch. You mentioning a watch. No one outside this office knew that the watch was missing, until this morning."

"Bradshaw must have known."

"Of course. I told him. But I told him not to mention it. I didn't want anyone but the actual murderer to know about its being missing."

"Why was that?"

"There was always a chance of the murderer giving himself away."

"How could he do that?"

"In several ways. There are so many ways in which he could slacken his vigilance. He could say for instance, 'I wonder if they've

344

found the wallet yet.' How would he know there was a wallet missing?"

"Isn't that a million to one chance?"

"Of course, but that's what one relies on, throwing out as many million to one chances as one can. The meshes of the net, you know."

"Did it serve any purpose?"

"No, I'm afraid it didn't."

He was smiling as blandly as ever: his face wore its habitual vacuous expression. Maxwell's irritation mounted, with it a sense of fear; he felt that he was being encased by some vast, flabby substance, whose hold would gradually suffocate him in its warmth and thickness. It exasperated him into action.

"Why did you say that it was curious my mentioning the watch?"

"Because you couldn't have known then that a watch was involved, yet you would know within two hours. Have you read Dunne's *Experiment with Time*? You should. It's very interesting. This case is a good example of it. Dunne's theory, as far as I could get it, is that the future and the past both exist simultaneously, so that a man can find himself living in the future before it has, as far as the rest of the world knows, happened. In Dunne's book, there's the incident of a man dreaming of the eruption of Mont Pelée in Martinique three days before it took place. Now you apparently knew about this watch before you had read it in the paper.

"It may have been unconscious telepathy: as everyone in Jamestown knew, you may have picked it up subconsciously by telepathic wireless. Dunne's theory is different. Not that I understand his theory. It's very difficult, or it is to me. Priestley wrote some plays about it before the war. They were dramatic plays. But I could never see what he was trying to prove. He had some simile about life being one vast tapestry with the present moving over it like a spotlight. You only see that part of the tapestry on which the spotlight rests, but the rest of the tapestry—the past and future—hasn't ceased to exist because it's in darkness and you can't see it. Priestley seemed to think this was a source of consolation. I couldn't see that it was. If the spotlight is fixed on a dreary episode that happens to be your life at the moment, it's no consolation to be told that the past where you enjoyed yourself still exists. After all . . ."

He enlarged his thesis. Maxwell could have thrown his hat upon the floor and stamped on it. This was driving him out of his mind. There were things he had to know, things he had come in to learn and here was this tiresome old fool blathering about Priestley and Dunne and time.

Steady, he warned himself, steady. How often had he issued

that warning to himself in the last few days. How many more times would he have to issue it? How many more times would he have to say, "Patience now, patience. Don't do anything that is not completely normal."

Patience. Patience, he adjured himself. Yes, but was it normal for him to be patient, to sit here meekly while Whittingham prosed on? Wasn't he by nature difficult, cantankerous, ill-tempered? Weren't these imposed manners more likely to arouse suspicion than a breach of manners? Wasn't he overplaying his role of deception in Operation Carson? He was in a fog. Whatever he did seemed wrong. Why had he mentioned the watch? And why was Whittingham taking it as a proof of Dunne's theory of time? Shouldn't he have felt suspicious?

"Priestley's idea, as far as I can gather it . . ."

It was more than Maxwell could stand. No one expected such elaborate good manners from him. He waited for the next full stop, and although it came in the middle of an argument, he interrupted.

"Why did you tell so much to Bradshaw? Why did you trust him with facts that you didn't want generally known?"

Whittingham started.

"I'm sorry, I was boring you. I keep digressing. That's one of the troubles of middle age, that and repeating oneself and a faulty memory. You forget names and faces and you can't remember whom you told what story to. And one digresses, as you've observed. I apologize, my dear boy. I'm very sorry. I can't keep to the point any longer. Now what was it you were asking me?"

His apology embarrassed Maxwell. It made him feel in the wrong again.

"I asked why you told so much to Bradshaw if you didn't want it known all over Jamestown."

"Because, my dear boy, a journalist is in one respect the most trustworthy person in the world. He will only repeat gossip in a column. He keeps his cards up his sleeve. Bradshaw would not repeat one word I told him, until it appeared in print."

"But why did you tell him in the first place?"

"Because I wanted it in print, after a certain interval. To begin with, as I told you, I didn't want anyone to know: I wanted to keep the murderer guessing, there was a chance he might give himself away at once; but he hasn't done so. Then after three weeks or so I thought it would be useful to let him know that we were interested in the watch and wallet."

"But he already knows about the wallet."

"As it happens he does, but that was unexpected. I couldn't have foreseen, when I talked to Bradshaw, that we were going to find the wallet. That was a surprise."

"I wonder why you told the press about that."

Whittingham shrugged. "Possibly that was a mistake. It's very hard to tell. There was as much to say on one side as the other. As a matter of fact I tossed for it. I'm working in the dark, you see, waiting for a gleam of light. I'm confident that it'll come. It's simply a question of keeping my eyes open."

"Do you agree with Bradshaw about it?"

"On what point?"

"On its being done by someone who wanted to make it look like murder."

"Did Bradshaw say that?"

"I thought he did."

"Let's see the paper. I read the article in a hurry. But I didn't think he said exactly that."

Maxwell handed the paper over. Whittingham looked at the last paragraph.

"No, as I thought, he didn't say quite that. I'll read you what he says. 'Everything points to the murder having been done by a housebreaker who was interrupted by Carson's early return, but the police are alive to the possibilities of the murderer having attempted to make it look like a thief's handiwork.' Not quite the same thing, is it?"

"No, no, indeed not. I read it quickly."

"Of course, of course."

There was a pause. Whittingham appeared to be in no hurry for him to go. Whittingham never seemed to have any work to do. He was always in when you called. The telephone never went. Nobody brought in files. No visitor was announced. It was hard to believe that this office was the center of security in the island. The pause lengthened. It made Maxwell awkward. He had got to say something. He had not had any answer to his last question.

"Do you yourself think it's likely that the murderer tried to make it look like theft?"

"My dear fellow, how should I know? It is a possibility. There are fifteen possibilities. I am in the dark."

"But you must have a theory?"

"Why should I?"

"When you were enumerating those fifteen possibilities, you must have considered which was the likeliest."

"That's the last thing I'd do."

"Why?"

"It's a mistake to have preconceptions. You must keep an open mind."

"It seems a curious way to track down criminals."

"You read too many detective stories, my dear friend."

"But..." Maxwell checked, baffled. He had the sense of that warm, soft flabby substance closing suffocatingly round him. He had to hit back against it.

"I've read the Freeman Wills Croft stories. You seem to follow the example of Inspector French."

"In what way?"

"You check on everything. Your inspector's been making a check in our district."

"He's been making a check in every district."

"That sounds like Inspector French thoroughness."

"You don't expect us to sit here idle, do you?"

"I was wondering after what you said."

Again the colonel smiled, that lazy, friendly, basically uninterested smile.

"You didn't play rugger football, did you?"

"I didn't, no."

"I did. I played under two coaches. One had been a three quarter, the other had been a forward. The three quarter coach was always devising new methods of attack, training the forwards to take part in three quarter movements. That was at school. The papers said that we were the best side to watch in England. We ran up big scores, but we got beaten now and again through having gaps in our defenses.

"The other coach was a forward. He coached our police college. He concentrated on defense. If you don't let the other man through, he'd say, you can't be beaten. Sooner or later the other side will make a mistake, jump on it and you'll score a try. We weren't a spectacular side to watch but we were rarely beaten and we won more matches than we drew. It was a good training for a policeman. He has to spend most of his time waiting, a spider at the center of his web."

"It sounds dull."

"You say that because you've been reading detective stories. It's fascinating. Things have to happen quickly in a detective story, and in a detective story the policeman is working on one case only. In real life he's working on a dozen simultaneously; so many pots simmering; I very often know who is the criminal, but I have no proof. I sit here and wait. He probably plays into my hand someday. Very often I don't know. But I'm in no hurry. Wasn't I saying

348

this to you before or was it to Bradshaw that I said it? I can't remember whom I say what to nowadays. Middle age, past middle age, it's hell. No, it's not dull, far from it. Look at the steel cabinet over there. It's full of files. I know at least twenty people in this town who would give ten years to have ten minutes inside that cabinet. I sit and wait and lay my little traps. Nine times in ten they give themselves away."

"In what way, give me an example."

"Let's see, can I think of one? It's usually something very trivial; something that isn't evidence at all, a look, an intonation, the use of one word rather than another. There was a case now in B.G. a long time ago, I wish I could remember the exact details. I ought to have kept a diary. I shall never be able to write my reminiscences; they'd have been worth reading. This B.G. case now. It was forgery. What put me on to my man was his saying 'afterward' instead of 'after.' What was the context—no, I can't remember. The key point was that the word 'afterward' gave the suggestion of something happening after a definite event. I wonder if you get the point.

"Suppose for instance you were telling me that you called round at the tennis club on your way back home. You'd normally say, wouldn't you, 'I looked in there after lunch,' but if you were to say 'afterward I looked in at the tennis club' that's somehow different. It gives the impression that something definite and dramatic happened about lunch time. 'Afterward'—it's a powerful word. Do you get my point? No, probably you don't. I haven't explained it properly. I've forgotten the details. It's a terrible thing to be old, one by one your faculties desert you, but the use of the word 'afterward' instead of 'after' did the trick in that forgery case. I wish I could remember the whole story, it would interest you. That 'afterward' put me on the scent."

The warm, soft flabby substance was closing inexorably on Maxwell. He was being stifled, yet he shivered too. "After," "afterward": hadn't he himself confused those words in this very room three weeks ago? Hadn't he said "afterward" instead of "after I passed the house"; "afterward" must have given the impression that he had seen that car in the road after some definite event. Wouldn't it have been normal for him to have said, "after I passed Carson's turning," but instead of that he had said "afterward"? Hadn't Whittingham caught him up, asked, "after what"? He had barely noticed the slip at the time, but now it all came back, vividly, startlingly.

"We set our little traps. We lay our ground bait. We sit and wait," Whittingham was repeating.

His face looked as innocent as a child's. It was impossible to think of him as a malevolent spider, watching from the center of his web. "If you are worried about the people in your district, get in touch with our officer. He's got his orders. He'll look after you," he said.

5

"We set our little traps. We lay our ground bait."

Maxwell sat at the wheel, trembling, unable to release the clutch. His hands were shaking. "After," "afterward." What other slips had he made? The watch, how could he have known about the watch? Whittingham had pounced on that: all that long spiel about Dunne's theory of Time was a pretense. Whittingham was an astute old bird. He did not let you know when you had made a slip. What other slips could he have made? The Belfontaine Committee, what on earth was that? Why had Whittingham started? He had been suprised then. Why, why, why?

"We set our little traps, lay out our ground bait." What traps had Whittingham set for him? The wallet. Had he held it in his hands purposely, to see how he would take it? Had he calculated its position on the desk, so that his victim could not look simultaneously at the wallet and at the policeman? Had Whittingham wanted to see whether he would keep looking in its direction? If Whittingham had, he had been disappointed. I gave nothing away, Maxwell reassured himself. I never looked once at it. Ah, but might not that in itself have been suspicious? A normal person would have looked at it, would have been inquisitive about anything he saw in a policeman's office, would have made some comment. Mightn't he have been over clever? And hadn't he this morning betrayed himself by showing that he had noticed the wallet? He had remarked on its being pigskin, because he had known already that it was pigskin. Had that been a mistake? Could he have known that it was pigskin by glancing at it from three yards off? It had been in the sun and rain three weeks. Whittingham had said he hadn't known that it was pigskin. He had said it did not matter. But that must have been pretense, said to embarrass him. You couldn't tell where you were with Whittingham.

Why should he have tried to fuss me with the wallet? Maxwell asked himself. It was my first visit. I hadn't made any mistakes then. Perhaps he had had that wallet on view for every visitor. Another of his traps and I fell into it.

He shivered. He was in a fog. He did not know what was being

350

plotted against him, nor by whom. But I'm safe, I'm safe, he told himself. I left no clue. There's nothing they could find out now. Even if he suspects, even if he knows, there's nothing that he can do. He must have evidence. This isn't Russia or Nazi Germany where you can torture a suspect into a confession. This is a free country. He must have evidence. Even though my subconscious trips me. As it did today, as it did twice today. Once over the watch, once over the Belfontaine Committee.

You could not control your subconscious any more than you could control your dreams. Any moment it might betray him into some admission. The more he worried, the more he brooded, the more likely it was to trip him. He must clear his mind, think of other things, of the elections, of Sylvia, of the estate, of Jocelyn's marriage; banish that dark chapter from his memory. He would go to the club, stand a round of drinks, swap some off-color stories, behave as though he hadn't a trouble in the world.

The club was crowded. Twenty-five to thirty members. There seemed to be some celebration.

"What's this in aid of?" he inquired.

"Bradshaw's farewell party."

"Is he going back to America?"

"No, round the islands."

"Then he's not leaving for good."

"I don't think he is, you never know."

Maxwell looked round him: it was the usual group; only one person's presence suprised him, David Boyeur's, but perhaps he wasn't here as Bradshaw's guest but as a member who had happened to have looked in that morning.

The sight of Boyeur roused his irritation. He could never forget how Boyeur had strolled on the evening of his humiliation into that path of light. He had a score to settle there. As he stared at Boyeur, his temper mounted. Boyeur was so sleek, so smooth; his jacket fitted so snugly over his shoulders. It was one of those new corded suits, with a thin blue stripe. When anybody else wore that kind of suit it looked exactly what it was, something that had been bought off the peg for thirty dollars, but worn by Boyeur it had the air of having been tailored in Saville Row. A white flowered bow tie caught up the blue of the coat. He looked fresh and cool on this sultry morning.

Boyeur turned his head and met Maxwell's stare. He smiled, a familiar, patronizing smile. Maxwell clenched his fists. It embarrassed him that Boyeur should have seen him staring; it would make Boyeur feel important. Never mind, he could afford to wait. He'd settle his score with him one day. He'd have his chance when the Leg. Co. met. He turned away, a club waiter was at his side.

"Mr. Bradshaw's order, sir."

"Pony rum and ginger."

He crossed over to his host.

"I'd no idea that you were leaving; isn't this very sudden?"

"Journalists always operate at a moment's notice."

"You've got tired of us so soon."

"It isn't that. I need to see the other islands. I'm told that every island is a little different: I shall understand this island better when I've seen the others."

"That's very true."

But that was only in part Bradshaw's reason for setting out upon this trip. He had come to the conclusion suddenly that he had overstayed his welcome, or at least was less welcome since his article on the color question. He had been congratulated on the article. Everyone had agreed that he had said something that had needed saying, but as individuals they were apprehensive about what he might have to say about themselves. He was aware that conversation tended to cease when he joined a group.

Moreover he had come to suspect that nothing very dramatic was likely to happen in Santa Marta for several weeks. The stage was set, the characters were in the wings, each had his script, but the curtain was not likely to rise till after the elections. When the new Leg. Co. was elected under universal suffrage, then sparks would fly. How would young Boyeur comport himself? That would be worth watching, but until then a state of suspended animation would prevail. He might as well be somewhere else. He would see Santa Marta with new eyes on his return. He was also curious to know how the other islands were reacting to events here. Were they even interested? He needed to get current events here into focus. If you stayed in one place too long, particularly if it was a small place, you lost your sense of proportion. You became parochial. His stateside readers would soon be feeling that. He had in mind a couple of general articles with the title "So Many Volcanoes."

"I'll be away about ten weeks," he told Maxwell. "That'll give me a week in each of the smaller islands, and a couple of weeks in Barbados; no, I shan't attempt Jamaica. It's too big, too complicated. I shall finish with a day or two in Trinidad. As perhaps you know there's a meeting there of the Caribbean Tourist Board. Several American reporters will be there. I'm persuading a few of them to come on here. I want them to write up Santa Marta as a summer resort: a bargain Paradise; that'll be the line. I'll collect them there and bring them back with me. They might do something for the island. I don't see why not."

He was in a benign, expansive mood, excited about his trip.

"Have you heard anything about the Belfontaine Committee?" Maxwell asked him.

Bradshaw started as Whittingham had done.

"I shouldn't have thought that you'd have heard anything about that," he said.

"Why not?"

"Do you know what it is?"

"As a matter of fact I don't."

"Where did you hear about it?"

"I can't remember now. I heard it mentioned somewhere. I asked what it was, and people laughed."

"I'm not surprised. People can be very indiscreet. It's meant to be a secret."

"As I've heard so much, you'd better tell me the rest."

"I suppose I might." Bradshaw paused and looked about him.

"A fund's being raised to give your father a present; it's ostensibly because he's going on the Leg. Co. as a nominated member. Actually it's a tribute to all that he's done, one way and another, for the island. It's intended to be a complete surprise for him: everyone's been told to be very careful about referring to it when the family is about. So you see . . ."

Maxwell saw all right. No wonder Whittingham had started. Had his knowing made Whittingham suspicious? How could it have? Why should it occur to Whittingham that he had heard it from Carson on that fatal evening? His knowledge of the committee could not possibly suggest that he had learnt of it from Carson and on that day. Unless . . . a sudden alarming thought had struck him.

"Who's the chairman of the committee?"

"The Archdeacon, as of now."

"What do you mean by 'as of now'?"

"Originally it was Colonel Carson."

353

# CHAPTER TWENTY-ONE

*1*

Bradshaw's eyes were heavy. In another hour he would be in Trinidad. He was on the last leg of his trip. For ten weeks he had been island hopping, and his attaché case bulged with travel folders. He was well content. He had dispatched one article and had accumulated the material for a second. He was well documented now about the Caribbean. If any of these small volcanoes were to erupt—St. Lucia, St. Vincent, Nevis, or Antigua—he would have his material ready. It was very true that each island had its own special characteristics, the outcome of history and geography. In some, St. Kitts in particular, the color bar was marked; in others, Grenada for example, it was practically nonexistent. Some were prosperous and some depressed. In some wealth and power were in the hands of a few feudal families, in others the land was divided among small peasant proprietors. In some there was political unrest, in others there was a working, workable basis of democratic government. Some islands were Catholic, some were Protestant. Some, such as Barbados, owed a deep loyalty to England, while St. Lucia was more excited over the arrival of a French than of a British battleship. He had tabulated the separate differences; he had met the officials and notables in each island. He would be able to follow their news through the papers. While he was in Barbados an idea had occurred to him. For half the year he could make this island his headquarters. He could spend the fall and early winter in New York, come down at the start of Lent, and keep the paper posted about the social currents in the Caribbean. He would have to take in Jamaica; but there was so much in the press already about Montego Bay and so little about the American colony in Antigua, at Milreef. He would have no lack of material, and Barbados would be his base.

Barbados was his place, as the Archdeacon had prophesied. Barbados had everything for a person of his tastes; antiquity, tradition, brick-built estate houses, rectangular, with dignified eighteenth century lines, old silver and old china and old furniture. It had reminded him of Charleston; but whereas Charleston was the symbol of a life that no longer existed, in Barbados the feudal tradition was still maintained. There was all that in Barbados, but there was something more: a new, entertaining, enlightening collection of expatriates—English, Canadian and American—had settled since the war on the St. Edmund's coast. They were witty, affluent, unprejudiced; cultured in the fullest sense. The Archdeacon had given him letters of introduction. He had been amply entertained, he had been made to feel one of them. He had left with many promises to return. From Antigua he had written to Baltimore, outlining his scheme for spending half the year in the Caribbean, with Barbados as his base. An answer to that letter should be awaiting him in Trinidad.

His plane was scheduled to land in Port-of-Spain at nine o'clock. It was a tourist Pan-American flight to South America and every seat was occupied. But it was an hour late and its arrival had coincided with that of a north-bound tourist flight. A Dutch plane bound for Curaçao had docked a quarter of an hour earlier.

The chaos in the small airport was fantastic. There was no system for separating transit passengers from those who were disembarking. The northbound passengers from South America had to present vaccination certificates, whereas those who were southbound did not. The medical office opened off the waiting room and there was no demarcation between those who were trying to line up to reach it and those who were pushing their way to the emigration desk. There were no lines: there was no space for lines. The waiting room was very small; it was raining and no one could stand outside. On the stretch between Puerto Rico and Trinidad, passengers had been issued with cards carrying a standardized autobiographical questionnaire. They were now issued with further forms, for the customs, one stating how much foreign currency they were carrying, another concerning the contents of their baggage.

Bradshaw had filled up a number of these forms during his ten weeks of island hopping. They had to be filled up even by Britons traveling between one British colony and another. They seemed, Bradshaw judged, to be a survival of wartime restrictions, with inquiries about "munitions of war." Each island had a different form, and in St. Lucia there was an odd survival of censorship in the inquiry "Are you carrying letters to any residents?"

The present questionnaires were made out in English and many of the passengers could not read English. A large proportion of them had no pencils with which to fill them out, so that this had to be done at the customs desk itself: the currency questionnaire had to be filled out in duplicate and a carbon paper was provided. Most of those who filled out these forms with pens failed to realize that the pressure of a pen was not strong enough to produce an impression on the carbon. Many of the questionnaires that had been filled out in the plane had been done so incorrectly, and the emigration officer had to check each card against the passport.

The customs officials were punctilious in their examination of every suitcase. Many packages were tied up with string. A couple of airline representatives who were bilingual hurried back and forth trying to check future reservations. They were sweating and harassed but polite. No airport official was doing anything to organize the traffic. Such officers as were on duty expected to remain there for several hours and saw no cause for hurry. They knew that eventually everything would get sorted out. Were these people really ready for federation and dominion status, Bradshaw asked himself. Yet even as he asked it, he was amazed at the cheerfulness and the good humor everyone displayed. In New York or London a crowd exposed to such inefficiency, and late at night, would have been highly vocal with indignation. Yet here no one had lost his temper. Crowd psychology was very curious. No crowds were more inflammable than the West Indian. Yet they could accept irritations of this kind with equanimity.

It took Bradshaw nearly two hours to get through customs. It was midnight before he checked into his hotel. A large pile of letters awaited him. He flicked through them quickly, searching for the one from Baltimore. He tore it open impatiently.

"Dear Bradshaw," it said, "Let me first of all congratulate you on your 'So Many Volcanoes' piece. It is first class. I look forward to its successor. You have done a wonderful job for us during this last four months and we are all most appreciative. I am considering carefully and sympathetically your suggestion that you should spend half your time in the West Indies. We all of us have to recreate ourselves in middle age, as writers and as human beings, and you seem to me, to us, to have discovered a new self in the Caribbean. Your work has much deeper implications, and very likely on your return to New York, seeing New York with new eyes, your work there will have a fresher appeal. We have all to watch against the danger of getting into a groove and I am sure that we shall be wise in the future to develop your undoubted qualities as a travel writer, qualities that I must frankly admit I did not know you possessed in such full, rich measure.

"For that reason I am not anxious to limit you to the Caribbean. I see a new slant for your column. Let us call it *A New Yorker at home and abroad*. This will give you a wide range of movement. You can visit London, the South of France, Paris, Rome, all the pleasure grounds in fact that New Yorkers frequent. With your social links you will be able to report on the world of fashion, and you will also be able to throw interesting sidelights on political conditions. I want to enlarge the scope of your work and I suggest that you come back here as soon as is convenient so that we can discuss the details. The weather will soon be getting uncomfortably hot in the West Indies and the hurricane season is imminent. I believe you would be very wise to spend September at the Cap d'Antibes."

The Cap d'Antibes, Eden Roc: Bradshaw repeated the words like a charm as he undressed. The large pile of letters lay on his desk untouched. He was in no mood to read them. He would not be able to concentrate on them. A new world was opening before him.

He pictured himself, on an expense account, giving smart little London dinner parties, receiving in return invitations to fashionable villas in Cannes and Capri, talking in Florence of the Colony and 21 and back in New York telling them at the Coffee House about Elsa Maxwell. His world had been refashioned and only four months ago he had flown south from New York, desperate and afraid; how quickly fortune's wheel had turned. He was tired after his flight, but his brain was racing. He lay on his back in the dark, his hands clasped behind his head, brooding on his future.

2

Next morning in the library Bradshaw studied the back files of *The Voice of Santa Marta.* He had seen occasionally issues in the other islands, but he needed to get a clear consecutive all-in picture before his return. He had arranged to meet his fellow journalists at lunch. Three hours in the library would give him all he needed.

As he skimmed through the back numbers he congratulated himself on his good judgment in having left when he had. Nothing much had happened in his absence: or at least in retrospect it did not seem that very much had happened. The Santa Martans themselves no doubt had considered it a dramatic period. The elections had taken place, and both David Boyeur and Maxwell Fleury had been elected. That he already knew and had incorporated the news in his first "So Many Volcanoes" piece. There had been the opening of the new Leg. Co. with His Excellency appearing in his embroidered coat and cockaded hat with ostrich plumes. There had been only formal business then, the equivalent of the address from the throne; the real tension would not arise till the first general meeting when Boyeur crossed swords with authority. That should be worth seeing and he would be there to see it.

At the St. James Hotel on the night of the first meeting, the Belfontaine Committee had presented Julian Fleury with a silver cigarette box in token of his services to the island. There was a short article about the new Attorney General, listing Grainger's athletic feats in England; at the foot of the article was a paragraph that made Bradshaw raise his eyebrows; it announced the engagement of Grainger's younger sister Muriel to David Boyeur. David wouldn't like that, Bradshaw thought, appearing at the foot of a column, as the future brother-in-law of the Attorney General. He'd prefer to have the story, *Boyeur's future brother-in-law is H.E.'s choice as Attorney General.*

Bradshaw flicked the pages. Two entries made him smile. One announced the return of H.E.'s son by B.W.I.A. from Trinidad. Two days later Jocelyn Fleury's return was listed from Barbados. Bradshaw had seen them dancing together in Barbados. He wondered how many Santa Martans were aware that the engaged couple had registered in the same hotel. It was a piece of information that might come in useful one day; like Archer's relationship with Margot Seaton. Nothing that really mattered had taken place while he was away: within a morning he would have picked up all the threads.

3

As the plane circled over Jamestown, Bradshaw noted with affection the familiar landmarks, the Union Jack flying from the terrace at G.H., the curve of the *carenage*, the dark stonework of the fort, the great sweep of *Grande Anse*, the bright yellow of the sand and the palm-grove flanking it, the broad river of sugar cane winding between the foothills. How differently he had felt four months ago when he had first landed here. He quoted the last song of *The Beggar's Opera*—"The wretch of today shall be happy tomorrow." Then he had faced the ruin of everything that he had lived and worked for. Here he was now, with an assured and ample future, the doyen of a group of journalists. Now don't be officious, he warned himself. Norman and the Tourist Board would be here to welcome them. Wait and listen, and if anything's been overlooked you can put them wise. Don't be self-important. Let them learn from the way that others treat you that you are important.

He was right in expecting that the Tourist Board would be there to welcome them. But not only was Norman there, but Denis Archer.

"H.E. wants to see you all as soon as possible," he told Bradshaw. "He wants to welcome the press boys and find out what he can do for them. Can you bring them up for cocktails tonight? Informally, just yourselves. When we find out how long they'll be here and what they want, we can make our plans. We've booked them into the St. James, but I gather you'd rather stay on at the Continental."

"I certainly should."

He had explained his position to his colleagues.

"You'll all be much more comfortable at the St. James. The Continental is a crummy place. But the people who run it have put themselves out for me. I don't want to hurt their feelings."

That was partly true: but he also wanted to be on his own, to show them that he was independent, so that when they got back to America they would say in Bleeck's "that fellow Bradshaw on the *Baltimore Star* is quite a person in the islands."

That night at G.H. he kept himself in the background. He could rely on the Governor to bring him into the center of the conversation. His reliance was not misplaced.

"I've one pleasant surprise for you," the Governor said. "I expect your distinguished colleague whose company here we so much enjoyed earlier this year, will have spoken to you of the excellence of our rum punches. You will find them not only excellent, but cheaper than they are in any other island. I have decided as from today to reduce the duty on rum by thirty-five per cent. Now I shall be very surprised if any one of you except Mr. Bradshaw can guess the reason for my philanthropy."

They all of them made their guesses. The general presumption was that the duty was so high that it discouraged consumption and that the change had been made to pleasure the sugar planters.

The Governor chuckled. No, that was not the reason. He had done it to discourage smuggling. Comparing the per capita consumption of rum and cigarettes here and in St. Kitts he had found, to judge by the export and import revenues, that twice as much rum and twice as many cigarettes were consumed in St. Kitts as in Santa Marta. "Gentlemen, I could not believe that we, on this island, were twice as temperate as our friends upon St. Kitts. I believe the Santa Martans drink and smoke as much as anyone. Only they do not pay duty on their tobacco and their rum. I came to the conclusion that too large a proportion of the populace was engaged in smuggling, so I reduced the duty to a point where smuggling is uncommercial."

Where did the cigarettes come from, he was asked.

"From the French islands, St. Martin's a free port: as for the rum, I fancy they take it out of bond from our own warehouses, transfer on to small boats, and run it back into one of our own bays. As you'll see, gentlemen, when you drive round the island, we have a

359

bay every second mile. I can't have our police launch wasting its time patrolling them."

The story put the meeting onto easy terms with its host. Bradshaw turned to Archer.

"What are young Templeton's plans?" he asked.

"He goes up to Oxford in October."

"What about his fiancée?"

"She'll follow after Christmas and have an April marriage. H.E.'ll have been out a year by then. He'll be able to take ten days leave."

Bradshaw nodded. The old boy had played his cards cleverly. He had a tricky problem. Officially committed to a policy of racial equality, he could not have objected to his son's engagement to a girl who had colored blood, yet at the same time he could not have welcomed the possibility of a dusky grandson waiting to take the Templeton seat in the House of Lords. H.E. had played for time, as the British always did, in their confidence that they would muddle through, that they could lose nine battles and win the tenth. Had H.E. learnt about that meeting in Barbados? He probably had, from one source or another. Possibly he had learnt of it with relief. Absence might be likelier to cure a realized than an unrealized love. At any rate that was what a man of the Governor's generation might be inclined to think.

"What about that pretty secretary of his, the one who used to work in a pharmacy?" he asked.

"She's fine. Is she a friend of yours?"

"Unfortunately not. I've never spoken to her. But I remember noticing her at the Nurses' Dance. She's very pretty."

"I think she is."

"Does she still work here?"

"She does."

His voice could not have been more offhand. Bradshaw switched the subject.

"What about the Carson case? Any developments?"

"You'd better ask Whittingham. He's more likely to talk to a newspaper man than to an A.D.C."

How uncommunicative could you get, thought Bradshaw.

That night there was a dinner party at the St. James for the visitors. Boyeur was one of the hosts. Bradshaw shook him warmly by the hand.

"This is most happy news," he said.

"It is for me."

"Congratulations on your election too."

"That was never in any doubt."

Boyeur was sitting on the opposite side of the table from him and two places down. Bradshaw glanced at him several times when his head was turned. Ten weeks had effected a change in him, or so it seemed. He was more assured, less belligerent. It was hardly being in love in Boyeur's case, he fancied. For Boyeur, surely, marriage was a stage in a career, a step to self-advancement. He was marrying into a good family. That was what counted with his kind of man. His ambitions were the nearer now to being realized.

After dinner, when the party moved on to the veranda for liqueurs and coffee, Bradshaw placed himself next to Boyeur.

"When I read the announcement of your engagement, I remembered our talk the time you came to tea."

"Ah?"

"That afternoon you had your plans prepared. You were going to run the island, through your control of the Trades Unions."

"That's right."

"I wondered if you've changed those plans."

"Why should I?"

"Because you're in a different camp. Your future brother-in-law is the Attorney General. He's the representative of order and tradition. Your father's a capitalist, in a minor way. Your wife will inherit capital. Your children will be left a share of the estate. You don't want, do you, to undermine the value of their inheritance?"

He paused; he was watching Boyeur closely.

"Perhaps you haven't seen it from that point of view," he added. "Do you want to destroy the power of the class to which you are now allied?"

Boyeur made no answer. Exactly, Bradshaw thought. He never had seen it in that way before. It was surprising how often obvious truths did not occur to people. He had recently read Tom Driberg's reminiscences. Someone had remarked to Driberg casually, "Why don't you run for Parliament?" It had been a new idea to Driberg. He had run for Parliament as an Independent, won a seat and been a great success. John Galsworthy had had a similar experience. The woman who later became his wife remarked, "Why don't you write? You're just the person." Of course in both cases the seed had been growing, under the soil—in the subconscious for many years—but it was always a haphazard day of sunlight that brought the flower to the surface. Galsworthy was a born writer. Driberg, though he had been trained as a journalist, had with his social sense a flair for politics. Someone else with some other remark would have given them the key to their own nature. Sooner or later it would have occurred to Boyeur that the axis of his interests had changed.

The shape of that final article began to form. The volcano was not extinct, but it was quiescent. On that note he would say good-by to Santa Marta.

On the following morning Bradshaw toured the island with the other journalists. They took a picnic lunch. Four cars were booked, and several of the local girls were requisitioned to act as hostesses. Bradshaw was placed in the same car as Doris Kellaway. One of the journalists was a bachelor in the middle twenties. Clearly it was to be quite a day for Doris. Bradshaw had rung up Belfontaine after breakfast, and arranged that his carload should look in for a punch after their bathe. He regarded Maxwell as a pipeline. That first election meeting had been one of his best stories.

"You wouldn't mind stopping there, would you?" he asked Doris.

"On the contrary, I was going to suggest it myself. I want to see Sylvia particularly. You've heard her news?"

"I only got back yesterday."

"I know, but you might have heard. It's marvelous. She's going to have a baby."

"You're right, that is marvelous."

It should make all the difference to Maxwell. He had been such a problem child, by all accounts; surly, with a chip upon his shoulder. He was a different person now, everyone said the same thing about him. That article about the colored blood in the Fleury family had done the trick. Maxwell had nothing to be secretive about any longer.

Certainly he could not have been more gracious in his welcoming of the journalists. He took them on a tour first of the grounds, then of the *boucan*.

"I don't know how it'll strike you," he said. "You've seen so many more of the islands than I have; you can compare one island with the other, but from what I've been told and from what I've read, there are certain things here that you can't get anywhere else, at the same price that's to say. We've a real sense of the past here. And there's no better bathing in the Caribbean. What's your candid view about making this a summertime resort?"

Four months ago he would have been a poor advertisement for the island, now he was a good one. He was a salesman without appearing to be one.

"It's an easy flight from New York," he said. "You have to change planes at Puerto Rico, but maybe we'll be able to get that altered. Pan Am. might stop here if there was sufficient demand. The airstrip is adequate. And, as you see, the climate stays good right through into September. The countryside may look parched; it may have been greener farther south and you may have seen more flowers and more trees in flower, but in a way that lack of rain is to our advantage. You can rely much more upon the weather here. I wouldn't recommend Grenada or Dominica for a summer holiday to a family that has only three weeks off a year and needs reasonable weather."

He discussed the issue with an impartiality that was effective.

"I'll be very grateful if before you leave you'll tell me exactly how this place strikes you," he said. "As probably you know, I'm on the Leg. Co. and we'll be discussing at the next meeting the possibilities of developing this island as a summer resort. We don't want to invest a lot of money in hotels and tennis courts and find them empty on our hands. I'll be most grateful for your advice."

Three months ago, Bradshaw thought, if Maxwell had talked to journalists on such a subject a sneer would have come somewhere into his voice. He would have belittled the island, or himself; he would have been truculent toward these emissaries from a larger world, ready to take offense, putting the others' backs up. Today, without being in the least ingratiating, he so put his point that the journalists wanted to be able to do something for him.

Bradshaw turned to Sylvia.

"Success has made him quite a different person. It's a point that Maugham has made more than once. We're all pleasanter people when the sun is shining. Your husband does not seem the same person that he was when I came here first."

Sylvia smiled. "I have to thank you for that."

"You genuinely believe that article made all that difference?"

"He admits it himself. He draws a parallel with psychonanalysis. The psychoanalysts maintain that all our troubles are caused by a hidden worry; something that happened in childhood put us onto the wrong road, but as soon as we know what that worry is, we can start to cure it. Till we know, we are in the dark. Maxwell always had a feeling that people were against him, that people despised him; he thought he hadn't been given a fair chance, he was jealous of his brother. He was an awkward person; to be quite frank, I couldn't relax with him myself. I didn't at the time admit it to myself. I can only speak of it now because everything is different, but he was a person whom it was very difficult to love. And in addition, he had that insane, ridiculous hatred for the colored people. He was no good on that account at running an estate. The peasants wouldn't work for him. They knew he didn't like them. He didn't know how to handle them. You were at that first meeting of his.

363

He hit the wrong note every time. Then your article came out; he realized that he was one of them: it's made all the difference.

"What he himself thinks is that subconsciously he knew it all along. A nurse or a housemaid when he was a child made some remark about the Fleurys having colored blood that lodged in his subconscious. Your article was a violent form of shock treatment."

"The change really started with that article."

She nodded.

"The very day. I remember the morning it came out. He was furious. He was swearing all manner of vengeance against you: he was going to sue you for libel: heaven knows what else. He drove into town, to see his father, directly after lunch. He came back a different man."

She smiled, a fond and tender smile that sprang from a deep well of happiness. That night had been her real wedding night.

Bradshaw too smiled, for very different reasons. Journalists were always accused of making copy out of their friends; particularly a gossip columnist like himself. He resented the criticism. It was his job to write about personalities. Everybody knew that. People asked him to their houses at their own risk. He could not afford to go to parties that would not provide him with a paragraph. And indeed hostesses for the most part considered themselves ill-used if no reference to their hospitality appeared in print. At the same time he had his conscience. He exercised discretion. On occasions he had abused a confidence. He had done it knowingly, remembering Maugham's remark that it was hard to be both a writer and a gentleman. When the temptation was too strong, when the copy was too good, he yielded. He consoled himself with the casuistry that the sin was much less when you were still able to recognize it as a sin. It was when you could not distinguish between right and wrong that your soul was in dire peril.

He had known that he was betraying a trust when he had revealed the secret of the Fleury ancestry. The Archdeacon should not have told him; but the Archdeacon had. He had been ashamed of himself. He would never have written the article if he had known that it would be reprinted in Santa Marta. He had shivered when he had seen it in *The Voice*: yet here lay the irony of the situation, the one act of which he was ashamed since his arrival in Santa Marta had unquestionably, irrefutably done good.

He enlarged on the topic on the following day to Whittingham. He had gone there to check over his impressions before writing what he planned to be his farewell article on Santa Marta.

"Out of Evil, Good," he said. "There's no doubt that Maxwell

364

Fleury is a reformed character, and it's entirely due to that article. At least that's what his wife assures me."

"There's a change all right; we've all noticed that."

"And it started on the day that article appeared."

"Are you sure of that?"

"Quite certain. I was at the club that evening. I confess that I was shy of going there. I did not know how I should be received. Luckily perhaps for me, a good deal else was happening that night. Carson had that scene with Leisching."

"Did he now? Yes. Of course he did. I'd forgotten that. It's a long time ago. As you say, a good deal happened that night."

He pursed his lips.

"Your article comes out in the morning. Young Fleury reads it at lunch time. He hurries straight up to see his father; he then learns that there's no case for libel; he goes round to the club, to make, as he called it, a gesture; to show everyone that he doesn't give a damn. He goes on foot so as to clear his mind. He passes Carson's house, just after Carson must himself have reached it; he may have passed it at the very moment when Carson was being killed; he arrives at the club, in such a state of excitement that he never learns that Carson has had that scene with Leisching; he makes a long speech to you." Whittingham paused again. He looked very thoughtfully at Bradshaw. "Looking back, in what kind of a mood would you have said he was in that night?" he asked.

"He was very self-assured. He took me aback. I'd never seen him like that before."

"The phrase is a cliché, but would you say he was bubbling over with some inner, I don't know what the word is, I'm losing my vocabulary as well as my memory. But you know what I mean."

"I do. I'd say that's how he was."

"And after he'd made his speech, and stood drinks all round, he's still so absorbed in this discovery about himself that he doesn't listen to any gossip. He does not know about Carson's scene with Leisching. It's ironic that he was the one person at the club that night, I might also say the one person in Jamestown who wasn't discussing Carson over his dinner, yet he was near as dammit to being the man who discovered Carson's murderer. And then when he's stood his round, he hurries back, still on foot, past Carson's house, notices incidentally that there are no lights on in the bedroom; you'd have thought he was too busy with his own thoughts to have noticed that; he's in such a hurry to get back home that he forgets to give his sister a message that young Templeton left for Jocelyn—and a message from young Templeton that night must have been important. Jocelyn can't have known how the Templetons were going to take this news of yours. He's bubbling over inside himself, he drives straight out to Belfontaine. And his wife tells you that from that evening on, he's been a different person. There must be more in this psychoanalysis than I'd suspected. Yes, it's quite a business. You certainly provided, what was his wife's phrase for it, shock treatment. For all that to have happened in one evening."

"Are you any nearer to finding out who did kill Carson?"

Whittingham hesitated. Bradshaw was proving a useful catspaw. There was no reason why his usefulness should not be exploited further. He nodded.

"Are you any nearer to an arrest?" Bradshaw asked.

"You've been away ten weeks. That means I'm ten weeks nearer."

"You're confident that you'll get him?"

"Quite confident."

"I suppose you can't tell me anything."

"Nothing that you could use. I'm afraid that you'll have to do what I do, sit and wait."

# CHAPTER TWENTY-TWO

## 1

That evening Bradshaw settled down to compose his final article. He wrote in a carefree almost a valedictory mood, with the confidence that is born out of success. In a sense he was going back on what he had said four months earlier. He was prophesying smooth things now: but it was the privilege of journalists as of politicians if not to eat their words at least to set up a different menu. The memory of the public was mercifully short. You had to titillate their interest from day to day. They were grateful if you kept them alert and interested.

Volcanoes can remain quiescent for several years. That was his general thesis. Santa Marta had rumbled, had sent up clouds of smoke, there had been flashes of fire; a planter had had his cane fields burnt, a colonel had been killed. But for the moment there seemed no immediate anxiety. The elections had passed off quietly. David Boyeur was now a person in authority: he was also engaged to be married. Two such simultaneous events could be expected to have a tranquilizing influence. The best way to disarm a revolutionary was to give him public office. In a few years' time there would be another David Boyeur; or rather an equivalent for David Boyeur; there was still discontent under the surface, but at the moment nothing very alarming need be feared from Boyeur.

Bradshaw drew a parallel between the political situation and the apparent inactivity of the police in connection with the Carson case. The murderer was at this moment congratulating himself that he had got away with the perfect crime. Twelve weeks had passed, no movement had been made by the police, yet it would be as unwise for that criminal to become complacent as it would be for the Colonial Office in Westminster to look on Santa Marta as a file that could be shut away. The police were accumulating evidence: they were not yet able to justify a warrant for arrest, but they had their man under their eyes. Sooner or later he would play into their hands. In just that way, time would set a match to the essentially inflammable material that comprised the social structure of Santa Marta.

Whittingham chuckled when he read that article. Bradshaw had played his cards for him very satisfactorily. Whether anything would come of it, he could not tell. But he liked to think of "his man" wilting as he read that piece.

Boyeur also chuckled when he read it. So they had got that idea of him, had they? He read the article out loud to Muriel.

"They'll see at the next Leg. Co. meeting whether my teeth are drawn," he told her. "I've got a motion down on the condition of our school building. They'll see if I'm tamed."

She watched him with adoring eyes. He was so definite; he spoke with such authority. At home everyone was so mild; everyone accepted everything, even Grainger, clever though he was. She was marrying a real man, thank God.

2

Maxwell read the article in the club. He had come in for the day to stock up on groceries. He had left Sylvia behind. He did not want to have her traveling on that bumpy road more often than was necessary. The fourth month was the danger time as he had always heard. He had finished his shopping quickly and was alone in the club. He thanked his stars for that. He sat by the window, staring at that final paragraph. He read it a second time and then a third. The steward stood beside him, with the lime squash that he had ordered. It was cold and sweet. He drank the half of it in one long swallow. He wished that it were rum and ginger. He longed to order a strong hard drink that would warm his blood, restore his courage. But he mustn't. He knew that. Alcohol would be fatal. He must keep his head, watch himself: maintain that latchet on his tongue.

For the fourth time he reread the article. Was Bradshaw right? Did the police know? Was it only a journalist's guesswork? He turned over the paper: there was a paragraph about the meeting of the Leg. Co. on the following Tuesday. There was a proposal that patients to hospital should be allowed to wear their own clothes without payment, if they wanted. What on earth was this about? He'd have to find out the facts, it was the first he'd heard about it. He wasn't going to sit there silent; there was a proposal about developing a section of *Grande Anse* as a resort for tourists, with bungalows and tennis courts: there was also a proposal about repairing the school building in St. Patrick's; that was Boyeur. He'd better have a look at that school and also at some of the other schools: find out exactly what had been done, what was being done, what it was planned to do. He'd put a spoke in Boyeur's wheel if he could. Repairing of schools indeed; a typical Boyeur plan to impress his own constituents.

He turned to the back page. Next week the new version of *Show Boat* was coming to the Carlton. He mustn't miss that. It would be good to hear those songs again. "Can't help lovin' that man," and "Ol' Man River." He hummed the tunes. He looked through the window onto the *carenage*. A schooner from Guadeloupe was being loaded with sacks of copra by a couple of longshoremen. They were bare to the waist; their blue jeans were patched; their damp shoulders glistened under the sun; their biceps swelled and sank as they heaved the sacks onto that deck. "Lift that rope, heave that bale . . ." Had their lot really changed, in its essentials, since emancipation? He was in part repelled by their instinctive animal existence, in part he responded to a kinship with it. He had a chance now of doing something for this people. Far more than Boyeur. Boyeur was a demagogue. He didn't care about the people: only about himself: the misfortunes of the proletariat were for him so many private stepping stones. He must find out the facts about those schools.

He laid down the paper. As he did so, his eye fell on the leader page, on Bradshaw's article. He blinked at it. Why was he worrying about schools and cinemas and Boyeur? How did he know that he would be a free man on Tuesday, that he would ever see another film? For ten weeks now he had let himself forget about that dark half-hour in that hidden house. There had been so much else to think about. There had been the excitement of the election, then there'd been Sylvia's news. So much had been happening; everything had gone so well. He had been so happy. Love, reciprocated love; he had known it for the first time during these weeks. His sky had been unclouded. Yet all the time the enemy was drawing closer.

He rose. It was ten past eleven. In a few minutes the first of the planters would be in here for his morning punch. When he had left Belfontaine he had pictured himself standing round the bar, swapping stories, picking up the local gossip. That, after all, was his job now, as a councilor, to know how people were thinking, what was on their minds. But he was in no mood now for that kind of morning. He'd have no peace of mind till he'd seen Whittingham.

He drove straight round there without ringing first. As usual Whittingham was in.

"Forgive my barging in like this," he said. "But our telephone's impossible. You know the way it is with a party line. Probably you'd have got the message wrong, and that would have been a pity, because what it was is this. Sylvia won't be coming into town more than she can help, these next few months. You've heard our news, haven't you?"

"I have indeed. I was delighted."

"But she doesn't want on that account to lose touch with her friends, and I'm very anxious that she should not be bored. So I'm arranging to have people out regularly to dinner. Not big parties, that would mean her standing about: never more than six: usually only four. And we should so like it if you and your wife could come out one evening. Sylvia often talks of the kindness your wife showed her when she was a child. What day would suit you best? We'd like it to be soon."

Did it sound convincing, Maxwell wondered. He had only thought up the scheme on the spur of the moment. But the ideas that came to you in a flash were often the best. First thoughts rather than second thoughts. Like love at first sight. Mrs. Whittingham had run the Girl Guides when Sylvia was at school. It was reasonable that Sylvia at a time like this should need the company of those who had been her mentors when she was finding her feet in life. Anyhow Whittingham had not seemed surprised. He was looking at his diary.

"Nothing I should enjoy better," he was saying, "and the old hag'll love it. She gives a lot to those kids. Never had any herself you know. Misses them when they grow up. She's touched when they remember her. Sylvia was always a favorite of hers. This'll genuinely please her. How would Monday suit you?"

"Monday's fine."

"It's the day before the Leg. Co. meeting. Sure you don't want a quiet evening before that."

"I shan't be igniting fireworks, I promise you."

"Leaving all that to Boyeur."

"That's the idea."

"Then I'll ring up the old hag now."

He spun the handle and picked up the receiver. Maxwell was taut, excited; very much as he felt when he was playing golf and on his game; alert, concentrated, nervous, but not apprehensive.

Steady, steady now, he warned himself. This is only half your job, quarter of your job. You must now organize a succession of these parties. It will look suspicious if you ask only Whittingham. Particularly after what you've told him. You must go back to your father's house and start telephoning. Ring everyone that you can think of; so that they'll be talking about it this evening at the club; do nothing that won't seem normal.

"Confound this telephone," Whittingham was saying.

He put back the receiver, paused, spun the handle, lifted the receiver.

"Call Mrs. Whittingham," he said.

He put his hand over the mouthpiece.

"At any rate I'm through to the exchange."

There was another pause. Was anything more exasperating than waiting while someone else was trying to put through a call? One's instinct was so strong to grab at the receiver, to say, "Let me have a shot."

Maxwell looked away. A copy of *The Voice* lay on the desk; it was open at the leader page, with Bradshaw's article staring at him. Whittingham must have been reading it when he came in. He had not meant to mention the case this time: he did not want his invitation to dinner to look like an excuse for discussing the Carson case. But with the article on the desk between them, it would be suspicious if he did not mention it; in view of those earlier talks of theirs.

"At last," Whittingham was saying. "I've been trying to get you for the last ten minutes. Can you remember, darling, if we're doing anything next Monday? We're not: that's splendid. Young Fleury has very kindly asked us out to dinner. His missus doesn't feel like traveling and she thought she'd like to reminisce about those old days in the troop. Wants to know what she was like as a kid I suppose so that she'll know what to be on guard against now she's about to have a kid herself. Yes, I suppose that's it. Monday's all right then. Good. I'll be home early this evening. No, I'm not looking into the club. I can't drink with these young fellows any longer; two nights a week is all that I can take. See you around six."

He had been looking at Maxwell as he talked, including him in the conversation, talking at him.

"That's that," he said. "What time shall we get out? Half-past six suit you? Time for a chat before we eat. I don't want to stay up late. I don't expect you do either."

Maxwell half rose, then as he had that earlier time, checked and sat down again.

"I see you've been reading that article of Bradshaw's."

"I was finishing it when you came in."

"I suppose he got his facts from you."

"He had a talk with me the other day, but you know what journalists are like; they paint with a broad brush."

"He says you know who did it."

"I know certain things. I can guess at certain things."

371

"What things?"

"You can't expect me to tell you that."

"No, but . . ."

Maxwell paused, embarrassed, putting himself once again in the confessional. Was he being too eager? Was he being impertinent? Whittingham was nearly three times his age.

"I'm sorry. I apologize. I shouldn't have asked you that."

"My dear boy, you can ask me what you like. I can't tell you everything, but I can tell you quite a lot. I know that you're discreet. And even if you weren't discreet, it wouldn't matter. There are one or two things I'd be quite happy to have that fellow know. I like to remind him now and then that I'm still watching him. That's my strong point, and it's a point that the layman forgets; that somewhere in this island there is a guilty man, a man who is conscious of his guilt, and who knows that I'm here, in the center of the web."

His voice had a drowsy hypnotic quality. As always the right hand bottom drawer of his desk had been pulled out; he now put his foot in it, and began with its leverage to rotate his swivel chair, his head remaining stationary while the trunk of his body swung.

"You may think I'm looking for a needle in a haystack; but this island is in proportion much smaller than a haystack and the man is a great deal larger than a needle. I've been able to limit the field considerably. I have ruled out a large section of the community. Didn't we discuss some time back, I think it was with you but I'm a garrulous old codger I know, and I can't remember whom I say what to; the old hag keeps telling me that I repeat myself, but I believe we were discussing deception tactics."

"We certainly did. You talked about *Operation Cicero*."

"Then it *was* to you that I was saying it. It comes back now. We were wondering whether it was a question of a thief interrupted at his work, or a clever man wanting to make it look like an interrupted theft. I told you as far as I can remember that I had an open mind."

"You did."

"Now I've made up my mind. I've decided that it was a clever fellow who wasn't quite as clever as he thought."

Maxwell wanted to close his eyes, as you do when a cloud of dust blows at you. But he mustn't; he knew that: nothing out of the ordinary.

"What made you come to that conclusion?"

"Quite a few things. First of all I became convinced that the man who had the wallet was speaking the truth. I couldn't explain to you how I knew. But after a while if you're in my game you get a second sense of when you're being told a lie. I believed that he was speaking

372

the truth, that he did find the wallet in a cane field as he said. I went out with him to the spot where he said he found it. I'll tell you about that. It'll interest you."

He spoke very slowly, repeating himself, taking a quarter of an hour to explain how he had thrown the wallet out of a car that was being driven northward, along the windward coast.

Maxwell fidgeted as he listened: he wanted to interrupt, to break in on this dawdling exposition.

Yes, yes, he longed to say, you're absolutely right. That's the way it was and two miles farther on if you look you'll find the watch.

It was difficult to look interested in the recounting of an incident with whose each least detail he was familiar. It was hard not to prompt him, to hurry up the telling, hard not to be impatient. He must not look bored. He ought not to be bored. He should be fascinated. What wouldn't the ordinary person give to be taken behind a policeman's mind, to be shown how that mind worked, and in the most exciting of all cases, a murder case? He ought to be thrilled. Yet he was bored, exasperated, irritated. He wanted to scream. Yet at the same time he was mesmerized, fascinated; outside himself, watching himself, thinking This is how a murderer gets caught.

At last Whittingham reached his climax. "You see how that narrows the field?" he said.

Maxwell started. The cessation of that slow monotone shook him out of his trance. He must now be intelligent, ask questions, the right kinds of question.

"How does it do that?" he asked.

"A clever fellow, who thinks he's cleverer than he is. There are not so many of those in Santa Marta."

"But is that all you know?"

"Of course not; not by any means."

"What more then do you know about him. I'm assuming that it's him not her."

"Yes, I'm assuming that."

"A woman wouldn't have been strong enough."

"I don't see how she could."

"Though I have heard that a person who is really roused has the strength of ten."

"I have heard that."

"Have you read Kipling's story about a man who killed a baboon with his bare hands?"

"I've read that story."

"Mightn't a very jealous woman have had that strength."

"She might."

373

"Or a very heavy woman."

"I'd thought of that."

"If she knelt across his arms, so that he couldn't throw her off."

"Knelt across his arms?"

"Suppose that he had slipped, and fell with his arms spread wide and she knelt across him, a knee on either arm, then she'd have her hands free at his throat."

"Knelt across his arms. Yes, that's how it might have been done, that's how it probably was done."

"And that's why there were no marks upon his face."

"On whose face."

"His or hers, the murderer's."

"Yes, that would explain it, if there were no marks."

"But there were none were there?"

"That's something I don't know as yet. How could I?"

"Oh, I see. I thought, I mean if anyone had had marks, someone would have noticed them and wondered how they got there."

"That's true, of course."

"So I'd assumed there were no marks."

"Naturally, naturally."

"So that in that way it might have been a woman mightn't it?"

"It might, but I'm sure it wasn't."

"Why are you so sure."

"There was no woman in his life, light or heavy."

"Can you be sure of that?"

"In a place like this I can. Have you heard of anyone keeping an intrigue secret, here where there are no locks on doors, and half the time no doors to lock."

"That's true."

And it was because he had forgotten that, refused to realize that, that he was sitting here now ferreting out what Whittingham knew and what he didn't know. How could he have been so crass as to have suspected Sylvia and Carson on account of a Turkish cigarette, and a raised toilet seat. How ridiculous it seemed in retrospect.

"If it wasn't done by a thief who was surprised," said Maxwell, "and if it wasn't done by a jealous woman; if it was done by a clever man who wasn't as clever as he thought, why on earth should that kind of man want to murder Carson?"

"It was not premeditated."

"Then why on—"

"It was an accident. That's what I've concluded. Carson was in a strange mood that night. He had drunk a great deal. He had been humiliated in the club. He was a choleric man. He might have found an acquaintance waiting for him when he got back, or he might have met someone in the street, and asked him to come in for a drink. He did that kind of thing. Then when they got back they had a quarrel, and Carson took a slug at the chap and slipped, and as he fell, he flung out his arms and the other fellow was across him, pinioning him with his knees; he was seeing red, his hands were at Carson's throat; you're right: that's how it must have been. In two minutes there was Carson dead. It was the last thing that the poor devil had in mind. If only he'd come to the police station right away, we might have smoothed it out. What a fool he was."

"Indeed."

It came, that "Indeed," from his very heart. What a fool he'd been. What a crazy fool.

"So that's the way it was," said Whittingham. "You see now, don't you, that I've narrowed my field considerably."

"You've got a great deal to find out still, though, haven't you? Simply to know that he's a clever fellow who isn't as clever as he thinks, doesn't get you far."

"I know more than that."

"Yes?"

"I know a great deal more than that. He's a man of a certain position."

"How do you know that."

"He owns a car, or at least he drives a car."

"Can you be sure of that?"

"I can be sure of nothing. But it seems to me most unlikely that a man would throw a wallet into a cane field, and such a wallet, when he was being driven by someone else. Do you think it likely?"

"I can't say I do."

"You see how this limits the field."

"I'm beginning to."

"There are three hundred and seventeen cars in Santa Marta. There are a hundred and twenty-seven trucks. Six hundred and three driving licenses have been issued. I have told my constables to check on the whereabouts on that night of each of those six hundred and three persons."

"Can you expect them to remember what they were doing on a given night."

"I can't. I don't. In fact if some of them did I should consider it most suspicious."

"Some of them must have lied."

"As you say, some of them did lie. They lied automatically. They didn't know what I'm after, but they felt it was as well I shouldn't get the truth and so they lied. Actually their lies told me more than the truth would have done. That old point in psychoanalysis again. The first thing that jumps into a man's head. It's very useful to know what sometimes."

"So you found out things that helped you."

"I found out a lot of things, altogether independent of the Carson case. It's surprising how often when you're fishing for pilchard you catch a sole, but oh yes, I did find out at least half of what I needed. I've a pretty shrewd idea which cars were on that road that night."

"You know that mine was, for example."

"I do."

"But can you be certain that it was on that same night that the wallet was flung away?"

"I can be sure of nothing. But it's probable. If you'd been in his position, wouldn't you want to get rid of it as soon as possible."

"I suppose I would."

"Of course you would, and so did he."

And you suspect me, don't you, Maxwell thought. Or you think it's possible. And you're right, damn you, but you can't prove it. You've got no evidence. You never will get it. How can you hope to. You've got all the tangible facts. There'll be nothing more. You may find the watch but will it help you. How can it? You've nothing to go on. You'll never have anything to go on.

"But all this is supposition, isn't it?" he asked. "It's not even circumstantial evidence. It's only guesswork."

"That's what it would look like in a court of law; but you can't think what a difference it makes to the policeman when he knows who his prey is, and what a difference it makes to the criminal when he knows that the detective knows. There's a very curious cat and mouse relationship between the two. Have you read *Crime and Punishment*?"

"No, what is it?"

"It's a novel by Dostoevski, about a young student who needs money to continue his studies and kills an old pawnbroker, then robs her. It is a curious book; it was written by an intellectual that highbrows rave about, yet he wrote the best detective story I've ever read. He understands both the criminal and the detective. I was rereading it the other day. I go back to it to remind myself of the essentials of my profession. As a matter of fact I've got my copy here, I'll lend it you. It'll show you how the game is played. A person who can't imagine himself committing a crime, a person like yourself for instance, can't realize the curious affinity that exists between the policeman and the criminal. The criminal lives in a prison of his own devising; he can't speak openly to a soul: he inhabits a secret world: the only person who understands him is the policeman who is chasing him. They share a secret; they have a deep-based bond: there is a curious collaboration: it is like a love affair. The criminal is drawn to the detective because the detective is the one man in the world who understands him. Ordinary people, his friends and family, are foreigners. He is only himself in the detective's company. You read it. It makes all these thirty cent whodunnits look like milk and water. You won't be able to put it down when you've once started. I'll collect it when I come out on Monday. You'll have finished it by then. You won't be able to put it down, I promise you."

3

He knows, Maxwell told himself as he drove that afternoon along the windward coast to Belfontaine. He knows. And he knows I know he knows. But there's nothing he can do: nothing, nothing. He's got no evidence. He'll never get any evidence. But he knows all right.

It was pointless to have invited all those people out to dinner. It wouldn't fool Whittingham. The parties would bore Sylvia. She didn't want to be pestered with acquaintances; she didn't want to be bothered with arranging meals. She was perfectly happy sitting on the veranda talking, reading, listening to the radio. She had wanted parties a year ago. She didn't now. She was dreamily content, brooding about the future. Why on earth had he asked all those people out. Why hadn't he had the courage to have a showdown with Whittingham: to lay his cards upon the table. I know and you know but you can't prove it. That's what he should have said. Why was he continuing this insane pretense, ringing up all these people, putting up this blind.

He knows, he knows. He repeated it like a refrain, in tune with the throbbing of the engine. He knows. He knows.

He passed the cane field where he had thrown the wallet. What a fool he had been. Why hadn't he destroyed it, burnt it, cut the leather, ripped the lining. It was the wallet that had put Whittingham on the track. But for that wallet, Whittingham would never have been given the clue. The wallet and his own behavior. All those slips of his. The Belfontaine Committee. How could he have known that. Wasn't Carson, in his cups, the likeliest person to have told him. Carson had been in his cups that night.

By itself the Belfontaine Committee slip meant nothing, but taken with all those other slips, it formed a tally. There had been so

377

many slips. That "afterward" instead of "after." Slips that he hadn't himself noticed. There must have been so many for Whittingham to note down in that filing cabinet memory of his. He talked about forgetting things, about being middle-aged. That was his blind. He didn't forget anything he needed to remember.

He passed the cane field where the watch lay rotting. Why couldn't the wallet have been like the watch, lying there hidden in mud, exposed to rain and sun. The watch, that was another slip that he had made. Referring to the watch before he could have known about it. One of his worst slips that. Every step of the way he had led and guided Whittingham. He knows. Of course he knows: but he can't do anything, Maxwell reassured himself.

The sun was low in the sky when he reached Belfontaine. Sylvia was sitting on the veranda. She was wearing a white off-shoulder blouse. She rose to welcome him and he held her close but gently. She leant against him; raising her face, letting her kiss linger against his, fondly, deeply, tenderly. She sighed as she drew away.

"I didn't expect you back so soon. I thought you'd be going to the club," she said.

"Leaving you all alone here?"

"I'd have been all right. I'd have been happy with my thoughts. You mustn't cut yourself off from things on my account."

"I wasn't. I was being selfish. This is where I want to be. I'm going to hate that Leg. Co. taking me into town every month."

"Ah, darling."

She had never seemed more beautiful. He had read that women lost their looks in the first months of pregnancy. Sylvia hadn't. Her eyes were bright, her skin had a new gloss and glow: her hair seemed alive. He had never been more in love with her: every day, every night his love went deeper.

They sat on the balcony, watching the sun sink into the sea. She wouldn't have a drink, she said, only a lime squash. She was cutting down on alcohol. She would soon have to give it up altogether. "But you have one, darling," she insisted. "I'm not a spoil-sport."

He sipped his whisky soda slowly, appreciatively. Six months ago he would have felt awkward and ill at ease, drinking whisky when someone else was taking a soft drink through a straw; he did not now. They talked, casually, with pauses drifting into their talk; six months ago he would have been embarrassed if there had been any pause in the flow of talk. He was not now. Was it not the ultimate stage of intimacy to be able to sit silent with another person?

"I never knew I could be as happy as this," she said. "I didn't know such happiness existed. I haven't got a trouble in the world."

He stretched out his hand, laid it over hers and pressed it. If only he could have said, "I too." He ought to have been able to say "I too." He had everything now that he had lacked four months ago. He was a member of the Leg. Co.: his wife miraculously had changed toward him: to be loved by a woman whom one loved, what had life more to offer. He had shaken a lifelong chip from off his shoulder. He too should be without a trouble in the world. If only there were not this shadow over everything.

But he can't do anything, he tried to reassure himself: even if he suspects, even if he knows, he can't do anything.

"I wonder if it'll be a boy or if it'll be a girl," she said.

"Which would you rather?"

It was a question that they had asked each other every day. They had drawn up a list of names, sorting them out: one day preferring one name, the next another.

"I don't really care," she said. "I shan't be disappointed either way, will you? I'm so happy there is going to be one. That's all that matters."

She paused and her eyes went seaward.

"I'm so glad we're having one now, when we're so happy. It must make a difference to the child."

She paused again. She might have been talking to herself; except that they were now so much one person that when she was talking to herself, she was talking to him too.

"We're lucky, more lucky than we can guess. I'm glad we didn't plan it. Don't you feel there is something unromantic about a couple saying 'Let's have a gay time for three or four years, make a love affair of marriage, then we'll settle down and raise a family.' That sounds as though . . . I should hate, I mean, to look at my child and think 'that was the finish of a love affair.' I should so hate that. But the way it is with us, feeling the way we do, it must make a difference to the child; our child ought to be something rather wonderful."

Pauses drifted into her conversation. She skirted round the subject. She had lost all shyness with him now. Strange love grown bold had become simple modesty, but she had a reluctance, a hesitance to put her thoughts in words. "They always say, don't they, that a love-child is something special."

Maxwell closed his eyes. If only, he thought, if only . . . But even if Whittingham knew, what was there he could do. He'd no evidence. Not a shred of evidence.

"What are you reading?" Sylvia asked.

He held out the book. She took it and read out the title. "*Crime and Punishment*. Feodor Dostoevski. I've never read it. Any good?"

"Terrific."

She opened the book. "H.C. Whittingham. How did you get hold of this?"

"He lent it me. We were talking about the way a detective could lure a criminal to give himself away. He said this novel gave the best example of it."

"How did you get onto that subject."

"We were discussing the Carson case."

"The Carson case. I'd quite forgotten that. I'd thought of that as shelved."

"It isn't as far as Whittingham's concerned. He's hot on the trail still. Didn't you read Bradshaw's last article in *The Voice*?"

"Darling, I never read anything now, except poetry and sloppy novels. What did Mr. Bradshaw say?"

"He hinted that Whittingham knew who it was, but hadn't the evidence yet, that he was biding his time."

"Is that what Colonel Whittingham says himself?"

"He didn't commit himself. You know how he is. Looks a silly old codger, but he's a watchful bird."

"We must ask him about it when he comes out on Monday."

"We must."

They would too, of course. It was impossible for him to be long in Whittingham's company and not bring the talk round to it.

"He might be a little more forthcoming when he's got the 'old hag' with him."

"He might."

Her voice was interested, but not more than interested. She had probably not thought about the case twice in the last two months. Yet her future as well as his was bound up in it. Oh, but so closely bound.

He looked at her thoughtfully. "Carson wasn't a particular friend of yours, was he?"

"I scarcely knew him."

He laughed. "It may sound curious now, but do you know I was jealous of him once."

"Jealous? Of Colonel Carson? Why?"

"On account of you."

"Of me!"

The astonishment was too utter to be feigned.

"It must sound silly now," he said. "But in those days, when things between us weren't so happy, I was ready to fancy anything, to suspect anyone."

"But Colonel Carson, darling. Why ever him?"

"Do you remember a day when we'd gone into Jamestown, it was the day of that party to welcome Euan Templeton. I was with my father going over the accounts. Carson came up to the house to see you."

"Did he? I must try and think. Colonel Carson; oh yes, I do remember now. It was to do with the Belfontaine Committee. He had to find out what your father would really like. Someone in the family had to know about it. He did not want to ask your mother: it was meant as a surprise for her as well. He did not ask you because you were at Belfontaine. It wouldn't be as easy for you to sound him out. It might have been apparent. So he decided to ask Jocelyn. He came up on a morning when your mother was away. I remember it very well because he had not expected to find me there. He looked embarrassed. He said to Jocelyn, 'I know this will sound peculiar, but this is a private matter. Could I see you alone.' So I went out of the room. They were alone together for about twenty minutes. She was very mysterious about it afterward. 'Whatever you do, don't mention it to anyone,' she said, 'particularly to Maxwell. I'll tell you as soon as I can.' She told me on the day of the presentation."

"So that's the way it was."

"Yes, that's the way it was and whatever has it got to do with me and Colonel Carson?"

He laughed, ruefully. What indeed had it got to do with her and Colonel Carson!

"It'll sound ridiculous to you. It sounds ridiculous to me now, but it didn't at the time. When I came back to the house that afternoon the house smelt of a heavy cigarette. Turkish or Egyptian. I wondered who'd been there. There were no cigarette butts. The scent was very strong in the lavatory under the stairs. The seat was raised, so that I knew a man had been there. Then you and Jocelyn came back. You didn't mention your visitor. You must, I felt, have been keeping it from me deliberately, as of course you were."

"But what made you think the man had come to see me, a married woman, instead of Jocelyn. That would have been much more natural."

"Precisely. That was the trouble. If a man had come up to see Jocelyn, you'd have mentioned it to me. We'd often talked about finding her a husband. You couldn't not have made some comment. You'd have said, 'Frank Mason or Charles Hewlett was up here this morning to see Jocelyn. Do you think that would be a good idea?' Something like that. But you never mentioned it. It was the one thing in the whole day you didn't mention; so I knew it was something you didn't want me to know. What else could it be but that a man had come up to see you."

"Oh darling, how absurd."

"But wasn't it natural of me; we weren't happy then, remember, not the way we are now. I was crazy over you. . . . While you—I remembered that remark of the French cynic 'one loves, the other submits to love.' And I knew, I was certain that you weren't cold. Sooner or later you were bound to fall in love, the way I was in love with you. Then when Carson offered me his cigarette case at the Nurses' Dance, and I saw that it had two kinds of cigarette, Du Maurier and Egyptian for, so he said, special occasions, I saw red. He was everything I wasn't; the opposite of me in every way. I couldn't go into competition with him. There was no common ground where we could meet. If that was the kind of man you wanted, there was nothing I could do. It drove me mad."

"Darling, what did you do? Were you melodramatic over it? Did you forbid him the house?"

"It didn't get as bad as that. He never knew, in fact. I hadn't any proof. I was waiting for a proper showdown. When there was that talk of our coming into town and Preston running Belfontaine, I was torn between two choices; on the one hand it would give you chances of meeting Carson, on the other I'd have a chance of watching you, spying on you if you like, checking on your movements and on his, preparing for the showdown."

"What did you plan to do, challenge him to a duel?"

"I hadn't thought it out as far as that. I was in the dark."

"I'll say you were."

She rose, came across to him, put an arm round his shoulder, leant her cheek against his.

"Darling, I'm touched. I'm flattered. I wouldn't like it for you not to be jealous, but next time, angel, will you promise me, before you start working yourself up into hysteria, you'll have it out with me."

"I can promise that."

Her voice was soft and there was in her eyes a loving, protective, almost a maternal look.

"I'd no idea you could work yourself up into such a kind of frenzy. How you imagine things," she said.

382

How he imagined things. A state of frenzy. He had done that once; was he doing it again? The case against Carson had seemed such cast iron. No room for doubt, no loophole. And yet how easily the whole structure of suspicion had collapsed. Might not this present hysteria of his be equally a child of fantasy. What had he to go on after all? What had Whittingham said, what had he himself done to make him believe himself a suspect?

He reviewed the case. Whittingham had had the wallet in his hands when he came in. Why shouldn't he? It had only just been found. Later he had a copy of *Crime and Punishment* upon his desk. Why not in heaven's name? Why shouldn't a policeman want to refresh his mind by reading a classical crime story? It was ridiculous to fancy that Whittingham had had the wallet on his desk to trick him into some admission or that he wanted to frighten him with *Crime and Punishment*, showing how the dice were loaded for the police. Fantasy, what else was it but fantasy.

What could be more absurd than his idea of Whittingham's connecting his knowledge of the Belfontaine Committee with an indiscretion of Carson's on that very night. How could that two and two have been put together? It was absurd, ridiculous; the criminal's traditional hallucinations. Is this a dagger that I see before me? Don't shake those gory locks at me! He had had far more logical reason for suspecting Carson than Whittingham had for suspecting him, and of what a flimsy fabric had those suspicions been composed.

"Do you think that you've a suspicious nature?"

Sylvia's question cut so appositely through into his introspection that he looked up with a start.

"It looks as though I had, doesn't it?"

"But that's only on this one occasion, and you did have a reason. I wonder if you are by nature. We shall have to be on guard shan't we, against our child inheriting our tiresome characteristics."

"We can't stop him inheriting them."

"But we can stop them developing, or we can check them developing. We can look out for them. Environment is as important as heredity. If your father's not suspicious, and if you are suspicious, it's because you'd been brought up feeling you'd not been given a fair deal. Now that's something we mustn't let our child feel."

"We must not."

"And it's very true what you were saying some time ago, that it will be very useful for him to have his aunt a peeress. He'll have all those doors open to him when he goes to England. Isn't it funny the way I talk as though I were quite certain that it's going to be a son? You know on the whole I do really think I'd rather it was a son."

A son, who would inherit his name, his position, his reputation; in whom would be blended his features and Sylvia's: his character and hers; with certain characteristics of his own, individual, grafted, superimposed, the product of environment: and in twenty-five years that son would be sitting on this balcony, perhaps, wondering with his wife in what ways the child shortly to be born would be like his grandparents. His own daughter-in-law would perhaps be saying, "We shall have to be on our guard against our son growing up as you did. Your father after all . . ."

In what way would that daughter-in-law be wanting to guard her child against heredity. That would be the real verdict on himself, his daughter-in-law's judgment of him. Was anything more important than to have his son say "If I can give my son the chances that my father gave me, he'll be a lucky fellow."

If only his son were to be able to say that.

# CHAPTER TWENTY-THREE

## 1

By the Monday evening Maxwell had only sixty pages of *Crime and Punishment* left to read. He looked forward to discussing it with Whittingham. He could see why Whittingham had lent it to him. It bore out the old boy's theory, but he could not see that the lending of it need alarm him. There was no reason why he should not bring up the subject. It would be more natural for him to do so. You normally began a conversation with a reference to the last meeting. You said "We had a good time at your house the other day" or "What fearful nonsense old Bill was talking."

He opened with the topic right away as he prepared the swizzles.

"I'm very grateful to you for lending me *Crime and Punishment*," he said. "I'd probably never have read it if you hadn't. I'd have missed a treat."

"I've never seen him so absorbed in a book before," said Sylvia. "I've almost felt jealous of it. He's been reading it every spare minute. I've had no conversation out of him at all this weekend. I shall be relieved when he's finished it."

"I've only another sixty pages."

"That won't take long at the rate you're going."

"Have you read it, my dear?" the Colonel asked.

"I haven't, no."

"Then you must. Don't bother to bring it back, Maxwell, till Sylvia's read it. It'll make the time pass very quickly for her. Good books are so often heavy reading. This is more exciting than any detective story. I was told to read it by my first chief. He said it should be on the manual of Scotland Yard. Whenever I'm up against a ticklish proposition I reread it."

"Was that why you had it on your desk?"

He nodded.

"I'd brought it down from the house a week before. I'd been turning the pages whenever I hadn't anything to do."

A week before, Maxwell thought; then he couldn't have brought it down on my account. He can't have known I was coming in to see him. That lets me out. It's fantasy, all of it, nothing else. Fancying things again.

"What case was worrying you?" Sylvia asked.

"The same old headache, I'm afraid. The Carson case."

"I thought that had been shelved a long time ago."

"That's what one particular man is hoping, but it's a hope that'll never be gratified, I'm much afraid."

"So you're still hopeful."

"Never more so. I watch and wait. That's the point this book brings out so well. As long as the criminal's alive, so is the cat and mouse game. You think the case is forgotten because no one talks of it any longer. I don't suppose that you yourself have thought or talked about Carson for two months."

"It's curious that you should say that," Sylvia answered. "As a matter of fact we were only talking about him last week; in such an odd way too. I've been chuckling over it for the last five days. Darling, you don't mind me telling the Colonel do you?"

"Of course I don't."

She recounted the episode of the cigarette.

"Have you ever heard anything more hilarious? Colonel Carson and myself, and Maxwell was so jealous: he was off his head about it. I'm surprised he didn't challenge him to a duel. The things that men think up. Doesn't that astonish you, even with your experience?"

The Colonel smiled. He had been watching Sylvia as she talked, but now he turned toward Maxwell. There was a conspiratorial quality in his smile as though he and Maxwell shared a secret, as though the incident had for them an inner significance it could not have for the others.

"No," he said, "not altogether."

He paused: his smile became ironic; then he turned back to Sylvia.

"If I were married to anyone as attractive as you, my dear, I should be jealous of every male that breathed."

It was the kind of lumbering compliment for which the Colonel was notorious and for which "the inseparables" had invented their own counteroffense of Victorian coyness.

"Oh Colonel, come now," Sylvia said.

He knows, Maxwell thought, he knows.

2

He knows, he repeated to himself as he drove on the following morning to the Leg. Co. meeting.

The meeting was to be held at ten in the Court House.

Bradshaw arrived there at quarter to. He had persuaded two of his fellow journalists to accompany him. They came reluctantly. They were here, they argued, to describe the tourist potentialities of the island. They wanted to find a nearby beach and work upon their tan.

"You can't have too much background material," Bradshaw had assured them.

They had gone grumbling: Bradshaw, whom in Trinidad they had thought of as a pompous old Mr. Know-all, had managed since their arrival in Santa Marta to establish an ascendancy over them. They were having a good time and they had been forced to feel that the continuance of that good time was dependent on his good will. They supposed they had got to go to this damned meeting.

By the time they arrived the road outside the court was lined with cars. Policemen were patrolling the entrance to the courtroom. They were in full uniform; white spiked helmets, white tunics, dark blue trousers with red piping. They wore their medals. The stripes on the sleeves of their coats were embroidered in red and gold. They carried swagger canes.

"The British certainly know how to put on a show," said one of the journalists.

In the colonnaded passage way outside, the councilors, self-conscious and self-important, were standing in groups waiting till the last moment to take their places. From the court came a loud murmur of voices.

"Sounds like a lion house in the zoo ten minutes before feeding time," a journalist remarked.

Bradshaw looked through the entrance. At the back of the hall two rows of benches were reserved for the public. There was seating accommodation for about forty. Usually there was an attendance of a bare half dozen. Today the benches were crowded and men were standing against the walls. They were all very dark; most of them were coatless; they had the look of field laborers and longshoremen. Young Boyeur's fans, Bradshaw supposed. He looked round for Boyeur and saw him in conversation with Grainger Morris. Boyeur was wearing a dark blue suit, a white shirt, a plain burgundy red tie, and his shoes were black. He was starting to dress the part. Bradshaw caught his eye and came across.

"Is all this in your honor?" he asked.

Boyeur grinned.

"I guess some of the boys wanted to see how I made out. I thought they might. I warned Whittingham. As you'll see, he's put out some extra chairs for the elite."

387

There were a dozen office chairs in front of the benches. They were empty.

"We might as well sit down," Bradshaw said. "It's five of ten. They'll be here any minute now."

He explained the setup to his colleagues. The Judge's chair had been brought down from its dais and placed in the apex of two curved quarter circles. Five seats were set on its right side, seven on its left. In front of each chair was an inkpot, a blotter with a weight to keep the papers from being blown about by gusts of wind, and a glass of water.

"The official and nominated members sit on the right, the elected members on the left," Bradshaw explained.

The big hand of the clock had reached the edge of the roman numeral. In twos and threes the councilors moved in to take their places. Maxwell Fleury faced his father with Boyeur two places away on his left. Maxwell was taut, excited: his senses quickened by the dramatic irony of the situation. Here he was one of the island's legislators, the honorable member for Belfontaine. And only thirty yards away in the police station, Whittingham was spreading his net, hoping to trap him, hoping to place him in the dock that faced him against the wall, behind his father's head.

"Look, here they come," Bradshaw whispered.

A policeman came first, bearing over his shoulder the gold mace. The Governor followed. He was wearing a khaki bush shirt with a Sam Browne belt. He was three inches shorter than the constable, but that did not diminish his impressiveness. He looked very imposing as he stood under the royal coat of arms with the red tabs at his collar and four rows of ribbons above his left breast pocket. He recited a prayer hoping wisdom might be granted to the Council. He bowed to his councilors, and as he took his seat, the policeman laid the mace on its stand facing him.

"As you remarked, the British certainly know how to put on a show," said Bradshaw.

As the hall settled into its seats, Bradshaw was conscious of a rustle beside him and a wave of scent. He turned and there was Muriel Morris, flushed and breathless, embarrassed at being late. He saw Boyeur turn to her, Boyeur's face light up as he smiled. There was a fondness in that smile that was new to Boyeur. There was pride there and gratitude and friendliness, a look of belonging, a recognition of being belonged to. It warmed Bradshaw's heart. He had thought of Boyeur's marriage in terms of self-advancement. The experience of his life had taught him to think of most marriages in those terms, an angling for position. Perhaps this was more than that.

Perhaps this was the thing that novelists and poets wrote about. He shrugged. He did not know. How could he know? It was something that lay outside his own experience.

"Excited?" he whispered to her. She nodded her head twice quickly. This must be a big day for her. He hoped Boyeur did not make an idiot of himself. He turned back to his colleagues. "There's quite a little routine stuff coming now. We may get fireworks later. We may not. You can never tell."

The ordinary business of the meeting took its course. A member who had been absent for the opening meeting took the oath of allegiance to the throne, swearing that he would be faithful and bear true allegiance to His Majesty, his heirs and successors, according to law, so might God help him. The minutes of the previous meeting were then read; two announcements were delivered: were any petitions to be presented? No, none were. Were any papers to be laid before the house? Yes, there was a report from the Housing Commission. Copies were issued to the councilors for their information and if necessary, action. The whole procedure took twenty minutes. It was time then for the first motion. "We may have fireworks now," Bradshaw whispered.

"The first motion," the Governor announced, "is that hospital patients should not have to pay to wear their own clothes; it is proposed by the Honorable Member for St. Augustine's."

"What on earth is all this about?" asked Bradshaw's colleague.

"Probably a private quarrel with a matron somewhere. But we shan't know that."

The Honorable Member for St. Augustine's rose to propose his motion. He was an elected member. He was short, dapper and quarter colored. He was dressed in a black cloth suit with a high butterfly collar and a black and white polka dot bow tie. He looked as though he were dressed to take part in an Edwardian comedy. He spoke slowly, articulating his words carefully as though he was speaking in a foreign language.

There were standing instructions, he explained, that patients in the Jamestown hospital might only wear their own clothing on payment of a shilling. This was an antediluvian instruction. He did not know how long it had stood upon the books or for what reason it had been put there, but it was hard to conceive of a more ridiculous regulation. It was obviously in the interests of economy that patients should wear their own clothing; it represented a considerable saving in wear and tear of nightgowns and pyjamas; there were some people who had an affection for their own clothes; sick persons have their little fads and those little fads should be humored; the speed of

389

recovery might depend on it. A shilling a week might not sound a large sum to the members of this Council, but it was a large sum to certain sections of the public. What, he asked, was a laborer's wage. A dollar a day. A shilling was quarter of a day's work. Would any planter be satisfied to pay away every week one quarter of a day's profits for the privilege of wearing his own pyjamas when he was sick? Besides, apart from the money involved, there was the principle of the issue. Was it not manifestly unjust?

"There must be some private feud involved," said Bradshaw. "That's how things happen here."

The proposing speech lasted thirteen minutes. It was seconded by a five minutes speech. Its supporters on the elected side were brief. Boyeur retained his seat. He did not want to speak for the sake of speaking. He did not want to echo the others. A Boyeur speech must be an event. It paid not to speak too often. That was how to be effective. Let the others speak every time there was a motion so that they could see their names in the papers. Better to be shock troops.

"Has any other Honorable Member anything to say."

Julian Fleury rose.

"I was unaware, sir, of the existence of such a regulation. I do not know when or how it came into effect. But it does seem to be a case in which the opinion of the medical authorities should be invited. I can imagine several reasons why this regulation was made. Many of the hospital patients come from very humble homes. Many, unfortunately, live in squalor. Such patients may arrive in a verminous condition. It is essential for the sanitation of our hospitals that their clothes should not be brought into the wards. The charge of a shilling, when this regulation was made, must have been designed to prevent such clothes being brought into the wards. Thirty years ago a shilling was a large sum of money and the kind of person who would arrive in that condition would not be able to afford a shilling a week for the satisfaction of wearing those clothes. A shilling is possibly too small a sum today."

He was not, however, he continued, going to propose that the charge should be raised to a dollar, a proposal he had incidentally considered; but he was going to suggest an amendment to the motion: he suggested that the charge of a shilling should be removed but that the medical authorities must be satisfied that the sanitation of the hospital was being at all times maintained.

Maxwell, watching and listening from across the table, was touched for a moment by that old sense of self-inadequacy, of resentful jealousy. His father carried off this kind of thing so well.

390

Why couldn't he? He had been sitting silent for forty minutes, wanting to say something, but lacking the confidence, the assurance. If his opinion had been invited, he would have been able to make some contribution, but when the pause came, when a speaker finished, he lacked the experience to interpose his comments. Why couldn't he be more like his father? But it was only for a moment that he thought that. It was a matter of practice; that was all; he'd soon learn.

This afternoon they were to discuss the tourist potentialities of the island. He had ideas on that. He had made notes, memorized his key sentences. It would be his first speech and it would be effective. It was the first step that counted. Within a year he would have acquired his father's poise. Within a year . . .

He checked his thoughts. Where would he be within a year? Only three rooms away Whittingham was spreading the meshes of his net. Where would he be within a year?

"The amendment to the motion reads—" the Governor was announcing.

Would the day ever come when a Governor would read out *his* amendment to a motion.

"Will all those in favor say aye."

It was carried unanimously. How easily his father got his way.

"The next motion is 'That immediate steps be taken to vote an adequate sum of money to repair the schoolhouse in St. Patrick's.' To be proposed by the Honorable Member for St. Patrick's."

There was a stir, a shuffle of feet from the crowded benches. This was what they had been waiting for. There was a pause. Boyeur was in no hurry.

"Sir."

From the other side of the House had come an interruption. Julian Fleury was on his feet.

"I hope, sir, that I may be forgiven this interruption, but before the Honorable Member for St. Patrick's addresses us, I would like to remind the House that the priorities for the rebuilding and repairs of schools lies in the control of the Board of Education. There is an urgent need for repair in a number of school buildings. St. Patrick's, no doubt, is one of them. But is it desirable that this House should debate an issue that is being discussed and decided upon with the full authority of this House, in another place? I venture to make this interruption because I am not sure whether the Honorable Member for St. Patrick's is aware of the situation."

The interruption did not discomfit Boyeur. His voice in reply was firm and confident.

"The Honorable Member for St. Patrick's is perfectly aware of the fact. It provides an example, a typical example, of what we in this new Council must be prepared to fight, what we must fight. The board is our servant, not our master. It has been allowed to think of itself as our master, because up to now this island has been run on an antiquated system. If we had a ministerial system such as exists in England and indeed in Trinidad . . ."

Bradshaw leaned over to his colleagues. "I'll explain this," he whispered.

He wrote on a sheet of paper, "The system in Britain is to have various Civil Service departments, Fuel, Transport, Post Office, Treasury, over which members of the cabinet are made ministers, responsible to Parliament for the conduct of these departments. Some West Indian Islands have that system too. But not Santa Marta yet."

He paused, then continued, "Each island has its own distinct system. In some islands the administrator presides over the council. Some councils have a speaker. Santa Marta is the only island where the Governor presides."

He paused again, then added: "There's an Executive Council that carries out the instructions of this Council. H.E. presides over that."

It took Bradshaw two minutes to explain the situation to a man ignorant of the political formula; it took Boyeur ten minutes to attack a system with whose working every member of the Council was familiar.

The Governor sat back with his elbows rested on the arms of his chair, his hands clasped on its round knobs. As Boyeur's jeremiad grew more perfervid, his hands tightened their hold. This had got to stop. One had to allow councilors a certain latitude. It was traditional for elected members to shout, wave their arms, exaggerate. West Indians were naturally oratorical, and councilors talked to impress not so much their fellow members as their constituents in the districts. They wanted to be quoted in *The Voice*, they wanted to have the districts discuss the vigor with which their interests had been defended by their representatives. Councilors must be allowed some latitude. But Boyeur had passed the bounds.

The Governor looked at the crowded benches. Every face was turned to Boyeur; the eyes wide and gleaming; sometimes the lips moved, following his words in a mesmeric trance, as Boyeur harped back on that refrain "The Board is our servant. We are its master." No, this was too much. The Council could not be turned into a circus. Boyeur must be brought to heel.

The Governor tapped the table with his gavel and stood up. Boyeur surprised, checked in the middle of a sentence. He gaped, staring at the Governor. H.E. sat down and turned to Grainger.

"For the benefit of the Honorable Member who is not, apparently, familiar with our procedure, I will ask the Attorney General to read out Standing Order 7 c."

"Standing Order 7 c," Grainger read. "When the President rises to his feet, any member who is standing will resume his seat."

The Governor bowed, "Thank you," then tapped again upon the table. As he rose, Boyeur sat down.

"I must remind the Honorable Member for St. Patrick's that his present duty is to propose the motion under his name, namely that immediate steps be taken to vote an adequate sum of money to repair the schoolhouse at St. Patrick's. The system of Government in this Crown Colony is not under discussion. The time at our disposal is limited."

He sat down and Boyeur rose.

"I apologize, sir, to you and to the house. I was carried away by my enthusiasm, by my anxiety to serve my people. I had thought what I was saying was relevant, as a prelude to what I had to propose, in view of the intervention by the Honorable Nominated Member. But I was carried away. I spoke at too great length. I will confine myself strictly to my proposal. Gentlemen, I was carried away. In my place you, too, might have been. I speak of a blot upon our colony. How many of you have ever visited the school house at St. Patrick's, where the children of my people, my poor, poor people are learning to be worthy and loyal citizens of the British Empire? Have you seen the crumbling steps that lead to it; have you seen its leaking roof and the rotting timbers that support it? Once it was the house of a rich planter: for many years now no planter has deigned to live in it. It is not good enough for him; but it is good enough for the children of my poor people."

His voice was under control, it had a rich fierce vibrancy. How sincere was he, how much was he a self-seeking demagogue the Governor asked himself? Did Boyeur at heart care for the welfare of his people or was it only that it paid him to appear to care? Mentally the Governor shrugged. You could not split hairs like that. In the last analysis the great patriots were those who identified personal ambition with the welfare of their country. The traitor, as often as not, was one who, failing to recognize where the true interests of his country lay, identified his personal ambition with the less noble aspirations of his people. That was what Lord Acton had meant when he had remarked in a cynical moment that all great men were bad

393

men. There was no such thing as an unselfish patriot. Every man in public life worked for his own ends. But the statesmen whom history respected were those who out of a genuine and basic virtue in their natures, had identified themselves with noble instead of base aspirations. Hitler had become the focus of everything that was ignoble, every braggart, bullying, acquisitive, self-righteous, authoritarian, aggressive instinct in the German temperament. Churchill on the other hand, the subject of intense personal ambition, had been at the hour of his country's greatest danger the spokesman of its highest courage. Who could tell what figure Boyeur would cut in the eyes of history? He was out for himself; but so were most young men who were anything. If Boyeur had identified his need to better himself with the ambitions of a backward and originally ill-used people, history might venerate him as a patriot.

It might. But that, Templeton reminded himself, was forty years away, and his own immediate problem was to keep this young firebrand under control. Boyeur must not get the bit between his teeth, and a good deal depended upon how he handled him today. Boyeur must be made to realize that he was one of a team, here to do a job.

"We were brought to this island, we the people of Santa Marta, from our huts beside the rivers of West Africa. We were deprived of everything that made us superior to the beasts of the field, our language, our laws, our faith. We were shipped in slavers from the Guinea coast. We were sold in the open market. We were treated as cattle; we became cattle. Gradually through the centuries we evolved again into human beings with our own language, our own laws and our own faith. And how have we done that, gentlemen? Through education."

Yes, it was well enough done, the Governor thought. It had all been said a hundred times before: but the success of oratory lay in the speaker's power to pronounce with conviction what an audience already knew. Conviction, that was the key word. Confirm people in their beliefs, in what they wanted to believe. That's what Boyeur was doing; and he was doing it well and cleverly. Conscious though he must be of those crowded benches at his back, of the girl sitting beside Bradshaw, he never looked toward them, never gave the impression of appealing to them. He faced the chair. He was addressing the chair on behalf of those crowded benches. He was their spokesman, their champion, their defender. All the same, he had been talking now for thirty-seven minutes. There was a limit. The Governor tapped the table.

"I must remind the Honorable Member for St. Patrick's that our time is limited. He has been speaking now for thirty-seven minutes. For the last nine minutes he has given the House a lecture on the value of education which is irrelevant to the motion which is entered under his name. I must request that he confine himself more closely to the subject."

Boyeur rose, stood very straight, in silence, then bowed to the chair.

"I am sorry, sir. I am sorry, gentlemen. I was carried away. I will control myself. My old schoolmaster in that very building about which I am speaking to you, quoted to me a couplet from a poem about Savonarola. I shall always remember that couplet. Savonarola, it said:

> was one of those who knew no rest
> Because the world's wound ached so in his breast.

That is how I feel about my people, my poor people. I am carried away. I apologize, gentlemen. I will be very brief. I have little more to say."

He took, however, a long time in saying it. The Governor fidgeted. Boyeur appeared to have reached his peroration, yet he went on and on. It was like that Eastern music which he had found so exasperating during his service in India that had always seemed to be about to resolve itself into a rhythm and never did. Every sentence Boyeur began had the air of being his last, but always another followed. His voice had assumed the particular valedictory intonation that is associated with a peroration, but the final full stop was never reached. Boyeur had now returned to his attack on the Board of Education.

"Gentlemen, I must again remind you that the Board is our slave, our creature, not our master. Santa Marta belongs to us. Men come, men go. Administrations come and go. Governors come and go. Santa Marta goes on forever."

No, this was too much. His Excellency's patience was exhausted. Boyeur had been speaking for six minutes since his last interruption; for five minutes, at least, he had been off the point. The Governor was accustomed to military discipline, where the word "please" was an order. Boyeur had to be taught a lesson. The Governor rapped for the third time.

"For the benefit of the Honorable Member for St. Patrick's who is not familiar with our procedure, I will call upon the Attorney General to read Standing Order 9."

Standing Order 9 dealt with breaches of order. It stipulated that if a member showed disregard for the authority of the chair or

abused the rules of the council by persistently and willfully obstructing the business of the council, the President should direct the
attention of the council, mentioning the member concerned. A
motion might then be put that such member be suspended from the
council, no debate being allowed upon the order.

"I am forced," the Governor said, "to call the attention of the
Honorable Member for St. Patrick's to the wording of that motion.
If he continues to occupy our time with dissertations that are
irrelevant to the motion I shall be forced to conclude that he is
wilfully obstructing the business of the Council."

This time Boyeur did not apologize. "Gentlemen, I have said all
I have to say. I will now propose my motion."

As he sat down, he turned for the first time to Muriel. She raised
her hand shoulder high, fluttering her fingers. Her face was flushed.
Pride was there and happiness. She was unaware, evidently, that he
had been rebuffed. The episode was to her an official technicality.
If she had missed its point then surely his followers had done. They
would have gathered the general drift of what he was saying. They
would have seen him, on his feet, haranguing the notables of the
colony; they would have seen the Governor sitting in that high-
backed chair, listening. They would have recognized that their
representative was a man of consequence; that was all that mattered.

He took a sip of water and lolled back in his chair. On his right
the member for St. David's was seconding his motion, but in such
a way as to be offering an amendment. He was in complete agreement, he was contending, with the Honorable Member for St.
Patrick's. The schoolbuilding there was in a lamentable condition.
It should be repaired; it must be repaired; but at the same time he
must point out to the Honorable Members of the Council that the
schoolhouse in St. David's was in an equally lamentable condition.
That too must be repaired.

Boyeur smiled. He knew how it would go. He had sat in the
audience for many meetings of the Council. He knew the form.
Each man had to fight for his own district. One by one the elected
members would stand up and testify to the dire condition of their
own school. Finally an amendment would be moved urging that
immediate steps be taken to modernize and repair schoolbuildings;
and though immediate steps would not be taken, steps of some kind
would be, and sooner than would have been possible if he had not
proposed his motion. And when those steps were taken, the credit
would go to himself, to David Boyeur; not only in his own district,
but right through the island. He'd see to it that *The Voice* presented
the issue accurately. He'd give Bradshaw the tip. And *The Voice*

would print it the way Bradshaw wrote it. He could feel well satisfied with the way that things had gone, were going.

Next time it would be even better. Next time he'd be more careful. There were rules that he must remember. It was all the fault of Fleury: why had he interrupted him with that statement about the Board of Directors? That had put him off his stroke. Of course he knew about that damned board and its damned priorities. It was so like Fleury to have brought that up: typical of the whole Fleury point of view; trying to retard progress, to put a spoke in the wheels of progress.

He looked at Fleury sitting across the room, doodling on his pad. How smug he looked. Boyeur's temper rose. Father and son: made in the same mould. They stood for everything he hated. Arrogant, supercilious, self-sufficient. He remembered how Maxwell had spoken to him the other morning and in front of Muriel. He had some unfinished business there.

### 3

"Gentlemen, it is now quarter-past twelve," the Governor said. "I suggest that we adjourn until a quarter to two."

There was a murmur of agreement. It was a good time to pause. Boyeur's motion had gone the way that Boyeur had foreseen. All the elected members except Maxwell—I suppose he considers himself too grand, Boyeur had thought—had risen to plead the cause of their "own poor people." Finally an amendment had been agreed upon and passed with Julian Fleury alone voting against it.

Council meetings usually adjourned at half-past twelve, but the next motion, proposed by Norman, requesting the appropriation of funds for developing the tourist industry, would need lengthy deliberations. This was the time clearly for an adjournment.

The policeman strutted forward, lifted the gold mace and sloped it like a rifle on his shoulder; the assembly rose as the Governor followed the policeman to the Judge's chambers. The moment he left the room a burst of chattering broke out from the crowded benches. It was like a monkey house, Maxwell thought.

His father came across to him. "You're lunching at home, aren't you? Can I drive you down?"

Maxwell shook his head. "I'll follow you. I've some eggs and fruit and vegetables in my car. I'd better bring them now. I won't be long."

He had parked his car in the road leading to the tennis club. The crowd from the courthouse was thronging out into it: he

397

hesitated then took the narrow footpath that opened into the path leading to Carson's house. It was the first time that he had been here since the night. He paused, looking first one way then the other, remembering how he had walked up here, at Carson's side, his blood afire, his fists clenched: remembering how he had stolen back, a quarter of an hour later, alert, cautious, apprehensive, his nerves tingling, more conscious of being alive than he had been in his whole life. A quarter of an hour. That so much could happen in so short a time. He paused, pensive, in a reverie.

A hand fell upon his arm above his elbow; a familiar voice sounded in his ear. "He must have paused here on that night, wondering if there would be anyone to see him when he crossed this footpath. He may have stopped here for several seconds, listening: it was very dark. There was no moon that night as far as I remember."

"There was no moon."

Whittingham's voice had fused into his reverie so completely, so harmoniously, that for a moment he had not been conscious of the interruption. Then he started.

"You made me jump," he said and laughed.

Was it a nervous laugh? Had he given himself away? But it should, shouldn't it, have been a nervous laugh? It would have been unnatural if it hadn't been.

Whittingham did not appear to notice his start, his laugh, his interjection.

"It's strange," he said, "on this sunny morning to think of what happened here, three months ago on a dark moonless night. The man must have tiptoed out of the house, come through into this narrow path. At the end of it he could see the roadway, but he himself could not be seen. I'll tell you a curious thing about this house. It's a thing I've not told anyone, but it'll interest you. Do you know why Carson took this house? Because he wanted a place to which a woman could come and which a woman could leave without being seen. It wasn't a convenient house for him in other ways. He had to garage his car at Simpson's. But he was prepared to endure inconvenience for the sake of privacy. He had the regular soldier's respect for appearances, for not being talked about.

"After his death I made inquiries. I couldn't find what women had been up here, though I know some had. That's a feat in a place like Jamestown. It's ironic that he should have had this passion for privacy. It was his undoing. If his house had not been so hidden, his killer could not have got away. Perhaps whoever it was killed him, might not have risked getting into the house at all. Perhaps Carson might be alive today, if he hadn't chosen the kind of house where he could indulge his fancies privately. What an ironic revenge of fate's. Isn't there something in *King Lear* about our pleasant vices becoming thongs to scourge us? I can't remember how it went. My memory's hopeless."

His voice had a slow, tranquilizing, languid quality. His hand still rested upon Maxwell's arm above the elbow.

"It's strange, isn't it, to think of that dark night? Can't you picture him pausing, there where the paths join. He's fifty yards from the road. 'If I can make the road, I'll be safe' he must have told himself. 'No one will notice me, no one will suspect me. It'll be natural for me to be in the road. No one would question it.' That's how he must have thought; fifty yards to safety. Such a short distance. If only he could make it. I wonder how long he stood there waiting. I wonder if he saw you go by. Do you think he counted the cars; gauging how long the interval between them was; deciding to start as soon as the next car passed: or did he make a dash for it? I wonder if he remembered this footpath, leading to the courthouse: perhaps he didn't. It's very little used. What do you think?"

"I dare say he didn't."

"That's what I think too. He forgot all about it. There's always something that the criminal forgets; that may have been one of the things he overlooked: one of them."

"Were there other things then that he forgot?"

"Of course there were. There always are. But there, he was lucky; if he did forget, and we don't know that he did, anyhow no one saw him. He may have stood, at that exact spot there, waiting, listening: or he may not. We can't tell that. But what we do know, what we can guess at is the surge of relief he must have felt when he turned the corner, there, into the roadway. 'I'm safe. I'm safe,' he must have told himself."

Maxwell closed his eyes. That was how it had been. How clearly Whittingham understood him. Whittingham's voice was kind and tolerant. The pressure of his hand was reassuring. What a relief it was to be understood. If only he could relax completely: pour out the whole story to the one man in the world who would understand. It would be so easy to tell Whittingham. Whittingham knew so much, had heard so many confessions; he wouldn't be shocked, or startled. He would make it easy for you, like the priest in the confessional: if only he could say, "Yes, that's the way it was." Whittingham was the one man in the whole world who could understand.

"When I'm investigating a case," Whittingham went on, "I always put myself in the position of the man who did it. Like an actor. It's a great help to me."

Maxwell nodded. That was Whittingham's strength. That was where his skill lay. He knew how the criminal felt. Maxwell felt mesmerized; weak, helpless, hungry for surrender. If only he could discard this burden of personal responsibility. Another minute and the temptation to confess would have become unbearable. But in that half minute Whittingham had changed the subject.

"What a charming evening we had last night," he said. "I've never seen Sylvia looking better. The old hag was saying the same thing. You've wrought a miracle in that girl. She's become another person, so warm and out-giving. She always seemed frozen and shut in: you've unlocked the door. She used to seem happy on the surface, but now she seems happy in herself. By the way, I meant to ask you and forgot. Are you having any trouble with that man Montez who had the case with Preston?"

"I've seen no signs of trouble."

"That's fine. I was wondering. A chap like that, you see..."

They discussed Montez for a couple of minutes, then Whittingham turned to go.

"Time for tiffin," he said. "By the way there was something I wanted to ask you about *Crime and Punishment*. It's a long time since I've read it right through; there was a point I'd forgotten. You remember that man who waylays Raskolnikov and mutters that one accusation 'murderer': was it ever cleared up who he was? Was he one of those mysterious sleepwalking characters that Dostoevski sometimes introduces, like the man who bows down to that wild Karamazov brother, what was his name—Dmitri, Michael, I can't remember, the one who was accused falsely; or was he a police stooge, planted so that the detective can see how Raskolnikov reacts to the accusation? Was it ever cleared up which it was? I can't remember."

"I haven't finished yet. There's been no explanation so far. But I'll look out for it and I'll let you know."

"Fine. Do that. I was thinking about it the other day. It was a trick I've not known in English detective practice and it's a good one. Those Russians are no fools, where police methods are concerned. Their secret police could teach us a point or two."

He knows, Maxwell thought, he knows.

### 4

He must know. How can he not know? Yes, but what can he do?
So Maxwell argued with himself as he sat with his family at lunch. Euan Templeton was there, seated next to Jocelyn. He ate with his

right hand, she with her left. They did not talk a great deal but there was an air of repose, of calm about them; of fulfillment. Jocelyn hadn't a trouble in the world. He envied her, but not aggressively: not as he would have done four months ago. He did not resent her being happy. He did not even feel he had himself been cheated. He had no one but himself to blame.

His father at the head of the table was discussing the morning's meeting. On the whole he did not think Boyeur had made himself ridiculous. He had said his piece, established himself as a force among the other councilors.

"But he'll have to be careful," he insisted. "He's put H.E.'s back up. Your father's a disciplinarian, Euan. A no nonsense man. He's not going to have his authority flouted."

"It's not a job I'd care to take on myself," said Euan.

There was a laugh at that.

Jocelyn asked Maxwell if he had spoken.

"No, I'm waiting till this afternoon. I didn't want to echo Boyeur, that's all I could have done."

This afternoon he would as likely as not be on the other side. He had thought out his argument. He had telling things to say. His first speech would be as effective as Boyeur's had been, more effective actually, because he had kept silent that morning. If he played his cards carefully he would earn the reputation of being a man who only spoke when he had something of consequence to say. Not like Boyeur, jumping to his feet at every opportunity; speaking for the pleasure of hearing his own voice. Boyeur, how he hated him. He saw him in memory striding into that avenue of light, looking up to the platform with supercilious triumph: heard again the contempt in his voice as he had said, "Come on, there's nothing to amuse us here"; saw himself standing speechless while the crowd dissolved. Boyeur stood for everything he detested. Boyeur: he'd get his own back in the council.

5

"I therefore suggest, sir," Norman concluded, "that a subcommittee should be formed to examine the possibilities of developing *Grande Anse* as a tourist resort and to report on the amount of capital that it considers necessary."

He had been speaking for a quarter of an hour. Julian Fleury rose to second the motion.

"I will be very brief, sir. I am in such complete agreement with what the Honorable Member has just said that I have little to do except endorse his opinions. There is one point, however, that I should like to make. We need, in my opinion, the advice of an expert. We are all of us here amateurs in these matters. We do not know what kinds of entertainment Canadian and American tourists will expect in a place like this. We have to give something that other islands have not got. We cannot go into competition with Jamaica, Bermuda, Nassau. Nor for that matter can Barbados, but Barbados has found the means of providing special attractions of its own, and we in Santa Marta ought to be able to do the same. But we need the guidance of an expert."

He elaborated his thesis briefly and with effect.

"The first duty of this subcommittee should be to select that expert," he concluded.

The Governor tapped with his gavel. "The following motion has been moved and seconded." He read out the motion. "It is now open for discussion by the House."

Maxwell and David Boyeur were on their feet simultaneously. The Governor looked from the one to the other. Maxwell had not spoken yet. He was entitled to speak first. But Boyeur had been subjected to reproof. It was better that he should not be allowed to feel that that reproof now entailed reprisals. A reprimand was a punishment and the slate was clean now. He caught Boyeur's eye. Maxwell sat down. Hell, he thought. It was his turn surely.

"May I say, sir," Boyeur started, "that with one remark of the Honorable Member who spoke last I am in complete agreement. We are, he said, amateurs in this business. We are, and for that reason we should move with the greatest caution."

He spoke with an easy fluency. Maxwell glowered, envious and resentful. Why had he not himself this gift? Of all the capacities in the world it was the most superficial, the most trivial yet the most valuable. Good plans sound inefficacious if they are presented clumsily; a persuasive speaker could gain attention for the most flimsy schemes. It was such a minor talent. The pitching of a voice, the turn of a phrase, a smile at the right moment, a gesture, a movement of the head or hand; they counted for so much. Why should they? It was not fair. Why should a glib tongue achieve more than solid arguments backed by research?

"I will say, frankly, at the start that I shall vote against this motion," Boyeur was announcing. "I say that to make my position clear. We are amateurs in this business and we have not the right to ask Government to finance a venture run by amateurs. We have been assured that the development of *Grande Anse* will prove a good investment, will bring hard currency into the colony. But if

402

that is so, why has not private enterprise developed *Grande Anse*? There is a great deal of capital in this colony. There are many capitalists. We are always being assured, we socialists, that private enterprise is infinitely more efficient than a State-run proposition. In a State-run proposition no one cares about making profits. 'Jobs for the boys' that is all that matters. I disagree most heartily with that contention, but the Honorable Members on the other side of the House endorse it. Why then are they suggesting that Government should finance this venture? If the development of *Grande Anse* is such a gilt edged proposition why have they not formed a syndicate, invested their own money in it, organized it with that extra skill, that extra energy that are, so they tell us, the essential accompaniments of private enterprise, and in the process not only brought hard currency into the colony, but earned rich rewards for themselves.

"Sir, it is my suggestion that private enterprise has been warily noncommittal because it has no confidence in the dividend-earning prospects of this scheme. The capitalists of Santa Marta are not simpletons. Let Government put up the money, they say to themselves, and we will make our incidental profits as middlemen, supplying goods and services; cinemas, bars, hotel rooms, taxicabs; then when the balance sheet shows a deficit we can shrug our shoulders with a 'What can you expect when Government runs a show? Think of all the boys who have to get their rake-off.' No, sir, I am convinced that if the capitalists of the colony were convinced that money could be made out of developing *Grande Anse*, they would not at a boom period such as this have handed over to Government this chance of lining their own coffers."

He smiled as he made his speech. There was no note of anger or indignation in his voice. He was not being the demagogue, as he had that morning when he had talked on his motion of "my poor people." His self-control made him the more effective. He did not give the impression of having any personal ax to grind. Maxwell was acutely conscious of Boyeur's success. His resentment was quickened by the fact that Boyeur was using many of the arguments that he had planned for his own speech. He too had meant to oppose the motion; why could he not have been given the first innings? It was not fair.

"There is another point which I want to make," Boyeur was continuing. "I want to ask, sir, whether an influx of tourists is really desirable in a small island such as ours. It would bring prosperity to individuals, it would bring hard currency into the colony, but there are things more important than a balance sheet in the black.

I would remind the house that the once French island of Haiti was never more prosperous in terms of bullion than it was during the months before it collapsed into anarchy and civil war. In those plush days a canker was eating at its heart. A balance sheet in the black is of less importance than a system that is free from canker. I would remind the house, sir, that at the present this colony is paying its way. We have no immediate cause for concern on that account. But our internal health is a plant we must tend carefully. We have, and we must admit that we have, a color problem here. Let us consider how the sudden influx of a group of Canadian and American tourists will affect that problem."

Maxwell clenched his fists. This was another of the points that he had meant to make. His speech was being pulled apart. There would soon be nothing left of it. And he had planned it all so carefully, written it out, memorized the phrases. He might not have been able to deliver it with Boyeur's ease of manner; but the arguments were sound enough to have told even if they were not mouthed by a rhetorician. He should have made his mark with this speech. As it was he would be left with only a few scattered comments. All the best points, the opportunities for punching phrases, had been stolen.

How he hated Boyeur. Boyeur typified everything he detested in West Indian life. In the same way, though in an obverse, exactly opposite way, that looking at Sylvia across the table he would note adoringly each loved feature, so now he marked with fascinated repulsion each detested feature: the black skin, the short crinkly hair, the wide purple dark mouth, the dazzling white even teeth, the widespread nostrils, the flattened nose, the naked-looking eyes; he watched the long-fingered hands gesticulate. What an animal Boyeur was, with the arrogance, cunning, cruelty of a panther. He remembered Boyeur swaggering into that long avenue of light. How he had longed at that moment for revenge: how impotent he had felt, standing on that platform, with Sylvia an indifferent and disdainful witness.

His blood had boiled that night: it had been boiling on the next morning when he had read that article in *The Voice*, had boiled as he had driven into Jamestown to demand reparation. It had been still boiling that night as he had strode toward the club, as he had checked in the street to talk to Carson. How much of his fury was not due to the humiliation he had endured the night before at Boyeur's hands. Who could pinpoint the exact source of one's moods, one's actions? But for Boyeur, he might have been spared this torturing

404

doubt, this invading menace, this blight that soured what should have been his sweetest hours. Boyeur.

"It is a delicate situation that we must handle delicately," the speech continued. "On the whole we may consider ourselves lucky here. We all know each other. We have known each other all our lives. We are bound by the bond of being Santa Martans. We go our separate ways; we have our separate clubs; we know how to avoid friction. But let us consider, sir, the very different people who will be coming here from America and Canada. They too have a color problem; at least in America they have, but it is a very different problem from our own. They boast in America that they have no racial discrimination, and perhaps they haven't, before the law. But there is complete segregation of the races. White and colored groups do not meet socially. How will these visitors react when they find colored families using the same bathing huts that they do, and sitting at the same bar? Jamaica is so large that the visitors to Montego Bay are not socially aware of the existence of African Jamaicans; and in Antigua there has been created at Milreef a club that is cut off so completely from the life of the visitor that members there might fancy themselves in Florida. But here it is very different. We are a small island. We see each other all the time."

It was another of the points that Maxwell had proposed to make. What was left now of his speech? His temper mounted, the same black ungovernable temper that as a child had made him scratch at his nurse's face, stamp on his toys, throw a lesson book across the room; the temper that had flamed up in him through boyhood into manhood, that after the Governor's party for his son had made him fling Sylvia through the mosquito net; the same black blind frenzy that on that moonlight night had driven him, kneeling across a pinioned body, to batter a head against the floor: a fierce blinkered atavistic frenzy that knew no mastery beyond its own blind need for self-assertion.

"It is for these reasons, sir, that I shall vote against the motion."

Maxwell was on his feet before Boyeur had sat down. His blood was boiling; he was passionate for revenge, in a need to hit back, to wound, to cause pain. He sought for the searing words and in the inspiration of hatred came on them.

"Sir, I must warn the Honorable Members of this Council against being swayed too easily by the eloquence of the Honorable Member for St. Patrick's. May I congratulate him on his speech. We are indeed fortunate to have the privilege of listening to such oratory. His presence here, and his contributions to our deliberations will make our attendance not only a duty but a pleasure. At the same time, sir, we must be on guard against his eloquence, particularly on the question of color.

"It is a very tricky situation for all those of us, and we are the majority, who have African ancestry. Such ancestry in many parts of the world is looked on as a stigma. It is not here any longer, but because it is elsewhere, we are liable to take a biased, a parochial view of the subject. We imagine slights where no slight was intended. If we fail in any enterprise, we attribute our failure to that African ancestry. We have been passed over, we tell ourselves, because we have colored blood. Whereas in fact we have been passed over because we were the wrong man for the job. We have all of us got to be on guard against this tendency, in ourselves and others. The Honorable Member for St. Patrick's is as vulnerable on this point as the rest of us. He made, sir, a particular point of the attitude that might be adopted toward our womenfolk by North American tourists who do not realize that the young women of Santa Marta have to be treated with the same respect as their own sisters and daughters are back north. Now that is a point that bears out precisely what I have been saying."

He paused. Now is my chance, he thought. Now for the phrase like a knife. He was still turned to the Chair.

"A traveler may condemn an entire town because he has been insulted by a waiter or cheated by a taxi driver. In the same way a man of color—" he paused, he turned his head and looked at Boyeur. Now, he thought, now—

"A man of color who has been abandoned by his mistress in favor of a handsome young English officer . . ."

He said it slowly. There was venom in his voice, contempt in his voice. It was a challenge and Boyeur knew it. Boyeur jumped to his feet; his fist banged on the table, rattling the inkpots.

"You dare to say that. You dare to say that to me," he shouted.

The gavel beat upon the table. The Governor was standing. Maxwell sat down at once: his heart was pounding. He had succeeded beyond his dreams. Boyeur looked round him, dazed, flabbergasted: opened his mouth, changed his mind, sat slowly down.

"I will call upon the Attorney General to read Standing Order No. 6," the Governor said.

By Standing Order No. 6 a member was not allowed to address another member unofficially, or by name.

"I will now ask the Attorney General to reread Standing Order No. 7, which he has already read to us this morning."

It was the order dealing with the disciplinary action which might

406

be taken against a member who disregarded the authority of the Chair.

"I will now," the Governor said, "call the attention of the Council to the behavior of the Honorable Member for St. Patrick's. Mr. David Boyeur."

As he sat down he looked toward Julian Fleury. Julian Fleury rose. Within ninety seconds it had happened. The motion had been proposed, seconded by Norman and carried without a dissenting voice, that Mr. David Boyeur be suspended from the service of the Council.

Heavens, Bradshaw thought, when the British move fast, they certainly move awful fast. He watched Boyeur gather together his papers, rise, bow to the Governor, turn and walk toward the entrance. Boyeur did not look at the crowded benches nor at the girl at Bradshaw's side. How was she taking it, Bradshaw wondered. Purposely he did not look at her.

The gavel was tapped upon the table. "The business of the Council will now be resumed," the Governor announced. Maxwell stood up.

"Sir, as I was pointing out, a traveler judges a town . . ."

Bradshaw heard a rustle at his side. His eyes followed Muriel Morris as she tiptoed to the entrance. She paused at the policeman's side, turned, bowed to the Governor, then hurried down the colonnaded passageway to where Boyeur waited. She slipped her arm through his, and they walked together down the steps.

"What does this involve?" Bradshaw's colleague whispered.

"Nothing very drastic; an apology from Boyeur next time the Council meets."

# CHAPTER TWENTY-FOUR

*1*

His Excellency had been trained under a system of "On parade, on parade: off parade, off parade." You did not talk shop in the mess, and the fact that your adjutant or company commander had abused you to high heaven that afternoon for a breach of procedure at the rifle range would not prevent you from sitting next him that night at dinner and arguing over Middlesex's chances in the county championship. Templeton bore no more ill will to Boyeur than he would have to a subaltern he had reprimanded. He considered that Boyeur should look on the incident in the same light. But he was aware that Boyeur had not been acclimatized to that atmosphere. It would be as well to show him that no personal relations were involved and that when he reappeared at the next meeting of the Council, the incident, after the preliminary apology, would be considered closed. It was up to himself to make a gesture; and the fact that Boyeur had recently become engaged to the Attorney General's sister seemed to provide an appropriate occasion.

"I want Boyeur and his fiancée up here to dinner," he told his A.D.C. three days later. "Fix a date with them for next week. Put it to them as though it were a party in honor of their engagement; no perhaps not quite that. Say I want to wish them luck. Make it look like a party for them. Let them choose their day; but the real purpose of the party is that Boyeur and young Maxwell should make up their quarrel. You've heard all about it, I suppose."

"Yes, sir."

"From anyone in particular or simply general gossip?"

"I had a talk with Bradshaw, sir."

"That man gets everywhere. Did he tell you exactly what young Fleury said?"

"Yes, sir."

"What did you make of it?"

Archer flushed and hesitated. How much did H.E. know, how much did H.E. suspect? There were quite a number of things that you would expect him to know about, of which he was completely ignorant, but very much more often he surprised you both with his percipience and the range of his information. He was a downy old bird.

408

"Well, sir, I don't quite know . . . ." He paused, waiting for a lead.

"Do you think that remark about the colored man being chucked by his girl referred to some actual fact, something I did not know about myself, but which a great number of people in that room did? What I'm saying is, did Maxwell deliberately taunt Boyeur?"

"I believe he did, sir."

Archer had listened to the unfolding of that long sentence with relief. It bore out to a T exactly what he had been thinking about the old boy half a minute earlier. The things he knew and the things he didn't know. He'd presumed that by now his chief had some inkling about the relations between his secretary and A.D.C., but had accepted the traditional English credo "a row's a row and damned disgraceful; when there is no row, nothing is disgraceful." Archer had been at great pains to preserve appearances, and few men noticed what was right under their nose. All the same without the facts to guide him, H.E. had accurately diagnosed the case. Men like the General fooled you. You always thought of professional soldiers as being stupid; but the old man was a much more acute psychologist than most Bloomsbury intellectuals.

"That's what I suspected myself," the Governor was saying. "Have you any idea what caused the ill feeling between these young fellows?"

"You heard about the demonstration at Belfontaine at Maxwell's first election meeting."

"Yes."

"Boyeur was responsible for that. He may have been responsible for the burning of the cane at Mardi gras. Boyeur had been backing that man Montez who brought the case against Preston. There was some idea at the time of Preston taking over Belfontaine. Boyeur may have thought Mr. Fleury's position influenced the judge. Things get very involved here, sir."

"I know, my boy, I know. We can't always get to the cause of things. Sometimes best not to trouble. When you get a spot, prick the yellow head and hope the damned thing clears up. That's what we'd better do now. I want both the Fleurys here on the same night as Boyeur. Make it a command. As for the rest . . . Well, let me see. We'd better have it a young people's party. Not Grainger Morris. His sister would be more at ease without him. Boyeur would too, probably. That young Kellaway's amusing. Who else would you suggest? Mavis Norman? We might have her: particularly as her father seconded the motion against Boyeur. Mavis Norman. I seem to have heard something about her recently?"

He had in fact heard nothing, but he had found that one of the best ways of obtaining information was by appearing to possess it. And he was curious to know what was happening to Mavis. She might so very well have been his future daughter-in-law.

"Have you heard what I've heard?" he asked.

"No, sir, I've heard nothing."

"Possibly it's only a rumor then, forget it. Let's have her up here anyhow. And get this dinner fixed as soon as you can manage it. Come back and tell me as soon as you've decided on a day."

Archer returned to his office pensively. It was no business of his, he supposed, but all the same . . .

He sat at his desk staring at the telephone. Boyeur would be in his office now. He had his orders. But . . .

He picked up the receiver of the house telephone and spun the handle. Margot answered him.

"Are you alone?" he asked.

"No."

"Could you come here a minute, then?"

"Right away?"

"Yes, please."

He did not get up when she came in. That was part of their campaign. He maintained an office manner to the point of rudeness. They acted their parts, even when as now there was no need, so that it would come naturally to them when they met in public. He pointed to a chair. She sat down and opened her dictation pad.

"He doesn't know about us," he said.

"That's good."

They had discussed it together yesterday. They had been afraid lest Maxwell's public reference to their private lives would make things difficult for them.

"We don't have to worry about anything," he said.

"I'm free tomorrow early."

"I can manage that."

How calm that sounded, how matter of fact she seemed. Yet her placid announcement made his blood tingle as those two others for all their protestations never had.

But it was not to discuss their own plans that he had summoned her during a working morning.

"H.E.'s going to have David Boyeur up to dinner," he told her. He outlined the Governor's scheme.

"Do you think that's a good idea?" he asked.

"I think it's a very bad idea."

"Why?"

"Because of David's vanity. That's the first thing about him. His

410

pride means more to him than it does to any Jap. He has been shamed in public. He is angry and bitter. It is very necessary when he is in that mood to handle him in the right way."

"What is the right way in a case like this?"

"Ignore him."

"Leave it to simmer down?"

"Hope that it will simmer. When his vanity is hurt, he is danger-ous. Unless you are absolutely certain what is the right thing to do, it is wisest to do nothing. Let him make the move. It might be fatal to make a wrong move yourself."

She talked as though she were discussing the behavior of a casual acquaintance. It was strange that she should be able to discuss with such detachment someone who had been once so close to her. It was strange for that matter that he should be able to hear her talk of his predecessor with such indifference. They had barely mentioned him, until yesterday his scene in the Leg. Co. had created the possi-bility of a situation for them.

During his two love-affairs in England he had been intensely curious to know about each woman's past: not out of jealousy but because he wanted to know by what steps they had become the women that they were: each stage of their past had been a landmark on their road to him. He felt no such curiosity about Margot. It surprised him that it shouldn't, since Margot's past, her whole for-eign background, might have been expected to be of absorbing interest to a writer. She could have taught him so much about her race, about the problems and aspirations of her people. But he had felt no instinct to probe, to dissect, to treat her as copy, as exhibit A. He had not even bothered to examine his own feelings to her. Was he so detached that he did not care, or was his capitulation so complete?

"David's vanity is so great that a man like His Excellency could not measure it," she was saying. "The chances of his making a mis-take in this case are ninety-nine to one."

Was it a deficiency of emotion in himself that he could hear her talking so casually of a former lover, without drawing a parallel between her indifference to Boyeur and her own feelings for him-self. Why did he feel no jealousy? Jealousy moved in such devious forms. He could understand the intellectualized jealousy of Swann and the tyrannical masculine jealousy of Othello. Should he not have read a warning for himself into that calm, level voice. Might she not one day talk of him in just that way to his successor? Betrayed she not another loving him. Why should he be so calm?

411

Was it indifference, or was it a faith so utter that he could not doubt her: that he could doubt the universe before he doubted her?

"Do you think I ought to warn H.E.?" he asked.

"If you think you can, tactfully."

"Even if it means mentioning you?"

"Why should I care?"

"I'll think about it then. You've been a great help. Thank you very much."

"Will that be all then?"

"Yes."

She rose.

"Will half-past five be all right?" she asked.

"It'll be fine."

His nerves were tingling as he heard her soft footfall down the passage. How could it be indifference?

In front of him the telephone waited, symbol of his orders. It was not his business to query his superior's command. That was why soldiering was such a relaxation mentally. You never had to plan out independent action. You found out what your superior wanted and carried out his instructions. The responsibility was his. But I'm not in the Army now, Archer told himself. Even if my chief is a General and wears uniform.

He stared at the telephone. Had he any right to telephone Boyeur until he had told his chief what Margot thought? Margot knew Boyeur better than anyone in the island knew him. It was his duty as A.D.C. to convey to his chief any information that might help him to carry out his job. He had never known Margot's judgment or rather instinct to be at fault on any issue where she held a definite opinion. The old boy might think him a fool; might consider his intervention an impertinence, but his own conscience would not be clear if he did not warn him. He returned to his chief's room.

The Governor was holding the receiver of the telephone to his ear. But he had called out "come in" when Archer knocked.

"No, don't run away," he said. "I've no secrets from you, not official ones at least. London's on the line. Take the weight off your feet."

He pointed to a chair.

Seated, facing his chief, Archer's nervousness began to mount. The old boy would think him crazy, and by the time he was through with his explanations, would know not only about Boyeur and his secretary, but about his secretary and his A.D.C. I must be mad, he told himself, but it was too late now.

"Yes," the Governor was saying, "yes, this is the Governor of

Santa Marta: Ah, hullo, Bobbie, my dear fellow. What can I do for you?"

There was a pause. The Governor frowned. He looked very formal and official. He was not one of those who when they are talking on the telephone, include in the conversation those who may be in the room. He was tense and concentrated.

"No," he said and his voice was firm. "There is no need to feel any alarm. You know what journalists are. They only hear half the story. They exaggerate and minimize. They think in terms of head-lines. I am having the young man up here to dinner next week and I am inviting to meet him the group that was responsible for his behavior. In my opinion he was goaded deliberately into that out-burst. He is not as much to blame as the newspaper report may have led you to suppose. No, no, there is nothing in the least to worry over."

The certainty in his voice must have carried conviction to the man who was listening three thousand miles away. Templeton was not the man to loiter on a telephone. He cut off the call quickly.

"That was the Secretary of State for the Colonies," he told Archer.

Archer had guessed as much. He had listened to the conversation with relief. This let him out. There was nothing he could do about it now. It was a settled thing.

"There've been paragraphs in the London papers about that scene in Leg. Co.," Templeton was continuing. "The Minister expects questions in the house. He's getting very jumpy. I wonder what's happening over there. Perhaps there's going to be a cabinet reshuffle. He's got his eye on a promotion. What was it you wanted, Denis. Have you fixed that date with Boyeur?"

While the Governor had been talking on the telephone, his A.D.C. had readjusted his program.

"No, sir, not yet. He wasn't in when I called just now. I came to remind you about that dinner of the cricket club next Wednesday."

It was with mixed feelings that Archer returned to his own office. He was glad to have been relieved of an awkward interview but his conscience was not completely clear. The chief should have been warned. Yet what could he have done after the Minister had been given that assurance? It was a *fait accompli*.

3

Archer left his call to Belfontaine till last. It was always difficult to get through there and the line was less likely to be busy at lunch.

Maxwell had just got in when the call came through. He was hot and tired, anxious for a shower, and for a punch, for the peace of Sylvia's company. The last thing he wanted was a G.H. dinner. All the business of packing.

"No, really. Have I got to? Can't I be excused?"

"I'm sorry. It's a command."

"Why, what's in the air?"

"I can't tell you on the telephone."

"Oh, I see, of course not. All the same, H.E. does know about Sylvia, doesn't he?"

"We all know. It's fine news."

"You can see why I'm not anxious to bring her in. It's a bumpy road."

"There's no need for her to come if she'd rather not."

"Oh, so it's me you want."

"It's you we want."

"In that case," he hesitated. He had only used Sylvia as an excuse. The road was not all that bumpy. Sylvia would have no qualms about it. Sylvia enjoyed the parade atmosphere of G.H., she would welcome the opportunity of dressing up while she still had the chance. She would resent it if he refused for her. Besides it would be very lonely for her out here by herself.

"All right, we'll make it. Eight o'clock I suppose."

"Yes, eight o'clock."

Him and not her. What did that mean? He could understand H.E. wanting them as a couple for an official party, to welcome some visiting fireman. Sylvia was pretty and amusing. She dressed a table well. But why should H.E. insist upon his attendance? What was behind it? Whittingham?

That sense of doom, of menace was again upon him. Did Whittingham want to watch him, to remind him that he was never out of his scrutiny, to goad him to his final breakdown, his moment of confession? Whittingham's vigilance never relaxed. Whittingham had warned him on that very point. In the end the criminal broke down in self-defense. He longed to be in harbor. Him and not her. It must be Whittingham.

She raised her eyebrows interrogatively as he came onto the veranda. She had probably heard the greater part of the conversation.

"That was G.H. They want us to dine there on Tuesday."

"And did I hear you trying to refuse?"

"It's a bumpy road."

"Now, darling. That's ridiculous. I won't be coddled. It's very bad

414

for me, the doctor said so. I'm not an invalid. You're not to treat me as one."

"I know, I know."

"I'd have been furious if you'd robbed me of the party."

Her words were stern, but the ring in her voice was tender.

"I never want to go into town," he said. "I'm so much happier out here with you."

"I much prefer that reason to the bumpy road."

"I can't tell you how happy I feel when I wake up in the morning and look at you beside me, and think that we haven't got to do anything all day; no one to visit, no one to entertain, just ourselves, and the estate to potter round. I wonder what I've done to deserve such luck. I feel so happy about it all, that I have to wake you up to tell you."

"You say that as though you really meant it."

He was standing beside her; his hand resting on her shoulder; he lifted it and stroked her cheek. As though he really meant it. If only she knew how utterly he meant it. He felt so safe here, looking forward to an eventless day. Nothing could touch him, no one could get him. Was that how rabbits felt in the center of a corn field at harvest time, while the reaping machine working in a narrowing circle drew closer every minute? It was safe and dark and warm there in the center: but soon the sharp blades would drive them to that dash into the open where the harvesters with sticks and stones were waiting. For the moment they were secure; but the moment was set, inevitably, inescapably when they would have to risk that dash for freedom. Was this his position now?

4

Always now during her siesta, Sylvia slept in Maxwell's arms. "Darling, don't I stop you sleeping?" she protested.

He shook his head. "The moment I see that you've gone off, I go too."

He did not, though. The moment he began to doze, and his muscles relaxed, her body became a dead weight, numbing his arms. He enjoyed in a vague masochistic way this loss of sleep.

Afternoon after afternoon he lay beside her, luxuriating in the denial, the defeat of sleep; but today even if he had been alone in his dressing room, sleep would have been impossible. His mind was racing. Him and not her. Was the Governor privy to the trap? What was the trap? A tape recorder behind his chair? How easy everything was made for the detective nowadays. All the aids of science; drugs that sapped your powers of resistance, lie detectors. They were bound to get him. He understood now how those Russian Generals broke down under cross-examination, they longed to be let alone; anything for peace of mind.

He'll never let me alone, never, never, Maxwell told himself. He'll hound and harry me. He knows, he must know. I've made so many slips. "Afterward" instead of "after": the Belfontaine Committee: the watch: then how his arms were pinioned: the knees on the elbow joints, no marks on the killer's face. How could I have guessed? He must suspect, even if he does not know. As long as he suspects, he'll haunt me. As he did at that Leg. Co. meeting, coming silently beside me, recreating the crime. That's how it'll always be, suddenly I'll find him at my side. I'll be never safe from him, never, for an instant. My shadow, that's what he'll be, my shadow.

I'll have to be on my guard all the time. I'll have to fight him off, for Sylvia's sake, for the child's sake.

That was the key point. He had come to see that now. He was fighting not in his own defense but in defense of Sylvia and their child. He could not bring shame on them. How could a child face the world if its father was a murderer? The knowledge would haunt it all its life. It must be spared that shame. On the day that he knew for certain that Whittingham knew, he must find the remedy. What else could he do? His was not "an ill for mending."

Her shoulder pressed above his heart, her breast lifted and sank slowly as she breathed, her hair scented with jasmin was against his cheek. Her nearness was a delight beyond words' measurement. Why should fate have given him such delight only to imperil it? Why had this torture had to visit him? Why could it not have struck at someone who did not value life, who did not care whether he lived or died, who could have shrugged off his grim necessity? To many men life meant little. Why could not fate have attacked one of them? Why had it chosen him?

What were they plotting for him, down there in Jamestown, Whittingham and the Governor, with their traps and tricks? But they won't get me alive, he vowed; never, never, never.

# CHAPTER TWENTY-FIVE

## 1

David Boyeur stood in front of his mirror and turned slowly round. He was wearing evening clothes for the first time. He had bought them in Trinidad, three months back. They had been made by an East Indian tailor. They had cost a hundred and thirty dollars. He had charged the cost against Union Funds. His conscience was clear on the morals of the transaction. The Union's representative needed to be well dressed. He must not appear at a disadvantage when he met the Sugar Barons. Every morning when he dressed he would look at his white dinner jacket on its hanger and the black trousers with their broad braid stripe, wondering when the day would come for him to wear them.

He had read that some of the British Labor politicians had appeared at Court in ordinary lounge suits, refusing to wear the livery of social servitude. He had thought that ridiculous. Beat them at their own game. When the A.D.C. had rung him up, he had not asked what he should wear. No doubt Archer had expected him to say, "But I'm afraid I've got no Tuxedo," and Archer had no doubt had his answer ready. "H.E. doesn't bother about that kind of thing. It's you we want to see."

Probably some of the other guests were wondering at this moment how he would appear, saying to themselves, "Poor fellow. He won't have a Tuxedo. He'll feel embarrassed. We must put him at his ease." Put him at his ease, my foot.

As he turned slowly round he twisted his head first over one shoulder, then over the other. My, but it was something. The high squared shoulders, the tight fit over the hips, the narrow waist, the long skirted coat; that East Indian had known his job. And then the accessories; the long tie like those he had seen in the Hollywood movie papers, the semi-soft poplin shirt with its crisscross piqué, and the black satin waistcoast embroidered with flowers in gold thread. He'd show them.

He had arranged to call for Muriel at ten to eight. He arrived at half-past seven. He wanted to see Grainger first. He was not sure of his exact position at the Leg. Co. He needed his future brother-in-law's advice. But Grainger was not in. He had gone out directly after supper. Wasn't that unusual, didn't he always after an early meal work on his cases until ten? Yes, that was usual. But tonight he had gone out. He had not said where he was going nor when he would be coming back.

Afraid of meeting me, Boyeur thought. Mrs. Morris looked embarrassed. She talked about the Test matches in England, then about a film that was to come next week. She was making conversation, avoiding any topic that might lead to a danger issue; and any ordinary local topic would. In a small place like this everyone was discussing the same three or four topics of the hour. And he himself, right now, had ousted every other one.

At the end of the veranda the youngest Grainger boy, with his heels tucked under him, stared at the visitor with wide fascinated eyes. He was awe-struck by Boyeur's elegance. The white dinner jacket, the piqué shirt in contrast to his brother's armor, the satin embroidered waistcoast. He was more impressed by Boyeur's clothes than by his brother's. He had remembered his brother's homily "work hard, that's the only way." He had been working with fierce concentrated vigor ever since. Boyeur could not tell that he was thinking that. Boyeur supposed that that unwavering stare was inspired by horror, that the child saw him as some black ogre come to steal his sister.

Mr. Morris came onto the veranda; he was out of breath and over-apologetic at having kept Boyeur waiting.

"I'm very sorry. You came a little earlier than we expected. We keep early hours. Supper at half-past six. Fell into the habit for the children's sake and kept it up."

Why was he so flustered, so apologetic?

They were all of them ashamed of him, Boyeur thought. They didn't know how to treat him. They were regretting that they had agreed to the engagement. They were wondering how they could get out of it. He could give them the answer to that one. They couldn't.

"What can I offer you," Mr. Morris asked. "A swizzle?"

Boyeur shook his head. He rarely took alcohol and only on occasions when he was certain that he would not need to be upon his guard. Alcohol was an extravagance, so was tobacco. He would rather spend his money upon clothes. Alcohol was a betrayer. You committed yourself to things, were indiscreet and injudicious. He made enough mistakes without alcohol. Besides, he did not like the taste of it.

"Will Muriel be long?" he asked. "I'd like to have a talk with her before we go."

At the sight of her in the doorway Boyeur started. It was an off the shoulder dress. White with a small pink and green flower pattern.

418

She was so young, so fresh, so unaware: and his to mold, to fashion; his and his alone. He pictured himself walking with her at his side into smart hotels in Trinidad. He would wear her like a buttonhole. No one would suspect that she was colored. Their children would pass as white. They would go to school in England. The future dazzled him. His future was symbolized by this tall, slim girl, with her delicate features and firm, pliant figure.

"You do look beautiful," he said.

There was a ring in his voice that sounded like a film star's. How often, as a schoolgirl watching from the stalls entranced, had she not dreamed of the day when a man's voice would sound like that for her. How long would she have to wait? Three years, four years, two years. She had read the movie magazines. All the heroines of the screen had had their first dates when they were sixteen. Many of them had married before they were twenty. How long would she have to wait? Then she had looked from the screen idol to the heroine who had inspired that glint of the eye, that hunger in the voice. No wonder a man felt like that when that kind of a woman beckoned. On her return she had faced her reflection in the mirror. She had noted her scraggy arms, the hollows under her shoulder blades, the unformed breasts, the flat hips, the coltish legs. Would any man feel like that about her when the world was full of women like Lana Turner? She would never see that gleam in a man's eye, never hear that tremor in a man's voice. She had cried herself to sleep in impotent despair.

And that was only a year ago, and now here she was, a circlet of diamonds and rubies on her left hand, facing a tall young dashingly handsome man; his eyes were shining, his voice was echoing in her ears. A year ago she would not have dared to wear a dress like this. She would have wanted to cover over her skinny shoulders; now she wanted to display them. They were round and smooth. A miracle of transformation had taken place.

"I'm early," Boyeur said. "But I wanted to see you for a moment first. Although the party is being given for me, I shan't be allowed to spend one second with you. They'll separate us the instant we arrive. Let's go for a drive."

He took her by the arm, above the elbow. She was breathlessly conscious of the electricity in his finger tips. It made her knees feel weak.

She sat away from him in the corner of the seat. She could not trust herself to be too close to him. Later, when he drove her back, not now.

"Is this party really for you?" she said.

"That's what the A.D.C. said. He asked me to pick the night. That means it must be for me. Or rather I'd say it was for us, in honor of our engagement."

A party at G.H. for her. It was the first time that she had dined there. And to have on that first time a dinner party in her honor. It was wonderful to be engaged to David, to someone who was both young and vivid and was crazy over her; and so important too. Yet the most wonderful thing of all about it was that it would not have made any difference to her if he had been poor and obscure; a minor Government official, say. But it was wonderful, there was no use pretending that it wasn't, that he was one of the chief figures in the island. All this and heaven too.

"I reckon that H.E. is trying to kill two birds with one stone. He wants to honor our engagement, and he wants an opportunity, I won't say of apologizing for that scene in the Leg. Co., but explaining to me that it was only a routine affair. Nothing to be taken seriously. He knows that he's got to keep on the right side of me. Otherwise we'll have the Trades Unions down on him like a ton of bricks. At the same time he has to maintain appearances in the Leg. Co."

He was talking to impress himself as much as anything; to convince himself of his own importance. She listened, entranced not so much by what he said, as by the force and vigor of his voice. He was such a man, so confident, so forceful. That he should want to marry her.

2

Boyeur arrived at G.H. at eight minutes to the hour. Julian Fleury was at that moment calling impatiently to his son.

"Hurry up now, Maxwell, for heaven's sake. We're going to be late."

"Two minutes, Father, not a second more."

It took five minutes to drive up to G.H. His father always fussed about the time and Maxwell was resolved to arrive last. He wanted to see how the stage had been set out for him; how the enemy's forces were disposed, and who the enemy were. His nerves would not have stood the strain of waiting, of watching the arrival first of one adversary then another. He might have given himself away, before the eyes of one who had been deputed to observe each gesture. He wanted to see the whole order of battle set out before him in a glance.

They arrived at two minutes to eight.

"I thought you weren't going to make it," Archer said. He did

420

not appear, however, in the least bit flustered. That, Maxwell reflected, was one of his chief merits. He never panicked. If a guest was late, it was the guest's fault not his.

"What was all this mystery about?" Maxwell inquired.

"You'll see."

Archer led the Fleurys into the room.

"This is one of the fortunate occasions when I don't have to bother about introductions," Archer said.

Maxwell looked round him. He saw young Templeton and Mavis Norman and Doris Kellaway. The usual group; what was the mystery? His eye ran on, to be checked, in sudden relieved recognition. David Boyeur. Of course. Now he understood. He had had no cause to be alarmed. Boyeur started too. He, on the other hand, was puzzled. What did this mean? Why was young Fleury here? He met Maxwell's stare and held it. Young puppy, damned young puppy. A door slammed upstairs. The Governor stood at the head of the stairway, paused, looked down at his guests, then slowly came down the stairs to welcome them. He was dressed informally in tight fitting dark blue patrol trousers with a white tunic high buttoned at the neck. Muriel found it hard not to gasp. She had never guessed that he could look so impressive. She had thought of him as a little man.

As soon as the Governor had shaken hands with his guests, cocktails were served. Boyeur shook his head, but at dinner he allowed the butler to fill his glass with wine. He was feeling nervous. It was the first time that he had dined at G.H. Its mixture of informality and ceremony made him feel awkward. In a sense it was a family party, yet he was conscious of being entertained by the representative of the British Crown. There were twelve places laid. General conversation was impossible. He could not impose his presence and personality. Mavis Norman was on his left. He did not find it easy to talk to her. He had always been told that she was the liveliest of the unmarried Country Club set. But she did not have much to say for herself. Small talk was not his line. A pause between them lengthened. He was seated near the end of the table, and Mrs. Fleury who was occupying the hostess's position at the table's foot, addressed a remark to Mavis that started a triangular conversation, with himself excluded, with Mavis's back turned on him. On his right Mrs. Norman was occupied with Julian Fleury. The talk had divided on either side, turning away from him. He looked round the table. He felt conspicuous sitting silent while everyone else was busily engrossed in talk.

Muriel, placed on the Governor's left, was talking easily, it seemed, to Maxwell Fleury. Her skin looked very dark against the

Governor's white tunic. She had seemed white enough against her family's darker coloring, but what a difference there was between Maxwell's skin and hers; and Maxwell had African ancestry. Maxwell would pass anywhere for white. It had never occurred to anyone that he was not white till Bradshaw's article appeared. While as for Jocelyn with her fair skin and blue eyes and light blonde hair—the very replica of her mother—no one would have thought of her as being anything but white. It would be a long time before his children could pass as white, whereas Maxwell's and Jocelyn's children . . .

He looked resentfully at Maxwell; resentfully and enviously too. Maxwell had put Muriel at her ease, whereas he himself had failed to hold Mavis' interest. Maxwell had put Muriel at her ease, because he was at ease himself. Maxwell ate his food without appearing to be taking nourishment, eating as he talked, yet never seeming to eat when he was listening, or when he himself was talking. His entire attention was concentrated upon Muriel, yet the volume of food upon his plate diminished. How did one do that? He had read about young men dining for the first time in grand houses being embarrassed by the number of forks and knives and spoons confronting them. He wasn't. He knew all about that. He had bought a book on etiquette. But this business of eating while you talked, that puzzled him. He liked to talk, then eat, then talk again. How did you do two things at the same time.

Doris Kellaway was sitting next to Maxwell. Young Archer was on the other side of her. Archer too was thoroughly at his ease; eating and talking and laughing and emptying his glass. A series of automatic movements. Boyeur concentrated on Archer. He preferred watching Archer. He liked Archer. Margot had created a bond between them. Archer never attempted to high-hat him. He was just another guy; he would not mind taking lessons from Archer. Archer was, in one way, indebted to him, had reaped where he had sown. Young Fleury was a bastard, neither fish nor fowl nor good red herring. Archer was different. He was the real thing; in the way that the Governor was.

Boyeur looked at Archer enviously, but not resentfully as he had at Maxwell. He noted the cut of Archer's dinner jacket, it was white, single breasted and hung loosely on his shoulders. It had been bought off the peg most likely. Archer was wearing a soft shirt: it was not an evening shirt at all but it was made of silk. His tie was of a butterfly wide-ended style, a prewar tie judging from the movie magazines. It was slightly aslant upon its axis. Yet at the same time Archer looked well dressed. He made Boyeur, with his padded shoulders and fancy waistcoat, feel overdressed. Wasn't the test of a gentleman the way he wore evening dress. That was what he had always read.

Boyeur turned his attention from Archer to Julian Fleury, who was wearing a high wide-winged collar and a plain stiff shirt fastened with a single black pearl stud. You never saw a collar and shirt like that in the movie magazines. Yet Julian Fleury looked well dressed, in the same way that young Archer did. Whereas I don't. I'm over-dressed. I've got a lot to learn.

Boyeur felt awkward, embarrassed, sitting there silent, while everyone else was jabbering away. He felt hot and uncomfortable. His skin was damp under his padded shoulders. A lot to learn, yes, but he would learn it. He was disdainful, truculent. He'd show them.

The fish plates were cleared away. The Governor turned to his left, to Muriel.

"Now I want to hear all your plans: when you are going to be married, where you are going to live: everything. May I say that I think you are a very clever young lady to have captured our most eligible bachelor. He has been, from what I gather, the despair of designing mothers-in-law for several years. Now that I see you, may I say that I am not at all surprised."

Muriel flushed with happy pride. It was the kind of little speech that she had heard British Diplomats make on the screen, old-fashioned, mannered, courtly. The whole evening was like a film. The Governor coming down the stairway, the A.D.C. making the introductions, the long candle-lit table, the silver candlesticks and flower bowl; the china with the royal arms, the servants in uniform; the whole dressed-up atmosphere of it all; Mavis and Jocelyn and Doris Kellaway in their pretty frocks, with herself on equal terms with them; and all the men so handsome and so smart, with her David so much the smartest; look at Captain Archer's tie, all swiveled round; no one else had an embroidered waistcoat. She felt so proud of him; so proud of herself because of him. This was the loveliest evening of her life and at the end of it all, the crown of it, they would drive out past the fort to St. James's point and park the car there, high above the sea, to talk it over, and that rich tremor would come into his voice. Oh, but it was lovely to be in love; and to be loved.

Mavis turning back to Boyeur, saw Muriel as she leant forward across the table. She looked very young and happy and excited. It sent a pang not of envy but of nostalgia along her nerves. This was what as a schoolgirl she had wanted for herself, to be in love and to be engaged and to have a party given for her. It was something she would never have, not in the same way. To be engaged to the first person that you were in love with, what a dream that must be: you only realized what a dream it could be when you had passed the possibility of its realization.

Muriel was lucky, but then Muriel had stood more chance. She had had a much wider choice of men. Muriel was not walled in, as she was, by this color conflict. David Boyeur was many degrees darker than Muriel. By Moreau St. Mery's reckoning there was more difference between Muriel and David Boyeur than there was between Muriel and herself, yet whereas everyone welcomed and honored Muriel's engagement, she herself could not meet socially a man like Grainger Morris. Grainger could not belong to the Country Club.

What was going to happen to her, she asked herself. She was young, she was warm blooded; since that silly business with young Templeton she had avoided complications, but it couldn't last; she wouldn't want it to. She was not that type. She knew herself too well. Sooner or later it would all begin again.

Where was she headed? What could she look forward to? What was she making of her life? She was not the career woman, not the "good works type"; she was meant for marriage; to merge her life with a man's, make a home for him, bear his children, create a background for him, help him to play his part in the world's work. Did that sound dull and sophomoric in this modern day? It might do, but it was what she needed. And what chance did she stand of finding it out here? There were so few men and she was bound to one type of man, one class of man. In Europe you weren't bound by class. The son of your father's chauffeur might become a first-class engineer, earning a large salary, on his way to prestige and prominence; your engagement would make people say, "How things are changed. Her father's chauffeur. What a democratic age. Fair chances for all. A good thing too." But here your father's chauffeur was a colored man, so his son was out, no matter how brilliant he might be. There was no choice here.

Five years ago she had spoken lightheartedly to "the inseparables" of having all the fun that came your way and relying on one of your escapades turning out seriously. But she was eighteen then. Now she was twenty-three and time was hurrying past. The writing on the wall. The months had gone by, the escapades had proved short-lived. A boat had sailed. There had been letters and cables for the first two months: then a long pause and a card at Christmas, promising "a real letter soon." Then silence and a press clipping with a note attached, "As you see I'm going to be married soon.

Please wish me luck." That or something like that: except that once, with Rickie; well, she'd got over that.

And that's the way it had been. And that's the way it would be; and when someone really eligible turned up, she'd let him slip through her fingers. Not that she'd regretted that: Euan wasn't right for her. She'd known that inside herself from the start. And if she married the wrong man she would be impossible; she'd *tromper* him right and left. All that sophomoric talk of marriage held good for the right marriage with the right man; a man whom you could honor, whose work in the world you could respect; someone whom you could serve. Where could she find that here, encased as she was by this rigid protocol of color?

She looked away from Muriel. Whatever might lie ahead, her present job was to be a good guest and entertain the guest of honor. "We've hardly exchanged a word," she said to Boyeur. "What are your plans? Is there a house you've got your eye on yet?"

Sylvia, too, looking across the table, noticed and was touched by the look on Muriel's face. The kid was in love all right. She recalled her own engagement party. She hadn't been in love then, not as she knew love now. Had an experienced woman looked at her and wondered: saying to herself, "There's one who's missed it." Would that same woman looking at her during these last weeks have changed her mind thinking, "Something has happened there." She felt different, she must look different. Surely she had been transfigured, in the way Muriel had.

She looked away from Muriel and as she did so she realized that Maxwell had been looking at her. He smiled as their eyes met, warmly, tenderly, adoringly. As she smiled back her lips framed a kiss. It was he who had achieved that transformation. It was a debt that she could never repay to him. He had revealed her to herself.

Maxwell half closed his eyes. It was the first time that she had looked at him like that across a table. Four months ago he had not believed it possible that she could look at him in such a way. Four months ago he had been blind with jealousy, ready to fancy Carson was her lover. How incredible that seemed. In another four months would it seem as incredible that he had fancied Whittingham suspected him as a murderer? Here he had been fretting himself into sleeplessness because he had suspected that the party was a trap concocted between H.E. and the policeman. Instead of that it was a trap for Boyeur. The old boy would give him the works after dinner, he supposed.

425

Maxwell had guessed correctly. The Governor did not move down to take the seat that Mrs. Fleury had vacated, he beckoned Boyeur to his end.

"Come here on my right, David; Maxwell, you move up. And pass the port round, Julian."

The Governor paused, looking round him; there was silence. He was about to execute tactics that he made use of when he was a colonel, when two young officers had quarreled.

"Look here," he said, "you two are at outs, I gather. I don't want to interfere with your private matters. I don't want to know the 'ins' and 'outs' of it. There are rights and wrongs on both sides. There always are when two decent young fellows are concerned; and your private quarrels are none of my business, normally, but they are in this instance because they concern the welfare of the re——colony."

He had almost used the word "regiment," the scene was so familiar. Archer, noticing the slip, felt guilty and apprehensive. These tactics would work well enough in a regiment: invite the two young officers to your house, along with one or two of their seniors, treat them as friends, make them feel important, yet at the same time overawe them, give them a sense of duty and obligation. Such tactics would work admirably with regimental officers who had been groomed by a Public School and Sandhurst to this kind of discipline. He doubted if it would work with these two West Indians who had a basic hereditary distrust of themselves and of their neighbors. He looked at Maxwell and at Boyeur. Their expressions were impassive. It might be working. It might seem to have been worth trying, but he remembered Margot's warning. He would rather trust her instinct than the experience of a high officer of state.

"The colony needs you, both of you," H.E. was continuing. "You're the two youngest councilors. You have great influence, great futures. The fortunes of the colony depends on you and on young men like you. You set the others an example, and we cannot, I insist, we cannot have a repetition of last week's performance in the Council. You will, of course, David, have to make a statement at the next meeting of the Leg. Co. That's a matter of form, the mere drill of the thing, but that's beside the point, that's a minor matter of routine: what I want now from you both is a promise that you'll try and forget your quarrel. I don't want you to promise to become bosom friends right away, though I do want you to respect each other's point of view, to recognize that each in his own way is working for the island's good, for I know that you both are;

what I want you to do now, in earnest of that, is to shake hands across the table."

It was by no means unimpressive, Archer thought. The General was himself an impressive figure, particularly here in his white tunic, with his row of medals, his crown and crossed swords on the shoulder, at the head of this long table in the high-backed chair with the royal portraits above the mantelpiece.

The Governor looked to his left hand and to his right.

"David, Maxwell."

It was in part a question, in part an order. Automatically the two young men stood up, their hands stretched across the table; as their eyes met, the A.D.C. would have given a great deal to have been able to know what manner of expression the eyes of each held for the other. Their profiles told him nothing.

"Fine. That's settled now," the Governor said. "Keep that port moving, Denis. I don't know what an A.D.C.'s for except to keep the port in motion. One more glass, everyone, and we'll join the ladies."

### 4

A quarter of an hour later the Governor pushed back his chair. Archer shepherded the guests. "The lavatories are at the end of the passage, or there's the garden."

Maxwell was the last to leave the dining room. He turned into the garden. Boyeur was facing a hedge of crotons a few yards away. Maxwell was subject to an irritating and embarrassing disability. He was often unable to relieve himself in public. This disability was a great inconvenience to him at the races when queues were formed behind an open drain. He walked past Boyeur to the end of the hedge and faced in the opposite direction.

Swine, Boyeur thought, turning his back on me. That settles him.

Maxwell walked across the lawn to the garden wall. The air was soft and scented with jasmin. A large Dutch cargo was at anchor, its portholes were reflected in the water. It was its maiden voyage, and the gangway was festal with electric bulbs. The dark hills above the *carenage* were sprinkled with lighted windows; there was no moon, but the sky was cloudless: he could see the white wash of breakers on the reef. Men who had traveled far had told him that there was little as lovely in the world as this. He stood there, his mind a blank in unreflecting enjoyment of its beauty. From the drawing room came the sound of music. A gramophone. Perhaps they were dancing. He must be getting back; through the uncurtained windows he could see Sylvia's blonde head in profile against

427

pale green panels. He remembered how across the table her lips had framed that kiss. No shame must ever come to her through him. If the law's hand was about to fall on him, he would know how to avoid its clutch.

There was no dancing after all. Not enough young men, Maxwell supposed. The gramophone had been turned on softly, so that conversation could be continued through it. Jocelyn and Archer were together and he joined them.

"Do you write novels as well as poems?" he asked.

"I've done some short stories. I'm meaning to get down to a novel soon."

"Your characters commit suicide, don't they?"

"Now and again, of course."

"How do they do it?"

"It depends where they are. If they are in Canada, I'd make them walk out into the snow. That's painless, almost pleasant I believe. But that wouldn't be a good idea if I were writing a West Indian novel."

"If you were going to commit suicide yourself, how would you do it?"

"The easiest way, with sleeping pills."

"What about taking too many? Isn't there that danger?"

Archer shook his head.

"Not with pheno-barbitone. That's the merit of it. Morphia can trick you but not pheno-barbitone. Thirty grains and home you go. Of course if you've been in the habit of taking it regularly, you'd have to give yourself a larger dose. 'Mithridates, he died old.' "

"But everyone would know that you had taken it."

"Naturally."

"That might defeat your point. It would cause scandal for your family. The whole point of the suicide may have been to avoid scandal for your family. Suppose, in a novel, one of your characters wanted to commit suicide so that no one would suspect that it was suicide. How would you make him do it?"

"It would be easy if he was a man," Jocelyn interjected. "He could book a passage on one of those Dutch cargo boats that take only twelve passengers and don't carry a doctor. He could take sleeping pills and be found dead in the morning. No one would know what was wrong and they'd have to bury him right away. He'd be reported 'died at sea.' "

"Why couldn't a woman do that?"

"They won't take a woman passenger on that kind of boat, unless she's with her husband or another woman. If she is, that makes complications."

Archer looked at her with surprise and interest. She must have thought about suicide a lot. He, as a writer, had to know something about the various fates that might befall his characters. He had to know about suicide and illness and law court procedure. She had not got to. She must have considered suicide as a serious personal problem. She would only consider suicide seriously in relation to herself. "If it comes to the worst, how shall I get out of it?" She must have been desperately unhappy before Euan had turned up. She must . . .

He checked. A sudden thought had struck him. The Dutch cargo boats with limited passenger accommodation had only been running this last month. The boat now at anchor was on its maiden voyage. The first ship had called two weeks ago. They worked on a fort-nightly schedule. There were no other such boats. That had been one of the problems since the war for the smaller islands. There were no direct services to Europe. You had to pick up a French Line boat in Trinidad, or an Elder-Fyffe banana boat in Jamaica. It must have been in this last month, perhaps in this very fortnight that she had been thinking, "Men are lucky. A man could go in that boat and take an overdose of pheno-barbitone and no one would know. Found dead at sea." Why had she thought that, now, when the future was spread out for her so brightly? She ought not to have a trouble in the world and yet she was brooding about suicide. How little one knew about other people. Perhaps one should always write novels in the first person; then one could confine oneself to what one knew. Better not to attempt to identify oneself with another character, seeing through his eyes, speaking through his voice; best to admit as one told one's story that one relied on guesswork. You could report on what your characters said, how they behaved, what they were, how they looked, but the why and wherefore were beyond your scope. If you wrote in the first person you could avoid the responsibility of omniscience. Surely . . .

He pulled himself together. Off again into a daydream. The writer's occupational liability. This was no time for ruminating on the craft of fiction. He was an A.D.C. and his present and immediate job was to see that the party fulfilled its function. And there as the proof that he was not doing so, was David Boyeur, glum and silent on the wing of a group of four, who were talking inward to their apex. He excused himself and went across.

For a minute or so he too sat silent while Mr. Norman enlarged on the necessity for more tennis courts as a bait for tourists: then he touched Boyeur's knee.

"I wonder if you've seen the G.H. collection of West Indian prints. They keep them upstairs. I can't think why. They might amuse you."

He took Boyeur up to the Chief Guest bedroom. They were eighteenth and early nineteenth century color prints. They had a charming period quality. They had not the accuracy of a photograph but they had "the feel of the place." There were one or two of Santa Marta. There had been much construction since the drawings had been made; a swamp had been reclaimed, wharfs had been built; the hillside had been dotted with new bungalows, but there was no doubt that it was the *carenage*. With a modern photograph you might have had to look more than once.

Boyeur peered into it, noting this change and that, pointing out this inaccuracy and the other. The fort was not as large as that, the bay was not as narrow. "And look at the church, the spire's half that height."

Boyeur took a pride that was touching in the island of his birth. He resented any distortion of its landscape. He examined a print of Trinidad. Yes, the Queen's Park Savannah was well enough, but it was too big. It lacked the coziness of Jamestown.

Archer could not help liking him. There was something ingenuous about him. It was the first time he had been alone with him. He wondered if Boyeur knew about himself and Margot: he presumed he did. No one at the Country Club might suspect, but it would be common gossip at the Aquatic. He did not feel embarrassed. On the contrary, he felt that they could talk in shorthand, he and Boyeur. He wondered if there was anything that he could say to make Boyeur feel better about the evening. But he remembered Margot's warning. "If you have any doubt when you're dealing with Boyeur about what's the right thing to do, do nothing." He trusted her instinct. Best say nothing.

He pointed to a print of Antigua.

"That's my favorite of the lot," he said.

It showed a red brick, two storied estate house, beside a windmill, against a background of low, rounded hills with a team of Negroes bare to the waist cutting the cane with thin, long, curved cutlasses, while long-skirted Negresses with bright shawls and headdresses piled the stalks onto a cart. In the near distance were the low barrack-like slave quarters, with naked children tumbling over each other on the steps and a woman suckling her child. It had a pastoral charm, an air of happiness like a Morland farm scene.

"On a well-run plantation they did not have too bad a time," he said.

"Probably a better time than they have now. They had no worries. They were looked after. A wise farmer looks after his own cattle. But it can't stay that way. They've been given freedom. They've got to use it. They've got to be taught to use it. They've got power now. They've got a vote. They're the top dogs. They've got to realize it. That's what I'm doing for them, showing them how powerful they are. The right to strike. That's more important than a vote."

He spoke, so it seemed to Archer, with a mulish, stupid stubbornness. None of it hung together. One thing alone was clear. Margot had been right. It was best to do nothing with Boyeur if one had the slightest doubt of what was the right thing to do. But perhaps the old boy had had no doubt. That might well have been the trouble. He saw everything in terms of the cricket field.

"A slave mentality. That's what's wrong with these people," Boyeur was continuing. "They were slaves, the half of them, in Africa before they were ever shipped here. They don't understand freedom. I'll give you an example. Find a man who's never seen a revolver fired. Give him a revolver. Tell him that if he pulls the trigger, there'll be an explosion, that a bullet will fly out that can kill anyone it hits. He'll nod his head, say 'yes, yes' in agreement. But he won't understand what you're talking about till he's seen a revolver fired, till he's seen the damage it can do: till he's seen someone fall down with a wound in his shoulder, bleeding. We've given the Negro the equivalent of a revolver, but he hasn't seen yet what damage he can do with it. The vote, the right to strike; teach him his power. That's what we've got to do."

That's what I've got to do, Boyeur told himself. Teach these stuck up prigs a lesson. They had tricked him, brought him here on false pretenses; led him to think a party was being given in his honor, to celebrate his engagement. They had encouraged him to think that: it's what the A.D.C. had told him.

"When you rang me up, you said that H.E. wanted to have the dinner on a night that I could come. You did say that, didn't you?" he challenged.

"I did."

"And you said that H.E. wanted an opportunity of wishing Muriel and myself good luck. Did H.E. tell you to say that?"

"Yes."

"But that wasn't the real reason for the party, was it? He wanted to get me at the same table as the Fleurys. He wanted a showdown about that Leg. Co. meeting. That was the real reason for the dinner, wasn't it?"

431

"Yes."

Archer did not hesitate over that "yes." There was no point in lying, when you were unlikely to be believed.

"As I thought," said Boyeur. "As I thought."

They had tricked him here; taken him off his guard, staged their showdown and made him shake hands with that conceited puppy. Maxwell Fleury; turning his back on him indeed, refusing to sully his eyes with the sight of him at such a moment. He'd show Maxwell Fleury where he got off. And the Governor too, and the whole pack of them. Bradshaw: making out that his teeth were drawn because he was now a councilor, because he was marrying into the local aristocracy. The Fleurys, Bradshaw, General Templeton, His Excellency Major General the Lord Templeton: he'd show them all. He'd demand of the Planters Association a twenty per cent rise in wages for field laborers; he'd give them a three day ultimatum. And if they didn't come to heel he'd call a general strike. He'd held his men in long enough. They were impatient, straining at the leash. And in the temper that they were in, that they would be in when he gave the word, a general strike wouldn't be a mere staying away from work. Men like that wouldn't sit idle before their huts. There'd be incidents, slashed tires, flaming cane fields, gutted *boucans*. He'd show his men what a revolver could do when you pulled the trigger.

## 5

The party broke up at eleven. Templeton came out on the doorstep to bid his guests good-by. To Muriel he was particularly cordial.

"This has been a great pleasure to me. I hope that this will prove to be the first of many visits to this house. Once again I wish you the best of luck."

His smile was friendly and benign. Boyeur noted it with a satisfying appreciation of the moment's dramatic irony. The General would be smiling the other side of his face tomorrow. His jaw was set as he released the clutch. He drove fast. He did not speak one word on the way back. He was unconscious of Muriel's presence at his side. He was following his own thoughts. He kissed her goodnight negligently, outside her parents' house. He did not get out of the car. He was impatient to be at his desk, drafting his ultimatum.

432

# CHAPTER TWENTY-SIX

## *1*

Boyeur's ultimatum was delivered at ten o'clock next morning. It was the sole topic of conversation two hours later in the Jamestown Club. Bradshaw happened to be there.

"Is there any chance of the planters agreeing?" he inquired.

"None at all," they told him.

"Will Boyeur call the strike off?"

Heads were shaken.

"It's very doubtful. He's bluffed before. He's doing this to impress the gallery. He'll find some way of saving face. There'll be a conference. We'll concede him something. He'll tell his followers that a wise shopkeeper always puts a high price to start with, so that he bargains down not up."

"I see."

But himself he did not agree. Certainly if the issue was put to Boyeur in a way that challenged him. He called upon Boyeur after lunch.

"Do you know what they're saying about you in the club?"

Boyeur laughed when Bradshaw told him.

"What did you say?" Boyeur asked.

"I didn't say anything, but I know what I thought."

"What did you think?"

"That you can't afford to call 'Wolf, wolf' again."

"Have I ever called it?"

"They think you have. They say you've kept this strike like a joker, up your sleeve. They're beginning to say that it isn't a joker at all: only the deuce of diamonds."

"They say that, do they?"

"They say more than that. They say that you are trying to make the public forget that you were expelled from the Leg. Co."

No one had said quite that, but Bradshaw knew Boyeur well enough to suspect that that had been in part one of the reasons for his action.

"Thank you for telling me," Boyeur said.

Bradshaw went straight to the cable office. He had already written out his copy.

Thirty-six hours later it appeared in the *Baltimore Star*.

"I was wrong," it ran, "in believing that the threatened eruption of the political volcano in Santa Marta has subsided. Far from it. David Boyeur, who was expelled from the Leg. Co. meeting for breach of manners has taken his revenge by issuing an ultimatum to the Planters Association. A 20% wage increase for all field laborers or a general strike in three days time. The planters believe Boyeur is bluffing, but he is not. Though no one believes it in Santa Marta, the general strike will begin on Friday. Friday is pay day. It is doubtful if the men will receive their pay, since they will be on strike. They will consider they have been cheated. There will be incidents. Those incidents may lead to serious disorder. No man can tell what will happen. Boyeur's prestige is at stake. The Governor is a soldier. He is accustomed to striking swiftly and striking hard. There have been many equivalent situations in British colonial history—Amritzar is the most recent—when a military governor has opened fire on the mob. This may happen here. No one can tell. But without any doubt the volcano is erupting."

Twenty-four hours later the article reached the Colonial Office in Westminster. The Minister read it with irritation. These wretched little West Indian islands were like mosquitoes, trivial and maddening. He wished a tidal wave could submerge the lot of them, leaving the big three islands and B.G. as a manageable proposition. The Windwards and the Leewards were a nuisance and a liability: taking up all this time when there were problems of real importance to be decided in the other colonies.

Templeton had complained that the Minister was getting jumpy. He was. A Cabinet reshuffle was imminent. No one knew whose head would fall. This was a crucial point in his career. If he once lost Cabinet rank he would be unlikely to recover it, but he might in the reshuffle be sent to the Foreign Office. The road led straight from there. Everything depended upon the next few weeks, and anything might happen in the next few weeks in Kenya or in Malaya.

The situation had changed since he had given Templeton his instructions last September. The wave of nationalism was getting out of hand, not only in the British colonies but in the French as well. Morocco was a tinder box, and events in Morocco were influencing the nationalists in British Africa. A go-slow directive had been issued to the Colonial Office. "We don't want any more trouble," the Minister had been told, "but if there is trouble, we want you to come down hard on it." Damn Santa Marta, thought the Minister.

He reread Bradshaw's article. Bradshaw was no fool. Bradshaw had guessed right before. And Templeton was the kind of man who might open fire on a mob. Nothing like that must happen. Better forestall the danger by a premature show of force. There

434

was a destroyer in the Caribbean, the *Cheltenham*, on a training cruise. Best send it straight to Jamestown. Revolutionaries knew what a destroyer meant. You couldn't fire back against long range shells.

The Minister rang for Purvis. "Get in touch with the Admiralty, tell them that we are expecting trouble in Santa Marta, we want the *Cheltenham* there straight away. It'll mean my having to speak to someone personally. Find out who that someone is. Perhaps the First Lord will do. Anyhow find out; then cable Templeton not to worry, tell him the *Cheltenham* is on its way."

When the cable reached Santa Marta its recipient smiled. Poor old Bobbie. What a panic he was in. Still he supposed it didn't matter. It would be pleasant to have a Man-of-war at anchor. It would be a diversion for the islanders. He would give a dance for the officers.

That morning there was a meeting of the Executive Council. "I have what I am sure will be happy and reassuring news for you," he informed them.

To his surprise the news proved anything but welcome, particularly to Norman.

"Nothing could do more harm to our plans for attracting tourists to the island. We shall undo all the good that we have done in entertaining those journalists. They are back now in America; we cannot explain to them what the true situation is. They will welcome the opportunity for an effective headline. They will present an alarmist picture of conditions here. They will scare tourists away. Look what happened in Grenada."

In Grenada recently there had been a general strike. There had been incidents on the estates, stones had been thrown in the streets, a warship had been hurried to the rescue, bluejackets had been landed, tourists had been evacuated and it had taken the tourist trade in Grenada several seasons to recover from the consequent bad publicity. "We don't want that to happen here," said Norman.

He spoke with such vigor that the Governor was impressed. When the meeting was over, he sent for Whittingham.

"I'm speaking to you off the record. I should like to stop that warship coming here. I am assured that it will be bad publicity for the island's tourist trade. It was a point that I will admit hadn't occurred to me. I have always believed in the motto, if you wish for peace, prepare for war. I like the security that comes from a well-stocked armory. And so do you. But I see the point of the Tourist Board's argument. How much actual danger is there?"

As Whittingham hesitated, the Governor produced his final selling point, the one that would be most likely to influence Whittingham.

"I'll tell you how it strikes me: we ought to have sufficient forces in this colony to maintain order ourselves. If we haven't, then we should strengthen our police forces. We ought to be self-sufficient. Are we? But remember I'm not going to hold it against you if there is greater trouble than we have a reason to expect."

To that question, Whittingham could only give one answer.

"I should have welcomed a Man-of-war in the harbor, sir, because its presence would have acted as a deterrent, but I'm sure that we have enough forces to deal with any trouble that can arise."

"Thank you, and remember, I promise you that this is off the record."

The Governor drafted his Whitehall signal.

"Tourist Board convinced that unexpected arrival of battleship will scare away tourists as happened Grenada. Chief Police officer unofficially considers local police adequate any local emergency. Earnestly request you cancel orders *Cheltenham*."

The Minister shrugged when he read the message. Trust the man on the spot; yes, that was all very well in principle. But it was the man who appointed the man to the spot who was ultimately responsible for that man's behavior. He had taken a risk when he appointed Templeton, a soldier and a cricketer, over the heads of career colonial officials. He had had a good press at the time. The Government had been congratulated on its wise appointment. But that was nine months ago. The honeymoon period was over. The new administration was open to criticisms from its own supporters. He couldn't afford to make a mistake about Santa Marta. Better to have trouble in Kenya, better to have trouble in Malaya. The responsibility there would be less directly his. The appointments there were not of his making. The officials had not broken with tradition.

The telephone bell at his elbow rang.

"It's your wife, sir, shall I put her through?"

"Yes, please."

Marjorie's voice was cool and calm and friendly.

"I'm sorry to interrupt you at your work. But I think it would be better if you didn't pick me up here this evening. I may be a little late. Will you go straight to the Forresters'?"

He replaced the receiver thoughtfully. Why should she be a little late? The Forresters were in Hyde Park Gardens. Brompton Square was on the way there. Wouldn't she want to be at home, to fix herself before going to the cocktail party? From where would she be coming? What might keep her? Was it his fancy, or had he

436

detected during these last weeks that same kind of vagueness that had worried him eighteen months ago before he was in office? Was the novelty of being the wife of a minister wearing off? Was she becoming irritated by the frequent demands upon his time? Was she bored at having to meet so many politicians? That weekend at Chequers for example, where no one had talked anything but shop. He was overworked, worn out with detail; he did not give her the attention that she deserved, that she needed at her age. Maybe his only hold on her was the respect that she believed was owed to his position. If his head were to go in the Cabinet reshuffle— No, he couldn't have trouble in Santa Marta.

He compromised. He sent Templeton a savings telegram, "Accept your man on the spot decision, *Cheltenham* will be within half day sail for next two weeks. Summon if situation worsens."

He got on to the Admiralty by telephone. He explained the situation.

"But I don't want trouble," he insisted; "tell the captain of the *Cheltenham* not only to keep within half a day's sail of Santa Marta, but in radio communication with the Governor."

He then sent another signal to Santa Marta. He asked for a daily bulletin of events, and requested that G.H. should keep in touch with *Cheltenham*.

If the situation got worse, he himself would act whatever the man on the spot might say.

2

On the first Monday of the strike Carl Bradshaw sat on the veranda of the Continental Hotel after breakfast in a mood of irritated doubt. He had canceled his passage to New York on the Friday morning counseled by his nose for copy to stay on, but nothing seemed to be happening. Life was going on as usual. School children had loitered by with their books under their arms. Buses had come in from the districts crowded with chattering peasants. Empty lorries had set out for the districts, presumably to collect cane and copra. The shops were open; cars went honking by. It looked like any other day. His flair for news appeared to have misled him.

That was what he was thinking at half-past nine. Ten minutes later he was alert, curious, his antennae stretched. A station wagon had drawn up outside the hotel. Mr. Preston was at the wheel. His wife was beside him. Their two children were in the back. They were carrying a great deal of luggage.

Bradshaw left the veranda and sauntered to the reception desk.

Mrs. Preston was demanding accommodation for herself and for her children.

"No," she was saying. "One room will not be sufficient. Two double rooms, if you please. My husband is returning to his estate this afternoon. It is very foolish, but it is not my business to interfere. A wife should let her husband make his own decisions on such points. But I am convinced that he will be back by Wednesday. It is not safe out there. Yesterday was Sunday, and everybody went to church. But tonight after an idle day, no, it is no place for a white woman and her children."

Bradshaw was relieved. So his hunch had been right.

"What's happened?" he asked.

"Nothing so far: but I heard those drums in the hills. I could hear them all round me. And there were fires in the cane fields. Don't tell me that that's a coincidence. Yesterday was Sunday. They had occupation. Whatever they may say, I continue to believe that there's cockfighting every Sunday. You could not expect anything to take place on Sunday: but later in the week after three days idleness, you know how hunters get when they are not exercised, there'll be trouble right enough. No doubt about that.

"I'm not going to risk having my children out there at a time like this. Something might happen that would warp their minds for life. Frank can go back there if he wants. He tells me it's his duty. He may be right, I'm not contradicting him. I've been brought up to believe that a man stays at his post. A captain goes down with his ship. But a woman's duty is to her children, to the next generation. A man sets the example. A wife trains the children in the light of that example. That was what we meant by *noblesse oblige*. Frank returns tonight. But I shall not be surprised if he is back within a week, with the house burnt down. Yes," she insisted, turning again to the woman at the desk, "I must have two rooms."

"What about the Fleurys?" Bradshaw asked.

"They haven't made their minds up yet. We discussed it with them as we drove in. I believe they're going to wait a little and see what happens. It's very foolish of them, in view of Sylvia's condition. You knew of that of course. Yes, of course you did. There's no secrecy in a place like this. As I say they may wait too long: that's what I told them this morning when we drove past. It's no good being wise after the event."

Wise after the event. It was what Maxwell himself had felt as he watched the Prestons' station wagon curve down the road.

"I suppose they are really right," he had said to Sylvia.

"I suppose they are."

In his own mind he had no doubt they were, yet he was chained by a complete inertia. He did not want to move. Danger might be imminent, but it was still several hours distant. There was a ghostly silence over the estate. He had gone out as usual before breakfast to the *boucan* for the morning roll call. Nobody had been there but the manager. They had discussed the various problems incidental to the strike: the animals were the chief. The pigs had to be fed and the horses watered. There were a few estate boys who were not union members, but they would knock off work on the least provocation. They had to be closely supervised; Maxwell and his manager had worked out a division of responsibilities. Beyond that there was nothing to be done. The coconuts would lie where they fell. The cocoa pods would rot. They could only wait. He had returned to breakfast with the prospect of an idle, empty day ahead of him. It was a pleasant prospect. Nothing to do and Sylvia to idle with.

"Why don't we take our lunch down to the beach?" he said.

"Why don't we?"

It was something they never did, something they never had a chance of doing. They could only picnic when they were on holiday in Jamestown.

They sat on the veranda after breakfast. They turned on the radio and picked up dance music from Puerto Rico. Sylvia had her knitting. He rocked himself slowly back and forth. It was utter peace. Then the Prestons had driven up, honking their horn, and they had gone down to meet them, and Mrs. Preston had talked and talked in her slow, persistent, unhurried way. She did not urge them to leave Belfontaine. It would have been beneath Mrs. Preston's dignity to urge anybody to do anything. Other people's affairs were their own concern. Herself, she was independent of them, superior to them. Yet she considered it her duty to give her friends the benefit of her wisdom and experience. She made it very clear that in her opinion it would be very foolish, very nearly criminal of Maxwell not to send Sylvia into town.

As the station wagon drove away, Maxwell passed his arms about Sylvia's shoulders.

"I suppose they are really right," he said.

"I suppose they are."

"Let's not think about it for the moment, though."

"Let's not."

"Let it wait a day."

"At least."

They turned back toward the house. "There's something I've always thought that this house needed. More flowers. Why not have an orchid house," she said.

"Why not?"

"Do you remember that house we were taken to see in Port-of-Spain, Mrs. Fitts' wasn't it? With that pergola of orchids. Something like that."

Back again on the veranda, she elaborated her idea. They'd have to find exactly the right place for it. Would it need sun or shade? Perhaps Santa Marta lay too far north. Perhaps orchids would be too ambitious. What about gardenias?

"And why not some more simple flowers; roses for example."

With one part of his mind while he listened, he thought of that station wagon raising its cloud of dust along the windward road. How glad he wasn't in it. Preston would be going round to the club to pick up the latest gossip. The club: they'd all be there, arguing, explaining the rights and wrongs of it: Whittingham would look in probably. Whittingham with that great booming voice and silly grin. Thank heavens, he was here, not there.

"What about zinnias," she was saying. "They're so pretty and they are easy to grow. We could have some seeds sent out."

It was the first time she had talked about the garden as something of her own, something to be worked upon by herself. Up till very recently she had been a stranger here; in this house as in her marriage, a sojourner, ready to fold up her tent; she was putting roots down now, here where she belonged.

The radio was turned low; it was background music, like the wash of the breakers on the reef. She did not have to raise her voice. How peaceful it was; if he had acted as the Prestons had done, he would be on his guard, taut, poised; watching Whittingham. Had the Prestons been right? He supposed they had, but it was hard to believe on a morning such as this that his laborers were planning their reprisals, any more than he could believe that down there in Jamestown Whittingham was laying out his bait.

He thought again of those rabbits in the corn field. When the machine was circling round their sanctuary, their ears were warning them of danger. Yet, at noon when the sun was high, the harvesters sat in the shade of the hedge and ate their cheese and drank their cold tea, and there was silence over the corn; the cowering rabbits could fancy themselves secure. Nothing disturbed eye or ear. But the sun would lower in the sky and the harvesters would return to their machine; and down there in Jamestown, Whittingham was sharpening his hooks and in the village a mile away idle men were sulkily growing restive: soon the wheels would revolve and the scythes slash; but not today, not yet. First there was this hour of armistice, of high noontide peace.

"We might go down to the beach fairly soon?" he said.

440

"Right now, why not."

The beach was empty. On the whole Santa Martans preferred bathing in the streams; many of them could not swim. It was for the most part only those who had been subjected to urban influence who enjoyed the beaches. In Jamestown Sylvia would not have worn a bikini. But here she did.

"I shan't be able to wear one of these much longer," she said laughingly.

No change in her figure was apparent yet. She was like a flower in the instant of its fullest bloom; she had never seemed more beautiful. She would never, he warned himself, look so beautiful again. The breasts would lose their firmness, and the stomach muscles slacken; the smooth skin would be ruffled by minute white flakes; her beauty was the present's sacrifice to the future; her beauty was being despoiled for the future's sake. It gave him a sense of awe. Let his eyes delight in this beauty, of which they would be robbed so soon. He had a "last time" feeling. Never again, he warned himself, never again. Make the most of it. The reapers will soon leave the hedge.

They swam, then sat on a rock and threw pebbles at a tree stump. Then they swam again. "Time for a rum punch," he said.

"I'll have one today. Just one can't do any harm," she said.

He sipped slowly, with that "last time" feeling not exactly haunting him but sharpening his enjoyment of the moment. Sylvia had prepared a chicken salad; mangoes were still in season. This was the only way to eat a mango, she maintained; on a beach, in a bikini, when you didn't mind how the juice dripped or what it stained. He watched her peel the skin and bite into the slippery fruit: a thread of its stringy flesh caught between her teeth, her mouth was smeared. A drop of juice fell into the hollow of her throat and trickled toward the division of her breasts. He bent his head forward, kissing it away.

"It's like a honeymoon today," he said.

"Every day is like a honeymoon now," she answered.

Lunch made them drowsy. They laid out their towels on the sand and fixed up their empty lunch bag as a pillow, but the sand flies began to settle and bite the moment they were motionless.

"It's no good," she said, "we'd best go back."

She curled into his arms under the mosquito net and for once the pressure of her head upon his shoulder did not disturb him.

It was the late afternoon sun shining in his face that woke him. He blinked, looked at the bedside clock: twenty to four. That he should have slept so long. How wonderfully one slept when one had nothing on one's mind. He laid his head back beside hers on the pillow. If only it could be always this way. This was what a honeymoon should be, what his own honeymoon had not been. How slowly the time had passed during those three weeks in Trinidad. Their friends there had avoided them, thinking they had wanted to be by themselves. "Next time you're here," they had said, "we'll give parties for you. But we know that's the last thing you want now." Actually it was the very thing they had wanted, something to do, something outside themselves, something to take them out of themselves. The time had dragged so that he had found himself counting hours to his return. It was now, not then, that parties would have been an intrusion on his privacy: now not then that he was living in a timeless universe. This, not that, was his real honeymoon.

It was in a honeymoon mood that later, after she had woken and they had showered, they sauntered together round the outbuildings to see if the pigs and chickens had been fed and the horses watered.

"It's nice without any of the workers here. It seems so much more our own," she said.

No sounds came from the village across the bay, no steel bands practicing. Was there an omen in that silence? He did not know, he did not care. Tomorrow could take care of that.

"What are we having tonight for dinner?" he inquired.

"A lobster, grilled."

"Then we'll drink champagne."

It was in a honeymoon mood that on their return he moved the bottle from the cellar to the ice box; in a honeymoon mood that he joined her on the veranda; he had brought out the gramophone. He did not want this evening to rely on the caprice of a conductor. He wanted to choose his own favorite records. Some new, some very old. "Small hotel." "You ought to be in pictures." "People will say we're in love."

"Do you remember," he asked, "that song you sang when we were driving into Jamestown?"

"I gave my love a cherry?"

"Yes, that one."

She began to sing it.

> I gave my love a story
> With no end
> I gave my love a baby
> With no cryin'.

He answered with the repeated queries,

> How can there be a cherry
> Without a stone?
> How can there be a chicken
> Without a bone?

Her reply came back clear and sweet

> The story of I love you
> It has no end
> When a baby is sleeping
> There is no cryin'.

"It seems to mean more now," she said.
"Yes, it means more now."

The sun sank toward the sea. The horizon was strewn with clouds. Every second a new shade of color flamed and faded. The ragged plantain leaves assumed a deeper color.

"This is the first day that we've ever had here, just ourselves," she said.

There could not be many more such days he told himself. The strike would not last for ever: and soon very soon there would be the incessant demands of a nursery.

"I've had a funny thought," she said. "Two years ago, three years, for as long as I can remember anything, when I've been to the cinema I've thought how wonderful it would be to have an immense palace kind of house—the Hollywood Long Island type, with a swimming pool and butlers and twenty people sitting down to dinner. But this last two weeks I've been thinking of the films that I did not notice at the time, that made no appeal to me; films that took place in some small town in New England, with a succession of wooden bungalows painted white and green, set back from the road with the grass very green and elm trees everywhere and at the end of the road, above the trees, the thin white spire of a church. And the houses inside are very simple, all except the kitchen which has wonderful gadgets for washing dishes and getting rid of garbage; with that kind of a kitchen you don't need servants, and the husband gets up first and fixes breakfast, and the wife comes down in trousers and a shirt, with her hair tied up in a handkerchief. And he has to go into the big town by train; they've only one car, so she has to go to the station with him, to drive the car back.

"Then she gets down to her household chores. Once a week there's someone who comes in to do the rough work and the ironing: but now and again things aren't going so well with them, and she has to do it all herself: and in the drawing room there's a TV set and when there's a program that she likes particularly, she watches while she does her mending.

"Then she drives into the village to do her marketing: and that's not at all the way it would be here. One store has everything you want, but everything. She takes a wire trolley and pushes it from one stand to another, and tosses into it all the tins and groceries and vegetables and fruit she needs. And there'll be friends to gossip with and she'll call the men who serve her by their christian names; and she pushes her trolley through a kind of turnstile to a man who runs up her account, and all she's bought gets packed into one large cardboard box and a boy carries it out into her car for her, and then she goes back home and fixes herself a sandwich and a cup of coffee.

"There's a lot to keep her busy through the afternoon. There's the TV and dinner to be prepared and a magazine to be read and friends to ring up. Then it's five o'clock, and that's her zero hour: that's the hour to which everything in the day has been building up: she takes a shower and puts on something that's very crisp and laundered and she drives down to the station and the sight of her sitting there at the wheel is his reward for all his hours at a desk.

"He's tired and he's hot and he's rather grubby and they don't talk much as she drives him back. 'I'll fix a drink while you get changed,' she says.

"And when he comes back into the living room in a casual open at the neck sports shirt, she's waiting with a cool frothing concoction, made with another of those gadgets, something she plugs in. And they sit and gossip over their cocktail and she tells him what she's done during the day and he tells her about the office and perhaps there's something on TV they want to see and perhaps there isn't. And perhaps they'll feel like a second cocktail and perhaps they won't. And they'll eat when they feel like eating, not when a maid announces dinner, and if they've anything to celebrate they'll have a glass of wine. They'll sit as long as they like over the table. It's their own life of their own, to do what they like with, and I've been thinking over that kind of life these last three weeks. And this evening, with everything so cozy here I've been feeling that if I could live the kind of life that people in films do, that's how I'd like to live, in a New England village; not as they do in Hollywood and Long Island with swimming pools and butlers."

She spoke slowly, in a drowsy, dreamy voice. It was her way of telling him she was in love with him. He replied in the same key, obliquely. He put on a new record. "If this isn't love, the whole world is crazy."

Maxwell was woken by the sound of drums. The room was dark; the moon had set. It must be some time after three. He raised himself upon his elbow and looked at the bedside clock. Five minutes to five. It would be light in half an hour. He was rested and refreshed. He had had all the sleep he needed. No wonder the drums had woken him. It was strange though that they should be being played so late. The men must have been up all night. The moon had gone down at three. They usually packed up when the moon went down. That, though, was when they were at work. Now they could sleep all day.

Slowly, rhythmically, with the maddening rhythm that never reached a climax, the dull thud of the drums beat across the cane fields. It tore one's nerves, fired one's blood; would it never reach a climax. Night after night of this, followed by long days of slumber, what effect might they not have on men who were used to long hours of manual labor in the heavy sun.

Sylvia had to go home. There was no doubt of that. He lay back on the pillow, his hands clasped under his head, waiting for the sky to lighten, for the thud of the drums to cease. He was in a mood that he had heard described as "happy-sad": the honeymoon was over, but at least he had known what a real honeymoon was like.

### 3

They left shortly before nine. Sylvia had little packing to do. She kept a wardrobe full of clothes in Jamestown. Maxwell was to return that night, as Preston had the night before.

"The animals would starve if I wasn't here to see them fed," he said, "to say nothing of how much would be stolen from the house."

He spoke lightly. It was easy to speak lightly now. Now when the sun was mounting in the sky it seemed impossible for any misfortune to befall Belfontaine. But four hours earlier in the dark, with the drums beating, that had been another matter. Night after night he'd have had no peace of mind, he'd have had no sleep, lying there waiting for the drums. It might have got on Sylvia's nerves too, and that was something that must not happen at a time like this.

"I'll try and work out something with Preston, so that we can work in shifts," he said. "Don't be surprised if you see me in town again tomorrow night."

But even as he said it, he knew that he would not be there. There would be no peace of mind for him in Jamestown with Whittingham waiting, watching. It was only at Belfontaine that there was peace. He had a "last-time" feeling as he drove along the windward coast.

They arrived in Jamestown at quarter to eleven. His eyes brightened as he drove over the saddle-back hill above the *carenage*. It was a clear sunny day with the trade wind blowing. A sloop with its sails furled was slowly steering through the pass. Groups of longshoremen were seated on the wharf, swinging their legs over the side.

They were on strike, but they came down as usual to loll and chatter by the bags and barrels. The *carenage* was their club, they had nowhere else to go. Nothing was changed. There was the habitual air of picturesque inaction. He drove to his father's house. His father was at the office, but his mother was at home. While Sylvia went upstairs to unpack, he stayed with his mother in the drawing room.

"I think it was wise, don't you, to bring Sylvia in?" he said.

"I'm sure that it was very wise."

"It's not that there's any real danger but she might think there was. She might start worrying. That would be the worst thing, wouldn't it?"

"The very worst."

"I shall miss her out there. I think she'll miss not being there. She's very happy out there now."

"I'm glad of that."

"You remember, don't you, when there was talk of my coming in to manage the office here, while you and father took Jocelyn back to England."

"Of course I do."

"You thought that she'd be happier in Jamestown, that she was bored and restless in the country; she isn't now you know." He paused; in the light of this "last-time" feeling, of this urge to make the most of each last minute he wanted to say something that would reassure his mother; that would make her feel happier about herself.

"I suppose you must have wondered sometimes during this last year whether you oughtn't to have discouraged us from marrying so young. It didn't look as though it were working out very well. But I'm so grateful to you now for not having discouraged us. A couple as young as we were is bound to take some little while to get adjusted, but now that we are, we're so much happier for not having got on so well to start with." He took his mother's hand. "I'm more grateful to you than I can say for everything. I'd never have had this happiness but for you."

His mother flushed. I was always her favorite, he thought.

"Don't say anything, Mother darling, but remember that. I must run round to the office now. I'll be back for lunch."

On his way to the office he met Denis Archer. Archer stopped.

"I heard you were in town; have you any news for H.E. How are things out there with you."

"They're all right."

"Yet you've brought your wife in?"

"Only because I don't want to have her worrying. In the condition she's in, you know."

"So you don't want me to alarm H.E.?"

446

"Good heavens, no."

"That's fine, he'll be happier after what you've told me. He's been told your district is the trouble area."

"I dare say it is, but it's calm enough at the moment."

"Good. I'll tell him that."

Archer was about to move on down the street, but Maxwell checked him. He had never seen very much of Archer. They weren't really each other's type, but Archer had always been friendly to him: he'd like to do something for him.

"Listen," he said, "I've thought of something. I'll be rather lonely at Belfontaine. Why don't you come out one night to dinner."

"That's very nice of you."

"It would be nice of you to come, and as I'll be out there as a bachelor, if there's any girl in whom you're interested, why not bring her out: I know how hard it is here to have any privacy. There's plenty of room there for you both; you could drive back in time for work next morning."

"That *is* an idea."

"Any time you say. Ring up when you feel like it."

"I'll take you at your word."

"Do that."


Julian Fleury was surprised to see his son.

"I hadn't expected you so early."

"I'm going back this evening. I'm on my way to the club now. I'll probably be falling among friends there. I thought that if we had any shop to discuss, we'd better talk it over first, when my head's clear."

But there was not a great deal to discuss. There were no immediate problems. Copra and cocoa were fetching a high price, and the estate was running at a handsome profit.

"It should be possible this year to plough back a large percentage of our profits into new equipment. Otherwise we'll be having trouble over income tax," his father said.

"I don't know why we should be doing so much better now than we were five months ago."

Julian Fleury smiled.

"I can give you the answer to that. You've got your eye on things in a way that you hadn't then. You've cut down waste. You can't think what a difference a two percent saving makes when it's spread over an estate's balance sheet."

"Is that really true, father?"

"Of course it is. What other explanation is there? The price of cocoa and copra are the same."

447

"You were pretty worried, weren't you, in the spring? If it was a question now of taking Jocelyn back to England and leaving me out there in control, you'd have no qualms, would you?"

"Of course not."

"You wouldn't put Preston in charge and bring me back to the office where I couldn't do any damage?"

"That's not the way I figured it when I suggested that. I said that I had to have somebody in Jamestown whom I could trust."

"You put it tactfully. But you were worried weren't you?"

"Well, yes."

"I've been a great trial to you, I'm afraid. I've been a disappointing son. But I'll be better in the future. I know where I am now. I didn't then. You don't need to worry."

He never really cared about me, Maxwell thought. But then how could he have. I was awkward, difficult, never knowing my own mind, ungrateful, unresponsive, so different from Arthur. No wonder he was impatient with me. It was probably only because I was so unamiable that my mother put me first.

He went from the office to the Jamestown Club. He did not mean to stay there long. But this curious "last-time" mood was still upon him. There were loose threads to be snipped off, a final impression to be left.

He arrived there shortly before twelve and the club was crowded. He paused in the doorway looking round him. Whittingham? No, Whittingham was not here. That was a relief. Whittingham could wait. He had brought in *Crime and Punishment*. He would return it to him in his office after lunch.

Whittingham was not here, but Boyeur was; standing aggressively self-conscious by the window, within full view of the street and of the library across the way. Maxwell went across to him. This was a loose thread all right.

"How's your strike getting on?" he asked.

"You should know better than I."

"How so?"

"You're in the trouble area."

"You wouldn't think so, if you came out there. They're as happy as clams—if clams are happy, and I can't see why they should be. They're having a holiday with pay. They beat those drums of theirs all night; then they sleep all day. What more could they want. It's paradise for them."

"This is only the beginning. It's like the start of World War II. Eight months of phony war. You wait."

"Wait till what."

"Till the Union funds run low."

"Then they'll come back to work."

"Oh no, they won't. Not at least on the terms that you imagine. They'll come back on their own terms, with a good many planters very sorry that they didn't accept my terms to start with."

His voice was raised. Attention had been attracted and a group was forming round them. It was what Maxwell wanted. He had known there were some loose threads here, but he had not known which.

"What do you mean by that?" he asked.

"That's obvious I should have thought. After a month or so, if the planters still hold out and I'm not convinced they will, the strike pay will be reduced. When the strikers have to tighten their belts you can expect trouble. They'll be hungry and they'll remember that the planters have stacks of food stored away."

"And they'll see you driving around in your M.G., wearing smart clothes: and they'll know that you're eating well at the Continental on their subscriptions. How'll they like that?"

He said it sneeringly. It was fun baiting Boyeur. He had only to shut his eyes to see Boyeur strolling into that line of limelight. Boyeur: all his troubles had sprung from that tainted source. The two young men faced each other, loathing each other with that basic unreasoning hatred that only those who carry chips upon their shoulders can feel for those who have hurt their vanity.

"My people know me, my people trust me. They know who are my enemies. And when the burning starts, they'll know which houses to set the torches to."

Maxwell laughed. "Now we all know where we are don't we," he said and turned aside. He had known there was some unfinished business. He had kept calm and Boyeur had lost his temper. What could have been more satisfactory?

4

Whittingham only went home to lunch on the very few occasions when his wife had guests. He brought down a small packet of sandwiches and ate them in his office and took a two minute siesta, rocking in his chair. All you needed, he insisted, was the mental relief of making your mind a blank. If you went to bed under a mosquito net, you found yourself sleeping for half an hour and needing a shower afterward. By lunching in his office, he put in, so he claimed, an extra ninety minutes work each day, "and ninety uninterrupted minutes too." That was when he did his thinking. Most men in the modern world never had time to think, he'd argue. They were caught up,

449

imprisoned by routine details. Because he saved that ninety minutes at noon, he had spare time at the end of the day to drink and gossip, the two things he most enjoyed.

Maxwell was aware of this routine. He hesitated, when lunch was over and the family scattered to their rooms. Sylvia looked at him, questioningly. He would have given much to have gone upstairs with her, but he wanted, during his long evenings in the empty house, to have as a last time memory that of the siesta when he too had slept.

He shook his head.

"I've too much to do," he said. "I'll be back for tea."

He reached the police station shortly after two. Whittingham was alone, with a heap of files upon his desk.

"I've brought you back *Crime and Punishment*," Maxwell told him.

"Fine. You see what I mean now, don't you."

Whittingham swung round in his chair, pivoting himself against the bottom drawer.

"You can understand now, why I've read that book so often. It's very comforting, very reassuring for a policeman. It reminds him that in the long run ninety-nine times in a hundred he's bound to win. The criminal gives himself away. He can never shake off the memory of his crime. It haunts him all the time. It is his shadow. He keeps looking over his shoulder for his shadow. That is what betrays him. You see how Raskolnikov gave himself away, fainting in the police station. And when he was recovering from his illness, lying on his sofa in a torpor, never displaying interest in anything that was discussed, except the murder; and then all those conversations of his with the policeman; his absorption in the murder. First of all the detective suspects, finally he knows."

"But he had no proof. Raskolnikov would never have been caught unless he had confessed."

"Ah, but that's the point; the criminal is always impelled to a confession, until he confesses he is a prisoner. I'm speaking, mark you, of the intelligent criminal. Not of the brutal thug who holds up a bank and shoots the cashier. That's an indiscriminate crime. I mean the man who kills a specific person for a specific reason; for jealousy, or to inherit an estate, or to marry someone else. Look at it this way. Most murders are committed as a means of escape, by someone who feels himself imprisoned by lack of money, a rival in love, a wife he no longer loves. He cannot live fully till he is free; with money, without a rival, rid of matrimony.

"That is what he tells himself. What happens though? The very opposite. He escapes from one prison into another, and a much worse

450

one. He is imprisoned by a sense of guilt, by a fear of discovery and worst of all by his loneliness. He has a trouble which he can confide in no one. That is a terrible thing, to have a secret that you cannot confide. Secret drinking is the worst form of drinking. Anything is tolerable that can be shared. We all of us have our troubles. And we all need somebody with whom we can share our troubles. That is why marriage is necessary for most of us, someone to share things with. There's a poem I read once with the lines

> You will die unless you do
> Find a soul to whisper to.

I don't think I've got it right. My memory lets me down all the time. Perhaps it's friend, not soul. It's something like that.

> You will die unless you do
> Find a friend to whisper to."

He repeated the quotation slowly. His voice was mesmeric. It made Maxwell feel drowsy; the voice ran on without a pause.

"The loneliness, think of the loneliness of it. Put yourself in his position. He has exchanged one prison for another. There is no one in the world to whom he can speak openly. He is enduring a penal sentence. Solitary confinement. He has no fellow prisoners in whom he can confide. Any other trouble he can share. Suppose he is in debt, there are plenty of friends with whom he can discuss the tantalizing knowledge that if only he had a little capital he could buy himself into the business that would lead to fortune. Perhaps he is jealous. He has friends who have known jealousy, with whom he can compare that feeling of desperate impotence when someone he adores is beguiled by some ridiculous physical trait, the sound of a voice, a way of smiling: he longs for vitriol to throw in the rival's face, to destroy that smile, to pour acid down the throat, burn out those vocal cords; he can compare notes on jealousy: as he can compare notes on the misery of being married to a woman who will not divorce him when he meets his soulmate: those are troubles he can share. But murder, no, he cannot speak of that."

How true, Maxwell thought, how true. The loneliness, the fear, the isolation; with the intervals of an occasional blissful day when you can forget; a day like yesterday.

The voice droned on.

"One prison for another, and a far worse prison than that other one. And remember this, the man who is in this position has a fetish about freedom. He cares so much for freedom that he will commit murder. Most of us can endure a little servitude: can compromise a little with necessity. But not this type of man. He has committed a crime for the sake of freedom."

"But he may not have committed a murder to escape," Maxwell interrupted.

Whittingham was wrong there, and Whittingham had got so much right that he must be shown where he had got it wrong.

"The murder might have been committed by mistake," he pointed out. "Suppose two men start a fight, suppose one of them falls and as he falls strikes his head against a sharp corner. You often see that happen in the films."

"Yes, you quite often see that in the films."

"It happens in real life too doesn't it."

"Why shouldn't it?"

"Or it might happen the way it did in Carson's case."

"And how was that?"

"The way we agreed, don't you remember? A man flinging his arms sideways as he fell; the other kneeling over him, his knees pinioning the arms, his hands at the throat, seeing red, beating the head against the floor, not realizing what he was doing till the man was dead."

"And is that how we agreed that it might have happened."

"Don't you remember?"

"Do I. Possibly. Yes I think I do. So that's what we agreed on, did we? Yes, of course we did. I remember now."

"And in that case it wouldn't be premeditated. It wouldn't be a case of escaping out of one prison and entering another."

"No, that's right, it wouldn't. But that case is far less common. It isn't usual, you know, except in books and films. When a man is killed in that way, it's manslaughter after all, and the man who did it could plead self-defense. He might get off altogether. If he had any sense, he'd go to the police right away. Every film with that kind of manslaughter is a warning against the folly of not doing that."

"I know, but suppose the man sets off to the police station meaning to give himself up, then on the way there realizes suddenly that no one has seen him leave the house, that he has passed no one in the road leading from it, that no one saw him go to the house, that he had no assignation, that he went there uninvited. He has left no clue. He realizes suddenly that no one can connect him with the act."

As he spoke, Maxwell could see himself four months ago, on that moonless night, hurrying down that dark pathway to the road.

"Don't you remember only two weeks ago, after the Leg. Co. meeting, how we stood in the path running from Carson's house; how we pictured to ourselves the man who had killed Carson, pausing at that very same point, wondering whether he could reach the roadway. You remember, don't you?"

"Yes, I remember."

"In that case then, if it had been like that, the man who killed Carson wouldn't have stepped from one prison into another."

"That's very true, but he would be in a prison all the same."

Maxwell nodded. How well he knew what it was like inside that prison. Who knew better than he did?

"He's in a prison," Whittingham's voice droned on. "And there's only one way out of it, confession. That's where *Crime and Punishment* is so sound. Raskolnikov is longing to confess. From the very start, within half an hour of committing the crime. He's not strong enough to carry the burden of his guilt. In his heart of hearts he prays to be found out. The police station is a magnet to him. He returns over and over again to the detective, for no need at all: not only because the detective is the one person who understands him, but because the detective is the one person who can set him free. That's how I think of that poor devil who killed Carson, I mean poor devil too—I don't bear him any ill will, I don't blame him, why should I? Who am I to judge anyone, who am I to blame him?—I'm sorry for him. I think of him, out there in the districts, or here in town, meeting his friends, going to parties; perhaps he's got a wife and children: perhaps he's a bachelor and engaged; or there's a girl in love with him, to whom he daren't propose because there's this burden on his conscience. Quite possibly he's someone of importance. He must be. If he's someone in a position to have been jealous of Carson."

"What makes you think he was?"

"Wasn't that one of the possibilities we considered the other day. Or was it with someone else, to someone else that I suggested the possibility of that?"

"No, it was with me. I remember now."

"It was. I thought as much. But I go over this case so often, with so many people, it's hard to remember who said what and when. But it may have been jealousy, and if it was jealousy, the betting is that the crime was done by someone of a certain consequence, a member of the Jamestown Club. It's not impossible. I picture that fellow standing at the bar, saying 'Take an order' to the steward, behaving like everybody else, looking like everybody else, yet all the time he's imprisoned in this lonely cell. Poor devil, I say to myself, poor devil."

Maxwell nodded. Poor devil. That was the way it was.

"And do you know what I feel, how I feel," Whittingham was continuing. "I want to go up to him and take him by the arm and tell him not to worry. 'I'll do my best for you,' I want to say to him. 'I'm not out to punish you. I'm not out to punish anyone. I've got to protect property and persons. I've got to maintain law and order. We have to set an example now and then. But I mean you no harm. Tell me the way it happened. We'll get it fixed as manslaughter. That might only mean five years and the sentence could be remitted for good behavior: it might only be three years. That may seem a long time now, but three years pass very quickly. Look back three years. Does it seem long ago? No, of course it doesn't. Three years isn't a big price to pay for your peace of mind. A prison of bolts and bars is far less bad than an invisible prison of the mind. Come now, tell me.' That's what I'd like to say to him."

Maxwell felt himself grow drowsy. What a relief it would be to relax; to throw off his burden, not of guilt, he felt no guilt, but of isolation. To meet human beings again on equal terms; even if he met them as a criminal: to break down this barrier of false pretenses.

One day the burden would become too great. Whittingham was right. He could see himself some day in this office, talking, talking while Whittingham pivoted himself against that lower drawer, listening, nodding his head, interjecting a comment or a question, "So that was how it was," "Ah yes, of course yes, yes." And he would talk and talk. Oh the relief of it. One day he would break free from this prison of his isolation. One day but not now, not yet. The burden was still supportable.

He stood up.

"I mustn't waste your time. Besides, I've things to do. I want to get back to Belfontaine before it's dark."

"How are things out there?"

"Like a long bank holiday. They sleep all day and dance in the hills all night."

"No signs of disorder?"

"There won't be till their funds run low."

"If I could be sure of that I'd find my job much easier."

They laughed together. Maxwell turned toward the door. As his hand stretched toward the handle, Whittingham called out.

"By the way, what was the answer to that point that I'd forgotten in *Crime and Punishment*."

"What point?"

"Whether the man who called out 'murderer' had been planted there by the police."

"I'm sorry. I didn't notice."

"You didn't notice?"

"No, I'm sorry. I forgot."

454

"Forgot. Now that surprises me."

"Why?"

"I should have thought that even if I hadn't asked, it's a point you'd have wanted to clear up."

"Why should you have thought that?"

"Because you are so interested in the way detectives work."

"Isn't everyone interested in that?"

"Not in the way that you are."

"Oh, I see."

Maxwell hesitated. He would have liked to have questioned the policeman further, but he did not dare. It was too big a risk. That was how Raskolnikov had given himself away, talking too much, asking too many questions, not leaving well alone.

"I probably didn't notice because the point probably never was cleared up," he said. "Didn't you say that was a possibility, that Dostoevski introduced mystical symbolic characters? I wouldn't know. It's the first book of his I've read. You did say that didn't you?"

"Yes, that's what I said. I'll have to read the book again myself."

Maxwell closed the door behind him. He was trembling. One day he would come here, as he had his afternoon: on some excuse or other, to return a book or discuss the security of his estate. But he would not leave this way. There'd be an escort, either Whittingham himself or a constable. In handcuffs? No, most likely not, since the confession had been given of his own accord. He would enter a free man and step out a prisoner. In the world's view that was to say. But in fact, in deeper fact he would step in a prisoner, and depart in freedom, his burden shed. The relief of that, the peace, the utter peace.

It was half-past two. He had said he had things to do, but he had not really. Only a few parcels to collect. He had half planned to go to the Country Club, but that would involve a three hour wait. He had nothing to do, there was no one he wanted to see: he collected the parcels and drove back to his father's house.

Jocelyn was reading in the drawing room.

"Is Sylvia down yet?" he asked.

"No."

He went upstairs. The door was held open by a wooden wedge. He tiptoed into the room. He was wearing crepe soled shoes. Sylvia was asleep, breathing quietly, her face turned toward him, he saw it veiled by the mosquito net. She looked very lovely and he yearned to join her, but he held back the impulse: Good-bys were best avoided. He looked at her, and his heart was heavy. Twenty min-

455

utes back, trembling in the passage outside Whittingham's office, he had longed for the day when he could step out of his encasing prison. Now, looking at his wife asleep, he recognized that never, never could he inflict that shame on her; he must spare her that: their child must not bear that stigma. Never, never could he draw the arrow from his side: even though the wound was festering. He must leave his child a name that could be honored. Sylvia, lying there asleep, looked so defenseless. Her life was his to mar. He must remember this, imprint this picture on his memory, to protect her when temptation came. He must carry his burden till he died.

He turned away, noiselessly trod downstairs. Through the open doorway of the hall he could see Jocelyn, her book upon her lap, looking toward the hills. He walked toward her.

"I didn't disturb Sylvia," he began, but she had started, her hand raised to her throat.

"Oh how you startled me. I didn't hear you. I was daydreaming."

Of whom? Of what? Of the happy future that stretched ahead of her with Euan Templeton. There were no clouds on *her* horizon.

"I'm sorry. I was so anxious not to disturb Sylvia that I can't stop tiptoeing. Will you tell her that I decided to go back to Belfontaine right away. I wanted to see whether the house-boy had fed the pigs or not. I wouldn't trust him not to eat the food himself. I'll ring through to her tonight. Will you tell her that?"

"I'll tell her."

Jocelyn picked up her book and began to read again. He hesitated. This "last-time" sensation that had haunted him all day made him wish to say something pertinent to his sister, as he had to his father and to his mother. But no words came. They had always been strangers to each other. He shrugged, remembering how he had stood in the hall on that February afternoon, thinking what good friends they ought to have been to one another. That February afternoon. Everything had started then. Yet when that day had dawned he had expected it to be like any other day. He had heard no warning: had felt no dread, no anticipation. He had woken up with a slight hangover, and a reluctance to go over the estate accounts with his father under such a handicap. Coffee. That had been his chief concern. Coffee, hot and strong, and a great deal of it. How little he had guessed when he came down the staircase of all that he was on his way to meet.

It would be good to get back to Belfontaine, to think the whole thing over, plan it out: throw up his defenses. For Whittingham knew: of that he had now no doubt whatsoever. Whittingham knew.

# CHAPTER TWENTY-SEVEN

## 1

Maxwell reached Belfontaine soon after five. He had told the maids that they need not prepare dinner: they could lay out a cold buffet meal. But one of them must stay in the house, on that point he had insisted. One of them had. A strange bicycle was leaning against the woodshed. A boy friend had been invited.

He went into his bedroom to change his clothes. There was a faint smell of gardenias in the room. Sylvia's scent. How long would it stay upon the air? How long would he be able to detect it. If he had not had such a strong sense of smell, he would never have noticed the smoke of that Egyptian cigarette and none of this would have ever happened. On what trivial things one's fate depended.

Sylvia's brushes and combs, her powders and face lotions and her scent were spread along the dressing table. She kept a duplicate set in town. He picked up her comb and held it against his cheek. With that scent against his nostrils, he could fancy that she still was here. The bed was reflected in the mirror. This time yesterday he had been lying beside her, waiting for her to wake. It had been one of the loveliest moments of his life. He should be grateful to fate that he had known that moment. He could not have lived a day more fully than he had yesterday. Perhaps if he had not caught the whiff of that cigarette, yesterday would have been less perfect. Payments canceled out. That's how he should think of it, he thought. Yesterday was the counter cheque.

Yesterday was the reward. As dusk fell he sat on the veranda, with rum and water by his side, living over that last day, hour by hour, minute by minute, detail by detail: remembering what he and Sylvia had done, remembering how Sylvia had looked, what she had said, remembering tones that came into her voice. Five months ago he had never heard those tones. He had only half known Sylvia; not that; not quarter known: and he himself had been half alive. Suppose that he had died six months ago before he had heard those tones, seen her eyes widen and grown tender. "Every day is like a honeymoon now." Had she really said that, said that to him, with that new depth, new warmth for him in her voice. Did not that pay for everything?

The moon waxing to its full had lifted between the division of the hills. Fireflies were flickering above the crotons. Bullfrogs were croaking in the ditches. The palm fronds rustled in the breeze. No sound came from the village. They were still tired after their long night's dancing: they were resting before the night of dancing that lay ahead. It was very peaceful: as peaceful as it had been last night when Sylvia was at his side. Tonight she was sixty miles away, but the telephone was in the hall. He had promised to call her up. It was early yet. She'd be at the club; she wouldn't be back till eight. He refilled his glass from the decanter. He sipped it slowly, then took a glass of water as a chaser.

It was good to sit by oneself, brooding over happy things while the rum ran warmly through one's veins. To drink alone. Whittingham had said something about secret drinking. But that was different. Secret drinking was stealing off to the bottle in the bathroom, slipping away six drinks to everybody else's one. To drink quietly by oneself, reflectively, that was another matter. It was something he had rarely done. He had hardly ever been alone. First he had been living with his parents, then he had married. This must be the first night he had spent away from Sylvia. Had there ever been another time when he had sat alone like this in an empty house, with a glass beside him. He thought back. He tried to remember one. He could not. He probably never had, and now he had a week, two weeks perhaps of evenings such as this. It would be good, very good sitting here, evening after evening while the moon ripened to its full, his mind abroad over that long day and night of honeymoon.

In the room behind him a table had been laid. But he was in no mood for sitting at a table by himself: he would make himself a sandwich, cut himself a slice of cheese and sit here, nibbling and sipping, waiting till it was time to telephone, remembering minute by minute what he had been doing, what he had been saying twenty-four hours back.

He went into the dining room to fix his sandwich. There were hardboiled eggs, cold chicken and piccalilli. He was slicing the chicken when the telephone bell rang, three times. It was Sylvia.

"Darling, I was starting to get anxious."

There was a genuine ring of anxiety in her voice.

"I thought you'd be at the club."

"If I had gone, I'd be back by now."

"Already?"

"What do you think the time is."

He glanced at his watch.

"Heavens, I'd no idea it was as late as that."

It was after twenty to nine. "I was so happy sitting there on the veranda, time raced away."

"Happy with me away."

"Happy thinking about you, reliving yesterday."

"Ah, sweet."

"It was lovely, wasn't it."

"It was a dream."

"We'll keep it that way, won't we?"

"Of course."

"I'm missing you."

"Me, too."

"Don't stop."

"I won't. Have you had dinner yet? How was it?"

"I'm fixing myself a sandwich now."

"A sandwich. Why on earth?"

"So that I can watch the moonlight."

"I see."

"It's more romantic in the mood I'm in."

"And what about the pigs?"

"They weren't starved either."

"Then everything's all right."

"Yes, everything's all right."

"Nothing for me to worry over?"

"Nothing, nothing at all."

"And you'll call every evening."

"What do you think."

"Good-night then darling."

He took his sandwich out onto the veranda. He sipped at the smooth, full-bodied rum and munched his sandwich, and the waxing moon sank toward the sea, turning the green of the cane fields to a silver blue, and at last from the foothills at his back came the beat of congo drums. Yes, Sylvia was better off down there in Jamestown. It was time for bed, he told himself. The pillow next to his was scented with gardenia. He held it in his arms, close, close against his cheek.

2

Maxwell woke with his mouth dry and his head throbbing, as he had done four months ago on the morning of the Governor's party. It was not a hangover, but he felt irritable. He walked onto the veranda and looked at the decanter. It had been three-quarters full when he had brought it out. Less than a third there now. Not much too much, but still too much. He must watch himself in future. It was easy to drink too much when you were by yourself. He must put the decanter away in future when he went in to dinner, and not touch it afterward. And he must eat a proper dinner tonight. It was easy to get into sloppy habits when you were by yourself. The servants got into sloppy habits too. A full three course meal tonight.

He went under the shower and felt better. He looked at the razor brush below his mirror. There was no need to shave and his hand might be unsteady. It was a temptation but he resisted it. Missing a morning's shave was the thin end of the wedge.

"Breakfast in ten minutes," he called over the stairs and went back into the bathroom. His hand proved to be unsteady and he cut himself three times.

The maid who brought his breakfast looked illkempt, but he could not tell in what way exactly. They'd tend to get out of hand with Sylvia away. He'd have to watch them.

"I shall be in for lunch and dinner," he said.

"Yes, sir."

She stood waiting for orders. This was something he had forgotten. He would have to order two meals a day for an indefinite period. He had never kept house before.

"A curry lunch," he said.

"What kind curry, sir?"

"Lobster."

"No lobster, sir, sea too rough, no men go fish."

"Chicken then, and what for dinner."

"What for dinner, sir?"

"Soup."

"What kind soup, sir?"

"Vegetable soup."

"What kind vegetable, sir?"

He felt his temper rising. Couldn't she think of anything for herself. Did Sylvia have to go through this every morning. But then Sylvia had nothing else to do.

"Potato soup," he said, "and after that, well, some kind of meat."

"What kind meat, sir?"

Her face wore an expression of vacuous amiability that was on a morning such as this infuriating. He could understand how in the old plantation days, a slave owner had strung up his property to a tree and watched it thrashed: anything to see that silly ignorant expression change, even if he damaged his own property.

"Go to the market, buy any meat there is and stew it. And after that some fruit, any fruit."

"Yes, sir."

She glided away on her hard-soled wide-toed feet. She had prepared him a dish of scrambled eggs, to follow a slice of pawpaw.

460

The fruit was soft and soggy. He pushed it away. He had no appetite for eggs. Coffee. That was what he needed, coffee hot, strong, and black. It was hot all right, so hot that it burnt his mouth, but it was neither black nor strong. A week of this will drive me mad, he thought.

He looked at the clock. Five minutes to eight. Four hours and thirty-five minutes to lunch. And then when lunch was finished, six hours to dinner. Ten hours and thirty-five minutes. What on earth could he find to do?

He sought his manager, whom he had not seen on the previous evening.

"What news?" he asked.

But he knew the answer to that question before he set it. There was no news, how could there be. Nothing had happened. Nothing could happen for several days. Coconuts were rotting on the ground, but on the whole the loss to the estate even if the strike continued for several days would not be very great. They had managed to ship all the copra that they had stored. The cane was cut. The cocoa was not ready yet for picking. The men during this month would normally have been employed on routine maintenance. That work could wait. From the planters' point of view, Boyeur could not have made his attack at a better time.

Normally after his morning interview with his manager, Maxwell would have ridden round the estate supervising the work in progress. There was no work in progress. There was nothing to supervise. The stables, the pigsties, and the chicken run lay within a few yards of the house.

"I'll go and see how things are at Mr. Preston's," he told his manager.

Preston too, as he had imagined, had nothing to report. There was no work to supervise. There was no point in riding round idle coconut groves. Nothing was happening in the village. Nothing would happen till strike pay was reduced. Then anything might happen.

"Have you any idea when the strike pay will be cut down?" Maxwell asked.

"Your bet is as good as mine. But Master Boyeur is impatient. He likes to have things happen fast. Inaction gets upon his nerves. He has to attack himself, he does not lure the enemy to attack him. I think he'll cut down the strike pay before he actually needs, to get things moving. When's the next Leg. Co. meeting?"

"Wednesday week."

"Then I prophesy that on the Friday before, there'll be a strike pay cut, so that something can happen over the weekend. He won't

461

want to go to the Leg. Co. meeting with empty hands, particularly as he has to eat humble pie and apologize for his behavior at the last meeting."

"I think you're right."

"In the meantime we can only wait."

"Exactly."

Preston was happy to be waiting. He was a handy man. He enjoyed fixing things. He was building a chalet where his wife could read and write and get away from the turmoil of a small house with children tumbling over themselves all the time.

"I've been looking forward for weeks to getting down to this," he said.

He was impatient to get back to it now. Maxwell could see that clearly.

"I must be on my way," he said.

"I wish I could offer you something. But it's too early for a punch. And I don't imagine that you are the kind of man who takes morning coffee."

"You're right. I'm not. And it's much too early for a punch."

It was ten o'clock. Eight hours more to be filled in. He might as well drive into the village, to the police station.

The constable in charge had the same report to make. No disturbance. Why should there be? The men weren't working but were earning money; who could ask more? Maxwell parked his car outside the station and strolled down the main village street toward the jetty.

It looked no different; naked and half-naked children tumbling in the dust before their huts; women cooking over their stove ovens at the back, shouting to their neighbors; now and again through an open doorway he could see a man stretched on a bed asleep; groups of men stood gossiping outside the liquor shop. They were not drinking, it was too early for that, and their idea of drinking was a series of quick shots of white rum. The liquor store was their club. Some of the men wore gaudy American beach shirts; some of them wore army khaki shirts that were torn and patched and tattered with their skin showing through the gaps. They laughed as they chattered, their big even teeth gleaming white and strong against their bright pink tongues. They looked very happy, and the dotted rows of shingle huts looked picturesque under the shade of palms and mangoes, against the light green of the cane fields and the dark green of the foothills. Visitors from Europe and America were appalled by the squalor of these one-room shingle huts, but they were adequate for the needs of simple people; in the tropics they only needed cover at night and when it rained. And at night all they

462

asked for was a small dark fortress whose windows they could nail up against evil spirits. They were well enough, these people, for the moment, till education developed different needs in them. Boyeur moved too fast; his appeal was not to their needs but to their cupidity.

Maxwell turned out of the main street toward the jetty. A boat-load of fish had been beached and the fishermen were selling off their catch. What on earth had that girl meant, saying that it was too rough to fish. She had probably only meant that no fisherman was going to sell to the big houses while the strike was on. They'd be acting differently when the pay cut came.

He walked across the sand toward the boat. The group divided making way for him. There was a lobster in the catch. Lobster was not a delicacy to the Santa Martans. They used it as bait. He picked up the lobster, holding it by his head: its tail thrashed against his wrist. "How much?"

There was a silence. The fishermen looked at one another. He had taken them off their guard. They were embarrassed. Lobster was cheap. Fifteen cents a pound. This couldn't weigh more than two pounds. He took out a half crown and handed it across. It was so much too high a price that the men dared not argue. That was exactly what he had wanted, to take without argument the lobster they had refused to sell. It established his superiority.

"Thanks very much," he said.

He was conscious of their eyes following him resentfully. He relished their humiliation.

He drove straight home. "Matilda, come," he called.

He pointed to the lobster.

"Why say no fish? Why say sea too rough?"

She gaped at the lobster, her mouth open like a cod's.

"Take it away," he said. "Lobster curry for lunch. Fried chicken dinner and bring now some boiling water; a cup, a spoon and a tin of *Nescafé*."

"Not the kind of man who takes morning coffee."

It was the one thing he did need this morning, just as it had been the one thing that he had needed on the morning of the Governor's cocktail party. If he had not been in that mood, in that condition then, would he have got so worked up about the smell of an Egyptian cigarette. The whole thing seemed so ridiculous in retrospect. It could all so easily not have happened. Nine times in ten Carson would have come to the son and not the sister. If he hadn't been married, if he had been living at home, if it had happened eighteen months before . . . but if it had happened eighteen months before, it would not have happened at all. There'd have been no Sylvia to be jealous of then.

How surprised those men who had formed the Belfontaine Committee would have been could they have foreseen to what their plans for Julian Fleury would lead eventually. The death of Carson and Julian Fleury's son the prey of justice.

The Belfontaine Committee. That was one of his first mistakes. How Whittingham had started when the name came out. The only time he had ever seen Whittingham start. The first mistake. The first of how many later ones. So many slips, right down the line. Whittingham knew: there was no doubt of that. Whittingham knew, and Whittingham was waiting: waiting and watching. Well, he could watch too. He must be on his guard, ruthless, relentless. Time was on his side. How many more years had Whittingham before retirement. Seven, ten: time passed quickly: Whittingham had been telling him that himself and only yesterday. He'd play out time.

Matilda was at his side with the *Nescafé* and boiling water. He put in three teaspoonsful: he needed it strong and dark. Ah, that was better. He could play out time. He looked at his watch: quarter-past eleven. How soon could he ring up Sylvia. She would siesta late. She would go to the club most likely, since she hadn't yesterday. She would be leaving around six. She might not be back till after eight. He must ring at half-past five then, or half-past eight. Six hours or nine.

Never had six hours passed more slowly. He had nothing to do, nowhere to go, nobody to talk to. Forty-eight hours ago that honeymoon day had ended before it had seemed to have begun. But now, with Sylvia away, what was the point of picnicking, of going to the beach. He turned on the radio, but after half an hour the succession of rumbas from Puerto Rico got upon his nerves. He tried to pick up the B.B.C. Overseas program, but there was a static interference. He had brought a couple of novels, but neither held his attention. They seemed tame after *Crime and Punishment*.

He lay down after lunch, but he could not sleep. When he pulled a sheet over his shoulders he was too hot; when he flung it off the intermittent wind struck coldly against his damp skin, whenever he was on the point of dozing off. He drove down to the beach where he had picnicked two days before. He could still detect the hollows in the sand that they had scooped for their hips and shoulders. He sat on the rock throwing stones at the tree stump. But it was no fun throwing stones by oneself; it was no fun doing anything by oneself.

The sun sank slowly. What was that he had thought five hours ago, that time was on his side, that time passed quickly. If he found five hours drag, how was he going to wait out ten years.

A sloop from Belfontaine was pitching and rolling on its way to Jamestown. The wind was behind it, and it was making rapid progress. It would anchor before nightfall. He wished that he was in it. What was happening in Jamestown? What was being discussed and planned there: at the club, at G.H., in the police station? If only he was invisible so that he could walk its streets, gauge the temper of its citizens, sit in on conferences, hearing and seeing without being seen.

What was happening in Jamestown? If he rang Sylvia before she went to the club, she would be unable to tell him anything. She would have heard nothing beyond what she had been told at lunch time by his father. That was not likely to be much. His father rarely went to the Jamestown Club. He sat in his office all the morning. He heard no gossip. Sylvia would not have anything to tell him at half-past five, but later she might have, when she was back from the club. He'd call at half-past eight.

What was happening in Jamestown? It was shortly after four. Suppose he went home right now and changed. If he drove fast he would be at the club by six, see and hear for himself and be back in Belfontaine before the congo drums had started their rhythmic beating. He could, of course he could. But wasn't that the very thing he mustn't do? Wasn't that what playing for time meant? Keeping away from Jamestown, keeping away from Whittingham, resisting the pull of that magnet. Keep away from Jamestown.

Matilda had set out on the veranda the decanter of rum, the ice thermos, the limes, the glasses and the angostura. He carried the decanter back into the dining room. Not again. Whittingham had been right about solitary drinking. You drank too fast when you were alone. You brooded and your hand went out to the glass beside you. You didn't pace your own drinking to another's. Never again. He couldn't afford to give away points in this game.

Out of the corner of his eye as he turned back to the veranda he saw the telephone in the hall. Quarter-past five. He could call Sylvia now. She was certain to be awake. He longed to hear her voice, he longed to hear any human voice. Somebody to talk to, anyone to talk to. But no, he couldn't call her twice; that would seem suspicious; and he had to hear what was going on in Jamestown.

He tried once again to get the B.B.C. Overseas program. This time he was more successful. There was no static. The voice came through full and resonant. The Minister of State for the Colonies was describing an average day in the life of a member of the cabinet.

465

Every week someone from a different walk of life gave a picture of his profession. It was a popular program, and Maxwell had listened to it more than once.

"One of my chief problems," the minister was saying, "is the putting of myself into the position of the Governor with whom I am in correspondence. He is living in a different climate, and—and this is a most important point—he is surrounded by men of a different race, bred very often to a different religion, speaking a different language; men at whose thought processes he can only guess. Each Governor with whom I am in correspondence is living in an atmosphere very different from my own.

"I am sitting for instance in my office in Westminster on a sunny September afternoon; there is a breeze, the sun is shining, the trees in my garden at home are starting to turn golden. I am at peace with the world. I am reading a report from, let us say, the Governor of Aden. Do I detect in that report a certain, shall I say, listlessness? I have to remind myself that the man who wrote that report has been living for the last five months on the edge of the desert with the temperature vacillating between one hundred and ten and one hundred and twenty-four degrees. He has had no weekend escape into the cool of the hills; he has been surrounded with Arabic speaking Moslems. He has been exposed to sand flies and dust storms. Is it surprising that toward the end of the summer his staff is exhausted and his own nerves are on edge?

"And then while I am considering this report, the telephone goes and I am informed that a question is to be asked in the house about a group of West Indian islands. I have to remind myself that the Governor of those islands is living under conditions that are every bit as trying but are completely different. The heat there is damp and muggy. It rains a lot. The hurricane season is beginning. In every decade one or other of these islands is the victim of a disaster that cannot be foreseen but that will demand from the Governor and his staff prompt and efficient action. I have to visualize that particular Governor's problem in terms of heat, damp, mosquitoes, and the constant apprehension that at any moment the telephone may summon him to an appalling loss of life and property. It is my business, therefore . . ."

The Minister explained what his business was. If it was hard for the speaker, Maxwell thought, to picture the conditions under which the Governors he had appointed were carrying out his instructions, how much harder was it for the West Indian like himself who had never left the Caribbean, to picture the conditions under which the destinies of his island were being administered by a man three thousand miles away in a city of smoke and fog and snow and open fires, things he himself had never seen.

What kind of a man was this whose firm and resonant voice was ringing through the West Indian air? How old was he, was he good looking, had he a wife, what kind of a home had he? He wished there were television here, so that he could visualize him. Did he worry about Santa Marta? Was it too small to occupy his interests? Had he ever heard of David Boyeur? Had H.E. reported the scene at the Leg. Co. meeting? Had his own name, Maxwell Fleury, figured in the report? It was strange to think that this man who was talking now from three thousand miles might have been wondering as he read the Governor's report whether there was a personal enmity between these two young councilors, and if so, what was it about?

What was it about indeed when it came to that? What had started this bitter quarrel between himself and Boyeur? Why had Boyeur organized that demonstration at his election meeting? That as far as he was concerned was the start of it. But why had Boyeur done it? There had been no feud between them as far as he knew. They had hardly ever met. Why, why, why? And how could this politician whose voice was now taking on the sermonic roll of an approaching peroration, understand the why and wherefore of an island feud when the persons concerned did not know the cause of it?

"Those, I repeat, are my chief problems," the voice concluded. "I do not start to claim that I have solved or am solving them, but it is something, nay 'tis much, as the poet said, to be able to recognize the nature and the dimensions of the task ahead."

There was a second's pause, then the announcer's voice, "You have just been listening to the Right Honorable Mr. Robert Marsh, His Majesty's Minister of State for the Colonies, speaking on 'A Day in the life of a Cabinet Minister.' Next week at this time you will hear Canon Edward Westlake, the Headmaster of Fernhurst School, address you on 'A Day in the life of a Headmaster.' We will now take you over . . ."

Maxwell smiled as the first bars of a symphony orchestra drifted from the radio. He turned it down, so that it provided a background to the mingled murmurous noises of early evening.

"A Day in the life of a Headmaster." "A Day in the life of a Cabinet Minister"; figures of influence and importance discussing the routine, the surface of their lives, avoiding personal problems. Would not it be more interesting to have obscure anonymous individuals, describing their own private hells, the private prisons that their misfortunes built for them? "A day in the life of a man who knows but cannot prove that his wife is unfaithful," "A day in the life of an unarrested murderer."

467

That now would be a subject. A day such as his today? No, not like today. A day like Wednesday, when he had driven into town with Sylvia, seen his parents, discussed the estate problems with his father, interviewed the police officer who was hunting him, then driven out alone to his estate to brood on his situation. What a theme that would be for a radio broadcast!

It would be unique. No murderer had told the truth about himself. Every other kind of criminal had done so. But in the nature of things no murderer could. Up till his last minute he had to protest his innocence, in the hope of a reprieve. Novelists without number had tried to enter imaginatively into the mind of a murderer. Several had succeeded. Dostoevski surely had. But no murderer in the history of the world had told the truth about himself. He had a unique piece of information to give the world.

It was a new idea to him. If he were to write down exactly what he had done, exactly what he had felt from the moment that he had risen from Carson's lifeless body, he would leave behind a document that would be read as long as books were printed. He knew something that no one else in the world knew, except other murderers, and they were silent.

What a story he had to tell. All through these weeks he had been carrying on, with his private life unchanged upon the surface. He had stood for election and he had won a seat; he had supervised his estate, and for the first time successfully. He had begotten a child and for the first time he had known what it was to be loved wholeheartedly. He had knocked his childhood's chip from off his shoulder. He had humbled Boyeur in the Leg. Co. Yet all the time he had nursed a gnawing secret, all the time he had been exposed to Whittingham's slow insidious campaign. Day by day he had felt his defenses weaken. How well Dostoevski had put that when he had made his detective say, "If I leave one man quite alone, if I don't touch him and don't worry him, but let him know or at least suspect every moment that I know all about it and am watching him day and night, and if he is in continual suspicion and terror, he'll be bound to lose his head. He'll come of himself or maybe do something which will make it as plain as twice two are four. With an intelligent man it's a dead certainty."

That's how Whittingham had been treating him, playing with him, reminding him that he lived in a private prison, walled in by fear and guilt. By fear and guilt? Ah, but that's where Whittingham, that's where Dostoevski had got it wrong. He had felt no guilt; not for a second. On the contrary he had had a sense of pride, of self-vindication. He had pictured himself making his announcement to the police; he had heard in his imagination the incredulous ejaculations at the Country Club, "What! Maxwell Fleury!"

He had felt no shame; why should he have felt shame? He had not plotted the thing. He had been inspired by no base motive. He had not killed out of jealousy, out of revenge. He had not killed to steal, to inherit, to supplant. He had killed in open fight; honorably; in a duel, one man's hand against another. How had it happened? He had seen red suddenly, he had been blinded by one of those spasms of ungovernable rage that had made him in the nursery scratch his nurse and stamp upon his toys, that had made him goad Boyeur at the Leg. Co. meeting.

All his life he had been subject to these fits of fury. Were they, he wondered—it was the first time the idea had occurred to him— a legacy from Africa: did that infinitesimal fraction of colored blood in his veins arbitrarily assert its domination; could it be that; was that too fanciful an explanation? What would Whittingham have to say on that point. Did Whittingham's experience include...

He checked, the corollary to his stream of introspection was suddenly terrifyingly apparent. The picture of himself at the microphone, at his desk, declaiming the record of what he only knew. From what source other than one, could it have sprung? The need to confess, the need to be absolved not of guilt in his case, but of isolation. A time would come when he must break out of prison. Sooner or later, he would be sitting in that chair at the police station, talking, talking.... He foresaw that moment as clearly as a leper sees on his skin the first flake of the sore, painless as yet, that will one day cripple him.

In the hall behind him, the telephone rang once, twice, three times. He hurried in to answer it.

"Yes, who is that?"

"Darling, why such impatience?"

She was going to cocktails with the Normans, and she was staying on to supper. She'd wanted to be sure of talking to him. How was he? Was he being properly fed? Was everything all right?

It was a lover's conversation. Her voice was fond and light and happy. The voice of a wife in love, confident in her husband's love, without a trouble in the world. His own heart warmed in response.

"Darlingest, I must rush. Sleep well. Keep missing me."

There was a click from the other end. He stood beside the machine, in a mood very similar to that in which he had stood there the night before; a mood of pride and gratitude; what had he done to deserve this of fate? But now there was an undercurrent of dissatisfaction. They had had their evening talk. She was not going to the tennis club. She'd have no gossip to report to him. What was happening in Jamestown?

3

Three hours later Maxwell was pacing restlessly the length of the veranda. The tennis club would be empty now. Who had been there? What had been said? How had the gossip run? His eyes were tired, but his mind was racing. Sleep was impossible even though he had taken no siesta. The rum decanter stood untouched upon the sideboard. Not again. He must keep his mind clear. He was not beaten yet. Whittingham did not know everything. Dostoevski did not know everything. If he could keep away from Jamestown, could keep away from that small hot room. Keep away from Whittingham. Make Whittingham come to him. Play the match on his own ground. But he had to know what was happening in Jamestown.

Quarter to nine. The Normans must have finished supper: or at any rate their cocktail guests would have gone. They wouldn't be sitting down to a meal. There'd be buffet food. He could call Sylvia now. She could report at any rate on the gossip at the Normans'.

He was a long while getting through. The party line was in use; when he did get through he first heard Mavis faintly against a babble of raised voices. It sounded like one of those cocktail parties from which no one went away. He had to shout to make himself heard. When at last Sylvia was brought to the telephone her voice sounded anxious. "What's wrong?" she asked.

"Nothing. What should be wrong?"

"You ringing up again."

"Are you surprised at my feeling lonely?"

"Oh, darling."

But there was in her voice a sense of being somewhere else, of not being attuned yet to the telephone. He ought to ring off, but he had rung up for a specific reason. Was it a large party, he asked. Yes, she told him, twenty to twenty-five: it sounded as though most of them were still there, he said. As a matter of fact most of them were, she answered.

"I don't suppose Whittingham was there?"

"Well, yes, he was."

"What had he got on his mind?"

"Would you like me to ask him, he's two yards away."

"Good God no, no."

"Oh darling, what a scream."

"I'm sorry, but hang it all I rang up to talk to you not Whittingham."

470

"I know, but since you mentioned him. Why did you?"

"Heaven knows. Who else is there?"

They gossiped for a minute or two, but talk was difficult against the noise of the party. He'd better ring off, he told her.

"Had you? I suppose you had. Oh, but there is one other thing, about Sunday. Couldn't you come in for the day, picnic at *Grande Anse*, then if you want to, go back afterward."

"I don't see why not."

"That's fine, only three days till then. I'll be counting hours. Good-night, my precious."

He leant his head against the woodwork. What a narrow escape. Suppose she had called Whittingham to the telephone. What could he have found to say to him. For that matter, had he escaped at all? At that very moment Sylvia might be turning to Whittingham with a "That was Maxwell. He was asking after you." And Whittingham would nod and giggle, like the fool he wasn't.

How could he have been so silly, but that, hadn't it, had been Whittingham's point from the very start. The subconscious took charge. That remark of his about the Belfontaine Committee. Why had that sprung out? You could never trust yourself. There was only one remedy. Keep away from danger. Avoid Jamestown and Sunday rum punches at *Grande Anse*. Cut that out.

He thought fast. Denis Archer. Why not remind him of that invitation, ask him and his girl out for the day? He'd jump at the invitation. No one ever followed up a vague, general invitation. But a second definite invitation: it was worth trying.

He called G.H. Yes, the A.D.C. was in. That was a piece of luck.

"You remember saying yesterday"—was it only yesterday—"that you'd like to come here for dinner. I've a better idea. Come out on Sunday. After breakfast and spend the whole day here. You can: now that's fine. Come out as early as you like. Go back next day."

That was a piece of luck. He could write a facetious note to Sylvia explaining that he had been cast unexpectedly for the role of gooseberry. There was no chance of her finding out that he had called Archer after he had promised her to come in on Sunday. He could say that Archer had taken up a vague invitation, that he did not want to disappoint him. He was safe for the moment.

But only for the moment. He could not keep this up for long. He could not keep permanently away from Jamestown. On Wednesday week there was the Leg. Co. meeting. He would have to come in for that. The strike would not last forever. This week or next, this month or next, the strike would end. He would resume the familiar pattern of his routine, exposed once again to Whittingham's incessant scrutiny: at the mercy of his subconscious self, exhausted

471

more and more by the longing to be free, the longing to confess, to get it all off his chest. I don't stand a chance, he thought. I'm licked.

He found a simile from the cricket field. The third evening of a six day match. A side has followed on four hundred runs behind, four wickets are down in their second innings for under a hundred runs. A stand has started. The fast bowlers are tired and have been taken off; the left-hand spinner has hurt his finger. Only a quarter of an hour before stumps are drawn. The batsmen should play out time. Defeat will not come tonight as ninety minutes ago seemed possible. The batsmen will be applauded when they return to the pavilion. But even so there is no hope; there are three days left. The fast bowlers will be refreshed by sleep; a doctor will have fixed the left-hander's finger. Three more days to play, a deficit of three hundred runs. Nothing can save the side but rain; torrential, three days rain. I'm licked, he thought.

He returned to his long chair on the veranda and flung himself full length on it. He was tired, mentally and physically, at the end of this one day, the first out of how many days. He was licked and knew it.

*4*

Only rain could save him.

That night shortly after one he was woken by a heavy downpour. As he lay, sleepless, listening to the drumbeat of the raindrops on the corrugated iron roof, thinking in terms of cricket, he remembered his father telling him of a Test Match long ago in Sydney when Australia had been set in the fourth innings a meager hundred and fifty runs. That night it had rained, as it only can in Sydney. No one in the city slept except one man, Peel, the Yorkshire slow left-hander who, anticipating a fast wicket the next day, had fallen among friends. He slept through it all. He arrived next morning at the ground, bleareyed with a splitting headache. He eyed the puddled asphalt with surprise.

"Looks as though it had rained," he said.

He was the one man in Sydney who did not know it had.

His captain eyeing him sternly, diagnosed the situation.

"It certainly has rained. There is a sticky dog out there. You go and bowl them out on it."

Peel did. England won by ten runs. But when the cheering had subsided, Peel was found sitting in a corner of the dressing room, his head between his hands, not yet fully aware of what had happened.

Only rain could save him. For three-quarters of an hour the rain beat upon the roof, rendering sleep impossible. Cricketers on the eve of a defeat would have gathered hope from it. Nature could always intervene. Fifty years ago, a hundred miles from here, in Martinique, the volcano of Mont Pelée had erupted, and thirty thousand people had perished in forty-five seconds. When the news of that disaster reached Fort-de-France, many secretly must have thought "That lets me out." Evidence of debt, evidence of guilt, records of loans had been destroyed. Sons had inherited estates unexpectedly, an unloved husband had made way for the young lover. To quite a few in Fort-de-France the disaster of Saint Pierre must have been good news. How would he feel sitting here at Belfontaine if a hurricane hit Jamestown. He would anxiously await news of Sylvia and his parents, but would he not also and in a very different spirit be awaiting news of Whittingham. Suppose a high-flung boulder crashed into the police station, hit a lamp and gutted it. Suppose a falling beam pinioned Whittingham beneath its weight. His own troubles would be over then.

It was not impossible. The hurricane season was approaching. It was many years since hurricane or earthquake had struck Santa Marta. Practically every other island had been hit. The immunity of Santa Marta could not last forever. It might happen. He indulged his pipedream, as the drum beat of the rain became a gentle patter.

He woke to a clear morning. The sea was waveless. The palm fronds were not rustling. There was no wind. Absence of wind was the first sign of a hurricane. He had never been in one. He had listened to those who had described it. The temperature went up or down. He could not remember which. You knew about an hour before it struck. It sent its warnings. Whittingham would know about it. He'd have the right security precautions in the station. He had a hurricane-proof shelter there, most likely: as generals had bomb-proof dugouts. Whittingham would not be in any danger. Whittingham would sit at the center of his spider's web, receiving reports of damage, sending out help when it was required. Whittingham was safe.

It was not the way he had pictured it in his last night's pipedream. It would not be Maxwell Fleury sitting safe at Belfontaine who would wait for news of Whittingham in Jamestown, but Whittingham secure in his dugout who would wait news of Maxwell Fleury in his exposed estate house on the windward coast. The roles were reversed. If the news came in that Belfontaine had been destroyed and Maxwell Fleury killed, how cheated Whittingham would feel. His cleverness had been foiled by nature. It would be an end....

473

Maxwell checked; a new idea had struck him. Rain could save him still. There was another way out of his troubles. A second pipedream began to form.

As he sat on the veranda, he imagined the news of the disaster being brought to Jamestown. He pictured Sylvia receiving it. She would be desolate, heartbroken; but she was young, she was attractive. She would get over it. She would marry again within a year or two. But nothing would efface his memory. He was the man who had taught her love, had revealed her to herself. She would never forget that, never. His child would be brought up to honor him. His grandchildren would honor him.

It would be the same with his parents. His mother would remember that last fond talk. "He was always my favorite," she would say. "Mothers always do have a favorite. But I was worried about him, I don't mind confessing it, now. He was difficult. But these last weeks he was a different person. It was Sylvia's faith in him. Yes, I'm sure it was that. And then the baby coming. He'd have been a fine father, I'm sure of that."

He could hear his father saying, "Yes, I'll admit it. I was worried about Maxwell. He was not running that estate the way he should have done. He was not getting the work out of the men. When I planned a trip to England in the autumn, I considered putting Preston in charge of the estate and bringing Maxwell into town where he couldn't do much damage. But these last months he's become aware of his responsibilities. Frankly I was against his running for the Leg. Co. I did not think he stood a chance of making it. But I was wrong; completely wrong. I see now that he was at the start of what would have been a very fine career."

He could hear them talking about him at the club. He knew how they had felt about him four months ago. On the eve of the Governor's cocktail party he had looked at himself in the glass, wondering what was wrong with him, what put people off, why no one liked him. It was different now. Silence did not fall on a group the moment that he joined it. Men came up to him when he stood alone. They would say friendly things about him in the club. Whittingham would be silenced. Whittingham would have been foiled. If, as some said, one lingered after death, an invisible presence, around the places and among the people one had known, he would chuckle over Whittingham's discomfiture.

If a hurricane or earthquake struck Santa Marta, he would welcome it. He would not take cover, he would sit here on the veranda waiting for the earth to tremble, for the house to split, for the boulders to tear down the hills, for an overturned lamp to pour its rivulets of flame along the floor; the way he had seen it in the films.

All day long he indulged his pipedream, hearing the voices at the club, picturing the look of disappointment on Whittingham's fat silly face.

5

Next day the wind was blowing, the sky was gray, the sea was rough. These were not the forewarnings of a hurricane. He must think again. For the sake of exercise, he walked into the village. It looked exactly as it had two days before, lazy, listless, picturesque. He went on to the jetty and sat at the end, swinging his legs over the side. The sea was rougher than he had thought, looking at it from his veranda. He was a strong swimmer, but he doubted if he would be wise in a sea like that to swim beyond his depth.

Suppose he swam out to the horizon, would not that be the equivalent of a hurricane's splitting the foundations of Belfontaine? It would be reported as an accident: no scandal, no shame would be attached. At first they would be surprised in Belfontaine, because they knew him to be a powerful swimmer. But on second considerations they would agree that it was simply because he was a powerful swimmer that he had outswum his strength, underestimated the power of the current. A weak swimmer would have stayed near the shore. No blame, no criticism would be attached. Whittingham would be silenced.

Another pipedream flowered. He remembered that conversation with Jocelyn and Denis Archer at G.H. on the subject of suicide. They had been discussing the easiest method of suicide that would give the appearance of an accident, since often the whole purpose of suicide was to avoid scandal for the family. Wasn't that his own position? But for Sylvia, but for his unborn child, he would be ready to accept Whittingham's offer, to throw himself on Whittingham's mercy. Five years, that might be reduced to three, was not too much for anyone as young as himself. He would not be twenty-five when he was free. He could go to England or to one of the Dominions, he could start afresh, he could change his name, if he had only himself to consider. But he had not only himself to consider. There was Sylvia and the child who would bear his name. A child of his must not know the shame of owning to a father who had committed suicide. That was the crux of the whole problem. It must look like an accident.

If he swam out in a sea as rough as this, who would suspect that he had swum out on purpose. He had only to change into bathing trunks and tell Matilda that he was going to the beach, but that he would be back for lunch; he would order a certain type of omelette,

475

he would leave a half finished letter on his desk, a book with a marker in it beside his chair; he would leave the house at half-past ten. Long before Matilda began to worry about his absence, it would all be over. He would be beyond the reach of any search party. He would leave an honored name.

How easy it would be. He could do it now, if there were any need. He held the remedy in his hand. He had no need to worry. The moment that danger threatened, he could take that medicine. When they had discussed suicide that evening at G.H. no one had suggested swimming out to sea—sleeping in the snow, pheno-barbitone in ships that had no doctor, but to no one had the obvious situation occurred, swim out to sea till your strength failed.

He raised the point next day when Archer came out for lunch. They had taken a picnic to the beach, the same beach to which he had taken Sylvia on that last day together. It was a warm, sultry morning, with occasional brief bursts of rain sweeping up the valley. The sea looked calm and friendly and inviting.

"It would be very easy to swim out there till one was too tired to swim any longer. Why didn't one of us suggest drowning that night at G.H. when we were talking about suicide?"

"I thought of it," Archer said, "but I don't think it's a good idea; it takes too long."

"Why's that a drawback?"

"You might change your mind."

"Is that likely? If a man's made up his mind."

"Do we ever do that, without mental reservations? The will to live is very strong. It can suddenly reassert itself: particularly when other impulses weaken. And when you are growing tired, the fear of punishment and of disgrace might lessen. I knew a stockbroker, a man in the late fifties; he was a gambler; he knew that one day he might be unable to meet his bargains. He was resolved not to be hammered on the Stock Exchange. He had evolved, he told me, a foolproof scheme of suicide, so that nobody could guess what had happened. He had two pills. He was going to take one and then a quarter of an hour later he was going to ring up his doctor and say that he was suffering in a certain way, asking him to come round at once, he would then take the second pill, and before the doctor could arrive the two pills working together would make his death consistent with the symptoms that he had rung up about."

"That sounds highly ingenious."

"It does. I've never quite understood how it worked. I've asked a couple of doctors about it. They couldn't help me. But my friend was confident. He told me about it more than once. He called it his death insurance policy, but the point is that when the time came, he didn't use it. Either it didn't work out, or he lacked the courage. At any rate he was hammered. My own belief is that he changed his mind between the taking of the first pill and the second. There was too long an interval. There's the objection about swimming out to sea. You'd start swimming back or you'd shout for help. I believe there's only one way to do it. Something instantaneous that gives you no time to think, jumping off a skyscraper, or taking strychnine. Think of all the people who start taking sleeping pills, but don't take quite enough."

"You seem to have given the matter a good deal of thought."

"Who hasn't?"

"I haven't."

The denial came from Margot. It was quite a while since she had spoken. She was a silent but an easy guest. Though she rarely spoke, she was part of the conversation. She was alert and interested, looking from one to the other as each spoke. Maxwell was pleasantly conscious of her presence, and much of the two men's conversation was addressed to her. They treated her as a chairman.

They turned to her now, with curiosity.

"Do you mean to say that you've never considered the possibility of suicide: that you've never wondered how you would do it if you found you had to?" Archer asked.

"No. Why should I? I've always known that things would turn out all right."

"Have you all that faith in your Obeah man?"

She shook her head.

"It isn't that. It's just that I just know."

She was seated on the sand with her heels crossed under her. Her smile was candid. It was probably perfectly true, thought Archer, suicide never had occurred to her as a solution for her problems. She knew that things would turn out right. She was a direct, straightforward person; so straightforward that when he thought of her in terms of mystery, of dark, jungle secrets, it was his own complicated self that was seeing its reflection in a mirror. He remembered a story of Maugham's in which a very simple woman earned the reputation of being a wit simply by telling the unvarnished truth. The truth was something that no one in fashionable circles had heard spoken for so long that they found it excruciatingly funny. Perhaps there was nothing puzzling, nothing mysterious about Margot; she only seemed strange to him because he had traveled so far from simplicity. Why should she ponder about suicide? She accepted life.

"I hope that nothing's going to make you feel any differently," he said.

They went back to the house after lunch. The sand flies would not let them sleep upon the sand. Archer chose a long chair on the veranda.

"I like my sleep to be unpremeditated," he explained. "If I go to bed and make a parade of it, I stay awake. But if I take a novel to a long chair after lunch, my eyes close and I fade out peacefully."

Margot curled up on the canvas swing seat. She could always fall asleep whenever she wanted and could stay awake as long as there was anything to stay awake for.

"I'm not as adaptable as that," said Maxwell. "It's a bed for me."

But though he undressed and changed into pajamas, though he closed the jalousies, darkening the room, his brain was racing. "Something instantaneous, that gives you no time to think"; but nothing like a revolver that would carry its rebuke of proof.

A suicide that did not look like suicide. What other solution was there? Whittingham held every card. Sooner or later Whittingham must win. There was no other way of foiling him. No other kind of rain could save him. The papers were talking about war, but that was the surest proof war would not come. The man who talked about committing suicide, never did.

What a solution war would be. Many men must have welcomed the declaration of that last war. A soldier enjoyed a special sanctuary. Whittingham would stay his hand. And how easy to discover in the field of battle a fate that was instantaneous, something that did not give you time to think. There was no equivalent for that in peacetime. Unless . . .

He checked; a sudden idea had struck him: a loophole, a possibility: no, not a possibility, a certainty. He felt of a sudden serenely jubilant. He had the answer; the way of settling every score, with Whittingham and Boyeur, with his past, his present, and his future. Why had he not thought of it before? It was all so very simple. He closed his eyes. For the first time in four months he knew complete peace of mind.

# CHAPTER TWENTY-EIGHT

## 1

Six mornings later Maxwell woke with his mind fresh and clear. He had gone to bed at half-past nine. He had drunk two rum swizzles before dinner and nothing afterward. He had never felt better in his life. He had never felt more conscious of being alive; of being able to enjoy the fact of living.

"Live this day as if thy last"; when he had sung that hymn as a schoolboy, he had wondered whether if he had known a certain day was to be his last, he would as the writer of the hymn imagined, have spent that day in prayer and meditation and good works. Wouldn't he rather have tried to extract from each moment the maximum of enjoyment, wouldn't he have done or tried to do all the things he was afraid of attempting, when his deeds would have an aftermath.

At different ages he had different ideas as to what he would choose to do. At one time he had wanted to ride his father's chestnut in the point-to-point: at another to drive the Colonial Secretary's Jaguar in record time round the island. There was a period when he had been curious to smoke marijuana. At another he had listed the three most attractive girls upon the island, to whom he had been timid about the making of advances. On his last day he would know no such shyness; and one of the three surely would submit.

But now he had no impatience to savor pleasures he had been afraid to taste. Was there anything he wanted to do that he had not already done? He had no wish ever to get drunk again. It was not particularly amusing, and marijuana as a stimulant would probably be no more than a heightened form of alcohol, bearing the same relation to brandy that brandy bore to wine. There were a number of young women whom he found attractive; but could one of them give him a quarter of what Sylvia had done? He would much prefer on his last day to brood over his last hours with Sylvia.

He was very lucky, he told himself. Here in a last day mood, there was nothing to nag at his curiosity or envy. There was nothing for him to do, but get the maximum of enjoyment out of each familiar detail of an average day, to treat his last day as though it were any other day: but to remind himself at each moment how good each moment was. He was lucky to be able to do that.

He stood on the brink of the cold shower, hesitating, as he always did before subjecting himself to the first slightly unpleasant shock of ice cold water, reminding himself that there was little more exquisite than the moment a few seconds later when his skin was adjusted to the chill, and tingled to the sting of it; when he was loth to step from under it, it was so refreshing.

Drying himself he walked to the stairs and called down to Matilda. "Tea in five minutes."

How good was that first morning cup of tea with a thin slice of white bread and butter, in the cool of the morning seated on a veranda with the cane fields fresh and green and sparkling, with the dew not yet dried out of them. It's the last time, he thought. I must make the most of it.

There were no workmen at the *boucan*, waiting for their roll call, but he saddled his pony and rode round there all the same. How long would it be before the workmen mustered again here in the morning light? Who would read the first roll call when they did? What would they be thinking when they heard their names read by another voice? Would they miss him, would they feel guilty?

He ordered a couple of soft boiled eggs for breakfast "and fry the bacon till it's so crisp that you can crack it."

It was American bacon, from a tin. He had been keeping it for an occasion. He had never realized how good bacon could be till he had eaten this kind of bacon, cooked this way. It had never tasted better than it did that morning.

"What about lunch and dinner now, Matilda."

Lunch would be the last meal that he would eat. He had often wondered what he would order if he were a condemned man taking his last dinner.

"I'll have cold fish soup," he said, "an omelette: stuffed with spaghetti, and afterward a soursop ice cream. Is that O.K.?"

"Yes, sir, that O.K."

"And then for dinner."

It was ironic to be ordering a dinner that he would not eat.

"Not too heavy a meal," he said. "Have we any pawpaw?"

"Yes, sir, we have pawpaw."

"Then pawpaw first. After that some meat; pork chop perhaps."

"Pork chop. I not think, sir: no one kill pig yesterday."

"What about kidneys?"

"Kidneys, maybe, sir."

"Good then, you find kidneys: grill them. Cheese afterward."

Who, he wondered, would eat those kidneys? Who and when? Perhaps he would be eating them himself. It was not certain yet

480

that this day was his last. That knowledge softened the sharpness of this last day feeling.

He rang up Sylvia. It would not be the last time he heard her voice, yet at the same time there was a chance it might be. That knowledge made him reluctant to hang up, made him talk with a deeper tenderness.

It had been arranged that he should come in on Sunday for rum punches at *Grande Anse*. He could find no excuse this time for staying out.

"Do you know that it'll be eleven days since I've seen you?" he was saying.

"That isn't my fault, is it? I'm ready to come out any time to see you."

"Not twice in a day, darling, on the rough road."

"I don't see why it should have to be twice. There's no danger, nothing's going to happen."

"I'll be a better judge of that after tonight."

"Why after tonight?"

"Boyeur's making a speech out here."

"He's making speeches everywhere."

"I know, but it's different here. I'm going down to hear him. I want to judge the temper of the crowd."

"You'll be careful, won't you?"

"You bet I will be, with Sunday only two days off."

"Ah, Sunday."

"Will anyone be joining us?"

"I haven't asked anyone. Jocelyn may have."

"Anyhow we'll have two cars. We needn't stay there too long. I'll be tired after my drive in. I'll be needing a siesta."

"Probably I shall be too."

She said it with a chuckle. She wouldn't have chuckled that way six months ago. Why must this have happened? That chuckle made his heart beat fast. It was very easy to go on talking.

"And then I'll be coming in on Wednesday for the Leg. Co."

"Of course. When Boyeur apologizes."

Boyeur's apology. How would he make it and to whom? Perhaps he wouldn't be there. His goose might have been cooked too.

"I don't see why I shouldn't risk it that night and stay up."

"Why don't you?"

"I shan't see anything of you unless I do."

Why am I talking like this, he thought. Pretending that next week would be like every other week. But that's what he had to do, hadn't he; make it look unplanned?

481

"I'll probably ring you late this evening. To tell you how the meeting went. Till then, my sweet, I'm missing you."

He stood, pensive by the line, drawing a double-edged savor from the situation. This might be the end, it might not be the end. He must behave as though it wouldn't be. He must make the most of every second.

After breakfast Maxwell drove round to Preston's. They discussed the temper of the village.

"They're all right now. But heaven knows what they'll be like tonight," said Preston, "after that damned man's been at them."

"I'd thought of going down. Will you be there?"

Preston shook his head.

"I couldn't stand it. I'd lose my temper."

"I'll be tempted too, but I feel I should go down, as a witness, to see the kind of thing he does say to them. It may be useful ammunition at the Leg. Co."

Tomorrow Preston would be recounting that conversation in the club at Jamestown. He would embroider the episode. "We nearly went down together," he would say, "but I felt that I couldn't stomach it. I wish now I had gone down with him."

Maxwell was outside himself, watching himself, picturing how everything he said and did, the way he looked, would be reported back to Jamestown. As he drove back to Belfontaine he pictured them in the club tomorrow, talking with lowered voices.

All day it was like that. He had never been more conscious of being alive, yet everything seemed unreal. This could not be really happening.

2

Boyeur's meeting was fixed for half-past five: the last hour of daylight. Maxwell planned to get there shortly before six. Boyeur would have warmed up by then, so would the crowd. He sat on the veranda, watching the sun lower in the sky. He was restless and impatient. Last night he had begun a detective story. He had a hundred pages still to read. It was an exciting story but he could not concentrate upon it. He could not read a hundred pages in half an hour and if he skipped it, he would miss the clues. It was tantalizing to read a book he would not finish.

It was quarter-past five. They would have started to collect now in the square before the police station, just as they had four months ago at his first meeting, when Boyeur had sauntered into the avenue of light. Why had he done that? Why had Boyeur instigated that demonstration? He had never done Boyeur any harm. Boyeur, it

482

was all Boyeur's fault. It all led back to Boyeur. If Boyeur had not humiliated him, had not fired his blood...Boyeur. Boyeur. He clenched his fists.... That at least was a score that would not stay long unsettled.

He rose and paced the veranda. Twenty past five. Where would Sylvia be? At the tennis club, or waiting to start for the tennis club. He looked at the telephone in the hall. Was he never to see Sylvia again? And yet he could speak to her. The apparatus that was nailed there on the wall could bring him close to her.

He walked across to it, spun the handle, lifted the receiver. There was a babble of voices. The party line again. He hung the receiver back. He returned to the veranda. He heard the sound of a car upon the road. Was it Boyeur's car? It was traveling fast. He craned his neck. At the turn of the road, between the palms, he saw a flash of yellow. Yes, that was Boyeur's new M.G. How did he afford a car like that; out of union funds: out of contributions wrung from laborers? Boyeur, that cheap upstart.

His temper rose again. His fists clenched. The black blind fury that had made him as a child fling his toys across the room was on him. He could use a drink, but caution counseled him against it. There must be no taint of alcohol upon his breath. He must allow no loophole for the defense of a drunken brawl. Drink. That suggested something. The kidneys he had ordered that night for dinner. His father had always told him that you should let a young red wine breathe for an hour or so before drinking it. He'd decant a half bottle of claret and let it stand in the dining room with the stopper out.

The wine was stored in a cool stone-built basement. His father had always prided himself upon his cellar. One of his earliest memories was of being taken down with Jocelyn on Sunday mornings to decant the port. Jocelyn had stood goggling at the ritual of muslin, the silver strainer, the candle beneath the shoulder of the bottle.

"I hope the cork doesn't break, oh, I hope the cork doesn't break." She would repeat it like a chant, but he had known that she was secretly hoping that it would break.

"You were glad it broke, you were glad it broke," he would rebuke her afterward, and she would burst out crying. They had never got on together, he and Jocelyn.

All the port was gone now; the last bottle had been drunk on VJ day, and the cost of laying down vintage port had become prohibitive; but his father had restocked his bins with adequate table wines. He took out a half bottle of what his father had described to him as "casual claret"; transferred it as his father had taught him into a wicker basket and poured it very slowly into the decanter, watching for the thin dark line of sediment to reach the shoulder. "I shall never do this again," he thought.

He sniffed the decanter before he placed it on the sideboard. It might be a casual claret, but it had a pleasant aroma. He wished he could have sipped it, but that might have seemed suspicious. Nothing must look suspicious.

It was twenty-five to six. Boyeur would have started speaking now, unless he was too grand to be punctual.

Maxwell crossed into the hall. The party line should be clear by now. It was. There was a silence, interrupted by a faint buzz-buzz. Then a high-pitched West Indian voice. No, mistress Sylvia was not at home. She go tennis club.

"O.K., Susan. Tell her I called. Master Maxwell. No, no message. I'll call later. Give her my love."

He pictured their thin scraggy little maid at the telephone. He could hear her repeating the message to Sylvia on her return. "He sends you his love, Mistress Sylvia." When would she get that message? Half-past eight? Would she know by then? He walked to the head of the basement stairway.

"I'm going out for a little while," he called. "I'll be back in an hour, but don't put those kidneys on until I come."

He walked to the stone stairway. The sun was very near now to the horizon. The clouds edging it were lined with orange; the sky was slashed with a succession of pale greens and blues and lavenders. His last sunset was certainly putting on a show for him. This isn't true. This can't be happening, he told himself.

He parked his car, a hundred yards from the meeting. He did not want his arrival to be observed. He stood at the back of the crowd. Boyeur must have been speaking for about twenty minutes. His voice had loudened and grown hoarse; his audience was shouting applause at the end of every sentence. He was like a bandmaster, with arms outstretched, his fingers spread apart, conducting the outbursts, spacing them, now calming them, now exacerbating them. The crowd had become a single person, obedient, mesmerized, his to do what he chose with.

"The planters have declared war on us," he was crying. "They have refused our demands, our just demands. We must return war with war. They forced us to strike. Because of them, the strike has lasted two whole weeks. Our funds are not exhausted. Our funds will last us for many weeks. But in order that they may last for several, we must use them carefully. If you were shipwrecked on an island with no chance of rescue for a month, what would you do with your food; you would divide it, would you not, so that it would last a month. So much a week, so much a day. You would not say, 'I am used to having so much food each day I must have this and that tomorrow.' If you did that, all your food would have been eaten before the ship arrived. For ten days you would have had no food. Many of you would have starved to death before the ship arrived. The food would have to be divided out, so much each day. And that is what we must do with our strike funds, divide them, so that no matter how long the strike lasts we shall have funds to fight the planters. They cannot hold out forever. Time is on our side. No one will tend their cattle, cut their cane, pick their cocoa, slice their coconuts. We may be hungry for a little, but they will be ruined and the land will become ours. We have worked the land: because of us the land is rich. By right the land is ours. Soon the land will be ours by law."

Boyeur paused and the screams became vociferous. As Preston prophesied, Maxwell thought, he'd cut down the strike pay so as to get quick results. He needn't have, but he hadn't the temperament for waiting. He wanted immediate action. Well, he'd get it. More than he expected, more than he bargained for.

Maxwell was acutely conscious of the crowd's mounting tension. His own temperature rose to meet it, in an adverse sense. His hatred for Boyeur was as electric as the crowd's hatred for the planters. Boyeur was wearing a white and blue tropical corded suit, in the latest style of which a few models had recently been imported from America. His shirt was white; he had a long thin-ended blue and white polka dot tie. He looked very elegant and handsome: very virile too. He was a natural leader: a man whom men would be proud not only to follow but to suffer for. He was an enemy worth bringing down, even if his own downfall was entailed. Samson leaning on those two pillars.

"The planters, those Sugar Barons, have declared war on us," Boyeur was continuing. "In war there are no rules. You make your own rules. An eye for an eye, a tooth for a tooth. Do not spare the enemy who will not spare you. Things are allowed in wartime that are not allowed in peacetime. In peacetime you may not steal, you may not plunder. But in wartime it is not stealing, it is not plunder to take the goods that an enemy is not strong enough to defend."

A shriek of applause went up. Yes, this was it, Maxwell told himself. Incitement to violence, incitement to robbery: there was no doubt of that. In the same way that West Indian politicians in a legislative assembly would indulge in violence that would be unheard

485

of in Westminster or Washington, so does a West Indian demagogue on the platform speaking to his followers use language that in Europe and America would demand police intervention.

Was there a policeman here? Maxwell wondered. Probably there wasn't. Local police had the sense to keep away from trouble. But there must be witnesses. Someone who would testify tomorrow. He was still outside himself, watching himself, thinking in terms of Jamestown, of Whittingham, and of the club.

"War is war," Boyeur was repeating. "There are no laws in wartime."

Another minute or so more, Maxwell told himself. Hysteria was mounting round him. Hysteria was firing his veins. It was going the way he had planned. "Something instantaneous. Something that didn't give him time to think." He'd settle his own business and Boyeur's too, and Whittingham's into the bargain. Another minute, only a minute more.

"The land is yours, the houses upon the land are yours. In wartime, you have the right to plunder, to destroy. In wartime you bomb open towns, drop atom bombs upon civilians. A strike is a war. Treat these fields, treat these houses, treat all that belongs to these Sugar Barons as in the war we treated the houses and the fields of the Japanese and Germans; take what you need, destroy what you cannot use. It is yours, yours, yours; to take or to destroy. Yours, yours, yours."

A scream answered each shouted "Yours." This was the moment. Something instantaneous. He drove his elbows sideways into the ribs of the laborers at his side. "Out of my way," he shouted.

His voice drowned the hubbub. With his elbows working fast, to left and right, he forced his way toward the table on which Boyeur stood, and jumped upon it. It was a long trestle table, such as is found in Army barracks, fifteen feet long and a yard wide. For a moment he faced Boyeur. There was astonishment and indignation in Boyeur's face. "You here," he said.

Maxwell laughed; the blood was pounding in his veins. He had done that something instantaneous. He had no time to think now, only to act. He had reached the point of no return. He had to go forward. Beyond Boyeur's shoulder he saw the local constable coming out on to the veranda of the police court. So he had his witness. All was well then.

He turned from Boyeur and faced the crowd. There were some hundred of them, staring up at him with stupid gaping mouths.

"Don't you believe him," he yelled at them. "There are plenty of funds. There is all the money that is needed. But he doesn't want you to have it. He wants to keep it for himself. He wants to spend it on himself, on his clothes, on his women: on that fast sports car over there. Look at him. Look at those clothes. Where does the money come from? From you. Can you afford clothes like that, of course you can't. But he can, though he is one of you. How can he afford such clothes, such a car, such women? Because he has your money; the five cents that you give out of your pay each week. That's how he buys that car, those clothes. That's where your money goes. Now when you need your money, you have not got it: because he has spent it, on himself. Look at him now. Look. . . ."

"Stop. Listen."

Boyeur pushed himself forward to the edge of the table; with his arms outstretched he appealed again to the inflamed temper of the crowd.

"Don't listen to him, don't believe him. He is one of your enemies. A planter. One of the Sugar Barons. He and his type have lied to you all their lives. They have tricked and robbed you. They stole you from your families in Africa. They brought you in slave ships across the ocean; out of every ten, three of you died in every crossing. They kept you in chains, they beat and tortured you. And when honorable men in Europe and America demanded that those chains be broken, they kept you still in slavery by paying you starvation wages. You had no rights, no property, no votes. They denied you human justice."

It was the familiar jargon of the West Indian demagogue. Maxwell made no attempt to interrupt him. Let Boyeur work upon the mob, and he, in his turn, would goad Boyeur, as he had in the Leg. Co. to the act of final folly that would be his undoing.

"This man has pointed at my clothes, at my car. But I point at that house of his upon the hill. How much did that cost? Think of the bricks brought out from England. Think of the furniture inside; the glass, the silver. Think of the rich food that has been eaten there, the sparkling wine that has been drunk there: think of the jewels and the silks that have been worn there by the Fleury women. How long has that been going on, for two hundred years: for seven generations. Think what that means in money, in two hundred years. And where has that money come from? From you, from your parents, from your great-great-grandparents, from their toil and sweat. Wrung from them, day by day, hour by hour, by their labor in the cane fields under the cruel sun. That was how Belfontaine was built, how the life at Belfontaine was paid for, out of your toil, your labor."

He paused at each full stop. And each time he paused a scream went up from the crowd. He had got them where he wanted them. Their eyes gleamed, their faces glistened; they waved their arms, brandished their cutlasses. Maxwell had seen them look like this at Carnival, but at Carnival they were mad with happiness, with good will; now they were inflamed by hate. They were Boyeur's chattels. A little longer, Maxwell thought, a yard or two more of rope. The contagious excitement of the crowd had caught him. The old black fury was upon him. He looked with loathing and disgust at the docile upturned faces. What slaves they were, following the loudest voice.

"He calls himself one of you," Boyeur was shouting, "because he has one minute particle of African blood in his veins. His grandmother came from Jamaica. She was slightly dark: but what is that minute trickle of colored blood compared with the long broad river of Fleury ancestry?"

Maxwell smiled wryly. A small particle indeed: so small that no one had ever known of it till Bradshaw broke the story, but small though it was it had been enough to bring him all this trouble. If he had been wholly white would that blind fury have taken control of him when his hands had fastened upon Carson's throat; that blind ungovernable fury that had made him throw Sylvia into the mosquito net? At certain moments he was a beast, not a man. It was in his blood to be. A thin, thin trickle but it had forced this desperate remedy upon him: had made him capable of swallowing the bitter draught of this desperate remedy.

"He says he is one of you," Boyeur was shouting. "He told you that at the election, and tricked you into voting for him; but he is not one of you: Look at him. He looks a white man. He is a white man in all that counts. He is on the other side. He is . . ."

Maxwell pushed forward. It was time to interrupt, time to goad the crowd, as he had goaded Boyeur. He had clenched his fists. He was held by the wild fury, but he was in control of it. It was a white hot passion that he could exploit for his own purpose. He looked with loathing at the gibbering faces. It was because of his kinship with them that he was in this trouble.

"He's right," he shouted. "I'm not one of you. I'm on the other side. I belong to the white people. But I have that fraction of colored blood in my veins, and because I have it I can understand you. I know what you are worth, I know what you are good for, I know and I can tell you. You were brought here to work as slaves: you were slaves most of you in your own country first. That's what you are; slaves. That's what you still ought to be."

A roar of fury greeted him. The shriek delighted him. It was what he wanted.

"You are idle, stupid, ignorant. You'll only work when a whip's cracked behind you. You can't think for yourselves, you follow any master: the man with the loudest voice. You all voted for me at the elections, now you listen to this cheap popinjay."

Shriek after shriek greeted every pause. He was following Boyeur's technique, pausing at each full stop. They were out of all control. Another minute, he thought, and they'll be ripe. I know them.

"Slaves you were and slaves you should be. Slaves you are, following a thing like this."

He turned and swung round facing Boyeur. You must keep your head, he warned himself. Picture the witness standing up in court. You've got your witness watching from the darkness of the station. This mustn't be reported as a brawl. All the responsibility must lie upon the other side.

He glanced back at the angry faces.

"The white people flatter you," he shouted. "They tell you that you're as good as they are. They give you a vote, they give you self-government, they finance your projects. I know how wrong they are, because I've that small dark part of you inside me. You're idle, dishonest, stupid; listening to the loudest voice. Take no notice of what this man says. Get back to work while you still have the chance. Before troops are landed and you're sent back in chains. Don't you forget it, you're still slaves at heart."

The crowd was like a cageful of beasts at feeding time. Now, he thought, now's the moment. He swung round to Boyeur. Boyeur had lost control, just as the crowd had done. He only needed the final prick of the goad. Maxwell leant toward him. No one but Boyeur must hear what he said. There must be no extenuating circumstance. He dropped his voice.

"You," he said, "whose girl walked out on him the moment a white man raised his little finger. How long do you think you'll hold that Muriel of yours? Only till something better comes along. Someone with a better skin."

He hissed the final word. He saw Boyeur's face contort, saw his right arm swing back. He made no attempt to duck, to guard himself. A blow struck without provocation, against unclenched fists.

The blow struck him below the eye. His cheek bone cracked. He staggered, off his balance, he put back his foot. It missed the edge of the table and he fell. He flung out his arms, and his hands clutched at a bare, damp shoulder, his nails gripped for a hold.

This isn't true, this can't be happening, he thought.

He was half stunned, he was only kept from fainting by the sharp excruciating pain below his eye. His fall was broken by a human wall: as his feet were grounded, he struck out. A huge hard knuckled fist crashed against his ear. He would have fallen had he had room to fall.

"Let him have it, boys." Boyeur's voice rang clear, breaking through the fog of pain that obscured Maxwell's senses. Maxwell gloated at the sound of it. Ah, that was what he wanted; the final testimony: Boyeur's score was settled and so was Whittingham's. The blows crashed in on him from every angle of the narrow ring that hemmed him. He swayed from one side of the circle to another, his equilibrium maintained like a top's as he spun from one blow to another. His knees were weakening. He was half-conscious; no human frame could endure this. Boyeur brought down, Whittingham foiled; Sylvia saved, their child's honor saved.

Sylvia, he heard her voice with its new note of tenderness. He felt her head's weight upon his shoulder, saw her hair scattered on the pillow. Why had this had to happen? Why, why, why?

Through half-dimmed eyes he saw the red glow of sunset on a cutlass, saw it and saw nothing more.

# CHAPTER TWENTY-NINE

*1*

"Maxwell Fleury is dead, killed in a strike riot. David Boyeur is under arrest. The Governor has declared martial law and the strike is broken. A British Man-of-war is anchored in the harbor."

Carl Bradshaw sat back in his chair and reread the opening paragraph of the last article that he would transmit from Santa Marta. Nothing that he had written in his whole life had given him greater satisfaction. Here was the evidence of his reestablishment. His prophecies had come true. How often could a journalist make that boast? He was returning to Baltimore on his own terms. The future stretched before him, rich and bountiful, with autumns in New York, winters in Florida, the spring in Paris, summers in Cannes and Venice; pauses in London, on the way back and forth. He could not ask more of fate. He did not consider its rewards unmerited. The cards had fallen luckily, but not everyone knew how to play a winning hand.

He resumed his article. He was spending a week in Virginia before his return to Baltimore. The plane that dropped him off in Miami could carry on the article. He had to mail it before six o'clock. It was his last article and he meant it to be his best. Since it was his last, he could be outspoken in a way that he had not been able when he was a resident. In all human probability he would never set foot again in Santa Marta. He would never see any of its inhabitants again. He could say what he liked about them. There was no need for discretion. He would not need to consider anybody's feelings. He could tell the truth.

"The news of Maxwell Fleury's death reached Jamestown at seven o'clock by telephone from the local constable who witnessed the incident," he wrote. "The Governor took the action to be expected of a general. He mobilized the police and drove out in person to the scene. David Boyeur was in the police station. The Governor carried a warrant for his arrest, and Boyeur was brought back in handcuffs. Boyeur was placed in the front of an open jeep, so that everyone along the road could see him. Before he arrested Boyeur, the Governor declared martial law, announced that the strike was ended and ordered all field laborers and longshoremen to report for work next morning. It is doubtful whether he had the legal right to do this, and it is possible that on some of the estates the peasants might have refused to return to work. But at four o'clock this morning a British destroyer steamed into Jamestown harbor.

"The arrival of the ship, coupled with the arrest of their leader has convinced the proletariat that the authorities intend to be obeyed. Men of African descent recognize the argument of force; they are also highly superstitious. They regard the arrival of an ironclad within ten hours of the riot as a miracle. Actually the ship had been cruising for the last week within a few hours' range of Santa Marta in case of emergency."

If this had all happened fifty hours later, Bradshaw thought, he would have missed the very story that he had been sent here to get. A lucky break. But luck went to the deserving.

That morning he had obtained an interview with the Governor. Templeton was anxious to have the facts of the case widely known.

"When I take action," he told Bradshaw, "I take strong action. I had Boyeur arrested on a charge of inciting to riot. But from what I have heard since, I believe that we can make out a case for incitement to kill. I shall discuss it this afternoon with the Attorney General, the head of police and one or two of our notables. Julian Fleury and Humphrey Norman for example. Personally I should like to see Boyeur tried on a charge of murder."

"May I state that, sir, as your opinion, or is that off the record?"

The Governor hesitated, then committed himself. "Yes, you can express that as my personal opinion. If the evidence is as strong as I think it is, I shall advise—no, I shall urge the Attorney General to prosecute."

Bradshaw reported the conversation word for word. Such was the Governor's wish, he wrote, but whether the Governor's wish was to be granted was another matter. The situation was impossibly entangled by personal relations.

"I will make no attempt to assess probabilities," he wrote. "I will content myself with a bare statement of certain facts. The Governor's son is engaged to be married to Jocelyn Fleury, the sister of the dead man. The Attorney General's sister is engaged to be married to David Boyeur. Humphrey Norman, one of the counselors whom the Governor proposes to consult, is chairman of the Tourist Board and chief shareholder in the St. James Hotel; it is in his personal interest that an example should be set that will reassure the tourist. He was also Maxwell Fleury's father-in-law. Four months ago the name of his other daughter Mavis was linked with that of the Governor's son. This correspondent reported a curious scene that took place between the two outside the courthouse when Mavis Norman angrily shook away young Templeton's arm. The

Governor's A.D.C. has been conducting for four months an intrigue with a young colored shop girl who obtained, through his influence presumably, a post in the G.H. secretariat. This girl, before she became Archer's mistress, had been for two years Boyeur's mistress. It may be presumed that this girl discarded Boyeur because the A.D.C. was white. It would be hard to find a situation in which the personal relationships were more entangled. High affairs of state are as often as not determined by the personal equation. As to the eventual outcome of the present situation in Santa Marta, anyone's guess is as good as this correspondent's."

And that was that, thought Bradshaw. Santa Marta was a closed chapter now: tomorrow at this time he would be high above the Caribbean, on his way "to fame and fortune."

2

In the Governor's study, in the house high upon the hill, five men were at the moment deliberating the issue that had formed the subject of Bradshaw's article. In addition to the Governor there were Whittingham and Grainger Morris, Humphrey Norman and Julian Fleury. The constable from Belfontaine was recapitulating his evidence. Whittingham set the questions.

"Could you hear what David Boyeur said in his speech to the crowd before Maxwell Fleury interrupted him?"

"Not the actual words, sir, but the general argument." The constable gave the gist of the speech.

"Was it very violent?"

"Mr. Boyeur is always violent."

"Was the crowd excited?"

"The crowd is always excited when Mr. Boyeur speaks."

"Was the crowd more excited than usual?"

The constable shook his head. No, on the whole he did not think so.

"Were you yourself watching all the time?"

The constable shook his head. No, he had stayed inside his office, listening. He had not come out of his office till Mr. Maxwell Fleury had made his interruption.

"How did you know he had interrupted?"

"I heard another voice shouting Mr. Boyeur down."

"So that until Maxwell Fleury made his interruption, you can give no evidence on anything that happened. You saw nothing. You only heard what Boyeur said and how the crowd received him?"

Yes that was so, the constable admitted.

"But after the interruption you saw everything?"

493

"Yes, I saw everything."

"How long was the table?"

"It was an ordinary issue table, borrowed from the station."

"How far apart did the two men stand?"

"As far apart as they could stand."

"Three, four feet?"

"About that."

"And what did Maxwell Fleury say?"

"He told the crowd that they were idle, sneaking, good-for-nothings; that they ought to be slaves."

"And the crowd got angry?"

"Very angry. They waved their arms."

"Did any of them have cutlasses?"

"Yes, sir, several."

"Do you remember which men had cutlasses?"

No, he could not remember.

"So that you cannot say that it must have been one out of ten or twelve men who had cutlasses?"

No, he could not say that.

"What about Boyeur? How did he take Fleury's interruption?"

"He got very angry."

"What did he do?"

"He interrupts Mr. Fleury. He shouts him down. He says that Mr. Maxwell Fleury is one of the enemy."

"Did he threaten Maxwell Fleury?"

No, the constable could not say that he had done that.

"What happened then? Did Maxwell Fleury interrupt again?"

"Yes and called him names; an upstart, a no-good fellow. And then Mr. Maxwell Fleury leans forward to Mr. Boyeur and says something I can't hear; and—"

"What's that? Something you can't hear. Was that the first thing you couldn't hear?"

"Yes, up to then each shouts, but this time Mr. Fleury leans forward and whispers something. And then Mr. Boyeur punches Mr. Maxwell, and Mr. Maxwell falls back into the crowd. And that's the last thing that I do see, the table is in the way. There is a lot of shouting and something seems to be happening, and then the noise begins to quiet and then there isn't any noise at all, and the people in front are pushing back to get away and those in the back are trying to push in front. And then I think I had better go and see what happens, and . . ."

"Please wait a moment. What was David Boyeur doing all this time?"

"Nothing, sir."

"Nothing?"

"He stand on the table all the time."

"Didn't he try and stop what was happening?"

"No, sir, I don't think so."

"Did he stand there, silent? That's not like him. Didn't he shout out anything?"

"Yes, sir, he shout something."

"What did he shout?"

"I can't tell, sir, there is so much noise."

"Now listen, Simpson, this is very important. You heard practically everything else that was said. But this one thing you could not hear."

"There was much more noise then, sir. I never hear so much noise. Everybody shouting."

Grainger intervened.

"I see your point perfectly. You cannot be absolutely certain of what you heard, so you prefer to say nothing. You are afraid of bearing false testimony, that's it, isn't it?"

"Yes, sir. That is it."

"And if you were in a court of law, giving evidence on oath, you would be quite right to say that you did not hear what Mr. Boyeur said. But you are not in a court of law, you are not giving evidence on oath. You are simply telling us unofficially what you saw and what you think you heard. What you think you heard may be of great value, because we can check by it something that someone else may have thought they heard. By comparing four or five different versions we may discover what Mr. Boyeur actually said. You see my point?"

"Yes, sir, I see your point."

"Then I think you should tell us what you think you heard. And I give you my word that what you say now will not be quoted against you in a court of law. We want you to tell us what you think you heard for our own information. You see my point?"

"Yes, sir, I see."

"Then what did you think you heard?"

Again the constable hesitated.

"You understand, sir, I cannot be sure."

"Yes, yes, we understand."

"Well then, I think he said, sir, 'Let him have it, boys.' "

There was a gasp from Humphrey Norman. The Governor glanced at Julian Fleury. There was no expresion on Julian Fleury's face. It was firm and set, with the lips closed tightly. Grainger looked across at Whittingham and nodded. It was the colonel's turn.

"When you reached the meeting, what was Boyeur doing?"

"Staring at the corpse, sir."

"He'd stayed on the table all the time?"

"Yes, sir, all the time."

"Did he say anything?"

" 'They've killed him,' that's all he said. He kept repeating it. He was dazed. He stood there staring. I asked him who had done it. He shook his head. 'They've killed him,' he kept on saying that, 'They've killed him.' "

"Were there a number of men there too?"

"Yes, and childun."

"What were they doing?"

"Staring at the corpse."

"You've got their names?"

"Yes, sir."

"You questioned them?"

"Not one by one. I had no time: so much to do, to ring you up, sir. Take photographs before it was dark. I had no one to help me."

"Yes, yes, I know. And you did your job extremely well. I'm very pleased with you. You didn't question the group individually. You asked them as a group who had done this. What did they say?"

"They say they didn't know. They couldn't see. They were at the back. The men at the front all gone away."

Whittingham and Grainger exchanged a glance. They could picture the scene. Boyeur on the table, dazed, and the men and children in a half circle gazing at the corpse with a fascinated, frightened horror. Maxwell Fleury lying face downward, his arms spread out, the trickle of blood congealing in the dust, and the daylight fading fast. How could you get evidence? There were fingerprints on Maxwell's coat and on his shirt: someone had caught him by the shirt and collar. But even if they fingerprinted the whole island, and how could they do that, what would they have proved? That such and such men had been there at that moment. That was all. It did not even prove that they had struck him. It only proved that they were witnesses, or might have been witnesses.

Who had swung that cutlass? That was the vital fact and how was that to be discovered? Boyeur might know. But Boyeur would not dare reveal it. The man would assert inevitably in his defense that he had been instigated, incited by his leader. "Let him have it, boys." Neither Whittingham nor Grainger had the slightest doubt that the constable had heard correctly. Boyeur in his own interests must stay silent. They would get nothing out of him. They would never find the killer. But a charge of incitement to murder against Boyeur might be maintained.

"You have told us," Grainger said, "that Maxwell Fleury leant forward and spoke in a low voice to Boyeur. The next thing that happened was the blow struck by Boyeur that knocked Fleury into the crowd. Was that the only blow that Boyeur struck?"

"Yes, sir."

"Before that happened had there been any threatening gestures made by either party? Had Fleury clenched his fists or framed up as though he meant to fight?"

"No, sir."

"Did you ask any of the men in the crowd if they heard what Fleury whispered to Boyeur?"

"No, sir. . . . Well, I no remember. . . . there was so much—"

"I know, I know. It's not important, but when you get back to the village see if you can clear up that point. It might be of interest. Up to that point there had been no sign of a fight, you say."

"No, sir."

"But young Fleury never struck at Boyeur."

It was Norman who interjected that. "Boyeur struck at a man who had not attacked him, who was off his guard, who was not even threatening to attack him. That is the main point."

A few more questions were asked, then the constable was dismissed.

"I trust," the Governor said to him, "you do not think because we have asked you all these questions that we are in any way criticizing you. Your conduct has been exemplary. It has been more than that. You acted with intelligence and initiative; it will appear upon the record."

As the door closed behind the constable, Templeton turned to the advisors.

"Now, gentlemen, I should like to hear your opinions. Julian?"

Julian Fleury shook his head.

"I've nothing to say. My son is dead. Justice must take its course."

"Mr. Norman?"

Norman had a great deal to say. An incident like this, following on Carson's murder and the publicity which it had received in the American papers would do an incalculable amount of harm to the tourist trade. Look how much harm had been done to Grenada by those mild riots, which had entailed no loss of life, and little of property. Young Fleury's death following upon Carson's would give American and Canadian tourists the idea that a white man was not safe here. There was only one way in which that impression could be dispersed. Drastic action must be taken to show that authority had been re-established.

"We must set an example," he insisted. "We have entertained a number of journalists here for ten days, at considerable expense.

Instead of having them say the kind of thing that we want said, they will write sensational 'we guessed it all along' articles. Santa Marta has barely been in the news till this last four months. Now it will be associated in everybody's mind with crime and pillage. It will be considered a place to avoid. Pan American will reconsider their plan to make a stop here and that is of prime importance to us. It may take us years to live down this damage. Our only chance of reinstating ourselves in the good graces of the world is by setting a disciplinary example. Boyeur is responsible and Boyeur must be dealt with as a criminal."

He spoke for a dozen minutes. The Governor listened, nodding his head from time to time; as a junior officer, after a tactical exercise he had listened to sergeants and corporals explaining the reasons for their actions. He had rarely interrupted. He had let them talk themselves out. He followed that technique now. He waited till Norman was about to cover the same ground for the fourth time, then without interruption, he amplified Norman's arguments.

"That's a very interesting point of view. That's something we must not lose sight of. A dollar shortage is one of the Empire's greatest problems. We must do all we can here to save dollars, and to make dollars. The tourist revenue is of great importance. You are absolutely right, Mr. Norman. At the same time the Attorney General will, I am sure, remind us that expediency plays no part in the demands of justice. We must govern this island in terms of its laws, even if the carrying out of those laws is opposed to our immediate interests. I would like now to ask Colonel Whittingham this question, do you consider that on the evidence you and your police can collect you will have a case that you can present to the Attorney General strong enough to warrant a prosecution on a charge of murder?"

"Yes, sir, I do."

"Then in that case, Mr. Morris?"

Grainger hesitated. There was so much that he had to say and at the same time so little. He could have talked on the pro's and con's of the case for an hour, but the issue was, in fact, a very simple one: a question of alternatives.

"There's one thing that puzzles me," he said. "Perhaps Mr. Fleury could help me in it. I have been back here in Santa Marta for only a few months: there's a great deal that I do not know about the personal relations existing between the various members of the community. I don't know what are the roots of the quarrels and friendships that determine social life here, therefore I don't recognize the danger signal. I am liable to make a false diagnosis. It has become quite clear for example that there was genuine ill feeling between these young men. I don't know what is the cause of it, I wish I knew what it was. Perhaps Mr. Fleury knows."

Julian Fleury looked surprised.

"Why do you say that? They hardly knew each other. What points of contact had they? They didn't play games together. My son's game was tennis, Boyeur is a cricketer. There's never been any rivalry between them in any field. Why should there have been ill will between them?"

Grainger gave his reasons. He spoke of Boyeur's demonstration at Maxwell's election meeting. He spoke of the Leg. Co. meeting.

"On that occasion, sir, Maxwell Fleury deliberately goaded Boyeur."

"How can you say that?" This came from Fleury. Grainger addressed the chair.

"Is your Excellency aware of the precise sting in the remark of Fleury's that drew Boyeur to his feet?"

"I'd like you to give me your interpretation of it."

"I can give you the facts, sir. You have working in your secretariat a girl called Margot Seaton."

"I have. She is a cousin of David Boyeur."

"Did she say that? I doubt it very much. But she was without any doubt Boyeur's mistress for two years. She is now the mistress of your A.D.C. Boyeur is very touchy about having been supplanted by a white man."

The Governor smiled. He had been taken off his guard; but he was accustomed to shocks. He was not going to show he had been.

"This is news to me," he said. "They always say, don't they, that a husband is the last person to learn of his wife's indiscretions."

The young scamp, he thought; getting his girl invited to that dance. It was at that dance that she had angled her post upon his staff. She had managed that herself. She must be quite a person. He did not know that Archer had it in him.

"At the Leg. Co. meeting," Grainger was continuing, "there was deliberate provocation. A few days ago they nearly came to blows in the club."

"I hadn't heard of that," said Fleury.

Grainger recounted the incident.

"There was very definite bad blood between the two," he said. "There's this too to be considered. What was young Fleury doing at that meeting? It's most unusual for a man in his position to go to that kind of meeting. It's below his dignity. And if he did go, why did he interfere? You may say he went there as a counselor to document himself on the temper of the crowd, and Boyeur's general behavior. But why did he interfere? It was unlike him. It was,

I repeat, beneath his dignity. It must have been a personal thing. That's why I want to know what he whispered to Boyeur. A great deal hinges upon that. How much was Boyeur provoked? I'd like to know the whole back history of those two."

He looked again at Julian Fleury, inquiringly, but the older man shook his head.

"I'm sorry. I'd like to be able to help you but I can't. It's a surprise to me. I didn't know the two had met other than casually."

"Can anyone else help me?"

No one could.

"I'd be very grateful if you could make inquiries," he said. "I'll do my best to find out myself, but my own information will not be coming from an impartial source."

He said it with a smile. It was the only indication he had given that, for him, this was a family affair.

The Governor asked Grainger to stay behind when the meeting broke up.

"Don't think I don't realize that this is very difficult for you," the Governor said.

Grainger made no reply. He waited for the Governor to continue.

"This is your first important case as Attorney General. It is of great importance in your career. I recognize that you couldn't have had an unluckier beginning."

Again the Governor paused, but again Grainger remained silent. He knew the value of saying nothing till one had made up one's own mind.

"This is your test," the Governor went on. "People are undecided about you. Many consider I made a mistake in appointing so young a man. You will be judged for many years by your conduct of this case. I know that you are in a difficult position. Whichever way you act, you will be criticized. You know that of course already. But I want to assure you of this. You have my complete confidence. Whichever way you decide to act, you have my support. I shall back you up. I have appointed you to this post and I stand by my own appointment. The colonel of a regiment fights the battles of his junior officers with the 'higher ups.' A colonel may abuse one of his company commanders in the orderly room, but he'll fight that officer's battles against the brigadier. Don't forget that, my boy."

"I won't forget it, sir."

### 3

Grainger usually lunched off a sandwich at his chambers. He had not yet found himself a flat and one meal a day in the atmosphere of his family was as much as his patience could take. His home had become a strain. Every week he became more conscious of the vast differences between his parents and himself. His years in England had made him foreign to them. They could not share his ambitions. But today was different. He needed to see Muriel.

She rushed to meet him, her eyes swollen and dark rimmed.

"What's happening?" she asked.

"I'll tell you afterward."

Or at least he could tell her partially. She would be of more help to him if she was not too completely documented.

"You'll be seeing David, won't you, this afternoon?" he asked.

"Of course."

"There's something I want you to find out for me. I want to know what the feud was between Maxwell Fleury and himself. I also want to know what Maxwell said to make David lose his temper. You know what happened, don't you?"

"Please tell me. I don't know the details."

He told her roughly. He did not want her to know too much. He did not want David to know how much he knew. He did not tell her that David had shouted to the crowd that fatal "Let him have it, boys."

She listened with a strained, uncomprehending look. She could not believe that this was happening to her David. Twenty-four hours ago she and David had picnicked on the beach. He had been tender, adoring, utterly absorbed in her, regretting that he had to go out to this boring meeting. He had promised to get back quickly, to take her to the second showing at the cinema.

She had waited and waited, first impatiently, then angrily; then anxiously. At last the appalling news had reached her. She could not believe that it had happened. Only six hours ago they had been on the beach, her head lying in his lap, his fingers stroking her cheek, running through her hair: such peace, such utter peace. Yet with the undercurrent of excitement, the knowledge that with one gesture he could set the blood pounding through her veins: she was his to do what he wanted with; she longed to be his utterly, yet she had been grateful to him for letting her savor this calm tranquillity a little longer. She looked at her brother with incredulous bewilderment.

"Nothing can really happen, can it?" she asked imploringly.

He shrugged. "It'll be for the jury to decide."

"But can't you stop it? Surely you must know that he never meant it. That it was all an accident."

"I hope that was all it was. Have you ever heard him mention Maxwell Fleury?"

"I can't say that I have. He never talked about politics to me."

"What did he talk about?"

"Love, half the time."

"And the other half?"

"About how we'd live. The house we'd have: the parties we'd throw."

Her brother nodded. Muriel had been a sounding board. Boyeur had built himself up while he talked to her. He had identified her with his ambitions. Muriel was the right person for him. She thought him marvelous, seeing him as he saw himself.

"Nothing can happen, can it?" she repeated.

"I hope it can't. It'll be a help if you can find out what the trouble was between him and Maxwell."

### 4

In two other houses, the case was being discussed on personal grounds, but in a very different way.

Humphrey Norman was discussing it angrily, with a sense of personal injury.

"I know how it'll be," he said. "Grainger'll find some legal quibble. You know what these lawyers are. And Boyeur's going to be his brother-in-law. They'll cling together, you see: you don't get one of them letting another down: at least not where a white man is concerned, and whoever thinks of the Fleurys as being anything but white.

"H.E.'ll realize now what a mistake he made in appointing Morris. Why couldn't he have chosen Baily; or if he wanted a colored man, one of the senior fellows. Carmichael for example. It's always the same. These men come out from England thinking they know everything. They meet a few intelligent colored men and fancy that there's no difference between an African and a European except the color of his skin. H.E. meets the West Indian cricketers and imagines that the laborers in the cane fields are no different. Morris'll fix it. You wait and see. He'll find some loophole, and the last chance of developing Santa Marta as a tourist resort goes down the drain. You mark my words. That's how it'll be."

Mavis listened in silence. She had heard her father talk in this strain a thousand times. She was resigned to this kind of rhetoric. But she listened now with a mounting irritation. Grainger wasn't like that, she told herself. He was a man of honor. He would do his best to see justice done. He was young, he might make a mistake, but he was honest. If there was one thing in the whole world of which she was certain, it was that.

In the Fleurys' house, too, a daughter was listening with impatience to a parent's tirade, but Jocelyn's irritation was not against her father, but her mother. Her father sat, with a tired, drawn expression, listening or appearing to listen.

"They've killed my son," Mrs. Fleury said. "First Arthur and now Maxwell. The Germans had to pay for Arthur's death. I never felt any sympathy for them when I read of their towns being bombed. It served them right. They started it. It was their doing. It's the same now with this David Boyeur. He didn't kill Maxwell himself, but he was responsible: just as Hitler and Ribbentrop and Goering were responsible for Arthur's death. You've got to see that justice is done, Julian. I rely on you. I trust you."

Her voice grew shrill. She was very close to hysteria. Vengeance won't bring her son back to life, thought Jocelyn. Why not mourn her son in private, decently.

## 5

Bail had been refused to Boyeur. It was not considered safe in the public interest to set him at liberty. There might have been rioting in Jamestown, but he was allowed to receive visitors, without police supervision. He had had his clothes sent round to him, and he looked smart and spruce that afternoon for Muriel's visit. He strode into the reception room as though it were a drawing room. His ease and confidence surprised and reassured her. At the same time it abashed her. She had arrived full of sympathy, intending to offer consolation, but that role was quite unsuited to her lover's manner. He was his usual ebullient commanding self, prepared to treat the whole thing as a joke.

"Isn't it absurd? Fancy arresting me. You might as well arrest a man standing on a balcony while a free fight takes place in the street below. I had nothing to do with it. How could I have? I was on the table the whole time. It happened so quickly that I couldn't see what was happening. One moment he was down there, struggling, hitting out right and left, the next moment he was dead."

"You didn't see who killed him?"

"How could I? There were twenty all at him at once."

"But wasn't it a blow with a cutlass that actually killed him?'"

"So they've told me since."

"But surely you saw that. A cutlass, after all—"

"You'd think so, wouldn't you? But when things are happening as fast as that, everything's unexpected. You aren't looking for anything like that. Have you ever seen a car smash?"

"I haven't, no."

"Well, I have, twice, and each time it was the same. It happened so quickly that I didn't know what happened. I couldn't have given evidence in a law court; I was walking along the pavement, thinking of something else, I heard a shout, I looked up, there was a scrunch of brakes, a crash, and there was a woman screaming. I couldn't say whose fault it was. Any more than I can say what happened last night. It's absurd of them to have arrested me, and to have refused me bail. I wish that brother of yours was a lawyer still. If I had him to plead my case I'd soon be out of here. As it is, I shall be out by tomorrow probably. We'll go picnicking. Wasn't it lovely yesterday?"

His assurance, his confidence, unarmed her. Her instinct told her to relax, to let him talk of love, and of their future. She longed to hear those rich tones in his voice. But she remembered her brother's warning. She had a duty to perform.

"Why did you knock him into the crowd?" she asked.

"I didn't knock him. I pushed him. The table was very small. He lost his balance."

"You didn't know him at all well, did you?"

"Hardly at all. Where should I have met him? He was no good at cricket. I've met him at G.H. once or twice, that's all."

"He wasn't an enemy of yours?"

"Of course he wasn't. I can't say I liked him much. Surly, stuck-up fellow. I hardly knew him. Why are you worrying on that score?"

She felt lost and helpless. She did not know what her brother had in mind, but she had faith in him and great respect for him. He must have a reason for having asked her to probe this problem.

"I'm sorry. I was curious," she said. "The story I'd heard was that Maxwell Fleury jumped up on the table and began to abuse you to the crowd, then he whispered something to you yourself, and you hit him hard in the face and he fell off the table."

"Is that what they are saying? You know how things grow, how each person who tells a story adds something to it. Yes, he did start abusing me to the crowd, and he did whisper something to me."

"What did he whisper?"

"I can't remember. It's unimportant. I saw that silly looking face under mine, and I pushed it away. You know the way one does in rugby football, handing someone off. I didn't punch him."

"And you don't remember what he whispered?"

"I've told you I didn't. It's unimportant anyhow. The whole thing's silly. I'll be out of here by tomorrow. Nichols was here this morning. He's the best lawyer in town after Grainger. He quite agreed with me. Don't worry about it any more. I still may be able to make tomorrow's picnic and if I can't, well, think of all the picnics there'll be waiting for us when I get out. I shall be so impatient, I shall want to eat you up. You don't know what you do to me when you look at me like that. You'll learn though. I'll be teaching you."

The deep tones had come back into his voice. She drew a long slow breath. Her knees felt weak again. She could not go on pestering him with questions about this silly case.

Her brother looked serious that evening when she recounted her interview with her fiancé. But he did not let her guess where the cause of seriousness lay.

" 'Pushed not punched.' And he can't remember what was whispered."

He did not like it. He needed Whittingham's advice.

"Boyeur's trouble is his vanity," he told Whittingham. "He's so vain that he'll cut off his own head rather than appear ridiculous. There's a lot more behind this than we can see. Maxwell Fleury was a problem too."

"He was a very peculiar man."

"I can scarcely remember him as a boy, our paths were different. But when I came back here a few months ago I couldn't help feeling that he justified everything that I had read in England about the no-good, effete, standoffish Sugar Baron type. He was arrogant, he was surly, he was anti-blackman and he wasn't any good at his job. Then suddenly he changed."

"As you say then suddenly he changed."

"He became affable, cheerful, a good mixer. And he also, so I have been assured, began to run the Belfontaine estate efficiently."

"Did you notice when this change began?" asked Whittingham.

"About three months ago."

"That's right. I remember the actual day: It was the day that article of Bradshaw's appeared about the Fleurys having colored blood. He came into the club, a few minutes after Carson had had that ridiculous scene with Leisching. We all wondered how he would take it. It was hard to see how a man like Maxwell would fail to hit the wrong note. To everyone's surprise he disarmed everyone: he was easy, gracious, charming. Then three days later he made an election address at Belfontaine that won the seat for him. Two days earlier he had been shouted down. He was a changed man."

"Do you attribute that change to Bradshaw's article?"

"It must have had some effect."

The two men looked at each other. Until he had become Attorney General, Grainger had seen very little of Whittingham. Even now he only knew him on the surface, as a noisy, genial bore, who in spite of his manner happened to be remarkably efficient. He had little idea of what he was like under the surface. He had the feeling very strongly now that Whittingham was holding something back.

"Have you any idea yourself as to the reasons for this feud?" he asked.

Whittingham shook his head.

"I've none at all."

"I think his father was telling the truth, don't you, when he said that he knew nothing?"

"It seemed to me he did. Why are you so anxious to clear up this point?"

"If Boyeur was provoked beyond a reasonable point, then I'm not sure that a prosecution would be justified. Maxwell was getting what he deserved. It may have been an accident. Maxwell may have been to blame. But if on the other hand, Boyeur having worked the crowd up to a pitch of hysteria knocked Maxwell over into them and shouted, 'Let him have it, boys,' it's like a lion tamer keeping his lions short of food, then pushing a man into the cage."

"I see your point."

"It's very important that I should know how much Boyeur was provoked." He paused, he looked at Whittingham inquiringly. But Whittingham did not help him out. He's like a clam, Grainger thought. Even though he is so garrulous.

"I suppose it would be against etiquette if I went down myself and saw him?" Grainger said.

"You know the answer to that better than I do."

"Do you think it would matter if I did?"

"I don't know who's going to complain."

Grainger went down that evening. Boyeur looked shy and apprehensive though his manner was flippant.

"Have you come to let me out?" he asked.

"Not yet."

"So I shan't make the picnic tomorrow afternoon."

"No, you won't make the picnic."

"Too bad."

"There are one or two things I want to ask you."

"Fire away."

"When Maxwell Fleury held his first election meeting, you organized a demonstration that made him look ridiculous. Why did you do that?"

506

"He was on the other side."

"A number of candidates were on the other side. Against how many of them did you organize demonstrations?"

"That was the only one."

"Why did you pick on him?"

"He was a bumptious bastard. Why should he interfere in politics? It was no business of his."

"At Carnival, his car was put out of action and his fields set on fire. Do you know anything about that?"

"I know a great deal about a great many things."

"Were you responsible?"

"I can't help it, can I, if my friends dislike my enemies?"

"So you admit he was an enemy."

"Not at all. But they may have heard me say he was a bastard, and that's enough for some of them. I have a business keeping them in control. I don't know what would happen if I wasn't there to watch them. The sooner I'm let out the better, if you want to keep this island quiet."

"You don't seem to have managed to keep it very quiet last night."

"That was Fleury's fault."

"How so?"

"Jumping up on the platform, shouting abuse at me, at them. No wonder they got out of hand. You know what a West Indian crowd is like. A man was killed in Trinidad last Carnival."

"It was you who pushed Fleury off the platform."

"He asked for it."

"How so?"

"Shouting out all that abuse."

"And then whispering that insult."

"I'll say so."

"What was that insult by the way?"

"What insult?"

"The one he whispered, when he put up his face close to yours."

"He didn't whisper anything."

"But you've just said he did."

"I didn't."

"Now listen, David, this is serious. I won't say your life depends upon it, but your next five years may. It's very important that you should tell me what Fleury whispered to you?"

"Why should it be?"

"I shan't tell you that. But the whole case might turn on it."

Boyeur did not reply. He was a little frightened. He respected his future brother-in-law and was in awe of him. Grainger was not the man to bluff. Grainger would not say a thing like that unless

507

he meant it. He ought to tell him what Fleury had whispered to him. But he still hesitated. To stand up in open court and admit that anyone had dared say a thing like that to him, even though the man had paid for it. How would Muriel feel? She couldn't think of him with the same respect again.

He heard the lawyer standing up in court and saying, "And now will you tell his Honor and the jury the exact words that Maxwell Fleury used." He could hear the titter in the court when he repeated them. No, he could not face that. Why should he? It could not be all that serious. Grainger was bluffing. If he found himself in real difficulties later on, then he could tell the whole story. But until then—no, he couldn't face the shame of confessing that an insult of that nature had made him lose his temper.

"He didn't say anything in particular. I can't remember exactly what he did say. I saw that silly face of his, gibbering up under mine. I pushed it and he lost his balance."

"And that's what you are going to tell the jury."

"Precisely."

"Then I've no more to say."

Grainger took his leave so abruptly that Boyeur was more than disconcerted. He was close to being frightened. There was something ominous and final about the closing of that door. He had the sense of a last chance gone. A constable tapped him on the shoulder.

"You must go back now," he said.

Boyeur followed him meekly to his cell. He sat on the iron bed with its rough straw mattress. This can't happen to me, he thought. I'm David Boyeur.

6

It was close on eight o'clock when Grainger returned to his father's house. Muriel was waiting for him with the same look of questioning anxiety upon her face.

He shook his head.

"I'm sorry. I've no news for you."

His parents were obviously embarrassed. They wanted to discuss the case, but did not know how to begin.

"I've kept you a hot plate," his mother told him.

"I'm not hungry," he said. "I'll make myself a sandwich."

He could not bear his family's company and questions. He went on to the veranda.

"I want to think things out," he said.

He was tired by the strain of a long day: he felt himself ill-used by fate. It was unjust that his first important case should have been involved with family consideration. H.E. had been right. He would be judged on his conduct in this case and he would be criticized whatever he decided. If only he could have had to deal the first time with a straightforward issue. He had never felt lonelier in his life. If only he had someone to talk it over with: if only he had here some of the friends that he had made in England: the men he had played football with, the men with whom he had thrashed out the problems of the universe long into the night at Balliol; friendships that had been proved. He had no such friends here. If only there was one person in the island to whom he could speak openly: one person.

The telephone was ringing in the hall. "It's for you Grainger."

He rose wearily. Was he never to be allowed a moment's peace. But it was not the official masculine voice he had expected.

"I shouldn't be bothering you now, but I wanted you to know that you have all my sympathy, that I know how difficult it must be for you."

The voice was quick, a little breathless.

Mavis Norman. And only a second earlier he had been thinking that there was not a person in the island to whom he could speak openly.

"Are you busy?" he asked.

"Busy?"

"I mean now, this moment."

"We've just finished dinner. No I don't think I am. Why?"

"In that case I'll be round within ten minutes. I'll take you for a drive."

The servant who opened the door was surprised to see him.

"Miss Mavis. Yes. I go tell her."

The maid did not ask him in. He was kept waiting several minutes.

"I'm sorry," Mavis said. "I had to change."

He drove her to the Morne St. James, above the fort. With his arms crossed over the wheel, he leant forward looking across the sea.

"At the moment you rang up," he said, "I was thinking there wasn't a person in the island to whom I could explain myself, to whom . . ." he checked. He was afraid that he might say too much. He changed his tack.

"H.E. said to me this morning that whatever I do now, I shall be criticized. If I prosecute, they'll say I've turned against my own people, that I've taken the white man's bribe: and if I don't prosecute, they'll say that I've let family interests influence me. But

509

whichever way I decide, I don't want you to misjudge me. I've not yet made up my mind, but I want you to realize this, that it would be far easier for me to do what looks the more difficult to do. If I prosecute Boyeur, if I put him behind bars, within a year colored people will be saying, 'That's an honest man. He puts justice first. He's not afraid of ruining his sister's future in the cause of justice.' I'd be established for ever as a man of integrity, but if on the other hand I feel there isn't a real case against Boyeur, as well I may, they'll say in the long run, 'He put his sister first.' Do you see what I mean. It's much easier for me to do the harder thing."

He elaborated the point. She did not interrupt. She sat listening, curled in a corner of the car, looking at his face in profile. There was a ring of sincerity in his voice that she had never heard in any man's before. She had been often wooed; and often her blood had responded to the deepening tones in a man's voice; but no man's voice had moved her in the way that his did now, when he was talking not of herself and him, but of abstract concepts, duty, honor, justice, the individual's obligation to the state.

"I can't tell you what it means to me, being able to talk to you like this," he said. "You're the only person in the whole island that I could talk to."

She had the sensation of something under her heart going round and over. Yet at the same time she thought Unless I'd rung him up, he'd never have thought of that. In part it irritated her, it should have been he, the man, who did the ringing up, who took the initiative. Yet at the same time the fact that he hadn't, made him special for her, made her special for him. He was not timid and bashful. It was because of his colored blood, because of his social separation from her that he had not called, that in five weeks now she had not talked to him. It would always have to be she who took the first step. Always.

7

Next morning Grainger again went round to Whittingham.

"I've no clue as to what really happened," he said, "or why it happened."

He had asked Mavis the same question that he had asked Julian Fleury with the same result. She knew no reason.

"Boyeur's lying," he went on. "And if I know him at all he'll lie in court and the jury won't believe him. He's sticking to the story that he only pushed Maxwell. We've got the constable as a witness that he punched him. I could get a conviction, I'm sure of that. At the same time I'm not certain. I've got a hunch. I don't know how.

510

I may be fanciful. It may all be moonshine. But I can't help suspecting that Maxwell deliberately planned this thing, that he wanted something like this to happen. I can't tell you why I think it, but I'm convinced that that's what did happen. It was the final scene in some feud between them. He goaded Boyeur on to do just that: he didn't expect to be killed, of course not; but he wanted to have something so shocking happen that Boyeur would be finished. I can think of no other explanation of his behavior. Why on earth should he behave so ridiculously, with such little dignity. It was unlike him. How do you feel about it? Is everything that I've been saying nonsense?"

Whittingham shook his head.

"It isn't nonsense at all. Maxwell Fleury was a very peculiar man. I've seen quite a lot of him one way and another during these last weeks. His behavior is, as you say, on the surface inexplicable. There must be some cause for it. People don't behave unreasonably without a reason; I don't say that you're right in your diagnosis, in concluding it's the last stage in a feud, that it was an act of vengeance, but at the same time, yes it does seem more than likely that he deliberately provoked Boyeur; that whatever he whispered was in the nature of a challenge, that knowing Boyeur as he did, he must have known that Boyeur would strike out at him."

"If you think that, it's good enough for me."

Grainger called on the Governor that evening. "I've come to hand in my resignation, sir."

He stated his reasons.

"I believe," he said, "that a prosecution against Boyeur would succeed. Boyeur would behave stupidly in court, and the jury would not believe him; which is what the other members of the Council want. They are demanding an example. They want to frighten the populace. They want to break the peasants' faith in Trades Union leadership. They want to convince the world that there is a strong government in Santa Marta, so that tourists can say 'There was trouble there once. But that's been all stamped out and there's no safer place than the one that's solved its difficulties. The reformed rake makes the best husband.' That's what they think, sir; and I believe that that's what you think too."

"And why do you think they're wrong."

"Because an injustice would have been done. And an injustice always results in a reciprocal injustice. Boyeur would come out of prison, eventually, full of hatred. The injustice that had been done to him would convince other young men that they cannot expect justice in our courts, that they would be smart to take the law into

511

their own hands. A heritage of hate would be created. That has been the root cause of all the trouble in these islands. One crime begets another. Violence leads to violence. In my opinion, sir, there's only one cure for the maladies that afflict this whole area; an impartial justice, respect for the law, a belief in the mind of every single peasant that he will get square dealing before the bench."

"That is what you genuinely believe."

"Yes, sir, that's what I genuinely believe."

"Then I'm not going to accept your resignation. You're the right man for the job. I've learnt to trust my own judgment where men are concerned. As a platoon commander I made very few mistakes in the privates I picked out for stripes. And as a brigadier, I can only say that I shouldn't have been given a division if I hadn't had the right men on my staff. I knew I'd picked a winner when I picked you. I'll back you up, my boy. I don't say you're right, but you stand for the right things. That's more important."

# CHAPTER THIRTY

## 1

Boyeur was released from prison on the day that Bradshaw's article was published.

On the following afternoon Bradshaw's siesta in Virginia was disturbed by a call from Baltimore.

"This is the Chief. Carl, I don't want to spoil your holiday. We'll take care of that later on. But I need you back at once. You won't have heard it, but that young colored agitator, the brash young man whom I met at the Governor's party, has been let out of jail. Your hunch proved right. And that's the second time. You've made a hit. The Time-Life boys have just been on the line. They want to feature you. They're giving you a cover, by Artzibasheff. Hit while the iron's hot. I shouldn't be surprised if you got hold of a Pulitzer. Fine thing for the paper if you could. I want to arrange for you to speak at the Dutch Treat Club. Come back here right away: hop the first plane and think out another article; it'll have to be the last one. Give it a big punch. Congratulations, Carl. It's great."

Bradshaw's hand was trembling as he hung the receiver back. His picture on a cover of *Time*, a guest of honor at the Dutch Treat Club. A Pulitzer award. He thought fast, searching for a telling title for his final article. The wind was at his back. An idea struck him. "It isn't cricket." Templeton, a soldier sent out to the West Indies for his cricket's sake, Grainger an Oxford Blue, Boyeur using cricket as a step to power. An Empire run on cricket. That was the precise type of satire to tickle the American sense of the ridiculous. He had only had ten minutes sleep in place of his usual thirty, but the divan with its dented cushions offered no temptations. He unpacked his typewriter.

## 2

The cable from Santa Marta announcing Boyeur's release reached Westminster on the morning before the arrival there of Bradshaw's article. The Minister read it with concern. There would be questions in the House on this. It could not have happened at an unluckier time. Kenya, Malaya, and now Santa Marta; British subjects being shot and no reprisals taken. The British Public was getting restive. So was the Opposition. So for that matter were his colleagues. He

513

had thought he was safe with Templeton. The usual trouble about generals in that kind of post was their tendency to rely on the musket as an instrument of discipline. He had raised his eyebrows when he had read Templeton's first cable: martial law and Boyeur behind bars. That was moving fast. But he had read the cable with relief. Action like this had come at the right time. But now this second cable . . .

He sat with it in his hand. Why this change of plan? It was so bare, the facts and nothing else. He felt helpless, sitting here at his London desk on a bleak September morning three thousand miles away from the scene of the events. The cable had been sent last night. Dawn had barely broken there. He had never been to the West Indies. He could not visualize the scene. He remembered in the war, in a foxhole in the Western Desert, how impatiently he had read the orders drafted in Cairo by staff officers who divided their days between the Gehzira Club and Shepheard's. What did they know about the desert; the freezing nights, the scorching days, the lack of water.

How could he, shivering a little in his unheated office—it was too early yet for a fire; he must put on heavier underclothes tomorrow— how could he in such a different setting appreciate the tempo and temper of existence in that remote, humid island, onto which at any moment now a hurricane might unleash its force. Yet sitting here, looking out over the roofs and chimney stacks of London, he had to make decisions, to arbitrate in the future of men and women alien to him in race and blood, in training and environment. He felt lost and lonely. If only there was someone with whom he could talk the matter over; someone whom he could meet on equal terms, who was neither his superior nor his junior. Was Marjorie lunching anywhere he wondered.

He called her on his private line.

"I'm sorry," she said, "I wish I could. But I'm playing bridge with Nora. Is it anything of desperate importance?"

"No, no. It's nothing desperate."

Playing bridge with Nora. That was what she was doing now three afternoons a week: or seemed to be. Was she? He didn't know. He didn't want to know. As long as he kept in office, she would play along with him. She was loyal. She wouldn't hit where he was vulnerable. He read the cable again. To impress his colleagues, he must make a show of strength. Templeton might have to go: but he must not be sacked. Templeton was too good a chap. He called his opposite number at the War Office.

"Can you at almost a moment's notice if it's necessary find Templeton a job that would look a promotion after being Governor of a

West Indian island? It must look above board. Whatever he may feel himself, it must look well on paper."

"O. K. I'll look around."

Two days later the minister received the last article that Bradshaw had written in Santa Marta. He read it with stupefaction. This was worse, much worse than he had feared. How could Templeton have been so blind. He'd got to come back. He couldn't be left there any longer. Himself he wouldn't know a moment's peace. He rang the War Office. "Have you thought of anything that's at all suitable for Templeton?"

"As a matter of fact we have. Commandant at Sandhurst. Archie Waldron's been trying to get away for months. It's right up your man's street. He'll jump at it. It's a Major General's appointment that confirms his temporary rank. That makes it a promotion."

"You've saved me from a fate worse than death. I'll get the P.M.'s confirmation."

The P.M. was in Paris on a conference. He could not be disturbed. The minister talked to his private secretary. The private secretary assured him that the P.M. had complete faith in the judgment of his appointees on routine matters such as this. The minister closed his eyes with relief. He was out of the wood. A lucky escape. He'd be on his guard another time. How could one tell, though. There were so many irons in this fire.

3

On the following morning Lord Templeton received two cables from London. The one he opened first was from the War Office. It offered him the appointment of Commandant at Sandhurst. It informed him that permission from the Colonial Office had been obtained. It hoped that in the interests of the service he would accept.

The other one was personal, from the minister. "War Office most anxious you accept appointment Commandant Sandhurst hate to let you go after your fine work for us but feel must not stand in way your obvious interest also national interest."

Templeton smiled wryly. Did they think he was a half-wit. He did not fall for that type of banana oil. He sent for Euan and handed him the cables. His son looked at him questioningly.

"What are you going to do?" he asked.

"Accept. It amounts to an order."

"Are you glad about it?"

"If I had had this offer made a year ago, I should have been delighted, but coming now, I hate leaving a job before I've finished it."

"Couldn't you refuse?"

"A soldier has to go where he is sent."

He would have liked to have said more, to have taken his son into his confidence; to have spoken of the knowledge of failure that was implicit in this recall. But a lifetime's training had taught him to conceal his feelings.

"When do you expect to return?" Euan asked him.

"Almost at once. I'll be needed for conferences at the Colonial Office. There'll be a good deal to tidy up before I can take over at Camberley."

"I see."

Euan frowned, pensively.

"In that case, Father—" he paused. "Is there any reason why Jocelyn and I shouldn't get married here before you leave? Then we could all go back together."

"We discussed that, didn't we, when you got engaged?"

"Yes, but it was different then. You'd have still been here."

"Does that make any difference?"

"In a way it does, or at least to me it does. There was a close link between us then, but with you gone . . . It's completely unreasonable, but I can't help feeling that if we don't get married now, we never shall get married."

"And you are very anxious to be married."

"Of course. Why not?"

"In that case then . . . if you can persuade Jocelyn. I'm sure I can persuade her parents."

"I'll see her right away."

Templeton watched his son hurry from the room, then began to draft his cables of acceptance. He wrote them sadly. He had not lied to Euan. A year ago there was no post that he could have welcomed more than that of Commandant of Sandhurst. It was like being headmaster of one's own public school. He had been very happy there as a cadet. He would have enjoyed looking out over the lake; watching exercises on Barossa, taking the salute at the steps. He would have regarded it as a high privilege to have been allowed to implant his ideas on a new generation of cadets, particularly at a time such as this when a new and democratic army was being trained.

In five months' time, once again in the saddle, he would be a happy man. He was well aware of that. But at the moment he was oppressed by failure. He had come out here so hopefully ten months ago. He had meant to do so much for Santa Marta. He had seen his three years here as the coping stone of his career. He was being recalled after ten months. There was a saving of face, but he had failed. There was no denying that.

He remembered too in what spirit he had awaited, seven months ago, his son's arrival for a summer holiday. He had thought that as a result of this visit he would come to understand his son, that they would become close friends. They hadn't. He had failed as a father too. He and Euan were strangers to one another. He had no idea what was passing in Euan's mind. Was Euan hastening on this marriage out of a sense of duty; because he had drifted into a situation and saw no way out. Was he in love with Jocelyn? Had he gone to her on the rebound from Mavis? He did not know, and there was no way of knowing. He was not in his son's confidence and never would be. He shrugged. He had learnt to take reverses in his stride. You attacked a position: only in part captured it, you reformed your ranks, brought up reinforcements: then attacked again with a different scheme. He wondered whom he'd have under him at Sandhurst, as "assistant commie."

4

On the following morning after breakfast, Jocelyn Fleury followed her mother into the small drawing room.

"I've some things to say to you," she said.

Her face was serious: it wore an expression that her mother had not seen before: an expression that seemed to be as much as anything one of triumphant enmity; as though she were about to deliver to an enemy a *coup de grace*.

"I'm going to be a nuisance I'm afraid." She employed a tone of voice which implied that she was delighted to be a nuisance. Her mother had never seen her in this mood before. Jocelyn was usually so docile, so irritatingly docile.

"What's all this about?" she asked.

"In about three months, I want to go to Canada," she said. "I shall need to be away four months. You had better start making arrangements now. I want it to look above board: a reasonable kind of thing to do."

"Canada. Why on earth should you want to go to Canada?"

"To have a baby."

"*Jocelyn!*"

They had been standing up but Mrs. Fleury now sat down. Jocelyn sat opposite on a high-backed chair and crossed her legs: she let her arms rest along its arms, her hands hanging loose over the ends. She leant back her head. She had an exasperatingly regal look, as though she were on a throne.

"Whose baby is it?"

"Euan's naturally."

517

"But I don't see when . . ."

"He joined me when I was in Barbados. But it had been going on a long time before."

"I've never been more surprised by anything in my life."

"Really. But then you don't know me very well."

"How long, I mean to say— Mayn't you be mistaken?"

"No chance of that. I've missed the second time, three weeks ago. There isn't any doubt."

To Mrs. Fleury, her daughter's calmness was the most astonishing aspect of the whole outrageous incident. Jocelyn showed no shame, no guilt, no penitence. She could not have been more matter-of-fact.

"I'd meant to go to Trinidad and get rid of it," she said. "I suppose I should have, but after Maxwell's death, it's quite illogical, but I felt I couldn't take a life. It seemed a murder. Canada's the best idea, don't you think? No one need know. I could have it adopted. There's a great demand for them up there. It should be easy. There's only one thing that really matters. Daddy mustn't know. It would upset him dreadfully. That's why I need your help."

There was an undertone of contempt in her voice, as though she were saying It won't hurt you at all although you are my mother. You're only interested in appearances, the look of the thing, what people will say.

Mrs. Fleury's temper rose. She was not going to be browbeaten in this way.

"This is the most ridiculous thing I've ever heard. You've been very foolish. You've behaved like a peasant girl in the cane fields. But that's neither here nor there. That's the past. It's the future that matters. You're engaged to Euan. You can get married in a hurry. You won't be the first by a long chalk. You haven't quarrelled with him, have you?"

"By no means, he wants to marry me at once. He wants to marry me right away before he goes back to England."

"Right away? But he's not going to England till October."

"He is, there's been a change of plan. His father has a new appointment, a military one. I only learnt it last night. That's why I've brought this up now. A certain amount of pressure will be brought to bear on me. You'd better know what the situation is, since you've got to work with me in this. We can even make this Canadian visit an excuse. You can say that you'd like me to have an autumn there, while Euan gets settled into Oxford. It's what his father really wanted. Then in the new year I can write from Canada that I've changed my mind. It's all quite logical, as long as you and I play ball."

"It isn't logical. And I won't play ball. You can't ruin your whole life for this. Are you still in love with Euan?"

"Yes."

"Then what on earth's to stop your marrying?"

"The danger of seeing a colored man in the House of Lords."

"Don't be ridiculous."

"I'm not being ridiculous. We say that there's no difference nowadays between a peer and a commoner. The age of the Common Man. But there is: otherwise there wouldn't be a House of Lords. A peer is different. It wouldn't matter for a soldier, or a lawyer or a politician. A slightly darker skin would make no difference. But a peer: think of all the jokes there'd be about it. Think of how the boy himself would feel. He'd grow up twisted. I wouldn't inflict that on my worst enemy, let alone my son."

"But there's not the slightest danger of his looking more than mildly dark. Think of how light-skinned you are. Nobody in England suspected about your father. It's only a very slight strain. And you know what the anthropologists say nowadays, that the strain gets lighter all the time, that there's no truth in that old story of the throwback from ten generations."

"That's what they say now. That's the modern theory. But how do we know they're right. There's a new theory of some kind every year."

"You might have thought of all this several months ago."

"I did. When I was first engaged to Euan I didn't know about that Jamaican ancestor. As soon as I learnt, I knew that marriage was out: but I didn't see why I should deny myself the kind of good time that Mavis and all the rest have had. They got off scot free. Why shouldn't I. But nature fools you. We haven't solved the world's problems with those little books. That's why I don't trust those theories of the anthropologists. Nature fools you, once in so many times. There's one risk that I'm not running."

"Is that the only reason why you're refusing to marry Euan Templeton?"

"It is."

"And if you had a chance, if things were different—"

"But they're not different."

"I know, I know: but suppose they were. Let's put it another way. When Euan was trying yesterday to persuade you to marry him right away, would you have given anything to have been able to say 'Yes'?"

"I would."

"Then in that case I've got to tell you. I owe it you. You need have no qualms about marrying Euan Templeton. You have not one

519

drop of African blood in your veins. My husband is not your father."

"Daddy not my father?"

"No."

"Then who—"

"That's immaterial. It's better for you not to know. He is completely English. You can rest assured on that point. I will tell Lord Templeton who he is. He has a right to know who is the other grandfather of his grandchildren. Telling him that will be the most difficult thing I have done in my life. It will be the price I have to pay for something I've regretted all my life. He has to be told. He may have the same old-fashioned qualms that you have. But I don't see why my husband need know. It would break his heart."

Jocelyn stared at her mother. She found it hard to believe what she was hearing. Her parents had seemed so devoted. She had never conceived the possibility of another man in her mother's life. So that was why her mother had seemed to be holding something back when Bradshaw's article appeared. Astonishment was mingled with a relief so intense that she could not face as yet the consequence for her of this revelation. Her whole life was to be transformed. She wanted to brood on it alone. But with that astonishment and relief was mingled something of the satisfaction she had felt in plays when a sanctimonious character had been exposed. Her mother had always seemed so correct, so aloof, so "county." That her mother should be capable of a thing like this.

"It's the last thing I could have expected of you," she said.

Her mother laughed; a short, bitter little laugh.

"You have a lot to learn," she said. "I was surprised myself. It was the last thing I would have expected of myself, two months before it happened. I had been married ten years. I was happy. I loved my husband. I was still in love with him. I hadn't a worry in the world: most people feel that they have been cheated by life, or that they have had to give up certain things to get certain others. I didn't. I felt I had had the amazing luck to pick up a hand that held all the court cards. And then this thing happened. It wasn't anyone that I respected: there was nothing glamorous about it: it was squalid, furtive, a hole-in-the-corner business. I despised myself for it. Yet I made no resistance. It was something that I had to have. There was a part of me, a very small part of me, not two per cent perhaps, of whose existence I had been unaware. It suddenly came alive. He brought it to life. It was a brief fierce lunacy. When it was through, heavens but how through it was. But I had to have it. I hated myself for having it. But if I hadn't, I'd be thinking now that I'd half lived my life."

She spoke with a fierce, masochistic concentration, as though she were relishing the pain that the opening of old wounds caused; at the same time it contained a vindictive sadistic undertone as though she were settling a score, were saying to her daughter, There's no need for you to be so smug. You're not the only one. You've got a lot to learn.

Jocelyn stared at her mother: she was seeing her for the first time as a human being.

"No wonder you've never liked me much," she said.

Her mother had resented her very existence, had looked for and been repelled by signs of the father in her. No wonder it had been the way it had.

"When do they expect to leave?" her mother was inquiring.

"They don't know yet for certain. Within a fortnight."

"And Euan wants you to marry him right away."

"Yes."

"Then the sooner this is settled the better. I'll see Lord Templeton this afternoon."

For a moment, with a minute malicious fraction of her mind Jocelyn pictured her mother's interview with the Governor. What a role for that stern woman to have to play. Malvolio crossgartered. But it was only for a moment that she allowed herself to gloat over the exposure. There was no need for it. She could spare her mother that. She shook her head.

"There's no need," she said. "I don't think he ever worried about that. And if he did, it doesn't matter since it can't happen now."

"But what about Euan? Won't he worry? He may look in his son or daughter for color. He may be unfair to them on that account: as perhaps I was unfair to you."

"I don't think he will. It's really only people with color themselves who worry about color. White people never worry about that kind of thing. Did you worry about Daddy when you learnt?"

"I can't say I did."

"No more will Euan about me."

"But what about your children? They may learn about it; they almost certainly will. It may give them an inferiority complex."

Mrs. Fleury's voice was anxious and insistent. How determined she is, Jocelyn thought, to drain the cup of sacrifice.

She shook her head again.

"We'll cross that bridge when we come to it," she said. "It's a long time off. I may have to tell them some day. But we've got quite enough on our hands at the moment decking me out in orange blossoms."

# CHAPTER THIRTY-ONE

## 1

Ten days later the bookstalls of the world carried Bradshaw's face on the cover of *Time* magazine. Artzibasheff had done one of his happiest cartoon portraits. The large cherubic fat cheeked face was bland and childlike but there was a look of sinister design in the network of wrinkles round his eyes and in the puckering of his lower lip. He looked astute and devious, like a worldly prelate. The caption below it ran "Cricket or Wasn't it. Baltimore's Bradshaw scoops the Ashes."

The portrait had a composite Caribbean background; it had the white colonnaded portico of a Governor's House: Negroes working in the cane fields; a liner swinging into port; a group of shingle huts and palm trees, with the whole pattern so designed that each separate activity was focussed upon a cricket match in which whites were playing against blacks.

In London, in the library of the Reform Club, the Honorable Esmond Price studied its wit and satire with disapproval. He was a tall, obese, cleanshaven man in the middle seventies. He wore a dark suit of heavy material; it was loose fitting, it looked as though it had been seldom worn, it had an unfashionable air, suggesting that its wearer was a countryman who rarely had occasion to wear city clothes. That however was not the case. Esmond Price had a service flat in St. James to which he came up every Tuesday, returning to Somerset on the Thursday night or Friday morning.

He had had a curious career. The younger son of a West country peer he had been elected to the House of Commons as a liberal in the Peers vs. People election of 1910. It was a period of intense ill feeling between the parties, but his speeches though effective and partisan won the respect of the Opposition. He was regarded not only as one of Asquith's most brilliant young men but a future statesman. In August 1914 he sailed for France as an ensign in the Grenadiers. In the same action in which he won an M.C. for gallantry in the field, his brother received wounds in the back that crippled him for life, and a wound in the head that made him a borderline case, in danger of complete collapse. Edmund Price resigned his seat at the end of the war, and made himself responsible for the care of his brother and the running of the estate that one day his own son would inherit.

No retirement from public life could have been more complete. Yet as a London clubman with vested interests in the country, he kept in touch with his old friends and his old interests. As the Liberal Party dissolved, and its brighter members allied themselves under other banners, he found himself with close and trusted friends in every camp. Men of consequence and position were glad to discuss their problems with him for the very reason that he stood "above the battle." He had no ax to grind, he was impartial, he was wise and he was well informed. Gradually he became a person of power and importance. The careers of many ministers had been advanced or retarded by his influence. He was unknown to the general public, but he was a power behind the scenes. He enjoyed the position that had come to him unsought, and was careful not to compromise it. He had early learnt that the best way to possess influence is by a sparing use of it.

He frowned as he examined the Artzibasheff cartoon. The frown deepened as he read the article on Bradshaw. It was a long and amusing article. It treated Bradshaw as the Innocent Abroad dropped without preparation into the confusion of colonial politics. It was sympathetic to Bradshaw, in a way it was sympathetic to the British regime that had to accommodate such conflicting interests, but nevertheless it poked a good deal of fun at it. Price shook his head; he did not like that kind of thing. The Colonial Office could not afford to have fun poked at it at a time when colonies were clamoring for dominion status or independence. Marsh had handled the affair clumsily. He was the wrong man for the post. Himself he had never felt happy about the appointment, but Freddie had been so anxious to give a chance to one of the younger men. Freddie knew better now: not that he could do anything about it. It was prudent sometimes to ignore one's own mistakes. And this was one of the times when it was. Wait for the cabinet reshuffle, then find Marsh a post where he could do no harm. The Duchy of Lancaster? No, that was too good. Agriculture and Fisheries perhaps: A gentle easing out. He'd have to think about it. The great thing at the moment was to give an appearance of solidarity, to act as though nothing untoward had happened.

He laid down the magazine and went into the morning room for a preprandial glass of sherry.

2

That was at half past six. The sun at that moment was high at Santa Marta as Denis Archer waited in the chalet for what well might prove his last picnic there with Margot. The last ten days had been his most hectic since the Battle of the Bulge. There had been the rush of good-by parties, the flurry over Euan's wedding; the arranging of passages, the forwarding of luggage. He pitied the A.D.C. whose employer had a wife as well for him to cope with. Never again, he assured himself, never again. He had been so rushed off his feet that he had very little time to wonder about his own future, for this change was going to affect him considerably.

He had anticipated that he would be in steady employment for three years. He had planned in terms of not having to worry about earning any money until his return. He had worked intermittently on a travelogue, had written half a dozen poems; there was plenty of time he had told himself. He would get down to something solid at the start of his second year and would return to England with a novel or travel diary to establish his literary identity. But here he was now, about to arrive in London, with a small balance at his bank and nothing to show a publisher.

The old boy had said "I'm afraid this will be a great inconvenience for you. Don't worry. I'll see that you are all right." Which was very decent of him and very typical of him. But there were limits to what the old boy could do. Anything practical he did, would involve a putting of his hand into his own pocket. And nothing he could do in that way would provide an equivalent for free board and lodging, leisure, and ample pocket money for thirty months. How could you live in London without spending money: and if you lived in a small country inn, what would you have to write about? He would have to think out a whole lot of problems as that clipper ship flew eastward over the Atlantic.

He had had no time to sort those problems; to classify and number them. He had been equally taken off his guard personally. What about Margot? He had seen her too in terms of a three years' appointment. He had never looked ahead. They had discussed nothing. They had lived from one day to the next. There was a timeless quality, a living upon another plane about their hours together. He had assumed that when his three years were up they would have reached a mood when it would be easy for them to wave good-by, having had the best of one another; each one ready for novelty. He had thought they were lucky to be spared the making of decisions. They would never go stale on one another. It would be the way things ought to happen, the way things did in books. He was utterly unprepared for this sudden break.

Impatiently he paced the room. This might be the last time. Did Margot realize that? What was going to happen to her? Would she be kept on here at the Secretariat? What was there that he could do for her? She was self-reliant. She had never asked for anything.

He had no idea what her home problems were. He'd send her something at Christmas, he told himself; something substantial, that she could keep in reserve for an emergency: though even as he thought that he knew that she was not the person who puts things by. She would spend whatever he sent in an orgy of new dresses.

I'll know what to do when the time comes, he told himself. He wouldn't put on an act. Maybe it wouldn't be the last time. They'd be able to squeeze in some last minute meeting, "the little grace of an hour," and if they didn't have that final meeting, he'd be able to say something consoling, reassuring about how lucky they had been not to have had a last time that they had known would be the last. "I couldn't have borne it, knowing it was the last." So he thought at hazard, confusedly: seeing it in terms of books he had read. Then she came round the curve of the narrow pathway and he forgot all that.

She was wearing a short-sleeved primrose yellow sweater, a wide sage green skirt, with a red belt that he had bought for her in Trinidad. She was wearing nothing that he had not seen a dozen times. There was no dressing for an occasion. He opened the chalet door for her and she paused beside him as she always did; placed her hands upon his shoulders, raised herself upon her toes, and kissed him, lightly, but letting her lips linger against his, the way she always did, then dropped back upon her heels and stepped away.

"I'm thirsty," she said. She pulled the cork out of the thermos flask and poured herself a punch.

"That's good," she said.

She sat on the arm of the long chair swinging her right leg over the side.

"I heard a funny story about the Archdeacon." She began to tell him.

Her voice ran gaily on. It was an amusing anecdote. He stood beside her; she was wearing a new scent that he had given her; a heavy one based on musk. The sweater fitted tightly across her breasts. He put his hands under her arms and lifted her onto her feet. She smiled. She lifted the glass to her mouth and tilted back her head; he could see the pulse in her throat throbbing as she swallowed the cool sweet liquid. The ice clicked against her teeth as the last drop ran over her tongue. She tossed the glass onto the divan and folded her arms about his neck.

She stretched back her arms among the cushions, and shook her head, blinking, as though she were rising to the surface after a long dive.

"I'm hungry," she said and swung her feet onto the floor.

525

"As I was telling you, when the Archdeacon saw what he was doing . . ."

She continued her story, as she munched her sandwich. As though there had been no interruption.

"I'm still hungry," she said, "and still quite a little thirsty. No, you sit still, I'll help myself. I like moving about."

A pile of manuscript was on the desk. She paused by it. She looked at the top page.

"This is new," she said.

She began to read.

"I like this," she said and turned the page.

Denis Archer, seeing her standing there, reading what he had written, had the sudden devastating picture of a life without her, of writing things she would not read. He blinked. He could not face that prospect. This had gone too deep. She was part not only of his life here in this room, but of his life wherever he might be. He could not leave her.

"Have you a passport?" he asked.

"Yes, I got one when I went to Martinique."

"How long will it take you to pack?"

"Two hours."

"The plane for England leaves on Friday at ten past eleven. I'll send a car for you at half-past ten."

"O.K."

"I won't be able to come myself. I'll be too busy shepherding the Governor."

"I'll manage on my own."

She had not looked round. She was still reading the manuscript. She lifted another page.

"I think this is the best thing you've done," she said.

Her calmness, even after all this time, astonished him.

"You don't seem surprised," he said.

"Surprised at your writing well. Why should I be? I think you will be famous one day."

"I didn't mean that. I meant your not being surprised at our going to England together."

Then she did turn round; and this time there was a surprised expression on her face.

"Where you go, I go."

He had in that moment a shattering sense of destiny fulfilled; a sense of pride, of exultation, of simultaneous triumph and surrender; an acceptance of life's challenge coupled with an acceptance of his fate. He knew in that moment beyond any doubt that there was only one thing for him to do.

"Are you a Catholic?" he asked.

She nodded. But even that, with his full recognition of the finality of a Catholic's marriage vows, the closing of that easy loophole of divorce, woke in him no premonition of disaster. Their lives were already linked.

"It would be simplest if we got married before we left," he said.

"You'd know that best."

She turned back to the manuscript. "I'd like to borrow this. There's too much to read now," she said.

She picked up the thermos and poured herself out a glass. She took a sandwich from the tray. She sat on a chair facing him. "I've no warm clothes," she said. "But I don't suppose it'll be very cold there yet."

"We'll hurry you straight from the airport to Debenham and Freebody's."

"I've heard of them."

She finished her sandwich and stood up. "You must be very busy. I should be on my way."

She crossed to the gramophone and turned it on, looking among the records for a successor. She found what she wanted and slipped it on. "Buttons and Bows." She hummed the words, her feet moving to the rhythm. He joined her and his arms went round her. As they danced, slowly, on the small square floor, his need of her, his delight in her, once again took control of him. But there were no protestations, no special vows of loyalty. That had been decided between them a long time ago.

# CHAPTER THIRTY-TWO

## *1*

Half the population of Jamestown and a large contingent from the districts had assembled to bid Lord Templeton farewell. The airport looked like the racecourse on Governor's Cup day, and Colonel Whittingham had mustered nine-tenths of his police force to control the crowd and supply a guard of honor.

It was a cool clear morning after two days of rain and cloud and the cane fields provided a fresh green background to the garish clothes of the chattering crowd. The fixed bayonets of the guard glittered in the sunlight. It was a gay and colored scene. The small BWIA plane that maintained biweekly a shuttle service with Antingua was reported to be on time. Templeton's hearing was good and his ears caught the drone of its engine before his eyes had spotted it.

This is it, he thought, and moved out of the waiting room. The plane would be grounded for half an hour. That would give him plenty of time to say good-by to everyone and to inspect the guard; plenty of time and not too much time. He disliked last words. During his service he had stood on so many platforms.

Everyone of any consequence had come to wish him well. Their handshakes were firm, there was a warmth in their voices. He could have easily assured himself that they were genuinely sorry to see him go, but he knew how quickly last minute emotions can be turned on and off. Were they being overgenial to conceal an undercurrent of embarrassment? Did they realize that he was being recalled? The thing had been well covered. His appointment as Commandant had been written up to look like a promotion and it did constitute a rise in rank. It would mean eventually a higher pension. But they must know. It would be too great a coincidence otherwise. Did some of them feel resentful, did some of them feel they had been let down, were being deserted by him? Grainger might well feel that.

"I shall be making a personal report about conditions here for my successor," he assured him. "I shall make a special point of the help that you have given me. He will, of course, know about you already. Your cricket and your football. But I shall see that he recognizes how complete was my faith in you."

"I appreciate that very much, sir."

The Governor paused; there was something more he might have said, about the inevitable checks that one receives in a career. But there were things better left unsaid, unless they were said at the right moment, in exactly the right way. And there was all this crowd about him. He put his hand on Grainger's shoulder.

"Good luck, my boy. I know you've a big future waiting you."

Above Grainger's shoulder he caught a glimpse of Boyeur. He had wondered whether he would come. He had hoped he would not, but had guessed he would. Boyeur was in a difficult position. The strike had collapsed; there had been no rise in wages. It was generally agreed that he had had an extremely lucky escape. He still held his place in the Council; but there was every likelihood that union membership contributions would need a lot of collecting. He would have to watch his step very carefully for many months.

Boyeur was standing beside Muriel Grainger. So she had stuck by him. Perhaps this might make their marriage a better one. Her loyalty might touch his heart, as well as his vanity. Templeton made his way in their direction. Nine months ago he had thought that Boyeur would be easy to handle because he was a cricketer. He did not think that any longer. Boyeur was one of those men who misinterpreted everything you said or did; he was a master of the fancied affront. It was sheer luck if you did not do the wrong thing. But even so cricket was as safe a card to play as any.

Templeton asked him about his marriage plans, then turned to Muriel.

"I'm sorry I shan't be here for it," he said. "Let me give you some good advice instead of a casual wedding present. Make him go back to cricket. There's always something to be complained about with any husband; there are worse fates than being a cricket widow."

He moved on to the Prestons. "Have you any messages for anyone in England?" he asked her.

"Please give my love to Lydia."

"Lydia?"

"Lydia Wessex. I owe her a letter. I really will write soon. Do tell her that."

"I won't forget."

The Normans were next the Prestons. Norman was certainly one of those who nourished a grievance over his son-in-law's death and over the blow to the tourist industry. He blamed it all to G.H. weakness. And he had been unlucky certainly. Someone had to pick up the bad hand in every deal. Mavis was standing beside her mother. But Sylvia was not there. Mrs. Norman apologized for her absence. "She sent you so many messages; she had wanted to come so much but she didn't feel equal to it. All the standing in the heat."

"I quite understand. She's very right. I've thought about her a great deal. At least she has the consolation of the future."

He turned to Mavis. She looked tired and drawn. Was she a little saddened by Euan's leaving, by Euan's marriage. What had there been between them? He would never know. She might so easily have been his daughter-in-law, the mother of his grandchildren. What was going to happen to her? The years were passing and she seemed headed nowhere. There were so many girls in the same position in the islands. He felt a pang of sympathy for her and for her problems. She might have become a close, integral part of his own life. Now she was going out of it along with so many others.

For ten months he had been seeing these people every day. They had become real to him. Their interests had been his interests. How few of them would he ever see again. Whom for certain besides Julian Fleury? Him, he would see often. As likely as not Julian and Betty would decide to sell out here and come back to England. With Maxwell dead and Jocelyn in England there was little to hold them to this island.

He wrung his old friend's hand warmly.

"I'm only saying 'au revoir' to you two," he said.

2

There is inevitably an anticlimax about the taking off of a plane. When a liner sails, streamers can be flung from deck to pier, and the colored paper strands snap one by one as the ship swings round into the harbor. On a railway station, a porter hurries down the platform, slamming doors; a green flag waves; heads lean through the windows as the train draws out. But there is such a long pause at an airport after the steps have been wheeled away; the passengers are belted in their seats; you cannot see them through the window though they possibly can still see you; the plane taxis to the runway and pauses, poised with the engines throbbing. You cannot disperse because your friends, though they are invisible to you, want to catch a last glimpse of you. They do not want to be reminded that you are about to enter, have in fact already entered a life in which they have ceased to have a part; so you stand there, gossiping together, impatient to get away.

Julian Fleury had passed his arm through his wife's as Jocelyn paused in the doorway of the plane, at the head of the steps, to wave good-by.

"We're just ourselves together now," he said.

She pressed his arm against her side. In many ways her heart was heavy. First Arthur and now Maxwell. Yet even so there was a new deep peace within her heart. She was alone again with Julian: after all these years. Maxwell and Jocelyn had always been a barrier between herself and Julian; they had involved a maneuvering for position, a necessity for scheming. All that was over now. To young things like Mavis Norman and Doris Kellaway she and Julian must appear old fogies, "all passion spent," packages upon a shelf. She was by no means sure that the best part of her life was not starting now.

A few yards away Doris Kellaway was chattering exuberantly to Mavis.

"I wonder what the new Governor will be like. I expect that he'll be married. But I don't suppose he'll bring his family out here. They appoint them younger nowadays. He'll be in the forties. That means his sons at school. I hope she's lively, a party giver. She'll probably choose the A.D.C. If she's gay, she'll choose somebody that's fun. Denis Archer was a dud, wasn't he? Fancy him marrying that girl. I suppose he had to, but even so. I do hope the next one's an improvement. We'll have loads of fun. It's always exciting when a new Governor arrives. All the parties that there'll be for him. It's a pity Sylvia won't be able to join in. We'll have to make it up to her when she's well again. It'll be like the three inseparables again, only with me instead of Jocelyn. It *will* be fun. I used to feel so envious of you, when I was at school."

Mavis smiled wryly. The three inseparables again. But you couldn't put back the clock. They had all been under twenty then, she and Sylvia and Jocelyn: Life had been limitless in opportunity; there was nothing they could not do. But Sylvia was a widow and would be a mother soon, and Doris looked upon them not as equals but as guides and mentors, and she herself, how the possibilities had narrowed for her, the horizon had shortened, with the bright faith tarnished. "The three inseparables" belonged to yesterday.

Her mother at her side was grumbling over young Archer's marriage.

"It's the most ridiculous and disgraceful thing I ever heard of. H.E. should have stopped it."

"How could he, mother?"

"Easily enough if he had wanted. He let enough things happen that he should have stopped."

Mrs. Norman as well as her husband considered she had a grievance against the Governor. She had been full of happy anticipations when he had arrived here with a young and good-looking A.D.C. and the prospect of being joined by his young good-looking son. What a chance for Mavis. Yet here, ten months later, not only was Mavis still unmarried but Sylvia was back upon her hands. She didn't imagine that she would be upon them long. Pretty young widows invariably remarried quickly; particularly if they had a dowry. And Belfontaine was entailed upon Maxwell's child. But that was some while off. There was all this business first of the child's being born. It was exciting to be a grandmother. But even so ... Mrs. Norman was disgruntled. She did not want to examine in too close detail the causes of her irritation. It was easier to focus that irritation upon some other point; Archer's marriage did as well as anything.

"It's the most disgraceful thing. What an example to the island. It'll make every girl in town feel that she's only got to set her cap at the right angle to capture one of us; and the young men are so feeble they'll let themselves be captured. They believe it's all right since an A.D.C. does it. And with the Governor's approval, in the same airplane as the Governor. It breaks down everything we've stood for. Well, they've got a bad time ahead of them, that's all I can say. They'll pay for it. What will his parents think? A daughter-in-law that's nearly black, a hole and corner wedding. He won't be able to take her anywhere. She'll ruin him professionally. A good thing too, I say. The only pity is that nobody here will know. The young people need a lesson."

Mavis made no reply. What was the point of arguing? She had heard her mother speak in that way so often. And it was untrue. It must be. Surely times had changed. They were living in the twentieth century. Good luck to them, she thought.

To her right the band broke into "Auld Lang Syne." The plane was beginning to move. Whittingham's voice rang out: "Present Arms!" There was the crack of wrists on magazines. A roar went up from the crowd. Someone shouted, "Three cheers for the Governor." A section of the crowd was singing "For he's a jolly good fellow." The playing of the band was drowned. The noise was a vast jungle roar. Templeton encased in his hermetic cabinet could hear none of it. He was waving his hand, but the crowd with the light shining on the windows could not see him. The plane lifted from the ground, soared high above the cane fields, slowly circled the airport and turned northward. The shouting lessened as the drone of the engines became fainter.

There they went, thought Mavis. Jocelyn and Euan, Margot and Denis Archer, and the big man himself. She watched the machine grow smaller: a faint and fainter flicker of silver against the pale blue of the morning sky. It had gone, it gleamed again; then vanished; she could hear it when she could no longer see it.

She turned away. The cheering was now a chattering, the crowd started to disperse.

"When do you think we'll hear about the next Governor?" Doris was inquiring.

The next Governor. With the last one barely out of sight. The next Governor. It would all have to begin again, and when it was over, the three years reign finished, she would be standing here beside some equivalent for Doris wondering what the next Governor would be like, waving good-by to Doris very likely, Doris whose turn it would be to return to England as a bride. Everyone seemed to be settling their fates, one way or another, everyone except herself.

She looked back to the G.H.'s garden party; it was only seven months ago. How many fates had been decided in those seven months—Sylvia and Jocelyn, Margot and Denis Archer, Boyeur and Muriel Morris: Maxwell and Colonel Carson and the Governor; that newspaper man, Carl Bradshaw, and with what réclame for him. His face on every bookstall. Even Grainger had made, hadn't he, his big decision during this half year? Everyone except herself.

Grainger was only a few yards away and she moved toward him. He welcomed her with that friendly smile that always made her feel that she was someone special.

"How does this affect you?" she asked.

He shrugged.

"I can't tell yet. But I shall resign my appointment when the new Governor arrives."

"Oh, Grainger."

"It's the only fair thing to do. A new regime needs new officers."

"Surely he won't accept it."

"He will in the way I put it. I'd only stay on if I was convinced he really needed me. But I'm sure he won't. I'd be an embarrassment to him. I couldn't bear being that, to anyone."

"An embarrassment. Why should you be?"

"Because Lord Templeton was recalled, and in part because he backed me up in my decision not to prosecute David Boyeur. I offered to resign then, but he refused. He'll speak up for me in London. But the new man will want to run things in his own way. He's a right to that. If after he's been here a little while he comes to believe that I'm the man he wants... but he must be allowed to make that decision for himself."

"That means the ruin of everything you've worked for."

533

He shook his head.

"It means a delay: that's all; and perhaps everything's gone too quickly and too easily for me up to now. Later on this will stand me in good stead."

He spoke with assurance, in an attempt to convince himself as much as her.

"At the moment," he went on, "the colored people are on my side, and the Sugar Barons are against me. Everyone thinks that I've taken the black man's side against the white. That isn't true. I've taken the side of justice. Later on there'll come a day when I take action against a colored man, on the white man's side. When that day comes it'll be remembered that I once took a colored man's side in a key case and resigned my appointment in consequence. They'll learn that I'm impartial. They'll trust me to administer justice."

He spoke in much the same way that he had spoken to the Governor. His voice took on again that deeper tone. He spoke with conviction, not so much of his own eventual re-establishment, as in the victory of the cause he stood for. Her heart glowed in response, warmed and fired by his fervor. What a man he was, how puny he made all the other men about her seem. How tawdry were their ambitions in comparison with his. And to think that he had selected her out of the whole island as his confidante.

"The one person in the island that I can speak to openly." The accents of that avowal would ring in her memory until she died. Five minutes ago she had been thinking dejectedly that during the last seven months everyone's fate had been decided, except hers. That wasn't true. She wasn't the same person that she had been then. His faith in her had restored her, had shown her that she was something more than an easy date for the visiting fireman. Her friends might see no difference in her, but she knew deep in her heart that there were now certain things that she could never be.

"Mavis, we're going now."

It was her mother calling. Mavis looked up questioningly at Grainger.

"Can you drive me back."

"Certainly."

They walked to the car park slowly.

"Did you know Margot Seaton?" she asked.

"Barely."

"What do you think of her marrying Denis Archer?"

"It may be the making of him."

"Why do you say that?"

"When young men marry the kind of girl who is as they say

534

suited to him in every way it often turns out wrong. If a man marries a girl whom the world thinks quite unsuitable, it means that he really wants her. That's the best augury isn't it?"

"Everyone thinks he's marrying her because she's going to have a baby."

"I'd doubt that. Archer's not the kind of young man to do anything quixotic. He's ambitious. He wouldn't saddle himself with a wife he didn't want."

"What'll his parents say?"

"There's nothing they can say. He's presenting them with a *fait accompli*. He's been very wise in that. If he'd taken her over as a fiancée, for their approval, they'd have done everything to stop it, but as it is they've got to welcome her."

"But what about his career? You say that he's ambitious. Won't it go against him to marry somebody as dark as that?"

Grainger shook his head.

"She isn't all that dark and they don't worry about that kind of thing in England. Which is something nobody realizes here. Color prejudice is confined to the countries that have a color problem, South Africa, the Southern States, and here. England hasn't got a color problem. Besides Archer's going to lead a Bohemian, ragamuffin life. Artists are expected to be irresponsible. They provide the color and contrast to existence. An artist would look silly with a rolled umbrella. An exotic wife like Margot will be an asset. She's very picturesque."

"It's a relief to hear that."

They had reached his car but the park was crowded still. Grainger's car was hemmed in. They would have to wait a moment longer. They stood together, waiting.

"Do you think that works the other way," she said.

"How do you mean, the other way?"

"In a girl's case. They say things are different for a woman. They say that even now. The double standard. Should a girl marry somebody unsuitable, if she really needs him, if she feels he's right for her... Denis Archer marries Margot. Euan marries Jocelyn. But when it's the other way around... Is there any difference?"

She was talking quickly, hesitatingly, with pauses between the clauses, with a dogged resolution. If she did not say it now, she would never get it said. She had to take the first step, hadn't she. "The one person I can talk to openly," but she had had to call him. All his training would assure him that he was outside her range....

Her toes curled inside her sandals. This course was opposed to all her instincts. Men should initiate. But this case was different. She looked up. He was so strong, so straight. He was such a man:

he was the one man who had believed in her; could he not do for her what Margot would do for Denis. This was her one chance, she must speak now.

Grainger stood looking down at her, it was utterly unexpected: he had never dared to dream that Mavis felt like this about him. The prospect dazzled him. But even so. . . .

"Why should there be any difference?" she was saying. The car behind his was backing.

"Now's our chance; jump in quick," he said.

He was thinking fast, desperately fast. She must be spared the humiliation of a refusal. She must be stopped from uttering the words that in her mind she had already framed. She must put that dream away forever, must be convinced of the utter impossibility of a shared life for them.

He set the car in gear and released the clutch.

"It's strange," he said, "that you should be asking me about marriage, a celibate like myself: though I suppose I shouldn't be surprised. Catholic priests express themselves strongly on matters on which they can never have any practical experience."

"What are you talking about?"

He was speaking lightly, almost flippantly; giving no indication that a few seconds before she had been talking with such fierce intensity. She was puzzled, upset, almost indignant at his tone.

"What do you mean, a celibate like yourself?" she asked.

"It's what I am."

For the first time he had fully realized, was able to formulate in words, what he had long in his subconscious suspected, that he was as much a celibate as any priest, since for certain dedicated persons, there is implicit in their acceptance of a calling, the denial of a right to personal happiness. He had as a colored man taken up a cause, a mission; and he must never accept responsibilities that could claim precedence over his allegiance to that cause: never, never, never. He must try to explain to her what had now become clear to him at last, the nature and obligations of his calling.

"I don't want to seem presumptuous," he said. "I don't want to make out that I'm more important than I am, or indeed that I am important, but there are certain people who can't carry out the work they've set themselves if they accept the privileges and responsibilities of marriage."

Slowly, carefully he guided the car out of the park, talking as he drove.

"I told you, didn't I, about that girl in England whom I would like to have married, whom I didn't feel it would be fair to bring out here. Since I've come back here, I've realized that it wouldn't be fair to any girl for me to marry her. I couldn't be a good husband and father and do my work the way I want."

He underlined the "and."

"Why do you say that? Why do you make yourself out to be a special case?"

"Because I *am* a special case, because I'm a fourth colored."

"Why should that matter?"

"Because I'd have colored children. They'd be special cases; every colored child is a special case. All my arguments would be affected by that case, and would be weakened. No matter what kind of woman I married, whether she was completely white or completely black, people would say the same thing, 'He argues like that because his wife is this and his children that.' They will say something like that anyhow. They'll say 'Of course he feels like that, look at the color of his skin'; but they'll say it much less if I stand alone, and in the end they'll stop saying it altogether if I continue to stand alone. Gradually they'll come to realize that I'm a man without an ax to grind, that I am impartial because I can afford to be impartial. That's how the people must see me, as a man without an ax to grind."

She made no reply. Her hands clenched. She stared at the road ahead.

What an escape she'd had. Another minute and she would have proposed to him. What a fool she would have felt. She'd never have dared look him in the face again. She'd never have dared look anyone in the face again. The story would have got round; stories always did in a small place like this. He'd have told someone else; one always had to tell someone else: one extracted the most dire vows of secrecy, but they were always broken. What an escape!

"Where would you like to be dropped, your house, the tennis club?" he asked.

"Is my house out of your way?"

"Not at all."

"That would be fine by me then."

He swung north along the bay. The tension was broken. The danger point was passed. But something more needed to be said. She must be in a desperate state to have reached such a point. Was there nothing he could do, nothing he could say to make her feel happier about herself. Surely there must be something.

Perhaps this was it.

"I had a letter from a friend in England two days ago that made me think of you," he said and his voice was gentle. "He said a rather curious thing. He runs an employment agency and he told me that he was finding it very hard to find for certain special and confidential jobs young women with pleasant voices. He said that there was

537

growing up now a uniform, standardized way of speaking that has no charm, no character: he used the simile of filtered water that has no taste. Young women from simple homes listen to the B.B.C., imitate the voices that they hear there, and iron out the small local differences of accent and intonation that once gave their voices charm. There are many jobs now, he said for the young woman with a pleasant voice who's prepared to work; so many of the girls who have pleasant voices aren't prepared to work. Their idea of work is a job where you meet interesting people, arrive at half-past ten, have two and a half hours off for lunch and go home at five. I thought of you. Why don't you take a trip to England and see what it's like. There's so little to do here that's worth the while of someone like yourself."

He had drawn up outside her house. His smile sent a warm feeling of self-confidence along her veins, that made her feel good about herself.

"You could surely manage a trip," he said. "Copra's booming. It's the time to go. I'll write to my friend if you like and get some facts. You'd enjoy working if you had a job that you believed in. Why not think over it?"

"I will."

England. Why not? It was an idea. Copra was booming. She'd got so used to thinking of hard times that she hadn't realized that the hard times were over: she hadn't got adjusted to the fact that you could now afford a trip to England. Why not, after all, why not?

3

That night once again Grainger sat alone upon the veranda of his father's house. He would not be sitting here alone so many more times. That afternoon he had found an apartment near his chambers that suited his requirements. He would sign the lease tomorrow. Very few renovations were required. He would be moving into it within two weeks. Afterward when he came to this house it would be as a guest.

Peace lay upon his mind. That morning he had felt despondent when he had watched the Governor step into the plane. His fortunes were at their lowest ebb. He was without a patron. He had had to speak boastfully to Mavis to maintain his spirit. In that tense five minutes by the car he had not only solved an immediate problem but seen into the heart of his own constant problem. He knew what that problem was, and how he would have to cope with it. He was ready to take up now, in pride, with courage, the challenge of his lonely destiny.